MW01064581

LAVENDER

an entwined adventure
in science & spirit

Copyright © 2010 Judy B. Gardiner
All rights reserved.

Cover photo by Lev Gogish

ISBN: 1439271046
ISBN-13: 9781439271049

DEDICATION

To the late Diane Peggy Brooks (*Peggymoonbeam*) and her coterie of resplendent friends who joined her in mentoring my dreams. They have shown me from afar how our lives unfold to reveal our destiny. I have been humbled by their teachings and their ability to manifest an endless stream of helpers along the way.

Like E.T., Diane held up her crooked finger, pointed it skyward, and said, "I will always be there." And so, she is.

෧෨

To the late, extraordinary humanitarian and teacher, Dr. Montague Ullman, I owe my largest debt of gratitude. While collaborating on our two contrasting bodies of work, his theoretical, mine experiential, we discovered that we were two halves of the same whole. He once wrote, "I feel as though we are both miners fumbling about in a dark enormous cave with only our small lights available to us, both driven by the conviction there is something here of enormous importance if only we humans can get a handle on it." When we merged, the wondrousness of the Universe sang out in a harmony known only to the angels. And a silhouette of that "something of enormous importance" began to take form. Of great significance to our work was the late twentieth-century physicist, David Bohm, who inspired Monte to apply his quantum theory of an underlying cosmic unity to dreaming. Many facets of this totality of existence have been actualized in the fragmentation, timelessness, interconnectedness, and wholeness found in Lavender's mission.

CONTENTS

vi

ACKNOWLEDGMENTS

This book was started in 1996, long before I even knew it would be a book. In the course of researching my dreams, miracles began to visit me. I had no idea what they meant, but still I recorded them. As my dreaming miracles seemed to multiply exponentially, so did happenings in my waking life. Soon they began to weave mysteriously together.

By the year 2000, I realized a story was being written.

My first debt of gratitude extends to my dear friend and editor, Richard Greb, husband of Suzette Greb, my best childhood friend. Rich is not only a superb editor but one with an amazing range of whiz kid knowledge covering nearly every piece of factual and human information in existence and, I might add, exactly what this book required. His myriad contributions in helping to shape the manuscript, often remembering details better than I, shepherding it through its various incarnations and conducting his own research helped make it a reality.

Heartfelt thanks go to my devoted friends, Karen Donohue Alden and Beverly Lovejoy, for their midwifery in bringing Lavender through the birth canal and for their implicit trust in the invisible. Their contributions will become evident as you turn these pages, for they have become important characters and travel companions on this odyssey of discovery.

To Gloria Purosky who asked me upon meeting her if I believed in miracles, to Dorothy Beach, Medea Eder, Mena Potts, and Myrna Rodriquez, abiding messengers of comfort in my loss of Monte and to Patrice Keane and Nancy Sondow of ASPR for providing an archival home for Monte's life work. To the wonder of Lois Farfel Stark who was often my candle in the dark …. and to Elizabeth Van Ness, perennial Santa Claus and friend for all seasons.

Special thanks to Nitsa Mattson for her efforts to decipher Greek writing appearing on my computer, its significance unknown at the time, to David Frankel who assisted in my research on Vision as I was trying to unravel this Gordian knot of dreams …. and to Guy Pascal who helped me navigate the academic sanctuaries of Paris.

Marion Adinolfi's unwavering healing and guidance can never be forgotten.

Enduring gratitude to Robert Bregman, close friend and accomplished portfolio manager, whose cautious investments enabled me to finish, to Ann Gregory for her continued support …. and to countless other dear friends and colleagues whose insights, encouragement, and inspiration have furthered the infinite connections that make up this story.

May the light be shining on my family in the hereafter and on my bosom buddy, Sandra Peters who is probably saying, "Crikey! It's about time!" A zillion hugs to my precious niece, Katherine Louisa Beck, and loving thanks to my cousin Bud for his astute and caring advice, and to the rest of my family who have been respectfully understanding of my commitment to finishing.

Inexpressible thanks to Melanie Starr Costello for her unshakeable faith in my quest, to Rita Dwyer of the International Association for the Study of Dreams for inviting me to tell my story publicly, to Sally Rhine Feather, for her every kindness and her indefatigable research into the mystery of psi .... and to Janet Sarno, speech coach extraordinaire, who helped me conquer a lifelong fear of public speaking.

To Lev Gogish, respected physicist and photographic artist, who conceived of and brought to life the mystical tree on the cover.

In having reached the portals of publishing, I extend untold thanks to Kayla Evett, who wears the label of designer but is actually one of those earth angels you'll read about in Lavender. As she midwifed Lavender through its final stages, I came to know the extraordinary combination of talent, professional commitment, perseverance and wonderful humor that make up this rare individual. Her contributions will long be remembered. Kayla's meticulous interior design coupled with Kerrie's exquisite cover design capture the story within. They have brought Lavender from chrysalis to butterfly into the light of day for you to read.

The profound knowledge and compassion granted me by Robert Keller, retired Cathwolic priest, were a beacon of strength when I needed one most. And now with the first volume ready to launch, I express eternal gratitude to my rabbi, a practicing cantor, Moti Fuchs, whose wisdom and illumination gave me the fortitude to soldier on through my darkest hours.

In conclusion, I must say that each of you acknowledged on these pages share the benevolence with the source of the work itself.

INTRODUCTION

by

Montague Ullman, M.D.

In Lewis Carroll's wonderful parable, Alice is hurtled down a rabbit hole into a very strange environment where everything is quite the opposite of her safe and secure waking life.

The protagonist in this book is a bright young woman, Penelope Peacock. Presumably, she has fallen through a "wormhole," a tunnel that connects this universe to another universe. In this realm, she finds herself in a heavenly abode peopled by humans and other life forms that have passed on.

Penelope feels quite at home in this place and happy to meet old friends, relatives, and her pet cat. Her trip was prearranged by four remarkable historical figures who, over the centuries, made ground-breaking contributions to science: Galen, on the neuroanatomy of the optic nerve; Ptolemy on astronomy; Steno on establishing the foundations for the science of geology, and Marie Curie, the French scientist who was awarded two Nobel Prizes, through her discoveries related to radioactivity. These four figures collaborated in a tutelary arrangement to impart their knowledge to a bright and eager student. They had an ultimate motive in mind, not known to Penelope until the very end.

Penelope turned out to be a serious and devoted student. She did extensive research on her own to keep up with the subject matter she was learning. Tu-whit, a wise old owl, came in on occasion as a heavenly archivist to elaborate on the data. It was not all serious study. From time to time, she made contact with relatives and friends who had passed over and who lightened the atmosphere.

A word about the setting at this point: This is not an ordinary classroom nor is the author an ordinary dreamer. Judy Gardiner has long and colorful dreams practically every night and awakens with excellent recall. She not only conscientiously records the dreams; they are accompanied by stick figures displaying the action taking place. In ferreting out scientific matter from personal matter, she has found that her dreams fall in two categories. In one, the personal, the dream is focused on private issues. In the other, the cosmic, the content goes beyond the personal and relates to large-scale natural events like earthquakes, volcanoes, tsunamis, and supernova explosions, events she could have no direct knowledge of. It is these dreams that Penelope and her four teachers focus on in her effort to identify the environmental references. Excerpts from her dreams, precisely as she dreamt them, were the homework she brought to the classroom. At times, Tu-whit helped to bridge the gap between dream and reality. The range of the external referents of the dream imagery includes the makeup and dynamics of the earth's crust as well as the stars and their constellations. Included in a series of dreams is the sinking of the Titanic, where her tutors hint at geological activity that may have played a role in that tragedy. Penelope is an apt pupil. Her teachers, aware of her lack of a scientific background, worked with her in small steps. Her dreams provided the raw material of the lessons. Her mentors helped her translate dream images into the various components of the earth's crust and their interactions. Tectonic plates bump into or slide over each other. Undersea volcanoes come to life. All impact the water above, and tsunamis are born. By the end of the book, she becomes quite an expert on undersea geology. She also learns a good deal about the movement of the stars and the formation of the galaxies. Somewhere between Heaven and Earth, she discovers the radioactive element uranium, quite by accident.

Her teachers are very thorough. In addition to connecting dreams to geological events, they also inform her of where to go to find substantive evidence for the existence of geological referents in her dreams. They cite two places in Canada: Newfoundland and Vancouver. The author is quick to follow through on this, and with a companion, she visits both. She does, indeed, find artifacts in each location that have a striking resemblance to specific images in her dreams. In some dreams, the color lavender was very prominent. They traveled to a small town in Newfoundland where all the fire hydrants were painted lavender. On another occasion on a walk through a small fishing village, they came upon a number of large rocks that were splashed with lavender paint. Her companions, knowing the purpose of the trip, were just as excited as she was. I was, too, when I learned about it. It soon became apparent to her that there was a distinct difference between the cosmic dreams and those focusing on personal issues surfacing in her life at the time. In contrast to the personal are the dreams noted in the book where the words or images seem strangely out of place, more impersonal and, when decoded, outwardly and environmentally oriented. Her mentors, living in a world outside of time and space, as we know it, continued to give her hints on where to discover the corroborative artifacts.

This book is a lengthy parable rooted in facts that suggest two possible directions our dreams take. The first is based on the fact that dreaming consciousness is a natural healing system. There is observational and laboratory evidence that dreaming is characteristic of the entire mammalian species and that dreams serve a survival function of some sort. In humans, our dreams serve a healing function by confronting us with hidden truths about ourselves, good or bad, that we have not yet acknowledged. Since we are creatures capable of abstract thought, we are able to capture feelings in metaphors made out of words in poetry, and while we are asleep and dreaming create images that tell the story. Both the poem and the dream capture truths about ourselves that we are not ordinarily capable of acknowledging in ordinary discourse. What is unique in this parable – pointing in the second direction – is the consistent way certain dreams confronted the author with direct hints about environmental events that involve us as members of a species. Thus, our dreams confront us with personal internal tensions that need resolution; as members of a single species, nature confronts us at times with an awareness of external environmental catastrophes.

In short, her dreams took two divergent paths. When the dreamer focused on personal data, the communication was rooted in the way feelings are either overtly felt or as embedded in metaphorical imagery that captures feeling residues both current and past. They have to do with the dreamer's life in the present, past, and expected future. When in waking life this exposes its meaning to the dreamer, there is a definite "Aha" feeling, a gut reaction that a hidden truth has been revealed. Dreams are creative events. We create pictures that talk to us, disturb us, puzzle us, but once their mystery dissolves, they speak to us very simply and truthfully. The strange involuntary images arising out of an environment unbeknownst to the dreamer do not carry a personal emotional charge and generally seem incomprehensible. This unfamiliar terrain can often be described as a cosmic dream where oceanic feelings of oneness and gratitude consume the dreamer.

In my writings, I have regarded dreaming consciousness as serving the unity of man as a single species by helping individual dreamers face issues that limit their sense of unity with each other. They do this by exploring the depths of the individual psyche that require attention. The message of this parable describes the way the dream has a wider purview of potential dangers to the species.

The story opens another door, namely, the relationship of dreams to the paranormal. Louisa B. Rhine noted that telepathy occurs more frequently in our dreams than when we are awake. The records of the British Society for Psychical Research have for over a century recorded impressive accounts of the paranormal which include telepathy, clairvoyance, and precognition. Beginning in the second decade of the last century, the American Society for Psychical Research has done the same thing. Scientific studies continue in laboratories in this country, England, Holland, and Sweden. William James, as well as Freud and Jung, each took an active interest in psychic phenomena (the older term for the paranormal). Jung wrote his doctoral thesis on the mediumship of a young woman. Freud was a corresponding member of the British Society.

To the extent the imagery of a dream in Lavender is initiated by external natural ecological events about which the author could have no firsthand knowledge, such a dream, would be paranormal. Just as Alice in Wonderland is more than a fairy tale, so is this book. When the eternal giants of Science have delivered a message to us mortals, there is no question that they are expressing their deep concern about Mother Earth. This book's fateful message is one that centers on the extent to which humans as a species have, ever since the Industrial Revolution, exploited and corrupted the physical environment that sustains them.

What is of special interest to me in Lavender is the realization that dreaming consciousness is bidirectional, pointing both to our inner and to our external environments. Dreamwork is generally assumed to be a voyage into the depths of our being and exposing the truth, good or bad, about ourselves. The author has described another direction our dreams take in facing not only the natural disasters but also the extent to which we have selfishly exploited nature.

Her experience has taught her the difference between dreams, calling attention to outer realities and dreams focusing on inner realities. More than that, she spent a good deal of time searching for objective evidence that linked the imagery to an external reality.

At story's end, she learns what the message was and why she was selected to carry it out. What brought her four mentors together was their common concern about the future of humankind because of the degradation of its own sustaining ecosystem through exploitation and corruption. Penelope validated their omniscient view that dreaming consciousness could serve as an early warning system not only for natural disasters but also for man-made ones. Just as dreams in pointing inward ferret out flaws in our individual character structures (as well as assets that we are not using), our dreams can point outward to environmental hazards. If Penelope is in touch with this feature of our dream life, probably all dreamers have this Janus-like bidirectional potential. The message is clear: dreams can reach a broader domain in monitoring our ecosystem.

Steno has taken the lead in this unique classroom that spans two different universes. He urges Penelope to go on to a postgraduate program they have planned for her. This throws her into a complete panic since his appeal threatens to shift her from the personal future she planned for herself to a task she is not sure she can handle. She ultimately registers in the postgraduate program with hopes that her readers will join her in unraveling the many loose ends of her cosmic mystery.

Reading Lavender is a voyage into a range of our dreaming psyche that reaches beyond the mundane, calling attention to the corruption of our environment, which has gathered speed during the nuclear age. The author has done with the intrinsic honesty of dreams what Al Gore and others have done with hard scientific facts. Gore's dedicated commitment has exposed one aspect of the dangers we face because of global warming. In its own way, this book complements his effort by calling attention to other environmental hazards.

The story is unique in both content and style. The bidirectional nature of its dreaming suggests the existence of a collaborative unconscious that alerts us to dangers both personal and global. It reminds us that our dreams are private events, but that we are also members of a single species and have a role to play in its survival. The seriousness of the message of Lavender is buttressed by the intensive research the author engaged in to verify her very rich and fascinating supply of dreams. This somewhat nonlinear adventure story of spiritual-scientific proportions becomes a refresher course in understanding the challenge we face both from nature and our failure to fully understand what nature expects from us.

Finally, the story is written in a lightly personal and eloquent style that gathers many threads together, piquing our curiosity about a universal unconscious and leaving us with a greater awareness of the role of industrial society in fueling the dangerous outbursts of nature.

FOREWORD

The story of Lavender will be unlike any other story you've read. It is true but unbelievable. It changes its address from a classroom on Earth to higher learning in
Heaven, from waking to dreaming and back to waking, from one subject to another,
weaving a glorious tapestry of the unity of Life. Time and space cross all boundaries
where the impossible becomes possible and the possible becomes real.

Simple yet complex, amazing yet commonplace, scattered yet ordered, visible yet
hidden, it took me a while to put all the pieces together. The seeds of this journey, unbeknown to me, had been planted in my dreams long before the quest began. I could not
know that its purpose was unfolding as I traveled on and that its full intention would not
be revealed until much later in the story.

Somewhere along the way, I realized that if I temporarily suspended the comfort of
knowing, I might learn more. My first insight into this mysterious puzzle came to me in
a dream: *A big net scooped me up very high in the air. After that, it dropped me in warm water
like a whirlpool, then it dropped me in colder water, and then it brought me back up again. The big
net felt like a safety net. It was an exciting feeling.*

(As you read, you will find dreams and their fragments italicized as above.)

This dream held the first of many lessons teaching me about how to approach my
everyday life. It was exhilarating but scary because I didn't understand the course set
before me, nor do most of us. I did not try to wriggle out of the net. Instead, I let it carry
me to safety. While being jostled through the ups and downs of this life-changing adventure, I experienced one wondrous discovery after another, each one taking me higher and
higher and gradually lowering me into colder more sobering water.

It is here where I ask you, dear Reader, to give Lavender a chance to unfold in its own
way and in its own time. Try to release from having to know where it's leading. Like the
Dream, let your own safety net transport you to your discoveries.

The road we are about to travel is circuitous, at times chaotic; the path is meandering,
and like Life itself, nothing makes sense at first. A blizzard of disjointed images and cryptic messages will bombard and overwhelm you, even disorient you, as it did me. Then
as the dream begins to unfold, a flash of insight sweeps over you and a long-forgotten
memory lights up, connecting to a deeply held experience or fragment in another dream.
Suddenly you catch a glimpse of the bigger picture. You are overcome by an intuitive urge
to turn the next corner, to find the next piece of the puzzle, to inch closer to the heart
of the mystery that holds your purpose. As you fumble about in the darkness seeking
answers to questions that have haunted you all your life, your most intimate truths will
come to light in the most unimaginable ways.

It has occurred to me that the dream is like a kaleidoscope which, with each turn, illuminates and reflects the prisms of our lives. Its multiple patterns and colors chronicle our earliest childhood experiences and follow us along life's ever-changing road. From one dream to another, aspects of our lives may appear to be new images but, on closer inspection, they are old patterns that have reassembled to reveal a broadening of experience. There's more on this process in chapter eighty-six.

While traveling the path of Lavender, you may contemplate your own life's path and discover that you were meant to share in this journey, for in connecting the pieces, you will have your own intuitive "Ahas" and without even knowing it, you will be connecting to something larger than yourself. After all, we are all swimming around in the boundless sea of Life searching for its meaning and for our place in it.

I hope you have the patience to stay with me on this incredible ride through the cosmos as it twists and turns its way toward wholeness.

෴

CAST OF CHARACTERS

Penelope Peacock	Seeker of Truth guided by celestial tutors.

Spirit Guides:

Charlesbigstar	Astrologer who introduces Penelope to the afterlife and the optic nerve.
Peggymoonbeam	Penelope's soul sister; liaison to the celestial mentors.
Agneswiseheart:	Penelope's beloved aunt and designer of the Oneiroball.

Celestial Mentors:

Lord Galen	(Claudius Galen) Greek physician/philosopher. Personification of light, vision, and healing, who illuminates Penelope's dreams with his timeless insights and second-century writings on the optic system.
Twink	(Claudius Ptolemy) Greek astronomer and Penelope's soul mate through the ages, who plants his second-century book on optical phenomena in her dreams.
Doc, Professor	(Nicolaus Steno) seventeenth-century Danish geologist/theologian. Protector of the Earth, who escorts Penelope through ancient rock strata.
Marie Curie	Nineteenth-century Polish chemist and physicist, who teaches Penelope about radioactivity.

Earthly Companions:

Karensurefoot	Investigator extraordinaire, Newfoundland expedition.
Beverlysmilingshadow	Chief of remote sensing; Egypt, Vancouver missions.

Animal Spirits:

Tu-whit	The Archivist Owl
Percival	Penelope's Grail Cat
Simon	Doc's Labrador Retriever

LAVENDER'S WORLD

Terracrust:
Satellite operation that oversees geology, paleontology, theology, physics, and chemistry.

Starsight:
Satellite operation that oversees mathematics, geography, astronomy, optics, medicine, and philosophy.

Paleosecond:
Time unit at Terracrust.

Lumensecond:
Starsight technology used to synchronize Earth Time.

Dominion of the Purple Scroll:
Time-honored society espousing ideology of the union of science and spirit.

Oneiroball:
Balloon aircraft holding the fragments of Penelope's dreams.

Oneiroglyphics:
The Dream's version of hieroglyphics.

Oneiromantics:
The symbolic language of dreams.

Oneiromancy:
Divination by means of dreams.

Psymometer:
Psychic compass with paranormal detection capabilities responsive to influences in magnetic fields of Earth and Heaven.

Telepathy:
Direct mind-to-mind communication.

Clairvoyance:
Seeing events at remote locations.

Precognition:
Seeing information about future events.

Retrocognition:
Seeing information about past events

Timelessness Glasses:
Provides vision with which to see the innermost nature of things and across all reaches of time and space.

DISCLAIMER

The dreams in Lavender are actual dreams I have recorded over the years. The journeys to Canada, Europe, and other locations actually took place, largely as described in Lavender although I created much of the dialogue to guide the flow of the story.

Individuals (living and dead) often appeared in my dreams as references in keeping with the methodology used throughout this work. Lavender's dream imagery uses archetypes in the form of given names and occupations as components to guide the message and are not intended to reflect personalities or historic traits of the individuals.

All electronic anomalies actually occurred.

An enormous amount of technical information came through my dreams and led me to in-depth research on a variety of topics. Scientific discussions in Lavender are thus the result of intuitive and inductive reasoning, and associative memory combined with well-researched data.

*There are only two ways to live your life.
One is as though nothing is a miracle.
The other is as if everything is.*

Albert Einstein

PROLOGUE

For one moment on earth, her finger touched a star above...
She pulled it from the sky and began to examine its many facets.

"It's like trying to lasso a swarm of bees," a friend once told me.

He was referring to the collecting of the years of dreams and the thousands of fragments it would take to tell this story. To turn chaos to order, to tell within time a story that manifested out of time — essentially, to transform a square into a circle — seemed indeed a feat beyond my ken, but I knew I had to try.

So begins the weaving of a seamless reality....

It began in the middle. I awakened one morning, turning over in my mind my dreams of the night before. Awaiting me was my morning ritual, in place for many years, of recording these messages. But, on this day, somehow, I drifted back into the arms of sleep.

> *There appears to be a star in the sky. At first, I have trouble making out its shape, for the image is quite fuzzy and seems to be billions of light-years away. Very gradually, it begins to travel closer, until I am able to focus. Indeed, it is a star — a very clear and lustrous star. It draws closer and closer — and then disappears. The scene goes black. A new star appears. It seems to have gauze covering it, but is larger and considerably closer than the first one. The closer it comes, the brighter it is, until it is practically in my bed with me. And then this scene, too, fades. A constellation appears; then the image of a stone embankment, stretching into infinity. I see a lion made of stone. He comes to life and moves his head. Next, I see the head of a young man, also of stone. He, too, comes to life, and following that, there appear more heads made of the same stone, three men and one woman, each one turning slightly as though taking a bow — like the finale of a play.[1]*

I could not know at the time that the statues who awakened within the dream would breathe life into all that followed.

Some weeks after this dream, I read that before man tried to count the stars, he grouped them into images.[2] The star-studded firmament became one of the most compelling picture books of humankind. This imaginative world led man toward the divine,

---

1   11/25/98.
2   Lurker, Manfred; *The Gods and Symbols of Ancient Egypt*, 1974.

to the meaning of existence and to portray this meaning through that use of images. It occurred to me that my dream images were like stars, and that such grouping of stars is what I had unwittingly been doing with my dreams for years.

A year later, I took my first trip to Luxor, Egypt, and visited the Temple of Karnak, one of the most spectacular places in the world. I was overwhelmed to see that its walls of brick were the same stone embankments I had dreamt. The statue of the sphinx, with its body of a lion and its head of a man was remarkably like the stone lion in my dream. I wondered about all the people in that dream who were stone and came to life. What part did they play? Were they the royal protégés of the sun god, Amon, to whom the temple was dedicated? Why would I be dreaming of them? Could the stone people in my dream in some mysterious way be related to the generations of pharaohs who left their marks on the stone of the sanctuary during the two millennia of the temple's use?

The sanctuary's walls are almost entirely covered with ornamentation and hieroglyphics; hieroglyphics that resonated with symbols I've seen, before and since, in my dreams; symbols somehow directing me to something higher while concealing that something until I was ready.

Threads joined my star- and stone-bound dream to Egyptian mythology and the age-old mysteries of reincarnation, resurrection, and an afterlife. I found the surface of my questions about my own microscopic existence still unscratched – even though my dreams were driving me on.

This was the first of many links. Threads spun out to the reaches of consciousness and beyond. They joined topics of human discovery and learning with mysteries people have pondered through the ages. And they became so all encompassing that I had to relate them.

With such connections is life's tapestry bound.

PART ONE

∾

LOOSE THREADS

CHAPTER ONE

BEGINNINGS

Relax. Stop wondering what it is all 'about'—like
many strange and familiar things, Life included,"
the story "isn't 'about,' it simply is … Don't try
to understand it. Let it try to understand you.

ee cummings

My dreams had been gently sleeping, awaiting the moment of triggering. Remembrances I was never aware of were overlain with messages seeming to come from a faraway place.

While I began keeping dream journals in my middle years, my experience of vivid dreaming goes back to my childhood.

When I was a little girl, staring up at the starry skies, I was fascinated by the ever-changing night, the stillness of the blinking constellations, the drifting of the clouds – there one moment, gone the next. I soon learned that I would never see the same patterns twice, though it was always the same sky. Dreams and stars, both made of matter so tightly condensed and so brilliantly complex, were a source of never-ending wonderment to me. They overwhelmed me, filling me with a curiosity I couldn't explain.

I remembered most of my dreams, but when I went to relate them, I soon learned there were few that anyone would listen to. As I grew older and looked skyward, I would imagine my rose-tinted dreams stretching endlessly across the heavens. My yearnings grew deeper. What if my dreams knew secrets that would change my life? What if I found out I was one of those stone people in my starlit dream? How would I ever know?

Through the years, I would occasionally see therapists. They half listened to my dreams, but mostly brushed them aside. When they did respond, their explanations were pat and unsatisfying. I knew there were connections between the planes of waking and sleeping that they didn't acknowledge. I'd seen a few. But I couldn't grasp the significance.

Footnotes contain dream dates and references to prior pages where the dream appeared.
Endnotes contain bibliographical references, are marked with "Ɛ" in the text, and appear at the end of the book.

Finally, in an unforgettably bleak phase of my life, living in a marriage where my only consolation was solitude, I began to delve deeper into these messages of the night. I thought that by trying to connect the myriad fragments of my dreams, I could find order and understanding. I thought if I put it all on paper, someone – perhaps even I – would finally hear and make sense of them.

My journals became a record of words and images, past, present, and future, which, often through startling juxtapositions of night and day, began to reveal truths that I, with my limited formal schooling, had no way to know. It became, at one and the same time, both a puzzle and the puzzle's key. My tentative exploration gained momentum, carrying me inexorably – evermore persuasively – to conclusions for which my waking life had never prepared me. The sorting began.

There were images that kept repeating themselves. By their frequent presence, they took center stage in my pondering. Somehow, I believed, they were the keys to meaning. I learned that, among those who study such things, these are known as "dream repetitions." I learned scientists had labeled many of these things I had experienced: "hidden stories," "ghosts," "dream narratives," "companion symbols," "metaphoric correspondences," "naturalistic observations." They used words like "interconnecting," "interweaving," "thin boundaries," "thick boundaries." The glossary went on. Dreams, I found, had become my field of interest while I was, literally, out in the field – dreaming.

Repetition – which otherwise might have been lost – encouraged a curious linkage as I paged back through the bevy of dream movies in the earliest pages of my journals.

> *A girl finds a hole in the sand, filled with human excrement next to which is artwork. She brings a strainer, a scraper, and various other aids, and gets most of the waste out.*[3]

> *The same girl comes up from an underground community, a utopian society where the air is pure, everything functions well, and everyone loves each other. In this idyllic place, conveyer belts carry gifts....*[4]

> *The girl comes up from the sand carrying very heavy things on a videotape. There is a sense of a hole being in the wrong place. She has a chair around her....*[5]

> *The girl climbs down into a hole. After a while, I can hardly see her but then I appear and am trying to hold down an umbrella with no top. I have only a*

---

3   10/12/92.
4   8/2/93.
5   9/28/93.

pole. The wind is blowing. Why, I'm asking, do I always have to anchor things down....[6]

Perplexing. As isolated pieces spread over two years, the dream images hadn't had the same bite as when I looked at them as a compilation. It struck me that the girl consistently passes through the Earth's surface, generally emerging; in the Earth there's always a hole.

What if the hole was a black hole from which only mangled information can escape? What if the hole was the black hole of the psyche[ε1] and it contained my own personal universe? What if the hole meant I was always in the hole, unable to emerge?

The fourth of these dreams – the one with the pole – was far and away the most seductive. The inscrutable pole. It was a deeply held mystery from which I couldn't shake loose, a mystery rooted in a photograph taken when I was a child. Though I was intent on finding the meaning hidden in the photo, it was often obscured by the ever-expanding roster of dream clips.

This theme of things being underground was appearing in my dreams in another way – in references to Macy's, the famous department store, once only associated with New York City. Macy's Cellar is a large emporium also known as Macy's basement. Dreams of Macy's basement pointed to two themes: one *a landscape and rocks from another time[7]*; the other embedded in multiple images of *crossing over, children coming from the other side, a subway, a crosstown street.[8]*

I was captivated by my subterranean dreams of unidentified openings, drawing me, so it seemed, to something underneath, something out of sight, something deeper with deeper meaning waiting to be discovered.

I faced my perception of the pole time and again, coming up blank. It was merely a pole. There was no other relationship at that time.

Many recurring dream images baffled me.

There were the roses. In my dreams, someone seemed to be sending them to me on a fairly regular basis. Sometimes they were by themselves, sometimes in bouquets with varieties of other flowers. In bouquets they seemed, somehow, less mysterious.

One night, my dream carried a string of strange messages, one of which would later reveal itself.

There are two attaché cases. Each has a lock: one a conventional lock, the other a combination. I didn't have the combination to unlock the second, nor the key for the first. The greatest adversary in

---

6   11/1/94.
7   11/26/97.
8   1/28/00, 8/26/99, 2/11/99.

my waking life at that time tells me the combination is "AVERS." I have no idea what that means. He says, "You'll know the real one someday."[9]

At odds with the suspenseful augury for "someday," and unable to connect *"AVERS"* with anything, my mind placed the dream aside as soon as I inscribed it in my journal. It would be three years before, as I searched for something else, that I'd come upon an Avens plant, a member of the Rose family. Memory of that dream returned, meshing Avens with those countless dream gifts. Avens. Not Avers. When I started to follow the image of a rose, the accuracy of the dream prediction became clear.

Avens was the "real one" – a key which would help me decode the message. But the combination was still missing.

The incorrect word drew my attention; a funny little habit the dream speller seemed to delight in. Often a word would appear, seeming so out of place, so strange, even wrong. Yet by the time it appeared again it was newly garbed and casting new focus on the "error" that it seemed to represent before.

Threaded in with the discovery of the Rose family was a lone leaf that had landed on the porch of my dreams, as if blown there by a gusty wind. In the early days, the image, buried deep in my dream story, was simply a profile of a leaf. With the gentle passage of time, it began to take on form until it finally matured to a complete leaf, stem and all. It was like a precious blossom hidden in the undergrowth, and I never knew where or when it might turn up. In retrospect, the gradual definition of the leaf was a good measure against which to gauge my progress in the unearthing of priceless dream nuggets.

During this sylvan interlude, I found a dream in which *a maple-leaf coin is buried deep in my purse. It is one of two, both silver with gold braided trim, and each bearing a nativity scene.*[10] This dream symbol hinted at Canada, the maple leaf, a well-recognized emblem of that nation since the 1700s and prominently centered on the Canadian national flag.

A short while later, another sylvan sequence depicted *evergreen trees against a pink background.*[11] The first flag to represent Newfoundland, I would discover, bore a green fir tree on a pink field. It was used in the early nineteenth century.

Aaah ....

The list of recurring images was growing, some with meanings; some still without. We had now the Pole, the Rose, Canada, Newfoundland – an odd medley to be sure.

At least I knew Newfoundland and Canada were in the same family.

---

9   12/9/95.
10   11/10/93.
11   3/1/94.

The profusion of dream blossoms continued, with pop-up flowers and plants. And they were not alone. My dreams showered me with metals – wrought iron in particular. There were repeated waves of black and white, of orange and yellow – the yellow taking on the doggedly stubborn symbol of a yellow slab. Its pale yellow hue was especially insistent.

Like Avens, with its mystery combination and its cryptic "You'll know the real one someday," the first Yellow Slab dream was the bearer of an equally mystifying message … *"Be patient. You will learn everything you need to know."* Other yellow slab dreams tagged along appearing to corroborate.[12]

There were dream images of *plates, walls, and sheets, echoes of things matching, spinning metals.*

There was lots of silver: *A silver key, silver platters, plates, bowls, and the like.* First among these was a dream of *a silver key that snaps in half and is put back together again.*[13]

Another category of images arrived in a flood of water dreams: *Strong tides, capsizing, pulling in rafts, going over waterfalls.* These I initially eliminated from my mystery, feeling they belonged to an emotional aspect of my waking life at the time, which explained them away. The more concrete images seemed to vie for center stage.

The color pink was ever present, managing to leave its mark wherever it could, but *the color Lavender* took first prize for most confusing entry in the palette. It masqueraded in an eclectic wardrobe of costumes, changing at every opportunity. Beginning as purple, it quickly mutated to Lavender attaching itself to unrelated icons from *paintings and goblets, to a blanket, a bicycle, a camera, a flash of light, an X-ray apron, a pair of heels, a chair, even eyeliner.*[14] Lavender covered everything, but its all-time favorite was *suede.*

After years of confusion as to why the amenities of home were so prevalent in my dreams, I finally discovered that *mattresses, pillows, sheets, plates, and bowls*[15] were taking on a definitively non-homey purpose, one rooted in geology. At the time they appeared, I wouldn't have known the difference between a dinner plate and a tectonic plate, so it appears that the royal tribunal of dream magistrates knew what they were doing, presenting me with icons I would recognize, and trusting that I would eventually connect the icons to their messages.

Armed with nothing but a stubborn streak and a strong sense of curiosity, I traipsed through this vast metaphorical campus without a guide for what seemed an eternity. Yet campuses have teachers and, eventually, some remarkably distinguished luminaries arrived on the doorstep of my dreams, completely unannounced and unexpected. I could

12 2/10/95, 9/19/97, 6/20/02.
13 9/22/93.
14 Lavender dreams: 1993–2007.
15 Bedding/dishware dreams: 1993–2005.

not understand how or why such superstars were interested in me, Penelope Peacock, an ordinary person from an average background.

Claudius Galen, prominent second-century physician, rang the doorbell first. Soon after, there arrived the notable Claudius Ptolemy who lived in Alexandria from around 85 to 165 AD and was known for his astronomical and optical contributions. The two Claudiuses were joined before long by Nicolaus Steno, seventeenth-century Danish founder of modern Geology and the first to explain the structure of the earth's crust.

The last person of such renown to join my nocturnal group of dream-tellers was the eminent Marie Curie, Nobel-prize winner for Physics (1903) and Chemistry (1911), the first woman to receive a Nobel Prize and the first person ever to be awarded this honor twice. She was also the first female lecturer and professor at the Sorbonne.

It was a virtual "open house" of unprecedented influence. What prestigious company I was in, but I couldn't help but wonder why.

The party grew to include dearly departed loved ones who had apparently been promoted to an ethereal court where their spiritual energy was now in the company of such distinguished contributors to humankind's understanding of our world. They arrived at random times, there being, I suppose, no clocks in Heaven. We will learn more when they join our story, but to the illustrious coterie were added Agneswiseheart, my beloved aunt and seer; Peggymoonbeam, my best friend and confidante; Charlesbigstar, my dear friend and astrologer. They guided me through my journey, and are among those who ghost my words.

As the teachers arrived, so, too, arrived more mysteries. One of particular note appeared one night as I stumbled around the dream campus looking for a class. I bumped into what appeared to be the cloudy traces of a shipwreck – the elegant 46,000 ton lady who met her tragic end on April 14, 1912, known then and still as H.M.S. Titanic. Now what could she possibly have to do with any of this?

My nighttime sojourns were so full they had no choice but to overflow into my waking world: Pole and Rose, Canada and Newfoundland, Yellow Slab and Silver Key, Lavender and Pink, along with a host of notable contributors to the development of humankind – and the Titanic?

This bewildering array of elements and celebrated persona could win a Nobel prize for chaos. I thought about jigsaw puzzles where the picture on the box reassuringly guides us through the maze. But the big picture in this story was buried among too many puzzle pieces to count. All I had was the growing belief that, somewhere and somehow, these jillions of pieces would someday come together. I knew a solution would eventually appear because the connections gradually grew, but the particulars of who, when, where, and what seemed largely held in a state of suspense.

Time was random. While it had become 1998, the dream image of the Yellow Slab had been hanging around since 1995, and I still didn't get its role. What I did get was the notion of suspense. When suspense becomes a way of life, it quite literally suspends all worries and disbelief, for in acceptance of the unexpected, we acknowledge that everything is possible.

It was, indeed, chaos. How could the pieces of this hodgepodge, this amalgam, align to become a unified vision?

Probably most astonishing is that during my years of intense dream exploration I never once questioned my sanity. I believed, for some strange reason, that my senses were intact and eventually the pieces would all commingle. To reach the destination, I knew, would require the willing suspension of disbelief. After all, dreams are the language of images and images are revelatory. They show us all we need to know. "Trust" is indelibly imprinted on every symbol.

With each symbol being a clue, one by one, in their own subtle way, they focused me on my endless dream associations. They prompted me to study and research on my own. At least, I thought I was alone with my computer as I wrestled with this gigantic puzzle. That is, until my mentors came to the rescue, sending mysterious electronic messages to my computer by day as well as baring their identities in my dreams by night. As associations began to gel, so did the contributions of each of the mentors. Their fuzzy appearances became clearer as I began to understand that the messages in my dreams were gifts pointing me toward new insights and explorations.

I didn't know until later that even the tiniest of symbols were gifts of Truth from my mentors. It would prove to be so – that the best things come in small packages.

CHAPTER TWO

SEARCHING

The deeper that sorrow carves into your
being, the more joy you can contain. Is not
the cup that holds your wine the very cup
that was burned in the potter's oven?
Kahlil Gibran

As your escort on this wild ride through the cosmos, I thought I'd tell you a little bit about me and what led to this unimaginable adventure. Talking about me has never been easy, but here goes ….

From the time I was seven years old, when I wasn't being a girly-girl dragging my Raggedy Ann doll with her sugar heart around with me everywhere, I was a tomboy climbing trees. At night, I'd sit for hours on the front lawn of my house in Coral Gables, Florida, wondering about God, Life and the Universe and how it all worked.

In this sleepy Spanish village and burgeoning upper-income neighborhood, my middle-class family occupied an ordinary ranch house. Keeping up with the Joneses was the theme.

I wondered what went on inside the Jones's house. In our house, a series of emotionally fraught operas were being performed nightly. As a child, I had been forced to accept a season's pass to this timeless drama where the characters invented and reinvented themselves with their every performance. Attendance was mandatory and there was no intermission or break other than when I could quietly sneak away.

I learned the nuances of family mediation at an early age. After my beloved father passed away, I inherited his role of peace-keeper between the battling wills of my mother and my little brother. A plate of scrambled eggs too well done was enough to stir up a Category 5 hurricane. To escape the clamor, I took to lawn sitting. This became a nightly ritual, consisting of gazing up at the sky repeating, "Star light, star bright, first star I see tonight …"

Footnotes contain dream dates and references to prior pages where the dream appeared.

Endnotes contain bibliographical references, are marked with "Ɛ" in the text, and appear at the end of the book.

Before finding the galaxies to converse with, I had talked to Bonnie, my Scottie dog, who was my constant companion, along with Raggedy, ever by my side. But Bonnie died when I was seven and I mourned her death for a very long time. I always thought she died of a broken heart because she was left up north when we moved to Florida. I cried for her every night and prayed she would magically reappear one day. Now Raggedy and I were on our own. There were times when I wished my little rag doll with her wrinkled knees and button eyes would come alive so I could talk to her the way I had talked to Bonnie. Then, one night I looked up at the Milky Way and realized I could talk to my precious doggie by sitting right there on my lawn. Just thinking of her wet little snout nuzzled up against me seemed to connect us and helped insulate me from the drama. I would never forget when I was miserable and scared and crying my heart out, how Bonnie would whimper, letting out her little doggie yelps, crying right along with me and licking my tears dry. I think she also liked the salt.

It didn't matter that Bonnie didn't answer with a bark; I knew she was there. All I had to do was to look up. One thing I knew I could always see anywhere were the stars.

A childhood memory that hardened like cement is the church that was next door to where we lived. Parking space for the growing congregation was at a premium then, so the spillover of churchgoers would park their cars right across from our house, the headlights angled directly at my bedroom window. At the end of every Saturday evening service, the spiritually restored worshipers came out to get their cars – all at once. It was an original sound and light show, Coral Gables style: first, the yakkety-yak of the car owners, then the roar of their ignitions and, finally, the blazing beams of fifty or so car lights flashing directly into my eyes. As I tossed and turned myself back to sleep, I was ever grateful for the week's reprieve until the next Saturday night.

As the sole survivor of those overwrought evenings, I made a pilgrimage several years ago to my old homestead to check out the persisting memories of being blinded by the light and awaking to the thunderous fifty-gun salute of the blasting engines. The jarring effect of that Saturday night countdown is forever imprinted in my brain and may have sparked the chorus of light and vision dreams that would perform in my sleep decades later. To my surprise, my house had been swallowed up by the church much as Jonah was swallowed by the whale. It had literally been annexed to and subsumed into the house of worship. The addition was so seamless that, unless you happened to have lived there, you would never know it was once the stage where a family of four played out its version of Elektra, revealing tragic flaws, unrelenting static and high drama that in childhood served me poorly (though in adulthood, well).

What had become of my bedroom – the place in which my childhood dreams came and went? Was it part of the chapel? Was it a lavatory? A pulpit? A ... what? Where had all the histrionics gone?

My house was no more; the uproar mute. Its memory-filled space had been occupied by an infinitely more harmonious and gentler strain of music. Yesterday's truths had become today's legends. So, I realized, everything does pass; nothing remains the same. Except, of course, for childhood memories, like the lights and my deep love for Raggedy Ann even after her eyes fell off and her clothes were in shreds. I had stopped talking to my mother for a good long time after I discovered my battered little whimsical pal with her happy face was thrown out like a piece of garbage. I retrieved her instantly; life was always sweeter when Raggedy was around.

Down the street, just biking distance from my house, was the old University of Miami campus, built like a Spanish fortress. For reasons that would remain obscure for most of my life, it had held a great fascination for me when I was ten. When the coast was clear — that is, when the grown-ups were nowhere in sight — I'd sneak away on my bicycle and peddle like mad to the mysterious yellowish stuccoed buildings. Secretly, I'd inspect the hallowed campus, a landmark that held an oracle I could not yet know. One day I was brazen enough to extend my tour and venture above ground floor to higher reaches. When I reached the floor of the psych department, I spotted a display case that housed brains floating in formaldehyde in different-sized jars. I noticed that the brains, themselves, came in different sizes and slightly different color variations. Well, that made sense. So do we.

I could not visit them enough. I'd stand and stare at these specimens for hours, almost as though waiting for them to talk to me. I wondered whom they once belonged to and what they once thought and why they were in these jars to begin with. Did their owners tell their families to put their brains in a jar or were these brains of people who died in car accidents or airplane wrecks that no one could identify? It was too weird seeing these disembodied people in jars. At that age, I somehow had the feeling they were the only really important part of the people to whom they once belonged, and that a part of this part was still alive. I knew it to be so, but couldn't explain it for the life of me. It was my deepest and most fervent wish to get to the bottom of this mystery before I, myself, went into a jar.

When I would return home, habitually late, from these cerebral excursions, I was routinely questioned about where I'd had been. I offered the pat response, "Oh, just out playing." But, as the visits became more frequent, I became gutsier, answering boldly, "Oh! To visit the brains." I really wanted to be found out. Looking back, I find it bizarre that no one ever questioned me. I wondered if the brain acts independently of the soul or if the brain dies and the soul lives. For some reason I've always thought that the soul has a memory; that some thinking, feeling, remembering part of us will continue. To this day, I find, most people tend to shy away from the subject of what becomes of our soul, the most important part of our being.

Entering adulthood in the '50s, I was expected to get married, raise a family, and have children. Eager to leave behind the clashing tempers and strident underpinnings of home, I married at nineteen, while at college. Finding it difficult to concentrate on my own studies, I left school after two years, shortly before I turned twenty, to follow my husband's educational goals to New York.

It would be many years before I left behind all effort to meet expectations, even though my hopes for a lasting marriage were dashed too soon. By the time I was twenty-one, I found myself changing my status on job applications from married to divorced.

But even as the '60s were beginning and I was making it as a working girl on my own, I wholeheartedly tried to conform to the '50s ethos, where the modus vivendi was dictated by the social immediacy of motherhood. It was a familiar prescription then. In many cases for young women college age or under – certainly in mine – it eclipsed the desire to advance through institutes of higher learning. The cookie-cutter Ozzie-and-Harriet, live-happily-ever-after family was carved in the expectations and activities of one's family and friends: birthing alternate genders (a boy, a girl, a boy) and acquiring the sought-after treasures of the day (a house in the suburbs, a white station wagon, a Dalmatian). What would become of me if I didn't conform? Would I be banished? Worse things could happen, but what about my friends? Would my popularity wane? Would I be branded a misfit? Would I be forever homeless and wandering? Scary thoughts.

By the early '60s, after two years of college, I plunged headlong into the madcap world of Madison Avenue, where stables of gifted writers were called on to create slogans and jingles for consumers whose lives would not be worth living without their products. The air burst with creative juices from which flowed a continuous stream of irresistible commodities. It was fun, actually heady at times, to be part of the fast-moving, fast-talking, fast-thinking advertising circles where the public's most private needs were anticipated long before they existed.

The veneer of advertising abracadabra soon wore thin. It was another bewitching dream you could buy into to live happily ever after. But if you dared to question all that was cleverly crafted as the norm, you were excluded. I loved magic, and advertising gave us the magic formulas for ultimate wish fulfillment, but for some reason they weren't fulfilling my wishes.

The crosscurrents of career building carried me from advertising to educational publishing. As the '70s rolled on, I revisited the hope that I'd have at least one of those prescribed children. Despite my time in the world of myth building, as a victim of the '50s my yearnings for motherhood overshadowed all else. I remarried with the promise of a bouncing baby in my crystal ball, but the other side of the looking glass reflected the all-too-familiar gloom of divorce.

I moved robotically through the repetitive and monotonous haze of legalities. I signed separation papers and an hour later presided over a meeting at work. Somehow, I pulled off the meeting, although I couldn't tell you five minutes later what had transpired. That night at home, I wailed and sobbed, mourning my lost motherhood. My body shook and rocked for hours as though in the throes of a religious rite. I beat my pillows so hard that all the feathers flew out. I sobbed and cried and cried some more for the sadness of it all. I exhausted my supply of tissues. I'd have to stop crying when I ran out of toilet paper, a fitting metaphor for what I then thought were the wasted years. I was sobered by the thought that I might have to go outside and buy more Kleenex or worse still, that my neighbors would hear the commotion next door, think someone had been beaten and they'd call the police.

When I dared to look in the mirror, I was a fright! My swollen face looked like a distorted reflection in a hubcap. My eyes were like laminated roadmaps, my overstuffed nose raw to the touch, my protruding lips, fat and deformed and, to make matters worse, all the sugar in Raggedy Ann's candy heart had dissolved; now Raggedy's sweetest body part would not be able survive any more mishaps. The "I Love You" candy hearts would be no more. This was not one of my better days.

This flood of tears, in cold storage for decades, assured me I would never again cry for what wasn't to be, for there were simply no tears left. Once more, the unknown powers hadn't seen fit to fulfill this piece of my fantasy. Disheartened by the stark reality that the biological part of my journey was over, I was ever so grateful for my career.

By the '80s, publishing merged with media. I was drawn into the black granite cavern popularly known as Black Rock, home of CBS Television, where a staff of notably talented magicians, aerialists, and jugglers performed the art of selling without seeming to be selling. I joined the media powerhouse, feeling privileged to have been selected. I soon learned that behind this magic curtain was a well-oiled machine that increased its speed and efficiency by cleverly convincing the troops that hard work equals glamour and prestige.

The image of the CBS Eye, imprinted on everything from the building's exterior to the letter openers, was tattooed on my cortex. Broadcasting's version of Cyclops followed me around like the eyes of the Mona Lisa, appearing years later in dreams about vision. Just imagine, dear Reader, what the power of a single image can do. The CBS Eye was an early insight into how far beyond a brand the magic of identification extends.

It was gratifying to be a member of this elite club known in the trade as the Tiffany of networks. CBS was the most exacting of the training grounds I'd experienced – a media boot camp that taught me discipline, forbearance, organization, teamwork and other basic survival techniques for corporate combat. Although training was rigorous, it was also morale building. Of the diverse exercises in basic training, working toward a common goal was the most defining. I was named drill commander to the corporate unit assigned me. Somehow, the concept of teamwork flashed back to my childhood.

Growing up as the only girl on the block, I was privileged to have been admitted to the all-boy's world of tree-climbing, baseball and, even, the game of War. The ultimate acceptance as an insider was when one of my buddies lent me his toy six-shooter and another one crowned me with his plastic army helmet to protect myself from the invisible "enemy." That measure of true love followed me through life. I dreaded the day when my tomboy cover was blown and the neighborhood rapscallions would discover I was a rare species, genus: Girl girl. I was gaga over baseball and the coveted position of shortstop.

My hidden girlish identity swelled in early adolescence and was fully exposed when I joined the Girl Scouts, placing my baseball career in instant jeopardy. I loved the Girl Scout cookies and waited on pins and needles for the yearly sale. Regrettably, the delicious morsels wound up in my stomach and I had no proceeds to report to the local chapter. I had to face the harsh reality that I'd never be a Girl Scout cookie entrepreneur, but somehow I compensated by earning a respectable collection of badges. The enduring principles and goals of the Girl Scout Promise opened my eyes to the value of teamwork and community service. Most instructive was our motto "Be Prepared."

On CBS's corporate playing field, I was on first base hoping to score a run by introducing a new strategy for developing team spirit. I got the idea to periodically rotate each player to a different position to learn its functions and goals. My brainchild was met with so much grousing you'd think these teammates were being led to the guillotine. Ultimately, it was a "win-win, which convinced me that it takes all the parts to make a whole – and to make it run well. This team experience drew on my early days as shortstop, catching pop-ups in the infield and as a Girl Scout, camping in the outfield. Be it the corporate ball field, the baseball field or the field of nature, the dynamics of team spirit would unexpectedly reappear in the field of dreams.

The '80s were topsy-turvy. The still warring factions in my family demanded my time and energy. Cosmic interference reached its peak. I would fall madly in love and it would prove to be a hopelessly impossible liaison. My apartment was in the highest decibel level area in New York City. Sleep was difficult. Between the late-night whistle calls for taxis from the transvestite club next door and the 5:00 a.m. garbage grinders chewing up the day's leavings, my dream cycle went retrograde. Putting in twelve-hour days on the CBS playing field, I was on the verge of burnout.

Accomplishment and roadblocks, hope and fear, the '50s and the '80s, stasis and change dating back to … when? What a mix of signals and messages! What confusion! Overwhelming? I had yet to meet my guides for I was still lost in the quagmire of life's ironies and could only muddle through the muck in some pretty flimsy footwear.

I had learned mental fitness along with corporate courtesy, but I tired of the "drill." Yet, it proved true that training is a mildly traumatic experience that produces a bond of shared experience, for it was at Camp CBS that I made friends who would last a lifetime, including one who is instrumental in guiding this journey.

After twenty-plus years, I'd graduated boot camp and decided to retire my corporate uniform. It took a real feat of magic for me to wiggle out of that seductive lair but I could draw on the tricks of illusion from the best of them. I knew I would move on to yet another school, though I had no idea in what field or what the course requirements were.

Corporate careers had painted my life's canvas with varied and colorful insights. I'd had a front-row seat in the creative laboratories of terrestrial magic-making. For three decades, I had watched the prestidigitators perform their sleight of hand, but when the tricks were over, what followed? More daring acts? More sophisticated magic? More consumer flimflam?

I continued to search for that inexplicable something that would dispel the confusion in the mixed messages and feelings. Perhaps it was a real rabbit in a real hat I sought. Although my acceptance of destiny prevailed, from time to time, a plaintive tune stirred memories of neither having children, nor finishing school, and that would smart. Having unconsciously enlisted in a survival course from birth forward I had, through the years, become more aware of the survival of the species and how we all go through this drill together, in one way or another. Holding my souvenir ticket from the land of illusion, I realized that an advanced magician would know how to extricate himself from the handcuffs that bind him, and that if he could find the real magic, he could escape from any locked container. (Starting with the word "ticket," the color changed "from black to pale blue to lavender involuntarily, the first of a string of intermittent surprises. In time, I came to realize that a creative and simpatico computer word painter had become a helping hand.) I later learned that lavender is called blue magic and is said to be ruled by Mercury, the great communicator.

Though I'd not yet begun serious journaling, from time to time, I would jot down a dream, puzzle over it, and file it away. I still longed for the answer to the mystery of dreaming. Then on one perfectly uneventful day in the fall of '92, I heard of a Dr. Noodle who was exceptionally skilled in the practice of dream interpretation. I couldn't wait to make an appointment. I arrived at his Manhattan apartment on October 14, 1992, for the first time and was surprised to find an open door with a sign on it that read "Come In." In the foyer sat a statue of Buddha, with his big belly and his beneficent smile, welcoming all mortals in search of Truth.

Dr. Noodle was a jovial man with a serene smile of his own and with whom I felt very much at home. I trusted him as he trusted those who entered his private sanctuary of dreams. Dr. Noodle also had a round tummy (he was reputed to be very wise and enlightened, like Buddha). I wondered if I studied with him long enough and let my stomach grow big enough if I too might gain some wisdom.

He extended his hand. "I'm Dr. Noodle and I take it you are Penelope Peacock." I nodded shyly and shook his hand. He then led me into his inner chambers and motioned to me to sit down. Tilting back in his big doctor's armchair, his hands forming a church that rested on his belly, he said, "So what brings you here today?"

"All my life I've been wondering about my dreams, Dr. Noodle, and I would like to understand what they mean. I have a feeling they're important."

He talked a lot about dream images being glyphs and explained that the pictorial symbols and words in our dreams tell a story, something like the Egyptian hieroglyphics. I said that I'd had so many dreams I didn't know what to do with them. Upon hearing this, he broke into an enormous grin and with great fervor began guiding me toward my first assignment. The air was tingling with excitement but I couldn't quite put my finger on why.

"Now, Penelope, to learn what all of this means, you must begin by recording your dreams. First, draw a vertical line down the center of an unlined page. Then record the dialogue on the left side and illustrate the dream on the right side."

"Illustrate? I can't draw."

"Oh, just stick figures will do."

"Dr. Noodle, I can't even make a stick figure lie down. I will write the dream but I really can't draw it."

"Just do it," he insisted, showing me to the door. He beamed a knowing grin and shook my hand. "You won't be sorry. I'll see you next week."

I left his office in a daze. That one short scene plays across the moving pictures in my memory to this day.

The dreams that followed were so revealing. They were mostly about healing.

In one of those dreams, *music is playing that I don't recognize. It's music from a younger generation. I hear two whispers in my ear. Someone is whispering my name and the words "Healing Power."*[16] In another, more mysterious dream, *I'm having a biopsy. There are black pieces of X-ray paper stuck to a piece of cardboard. One small piece keeps coming off. I have glue, but it isn't the right glue.*[17]

My little dream pictures were like the storyboards used in advertising in the '60s to depict the action and scenes in television commercials; the audio on one side, the corresponding video on the other.

As I wondered about the *X-ray paper*, it came to me that dreams are photographs we take without knowing.

While studying with Dr. Noodle, I had a dream in which *he handed me a piece of bark from a tree. It had a name that sounded Greek. I think this was good luck.*[18] I later learned that the Greek term for "tree bark" is cortex and so, like a learned mentor, my dream had introduced me to the cerebral cortex, which would lead me to study the visual cortex.

Dr. Noodle and I met several times before I moved on, unknowingly in search of other tutors. I had learned the basics and would unconsciously take my entrance exams in a celestial school of higher education where I would major in the field of dreams. The prerequisites were trust in one's intuition and a desire to decipher the secret metaphors embedded in our dreams.

----

16   11/2/92.
17   10/19/92.
18   2/24/93.

In December 1993, I decided, again, to marry, this surely for the last time. I had taken a short trip to Copenhagen. While at a social gathering crammed with an international crowd of partygoers, I sensed someone's eyes on me from across the crowded room. It felt flattering, yet strangely disquieting. The piercing stare belonged to a devastatingly handsome diplomatic attaché. It was love at first sight. Soon after, I would move to Copenhagen, where I envisioned, finally, living my '50s fantasy marriage, complete with the white picket fence in the fairy-tale land of Hans Christian Andersen.

Fooled again by the remains of my early yearnings, or by the hand of fate, I was to register this matrimonial adventure as yet another disappointment. The dream of love at first sight and living happily ever after was abruptly dashed, for my dream man morphed into another person overnight.

Animals are sensitive to being looked at by people. This is perhaps the evolutionary result of predator-prey relationships. An animal that sensed an unseen predator staring would stand a better chance of surviving than an animal without this sense.

Delving into my nightly revelations opened the door to consciousness during my darkest days in Copenhagen. Signs of a collision course had repeatedly crashed into my dreams, but I had casually dismissed them. Having suffered through the shock and trauma of marrying a total stranger, I finally got it! My higher consciousness was the victor and I had no choice but to surrender.

I began to search my dreams purposefully, determined to understand why I sensed the gaze but overlooked the danger. This time, the delusion had a life-changing twist. I could not yet know that a higher purpose was being written.

Where should my search begin? From the beginning, they always say, though after a while I discovered that it's hard to pinpoint where the beginning is.

Serious excavation of my first journal uncovered amazing parallels among all the relationships in my life, beginning with my family matrix. I came to realize that I was like the cream in an Oreo, squished in between two very crunchy cookies: my mother and my brother, players in a daunting and emotionally loaded melodrama.

My every hair stood on end when, in my dreams, I recognized my husband exhibiting characteristics etched in my family template. How could that be? Was I reinventing my job as childhood mediator by attracting a personality type that fostered this repetitive dynamic?

This came as a monumental revelation, for the behaviors were so alike they were almost interchangeable. Many will yawn and ask, "What else is new?" but to someone who had lived her life in a metaphorical blind alley, it was nothing short of miraculous.

As piece after piece of my family puzzle fell into place, I fell more deeply under the spell of the Dream's profound ability to produce answers to questions I dared not ask in waking.

Thus my commitment was born. Driven to unlock the secrets in these nightly mysteries, I wholeheartedly began to record and illustrate my dreams. This was nearly every day. The little stick figures I drew, though they still wouldn't lie down, took on personalities of their own, like characters in a cartoon strip. Pictures and words. Words and pictures. The words tumbled in, one atop the other. But it was the pictures, the innocent charades in the Dream that really told the story. How would I find the words to describe a language expressed in pictures? Time would tell.

Dedication and an inexplicable perseverance hatched what is now a substantial collection of dream journals and my efforts to bring order to years of waking confusion.

One observation that took my breath away was that my waking life experiences were becoming more illusory than the dreams, which were becoming more concrete. "How ironic," I thought. "Which is real? Waking or dreaming?" A waking life relationship would in its aftermath prove to be an illusion, but the once faint outline of the Dream was pouring a foundation cast in stone.

The weaving together of strands began.

As I tried to make some sense of the chaos, two categories of dream symbols popped out immediately: Light and Seeing. They were hauntingly repetitive and shared a common reference. Actually, "Seeing" was "not" seeing, for there were repeated dreams of me not being able to see.

I was perplexed and questioned what it could be that I wasn't seeing. I assumed it was my inability to read the warning signs when making personal life decisions. I remembered one dream where *I am blinded by the headlights of a car*[19] – literally blinded by the light. Was this a replay of the Saturday night churchgoers? Were the headlights that flashed me awake for what seemed like an endless childhood, repeating in my dreams nearly fifty years later? My life was quiet now. I no longer had to contend with ignitions blasting, either inside my family of origin or outside of myself. I soon learned that quietness is a friend to vision.

My interpretation of these dreams was that I couldn't see the light, and that was true up to a point. However, a deeper purpose was revealed, one that began with a microcosm in which the singular expression of one's dreams, in some magical way, whirled far beyond, scattering its particles of thought through the macrocosm. The scope of this was unfathomable. If some mystical dream wizard granted me sight through which I could perceive everything, how would he do it? Would that be a good thing or bad?

Out of the blue, in drifted a dream in which I have two coins. *One is a dime and one a penny. I fit the dime, after some difficulty, into my left eye. The penny is an easier fit and goes into the right eye like a contact lens.*[20]

---

19   10/27/92.
20   11/13/94.

Sun. Nov. 13, 1994

I had put a penny in my right eye (like a contact lense). Then I put a dime in my left eye, but it didn't fit right away. I had to keep fiddling with it until I finally got it to stay in.

DIME 10   PENNY = 1

COPPER

I had learned from Dr. Noodle that in dream speak, left signifies past and right, future. I translated this, rating the imprint "Liberty" on the dime, as the more difficult fit since it symbolized freedom. I reasoned, "If left means past that must mean hard-won freedom from the past." The penny's engraving was embossed "In God We Trust." This would be my vision for the future, though I was not yet fully aware of its magnitude. Of course, the metals the coins are composed of had to do with the meaning as well, but I could not yet see that thread.

Why were the coins in my eyes, and why in the guise of contact lenses, which I don't wear?

How is it that we can see with our eyes shut?

Connections that might seem farfetched became possibilities in the multidimensional logic of my dreams.

CHAPTER THREE

THE POLE

One aspect of serendipity to bear in mind is that you have
to be looking for something in order to find something else.
                                                    Lawrence Block

While transiting through life's unknowable passages, I sensed, as we all do, things in my early childhood that had gone unexplained and about which I hungered for answers. In addition to the brains, one such enigma centered on a pole.

The pole in my dream resonated. It took me back to a picture I first saw when I was five or six, but which really didn't register or pique my curiosity until I was in my teens.

The picture is of me, a photo – perhaps two photos – taken when I was two. There's but one background in this picture. Is it a double exposure? Perhaps. There are two little girls, one slightly less distinct, both apparently the same person – me. The little girls are in different positions. One of my images is holding onto a pole and the other is not. Two little girls; one pole. Was the more faded image indeed mine? If not, whose?

The picture began to haunt me. What started as mild curiosity edged toward obsession.

Every few years, the picture would turn up again. I would look at it and wonder. In between, and especially as I grew older, that single pole continued to nag at me, dreaming and waking, until it pointed me toward a cavern of knowledge arcane. Or, at least, arcane to me.

Some five decades after the photo was taken, I dreamt I was going through pictures and came upon my double exposure. The dream had changed it, however, with the pole absent. *One of the girls had become me as a baby and the other was my niece* who often is a dream characterization of a younger me. *I am holding the picture and a corner of it suddenly catches fire. My heart is racing because I'm afraid the fire will catch my niece's hair and, even though it's just a picture, she will be hurt. Without warning and just as suddenly as the fire began, it ends.*

Footnotes contain dream dates and references to prior pages where the dream appeared.

Endnotes contain bibliographical references, are marked with "Ɛ" in the text, and appear at the end of the book.

I awakened for a minute knowing this was a significant dream. The photo catching on fire by itself really scared me. I fell back asleep and dreamt a new gentler scenario about *a hollowed-out book.*[21] As the morning light forced me awake. I reached for a pencil and warily drew the image of a flame at the corner of the picture.

The flame jarred my memory of the actual twin image. I knew I had to take it to someone who could explain the mechanics of a double exposure. I found, as I showed it to a variety of photographers, that the answer depends on whom you talk to. The opinions ranged from "The film must have slipped. It's a double image" to "That's impossible. It can't be a double image" because of missing elements against the same background.

Spiritually attuned individuals and those of the Kirlian school of photography, known for capturing auras on film, negated the double image theory, postulating the second image as the semblance of a guardian angel. Others pondered the aura of a twin sister who might never have made it through the birth canal but was somehow revealed in the photograph. I'd heard about the vanishing twin syndrome and wondered if I might be a surviving twin.

I was born three months early weighing a little more than a pound. The odds of survival for a premature baby were slim at that time. Years later, I learned from my Aunt Belle that there were sets of twins on both my maternal grandmother's and grand-father's sides. My grandfather survived his twin brother who, while ice-skating in Russia, knocked over a crucifix by mistake, was picked up by the police and never again seen. My grandmother had a sister and brother who were twins. So the twin theory gained in plausibility even though the mystery of the photograph was still unsolved.

Since then, I've come to understand that we don't always have to have an answer to everything. What's more, we often can't get one. But amazingly enough, dear Reader, this serpentine trail on which I was embarking would eventually lead to an answer regarding the ubiquitous pole.

The specter of the two little girls in the waking photograph followed me to Copenhagen. There, I met a woman named Winnie, who had discovered a calcium sup-plement called Osforte, meaning strong bone.

When Winnie first saw me, she greeted me effusively, arms open wide, exclaiming, "I know you." I was surprised by her familiarity. Moments later, she showed me a damaged photograph of a small Indian boy kneeling before an elephant while reading a story. She shared its story. One day, while she was gazing at the picture, the noonday sun filling the room, the center of the photo suddenly caught fire. It was not consumed, but the incident left a hole in the elephant's stomach. As she was relaying this amazing story, she handed

21   9/12/93.

me the photograph so I could look more closely. When I gave it back to her, it split into two layers, and I was left holding the back, which, I noticed, was imprinted with the same image as the front. Now there were two holes in the elephant's stomach; one in the emulsion and another in the layer beneath it. I couldn't understand what I had done to cause her treasured picture to come apart.

I flashed back to my powerful dream of the *photograph that suddenly caught fire* and to my image of the two little girls who were only one. The connection startled me. "Why," I wondered, "did Winnie's photograph of the elephant also suddenly catch fire, and why did it now produce two elephants?" It crossed my mind that I had always used the expression "I'm just beside myself" when I felt anxious or excited, scared or elated.

The elephant picture (personifying memory) rekindled my already gnawing curiosity about the double image and led to the pairing of memory and vision threads. Who was that child next to me who looked just like me? Was it literally me beside myself? Why did the sudden outbreak of a fire occur twice – once while sleeping, once while waking – and relate to a double image each time?

Later that same day, I shared with Winnie a dream account in which I'd drawn some *pastel colored plastic keys*.[22] Looking at my drawing of the dream she shrieked, "Penelope! The keys are femurs!!" And that's exactly how I had unknowingly illustrated them. This unexpected interpretation would prove to have great meaning in the future.

After I left Winnie, I turned the mystifying puzzle of the double image over and over and, that night, before I fell off the concrete ledge of day into the deep abyss of sleep, my last conscious snip of thought was …" Fire is a supernatural force."

The sequel to the burning picture dream produced a new set of images with a cryptic message about a book. *There's a cork and the bottom of a branch in a hollowed-out book. Someone is giving me detailed instructions about finding the yellow lexicon, and the name Ramos keeps repeating. Jacqueline Onassis also appears.*[23]

The mysterious Ramos message lingered in the back of my mind for years while my only conscious link to Jackie O was that we were born on the same day, July 28. I flashed back to her marriage to Aristotle Onassis, the shipping magnate. Would this have any meaning, I wondered.

On my birthday in 1999, six years after my experience with Winnie's photograph that became two, I awakened at seven in the morning, compelled to jot down a thought that had come to me. I searched for something to write on. The only thing around was a small paper bag from a greeting card store. The message was:

---

22   10/15/92.
23   9/12/93.

July 28, 1999

Life's experience departs with the enteric soul. This may be called enteric
memory as it returns to Earth when the soul once again is physicalized.
It then becomes cellular memory and resides within the visual cortex,
which is activated by the visual reminders of past lifetimes.

I shared this message with a dear friend who asked, "What does enteric mean?"

I answered, "I don't know." She looked it up in her dictionary and read me the
definition:

"Enteric – relating to, or occurring in the intestines. -origin early nineteenth century:
from Greek enterikos, from enteron 'intestine.'"

I dug a little deeper and found there actually is an enteric nervous system embedded
in the lining of the gastrointestinal system. When I read that sensory neurons have cell
bodies in the gut wall, I couldn't believe that the word "enteric" came to me unknowingly.

"Hmm," I thought. "It's our gut feeling. It's instinct – a knowing without learning."

Pieces of the mosaic were coming together, and to life.

The enteric-gut connection returned me to a revelation I'd had about Winnie's
elephant picture. I had noted it in my journal:

December 9, 1997

Awakened at about 4:00 a.m. when a blinding glare brought back the
picture of Winnie's elephant, which had two holes in the stomach. I
connected that with the twins (in my photograph), the elephant with
memory, and the picture separating in two with the double image.

Is my gut telling me the double image of the elephant links in some way to the
double image of the little girls in my waking picture?'

Recorded on the same page with my elephant notes was an illustration of the dream
I'd had that night. It was about *branches coming out of my head*.[24] The drawing of me with *a
branch projecting from either side of my head* was the only image on the page. Only one other
time had I consolidated two dream entries on one page. That was when *I drew a circular
key ring with a message about the optic nerve and combined it with a dream where I was serving
people in a hospital*.[25]

Was this dream with the branches in my head, four years after the Ramos dream, a
reminder of the message about a branch in a hollowed-out book? If it was, I thought the

24   12/9/97.
25   11/11/94.

dream masters upstairs had certainly cornered the memory market. There were usually two floors in my dreams – the first and the second, the latter steering toward the domain of the unconscious – or maybe the superconscious.

I turned back to enteric. If it means gut, are we talking gut memory?

Could the question of a second image be a "key" to visual and cellular memory? If we suppress a second image, does this mean we see less optically but know more intuitively?

If instinct resides in the intestines (our gut feeling), how does it get from there to the visual cortex? Or is that too literal?

Well, this was "just the tip of the iceberg," so to speak, for a dream would soon be floating an immense tip of a long-forgotten iceberg our way. It took me back to a time when I had repeated dreams about "not seeing": dreams of my *hair being in my face*,[26] *crossing the street with blinders on*,[27] when *my dream doctor gave me a prescription for eyeglasses*.[28] As I retraced my steps back to my symbolic blindness, I traveled even further back into my childhood, when one thing I wasn't blind to was the enchantment of the star-studded heavens.

---

26   3/4/93.
27   10/29/92.
28   4/24/94.

CHAPTER FOUR

CHARLESBIGSTAR

Enchanting. Miraculous. Hypnotic. Fascinating. Such were the stars to me from the time I first focused on the night skies. They were magical for me. I was always on the lookout to learn more about them.

When I was older, I had a unique and very special relationship with a brilliant and celebrated astrologer, evidenced by the connection that has continued even after his death. He now appears in life-changing dreams as Charlesbigstar. In life, he was Charles Emerson, one of the founding fathers of the National Council for Geocosmic Research, an organization dedicated to exploring the interaction between Man and the Cosmos.

When I called him in 1987 for my first reading, he asked for my birth date and time. I said I didn't know the time. He asked me to compile a chronological list of milestones in my life so he could rectify my chart. I was skeptical but complied, mailing him the list about a week before our appointment. As luck would have it, I found my birth record with the recorded birth time before our scheduled date. I sensed he had already done the work so I chose not to call with the information.

When I arrived for my appointment, a courtly gentleman standing over six feet tall met me at the door. Bending down to shake my hand, his wide smile welcomed me in. A rare breed of thoroughbred and overgrown puppy dog, his incipient warmth eclipsed the shabby surroundings. He escorted me to his table strewn with files and astrological charts. I couldn't know then that my future would be mapped out in this impoverished little apartment with the sunlight straining to trickle through the soil- stained windows. It would be several years before Charlesbigstar would become my talisman.

I anxiously awaited his reading. His charts showed I had been born at 12:06 a.m. I gasped! I explained that I had found the birth record and showed him the note on which I'd written the birth time: 12:04 a.m. "No matter," he said. "There are two different schools of thought on time – whether at the point of separation or at the birth cry. There can be a little variance." Astrological chart rectification was one of his specialties, using the ninety-degree dial and other Uranian techniques. His readings were fascinating. I learned that my most recent past life was one of complete harmony and that I came into this life to struggle. I hung on each word of his reading as he retraced truth by truth, the

---

Footnotes contain dream dates and references to prior pages where the dream appeared.
Endnotes contain bibliographical references, are marked with "ℰ" in the text, and appear at the end of the book.

tragic flaws and reversals of what he called my "present life." As I was sinking into a black void, he immediately switched course by pointing out that I was in good company sharing the same astrological position as Abraham Lincoln. He reminded me that Lincoln's life was one of struggle, and like me, he did not complete his formal education.

He comforted me with stories of Lincoln's strength and told how he beat back marauders on the river, and fended off a gang of bullies in one of the most famous wrestling matches in history. He concluded the reading by urging me to remember the famous words from Lincoln's second inaugural address ... "With malice toward none; with charity for all..."

Charles and I soon grew close. Unfolding parallels in our lives created a deeply intimate bond. Our profoundly soulful relationship was never declared but was clearly manifest as similarities in our childhoods. We knew we shared something special, for we confronted the same challenges; we had learned the language of acceptance.

During what would be my last reading with Charles, he projected into the future, telling me there would be people around to guide me. What did he mean? He was my Gibraltar, always there with an outstretched hand and a broad fatherly shoulder to lean on. He would never abandon me. Shortly thereafter, he passed over. He left this Earth on the same day that I took my first trip to Copenhagen. That was September 19, 1992. I've always wondered if he knew he would be passing.

Devastated by the enormous loss of Charles, I flew to New York for the memorial a month later. I was one of few who wept, not yet having made the leap into the acceptance of death as a continuum of life. The lack of tears among the other mourners was not due to insufficient feeling or admiration for Charles but rather to a tacit understanding that their beloved friend and teacher had ascended to a higher plane where he had aspired to be.

I remembered his words, "The real hell is down here." I still had so much to learn.

And so, more than two years after Charles's departure, along came Charlesbigstar in a vintage dream that would one day yield knowledge beyond my wildest imaginings. He had not forsaken me.

It was on November 11, 1994. He floated in on this bewildering vehicle, much different from all the rest because it contained a medical term. It was a two-part dream about the optic nerve.

When I tried to illustrate the optic nerve, I depicted it as coming from the eye. I remembered the dreams of *not being able to see*,[29] the dream of the *penny in my eye*.[30] Had Charlesbigstar sent the optic nerve dream so it could join earlier dreams about vision? Perhaps, but this dream was qualitatively different.

---

29   See Ch. 3, The Pole, p. 27
30   See Ch. 2 – Searching, pp. 20–21

In the first part, I see an image that resembles *a circular key ring with about five straight pieces hanging from it. There's a message that the same key fits all the apartments (I think there are six), but no one knows it.*

In the second part, following the same cryptic note, *I am in a hospital serving people tea. Many of the people there have passed over. I'm happy to see them again. Charlesbigstar is there and announces that he is working on a major contribution for mankind. He mumbles something about the optic nerve. I say it is "a major breakthrough." In the end, I sadly have to leave my friends and return to a refrigerator stocked with lettuce, strawberries*[31] – things of the temporal world.

This was the first dream in which I paid a visit to the other side; it would be the first of many. Visiting with people who had passed on was an incredibly lifelike experience, so much so that I was always astounded, after one of these pilgrimages, to awaken in my own bed. The commute was swift and the impressions clearer than those of any trips I've taken on Earth. It actually took longer to go from New York to New Jersey.

It was my earliest realization that we don't have to wait to die before we can see Heaven. As time passed, my visits became profoundly richer and more frequent. Years later, when a friend looked at my drawing of the mysterious circular key ring, she commented that it looked like aboriginal art. Another connection was born. The aborigines! Their visits across? Their Dreamtime. During the Dreamtime, "ancestral spirits came to Earth and created the landforms, the animals, and plants. The stories tell how the ancestral spirits moved through the land creating rivers, lakes, and mountains. Today we know the places where the ancestral spirits have been and where they came to rest."[32] Their mythical age of the past is at the same time the present in which each individual must do what the great heroes did in the "Dreamtime."[33] Great heroes of the past? Galen and Ptolemy would fit that. "Myths are public dreams, dreams are private myths," said Joseph Campbell.

This dream of serving tea in a hospital was the harbinger that signaled what would be my frequent presence in worlds I had never before visited, ultimately launching my search for the meaning in all my dreams. Its medical connotation set it apart from previous dreams. It marked the beginning of research that would reach far beyond my own dreaming and, indeed, far beyond anything I had learned in my years to then.

To spending time chasing writings on dreams in the New York Public Library, I added hours in the various medical libraries in Manhattan. I spent days on end in the months ahead scanning their computer systems and immersed in book and magazine stacks. Following the medical hints in my dreams connected with many areas of research that verified sleeping messages and directed me back to points I had previously missed.

---

31 11/11/94.

In mid-'96, about a year and a half after that first visit to the other side, I had a dream about *a cat named Percival whose head is perched atop a woman's head. The woman is telling the cat to go away. I ask her to "listen, because the cat has something important to say."*[32]

Why would a cat in a dream have a name? I couldn't know what meaning the name "Percival" would have for me but I knew the dream was important. As for the cat, I had learned that animals represent the instinctual aspects of our nature. Thus, the feline known for its night vision, excellent memory and an aptitude for learning by observation and experience would be a fitting character to unravel the yarn of a dream. That was only one clue in hundreds. I had to decode the rest of them and try to understand why I felt so compelled to follow what appeared to be a riddle. What did Percival have on his mind?

I was lost as to where to begin or how to make these connections. It was another maiden voyage. The next time I was at the New York Public library, I began searching the World Medical computer under "Dreams." There appeared a category entitled Vision Sciences, listing a seventeen-volume work on Vision and Visual Dysfunction by B. Dreher. There I was, looking for Dreams, and I got Vision. But given the connection to my research on the optic nerve, my intuition told me I must be on the right track. While scanning the contents of each of the seventeen volumes, I found my eye focused on Volume Three, Neuroanatomy of the Visual Pathways and their Development. I knew that I had to pursue this volume and was overjoyed when I found it straight away at the Columbia Psychology Library. What had come over me? Why such excitement over finding a book I couldn't understand? Though it was highly technical and academically forbidding, information on the ganglion cells in the cat retina provided enough incentive for me to try to make it digestible. I decided, at that point, to tough it out in the Visual Sciences, concentrating for that time on an area completely foreign to me. I put direct studies of dreams on hold.

I camped out at every institute of higher learning I could find. I felt like an imposter frequenting the New York medical libraries where certain officious receptionists looked askance at my failure to identify myself with an institutional affiliation. No matter! I was driven by the scent of the clue. A snotty glance, unpleasant though it was, could not deter me.

When I learned of work done on REM sleep behavior in cats and the extensive studies of ganglion cell classification in the cat retina, the Percival dream began to make sense. Was the cat retina transmitting, through the optic nerve, the visual information to the brain? But vision was only one sense. The key ring had five keys.

I kept turning it over … *the same key fit all six apartments, but no one knows it.* Hmm. Five keys … six apartments. Another puzzlement.

---

32   5/28/96.

I stepped back into the vast caverns of dream research a few months later. Daily visits to the New York Public Library were friendlier and reminded me of my many years of reporting to work, but now with a far greater, yet unidentified purpose than ever before. Of thousands of books on dreams, the one that caught my eye was an encyclopedic bibliography entitled "The Dream. 4,000 Years of Theory and Practice" by Nancy Parsifal-Charles. "Parsifal" leapt off the cover.

I opened to a page that had listed "The Dream Book by Gardiner (Alan H.)." This annotated version of the first recorded dream book was described as dating from seventeen hundred to two thousand years before Christ.[E4]

"Gosh. Dreams have been fascinating people forever," I thought. I glanced at the preceding page and appearing there was:

> "Galen. On the Usefulness of the Parts of the Body....
> "While formulating a detailed description of the physiology of vision, Galen dreamt that he had 'committed an outrage ... by leaving work unexplained ....' He promptly rewrote his 'The Geometrical and Physiological Concept of Vision,' which stands today as the first great study of the optic nerve. A classic example of problem-solving while dreaming."[E5]

The Optic Nerve! The Cat Retina – Nancy Parsifal-Charles – Charlesbigstar – Parsifal – Percival – Galen – The Optic Nerve!

It was a string of miracles starting with the Percival dream leading to the cat retina leading to the optic nerve. "The Dream Book" authored by Nancy Parsifal-Charles led me to Galen's great study of the Optic Nerve. Parsifal – Percival – Perceive. Such similar sounds. It completed a path as circular as the eye itself.

Percival, the cat, also led me to the Wagnerian opera Parsifal, about a mythical character who was anointed knight of the Knights of the Holy Grail. The Grail, the legendary sacred vessel used at The Last Supper is identified with the chalice of the Eucharist. According to Christian tradition, the Grail possessed many miraculous properties. It could provide spiritual nourishment to the faithful, blind the impure of heart, and strike mute the irreverent who came into its presence.[E6]

Now what did Percival the cat, have to do with Galen? Given the context of my dreams, they shared a quest and a vested interest in Vision and, as their stories go, a tenacity of purpose. After years of research, I concluded that this breakthrough dream of the key ring contained an explicit message about the interaction of the optic nerve with each of the senses. But how might that mesh with the aborigines?

FRIDAY,
NOVEMBER 11, 1994

I saw a key in the shape of a circle like a ring. There were 4 or 5 straight pieces hanging off of it. I thought it was for a certain apt. but it turned out to be the same key for all the apts. (6, I think). No one knew though that it was the same key.

SATURDAY, NOVEMBER 12, 1994

I was in a hospital and many people came to see me. I made ice tea for the first few, but then I ran out of glasses. There was a long table of people seated at it. In the center toward the back was Elsa Lewick (deceased). She was smiling. There were other people who I seemed to have known before and had not seen for a long time. There was a large man who I had become so close with (he reminded me when I awakened of Charles Emerson). He was working on a major contribution for mankind. It had to do with the eye. I think the optic nerve. I was going to have to leave and I was crying and crying because I didn't want to say goodbye to these people, I truly loved them.

The Optic Nerve Key Ring Dream

In the words of Galen:

"It is impossible to explain correctly the usefulness of any part without first finding out the action of the whole instrument."Ɛ7

CHAPTER FIVE

HONORED VISIONARIES:
TWO GENTLEMEN NAMED CLAUDIUS

Following the optic nerve revelations, a wealth of dream images characterizing vision and its functions began to infiltrate my nighttime meanderings. They eventually developed into a study exploring visual, emotional, and cortical connections in the brain.

The first part of my research was dedicated to Claudius Galen (c130-201AD), the Greek physician, and his doctrine on the Usefulness of the Parts of the Body. In this, he claimed utter disgrace because of the dream he had had in which he was "being censured because he was unjust to the most godlike of the instruments (the eyes.)"[E8]

Galen so profoundly believed in the validity of the prophetic dream that he diagnosed illness and performed surgery on its basis. He later wrote that advice received during dreams had allowed him to save many lives.[E9]

The sketch I had drawn of the circular key ring strongly resembled the image of an optic nerve illustration in Galen's seminal work.[E10]

I found in my journal another particularly mystifying dream, chockablock with clues that fit into Galen's work in Optics. The dream spells out the *word "Optico" and lists pages 16, 17, 18, 19, 20, 21, carrying a message that the blue rubbery logs contain the information. There's a missing piece of a board game and a hole at the base of a skull.*[33]

This Optico riddle had all the elements of a treasure hunt – elements I couldn't then conceive of. I wondered if the Optico information might be contained in one of countless books I had by then read on vision. And so I backtracked, checking pages 16 through 21 of every book I had consulted on the subject. There was nothing. Blue rubbery logs had me absolutely stumped as did the rest of this quixotic experience.

Frustration over the delays was mounting. Loose ends were out of control. The search had consumed my life but I was almost powerless to stop it. Should I quit while I was ahead? What was driving me? Where was this going? No matter how fatigued I was, no matter how exasperated I became, I couldn't stop chasing the clues even though most of

---

33   2/14/97.

Footnotes contain dream dates and references to prior pages where the dream appeared.
Endnotes contain bibliographical references, are marked with "E" in the text, and appear at the end of the book.

them didn't seem to be leading anywhere. At the end of each day, that tiny voice inside told me the journey had a purpose. This silent promise encouraged me to follow and try to remember each of the specific connections.

Eventually, I came across the works of Ptolemy. Born Claudius Ptolemaeus (ca. 85-165 AD) in Alexandria, he was an astronomer, geographer and mathematician who considered the Earth the center of the universe. The Ptolemaic System dominated academic thought until the Renaissance. Virtually nothing is known about his life.

His astronomical work was enshrined in his treatise, known today as the Almagest (meaning Great Book). The Almagest is divided into thirteen volumes, each of which deals with certain astronomical concepts pertaining to stars and to objects in the solar system – the Earth and all other celestial bodies that we now know revolve around the Sun.

My eyes fell on Ptolemy's work on optical phenomena – OPTICA! That was a thunderbolt! I wrote Optico, but it's Optica! The original edition, which consisted of five books, was the first recorded attempt at a solution to the problem of observing the refraction of light from celestial bodies. Optico? Optica? Pretty close, but what of pages 16 through 21?

Both Mediterranean luminaries, Ptolemy and Galen, began to appear to me in my dreams, each speaking his own metaphorical language, each remembering things past and beaming the light toward the future. My sudden attraction to older men had taken hold. Magnetized by their remembrances of bygone eras, I was ineffably drawn by their collective wisdom toward some unexplained Truth. They seemed to know everything about me – even those deeds which had yet to be realized. The eternal character of these second-century explorers – their intellectual prowess, their thirst for knowledge, their eclectic interest – stirred something deep within me. Why they were visiting my dreams was as profound a mystery as the messages they carried.

Lord Galen, as I came to this know this mentor, is the personification of light, vision, and healing. His imaginary lantern lit the way as he came forward to help me understand his optical and physiological theories of vision.

His essence exemplifies the Age of Chivalry: questing and righting wrongs, conquering worlds and following visions he didn't have time to capture while on Earth. In his eternal quest for all that is good, Lord Galen, the embodiment of Don Quixote led me to a spiritual awakening of unthinkable dimension. It would not be long before I discovered that Lord Galen was the emissary who sent my *Percival dream cat*. My truth-seeking mascot was indeed a personification of Parsifal, the knight in search of the Holy Grail. Two knights – two quests, each striving to combat the world's injustices. It was Lord Galen's splendid feats of vision and daring dreams of truth that in the end freed me from doubting that I might be seeing windmills as giants.

Lord Galen pairs with my Ptolemy, sharing with his Greek contemporary a remarkable facility with telepathy and great finesse in interpreting the mythical legends of the stars. Ptolemy, himself, tied astronomy to physics. I would nickname him Twink, for his personality matched that of a star. Bold, energetic, unpredictable, and romantic. He flashes streaks of brilliance as I see him dancing overhead, on my ceiling, near my bed, in my sight all through the night.[11] Whirling about in clouds of dreams, he materializes with a loud "Halloo … Penny," flexing his brightly colored suspenders. He reveals a bit of the "man of a thousand faces," often appearing as a magician, a detective, a poet reflecting prisms of stars in the spirit of Harry Houdini, Peter Sellers, Edgar Allan Poe. Yet he metamorphoses into the scholarly astronomer when the subject turns to physics, orchestrating dazzling scientific evidence with natural dexterity known to few. He charts the heavens with the grace of a concert maestro conducting his unfinished symphony with his astral baton. Like Inspector Clouseau, nothing escapes him – not manifestations of energy around him, not the foibles of playful spirits, or the grim behavior of wayward entities. A punster, practical joker, lover of limericks, and scribe extraordinaire, he often telegraphs me exactly what I need at the moment to understand a question at hand. It would come to pass that the rhythm of life and afterlife was not interrupted by the stopwatch of time. We knew each other well.

My mentors Galen and Ptolemy who scatter their mysterious imprints throughout my dreams have an endearing habit of reminding me that I'm supposed to match objects I find with things I already have, but what could those things be? I sifted through my journals unable to turn up those mysterious somethings. I had no idea – at least not yet.

One such finding took place within a dream I'd had in 1992 where *a very old book pictured a purplish flower* that looked like an iris. A voice tells me I have a larger painting of the same thing. At the time I recorded this in my journal, I was clueless as to what I was supposed to be doing with the riches of this cosmic extravaganza. Perhaps Percival, my loving feline who helps me ask the hard questions, would someday tell me.

I'd scratch my head and think out loud … "Iris. What do I have that's larger than this flower? Who do I know named Iris? IRIS is an acronym for the Incorporated Research Institutions for Seismology, but that is really far flung. Iris. In another dream, in 2002, *I am sorting flowers and throwing out the dead ones. I will replace the blue flowers with purple iris.* It's a lovely flower – but what does it mean?" The ten-year interval between these two iris dreams attested to their importance and to an elephantine memory whomever or whatever the source.

Now, I can proudly claim that most of the dream links have harmonized, but the first to come into focus was the iris of the eye. And that illuminated the initiation of extraordinary gifts to be presented by Galen and Ptolemy.

CHAPTER SIX

AVALANCHE

The trumpet of clues sounded from near and distant: voices extending to the galaxies, optical phenomena, the spectrum of flowers and plants and, in some ethereal way, to the fleeting shadows of memory, vision, and something ancient.

One of its simpler medleys was a dream repetition of elephants and ivory, usually against a backdrop of antiquity.

The compelling optical pull eventually drew me to study the function of the brain and reawakened my lifelong fascination that began with the pickled cerebra at the University of Miami. In June 1997, I completed the first part of my study, which outlined a neurophysiological pathway in the brain connecting vision, emotion, and our cognitive processes. My inclination then was that my dream images were relating to events in my own life, and that was so, but after I was finally able to disengage from my ego, I found that what I was learning about myself simply served as a photomap, clearly communicating in a universal language. This was reassuring but nonetheless inconclusive, for my questioning about the part of the brain that was immortal was still unanswered.

For example, since I had no formal training in medicine I was surprised to find that many of the findings growing from my dreams were highly technical in nature. Yet, when I went to scientific sources, these findings were, to my astonishment, validated. I quickly learned that dreams access information that far outstrips our conscious sense of what we know. I am convinced this experience is universal, but may be real only to those who are open to it.

Naively, I thought it incumbent on me to communicate my conclusions about a neurophysiological pathway that might reveal the site of intuition to those in the medical profession. Instinct or intuition? Which was it? I saw intuition as having evolved from evolutionary instincts for survival and adaptation but in my writings, I seemed to alternate between the two. In describing intuition, my responses were more reasoned; instinctual reactions were generally instantaneous. Either way, they both pointed to a gut feeling.

Footnotes contain dream dates and references to prior pages where the dream appeared.

Endnotes contain bibliographical references, are marked with "Ɛ" in the text, and appear at the end of the book.

Some professionals in the dream community were intrigued by the uniqueness of my effort, but trying to break through to medicine's inner sanctum was a feat too daunting for a mere uncredentialed mortal.

Regardless, I thought, "This is important! There are messages here for everyone – if only showing the affinity between waking and sleep, and the wealth of knowledge we all can find. I was learning so many things from dreaming. I felt that the subject of dreams as a form of scientific research and the connection of the optic nerve to the body's complex communication system was information to be shared," I sought an agent to publish those nascent medical revelations. But in 1998, this was not to be, so I turned my mind back to the mountain and kept sifting.

Part of the problem was that I clearly was not finished sifting through messages. The wealth of material in my journals grew with each passing night. There was much left to decipher: still growing mountains of loose dream fragments, a million-piece puzzle of which only a smattering, thus far, fit. I believed then that the loose ends would ultimately connect to the medical studies I'd undertaken, but I had not a clue how.

I soon found that decision was to the liking of the dream elves. I sensed they had their own schedule and that relieved my anxiety to publish – at least, for that moment. The message "In God We Trust" coupled with the striking dream image of *the penny in my eye*[34] stood as my bellwether, shielding me from oncoming bouts of confusion. Suddenly, I was in liftoff mode propelled into astronomy, chemistry, physics, geology, mineralogy, metallurgy, oceanography, genetics … and more – so many fields of which I knew nothing by day but much at night. The seeds planted under this nighttime tree of learning sprouted more branches than I could have ever imagined. It was a dream of a way to learn. I never had to prepare for an exam, take a test, or worry about being late for class. Missing a class in dreamland was no big deal, because these opportunities knocked more than once.

I was just beginning to get a handle on the medical messages from my dreams and now – this avalanche of directions, information and impressions. It was terrifying, yet thrilling, and consumed me beyond any measure of elation I'd ever known. It became my passion. Each night promised dream messages that fueled days of fascinating research. These days of learning melted together, holding me safely in an inner world cushioned in harmony and equilibrium. But at day's end, I faced a real dichotomy as I watched the television news and its hammering accounts of the gross injustices in the outer world. School killings were becoming rampant and the nation was entrapped in an unhealthy obsession with the sexual behavior of its President.

It was difficult for me to reconcile the optimism generated by dreams and scientific research with the disintegration of moral conduct in our country that was airing on the nightly news. I felt as if I lived, as Charlesbigstar would say, between Heaven and Hell.

---

34   See Ch. 2 – Searching, p. 20

CHAPTER SEVEN

BRANCHING OUT

It was during this time that Ramos was introduced to me and ceased to be a proper name. There are no points taken off for spelling in Heaven, I learned, and I now understood that I was looking at ramus, from the Latin, literally meaning "branch." Anatomically, ramus is defined as an arm or branch of a bone, and as a major branch of a nerve, vein, or artery.

What, however, was the lexicon in yellow? What was the cork in the hollowed book? And what was the message of this still cryptic "ramus"?

As my waking studies took me through all the brain functions and through myriad descriptions, in both the text and pictures I'd saved from my dreams, I was optimistic that the Branch was Medicine. But what was the nerve? All signs pointed to the optic nerve, not only because of the graphic dream[35] which Charlesbigstar transmitted but also owing to many months of research.

Yet, at night, when I was tucked safely in the womb of the unconscious, the midnight couriers continued parading before me, not only Medicine, but many of the lofty Branches of science that make up our world. It was the whole Earth! How could I, who knew so little, know so much that I didn't know I knew? The endless scroll of clues presented by the spirits was a scavenger hunt of galactic dimensions. It was a Quest, with a capital Q.

A dream I'd had about the Whole Earth came back to me ... *It opens with my desire to sell lights at CBS. People are marching, carrying placards that read "whole." I explain that it means "Earth." Then I learn that I have been assigned to the "shipping department." I think, "What a dull, unimaginative job." Sero — a mysterious word — presents itself.*[36]

I later discovered it represented Eero Saarinen, the architect who designed the penetrating Cyclopian Eye that followed me from CBS.

"People marching" drew my attention, for I had a vague recollection of another dream about *a march*. I checked my journal. Sure enough, it preceded the Whole Earth dream by ten

---

35   See Ch. 4 – Charlesbigstar, p. 31
36   11/9/96.

Footnotes contain dream dates and references to prior pages where the dream appeared.
Endnotes contain bibliographical references, are marked with "Ɛ" in the text, and appear at the end of the book.

months, but that "march" featured the book *"Meditations on the Tarot" and a cryptic message that contained four sentences in Arabic,*[37] which, since I don't read Arabic, sank into the swamps of unidentified dream mush. Meditations on the Tarot is considered by many to be a profound Christian meditation, revealing symbols of Christian Hermeticism in mysticism and magic, astrology and alchemy. Another puzzle added to the growing roster of hidden messages.

The shipping department and the CBS eye were two substantial threads that would weave together to create their own design in the center of my mammoth dream tapestry. Like an artist's rendering, the tableau would be reminiscent of shipping – linking to Onassis – connecting to cruising – and emerging at last as the legendary Titanic.

The Titanic. It had floated in little noticed via the *Ramos dream*, which highlighted *cork in the bottom of a book* and the *appearance of Jackie Onassis.*[38] Survivors described the ocean as a sea of cork the night that mighty ship went down. Some experts believe the cork was a result of explosions in the refrigeration holds, while some surviving passengers thought the great quantities of broken bits of cork covering the surface of the water came from the life preservers. I mused. "Could that be the *cork in the dream's hollowed-out book*?"

The Whole Earth dream had gone unnoticed for two years, from 1996 to 1998. I hadn't even included it in my master list of dreams, as it did not seem pertinent to the medical issues. While rereading it, I was interrupted by a phone call. As the call itself had no bearing on my musings, it derailed my train of thought for the moment. I took a break to check my e-mail. One message was ironic, given the graphic language in the Whole Earth dream. Amazon.com was announcing the "Whole Heaven Catalog."

I tried stringing the images together: The CBS Eye – Titanic – Whole Earth – People Marching– Meditations on the Tarot – Arabic – People Marching. Why would "people marching" repeat in this odd loop? Were people demonstrating for some reason? It was 1996. It didn't seem to fit, but then dream time did not match waking time.

Each of the images had bubbled up from the unconscious except for a conscious notice from the Whole Heaven Catalog. Had the waking world knocked on the door of my confusion for some reason? I sensed the shaping of a message, a miraculous message ... Whole Earth – Whole Heaven. Earth and Heaven. Heaven and Earth.

I laughed out loud. I silently said my thanks. I cried tears of reverence. Oh, that such connections were falling into place! Never had I felt such gratitude. I experienced my being as an integral part of the whole world. Ecstatic, in worlds both spiritual and terrestrial, I called a friend and jubilantly exclaimed, "I can't believe it! I can't believe what is happening!"

---

37   1/28/96.
38   9/12/93.

CHAPTER EIGHT

PEGGYMOONBEAM

I was just beginning to open my eyes to the subject of light and vision when my best friend and closest confidante in the whole wide world passed over. I thought probably the only one besides God who could understand my invisible purpose was my dearly beloved friend, whose full Earth name was Diane Peggy Brooks. I could not know through the years of her listening to my dreams and guiding me when I was lost that she would come back manifest as Peggymoonbeam. "Let me draw you a picture" was her maxim whenever I didn't understand something, which was often.

Peggy and I met in the mid-'70s during our passage through the corporate ranks of CBS. She ran CBS's Columbia Records East Coast recording and manufacturing facilities. I was manager of audio-visual production for Holt Rinehart & Winston, CBS's educational subsidiary. Peggy energetically pursued me as a client, wanting Holt to manufacture its audio recordings with Columbia. I agreed to a trial run, but due to endless production slipups, the deal was nearly aborted. She wouldn't hear of it. So eager was she to correct the errors, she hauled me off to the tape plant in Terra Haute, Indiana, where she sat me at the head of a huge conference table surrounded by her all-male management team and insisted I have my say. It felt strange facing off with this burly manufacturing crew but at the end of the day, all was right with the world. The contract was signed and I realized it was the first time in my corporate life that anyone really wanted to hear what I had to say. It appears she has not relinquished her role as my guardian. On Earth or in Heaven, her candle always lights another. It never goes out.

In life, Peggy was a waif of a being, all ninety pounds of her bursting with enough love and energy to light an entire planet. If you gave her an inch, she'd give you a ticket to Heaven. She remembered everyone and was never forgotten by anyone. She fit no mold, wore no label, and steadfastly marched to her own drummer.

Her greatest joy was in making others happy. She impishly kept witticisms up her sleeve and considered it a great day when she cracked a joke that magically dissolved your problems. Her hallmark was her gift of giving. Whenever she could, she would secretly plant a present. For her, anonymous giving fed the joy she got from the giving, itself. It was her addiction.

Footnotes contain dream dates and references to prior pages where the dream appeared.

Endnotes contain bibliographical references, are marked with "Ɛ" in the text, and appear at the end of the book.

In July of 1994, I dreamt that *I'd written a very serious letter to* Peggymoonbeam *about resolutions which I had left in her house. Shortly thereafter, she wrote me a letter and left it in my house. I had 2 sets of breastplates for my two best friends. One set was for* Peggy. *I made a toast …"To 1994 and Beyond. I started to say forever and then changed it to Beyond.*[39] The dream reflected our ritual of sharing New Year's resolutions but the breastplates were a mystery. *To 1994 and Beyond* both fascinated and disturbed me.

Peggy departed the physical plane in May of 1995. Though I thought of her every day and missed her physical presence fiercely, I knew she was around because she would show up in so many of my dreams. But little did I know that when Peggy became Peggymoonbeam, she had been given a very big job upstairs as head Puppeteer in Dreamland. My first clue should have been the dream I had the night of her funeral, in which I saw a *beautiful emerald green square that looked like a tablet.*[40] I later learned of an ancient artifact called the Emerald Tablet, one of the most revered documents in the Western World. The Emerald Tablet, also known as the Secret of Hermes is encoded with mysterious wording, but I didn't really understand why this would be in my dream. She had just departed and I hadn't yet arrived so it was very early in the day for such connections.

Peggymoonbeam's imprint was that of an advanced soul. Her extraordinary high-mindedness was visible in the way she placed others before herself. She did not have to be recognized by society but performed her good deeds silently with a contentedness known only to her. Her mantra, "Be Strong, Have Courage" was frequently expressed to others as she fought daily for her own survival. She radiated tolerance, compassion, and human understanding in exceptional measure. Indifferent to vain shows of ego, she was simply intent on making the world a better place, and that meant getting everyone to laugh.

Aside from her secret gift giving, she had other endearing qualities. Over the years I had given her gifts with an angel motif which oddly enough, she barely acknowledged. If I gave her something that didn't have an angel, she oohed and aahed, insisting I shouldn't have done it. This was a mystery. Why would the most grateful person on Earth be so dismissive of my angel gifts? Then, one day she admitted that she didn't believe in angels because they weren't in her religion. I was surprised because she was so knowledgeable. I said, "Well angels have been in every religion since the beginning of time and, as a matter of fact, angels are the cover story of Time magazine's current issue." "Really?" she said. Then I'll buy one today." That Christmas I received a beautiful angel sculpture. I was profoundly touched, for I knew she had defeated her earthly superstitions. She told me that when she bought this angel, she asked for "the other one," thinking they were a pair. "No dear, replied the saleslady, this is an original piece of art. This is one of a kind."

---

39 7/6/94.
40 5/19/95.

And so it was. One one-of-a-kind angel would make her entrance in Heaven a few months later. Soon after, her angelic presence would honor my dreams. Even as I write this, ten years later, my eyes brim with tears for the wisdom she brought and still brings into my life and for her illumination that ushers me through all my earthly trials. I often wonder if she left this world early to show us how high we can aim and how far we can reach.

The way I'm able to recognize her in a dream when she isn't being herself is that she sends a symbol to stand in for her. The most frequent avatars are wicker, the color peach, a picket fence, and a ficus tree, representing some of her earthly passions. Her lifelong dream of living in an ivy-covered cottage with a picket fence was realized when she moved into a charming cottage in the quaint town of Pacific Palisades embraced by the mountains and nestled above the ocean. Peach, wicker, abundant plants and flowers, and, of course, the picket fence were among the physical effects that adorned her California dream house. (Again, the color changed. This time it was grayed out, which in computer lingo means "ghosted" – disabled.)

A forest of dreams imaging trees and branches populated my journals but I hadn't made the connection until I remembered that the most important physical gift Peggymoonbeam ever gave me was her own lush ficus tree that thrives in my city apartment. Sprouting new leaves as though it were in its natural habitat, it is the recipient of streaming light, bright sunshine, and gentle winds off the river. It must know how loved it is, for it rarely drops a leaf. This very special ficus doesn't have a brain, but it does have a heart and is intent on surviving.

Peggymoonbeam's obsession with the story of A Tree Grows in Brooklyn came bounding back in a brilliantly radiant golden-white light. She must have been reading my mind because she chimed in as though she were there in the flesh, a practice my mentors engaged in more frequently as my research advanced:

"Penelope, do you remember my yearning – my dream that someday someone would make a sequel of A Tree Grows in Brooklyn?"

"Yes, Peggymoonbeam. You always talked about it."

"That's because I so identified with Francie, the protagonist. When she looked down from the fire escape, the tree looked like the tops of green umbrellas and now when I look down at you, I see the lush green of the Earth. Well, no one ever made that sequel, so now that I'm in a place where we spin the essence of dreams it is my eternal wish to bring back to life that story so dear to my heart. I finally figured it out, Penelope! I can do it through your dreams! All you have to do is remember them and write them down."

"Well, my imaginative little moonbeam, I know that you're capable of just about anything, but how on Earth are you going to pull that off? After all, a tree grows in the Earth and you are in Heaven."

"How observant of you, Penelope.

"You see, it works like this. The tree has many roots, just like the ficus I gave you, but this particular tree will grow in Heaven and reach all the way down to Earth where it will plant itself in your dreams and you will be the recipient of its many branches."

"This is silly, Peggymoonbeam! How can a tree be planted in my dreams? How can I receive imaginary branches?"

"Imaginary, Penelope? You have already had dreams of *branches*.[41] And loads of dreams about trees — flowering trees, palm trees, Christmas trees, and endless dreams about leaves that grow on trees and plants. Your first teacher, Dr. Noodle, even gave you *a piece of "tree bark" in a dream that signaled good luck. The name sounded Greek.*[42] You discovered that cortex is the Greek term for "tree bark" so I know you have an inkling of what is developing even though you're resisting it. The work was in progress before I transitioned to the astral plane, Penny. I'm only adding to it."

"The astral plane? Where's that?"

She giggled. "Well Penny, it's very hard to explain where because it's kind of everywhere. It will become clearer as we go along, so for now I'll just say it's an ethereal realm where we're able to transfer information from one realm to another. Your physical realm on Earth is penetrated by energy substances in our realm, which are far beyond your range of perception. When you open to our vibrational frequency you will find that your dream branches are not imaginary at all but that discovery will take some time, for you have much to learn. You will actually see these branches come to life, for this is a story of survival and immortality and will symbolize the tree of science, each branch depicting a different branch of science. Of course, the most important part is that the Earth sustains the tree and makes it grow bigger and stronger and as this tree begins to flourish, so will you. You will actually be amazed at what this tree is able to produce."

"Oh no, Peggymoonbeam. I fear you are the one who is dreaming, not me. You know I don't know anything about science. I think it's boring and hard to understand and all those theories give me a headache. I do wish you'd let go of your fixation about A Tree Grows in Brooklyn. You're in a much better place now and your spirit should be free to roam the heavens and not be saddled with past yearnings. True, it was a good story while you were on Earth but I think you're going overboard taking it all the way up to heaven with you. I do hope you haven't discussed this with anyone."

I sensed Peggymoonbeam giggling through her frustration.

"Penelope, you're stubborn as ever. Just calm down and listen. If you'll only open your eyes to what I'm trying to show you, you will find that at the heart of the story Heaven

41   9/12/92, 12/9/97.
42   2/24/93.

and Earth are really not strangers to each other. In fact, they are very much a part of each other; almost like an old married couple.

Hmm. I thought back to all those messages I was getting about Heaven and Earth.

"You must remember how I loved to read and that learning to read was my first step toward becoming educated. Well, I've been doing a different sort of reading over here in Heaven."

"Oh really! Exactly what is it you're reading now? I know you were especially drawn to stories about hope and overcoming hardship like the story of a Tree Grows in Brooklyn but you don't have any hardship now."

Peggymoonbeam's spirit blushed pink. "Well, I've been engaged in an astral course called dream-reading. I can see, my little buddy, that having learned some of life's hard lessons you are coming of age. You are now ready to absorb a substantial knowledge base that extends beyond your own personal world of people, places, and things to global issues which affect humanity. You'll get over your fear of science in time. Trust me. You will.

Remembering Peggymoonbeam's idealistic bent and not wanting to dampen her spirits, I reluctantly asked, "Well, what is dream-reading, anyhow?"

"It's tuning into your unconscious, Penelope, where your dreams are lodged. I sense both your skepticism and your curiosity, but don't even bother asking how I do it. Just trust that it's a higher form of thought requiring astral light, which does not exist on your plane. Think back, Penelope, to the day of my funeral when you received a dream about an *emerald green square that looked like a tablet.* The wisdom in the Emerald Tablet is the foundation of the ancient mysteries. And if you follow this dream message with open eyes and mind, you will learn that your insight will be increased a hundredfold.

"Gosh, Peggymoonbeam. How could you have sent that dream the same day you departed Earth? I would think you'd have to get settled before you began your dream-reading course."

"I am not your only benefactor, dear Penelope. Over time, you will come to know where each gift is coming from.

"Because you are my bestest friend in the whole wide world, if you will set aside your doubts and fears and indulge me in my passion of gift-giving, I have some twenty-first-century gifts that will knock your socks off! For now, all you have to do is to continue studying the symbolic nature of your dreams and oh, – don't forget to keep a pen by your bedside."

Hmm. This was sounding pretty mysterious – and exciting! But science?

(Gulp.)

CHAPTER NINE

SPINNING DISKS

On the lookout for Peggymoonbeam's heavenly offerings, I wasn't surprised when, in 1997 she appeared in a dream that – naturally – centered around a gift.

A machine is making something and spinning at ultra-high frequency. Next to it is a disk, like a 7-inch record player going at many rpm's per minute. It looks like it's spinning a record of metals. It's not flat and it's not a combination of metals. It has a mound in it, described as a breast implant, which is all silver. Another is all gold and still another that may be of copper or another metal. It's a gift from and for Peggymoonbeam, coming from her and being for her if it can be realized. While I'm looking for my purple glasses, I open the freezer and find a bunch of frozen butter bricks I forgot I had.[43]

I have reflected endlessly on this dream and have continually asked, "Is it a gift from her or for her?" Eventually, I was inclined to think it was both.

I flashed back to the dream *"1994 and Beyond"* and *the mysterious breastplates.*

It occurred to me that breastplates are metal. *We had each left something in the other's house.*[44] Was this marking some sort of exchange? Of resolutions? Was the one house Heaven, the other Earth? Was Peggymoonbeam right? Maybe they weren't strangers.

I noted that the *Spinning Disks* dream contains both metal and a breast (implant).

This was the first toe in the door to the Galaxy. As astronomers presently understand the Milky Way, every star falls into one of four different stellar populations. After much study, I surmised that the spinning disk was analogous to the stellar aggregate called the "thin disk," which is metal rich and of various ages. Those stars in the thin-disk population, to which the Sun and 96 percent of its neighbors belong, are the brightest. The stars revolve around the Galaxy fast, having fairly circular orbits, ε_{12} like the motion of the spinning machine making its metal disks – much like those which Peggymoonbeam had spun my way.

---

43   3/23/97.
44   7/6/94.

Footnotes contain dream dates and references to prior pages where the dream appeared.
Endnotes contain bibliographical references, are marked with "ε" in the text, and appear at the end of the book.

Initially I thought the *mound described as a breast implant* in the dream to be silicon since the most common implants used until 1992 were silicon. However, when I discovered a stellar population called the Bulge which is old and metal rich and lies at the center of the Galaxy, it seemed to fit Peggymoonbeam's tidings: a mound, rich in metals.[E13] Then I learned that iron meteorites occasionally have silicate inclusions, which can be so common as to make up nearly half of their bodies.[E14] It was coming together. Silicon was connecting to iron.

"Aha!" I wondered. "Rich in metals. Silver is a metal. Could this tie to the Silver Key?"

Most of the stars in the Bulge lie within a few thousand light-years of the Galactic center, so few if any exist near the Sun. This makes the Bulge the least examined stellar population in the Milky Way.

Peggymoonbeam's *spinning disks* led me to do more research. My questions mounted as it led to potential connections:

"Could the dream symbol of *the mound described as a breast implant which is all silver* be alluding to an ancient supernova explosion where the last process of nuclear fusion in a star is from silicon to iron?[E15]

"Could the spinning record player be suggesting that the history (recording) of elements formed in the early solar system can be found not in one but in three different metals, as told in the dream?

"Might some of these metals relate to original material in the solar system such as amino acids – the building blocks of life?"

Crikey! There are over one hundred billion galaxies in the universe! Before I was able to figure out which galaxy this spinning metal dream came from my dreams pulled me as though by an invisible string into the province of Genetics, where strands of jewelry became the next nocturnal theme.

CHAPTER TEN

THE STUFF OF LIFE

In July of 1998, my medical studies resumed as jewelry: a rousing dream volume of necklaces and chains that led me to DNA and the amino acids that are the chains binding genetics.

Thematic repetition in my dreams grouped things in threes along with repeated images of *chains and necklaces, some single stranded, some double stranded, and one quite striking triple-stranded necklace of jet, which once belonged to my dearly departed Aunt Agnes.*[45]

These caught my eye since I seldom wear jewelry.

As I began to skim the surface of DNA, my first impression was that the *triple-stranded necklace* would make a likely partner for the genetic code in which sequences of nucleotides are read in sets of three and translated into amino acids.

The key that unlocks the genetic code is the order in which the bases are arranged in sequence along the double or single strands of DNA or RNA.

Might *the single-stranded necklace* portray the single-stranded messenger called mRNA? Following this line of questioning, I wondered if the *double-stranded necklace* might be a metaphor for the double-stranded helix of DNA.

I either was in view of exciting new horizons or had taken a leave of absence from the real world. In my hours of greatest doubt, research was my supporter helping to match the clues and authenticate my detective work.

The genetics theme was flirtatious in the beginning, winking a subtle interest in getting to know me, but as at the end of a fuzzy dream, it was anyone's guess if I'd see it again.

The contrast between vision and blindness was paradoxical. I was to follow a blind path before being granted sight. The hazy images gradually crystallized and magically interlocked through some inexplicable cognitive wiring all the while searching for their place in the puzzle. The unfolding of what was to become ironclad logic echoed a lesson: at the end of the day, Trust was to be the Seeing-Eye Dog.

Thinking about the *repetitive chain dreams and the triple-stranded necklace*, I realized that three could mean anything and so could chains but – when folded in with a dream

---

45   2/4/95.

Footnotes contain dream dates and references to prior pages where the dream appeared.
Endnotes contain bibliographical references, are marked with "Ɛ" in the text, and appear at the end of each Part.

series in which peas were the entree du jour – it seemed a plausible feature on the genetics menu.

In the pea series, for example, there was one dream where *I'm carrying a bucket of peas,* and another where *a pea pod comes to life and is breathing.*[46] This pulsing pea vignette linked to Gregor Mendel's experiments with the garden pea, which developed in 1865 into his theory of inheritance that formed the basis for today's science of Genetics.

The peas in the bucket dream waltzed in with another bucket dream where *I find two very long strands of amber in a gray metal bucket. Metal and amber.* Hmm. I wondered what these ingredients signified, even though it seemed clear that the two strands wound back to the double-stranded helix of DNA.

While in the jewelry district of dreams shopping for necklaces, one of the DNA dream fairies presented *an amethyst necklace on a chain coated with peanut butter.*[47]

Yuk. *Peanut butter and amethyst.* A tacky piece of jewelry no doubt, but I thought it might have some other value. A fast appraisal revealed that amethyst was the purple variety of quartz, but the peanut butter was up in the air – literally. Trying to untangle this gooey mess wasn't only sticky, it seemed downright impossible. In the end the good fairy of protein synthesis would trip down a spiral staircase called the double helix to tell me that peanut butter symbolized the sugar phosphates on the outside of the DNA helix. They were as compatible as peanut butter and jelly but I just didn't get it at the outset.

Moving from the sublime to the ridiculous, it appeared that the more absurd the dream, the more conspicuous and conclusive the link. What a notion! The concoction of amethyst and peanut butter said it all: neither an edible nor wearable ensemble, in all likelihood, they had some place in the story.

As time would tell, there resided a whole Branch of Genetic Engineering up there in the penthouse of puns. Many dreams spun a recurrent *yellow and green color combination, sometimes attached to leaves or plants.*

I was like an infant cutting my teeth on the nuances of this language, with its visual and verbal metaphors, idioms and slang, when I heard a little fly buzzing around Mendel's experiments with the garden pea. He had found that when two peas that contained both green and yellow information, were crossed, the dominant trait was green and the yellow was recessive. That seemed to explain the virtual garden of yellow and green leaves and plants in my dreams. In Mendel's garden, it was cross-pollination of pea plants. In mine, it seemed I was supposed to cross-pollinate the seeds of dreams.

The sheer magic of elements combining was intoxicating. The quirkier it was, the louder that wee inner voice sounded. I knew it was important if it made no sense.

---

46   3/18/96, 1/14/95.
47   10/28/95, 3/27/98.

Imagine my surprise when the botanical name of the Three-Flowered Avens turned up in my research linking to the *Avers*-Avens secret combination code. Avens is also called Old Man's Whiskers! And whiskers in another dream took form *of an older man disguised as a scientist with white whiskers under his hat. I had the feeling of a metal thing on my back.*[48] It seemed the *Avers*-Avens dream puzzle let slip a metal clue.[49]

And so plants and metal continued their pilgrimage, either individually or coupled. The force of metal was indomitable, for not only did I see it in my dreams, I actually heard it. "How does one hear metal?" you might ask. There's really no formula but I must have thought of an old beau, which oddly enough inspired the phenomenon of metal being audible.

This old flame with whom I had a symbiotic relationship shows up in a dream where *I hear the sound of metal twisting as on a chain and I see a double ring.*[50] Was there another light shining on the genetic code, this one signifying a chain of amino acids and the double-ringed compounds in nucleic acid bases?

In this metal twisting dream, *I see a measurement, like a ruler, with ruled lines of 3 on my boyfriend's foot. I comment that we could have been twins.* Peggymoonbeam's, "I'll draw you a picture" had materialized. And a picture it was, for I had sketched in my journal exactly what I saw in the dream. I drew *the number 3 on his foot.*

In genetics, there's a position referred to as the three-foot end of a DNA chain and — just in case I didn't get it – the dream elves slipped in the twins for good measure. I felt it just had to be genetics even though it arguably hints at a romantic component. The dream was so strong I even e-mailed my old beau the next day to see how he might react to the mention of metal. His response was a predictable wisecrack about me and my dreams.

The lengths to which I found I would go. I lost all inhibition. There was virtually nothing I wouldn't do to fetch a thread. Could the twisting metal link to the metal bucket where I got the amber necklace and to the spinning metal disk, both dreams inhabited by Peggymoonbeam? Hmmm. Spinning, twisting metal – with the genetic code in a metal bucket. To what limits would this reach?

Two interlocking ring dreams featured Gideon.[51] My meager knowledge of the Bible drove me to research Gideon who, with a servant, when summoned forth in the battle against the Midianites, gathered intelligence information – by way of a dream interpretation."Ɛ16

The Gideon story may be considered a stretch given the infinite possibilities of interlocking rings, but they were paired in the dream. The bell of Truth that rang with clarity was that Gideon received his information through a dream.

I continued to assemble groupings of repetitive themes and their variations.

The Yellow Slab was a theme unto itself but was it a puzzle piece for DNA?

---

48   6/14/01.
49   12/9/95. See Ch. 1 – Beginnings, p. 6
50   1/26/98.
51   9/30/95, 6/19/97.

One dream shows *a small girl standing on a staircase, second stair from the top. There are two pyramids; one pointing upward; the other pointing downward. She holds the downward pointing triangle under which is the number 14. It then changes to 16.*[52]

A second dream shows *two pyramid-shaped staircases; the upper stairway is facing downward, the lower, facing upward – like a mirror image. A yellow slab acts as a marker appearing on the second step in both pyramid-shaped stairs.*[53]

While hunting in the wilds of genetics, I was shocked to come upon something called pyridimine bases – a group of chemical compounds derived from pyrimidine. As I rounded the corner, another surprise appeared in my viewfinder and that was a paper written on two-step enzymatic coupling of pyrimidine bases.[E17]

The change in number from 14 to 16 piqued my curiosity. I checked the elemental tables and found that 14 is silicon and 16 is sulfur.

Pyramids – Pyrimidine – Second Steps – Two-Step Coupling.

Pretty fascinating, but when would the yellow slab fess up?

Amber! A cryptic dream medley of *amber stones, amino acids and a paper tied with a ribbon, one part blue and one part pink,* stymied me.[54] An equally mystifying fragment showed up in the dream with *the girl rising from the sand carrying heavy things on a videotape. She opens a door to a closet. She sees a huge amber vase and an urn behind it. The urn looks like a funeral urn. She thinks she remembers where these used to go.*[55] Were someone's ashes preserved in an urn?

This was driving me to distraction! I set out in hope of making some sense of this commotion and soon learned that the oldest sequenced DNA to be found is that of a nemonychid weevil trapped in amber from the Cretaceous period, and estimated as being between 120 and 135 million years old. Hmm. Metal and amber. Somehow the metal must relate to DNA – but how and in what form? The world is filled with metals.

I deliberated on ramus and the yellow lexicon. Could ramus have something to do with DNA? Could the fossil found mainly in sedimentary rock, asphalt, coal, and amber tie to this in some way? Fossils flashed me back to Winnie and my dream of the *pastel-colored plastic keys,* which, on sight, she said looked like femurs. I played the mental tape again: Winnie's calcium supplement was called Osforte meaning strong bone.

A femur is a segment of a leg. Maybe this is symbolizing a part of something.

Hmm. Fossils. Femurs. Bones. Calcium .…

52   12/28/94.
53   9/19/97.
54   4/3/02.
55   9/28/93. See Ch. 1– Beginnings, p. 4

CHAPTER ELEVEN

THE LEAF

Then there were the leaves. And more keys.

Toward the end of the doomed Copenhagen marriage, before retiring one night I asked two questions: Why was I sent here? and Why did I marry that man? A dream appeared in the early morning.

I see a bunch of keys lying on a bedspread. Under them is a solitary green leaf. Then I hear a man's voice whisper..."Judy," and I see a pen in a shiny black Lucite pen holder.[56]

TUES. MAR. 14, 1995

In the morning I saw a bunch of keys laying on a bedspread. Under them was a solitary green leaf.

Then I heard a man's voice whisper "Judy" and I saw a pen in a pen holder.

SHINY BLACK
LUCITE

At the time, I thought this was merely a message to record my dreams. I was too distracted to venture beyond that. Connection to the five keys in the optic nerve dream[57] occurred years later.

---

56   3/14/95.
57   11/11/94. See Ch. 3, The Pole, p. 26

Footnotes contain dream dates and references to prior pages where the dream appeared.
Endnotes contain bibliographical references, are marked with "Ɛ" in the text, and appear at the end of the book.

Early leaf auguries were as diverse as they were puzzling. Dream seedlings with *three leaves unfurling on a plant*.[58] A flashback to triplets in genetics!

Images of *pine leaves*[59] led me to amber-producing pines in the Baltic Sea basin. Genetics again. I learned that amber, when rubbed, takes a charge of static electricity, so the Greeks called it elektron. From this, the word "electricity" is derived.

A dream snippet *of interconnecting leaves on a belt*[60] refused to reveal its meaning for what seemed an eternity. My invisible tutor turned Ramos into ramose, from the Latin ramus meaning a branch, etching a dream *picture of leaves on a branch*.[61]

Again, I heard the whispering of plants and metal, this time in two dreams, almost two years apart. Taken together, they proved the pièce de resistance of the plants-and-metal course.

The first dream displayed an incongruous *grouping of plants and a peanut butter cookie made of iodized metal called Sunshine*.[62] What a strange mixture for a cookie, although a Nabisco competitor had actually named a biscuit, Sunshine. And peanut butter previously entwined in an amethyst necklace obstinately stuck as the symbol for the sugar-phosphate backbone of DNA/RNA.

The other dream, hosted by Peggymoonbeam, featured an equally unlikely assemblage of *Bill Moyers, my dentist, a messenger delivering a three-pronged sculpture of burnished metal, and a lot of green and yellow plants*.[63] The messengered delivery of the three-pronged metal sculpture was a surefire clue for messenger RNA and fit perfectly with the genetic code or triplet.

Whoever was presiding over this scavenger hunt must have known it would take massive doses of patience spread over untold stretches of space and time to collect all the pieces that would crack the code. Since Bill Moyers had appeared in the dream, I considered viewing his investigative documentaries in search of a tip, but just what we were investigating was anyone's guess.

I re-examined the dream of my *aunt's triple-stranded jet necklace*[64] and was washed back to my *dreams of driftwood*[65] when I learned that jet is a black gemstone formed by the submersion of driftwood in seafloor mud. Had the stormy seas of life washed me ashore? Or was this some oblique reference to driftwood, one I would have overlooked since it seemed so obvious. I couldn't imagine any permutations that would attach to driftwood. It seemed to be a one-dimensional symbol.

---

58 5/23/96.
59 6/20/93, 3/31/98.
60 2/13/96.
61 5/11/95.
62 7/27/94.
63 3/18/96.
64 2/4/95. See Ch. 10 – The Stuff of Life, p. 51
65 Driftwood dreams: 1993 – 2001.

At least, it seemed so until I happened upon "genetic drift," defined as "random changes in gene frequency ... esp. in small populations when leading to preservation or extinction of particular genes."[E18] I knew this was a good solid connection worth saving, but why? Was I looking for a lost gene? Wherever the secret might be buried, be it DNA or a piece of driftwood found in the sea, both shared the same landscape. Sea, sky, or brain, it was a confluence of natural forces.

The school bus driving genetics sounded a powerful voice in this great canyon of the unconscious, but where and why did genetics belong? Its family, with its triplets, necklaces, and peanut butter, actually took a backseat for quite a long while but reappeared as I sat down to write. This appearance as genetic drift told me it was confident of its justification and place in the story. No backseater on its revival, it came to be a most seductive, yet well-hidden, piece of the puzzle, so well hidden I would have to walk the Corridors of Time before its message came clear.

CHAPTER TWELVE

A FRENCH CONNECTION

My course in the complex language of day and night progressed, connections ignoring time as I'd been raised to think of it. If only I had had a waking teacher instead of relying on self-tutelage. Perhaps it would have been easier; perhaps I wouldn't have been as thirsty for insight.

Year in and year out, my desire to share my insights with others was deferred as I continued a process of unraveling and connecting that stretched into infinity. I wanted to stop but didn't know where or how. I was in a time warp. Unseen and silent companions tirelessly navigated the journey, oftentimes replacing my expectancy of completion with new and wondrous findings.

St. Paul de Vence in southern France was a vortex of connections. My first visit there was in 1984 with my brother and sister-in-law, expectant parents. One afternoon my sister-in-law and I decided to shop for baby clothes. It was lunch hour and the shops were closing. We leisurely strolled along the nearly empty cobblestone street. As we window-shopped, I casually glanced up and saw a woman, about a block away, walking toward us. She was waving, I thought, at me. She had a big smile and was fashionably dressed in white. I smiled and waved back.

"Who are you waving at?" asked my sister-in-law.

"At that woman in white. I must know her."

"There's no one there," she said.

"She was there a second ago," I insisted, looking at the place where I'd just seen her. My knees went weak. I was lightheaded. My brother found us moments later on that little side street, my sister-in-law holding me by my arm. He was unaware of what had happened.

"What's the matter with you? You look like you just saw a ghost!" he exclaimed.

I felt dizzy and disoriented. They guided me to a nearby fountain, where we sat until my dizziness lifted. I wondered about the reality of what had happened, but then dismissed it.

Footnotes contain dream dates and references to prior pages where the dream appeared.
Endnotes contain bibliographical references, are marked with "Ɛ" in the text, and appear at the end of the book.

Eight years later, when I started recording my dreams, a *woman in white appeared*,[66] albeit not often. When she appeared in a second dream, it sparked my memory of St. Paul de Vence. This dream figure had the same beneficent and ethereal manner as the woman I had seen there.

It was the memory of that woman that drew me back to the south of France. What's more, other curiosities seemed to play a part in the French puzzle … a dream featuring the French word BIARRITZ … among other dreams descriptive of Lourdes renowned for appearances of the Virgin Mary.

BIARRITZ.[67] What did it mean? Was it a place, a person, a thing? Two additional, but equally mystifying dreams occurred within days of each other. One featured *an A-frame house that looks like a pyramid, the word ROGER and a charming country scene of green fields, apple orchards, a little white church, and a gas station.*[68] The gas station seemed out of place. The other dream was extremely dramatic and took me on a trip *up a steep mountain with many hairpin turns. It has a secret place at the top of it.*[69]

When I learned that Biarritz is a city in the southwestern section of France, I asked my niece's (the baby's) French nanny, Solange, what she knew about it. We met one day for lunch and, as we sat in the restaurant, she sketched a map on a placemat. On it she drew a landmark – a steep mountain with a statue at its peak. Above it she wrote "Rocher de La Vierge" – the rock of the Virgin.

In sheer disbelief at recognizing the mountain as a near facsimile of my dream, coupled with the word Rocher, I bellowed ROGER! Roger in French sounds like Rocher. "Solange," I asked, "do they have apple orchards in Biarritz?" to which she replied, "Oh, but of course. There are apple orchards throughout the Normandy and southwest regions of France."

I shared this dream with Dr. Noodle who strongly encouraged me to follow my dream. He seemed to know long before I did that I had embarked on the journey of a lifetime. So follow I did and in August of 1993, I visited Biarritz, where I climbed the Rocher de la Vierge. However, contrary to the "secret place" described in the dream, the Virgin is a very public and popular statue which has graced the rock since 1865. The "secret" would remain so until the messengers decided it was time for me to know.

After spending four days in Biarritz, I traveled to Lourdes. I learned that the most famous sighting of the Virgin Mary took place in Lourdes in 1858 by Bernadette, a fourteen-year-old girl who Mary instructed to dig a hole in the ground, drink, and bathe in the water she would find there. The water flowed into a spring of healing and is now a major pilgrimage site where thousands have been cured. I wondered if Mary had traveled

66   11/1/92.
67   11/13/92.
68   11/21/92.
69   11/24/92.

over to St. Paul de Vence that day when I got so dizzy. I also wondered about the dreams of holes and the underground. I left Lourdes with an inexplicable yearning to return.

Drifting from the past, a driftwood dream fragment presented itself. I had drawn in my journal a sort of *twisted interplay of driftwood branches, reminiscent of brambles*,[70] which would bear an amazing likeness to an illustration of molecular cell function that I later saw in a genetics textbook. What was most memorable about this intertwining drift-wood was that I had redrawn it many times until I was able to capture the placement of each of the gnarled pieces I'd seen in the dream.

In September of 1993, I returned to the picturesque sixteenth-century hilltop village of St. Paul de Vence in France where the scent of lavender and enchanting stone walls transported one to another time. While ambling through the flower-studded garden of the charming Hotel Messugues, I passed a wishing well. Tied to a tree was a construct with an interlocking pattern, almost exactly as I had drawn it, though with one hitch: it was not driftwood; it was composed of gourds. I carefully sketched the entwined gourds on the back of a notepad. Growing more intrigued with it each time I saw it, I pho-tographed it. When I returned home and compared the waking images to the dream images, they were a perfect match.

What could this possibly mean? This turned out to mark the first of many waking-life materializations of dream images that I would experience.

Around the time of that second visit, I was researching the artist Victor Vasarely, the father of op art, after his geometrically abstract artwork had crept into my dreams.

The region of France called the Vaucluse joined in the patterned dance in progress. After the second trip to Vence, I looked at a map of Provence and was astounded to find a village called Gordes perched on the edge of the high Plateau de Vaucluse, and to learn that Vasarely had founded a museum of his own work there at the Chateau de Gordes. If the driftwood made of gourds in my dream matched the gourds in St. Paul de Vence, which took me to Gordes, France, what was in Gordes or in France that I still needed to see?

A flock of V's fluttered back through time ... Vence, Vasarely, Rocher de la Vierge, Vaucluse .... I was mesmerized by the V's . I knew they would ultimately splice some-thing together.

I felt I was looking through a kaleidoscope, the patterns ever changing, though some-times repeating. Destiny's mercurial nature loosened my grasp, but there was nothing to do but try to stay on course, wherever that might lead. Important clues, like slippery little fish, wriggled through the net of my mind. Only sheer unadulterated faith, infused

---

70   3/30/93.

with a surprising strain of tenacity led me to believe that if one slipped away from the now, it would be back.

Yet I vacillated. I would ask how I could possibly make any sense of this. In comparison, lassoing that swarm of bees would have been a snap.

Somehow, I was compelled to push forward along the dizzying and circuitous route through some very bumpy terrain. The destination of this leg of the expedition? I didn't know it then, though now it is clearly the creation of this book, and I can only hope that you, too, will have the faith and endurance to continue the journey, and perhaps even start your own.

Alas, my text contains seemingly uncountable detours, for which I feel I should apologize. On the other hand, the revelations of this odyssey parallel the road I traveled, and should come to you as they came to me … along twisting paths of revelation entwining in majestic thread, cord, swatch. In this, at least in part, lives the wonder. The adventure is in assembling thousands of assorted relics collected along the way, trusting that each token would eventually find its place in the tapestry.

My friends used to ask, "Why so many clues? Why don't they just tell you?"

Laughingly, I answered with a question of my own: "Why don't they just tell us how the universe was created?"

CHAPTER THIRTEEN

THE SCIENCES

Our species needs, and deserves, a citizenry with minds wide
awake and a basic understanding of how the world works.
Carl Sagan

Clearly, the secret of creation was taunting me in the wee hours of the night, harvesting dreams of treasures too curious to ignore. Before long, I was spending my waking hours studying crystalline substances, the quantum theory of particle physics, solid-state physics, the plum pudding model of the atom and more, while my sleeping vision continued to spin its guiding thread.

With not so much as a certificate in Home Economics and only two years of undergraduate college, I found wading through this web of physical sciences particularly daunting. No. To be completely honest, it was downright terrifying.

Nonetheless, I was compelled to journey on. I would wonder why there were so many dreams about calligraphy. Was it a calling of some sort? Or was it the elegant penmanship I associated with my dearly departed Aunt Agnes?

Another Peggymoonbeam-inspired dream, about a spinning stool with my elbow angled *upward,* translated to atomic spin and angular momentum, which connected to her earlier dream message about *the record spinning metals*[71] taking me to the Solar Nebula. Back to earth science.

Peggymoonbeam comes to me through a compact disc in the spinning stool dream, accompanied by the image of a crusty disc. A powdery quality is in the air. I'm in a school where an instructor spins a stool and teaches me to angle my elbow upward.[72]

The crusty disc was perplexing, tying to repeated images and messages of crust — usually piecrust — which I chalked up to being hungry at day's end.. Clue-finding was fast becoming an addiction and the perfect companion to unmeasured helpings of

---

71   3/23/97. See Ch. 9 – Spinning Disks, p. 49
72   8/25/98.

Footnotes contain dream dates and references to prior pages where the dream appeared.
Endnotes contain bibliographical references, are marked with "Ɛ" in the text, and appear at the end of the book.

Haagen-Dazs Vanilla. What, for example, would I ever match with heating elements and convection machines? I dreamed dreams of *a heating contraption operating on a convection principle.*[73] How could this be when my experience with such a heating contraption went little beyond a popcorn machine? It was some time later when I read that heat energy is conveyed through the Earth by convection[Ɛ19] and that it's possible for tectonic plates to move due to the convection currents in the earth's mantle, that zone between its crust and core. But how did this relate and why had I dreamt about it? I knew it was more than dessert on a plate. Or was it?

At some point, a parade of loops marched in. There were dreams of loops everywhere: *Loops atop my head, on a sheet, on a pair of socks, in a rug, as a ribbon, looping through a piece of fabric and a loop design in wedding attire worn by all.*[74] The loops, at that point, had become an apt metaphor for my mental state. I couldn't forget that Peggymoonbeam's handwriting was big and loopy. I wondered if the many cleverly placed loops might have been another of her signatures.

Stubborn little fellas whose perseverance won out, these nagging loops insisted, after years of interweaving and cross connecting, on registering as magnetic domains – electro spiritual signals which seemed to conduct the properties and behavior of Peggymoonbeam, reminding me of her notorious handwriting.

According to string theory, all particles of matter are tiny loops of vibrating string.[Ɛ20] Could that be what the loops implied? But the loop pattern also resembled the portal vein in a pathway in the visual cortex as well as a three-dimensional view of the RNA sequence. It could be whatever one wanted, but the key proved to be in knowing where it fit. It took me years to understand that the pattern fit everywhere. It was seamless.

Amid the mounting confusion over the mixture of so many different images, I sensed that somehow, there was an underlying order. Through the process of separating, mixing, combining, and then grouping the diverse pieces of this gigantic puzzle into themes, it seemed that all the themes would eventually join to reveal the full picture.

But was I up to the task? I honestly didn't know.

An eclectic arrangement of cone shapes was challenging beyond any known logic. The dream images were an absurd mix of *stacks of cones in my ear,*[75] *cone-shaped vases, cone-shaped desserts, skirted cone shapes – some presented as party favors.*[76] One bizarre arrangement had *pumpernickel muffins stacked in cone-shaped holders.*[77] But the most confounding of all was *a cone device that connected to a boat graced by the presence of Abraham Lincoln.*[78]

73　8/10/96.
74　Loop dreams: 1997 – 2000.
75　6/16/95.
76　Cone dreams: 1998 – 1990.
77　8/22/96.
78　1/25/98.

At first glance, it seemed that because of the work with vision, the cones must be representing the visual cones of the eye, and that was right as far as it went. However, following the path of its compatriots, it would soon evolve to something else that, endorsed by Honest Abe, carried the invisible seal of veracity.

Based on my research, I initially interpreted a dream image of *grids with lights* as the X-ray diffraction of crystals and it temporarily took its place as a piece in the crystal puzzle. A little dream birdie whispered that proteins are crystallized so their structures can be examined with X-rays, a connection that would help explain the hailstorm of minerals on its way.

While visiting online sites to learn about minerals and their properties, I fell upon the elemental tables where there appeared certain sets of numbers I'd dreamt. Never having an interest in chemistry, other than that magnetic draw to the opposite sex, I found it suddenly occupying my every waking and sleeping thought. Somehow, it felt like I was in the right place, though I understood none of it.

The odyssey was beginning to look like fractal geometry – patterns within patterns within patterns, repeating and stretching into infinity. At about this time I saw a television program about fractals entitled "Colors of Infinity" on PBS – The Public Broadcasting Service. It was my first inkling that our dreams behaved in much the same way. Indeed, the shapes of the universe and how they replicate our dreams fascinated me. My preoccupation with these connections returned me to thoughts of the stars. As my dreams expanded so too did my research and before long, I found myself immersed in material about our expanding universe.

Throughout this spectacular clue-finding mission, as each succeeding day delivered truths that reached for ever-higher ground, I was engulfed with gratitude at being drawn toward ultimate Truth. There seemed to be no limit, but I knew that, to arrive at a solution, I had to trust my instincts to the end. But was there to be an end?

CHAPTER FOURTEEN

HONORED EARTH GUIDE:

NICOLAUS STENO

One day, as a change of pace, I switched my attention from minerals back to vision, or so I thought. In my research, I came across a visual aid known as Stenopeic spectacles or pinhole glasses, which have opaque lenses perforated by a series of pinholes. They are used for both distant and near vision. When light passes through a small hole, it is restricted to rays coming straight from the object; these rays don't need focusing to bring them to a point. There are fewer peripheral light rays, which are responsible for blurring.

I thought back to the dream of the *coins in my eyes*[79] and again wondered how we can see with our eyes closed. When we dream, do we somehow peek through a pinhole that gives us infinite depth of focus?

In any case, while I was hunting for glasses, the subject of Stenopeic spectacles in some unknown way focused me on Nicolaus Steno (1638–1686) reminding me that another mentor would be stepping forward. Danish-born Steno was a man for all seasons: a physician, an anatomist and naturalist, and an ordained Catholic priest who believed the Bible recorded an accurate history of the Earth. He was the first to explain how the oldest rock strata in the earth will be at the bottom and the younger strata will be on top. From there, a time scale was created using rock sequences and the fossils contained within them to cover the Earth's entire geologic history from its origins to the present. This principle is called fossil succession. More broadly, it is known as Geologic Time.

Steno's name jogged my memory of a dream in which *I'm signing up for a course in shorthand. The girl reads off about 10 names of instructors. I choose the last name but that instructor isn't available so the girl tells me about an instructor (Japanese) who did not finish the course but was good. Both his names were impossible to pronounce. I'm wearing a woolen tam. The most dominant image is a single pole with a colorless rose on it, surrounded by the colors yellow and green.*[80]

---

79 11/13/94. See Ch. 2 – Searching, pp. 20–21
80 10/1/98.

Footnotes contain dream dates and references to prior pages where the dream appeared.

Endnotes contain bibliographical references, are marked with "Ɛ" in the text, and appear at the end of the book.

There they were again; the Pole, the Rose, and the prevailing color scheme of Yellow and Green.

I linked my first impression of shorthand to stenography and noted that trying to absorb the torrents of foreign dream content was like taking a crash course in steno. But what of the recurring Pole? It was still cloaked in secrecy.

Then I learned that Steno's examination of quartz crystals revealed that the corresponding faces of different crystals of a mineral all intersect at the same angle and that was called Steno's Law.[ɛ21, ɛ22] Amazing! Why would I be dreaming about this?

Quartz connected with the repeating chorus of roses. Rose quartz, my mind said, and from there on, the profusion of dream flowers symbolized crystals. At least I knew I was in the right family and had been able to identify that family as quartz.

The Avens plant, member of the Rose family, had morphed into the mineral Rose Quartz right under my nose.

The Pole. I was happy to have seen it again, even if I couldn't relate to it in this crystalline domain, standing, as it did, alone – without the company of the little girl. The surrounding colors of yellow and green cast a familiar hue, a duo perhaps cross-pollinating to connect to dominant and recessive genes, but how on Earth did they relate to the Pole? And why was I wearing a tam?

With a deepening trust in the universe, I learned that Steno championed the organic origin of fossils, having found fossil teeth far inland closely resembling those of a shark he had dissected.[ɛ23] That seemed to connect to the genetics piece. On the basis of his paleontological findings, he explained a view of geological history, contending sedimentary strata had been deposited in former seas.

This was beginning to fit with the "Whole Earth" messages, as well.

Dreams involving putty revealed Gypsum. In one, *I'm putting it on my face*[81] and in another *I'm using it as reinforcement for a four-cornered scarf.*[82] Gypsum, the primary ingredient of plaster of Paris used for making medical casts, seemed at the most elemental level to depict transformation from the abstract to the concrete, dreaming reality hardening to waking reality. The dream metaphor of a four-cornered scarf appeared to link to putty on the face or was it suggesting a plaster-like cast to mend the fractured face of the four corners of the Earth?

"Ah, Steno," I thought. "What a roundabout way of teaching. I feel like I'm spinning most days while fragments of a grand design are flying around me. But then, how else could worlds of knowledge be taught in a speed course such as this?" I would see him often, his spirit closest to God among my guides. He became the chief sleuth and the ordained theologian in the cast after spending three centuries in an otherworldly land

---

81   2/21/96.
82   12/31/95.

which I learned was called Terracrust. Driven by an intense passion to save our planet, he would become my devoted and erudite guide introducing me to Earth's multilayered and complex nature.

An inquiring detective and natural educator, he sensed me as a bewildered earthling, compelled to unravel the dream messages he sent. Though dream symbols are a kind of shorthand which can have many meanings and connections, Steno's clues would take me on real-time adventures into the workings of the earth. He judiciously waited for the right opening before he'd reveal the critical nature of the quest and its raison d'être. It was actually Steno, the Honored Earth Guide, who held out the Branch of Geology. Its many subbranches, such as volcanology, stratigraphy and astrogeology intertwined not only one with another but also with other branches of the earth sciences and with such fields as physics, chemistry, biology, mathematics, paleontology, anthropology, none of which I knew a trickle of.

Appearing with his steno pad filled with volumes of notes on the Earth and equipped with a detective's magnifying glass through which to peer, Steno somehow knew exactly when he was needed. He was passionately concerned about God's creatures and devotedly assumed his role as protector and guardian of the Earth. He taught me that God returns manyfold what you give to Him.

Steno's persistence proved a necessary and compelling force on my search.

CHAPTER FIFTEEN

A WONDERLAND OF MINERALS

The spinning metals, the gray metal bucket, the odd combination of metals and plants led me to the Internet. Surfing for metals, I wound up in a candy store of minerals called The Mineral Kingdom. It was magical and held a stash of hidden dream minerals, so many that I was convinced I had found the mainframe of my story. Clicking on to the Mineral Kingdom each morning, I felt like Alice in Wonderland following the White Rabbit down his hole. A childhood prism wedged in memory was my fascination with rock candy and how it was shaped like natural crystals. It came in an orange and blue box and you couldn't watch the movie without it. The natural crystal formations were as exciting as the sugar highs they produced.

Anyway, back to minerals of the present. First, there was *corundum*, an aluminum oxide, which signified a major and very puzzling theme. It had been delivered via a dream the first time by its mineral name with the message that it meant *a "new order or paradigm."*[83]

I thought then that the similarly spelled and pronounced conundrum, a riddle with a pun in its answer, would surely jibe, but the word in the dream was unwaveringly corundum. I was confused. Was that part of the riddle? "Which was it?" I mused. Was it a riddle within a riddle?

The dream scenario presented an *angel writing a script and a blue iridescent file, which held a game.* The blue iridescent file persuaded me to opt for the gemstone. Upon close examination of the dream, I noticed that one definition of "file" curiously impersonated emery (as in an emery board), a variety of corundum. In a dream five years later, *a chemist upstairs redelivered corundum, this time identified by chemical formula:* $Al_2O_3.$[84] This was a more deliberate knocking-on-your-door-to-remind-you dream and contained two characteristics of the mineral: *a black bead and a mention of sand blasting.* The *file* smoothed out another link for emery is black and used in sandpaper. In addition, erosion may cause emery to crumble and form sand, black sand.

---

83   4/13/94.
84   2/7/99.

Footnotes contain dream dates and references to prior pages where the dream appeared.
Endnotes contain bibliographical references, are marked with "ε" in the text, and appear at the end of the book.

This learning to pluck the nuggets from the slag, so to speak, was an initiation. Corundum was a perfect example.

After labored questioning of the corundum-conundrum dilemma and an engrossing wheel of connections, I was convinced the mineral was nestled in the puzzle. The fleeting message about the paradigm fit. A paradigm is an example or pattern, especially one underlying a theory. It was clear. The mineral corundum was the example underlying the language of dreams. Corundum was designated grand duchy of the mineral empire, one monarchy among many that would teach the nomenclature of the transcendental variety of dream experience.

That was its primary function – but, as I would discover, not its only one.

CHAPTER SIXTEEN

CALCITE

While scaling this multifaceted and glistening mountain of minerals, I next happened across Iceland Spar or Optical Calcite, which is transparent, colorless, and exhibits double refractions. "Back to the vision theme," I thought.

Sparkly babies[85] in one dream and *deformed twins*[86] in another matched the phosphorescence and twinning characteristics of Calcite and the deformation of mineral fracture.

Calcite, also the main component of chalk, directed me to a dream where *I am eating a chalky substance with hair in it from a spoon.*[87] Did the hair link to DNA? I knew they could analyze DNA from hair fibers. Chalk, at this stage, was blurry.

Researching calcium carbonate and how it's formed from hot springs, jostled my memory of a dream in which *geysers are the main attraction. I have to buy an 8mm cartridge to take a picture. I forget to turn on the camera but it still records on the cartridge.*[88] I seemed to remember something about geysers and calcite. I think after they have burst into steam and as the water cools, some form of calcite comes out of the solution.

There they were again: Calcium and Vision! What a handsome couple! They were definitely becoming more of an item.

In another dream, *I am carrying a parasol, walking through a heavy mist. There is turbulence, the air is thick. The winds are strong and I'm being thrown about but not minding it because it's part of that life. It's part of that costume. I am walking along. There is a black cloth under my feet. Suddenly, there is no ground beneath me. I begin to fall. I fall into a black hole – a void – there is nothing. I am falling and falling and tumbling and can't breathe. I am gasping for air. I think "This is it!" I struggle in the pitch-black hole. Suddenly there's a slab I can grab on to. I struggle and struggle and finally it's the unknowable slab that brings me up.*[89]

---

85   7/6/96.
86   10/23/97.
87   10/2/99.
88   11/16/97.
89   8/23/96.

Footnotes contain dream dates and references to prior pages where the dream appeared.
Endnotes contain bibliographical references, are marked with "ℰ" in the text, and appear at the end of the book.

There was that rabbit hole again, much too ambiguous to fill – at least for now.

Well, Alice found the Cheshire Cat, the Mad Hatter, and the King and Queen of Hearts. I thought I'd found an answer to the puzzling Yellow Slab after patiently waiting five years but this slab was not designated yellow. Did it belong to the yellow lexicon clue when Ramos dominated the picture? Yet, just as I was on the verge of what appeared to be an answer, I was learning that even the most gratifying discoveries were not conclusive. There were always more.

More and more I came to realize that even the obscurity of a particular dream image meant something. For example, in one of the yellow slab dreams,[90] there was emphasis on the *right change.*

For the time, the yellow slab, calcium, and vision were a companionable group.

The different levels of the cosmos began to resonate; the solar system, DNA, the minerals and plants of the Earth swirled in unison. Soon, I found they would launch the next quest, seeking a refined connection of minerals to metals.

---

90   See Ch. 32 – Mother's Apprentices, p. 141

CHAPTER SEVENTEEN

REAL ESTATE & ALCHEMY

While trying to transcribe the Steno discovery, a dream, from 1993, inventoried in the warehouse of my brain, carried a memory that I'd written it on steno paper.

The dream spotlighted *a piece of pink carpet floating around Rockefeller Center. I am a real estate agent. There's a glossy realtors' photograph of a house I am to sell. Someone asks if I'm an alchemist. I say, "We do more than one thing here. I'm in real estate and I'm also an alchemist." I have drawn a small house with a sold sign across it reading "5 Sold 250 cm."*[91]

Learning to crack this dream code was like navigating the crossword puzzle of the universe. Rockefeller Center symbolized rock, real estate denoted Earth, and alchemy conveyed transformation of matter and, perhaps, transmutation. Connecting the Steno piece, I noticed that the shape of the house resembled the basic symmetry of a crystal structure. While the symbols themselves were direct, their connections to each other were circuitous.

In the midst of this onslaught, *Peggymoonbeam turns up again, this time with a foot in each of two doors: one mineral, the other, genetics, where she appears in a gallery of family portraits. I register shock when I see someone who is dead. It's here that I see a gray metal bucket containing two very long strands of amber. I am wearing crystal beads and decide to replace them with one of these strands because the amber goes with what I'm wearing. At the very end, I'm given an orange cube, which I have to carry with me to about 10 different places. It is dark. I have to carry the cube with something else to each place. The other object changes at each place, but the orange cube remains constant.*[92]

The cube entertains a variety of meanings but the most striking is its representation of Truth as being always the same, however viewed.[E24] Another meaning closely reflecting my direction is that it symbolically squares the circle. And, within the mineral family, it could point to an isometric classification, a mineral equal in all three physical dimensions.

Early dream shadings hinted at transformation apparently starting with my own, but this was the first definitive appearance of metaphorical transmutation, where one element changed to another. This was in juxtaposition to the constant and unwavering

---

91   7/16/93.
92   10/28/95.

Footnotes contain dream dates and references to prior pages where the dream appeared.
Endnotes contain bibliographical references, are marked with "E" in the text, and appear at the end of the book.

Truth, characterized by the cube. Even in the dark, it would not change. The *"other object"* remained to be seen.

So went my foray into the realm of the "elements."

I raced through the elemental table seeking symbols of each chemical element and there it was, just as in my dream: Cm. Curium, named after the husband and wife researchers, Pierre and Marie Curie, was a real element, and the isotope in my alchemy matched: Cm-250 with a half-life of 9700.0 years. But the dream had gotten ahead of me. Curium, a silver-colored radioactive rare earth metal, may have been the signpost leading me to metals and pointing a finger to Earth. A rare earth metal. The Silver Key was echoing its unexplained presence.

Another dream beckoned. *I wanted to get my hands in the earth. Someone said it was conclusive*[93] and that was intriguing. The *Cm* dream seemed to be signaling a radioactive component connecting with the Curies' discoveries about radioactivity around 1898. Marie Curie actually coined the term "radioactivity." Going back to the dream with the *loopy headdress* and the magnetic domain, I wondered if the Curies were meant to be icons not only to advocate radioactivity but magnetism as well.

Now I was exploring Chemistry and Physics, more foreign tongues. I was terrified! How would I ever wade through this thicket of science?

I recall Dr. Noodle telling me it was not possible to dream anything you don't know. Though there's lack of agreement in the scientific community on this matter, that idea, together with the oft-repeated refrain that *I had something bigger that I was supposed to match* stirred my curiosity more than a little. In one dream I recalled, *it* looked like an iris, *a purplish flower*[94] but during my research, I wondered if it was the iris of the eye or an acronym for Incorporated Research Institutions for Seismology. I guessed that if I knew something about alchemy, as the cm dream said I did, I'd muddle through but would need to know more about Marie Curie.

She discovered two elements: one she named Polonium after her native country, and the other, Radium for its radiant blue glow. Having demonstrated her exceptionally strong desire to contribute to the welfare of others, she is known for her pioneering work in developing medical applications for radioactivity. Using tubes of a radioactive gas (now called radon) derived from radium, Marie brought life-saving X-ray equipment to the battlefront during World War I. Doctors used those tubes to treat wounds and to destroy diseased tissue, a foreshadowing of today's cancer treatments. Today, The Radium Institutes in both Warsaw and Paris continue the work Marie and Pierre began.

Why on Earth, I wondered, would her chemical element appear in my dream?

---

93   9/14/93.
94   11/23/92. See Ch. 5 – Honored Visionaries, p. 37

CHAPTER EIGHTEEN

HONORED CHEMISTRY GUIDE:
MARIE CURIE

Much like the interior of the atom, the soul continues to radiate,
living on from one lifetime to the next.

Marie Curie and the alchemist dream were the front runners of the metal delegation designed to carry out very important work. It appeared that Mme. Curie herself was charged with announcing it to me. The *Curium* dream telegraphed her future appearances and thereafter she appeared often, her entrance into my dream world often accompanied by a bright sprinkling of ions floating around her, various gases, ores, radioactive elements and weird chemistry talk – none of which I knew a whit of.

As a guide, she was the essence of simplicity and competence. Invariably cool and single-minded, she taught me the two main requisites for this work: balance and focus, directing me with steely determination exactly to the destination that had been charted.

At first, she appeared outwardly shy and retiring, but as I grew to know her more intimately, her great capacity for love and warmth blossomed. This had been profoundly demonstrated in her passion for her work and her compassion for humankind during her time on Earth.

Our Heaven-sent Earth-bound relationship became almost like that of mother and daughter. Fiercely protective, caring, and nurturing, she was affectionately receptive to my appreciation of her. She tacitly understood my fear in keeping up with her depth of knowledge and showed unfailing patience in guiding me through the complexities of chemistry – her native science.

Her idealism, her faith in science, her tenacity, her work ethic, and her pioneering spirit moved her to pursue and realize her dreams in Heaven just as she, and Pierre when they worked together on Earth, inspired the discovery of twenty-nine new radioactive elements between 1903 and 1912.

Footnotes contain dream dates and references to prior pages where the dream appeared.

Endnotes contain bibliographical references, are marked with "Ɛ" in the text, and appear at the end of the book.

Perhaps because some of the subject matter she was passing to me was outside her primary areas of interest, she offered her clues very selectively, and worked closely with my dream guide Steno since they shared an interest in crystallization.

With the metals duly announced, their filings in my dreams were transmitted on a new channel, reporting in a variety of formats. One strand came attached to a string of dreams showing metal as a frame: *Metal trim around a window, metal trim around a clock, a stainless steel picture frame around a word.*[95]

The lurking metal frame soon became a psychic magnet begging more: What was in the frame? The dreams, while reflecting the myriad uses of metal, began to show up more conspicuously in dream journals I had stashed away over the years. *A metal steering wheel, a metal cup filled with carrots, an encoded metal cartridge from a camera.*[96] How curious. Both the camera and carrots connected to vision. Hmm. Metal and vision.

Next tumbled in a jangling dream repertoire *of iodized metal, burnished metal, metal wrenches, coins made of metal, thin metal plates, metal flowers, metallic foil, brass, aluminum, iron, pewter, copper, stainless steel, a metal sphere, a metal slug, a metal compound, wrought iron parlor chairs, and lounge chairs.*[97] This long list of clanging metal icons finally served up silver – literally on a platter.

From an *etched silver slipper*[98] to *a floating metal wrench,*[99] silver's diverse resume showed great promise. Silver would certainly have its day but later.

The most baffling metal portrayals – *a gold ball appearing behind my ear*[100] occurred twice, the dreams coming about a month apart. In the first dream, I'm told that it's been there since birth. In the second dream, I'm remembering the first dream.

This made me wonder if the purpose of these dreams was to give me a personal warning, so I decided to have a complete physical to be sure I wasn't a carrier of excessive metal. When my test results proved normal, I understood that metal was indeed a dream force to be reckoned with, since its repetition stood it in a class of its own. The sheer volume of metals appearing in my dreams made them impossible to ignore.

The gold metal ball and the silver key … silver and gold. Gee, I thought, transmuting metals into silver and gold falls under alchemy. No longer floating, but rafting the whitewater of the unconscious were: alchemy – chemistry – Madame Curie – and the memory of moonlighting in the Rockefeller Center riddle: "We do more than one thing here."

---

95   5/4/96, 5/31/96, 6/1/96.
96   4/11/95, 4/14/95, 1/22/98.
97   Metal dreams: 1993–2004.
98   10/20/92.
99   10/12/98.
100 11/15/96, 12/24/96.

The first dream I was able to attach a real metal to revolved around a *lost piece of tin sculpture described as crude and jagged with hieroglyphics on it. It is emblazoned with a red insignia in the shape of a V.*[101]

V, despite its abundant presence in my dreams of France, at this juncture was symbolic of the metal Vanadium, which is used as catalyst, dye, color-fixer. It was discovered in 1830 and obtained from vanadinite, an ore that occurs with Galena, Barite, and Calcite, ores of lead, barium, and calcium, respectively. Hieroglyphics took me *to Egyptian hieroglyphics and ... the stone-faced people who came alive* in my dream[102] and mirrored those figures of stone at the Temple of Karnak in Luxor, Egypt, revisited.

Does everything in the universe, I wondered, connect with everything else? I was excited with the matches: Galena – Calcite. For the moment – I could go no further.

But the letter V is also a coming together – a joining.

---

101 1/3/93.
102 11/25/98. See Prologue.

CHAPTER NINETEEN

GALENA AND BEYOND

The cryptic codes of the penny in my eye and Peggymoonbeam's disk of metals sent me on a relentless search for copper that turned up an ore called Chalcopyrite – a copper-iron sulfide also known as Peacock Ore because of its iridescent blue color. That matched up with a dream of *beautiful blue iridescent peacock feathers on an exotic creature*. Was Peacock Ore returning me to the *blue iridescent file* in the dream riddle of *Corundum*?[103]

Corundum remained a conundrum in a labyrinthine vortex. Some days I wanted to morph into a lizard but I was powerless to stop the mining. This must be what it's like to be sucked into a black hole. Even so, I sensed a way out.

I found it curious that Chalcopyrite also occurs with Galena, since Galen's was the first ancient voice I heard among my dream guides. That seemed like lifetimes ago when I was trying to decipher the visual purpose of this odyssey.

I learned that Galena was used in crystal radio sets and is known as a "cat's whisker," which linked to Old Man's Whiskers and the Three-Flowered Avens plant.[104]

Galena, the most important ore of lead often found with silver, resonated with a variety of silver images in my dreams – bowls, plates, platters, and the like. But where did it all fit? With silver being one of the best conductors of electricity, I wondered if we're all like citizens band radios acting as conduits through which some metallic influence in the universe contacts us. Were the jillions of fragments of information I was receiving electronically transmitted? That seemed to jibe, but the silver component was still anyone's guess. It dredged up the dream of *the scientist and the feeling of a metal thing on my back*.[105]

I'd just have to wait it out until I could enlist some scientific know-how.

Is it any wonder that I continued to be attracted to Peacock Ore? It was so specific and among other things, my namesake.

And then the NBC, CBS, ABC connection struck. It was dazzling!

103 8/28/97, 4/13/94. See Ch. 15 – A Wonderland of Minerals, p. 71
104 12/9/95.   See Ch. 1 – Beginnings, p. 6
                    See Ch. 10 – The Stuff of Life, p. 53
105 6/14/01.   See Ch. 10 – The Stuff of Life, p. 53

Footnotes contain dream dates and references to prior pages where the dream appeared.
Endnotes contain bibliographical references, are marked with "Ɛ" in the text, and appear at the end of the book.

The NBC Peacock, the CBS Eye, and ABC as an analogue of the table of elements. It was a confluence of networks: communication networks, neural networks, retinal networks, mineral networks, chemical networks. A burst of insight flashed the word "communication." It had been transmitted and, finally, received. How ingenious of my guides to give me symbols related to the industry I was in for so many years!

The work was advancing with a celestial dispatch that would have rivaled NASA's. Never-ending surges of information were flooding my head, moving faster than the speed of light. Overtaken by the compelling forces of nature, my presence felt like a microscopic dot in a sea of foam. The magnitude of the experience was directly proportionate to the smallness of my being. The exhilaration was compelling, yet there was no danger. Never had I felt so safe.

At the same time, any attempt to direct it was impossible. I was on a virtual rocket ship blasting through space with barely time to eat or sleep. Cooking nearly vanished from my routine. With the exception of my nightly addiction for Haagen-Dazs Vanilla, I wasn't hungry much of the time. I was breathing my food.

Discovery filled my life. There was little room to spare for much of anything except to seize whatever information I could grasp. I knew countless connections would have to wait because the next night would bring new dreams, and the next day would hold new epiphanies.

CHAPTER TWENTY

AGNESWISEHEART

Somewhere, something incredible is waiting to be known.
Carl Sagan

If we're lucky, our lives are deeply touched by one unforgettable person. For me, this was Aunt Agnes, my mother's sister and the source, from the other side, of another epiphany. This woman of compassion, wit, elegance, and a host of virtues she'd never own up to, came to me as Agneswiseheart, a dream courier embodying infinite love and wisdom. It was only when I graduated adolescence that her strength, her values and her indomitable spirit became apparent to me. I watched in awe as she courageously faced trials in her own personal life, trials few knew about.

A mother to me in my early years, she was the only one who truly understood my childhood pain. In adulthood, she became my best friend, my majordomo mentor guiding me through life with the strength of her kindness and a knowing trust in the universe.

At the end of her time on Earth, she waged a strenuous fight against a cruel and spreading cancer, lapsing finally into coma. I stood at her bedside in her native Pittsburgh for what I knew would be the last time. As I leaned over the heartbreaking remains of her ravaged body, trying to breathe white light into her and praying that she be given the grace of peace, she opened her eyes, looked straight at me and uttered, "beep beep" before falling away.

It was extraordinary that this skeletal victim of cancer, who for days was in a coma, was able to come back if only for a second. Her final show of strength and pure spirit told me she knew I was by her side. She departed Earth in 1987 and since then I've thought often of those last words – "beep beep" – words not part of her vernacular; words I never before heard her speak and, though I knew she was trying to tell me something, I had no idea what.

That scene at her deathbed hung over me as a specter, permanently etched in my memory and in my heart. I'd often wondered what her mysterious "beep beep" could have possibly meant until...

Footnotes contain dream dates and references to prior pages where the dream appeared.
Endnotes contain bibliographical references, are marked with "Ɛ" in the text, and appear at the end of the book.

In 1996, I dreamt *I was running to catch a Delta flight.*[106] Then, I surely thought it was Delta airlines although, in retrospect I realized, Delta is an airline I'd never flown.

A deeper look into the dream revealed it was decidedly a flight aboard a spaceship, which I described as *a huge open space with open seating arranged in the round and highlighted with a spiral staircase. The hostess is telling me there are six different levels. A string of white and lavender balloons is blowing my way.* The spaceship scenario *concludes with a very long tube, like a telescope; the focal point of the exchange is with Agneswiseheart.* I had awakened feeling very happy that she was in my dream.

When I returned to this journal entry four years after the dream, it appeared at first to be a dream fantasy in deep space. However, on second thought, the particulars orbited toward a more scientifically stellar passage. One of the first symbols to catch my eye was the spiral staircase, which fit with "spiral nebulae," the name used for galaxies up until the mid-1920s. Exploring the nebulae, I discovered a star that breathed new life into the Delta dream. I found that Delta Cephei, a variable star, is the fourth brightest star in Cepheus, a large constellation in the Northern Hemisphere. From most northern latitudes in autumn, Delta Cephei is bright and high in the sky, away from the horizon and local light pollution.[E25]

Taking in the dreamscapes, my sleeping eyes seemed to experience the same varying brightness as that very famous pulsating star, the brightness of which expands and contracts rhythmically.[E26] I realized that a pulsating rhythm resonates with the movement of the dream which expands by unfolding aspects of our lives and contracts by combining those aspects. Some dreams were luminous while others were in shadow. I traveled back to my childhood pastime of stargazing in Coral Gables and remembered how the sparkly ones always seemed to blink at me.

Studies of Delta Cephei-type variable stars, usually known simply as Cepheid variables, have helped astronomers determine the size of the universe and the distances between various physical parts of the universe.

As I was typing the above sentence, an out-of-this-world kind of magic swept in.

While relaying to you dear, Reader, the story of my symbiotic relationship with Agneswiseheart and of her cryptic and final "beep beep," I took a break from my storytelling to further explore the constellation Cepheus on the Internet. I closed the file this page is in. I fetched what I needed from the Internet, returned to the file, and opened this page to continue the story. As I was scrolling to the place where I would continue writing, this line of symbols suddenly appeared exactly as you see it here.[107]

Υῶ´ϑΩ ´ ´ῶ ΥΩ χφ Υ˘ ΩΥ 's˘ ˘ΩΥ ´, ,ϑΩ

---

106 8/18/96.

107 This implantation occurred on March 18, 2000.

transformed to best friend in adulthood. Agneswiseheart was my majordomo mentor guiding me through life with the strength of her kindness and a knowing trust in the universe.

(This was the original text later edited to what appears in the second paragraph of this chapter.)

What is this! Where did it come from? What does it mean?

What I did not know at the time was this would not be the only instance in which such coding would appear.

I was dumbstruck. I just sat at the computer confounded. Weeping tears of gratitude and totally riveted to this page, I printed some paper copies, thinking no one on Earth would believe me. I tried to make computer copies to a new file and to a floppy disc, neither of which worked.

You may ask how it is that I could reproduce the letters here if nothing worked. I finally managed to convert the font from my later edited copy (a mother to me in my early years she[108]) from English to Greek, recreating the Greek code on the computer. It seems simple enough in the telling, but the translation proved to be something else.

At the time, I was confounded as to what these symbols meant, or what language they were in if they were letters. But I did have an overwhelming sense that in some inexplicable way they were from Agneswiseheart.

I was convinced that my aunt's departing beeps were precognitive and were telling me something, something being repeated some thirteen years later for the same reason, but this time in a mysterious computer code – ah, the marvel of digital electronics.

The wonder of this communication evoked in me feelings beyond what the spoken word can convey. The sudden appearance of those letters will be with me forever. I held this mystery close thinking about it day and night not uttering a word to a soul. It remained my secret for two years but finally curiosity won out and I just had to know if a similar experience had been reported anywhere. So two years later I asked a friend at the late John Mack organization[E27] if he had ever heard of this kind of thing happening on the computer. He said he hadn't but would check around. Sometime later, I received a letter from him suggesting I contact Mark Macy who researches transcommunication with spirits through electronic devices.[E28]

I screeched! MARK MACY! That's the password in my computer!

How did I get the name Mark? Mark was the name of my spirit guide in waking life and I'd been having strange dreams about Macy's underground, so I combined Mark with Macy and my password became markmacy! The plot was thickening, or as

Peggymoonbeam would say, "The thick was plottening." I ultimately contacted Macy who registered curiosity and surprise.

Back to the mystifying code. Risking my credibility, I asked a few of my friends about the symbols. One friend, schooled in ancient symbolism and cultures, matter-of-factly stated, "It's Greek."

Of course! The entire experience was Greek to me.

I exclaimed, "GREEK!" thinking the first symbol I recognized in the Greek code was Omega and that repeated five times. But the main thread was Delta and what was Delta, but Greek? Greek began to navigate my thoughts. Claudius Galen was Greek. Claudius Ptolemy was Greek. But how did that relate to the spaceship in the dream that began with a flight aboard Delta? Delta eventually sped me to Delta Cephei in the constellation of Cepheus.

Hmm. In Greek mythology, Cepheus (from the Greek word meaning "gardener") was the king of Ethiopia. Cepheus is one of the forty-eight constellations cataloged by astronomer Ptolemy in the second century AD, but it was delineated as a constellation many centuries earlier and is probably of Euphratean origin. "Ptolemy," I thought. "Astronomy — the dream of *the spaceship — the telescope.* It was back to vision."

Reaching back to the Delta dream that wound itself around a galactic theme, I wondered if the *string of white and lavender balloons* might be characterizing helium, one of the elements contained in a star.

Could Helium, the lightest of all gases except Hydrogen, be characterizing a gas unknown to me at this time? I wondered if, like so many other threads in the story, the introduction of a category like gas was presented so I could acquire the knowledge to uncover the particular gaseous element that would someday fit.

Then while exploring the stars and the galaxies, I stumbled across a name. It had floated in on a dream many moons ago and was one of few dreams I failed to record. I remembered a very long name that sounded Indian, but had been unable to conjure it up for years. Suddenly I had a tingling sensation, as if a faraway memory excited one of my neurons: Chandrasekhar. Yes. That was it – Chandrasekhar.

NASA's premier X-ray observatory was named the Chandra X-ray Observatory in honor of Subrahmanyan Chandrasekhar, the late Indian-American Nobel laureate. Known to the world as Chandra, which means "moon or luminous" in Sanskrit, he was widely regarded as one of the foremost astrophysicists of the twentieth century.

I learned that images from the Chandra Observatory have traced the aftermath of a gigantic stellar explosion in such stunning detail that scientists can see evidence of what may be a neutron star or a black hole near the center. Hmm… There's that hole again!

And where did the hole in so many of my dreams fit? It was an oxymoron. An empty space could fit nowhere or everywhere, but was it meant to be a black hole?

Heavy elements in hot gas produce X-rays of specific energies. Chandra's ability to measure these through an X-ray telescope allowed astronomers to tell precisely how much of each element is present. With this information, they can investigate how the elements necessary for life are created and spread throughout the galaxy by exploding stars.

Heavy elements? Light elements? Where was this going? I was in the dark but I had to forge ahead.

I returned to the dream having found in my research that among multitudes of meanings assigned to delta, it is also the code word used in radio communication to represent the letter D. Might the telescope that extends between Agneswiseheart and me in the dream be mirroring a radio telescope used to detect radio waves from the universe? Radio astronomers have mapped the spiral structure of the Milky Way from the radio waves given out by interstellar gas and have detected many individual radio sources within our Galaxy and beyond. They have also undertaken searches for intelligent signals from other civilizations in the Galaxy, so far without success.

In the words of Carl Sagan, "… a transmitting civilization could make it very easy for us if it wished. Imagine we're in the course of a systematic search or in the midst of some more conventional radio observations and suppose one day we find a strong signal slowly emerging. Not just some background hiss, but a methodical series of pulses … the numbers 1, 2, 3, 5, 7, 11, 13. A signal made of prime numbers (divisible only by one and themselves). There is no natural astrophysical process that generates prime numbers. We would have to conclude someone fond of elementary mathematics was saying hello. This would be no more than a beacon to attract our attention. The mean message will be subtler, more hidden, far richer. We may have to work hard to find it. But the beacon signal alone would be profoundly significant. It would mean that someone has learned to survive technological adolescence, that self-destruction is not inevitable … that we also may have a future. Such knowledge it seems to me might be worth a great price."[E29]

Hmm … I had received many of those numbers in my dreams. Particularly repetitive were the numbers 5 and 7. Were these pulses like beeps from Agneswiseheart? Were they signals from a transmitting civilization?

The message in the Delta dream was visibly rich in stellar elements: The "spiral nebulae" – *the spiral staircase;* gas – *the balloons;* X-rays and radio source – *the telescope.* Now I needed to scope out why the balloons were lavender and white and what the six levels might represent.

As though surfing a wave of adrenaline, recognitions would mount and then memory riding the next swell would surge and gently recede. Which perceptions were visual? Which were mental? I couldn't tell. I was carried back to a dream I had nearly forgotten. It was about *a circle I'd changed to a star. It looked like an eye so I drew points on it that resembled eyelashes.*[109]

---

109 6/10/95.

Those were some of Ptolemy's imprimaturs: The circle of the spheres, astronomy, and vision:

Ptolemy synthesized and extended Hipparchus's system of epicycles and eccentric circles to explain his geocentric theory of the solar system. Ptolemy's system involved at least eighty epicycles to explain the motions of the Sun, the Moon, and the planets. His view of the world was based on a fixed Earth, around which the sphere of the fixed stars rotates every day, carrying with it the spheres of the Sun, the Moon, and the five planets known in his time: Mercury, Venus, Mars, Jupiter, Saturn. His Ptolemaic system predicted the positions of the planets accurately enough for naked-eye observations.

My Optico dream riddle, Ptolemy's Optica, and the refraction of light drew attention to vision, light, and astronomy but gave me no further hints, except for one memorable experience.

The first of the *mirror image*[110] dreams of an *upside-down, right-side-up house* spurred me to research optics. Just at the time when I was studying light and vision, specifically the laws of reflection and refraction, I had to straighten out a matter with my health insurance. I called Blue Cross Blue Shield in October 1998 with a question about my PCP (primary care provider) number. A most courteous Mr. Dunham was trying to help me. He repeatedly tried to print out my record and it wasn't reading right. I sensed his exasperation and said, "I guess I'll just call back later."

"Wait," he said. "Something really 'cute' happened. It printed out backward so the only way I can read it is to hold it up to the light and read it from right to left – like a mirror image. I can now read it for you."

Poor Mr. Dunham must have thought I doubted him, for I was unable to contain myself. I squealed, "You really have to hold it up to the light to read it?"

"Yes, yes," and again, he excitedly told his story. I asked him to repeat it a third time. I could not believe my ears.

Somehow, it seemed Mr. Dunham had innocently tuned in to my studies of light and reflection. I was highly amused that he characterized as "cute" this colossal moment that led to one of my epiphanies. Of course, how could he know he'd been called upon to perform some optical magic?

It felt like Alice in Through the Looking-Glass when she discovers the book of nonsense poems which she can read only by holding it up to a mirror. This would mark the beginning of an endless stream of startling connections and coded messages that would probably seem like nonsense to a lot of people, but may possibly contain valuable insights for a few.

Stars ... Light ... Vision. A wondrous feeling of an intimate and unbreakable bond between my tiny self and the gigantic world about me was awakening me to dimensions

---

110 8/17/93.

beyond ordinary experience. How would I be able to increase my knowledge and aware-ness with my limited human senses? How could I feel so big and yet so small?

The bees were buzzing in full force. To quote the sound philosophy of Pooh:

"If' there's a buzzing-noise, somebody's making a
buzzing-noise, and the only reason for making a
buzzing-noise that I know of is because you're a bee."$^{\mathcal{E}}$30

There were more bees than you could shake a stick at, but essentially, I concluded that Agneswiseheart beeped beeped in with a banner of Greek letters just to let me know I was on the right track. Of course, I hadn't yet exhausted what a translation of the seven-teen Greek characters might reveal. Judging from past communications, there could most certainly be a code within a code and, perhaps within yet another code.

Had the telescope in the dream imaged a distant and very luminous starlike object in the form of Agneswiseheart? Was it confirming in a dreamlike X-ray, one of the most fascinating theories of modern times that we came from the stars? As Carl Sagan was fond of saying, "We are star stuff."

Just like the stars, my spirit guides must be there all the time, whether I see them or not. I guessed the only difference between them and us was a difference in altitude and maybe not even that.

I wondered if the *telescope* symbolic *of the exchange with Agneswiseheart* might also be a metaphor for the tunnel we pass through when we transit from one world to the next. The integration of waking and dreaming consciousness seemed to be opening the gates to the realm of interdimensional thought where the lack of fixed ideas allows for a mag-nitude of experience far beyond our ordinary physical concepts. As I pondered, I sensed a swirling current of intense nurturing light.

"Penelope, it is Agneswiseheart. You seem a bit overwhelmed with the abundance of knowledge we've sent. It is important that you be discriminating toward the profusion that surrounds you and do not allow that which you have desired to possess you. When this phase of the assignment is complete, you will communicate it as directed and then simply move on to the next phase.

"Your notations on delta are quite fitting, for every pattern that you see connects to another pattern in human history. I might add that delta is also the final and deepest stage of sleep where our messages are delivered to your unconscious. They patiently wait for the mentally active period of REM when they can surface in your dreams.

"Now, I want you to hold this helium-filled balloon for a moment and then release it. It is a very small movement. All we ask is that you let go of the string.

"When the balloon floats up to us we'll fill it with jigsaw pieces of a mammoth dream puzzle that holds the many answers to what you may think of as unanswerable questions. While your mind is at rest, pieces of dreams will drift down to Earth where they will enter the portals of your deep and regenerating sleep.

"You will observe fragments that stretch back to all of your days on Earth and even beyond. Through synthesis of the thousands of dream particles we're sending you, the big picture will become very clear.

"We call this balloon aircraft an Oneiroball. Oneiro derives from the Greek oneiromancy, which is a practice of dream interpretation that uses dreams to predict the future.

You will come to discover, Penelope, that the Oneiroball is the vehicle that holds your purpose."

I took the imaginary string and released it. And I wept. Tears of missing her flowed into tears of gratitude. As in life, Agneswiseheart steadfastly stood over me, protecting me with her ageless wisdom and her tender heart.

PART TWO

~

TIEING KNOTS

CHAPTER TWENTY-ONE

HALF CIRCLE - FULL STAR – CLOG

I wondered about the confetti nature of the dreams. Why did they come in such itty-bitty and seemingly disconnected pieces? The developing saga of the Solar System? DNA? France? Real Estate? Alchemy? Newfoundland? The Titanic? It was baffling. A few riddles appeared to have closed their loops, if only for a while.

Avens of the Rose family connected Rose Quartz to Nicolaus Steno. Avens, also called Old Man's Whiskers, was guiding us toward Galena, the first semiconductor used to extract an audio signal in the "cat's whiskers" of early crystal radios. And following the Galen trend was the linking of Percival to the Cat Retina to Galen to the Optic Nerve which encircled Vision. Whew. What a workout!

I would inhale and exhale a variety of unfamiliar smells rising from the potage many times before each element could be isolated and identified. But now a new essence, far less scholarly, gave off a mustier, aged scent. Departure from the already simmering mix of metals, minerals, and gases was confusing as this new aroma, although vague, conjured up another sense of the Titanic.

Taken with another cache of dream fragments that opened to the worlds of Astronomy and Astrology, I was nonplused by a repeating message that echoed:

"Half Circle, Full Star, Clog." I'm practicing the Girl Scout motto "Be Prepared," What did I see? I saw each of the images as a graphic depiction, so graphic that I illustrated the clog as a shoe with a wooden sole. *There is a resort. It has a bedroom at the end of a long narrow hall. There are three pairs of shoes outside the door.* This highly coded message with its *three pairs of shoes* would travel with me for a long time.[111]

I didn't know what to prepare for, nor did three pairs of shoes have any meaning. But there was enough material to give the galaxies their due so I decided to share this cryptic message with Chloe, an astrologer friend, who was especially adept at decoding. Seeking her opinion, I would present her with the jigsaw piece containing a message, which I linked to the stars.

---

111 12/1/97.

Footnotes contain dream dates and references to prior pages where the dream appeared.
Endnotes contain bibliographical references, are marked with "Ɛ" in the text, and appear at the end of the book.

"Half Circle, Full Star, Clog" resounded three times over the course of one year, each appearance the courier of a new and unforeseen clue.

As though on a maiden voyage, when they first appeared the full star and clog seemed to combine as they applied to discoveries of Danish and Dutch origin. The Danish astronomer, Tyco Brahe (1546–1601), was recognized for his accurate observations of the planets that enabled German born Johannes Kepler to prove that planets orbit the Sun in ellipses, now known as Kepler's laws of planetary motion. The Dutch physicist and astronomer, Christiaan Huygens (1629–1695), proposed the wave theory of light.

I thought, "If the shoe fits, wear it," but the image of the half circle did not fit and was still floating in the cosmic stew of loose puzzle pieces. I sensed that one pair of shoes might belong to Astronomy, but that was premature.

In the dream I shared with Chloe, *there is a man on a raft in the middle of the water. The raft has whitish stalks on it* which I described *as stalactites* (I really meant stalagmites). *I throw a rope to pull the raft in closer and when it is close enough, I will jump on.*

So entrenched was I in the subject of vision at that time, I perceived the whitish stalks to be the rods of the eye.

As Chloe was analyzing my collection of half circles, full stars and clogs, she muttered, "The star looks like the White Star from the White Star Line – the Titanic."

I thought, well maybe – but what about the rods of the eye?

I had no goose bumps or Ahas hearing Chloe's impressions of Titanic's White Star.

She continued, "The raft – these things you are calling stalactites look like icebergs, and the raft – the raft could be a lifeboat."

Well, it was food for thought, but what on Earth was the clog and what was it doing with a half circle? Fixed on an astrological theme I actually thought the half circle might represent a half moon, but that didn't quite work with the Titanic. The night of the disaster was reportedly a moonless night with little wind and a calm sea. With no moon, a half moon theory didn't carry much weight, but I wondered if the astrological aspect might have something to do with Peggymoonbeam's spinning disks.

Agneswiseheart interjected, "The night Titanic met its tragic end, Penelope, the stars appeared as brilliant points of light. In fact, it was reported that some of the survivors witnessed great numbers of shooting stars that night.

"Did you say 'points of light'?"

"Yes, Penelope. The stars, except for the Sun, appear as shining points in the night-time sky. They twinkle because of the effect of the Earth's atmosphere and the distance of the stars from Earth."

Hmm. The *dream of the circle I changed to a star* flashed back. *It looked like an eye and the points resembled eyelashes.*[112] I tried to illustrate it by fanning out the circle and shaping it into a star. I labored over making the points, which I thought looked like eyelashes.

The circle of connections was widening. Not long ago, I couldn't get beyond connecting the Optic Nerve, Percival and Galen. Having delved more deeply, I can add: Points of Light – Stars – Vision – to precede the Optic Nerve.

Unable to grasp the full intent of Agneswiseheart's latest message, I turned to another dream, one in which Chloe, my astrologer friend, appeared. I was so amazed at the likeness of her in my sketch I just had to show her. As I had told Dr. Noodle, I don't draw very well. I've never taken a course in art and struggle with it daily. When a drawing resembles its subject even slightly, it feels like a miracle.

This dream had *Chloe posed in front of a large ship, which is very, very white. Around her neck is a big boa made of plush, kept in place by a safety pin. It's as though she's posing for a photograph.*

In the next sequence, there's a *shuttle or ferry I have to take to get across somewhere. A small horse is in the front of the ferry. You cannot see the girl who is running the ferry*

When I get to the other side, I look around to say good-bye but the ferry driver isn't there. I say good-bye to the horse, who appears to be so human, he smiles. There, on the other side, I meet a friend who is a mechanic.[113]

When sifting through the riches of a bountiful dream, I've found it helpful to organize clusters of elements. To transform the scenario from dreaming to waking, I began with the first cluster.

The very, very white ship was another beacon directing me to Titanic's White Star Line.

The safety pin would prove a tiny icon with a huge intention, one that I was completely oblivious to. Chloe's reaction to this dream was even more visceral than her response to the white star dream. She exclaimed, "Penelope! That ship you drew looks like the Titanic and the safety pin could be a symbol for a life raft! That's ironic! The Titanic and the life raft are held together by a safety pin!"

"That's amazing, Chloe! The safety pin must be pointing to Titanic's safety features!"

The advertisements vigorously touted her watertight design and the claim that she was the safest ship afloat.

I thought it peculiar that the boa would be plush, the material used for fun fur, but it aptly described the Titanic, publicized as the world's most luxurious five-star floating

---

112 6/10/95. See Ch. 20 – Agneswiseheart, p. 87
113 12/5/97.

hotel. Nonetheless, I hadn't yet bought into the Titanic as a force majeure in the unfurling odyssey.

One of the more striking features in this novella is the dream picture of Chloe in front of the ocean liner, which *later becomes a photograph.* The mutation of subject to photography based on the principles of light, optics, and chemistry would appear in my dreams time and again, circling back to the theory of vision and memory – or photographic memory.

At dreams' end, this traveler is comforted by a spiritual message of protection.

The *invisible girl running the ferry* was most likely my spirit guide or higher self. Having learned that animals in dreams are representations of our instinctual nature, I believe the *smiling horse on the ferry* characterized a natural and pleasant transition from life on Earth to the afterlife, represented by *the other side.* I suppose he seemed so human to me because he was symbolizing my natural feelings about what it's really like on the other side.

The *friend who is a mechanic* was a director of a United Way Campaign when I worked at CBS. He is welcoming me to *the other side*: both sides working together, "united" the ultimate collaboration, Heaven and Earth conjoined, the mechanics of the union spelled out. Teamwork was a concept repeatedly enfolded in my dreams.

Mega hours of research coexisted with every new theme. At this juncture, with just a handful of possibilities that might link to Titanic, there didn't appear to be enough material to even consider the disaster a thread in the story. Like everyone else, I was aware of the catastrophe. It had never mesmerized me as it had some others, but I knew I had to remain open. The thought of reviewing some twenty-five odd journals to determine whether the Titanic was indeed an important thread was onerous. Time was at a premium. The office was already open 24/7.

CHAPTER TWENTY-TWO

WATER, WATER, WATER, AND MORE WATER

Ferreting out all the water dreams would be a feat, for water in dream language is generally a symbolic representation of the watery dimensions of inner consciousness and our emotional landscape. I'd never even included the water dreams on the master list. I had resolved that the subject matter may have been too personal and who would care, anyhow? With my curiosity piqued, this meant revisiting literally hundreds of dreams from 1993 on to see if there was any relevance to Chloe's suppositions. I would approach this with a discerning eye but was doubtful that anything more would transpire.

Buzzing around me was memory of the *Whole Earth* dream, *the shipping department and the CBS Eye.*[114] Somewhere in the crowded recesses of my cranium, shipping echoed a familiar chord that jingled *Ramos – ramus – branch – and the cork in the hollowed-out book.*[115] As I mentioned earlier, experts and survivors alike reported the ocean was a sea of cork the night Titanic met her watery death. Curiosity chased Percival, who was a paw away from getting entangled in this snarled piece of yarn.

What turned up was boundless repetition of dreams where *I'm being carried over waterfalls … rapids are carrying me along an elevated stretch of land.* Another description included *turbulent waterfalls, a dangerous omen, a strange invitation to a Circle Pond Road,* and still another, *depicted a water-covered path with waterfalls at high elevations, a secluded beach below* and images of *white rock formations.*[116] It occurs to me as I pull together this collection of water dreams that I'm always being transported with great speed. The rock formations stirred a ghost of a memory, for I had actually seen them in 1993 while I lay awake on an overnight train ride that made whistle-stops all the way from Lourdes to St. Paul de Vence in the South of France.

Continuing the waterfalls collection, *I'm walking through rushes; there is a ravine below with rocks and water and people acting something out in the waterfalls. There is danger.* Somehow, the *image of a pirate's hat* found its way into this dream.

---

114 11/9/96. See Ch. 7 – Branching Out, pp. 41–42
115 9/12/93. See Ch. 3 – The Pole, pp. 24–25
116 6/17/94. 11/11/96, 10/8/93, 11/11/96.

Footnotes contain dream dates and references to prior pages where the dream appeared.

Endnotes contain bibliographical references, are marked with "Ɛ" in the text, and appear at the end of the book.

Another dream story in greater detail revealed a raft that capsized. *I'm swimming in the ocean. There are other people in the water and a strong tide is carrying me to the left* (to the past). *I won't get on the float because "it always capsized." I see twinkly lights on the left, which remind me of the South of France.*[117] La Provence was the first vessel to receive Titanic's call for help. Provence was the region in France where the ethereal image of the lady in white came to greet me.

Still other fragments reminiscent of Titanic's splendor spun a long and mysterious tapestry of dream pieces, replicating the elaborate decorations and appointments on the great ship. Images of *brass railings* and *brass fittings* made their entrance on my dream screen as did *crystal chandeliers, wrought iron chairs, pewter lounge chairs, parlor chairs* – none of which matched my decorating taste. The centerpiece in one dream *is a gold-trimmed chandelier suspended in an open area with balconies surrounding it.* The grandiose fixture bore an uncanny resemblance to the twenty-one-light candelabra above Titanic's legendary main staircase.

The shower of old-world settings furnished with *antiques*, adorned with *candelabra*s and *ornate crystals* were suggestive of the Victorian period. This panoply of antiques merged with images of *brocade* and *embroidered fabrics*, all of it seeming to chronicle the period furnishings and ornate trappings that were the hallmark of Titanic's grandeur.

Clothing flashed across dozens of dreams, bearing the same rich and varied textiles as the furnishings: *Velvets, tulle, satins, silks, and filmy lingerie.* Period attire in the form of *knickers, parasols, mountains of shoes* flickered across my frontal lobe. Continuous flashes of *mother's jewelry, silver plates, bowls, platters* interconnected and locked into place. Could there be some other reference? Absolutely. There were many possible scenarios. Did it fit Titanic? I'll let you decide.

In an atypical chronological and linear sequence, the experiences seemed to gravitate from topographic and climatic descriptions to concrete imagery, such as a ship or boat and sometimes a raft. Then there were the inscrutable dreams that frightened me and contained matter-of-fact reporting of a disaster and being witness to a crime.

Since I'd previously had only sketchy knowledge of the tragedy, the driving force of my dreams and the waking discoveries they triggered generated everything I learned about the Titanic. When I began my research, I was completely unaware what part it would play or that the legendary ocean liner would become a major rope in my story.

---

117 10/7/93.

CHAPTER TWENTY-THREE

TRAGEDY

The Titanic was thought, in its day, to be not only the largest, most luxurious moving object ever made by man, but invincible as well. She weighed more than 46,000 tons, was nearly three football fields in length, and her 30,000 horsepower engines could drive her through the water at twenty-four knots. The elegant grand dame of Britain's White Star Line, Titanic set sail on her maiden voyage from Southampton, England, on April 10, 1912. Steaming west across the North Atlantic, seeking to set a record for speed to New York, she proudly carried the world's most aristocratic, wealthiest, and accomplished passengers.

On the fateful night of April 14 at 11:40 p.m., 409 nautical miles off Cape Race, Newfoundland, Titanic struck a large iceberg. She sank at 2:20 a.m., April 15, about two hours and forty minutes later. It took the Carpathia – the first rescue ship to arrive – four hours from the time it received Titanic's SOS to reach the doomed liner. Carpathia picked up 705 shocked and freezing survivors from Titanic's lifeboats and took them to New York Harbor. The 1,522 remaining passengers were lost forever as the icy cold waters of the Atlantic took them under. Titanic had become a mass grave – and a legend.

Many have thought there was a moral lesson in Titanic's sinking. Myths have been spun portraying the most famous shipwreck in history as symbolic of the evils of greed and luxury. On Titanic, the upper classes were afforded more than the lower classes, the obvious gap between rich and poor bespeaking the inequities of society. For nearly a century, Titanic served as the vessel that would contain prevalent beliefs on the human failings of avarice, arrogance, and incompetence.

I dreamt a variety of dreams before I had any conscious perception of Titanic's part in my story:

8/12/93: *I am in a hotel room (stateroom) with my husband. The wind is gusting, the rain, torrential. A baby and babysitter are sucked out the window. When it's over we talk about the number of lives lost. My breast is covered in mesh. There are 3 large Panda bears outside the window.*

Footnotes contain dream dates and references to prior pages where the dream appeared.
Endnotes contain bibliographical references, are marked with "Ɛ" in the text, and appear at the end of the book.

The man I'm with calls them to the window and when they get close he realizes he left the window open. He panics trying to close it and then is looking for a vent, which I show him.[118]

Titanic passenger Helen Loraine Allison, two years old, was the only child in first or second class to die. Her body was never found. She traveled with a nursemaid who survived. It was reported that when the stern finally pivoted and sank straight down, many were sucked below in its downward wake.[Ɛ1]

Bears Folly Mountains are located on Swift Current in the Eastern region of Newfoundland.

11/10/93: My dream characterizing *two coins as silver with gold braided trim, each imprinted with the nativity scene; one bearing the maple leaf.*[119] *I wanted to have them made into medallions.* This dream paired with another sequence that *displayed men's knickers,* popular attire in the early 1900s.

I'd been drawn to the maple leaf as a symbol of Canada, but there was another connection to Titanic. The coins bore a noticeable likeness to the gilt coat buttons on the uniforms of Titanic's officers. And what of the medallions? Molly Brown, the wealthy Denver socialite, presented medals to Carpathia's crew in gratitude for rescuing Titanic survivors from lifeboats. Despite their valor, most passengers could not be saved.

The synthesis of coins transforming into medallions, attire depicting uniforms, and the nativity scene paints a reverent tableau, enfolding birth with heroic service to ones fellow man.

2/10/95: *There's a big bay window and you can see the ocean in it. I call an operator (named Allison) to find out if my husband has checked out. Allison keeps saying "she" has checked out. I say, "No. He." Allison insists on calling him "she." I think there must have been a mistake. I look in the mirror. I wear no makeup.*[120]

This was the first time that the name Allison actually materialized in a dream.

10/2/95: *There are hundreds of kayaks or rowboats in the water. Each boat has four people in it except for mine and my friend's. We each have our own boat. A young man is giving instructions. The dream segues to a marketplace where there are sailboat cutouts in gold. Hoards of people are lined up. I say I'm glad I went earlier.*[121]

Only 705 people made it into the twenty lifeboats, which could have held 1,178 (only half of the Titanic's 2,228 passengers and crew).[Ɛ2]

I wondered if the *four people and the hundreds of boats* revealed that Titanic's lifeboats rowed away from the sinking with more than four hundred empty seats.[Ɛ3] If so, the celestial pundits had introduced a dream-styled number rebus.

---

118 8/12/93.
119 11/10/93. See Ch. 1– Beginnings, p.
120 2/10/95.
121 10/2/95.

Was the description *of sailboat cutouts in gold* marking a cutout as a pattern, a layout, a motif … an impression of the tragic story of Titanic? Was the gold emblematic of her riches?

Connecting the images of the *gold sailboat cutouts* to *hundreds of boats in the water* might portray the commercialism engendered by the Titanic catastrophe. Titanic novels and stories abound, as do a number of films. In 2000, investors in the 1985 expedition that had located Titanic's resting place retained permission to sell lumps of coal for $25 each. And in 2010 a letter from a first-class passenger on board Titanic was sold at auction for £55,000 to an unidentified British museum.

While combing my journals for Titanic-related reveries it occurred to me that, long before I began keeping dream journals, I'd had a recurrent nightmare. *I'm driving over a bridge. The bridge suddenly ends, there is a gap, and the car plunges into the water. I can feel myself in the car going down … down… down.* I would awaken terrified, wondering if it was a memory gap. This particular dream ended years ago, but my search for Titanic material turned up similar dreams.

10/14/95: *I take a wrong turn in the water. Ahead is a bridge which reminds me of the Ponte Vecchio. The water is very still and placid. A man appears and says I'm not allowed to go under the bridge. I will have to take the waterwheel, which is half in and half out the water. I think the car will capsize. He offers to drive but says it will take one to two hours to get over it.*[122]

My dream illustration resembling the Ponte Vecchio Bridge details the enclosures of the bridge lookouts typically found on a cruise ship.

At 11:40 p.m. April 14, 1912, William Murdoch, officer of the watch on Titanic's bridge, received the message from the crow's nest, "Iceberg dead ahead." He ordered the engines full astern and the helm hard a-starboard (right) to make a hard port turn (left) around the berg,[84] like a fishtail movement used to maneuver an automobile around an object.

There has been much speculation as to why First Officer Murdoch turned to port rather than starboard. Many authors and researchers believe a ship turns more easily to starboard,[85] and after all, according to the lookouts, the iceberg was "dead ahead."

That Murdoch turned to port indicates he saw the ice before it was seen and reported by the lookouts, and that he perceived the turn to port as the more advantageous course of action.[86] However, many agree that Murdoch's decision to order quartermaster Hichens to turn the ship "hard a-starboard" was probably the wrong one.

Did that turn to port connect to my dream where I take the wrong turn in the water? So many questions; so few answers.

---

122 10/14/95.

Some experts also agree that, had Titanic rammed the iceberg head-on, the first four compartments probably would have been crushed and some of the people in the bow may have died, but the ship would have remained afloat long enough for rescue ships to come to the aid of the surviving passengers and crew.[7]

Murdoch was last seen attempting to launch Collapsible Lifeboat A but was never seen again after Titanic disappeared into the Atlantic. His body, if recovered, was never identified.[8]

The dream's facsimile of the *Ponte Vecchio bridge* illustrates *six openings*. The Titanic employed six trained lookouts who took turns working in pairs.[9] Openings .... lookouts ... interlocking pieces meshing a fantastic revelation that Ponte Vecchio translates in English to "old bridge," a remarkably close fit for the old bridge of a ship.

The dream portrays the *water as still and placid*, mirroring the conditions the night of the tragedy. Second Officer Charles Lightoller had commented to Captain Edward J. Smith on the bridge at about 9:00 p.m. that in his twenty-four years as a mariner, he had never seen so calm a sea.[10]

The dream introduces *a man who offers to drive but says it will take one to two hours to recover.* This proffers a variety of scenarios. Could the man have been Murdoch offering to take the wheel, hoping that in one to two hours he could correct the difficulty? We, of course, will never know.

Another variation may rest with the ship's chief architect, Thomas Andrews, who was on board during the fateful maiden voyage. After evaluating the damage to the ship, he knew nothing could be done to save it; in less than ten minutes, there was fourteen feet of water in the first five compartments. When Captain Smith asked Andrews, "How long have we?" Andrews replied. "An hour and a half. Possibly two. Not much longer." The dream narrative says *it will take one to two hours to recover.* It also includes a chilling declaration that "*I think the car will capsize.*" Could *the man who offers to drive*, be a driving force? One more powerful than any of the players aboard Titanic?

Another awakening to the spiritual magnitude of such a disaster may be revealed in the timekeeping of a celestial clock. Given there are no calendars or timepieces in Heaven, the dialogue that *it will take one to two hours to recover* may be suggesting one to two earthly lifetimes, or perhaps one to two centuries. I started to think that time in Heaven must be a lot like time in our dreams. Dr. Montague Ullman, a renowned dream researcher, says our ideas about time and space, cause and effect in a dream cease to be because the dream has its very own logic. The celestial clock and the dream clock, therefore, have something in common: they are both timeless and they both span space.

Supposing that the age of the Earth is 4.5 billion years, if we were to scale one year down to one second, the average time on Earth for one human being would be about 1.25 minutes. Based on this innumeracy, the one to two hours might translate to 150 lifetimes or given the mysterious dream clock, one to two centuries in Earth time. At this writing, nearly one century has passed since the sinking of Titanic.

2/18/96: I'm meeting a friend in California. I decide to walk. I get to a center point and am confused about where to turn. I then remember you have to bear left all around the coastline. I get to where the waterwheel is --- that is the dangerous part. I get on a boat. There is a small place inside where people can stay if they don't want to get wet. I stay outside near the wall or core where there is a handle. When I get off, I try to locate my friend. I leave his name with the American Embassy in the section to locate people.[123]

This dream reawakened the impact of my nightmare about taking the wrong turn. California and waterwheels; this would take some doing.

Behind the glassed-off middle section of Titanic's Bridge was the Wheelhouse. In it was the huge wheel that the quartermaster turned to steer the ship. The Wheelhouse was completely enclosed because it also contained the compass, the master control to close the watertight doors, and other electrical equipment.[E11]

At 10:00 p.m., quartermaster Hichens relieved quartermaster Alfred Olliver at the wheel inside the shuttered Wheelhouse.

The connection with *a friend in California* gelled when I learned that the freighter, the Californian, was drifting near the Titanic as it sank. At 10:55 p.m., floating north of Titanic's course, its wireless operator had broken in on Titanic's operator "to report she was completely blocked by ice."

"Annoyed at the radio intrusion, Titanic's operator signaled back 'Shut up. Shut up. I am busy. I am working Cape Race.'" Cape Race was ignored. The Californian operator turned off his receiver and went to bed.[E12]

Forty-five minutes later Titanic collided with the iceberg. Mysteriously, the Calfornian's captain did not respond to distress rockets sighted by his officers. Forty-seven seconds had elapsed since the iceberg was spotted at 11:40. Titanic would only remain above water for another two hours and forty minutes.

I wondered about the dream imagery of *a small place inside where people could stay if they didn't want to get wet*. I was amazed to find that the wheelhouse serves as a shelter for the person at the wheel, in this case, Titanic's quartermaster. I then learned that a waterwheel is driven by water to work machinery or to raise the water. Both were relevant. Passengers sought shelter wherever they could find it; 25,000 tons of water reportedly poured into the front of the ship in the first hour.

A bizarre episode concluded this *"waterwheel"* dream.

123 2/18/96.

I'm in a coffee shop. I have no money so I don't order any food. Suddenly I realize I can charge on my VISA so I order a half cantaloupe. I really only wanted a quarter, but I <u>had</u> to order a half. There is something about a truckers' strike and a pricing war.[124]

The coffee shop scenario was chock-full of dream nuggets caught in a new web of industrial cues … cues resonating with Titanic's legacy. For example, the images of coffee and coffee shops, mainstays in my dream experience, point to caffeine … perhaps a wake-up call to the distress signals desperately transmitted by Titanic:

"Capt – SOS from MGY (Titanic's wireless call letters).
We have struck iceberg sinking fast come to our assistance.[Ɛ13]
Position Lat. 41° 46 N Long 50° 24 W"

The first distress signal is heard by La Provence.[Ɛ14] Wow! That connects to my dream where *a float capsized and I see twinkly lights reminding me of the South of France.*[125] While making that connection, I flashed back to St. Paul de Vence and the specter of the woman in white.

But back to the dream *VISA,* which may represent passengers traveling with visas aboard White Star Line's Titanic. Among famous American passengers who perished were John Jacob Astor, the real estate magnate, and Isidor and Ida Straus, the elderly owners of Macy's department stores.

The *half cantaloupe* turned out to be a tricky logogram for shipping magnets. I should have noticed how insistent the order was that it be half. *I only wanted a quarter* but the dream demanded that *I order half!* Actually, this is a wonderful example of our punning universe. Why would I have to order half when I wanted less? It was simple once you mastered the art of wordplay.

The *half cantaloupe* led to J. P. Morgan, owner of The White Star Line, the company that built, owned, and operated the Titanic. Shortly before buying out the British White Star Line, Morgan bought out the steel empire of Andrew <u>Carnegie</u> to form U.S. Steel.

And, after all, what is a *half cantaloupe* but a half of a melon … signifying Mellon .. as in half of <u>Carnegie</u> Mellon. Half Carnegie … half Mellon. It was the proverbial "leading the horse to water."

I admit that my dreams so often led me to puns and other wordplay that I entertained the thought that I "<u>can't elope</u>," that is to say, I can't escape from this unending tangle of yarn.

I would become frustrated when unrelated fragments, such as the *truckers' strike* and the *pricing war,* would slide into a dream out of left field with no apparent opening in an

---

124   2/18/96.
125   See Ch. 22 – Water, Water and More Water, pp. 97–98

already baffling story. That is, until I began research on the Titanic. These mismatched intruders were actually dutiful reporters who planted very leading doubts.

Could *a truckers' strike be* alluding to the long national coal miners' strike[E15] that started January 12, 1912? Several liners, including some of White Star's other ships, relinquished their coal to fill the Titanic's bunkers. How ironic that some of those passengers who had to cancel their departures on other ships embarked on the Titanic instead.[E16] And could the *pricing war* be symbolic of the intense competition stirred up in the shipping industry by Morgan's efforts to secure a monopoly in international shipping?[E17]

Yet, just when I thought I understood a dream clue, a new missive would drop from the Oneiroball and I'd be left scratching my head. One such clue was embedded in the ice and described as *"SURF pay."*

6/2/96: Someone asks me if I got SURF pay. I see a figurine of a man ice fishing. I am at a spa. I miss an 11:00 p.m. massage with a masseuse named Allison. I say, "Allison is the best they have"... she wouldn't just not show up.[126]

This dream is figuring *(figurine)* something out involving ice, in other words: "fishing" for something under the ice.

I hadn't the foggiest notion as to how to decipher *SURF pay*. Evidently, I was to "figure" that out. The word "massage" in my dream glossary had with regularity, signified "message." Eleven o'clock at night is a strange time for a massage appointment. I wondered. Was it another link to Titanic? The Californian was sending out ice warnings at 10:55 p.m.

Again, the name Allison, this time appearing as a *masseuse* was conveying a message and designated by the dream tellers as their best messenger.

The iceberg to this day has been blamed as the culprit that sank the 46,328-ton Titanic. But was it? And if so, was it alone or did it have an accomplice?

Ice fishing aptly describes the 1912 U.S. Senate inquiry, which remarkably was wrapped up in a little over a month and was followed by a British inquiry.

The search for answers – fishing under the ice – has exhaustively continued into another century of new technology employing robot submersibles with video cameras for eyes that scan Titanic's resting place for clues to the unknown. Discovery teams scan the wreckage and lingering curiosity persists in the public mind as it tries to understand how the invincible Titanic, supposedly immune to destruction by natural forces, was felled. If the cause were the iceberg and the iceberg alone, it seems the mystery would have been put to bed by the time we crossed the threshold into the twenty-first century.

Perhaps the unknown <u>was</u> put to bed ... to sleep ... to dream ... to awaken ... to be told.

---

126 6/2/96.

*6/3/97: There's a gash in the lower part of a six-foot long abstract painting which costs $2,300.
I unfold it from right to left. It is sewn together and comes apart. Because it's not in one piece, I
don't buy it.*[127]

Did the six-foot-long painting, correspond to the length of the Titanic, which was
one-sixth of a mile?

A first class parlor suite is reported to have cost $4,350 in 1912; therefore a first class
stateroom may have been in the area of $2,300.

The gash, reminiscent of the rumored 350-foot gash in the hull caused by the iceberg, was virtually undisputed until recently. Could the abstract painting be pointing to
an abstract theory of probable cause for the sinking of Titanic?

The unfolding of the painting from right (future) to left (past) may signify an
opening – a literal unfolding of the theory – by developing future findings based on past
beliefs.

Thanks to modern Science, there is a new theory about how the Titanic sank.

Sonar imaging has revealed that the collision did not cause a gaping hole. Instead,
there were six narrow noncontiguous openings in the starboard side of the forward hull.
Investigators now estimate that the total amount of iceberg damage to the ship covered
an area of only 12.5 square feet.

The decision in the dream not to buy the painting because it was "not in one piece"
is in accord with research that the ship was actually still in one piece when it plunged
underwater, contrary to survivors' testimony that the Titanic broke in half. For some
unknown reason, my unconscious did not "buy" the theory that it broke in half.[ℰ18]

Because it wasn't in one piece, I didn't buy it.

At the British inquiry in 1912, Edward Wilding, one of Harland & Wolff's naval
architects, proposed that the uneven flooding in the six watertight compartments meant
each had suffered unique, uncontinuous damage. Wilding also proposed that the actual
cuts might be relatively small. His testimony was widely ignored. Nearly everyone
believed the only thing that could undo a ship so big and well constructed was a huge
gash.

Why would I dream a "gash" surrounded by fuzzy details of Titanic when I'd no
conscious awareness of such detail? Memory and Forgetfulness were suspended over Past
and Future, seeming to form an infinite loop.

*12/7/98: I'm in the water with some other people. My friend disappears from sight. I was
working with a design in the water – it's a tiny diamond-shaped design and the colors around it
are green and yellow. I think I'm standing on a piece of rock and I slip. My boyfriend and I are*

---

127 6/3/97.

together. Suddenly the undertow carries us off. It happens so fast, we can't even speak — we're speed-ing as though we're in the rapids. Everything is dark — the water — the sky. We have no idea where we were going; we are being swept away. The force was overwhelming.[128]

This dark and menacing dream points out the green and yellow diamond-shaped design, a repeating icon. Its destiny would be revealed as I traveled onward.

Another bygone dream rang bells both in and out of sleep.

12/18/98: *Dreaming: Half Circle, Full Star is repeating and repeating.*

Waking: The chime in the living room was ringing. Then it was banging against the window frame.

Dreaming: The words "connect to foil" repeat and continue until I woke up and closed the window.[129]

I drew a bell ringing three times, over which I wrote "ding ... ding ... ding."

This was the only time I ever drew a waking image. Forcing myself awake from a dead sleep, I sought to find the source of the ringing. Was it in waking or in dreaming? I had no idea why I wrote three "dings."

I was flabbergasted to find that when lookout Frederick Fleet spotted an iceberg, he immediately sounded the crow's nest bell three times and relayed the message "Iceberg right ahead" to the officer of the watch, William Murdoch.

How bizarre that a ringing chime would actualize during a dream echoing the *Half Circle, Full Star* chorus repeating and repeating. The image of "foil" was brand new and would take its place at the back of the line.

It was like a game of hopscotch, jumping from one square to the next while all the bells tolled for Titanic even in as mundane a dream sequence as this:

2/9/99: *I'm parking a car on a side street in the Fifties -- maybe East Fifties. I parallel park so perfectly I can't see the tail sticking out and don't know if I'll be able to find it.*[130]

This short narrative illustrates how waking life experience sparks a dream, zooms into the individual's frame of reference, then pans to the world at large.

My neighborhood is the East Fifties. Considering that I haven't driven in the past five years, this puzzler was weaving another thread, which is why it found its way into the Titanic theme.

Generally, the car would represent a conveyance. In this story, the conveyance is the-matically a ship. *Parallel parking* may, as mentioned earlier, be identifying parallels of latitude. *Parking in the Fifties* may also be pointing to the fiftieth meridian.

---

128 12/7/98.
129 12/18/98.
130 2/9/99.

Prior to striking the iceberg, Titanic's captain had sought information from other ships on the sea that night.

"With ice drifting to the <u>east</u> as expected, a message from the Athenai, a Greek steamer, indicated Titanic's track was safe if she stayed north of the forty-second parallel until she reached at least the fiftieth meridian, which she did.

"Legend has ignored that every ice warning except the final warnings from Mesaba and Californian indicated to Titanic's master, with the knowledge of his era, that the ice fields were east of the fiftieth meridian by the night of 14 April."[19]

The last known position of the Titanic as relayed by the crew was:

Latitude: 41° 46' N and Longitude: 50° 14' W.

The dream account of *not being able to see the tail sticking out* may corroborate scientific findings about the stern, the rear end of the ship.

Despite film portrayals of Titanic's final moments above water, scientists say stress analysis shows that it would have been impossible for the ship's stern to rise upward at an angle approaching ninety degrees. Investigators now believe the stern never rose higher than a twelve-degree angle above the water.[20]

CHAPTER TWENTY-FOUR

AFTERMATH

*The swimmer becomes part of the element that supports him,
part of an ever-changing geometry through which he slices and
which then corrects itself as he moves past.*

Willard Spiegelman[E21]

Wandering through this labyrinth, I came to the next bank of haunting dream images both soulful and difficult to confront. Driven by the scent of curiosity, I began for the first time to actually question if I'd been part of the Titanic disaster. How else could so much of it be materializing in my unconscious? I knew it was not sheer coincidence.

Was the information transmitted from souls once aboard Titanic, or had I lived during that time but not traveled on the Titanic?

11/2/93: I'm taking my niece to the circus. It looks like the Colosseum in Rome, Italy. It is a semi circle of gray stone with little windows. I have to leave her there for a while to get a boat to go across to the other side. The distance seems too far to swim because I'm not a strong swimmer, but someone else goes without a problem. I realize the boat is on the other side and I will need oars to bring it back. I don't know how I can swim with the oars but I know I have to get the boat. The dilemma is unsolved.[131]

The dream produced a respectable facsimile of the Colosseum in Rome, but I was confused. Why was the ancient amphitheater woven into the burgeoning Titanic theme? The imagery of a circus resonated with the Colosseum; they are both circular.

Architecturally the arches of amphitheaters in the Roman period have been repeated in the design of its aqueducts and bridges. A Roman aqueduct dating to about 20 BC in Nimes, France, called the Pont du Gard, meaning old bridge, meshed with my dream[132] about the Ponte Vecchio. The Latin definition for bridge is *aquae ductis* (conduit) from *aqua* (water) plus *ducere* (duct – to lead).

---

131 11/2/93.
132 10/14/95.

Footnotes contain dream dates and references to prior pages where the dream appeared.
Endnotes contain bibliographical references, are marked with "Ɛ" in the text, and appear at the end of the book.

Hmm… I wondered, were "the oars" a metaphor for steering this boat of dreams? It would explain the anxiety over needing oars to bring the boat back – to review it once more.

Leaving my niece for a while had become a sad reality in my waking life, for my near slavish devotion to this Dream project eclipsed all facets of my life. I constantly thought of the day when my niece and I would reunite and my life would be restored to some normalcy, but it wasn't in the cards at the moment.

Was *swimming to get the boat on the other side* a nudge that the information was coming from the other side?

Getting the boat to go across to the other side, Peggymoonbeam would say, is "getting it across – putting the message across to the other side – to Planet Earth."

Caught in the intersecting tides of life and death, I was tossed back to a dream where again there was a crossing.

11/3/95: *I'm crossing a wide plain. It's like being in a forest with no trees. The ground is a sandy color. The word "irrigation" illustrates this crossing. A couple takes me to New York. Nothing of mine is left. I see all my baby pictures in an old photo album. I'm in front of a very large contraption (it could be a very wide swing). The ocean is to the right. The contraption disappears and fades into the distance. I think some people are inside. I know it happened because I already dreamed it.*[133]

The description of the terrain in my dream characterizes the bleak, treeless coastline of Newfoundland on the cold April night when Titanic went down. Using the word "irrigation" to illustrate the crossing of the wide plain suggests the connection of water to land.

Could *the couple who takes me to New York* be pointing to the rescue by Carpathia, which carried Titanic survivors from the lifeboats at sea to safety in that city? *Seeing my baby pictures* may allude to an inexplicable afterlife recognition (not necessarily my own).

Carpathia arrived in New York Harbor with her cargo of 705 persons rescued from the freezing sea at 9:30 p.m. April 18, 1912, some three days, nineteen hours, and ten minutes after Titanic sank.

Could the *"very wide swing"* be touching again on Murdoch's "hard-a-starboard" command? I wondered.

The narrative of the disappearing contraption matches accounts of how the ship sank lower and lower, fading from sight until the waves closed over it.

This dream posed the question of timelessness. *I think some people are inside. I know it happened because I already dreamed it.*

---

133 11/3/95.

The reports of the awful shrieking cries that arose out of the depths of the sea, the disappearing vessel, the unfortunates who found no means of escape and had dotted the ocean, the silence: the range of experience played across my dreams.

My recording of this dream experience was perfunctory, my early feelings about it dispassionate. As I unearthed more detail, a vague recognition began to stir as the Titanic theme strengthened. Oceanic waves of emotion that swept in from time to time eclipsed that fleeting spark of recognition, a spark that flashes under the lining of memory. I never knew if the peaks and valleys of emotion were coming from memory or the obligation of having received the message – or both.

As I finished this recording, I said to myself, "I dreamed a dream ... what could that mean?"

"Think about William Blake's Songs of Experience," coached Peggymoonbeam...

> "I Dreamed a Dream! What can it mean?
> And that I was a maiden Queen
> Guarded by an Angel mild:
> Witless woe was ne'er beguiled!"

"And don't forget the Bard," she chirped:

> "We are such stuff as dreams are made on, and our little lives are rounded with a sleep."[E22]

"Yes, Peggymoonbeam, but the stewards of science all have differing opinions about the significance of dreams. Physicists, paleontologists, psychiatrists, neurologists, philosophers, biochemists, and historians do not agree – let alone the poets."

What goes on in our consciousness is so fascinating and so hard to understand but one thing I'm certain of is that, whether awake or asleep, we're always observing and that must have something to do with vision. I thought about Lord Galen and wondered when he would step out of my dreams into daylight.

Peggymoonbeam shined her most brilliant light on that thought.

"We know up here that certain cognitive scientists and others on Earth have been looking for a neural basis of attention, about how the brain processes information. That is how Lord Galen's theories of vision came into your dreams. Don't worry, Penelope. We'll wind back to Claudius Galen and the optic nerve but we have quite a long journey before we return, so we best be on our way."

According to studies of Egyptian mummification, before the bandaging, and after the body was completely anointed with perfumes and oils, stuffing and pads, it was then colored. The bodies of men were often colored with red, the women with yellow. Next came the wrapping of the mummy. I wondered if the body paint on the mummies bled through the linen over the ages. That would account for a transmutation to the color orange in the dream.

Returning to the dream, I linked *sand with Egypt and the skinny tracks on the ground* with the ocean floor. A ship's track is the line of her true course. Was the dream characterizing the course over which Titanic traveled?

My dream drawing of the *skinny tracks* shows two parallel lines, which may identify parallels of latitude. The *driver speeding home* gelled with rumors that Titanic was on the shortest route commensurate, not with safety, but with the earliest arrival time in New York. It is said that had Titanic maintained a lower cruising speed, the iceberg could have been avoided.

The dream curiously tied *the metal slug* to the *Empire State Building.* There must be something to see from the observation deck, but what? It was bewildering. Percival, my ever faithful dream cat, knew when I was stuck. Purring madly, he would rub against me, letting me know he had something important to say; something I wasn't ready to hear.

The image of the quarter was becoming more familiar but remained an enigma for quite some time.

Flipping back through my journals, I found a windfall of connections that propelled me toward things Egyptian.

1/19/95: The dream opens *as I'm getting ready to go somewhere. At the last minute, there is something I want to see on the fifth floor. There is an old movie in black and white. On the left side is a screen depicting a scene from the movie. On the right is the real-life enactment of the scene. Then I'm on a boat walking past many windows. The object of the walk is to get to the outside ... to a sunny place.*

Then I see an image of a skull shaped like a mannequin's form. I silently say "Osiris's skull."

Black and white was a strong clue, for, over time, the dream tellers' "black and white" code translated to what was obvious – apparent – clear. Now, figuring out just what was so clear was another story.

The dream story, rich in metaphors of memory, myth, and immortality seemed to embrace the infinity of time. It is a look at the world with a remembrance of time past unfolding to time present. The *old movie on the left* (past) and an enactment *on the right* (future) depicts the scene that came alive. For me this dream embodies the legend of Osiris, the symbol of resurrection and eternal life.

The unseen and silent companions I had sensed earlier began to make their presence felt.

"Pardon my eavesdropping, Penelope, but the mere mention of eternal life activates my memory glands. It's Charlesbigstar, here. I know you are being propelled through the decades and into the lives and deaths of other humans. I want you to know that your custodians are nearby all of the time and you have nothing to fear. When I tuned to your observations on time past and time future, I thought I'd drop in, even though it's a bit early in your voyage for my two grains of salt.

"I just happen to have a special affinity for the story of poor old Osiris and his dutiful goddess of a wife, Isis. You know, Osiris is the oldest son of the earth god, Geb. If I may, I would like to recite the tale."

"Wow, Charlesbigstar! I can't believe it's you! Of course, I'd love to hear your recital. The worlds of knowledge you taught me when you were here on Earth are indelibly engraved in my mind. Your stories of Abraham Lincoln will live within me forever and I still do all I can to live by the motto – "With malice toward none; with charity for all..." You shone the light on the past and past lives and how we make pacts in Heaven to come back for our next lessons.

"Well, one never knows where a beam of light may fall. Now as the fable goes: Osiris was murdered by his brother Seth, who dismembered his body into fourteen pieces and buried each in a different part of Egypt. Osiris's lovely and devoted wife Isis re-collected these hidden pieces and brought Osiris back to life by re-membering him – by putting all the pieces back together.

"The legend of Isis reassembling Osiris mirrors the desire of man to learn from looking back – from remembering – and according to Egyptian mysticism, 'to guide the soul back through the inner darkness to the light of the higher dimensions, for those who seek to find it.'[24]

"Penelope, the story of Osiris, Egyptian God of the Afterlife and Underworld, is one of Egypt's most ancient myths, so old its origins have been lost in time. It was an important story to the Egyptians because of Osiris's role as the king of Egypt who is resurrected as the King of the Dead, the king that every Egyptian, from the mightiest pharaoh to the lowliest peasant, hoped to join in the afterlife.

"Now, this may have some bearing on your dream, for the cult of Osiris – also known as the God of the Underworld – started during the Fifth Dynasty when he was represented in 'human form. In your dream, you had to see something on the *fifth floor* before you left.

"You see, mummification techniques were not fully developed until the Fifth Dynasty when an elaborate cult of the dead was in full sway. Natural preservation of the body lying in hot dry sands is what slowed down decomposition and eventually led to the development of mummification.

"Your dream symbol of the boat and the effort to get to the outside, to a *sunny place,* just so happens to be symbolic of the Egyptian God of the Underworld, for the sun with its daily re-birth and death is also associated with Osiris. 'As ruler of the netherworld, Osiris was the night form of the sun; in fact, people even wanted to see him as the moon, in connection with which the lunar phases were interpreted, as being the death and resurrection of the god.'

"Another piece of the puzzle is that your dream image of *Osiris skull* connects to the legend of Isis finding the head of Osiris atop a pole at a local festival at Abydos, which became an important burial ground. Poor puzzling Penelope, you just can't seem to escape that pole. But to continue, the dream reference to the skull being shaped like a *mannequin's form* is meaningful."

"Charlesbigstar. I think I've made a connection.

"When I think of a mannequin, I envision a wax figure or a dummy. That rings the mummy bell: mummy – mannequin – dummy – mummy. It has a certain rhythm. The stuffing of the body in mummification to preserve it in a 'life-like form' resonates with the 'natural body form' of a mannequin.

"Charlesbigstar, it's amazing how our inner lives – our dreams – and our outer lives are a replay of how the world is constantly being re-collected in much the same way that, after scattering, Osiris' parts were gathered and reassembled by Isis."

"Yes, my friend. That is precisely why we at Starsight are bidden to the work of transient planetary study. Now I must depart for bluer pastures."

I paused. What was this mysterious place called Starsight? And transient planetary study?

I turned back to the fascinating legend of Osiris. The integration of waking and dreaming memory that the Osiris dream illustrated bridged the worlds of the conscious and the unconscious. My perceptual dimensions were soaring to heights I'd never known.

I couldn't help but analogize the collective ability on a conscious level to gather the parts into a whole; to an accomplishment that had already been demonstrated with Man's invention of the Internet. Imagine what could be achieved if we could gain a universally heightened perspective of unconscious awareness!

The mummy piece was a riddle and a half. First, the *bedded girl swathed in orange linen* and now the *mannequin.* Both mummies had threads that attached to a boat. Were they one and the same?

I circled back to the Optico dream which held a cache of hidden clues. To remind you, dear Reader, it was Claudius Ptolemy, the astronomical gremlin from the outer reaches who flashed *Optico pages 16, 17, 18, 19, 20, 21 – blue rubbery logs – a missing piece of a board game and – a hole at the base of a skull.*[135] I reminded myself that Ptolemy's treatise

---

135 2/14/97. See Ch. 5 – Honored Visionaries: Two Gentlemen Named Claudius, p. 35

was Optica – not Optico. Off by one letter but not bad considering the vast distance the information traveled.

While reflecting on the unfathomable hole, I sensed the oscillation of a luminous body overhead. "Psshooo..." Perhaps it was a spinning disk. No, on second thought – perhaps it was Peggymoonbeam beaming in. The radiant emission of light was nearly blinding.

"Oooh, oooh, Penelope, we're together. It's Ptolemy and me," vibrated Peggymoonbeam.

The spirits flitted around, continually transmitting their thoughts to me, as though no difference existed between day and night, waking and sleeping. No matter that I'm on Earth and they're in Heaven, they drift through the invisible curtain between us like thin wispy clouds that mystically bring their essence to life.

It's as though they are in the real world and everything they teach me here is like a shadow of their world – a world that knows no end. Their omnipresence in this garden of forever opens my eyes to the miraculous connectedness in my life. Through our communications, I see that my tiny life is a part of everything under the sun, everything in the entire cosmos, from a speck of dust to the infinitude of the galaxies – a picture so large, yet so detailed, it's nearly unthinkable.

Often unannounced, my spiritual mentors come and go. From time to time, their wing prints cause a riffling in the air and I can tell by the way the air stirs that they're clearing the path of any obstructions to my learning. They have many ways of letting me know they're around and one is a sprinkling of silvery dream dust containing scientific particles. This technique is easy to spot since most particles of science are foreign to me and are something I haven't seen before. At times one mentor guides me toward a particular science and when we graze another science, the guide assigned to that one appears. I know this is no accident because the appropriate guide materializes at just the right time for just the right reason. If I'm dreaming geology, which involves a heavier dusting, Steno emerges; when I'm dreaming about vision, Lord Galen is there; when it's about the stars and galaxies, Twink appears; and when it's time for chemistry, Marie Curie glides in for a landing. They work as a team flawlessly, resourcefully and so quietly, you can almost hear your own thoughts connecting with theirs. It's great fun when they all get together – like being at a big open house. Their presence during sleeping is stronger than in waking. I suppose that's when my unconscious is moving at a faster frequency in order to connect with them. They present a dream and then galvanize their formidable spirit power to help organize my work during "wakefulness."

Welcoming the first light of morning, I'm sustained by the inner peace that softly transports my mentors from their space to mine. I have a hunch that it's, oddly enough, the very same space.

I thought about the stars that blinked at me in my childhood and wondered if even then, some form of communication was taking place. Now in my dreams, these luminous stars of souls past have created an indescribable sense of lovingkindness and protection sending out visual associations that may be part of their divine memory. In what may be a superconscious mind, there seems to be no difference between my scholarly mentors and my dearly departed family and friends other than their levels of wisdom – the younger souls, still learning, the older, scholarly ones, teaching. As the younger souls advance, so too do their messages to me. The loving essence of Earth's great teachers, like Buddha and Jesus, seems to reside within the guides assigned me. I am always astonished at how their combined force continually recharges and revitalizes me even when I'm most exhausted. I wonder if they're building a bridge up there in the clouds between the conscious and the superconscious mind and if that isn't a vital part of the message.

"Yeah, yeah, yeah! Well, speaking of clouds, could you please get your head out of the clouds for a few lumenseconds and come back down to Earth. You've got work to do on the hole at the base of a skull."

"OK. OK, I hear you Peggymoonbeam. What are lumenseconds anyhow?"

"Oh, it's an advanced conversion scale used for tracking Earth time. Now, let's return to that dream that spelled out the word '*Optico*' and where you saw *the hole at the base of a skull.*"

"Hole at the base of a skull? What a strange puzzle piece!"

"It's strange all right," replied Peggymoonbeam, "but one that fits with mummification. The Egyptians removed the organs, starting with the brain. A common way to do this was through a large hole they made at the base of the skull. They couldn't remove every fragment with this or other methods, but perhaps this will help with your *hole at the base of the skull* riddle. Granted, it has been one of your most elusive puzzle pieces."

Interesting, but farfetched. *Blue rubbery logs* and *a missing piece of a board game* don't exactly follow.

But, what to make of the legend which holds that a cursed Egyptian mummy was actually on Titanic, and its spell is what caused the ship to sink. Of course, most authorities completely reject the story that there was a mummy on board Titanic at all.

"Penelope, my sources over here on the subject of the Titanic and the mummy are beyond reproach," interjected Peggymoonbeam. "You seem in a bit of a quandary over this so let me read you a well-documented mummy account from the Starsight Gazette:

"The tale of the Princess of Amen-Ra, cloaked in a specter-haunted mystery, tells of a string of misfortunes inflicted on those who handled her casket. The Princess lived some fifteen hundred years before Christ. When she died, she was laid in an ornate wooden coffin and buried deep in a vault at Luxor, on the banks of the Nile.

"As the story goes, she was presented at the British Museum in 1889 and displayed in the Egyptian Room as early as 1890. However, after almost twenty people who were involved with her discovery and removal met misfortune, disaster or death, no British museum would take her. So the museum sold the mummy to a private collector who also succumbed to the legendary curse.

"Eventually, an American archaeologist (who dismissed the injuries and deaths as quirks) paid a handsome price for the mummy and arranged for its removal to New York. In April 1912, the new owner escorted his treasure aboard the sparkling, new White Star liner about to make its maiden voyage. On the night of April 14, amid scenes of unprecedented horror, the Princess of Amen-Ra accompanied more than fifteen hundred passengers to their deaths at the bottom of the Atlantic.

"The name of the ship was Titanic."

I re-collected the dream nuggets – *fifth floor, boat, a mannequin's form, Osiris's skull* – and connected them to my waking research – Fifth dynasty – mummification techniques – the mummy – a natural form of a mannequin – Osiris. Osiris was dismembered; it was about remembering: putting Osiris back together; putting the pieces together.

Where was setting of the dream? I had to look back. It was on a boat. How strange. Why all this chatter about a mummy that was only rumored to be on Titanic? The Princess was buried at Luxor where the sun-dried bricks matched my dream of the stone-faced people who came to life.

Clandestinely hovering and echoing my spiritual mantra were Peggymoonbeam and Agneswiseheart: "Remember, Penelope, *Be patient. You will learn everything you need to know.*"

"Cheerio, girls," blinked Claudius Ptolemy, "I am off to Starsight Lab."

Claudius Ptolemy – I'd heard so much about him – read so much, and suddenly there he was; he hadn't even said hello. I guess social gestures aren't de rigueur in his neighborhood.

There it was again: Starsight Lab. What in Heaven's name was that and where was it? All my dream mentors seemed to know about it. I suppose I'd have to honor the "Be patient" mandate, so I turned to a page where the dream dust drifting around the Titanic was a bit more up to date.

CHAPTER TWENTY-SIX

THE DATE

Tweaking the syntax of a dream symbol often revealed a hidden meaning. Think of gazing at a painting every day for years, and then having its essence suddenly become visible in one hidden detail.

A groundbreaking dream grain produced an unimaginable seed of realization.

I discovered what appeared to be a useless scrap of a dream I had on October 27, 1993: *There are three people in a tub. It has a black sign that covers the outside with white lettering like a stencil. Then someone is making a big noise or a big smell. I have to insert some money into a machine and out comes a piece of wrinkled, wet brown tape with numbers on it. I have to let it dry out before I can do anything with it.*[136]

It looked like this:

> *Wet brown tape* 14
> 2
> 3

I had thumbed past this dream for five years, unable to relate it to anything.

The tape's puzzle had the feel of an anagram, but rearranging numbers instead of letters to form new numbers that might be holding a secret message. In this case, it was a question of simple addition and subtraction. These punsters of antiquity even gave us a black and white clue, meaning it was obvious.

In rearranging the single and double digits, numbers were formed that established the date of Titanic's sinking. The digit 4 symbolized April as the month.

$$
\begin{array}{ll}
\begin{aligned}
14 \\
2 \\
\underline{3} \\
19
\end{aligned}
&
\begin{aligned}
14 \\
-2 \\
\underline{} \\
12
\end{aligned}
\quad \text{(Date Titanic sank: Apr. 14, 1912)}
\end{array}
$$

---

136 10/27/93.

Footnotes contain dream dates and references to prior pages where the dream appeared.
Endnotes contain bibliographical references, are marked with "ℰ" in the text, and appear at the end of the book.

Could the tub, sometimes bandied as slang for a boat, have been pointing to the Allison family in which only baby Trevor was saved? Three of the Allison family perished: little Helen Loraine and her parents, Bess and Hudson Allison.

Might the tub and the black sign be a telling omen of Titanic's ill fate and the white stenciled lettering reminiscent of a pattern? This small satchel of clues configuring the date of the sinking was compelling.

Having to wait for the tape to dry out, invites a world of interpretation which I leave to you, dear Reader. But what was the big noise or smell?

The insertion of currency into a machine revisited the dream where I'd *inserted a quarter that looked like a metal slug into a coin machine; the machine looked like those on the observation deck of the Empire State Building.*[137]

Inserting money in a machine … inserting a metal slug in a machine…

The metal slug was anyone's guess. The thought lingered: "What a queer thing to dream of twice."

Around the thrilling discovery of the date, still circling the archives were dream images of the *maple leaf coin*, symbolic of the Canadian flag, and the *pink field of evergreen trees*, descriptive of Newfoundland's first flag.

The date – Canada – Newfoundland – the Allison family – the mummy – the water dreams – the boat dreams – the White Star Line.

The famed Titanic was stepping out of the dream and into the realm of waking.

The revelation of a piece of wet tape dating Titanic's demise demanded critical focus. Waves of uncertainty about what part, if any, I played in it swirled through the watery channels of the psyche. Crosscurrents of the transcendental forced me deeper into the murky abyss of the Atlantic. A cloud cover of mixed emotions floated overhead. Why was I dreaming this? Where would it take me?

Validating the date motivated me to forge ahead with the *"Half Circle, Full Star, Clog"* trio. *I'm practicing the Girl Scout motto "Be Prepared."* And adding to its mystery were *images of three pairs of shoes outside of a bedroom door.*[138]

I had for some time felt that the "full star" resonated with the White Star Line, but the "half circle" and "clog" were still a puzzle. I thought about meridians, halves of great circles which extend from pole to pole always at right angles to the equator. Consequently, meridians always run true north and south.

---

137 10/26/98.
138 12/1/97. See Ch. 21 – Half Circle, Full Star, Clog, p. 93

I was struck by the dream drawing in the first of the "Half Circle" series.[139] The circle was divided vertically. The next dream that grazed my pillow months later showed the circle divided horizontally.

Longitude and latitude streaked across the screen of consciousness: The vertical line, longitude; the horizontal line, latitude.

The first "Half Circle, Full Star, Clog" message contained a raft, which, in my interpreting brain, was bobbing toward the Titanic.

The second message was accompanied by an image of *a square divided in four*[140] resembling that of a "Punnett square," used in genetics to determine dominant and recessive ratios. Inside one very deep square were the words *"carrot soup,"* possibly denoting eyesight or perhaps another flavor containing karats, the measure used to weigh minerals.

The "clog," intent on revealing itself, taught me patience while Trust led the way. The almighty timekeepers would decide when we'd know where the clog fit.

Loose ends threaded a burgeoning pattern. *Half Circle* – longitude and latitude, *Full Star* – the White Star Line – Titanic, the *raft* – a life raft, *jumbled numbers on a wet piece of tape* – Titanic's date of demise, *a capsize* – La Provence – Titanic's call for help.

Still other telltale threads were weaving together: the *waterwheel* – the wheelhouse, *rowboats* – lifeboats, *the gash* – suspected damage to the hull, *a visa, a truckers' strike, a pricing war, the undertow, the American Embassy, a disappearing contraption, ice fishing.*

It all ran parallel to the legend of the Titanic, a subject that had previously been distant from my waking thoughts.

Determination, inspiration, and perspiration were in full force. I was sleeping on a mystery demanding to be unraveled.

139 Ibid.
140 7/24/98.

CHAPTER TWENTY-SEVEN

WITNESS

*S*omeone *is being tried for a crime I had witnessed. I'm brought into a courtroom and there's a big mountain of paper. They all know I'm the only one who saw the crime. It's something the man "didn't do." They also know I had to protect him and would not be able to speak. When I leave the courtroom the man in charge mentions that I am to cover for the suspect.*

Then there's another mountain of paper — strips of paper in different colors. Underneath it is a shelf and a sort of storage bin. I'm putting some of the strips in the storage bin and the guy whose strips they were wants me to put them on a narrow shelf. He says shelve it. I say store it. Then there is an X-ray pad with little narrow windows marked TV, Radio. I can't line up the colored strips with the pad.

At the end of this dream-encoded mystery which appeared in 1993, I awakened in the middle of the night to a blaring television. It had turned itself on in my den, a good distance away from where I slept. After years of turning this phenomenon over, it no longer seems presumptuous to think some form of electrical transmission in the wiring of my brain had activated an electronic device in the TV. At the time, I'd not a clue as to what any of the dream content meant. The different colored strips, the shelf, the dishes, and the bowl would reappear later. I followed the dream and *"stored it."*

The particulars had all the makings of a legal trial: *the crime, the courtroom, the man in charge, the suspect — even a mountain.* A mountain of evidence?

Footnotes contain dream dates and references to prior pages where the dream appeared.

Endnotes contain bibliographical references, are marked with "Ɛ" in the text, and appear at the end of the book.

CHAPTER TWENTY-EIGHT

MORSE CODE AND THE UPANISHADS

If one theme unites these writings,
it is the search for an underlying unity
linking everything we see and think.

Robert Hume[E25]

An inner radar system was collecting, scanning, ordering, and reordering the myriad pieces that would eventually reveal an apocalyptic, yet intriguing picture of Titanic in its entirety.

Precision and association, eye-catching hallmarks of the Dream, were instinctually and continually at work. What a process! When something fit, a built in sensor would revitalize an impression, inviting us to witness a piece of inner knowledge we never knew we held.

This time it energized a dream that spun out coded dashes:[141]

-- --- -- --- --

Could that be an abbreviated version of Morse code?

"SOS," telegraph shorthand for "Save Our Ship" or "Save Our Souls," translates to three dots, three dashes, three dots.

SOS would look like . . . - - - . . .

The wireless operator on duty failed to take one of the crucial ice warnings sent to Titanic to the bridge. Instead, he continued with the pile of personal telegraph messages he was sending. It has been said that the Titanic actually sent the very first SOS. There is evidence, however that other ships used the signal first that evening. In any event, Titanic's SOS did not match what the dream telegraphers had wired.

Perhaps the dashes that alternated in groupings of two and three didn't require further explanation. Perhaps they didn't need to match. Was the mere suggestion of Morse code enough? Even if it was, I was still driven to poke around in the encrypted chambers

---

141 1/20/94.

Footnotes contain dream dates and references to prior pages where the dream appeared.
Endnotes contain bibliographical references, are marked with "E" in the text, and appear at the end of the book.

of dots and dashes, clicks and pauses used for transmitting messages by telegraphy. The translation came through as MOMOM.

Holy Mackerel! Could MOMOM be a celestial hieroglyphic for Mother? Or ... mummy? Or Om, the sacred syllable uttered in Hindu as the spoken essence of the universe? Perhaps it was a combination.

- -   - - -   - -   - - -   - -   MOMOM

In the dream, the word or code - -   - - -   - -   - - -   - - was described as *extending every 2 and 3 lengths* and was placed under the word *Upanishad.*

I asked myself how the Morse encryption of MOMOM separated by dashes "every 2 and 3 lengths" could tie to "Upanishad." Intrigued with this veritable assortment of half riddles, the first thing I set out to do was find out what Upanishad meant.

Thus, I found the meaning of the term "Upanishads": the philosophical parts of the Vedas. "upa" (near) "ni" (down) "s(h)ad" (to sit) - the act of sitting down by one's Guru to receive instruction.

Veda is a generic name for the most ancient Indian sacred literature.

I had come to learn my Guru was the Dream and that it was shepherded by my loving mentors. I would listen devotedly to the inspired teachings, visions and mystical experiences of these ancient sages so that I might fully understand their message.

I discovered that Upanishads was a collection of Indian speculations, dating from around 600 BC, on the nature of reality and the soul, and the relations between these two. The Upanishads theme relates to everything we see and think. That unity is called Brahman – said to be the world soul – in which every individual is united with the cosmos and only needs to realize this to reach fulfillment.

The haze began to lift.

The Morse code of MOMOM accompanied by the word "Upanishads" was linking everything that I, as one human being on Earth, had unwittingly seen and thought. The interweaving and cross connecting far exceeded my own personal boundaries, uniting the masses who perished on the Titanic, the survivors, and all who have searched for an answer for close to a century.

The unfolding story of Titanic propelled me on a journey into the unknown, through the agency of the sacred and mysterious vessel of the Dream. Disordered though it was, for some inexplicable reason I never questioned it. From time to time, I'd reflect on a dream of *a begging cup, a cup that was begging and vibrating its way out of a brick wall.*[142] I thought of Percival the cat and imagined that Lord Galen, my professor of vision, had

142 12/12/96.

paired him with the prayerful cup. I wondered if the *begging cup* had anything to do with the legend of the Grail cup in the story of Percival and the Holy Grail.

With no rationale in sight, I was duty-bound to follow the invisible, not knowing where it would lead. Relentless in its pursuit, it stalked me, leaving no option but to blindly follow ... to trust. I was perpetually reminded of the penny in the eye dream: *In God We Trust.*

The Upanishads link began to shape new dimensions. The Dream as a universal vehicle could unite all peoples with the cosmos – with the purest and most instinctual ability we possess, our first voice.

The divine nature of man and God – the invisible higher power – was always there protecting and guiding us, visiting nightly, softly whispering the secret truths of our innermost thoughts during the peacefulness of sleep. Every culture on Earth, dreams. It is not for everyone to share the same driving passion that I have, not to mention the time to construct such an odyssey, but it is for everyone to realize his or her untapped potential – the vast storehouse of learning deeply buried in our unconscious. It is knowledge that far outstrips our sense of what we think we know.

While ruminating on the infinite concepts that this opus was silently imparting, a snippet of a dream floated in that displayed *a drawing of a needle and thread next to the ocean. The dream message is, "Mother needs attention."*[143]

Non sequiturs like the needle and thread had a way of bringing you up short. I just didn't get it ... what did Mother have to do with sewing?

The code - -   - - -   - -   - - -   - -, decoded in Morse, translated to **MOMOM**. Was I supposed to stitch something together?

---

143 6/20/97.

CHAPTER TWENTY-NINE

CLOCK A DOODLE DO

In dreams begins responsibility.
William Butler Yeats

Pressed for time and unable to dawdle over a single detail while mountains of others piled up, I turned to a dream forecasting the winds of change. Reminiscent of classic Newfoundland weather, it depicted *a big wind that comes and suddenly blows petals all over the place. The air is moist and sticky and I'm covered with white petals like feathers. They are stuck to my skin.*

The feather, symbolic of ascending Truth, became a recurrent theme in the voyage and had the quirky habit of materializing out of the blue.

One of the most deliberate messages in the same dream turned out to be a real "who-dunit." It pictured *a clock with a funny sort of doodle drawn on it. The time is 12:28 and shows a figure that looked like an "m." The message is that "he wants yellow ... pale yellow." I go to point at the clock with a pen, which I don't realize is a marker.*

It makes a mark with a curly cue by mistake. The person holding the clock is annoyed. Someone says, "you slipped." I say, it's "my mistake."[144]

The directive that *"he wants yellow"* flickered like candlelight through years of dreams, dancing in the dark, flirting and taunting, pulling me toward it. Like moth to the flame, I was drawn in closer and closer. Was the *yellow that he wants* part of the yellow lexicon?[145] Could it be the yellow slab?[146]

What was my mistake? Why did I slip? What was the meaning of the m? What was the curly cue and why was it on the clock? Moreover, who was the person holding the

---

144 2/24/95.
145 9/12/93. See Ch. 3 – The Pole, p. 25
146 9/19/97. See Ch. 10 – The Stuff of Life, pp. 53–54

Footnotes contain dream dates and references to prior pages where the dream appeared.
Endnotes contain bibliographical references, are marked with "Ɛ" in the text, and appear at the end of the book.

clock? Intuition, the eternal glowing light, subtly illuminated a foreboding association with the Titanic, but what could it be and why?

Feathers – a clock – a doodle – the letter "m" – a curly cue – pale yellow – a marker: would this jigsaw ever become whole?

Reverberations of the *Whole Earth* – *the shipping department* – *the CBS Eye* – *MOMOM* – were resounding in the diaphanous chambers of consciousness. What did it all mean?

The *shipping department* moved to the top of the docket with the arrival of Titanic's imperial presence. The *CBS Eye* was elected ambassador of communications, but that was pretty broad. What type of communication? What did the *Whole Earth* have to do with it? The rest would have to wait. It was crosstalk, but crosstalk with no static. If I listened to the first voice of instinct, it was static-free. The only interference was that second voice, the trickster of doubt who habitually derails our instincts.

The Half Circle,[147] Full Star, Clog trio was partially answered in the name of Titanic, though the jury was still adjudicating the fate of the Clog.

Sprinkled throughout were dream shavings of lavender, the silver key, the optic nerve key ring, and the pale yellow mark on the clock, which might or might not match the yellow slab. The centerpiece at this port of call was the grand lady of the sea, the R.M.S. Titanic, resurrected with esoteric hints of her legendary mummy.

Two new spheres began to form, one encircling the realms of the ancient past: Osiris – Memory – Resurrection.[148] The other, a more investigative circle, reined in: a Witness – a Crime – a Suspect[149] – a Morse-encrypted MOMOM.[150]

This homemade stew, brimming with ingredients from the night and spiced with findings of the day, was overflowing with flavors; some recognizable while others remained exotic and unexplained. Little did I realize, an essence that had been brewing was now bubbling to the surface. whetting the appetite for the next tasting.

---

147 See Ch. 26 – The Date, pp. 122–23
148 See Ch. 25 – Re-membering Osiris, p. 115
149 See Ch 27 – Witness, p. 125
150 See Ch 28 – Morse Code and The Upanishads, p. 128

2/24/95

A big wind came along and suddenly there were these little oblong shaped white petals blowing all over. We were being covered in white petals. Everyone was. At the end, it looked like a sea of white feathers.

COVERED WITH WHITE PETALS
(LOOK LIKE FEATHERS)

Then there was someone who had a clock and there was a figure in it... two M's. Someone gave an interpretation as though it was a dream. The one on the left was significant but I forget; the one on the right I said "That means he wants YELLOW". I pictured a pale yellow.

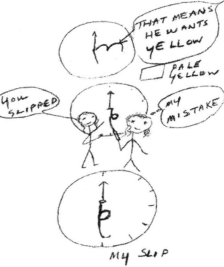

THAT MEANS HE WANTS YELLOW
PALE YELLOW
YOU SLIPPED
MY MISTAKE
MY SLIP

I had a pen & went to point at the clock. I didn't realize it was a marker & it made a mark with a curlycue by mistake. The person holding the clock was annoyed.

Then someone delivered a package to my room but it was mother's jewelry. They opened the package & started taking out the pieces one by one. I didn't want anyone seeing this and I told them to put it away. Then I noticed that a large coral dome ring was missing. One case was in a closet to the right; the other was more in the center (left) of the room.

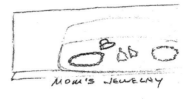

MOM'S JEWELRY

CORAL DOME RING
MISSING

CHAPTER THIRTY

MOTHER EARTH

When we heal the earth, we heal ourselves.
~David Orr
When we heal ourselves, we heal the earth.
~Penelope Peacock

Careful examination of the various frames in which another recurrent theme – mother – appeared, inspired me to think of the essence of mother as a quantum of mother energy. The image of my own mother, and the infinite set of memory units that constitutes did not match the structure that seemed to be motivating the dreams, or at least, then, it didn't.

It occurred to me that the dreams in which my mother appeared had characterized her in situations that completely clashed with her immaculate appearance and physical being. For example, she would be *wearing a scruffy wig that was on backward.* In one dream, *she had a deformed leg* and in another, she had *a veiny bulbous nose.* Her living conditions as portrayed in the dreams were suspect. *Acid on her carpets, urine on the floor, her place under construction* were all gross contradictions of her neater-than-a-pin household. The image of *mashed potatoes all over her floor* was especially bizarre.

In another dream *she was parallel parking in the East Fifties in New York* (as was I in an earlier dream; this one was a repeat) and in yet another reference to her floor, *she was laying on the floor of a car with a USA Today newspaper on her head.*[151]

What was the story with her floor?

This unrelenting refrain about my mother and her floor transcended the most fantastic flights of imagination. None of it fit. She had never worn a wig, much less backward. There was nothing wrong with her leg, she did not have veins in her nose, and it was not bulbous. She was a clean freak – compulsively so – especially where she lived. She hadn't driven for ten years, and as far as I can remember, had not taken to lying on car floors.

---

151 Mother Earth dreams: 1995–1999.

Footnotes contain dream dates and references to prior pages where the dream appeared.

Endnotes contain bibliographical references, are marked with "Ɛ" in the text, and appear at the end of the book.

None of it resembled her in the foggiest except for the continued images of loss and devaluation of her jewelry, for which she had a healthy appreciation. The outlandish distortions of her petite physical frame and the devoted attention to her floor finally pried open a door.

Was I revisiting the mother-daughter relationship? Or, I wondered, was the primordial symbol of my mother emblazoned in these images drawing on the weight of world experience? That is, Mother as in Mother Nature, the floor depicting earth as in ground. Hmm. Could this all translate to Mother Earth?

It was compelling, but it was too early to tell. And why would I be dreaming about Mother Earth? One of my dreams conjured up an image of *my mother and a yellow slab* that sprung like a tiny sprout from a very pregnant seed. What she was doing in the same dream with the yellow slab was a mystery.

My dream told me, *"Be patient. "You will learn everything you need to know."*

M O M O M!

I replayed the dream. The word or code - -   - - -   - -   - - -   - - was described as *extending every 2 and 3 lengths and was placed under the word Upanishad.*

M O M O M – the code was linking to Upanishads! A defining moment?

Could the Indian concept of Upanishads as an underlying unity be a metaphor for the totality of the Earth? For the mother lode of the story?

If MOMOM at this place in the story was symbolizing Mother Earth, what was the link between Mother Earth and the Upanishads?

Another Hindu concept, Vedanta, the search for self-knowledge, affirms the harmony of religions. Was this a reflecting pool for the harmony of humankind and its relationship to Earth, our terrestrial playground?

Considering that the Upanishads are symbolic of the divine nature of man and God, deductive reasoning led me to this rather simplistic end, though others might have another view: Man symbolizes God. God symbolizes man. God created man. God created Earth. But man is destroying Earth, destroying God's creation, destroying himself.

If God and man are ultimately subsumed into the Upanishads one soul which lives in the elements and is interwoven in sky and earth, then MOMOM – Mother Earth – would seek humankind's care of its hospitable home, a home pleading to be unified with God.

Lost in thought, I was reminded of the penny in the eye dream: In God We Trust. An ancient theme was unfolding, but what did it have to do with the Titanic, when a message the size of a cannonball discharged the answer: For Titanic, SOS signaled SAVE OUR SHIP. For this underground mission, MOMOM signaled SAVE OUR EARTH.

Above the surface, the spiraling of the natural mother-Mother Earth loop, connecting with my mom's peculiar behavior and eccentric features, was just the tip of that celebrated iceberg. I looked to see how much more lay beneath.

CHAPTER THIRTY-ONE

FLASHING LIGHTS! RINGING BELLS!

Two images that caught my eye while I was diving into the murky abyss of the Titanic floated back into view: *Mother needs attention* linked to *a needle and thread by the ocean.*[152] It was a sure clue that some mental needlework was looming and mother (be it my mother or Mother Earth) obviously had a hand in it. But how?

The whispering winds of Peggymoonbeam swept over me, directing: "Stitch it together, Penelope. Sew it up!"

The Morse-encrypted MOMOM flashed brighter. As on a string of Christmas lights, the starter bulb, "Mother," lit up the whole tree. Blinking in perfect unison, a string of motherly dream images was dispatched from the library of dream journals. *A bare-breasted woman nursing a baby* paired with *a series of wavy lines that look Japanese.*[153]

Another string of flashing lights: The woman nursing the baby was Mother, too! Why were these Japanese wavy lines paired with the image of a nursing mother? Was my unconscious reclaiming an emotional nursing experience? I wasn't breast-fed, but that aside, maybe the wavy lines and the mother's bosom didn't go together. But surely they did! They were together in the dream.

Why were these wavy lines characterized as Japanese? In trying to unlock the strange word-picture puzzle, I tripped over a science Web site where I found tsunami defined as a "Japanese harbour wave."[Ɛ26] I gasped!

Puzzled as to why I'd dream a tsunami, I was now compelled to understand how one behaved. A tsunami is a series of powerful ocean waves caused by large undersea disturbances such as earthquakes or volcanic activity.

While fleshing out a chronology of nature's work in the simplest of lay terms, I was deeply focused in geologic areas, then literally Greek to me. Completely uniformed as to strike-slip faults, energy mass, icebergs, landslides, tsunamis, earthquakes, and volcanoes, I'd have thought anyone who told me they'd become my basic intake, "mental."

---

152 6/20/97.
153 1/27/95.

Footnotes contain dream dates and references to prior pages where the dream appeared.
Endnotes contain bibliographical references, are marked with "Ɛ" in the text, and appear at the end of the book.

My morning ritual of gulping down handfuls of vitamins and minerals had been supplemented with daily excavations of the vitamins and minerals of the earth appearing in my dreams. The adventure of the day was retreating into the cavern of my computer to match the raw nutrients of terra firma to my dreams. All analogies pointed to the Earth.

Then came the bellringer! Oooh Wooo Oooh!

EARTH – MOTHER EARTH!! The woman nursing the baby was indeed MOTHER EARTH who was positioned directly under the wavy lines of the tsunami in the dream. Of course! Why didn't I get it? Beneath every tsunami, lies the earth. It was all in the detail and so simple once you saw it.

In one shocking moment, the epiphany of the tsunami became a freeze frame for this leg of the journey. I knew it was none other than Mother Earth steering the ship – a leviathan of a ship that she herself may have taken down. Together with the flickering of MOMOM, a brilliant flash with even greater luminosity shone through. It was none other than Peggymoonbeam beaming, "Nice work, Penelope!" Somehow, my hand was guided to draw a picture of a tsunami and Mother Earth nursing a baby. Wow! What if the baby was this project?

Completely overwhelmed by the depth and breadth of shreds and scraps and slivers of things bobbing to the surface, I sensed a connection to Titanic. But how would it all play out? What if I was wrong?

Given the buckets of clues so masterfully disguised in this unfathomable scheme, it seemed as safe a bet as any. But a tsunami? If a tsunami had occurred when the Titanic went down, wouldn't that have been common knowledge in unlatching the century-old mystery of Titanic's fate?

CHAPTER THIRTY-TWO

MOTHER'S APPRENTICES

Soon names of other family members trickled in, serving as Mother's apprentices while she devotedly carried, nursed, and designed for us the theory.

The repeated, and often ludicrous, mother dream impersonations unlocked the most startling recognition. Not only would my mother be the impresario for Mother Earth, but my Aunt Belle would play the straight man – that is the Strait of Belle Isle, an ocean channel near where Titanic went down. Added to the family circle was my cousin Andi, who would be cast as andesite, a volcanic lava. The geologic characteristics had latched on to my family members by name. Yet their everyday habits depicted in the dreams were completely outlandish.

Countless threads knit a family portrait that would reveal a virtual animation of my relatives, both living and deceased.

The volume had been turned up on what had literally become a 24/7channel, broadcasting all news, all the time.

The dream tide had turned to geologic tensions.

With the matriarchal tree solidly planted, other family connections clamored for recognition. Metaphorical bulbs were implanted far deeper than the roots of my own family tree.

The prologue to the Allison dream, where *the operator says, "She checked out,"* is part of a story that reveals a cluster of what appear to be unrelated clues.[154]

Mother is yelling and screaming and has a brown scruffy wig on backward. I have to pay 34 cents. I'm looking for change and come up with the right change, which I find in the dark. The yellow slab is there with the message "Be patient; you will learn everything you need to know." Aunt Belle is sleeping under a chenille bedspread.[155]

---

154 See Ch. 23 – Tragedy, p. 100
155 2/10/95.

Footnotes contain dream dates and references to prior pages where the dream appeared.
Endnotes contain bibliographical references, are marked with "Ɛ" in the text, and appear at the end of the book.

Another cobweb was being spun. The dexterous spider weaving its own complex network of fibers managed to ensnare a shadowy account of Titanic.

The players included two-year-old Helen Loraine Allison, a volatile mother/Mother Earth and the Strait of Belle Isle near where Titanic collided with the iceberg. As suspected, mother had become the conduit that would carry the dream and coax it along the ocean floor of Mother Earth's own abode.

Apart from the medley of disjointed clues, the most suspicious symbol that attached itself to my natural mother was that of the scruffy wig, which simply made no sense.

But, if staying true to the nature of geology, and the wig were interpreted as the lithosphere, the rigid outer shell of the earth, could Mother's tantrum then be suggestive of a volcanic eruption? An increase in volcanic activity worldwide would render an earth whose covering is tattered, torn – and scruffy.

Pairing mother's wig worn backward with looking for change may relate to keeping an eye on polar reversal, a change in polarity of Earth's magnetic field. Backward to me meant "in reverse." Remembering that my own mother never once donned a wig, much less a scruffy one, let alone wore it backward, I realized the scribes dared to test my boundaries as they segued from mother to Mother Earth.

I sensed they were waiting to see how far I'd venture on my own and if I took their message seriously. This was made clear in a dream at a time when I was distracted and had temporarily cast my research aside. I was asked *if I would be using my desk and am advised that if I wasn't, the desk would be removed.* Once I understood that my desk symbolized this body of work, I knew I had the option of not accepting the commitment to decipher my dream message, but my heart had been touched by my mentors. I had already sipped the elixir of cosmic knowledge ... how could I turn back?

My decision was made. I'd "use the desk" and accept its inevitable weight. I continued my struggle to decode the myriad fragments through my own studies. I knew that eventually, the mentors, both historic and personal, would come to help sift through the mountains of dreams that had accrued. It could not be too soon.

While thinking about the guise of the scruffy wig, I reflected on another dream that had hair at its roots. *American bills are being folded up because they are taking up too much room. There is a woman with a lot of hair piled up in a turban. I sense she has a fall in with her hair because there appears to be so much volume under the towel. She piles it up quickly.*[156]

I wondered if the "volume of hair" might be a metaphor for Pele's hair, which looks like long strands of greenish-gold hair, perfectly straight and as thick as human hair. Pele's hair is created when lava is ejected into the air during a windy day. When the wind is strong enough, it will cause the falling lava to thin out and harden into a strand of golden rock as it falls to the ground. It's like a glass fiber and very sharp.

---

156 3/3/99.

The "turban/towel" would become dream shorthand for terry cloth; terra meaning earth, cloth meaning covering. Voila!! The covering of the earth, the lithosphere was expressed twofold: first the scruffy wig; then the turban/towel.

Piling her hair up quickly may point to the sudden blast common to a volcanic eruption and the piling up of lava. The *fall that was in with her hair* would be untangled later.

The *American bills* converted to currency, not as in legal tender, but rather the currents of the ocean: Current-sea.

Characterizing Aunt Belle as the Strait of Belle Isle sparked a connection to the waters where Titanic met her horrific destiny in 1912.

Higgledy-piggledy pieces were connecting and reconnecting, falling into place in unexplained precision and with a weird sense that they all really belonged together. It was as though they were in all one piece to begin with, like a jigsaw puzzle that got separated and put back together again. The more they repeated, the easier it was to see the pattern and what piece went where. But what was the point?

The Strait of Belle Isle, historically a place of danger, separates the Great Northern Peninsula of the Island of Newfoundland from the mainland of southern Labrador. Hazardous navigation in the channel has been documented by writers who have reported that the Strait was frequently blocked by ice for eight to ten months of the year.

Thus, Aunt Belle being under a chenille bedspread, or under cover, may be depicting the Strait of Belle Isle as having been under a blanket of ice at the time of Titanic's collision with the iceberg. The chenille had a dual role. Not only did it appear as an undercover agent for Belle Isle; it emerged as a prelude to the lower berths of geology when I discovered it bore a remarkable likeness to a stratigraphic texture.

In 1912, mariners had not yet entertained the idea that field ice moves with wind rather than surface current, nor had they accepted that the direction of surface current could be deflected by a strong wind.

On Sunday, 14 April, 1912, the wind had been so strong out of the north that Titanic's usual daily boat drill had been cancelled.[E27] One would wonder if the strong winds the day of the sinking presaged some confluence of natural forces.

The eye of the dream needle threaded with the message that "Allison checked out" inspired me to gather some loose ends. A byzantine landscape was being painted by Mother Earth, polar reversal, the Strait of Belle Isle, and victims of Titanic's doom represented by the three members of the Allison family from Canada who perished in the disaster.

CHAPTER THIRTY-THREE

THE ICEBERG THEORY

For nearly one century, the blame for Titanic's sinking has been levied against the legendary collision with an iceberg. Underwater expeditions seeking the wreck, using site mapping, artifact recovery and photographic exploration, began in 1981. She was found on September 1, 1985, on the bottom of the North Atlantic Ocean, two and a half miles down.

Expeditions since have uncovered some remarkable findings, but have yet to provide a plausible explanation as to how a 46,000 ton vessel would have been brought to its end by collision with an iceberg alone. One of the experts in the 2005 expedition said, "Titanic may have side-swiped the iceberg." That's a lot different than colliding with it.

Scientists still ask, "How did flooding lead to such destruction?" "What occurred when the ship left the surface?" "Why is Titanic's stern radically damaged and twisted into a mangled mess while its bow remains in relatively good shape?" The mystery of long-held secrets and puzzling questions about Titanic's fate has captured public curiosity for nearly a century and answers still swing like pendulums slowly seeking the Truth.

Absence of light has long taken blame for Titanic's officers not being able to see the mountainous iceberg. Moonlight might have made what foam there was – or even the berg itself – easier to see. On that night, there was no swell or wind, so little surf would be generated around any icebergs that might be there. No moon, no clouds, no wind, stars as the only source of light, and a calm sea were the climatic conditions that night.

In 1996, a special acoustic device known as a sub-bottom profiler was used to look at the Titanic's hull through the muddy ocean floor. The long-held belief that there was a 350-foot gash was replaced with the observation that there was a series of six relatively small tears, some no more than an inch wide. The gash theory seemed logical way back then and many survivors of the Titanic said that they personally saw the gaping hole. Nonetheless, common sense should have discounted eyewitness accounts of the damage since the iceberg damage occurred below the waterline.

Despite discovery of the tears and the thousands of man-hours spent in research, testing, and evaluation, fundamental curiosity of how 25,000 tons of water could have flooded the ship in one hour has still not been satisfied. It defies logic. Even with brittle

---

Footnotes contain dream dates and references to prior pages where the dream appeared.
Endnotes contain bibliographical references, are marked with "Ɛ" in the text, and appear at the end of the book.

fracturing as a partial explanation, some unknown piece toward explaining the mammoth shipwreck has gone unfound.

The Titanic is now corroding. Some very interesting corrosion products have been discovered which are allowing scientists to gain insight into the geochemistry of iron and other metals that comprise Titanic's debris. The corrosion products are called rusticles and resemble stalactites.$^{\mathcal{E}28}$

This "current" finding returned me to an early dream of *a man on a raft in the middle of the water. The raft has whitish stalks on it that look to me like stalactites*[157] and appear to my friend as icebergs.

---

157 12/1/97. See Ch. 21 – Half Circle, Full Star, Clog, p. 94

CHAPTER THIRTY-FOUR

LABRADOR CURRENT

Icebergs, fog, severe storms, fishing vessels, and transatlantic traffic make the Labrador Current one of the world's most dangerous shipping areas. Officers of the Titanic were well aware of the risks.

The Labrador Current is a deep cold current which flows down from the North Pole around Labrador and Newfoundland to meet the warm Gulf Stream coming up from the Equator. It passes by the Arctic's greatest iceberg nursery in West Greenland. Freshwater bergs calve or break off from the glacier and form huge new icebergs that drift until they meet the Labrador Current, which carries them south in huge masses toward Newfoundland.

The iceberg that ravaged Titanic began its life in Greenland about 1100 BC as packed snow, or firn. It took about a century for it to compress into a glacier. Then slowly, over three millennia, this river of ice slid toward the sea, until the tides calved off the glacier's "toe" into a Greenland fjord about 1909.

As Titanic was being built in Belfast, the deadly iceberg sailed its circle tour of the Labrador Sea, first north, then back south and into the Labrador Current. Its deep keel, eight hundred to nine hundred feet below the water line, kept it in the strong current when shallower bergs eddied out into Fortune Bay at Newfoundland. Currents swept it against the prevailing winds past the Flemish Cap to trace the tail of the Grand Bank(s). ϵ_{29} In the two to three years the monster iceberg spent in the frigid waters, the majestic ship took form, was launched and steamed to Southampton to pick up its ill-fated passengers, the Current carrying it inexorably to their meeting.

Fortune Bay. Its name is believed to have come from the Portuguese word *fortuna* meaning either place of misfortune or place of good fortune. "Place of misfortune" seems the more appropriate description as it relates to Titanic.

While I reflected on the path of the iceberg, a swirl of light began to envelop me. From a distant galaxy, the twinkle of Agneswiseheart sparkled above.

"Penelope, you harvested a dream about a *money-water island where you were writing one check after another.*[158] Fortune Bay bears a strong likeness."

---

158 12/19/96.

Footnotes contain dream dates and references to prior pages where the dream appeared.

Endnotes contain bibliographical references, are marked with "ϵ" in the text, and appear at the end of the book.

Yes, Agneswiseheart. It really does. It's ironic that the crown jewel of ocean liners carrying the most prominent millionaires of its day went down only miles from Fortune Bay.

"Don't despair, Penelope dear. The souls of Titanic have all been healed and some have even returned to Earth."

Agneswiseheart, seated atop her angelic throne, then directed me to the Newfoundland map room where I spotted the Flemish Cap and suddenly remembered the dream in which *I am wearing a woolen tam and where I'm taking a course in shorthand from a Japanese instructor.*[159] The shorthand course led me to Stenography, and then, of course, to Nicolaus Steno. Japanese translated to foreign and foreign was the instruction I was about to receive, unbeknownst to me.

Hmm. *Woolen tam* – cap – Flemish Cap – *shorthand* – Steno? Steno was the first to posit that the earth is probably much older than originally thought.[E30] The thought of Labrador's cold ocean current awakened me to my studies of Newfoundland and Labrador, that little-known corner of the world nicknamed "The Rock" for its rocky and often very rugged landscape. Was this strange sort of shorthand leading to an abbreviated course of study mentored by the great Steno? If so, it was back to Mother Earth.

Supporting the Mother Earth theory were new themes weaving their mysteries into a geologic tapestry constantly bursting with new color and texture.

The angelical hierarchy had delivered this illusive puzzle. Through their luminous perseverance and concentrated repetition, a glossary began to spring forth. Growing like a vine, it needed plenty of untangling. Dream images of plates and bowls sent mixed signals. Some contained nuggets worthy of mining while others performed ordinary household chores like washing dishes.

In dream after dream, swarms of idioms, wordplays and illustrations crammed with depictions of bowls and plates, along with basements, belts, blocks, mattresses, pillows, platforms, refrigerators, sheets, wrenches, veiny body parts, vents, and more veered from the commonplace to a grab bag of metaphors and homonyms that would challenge the riddle of the Sphinx.

The oldest known physical puzzle was the labyrinth. Did the Dream have as many parts as the labyrinthine funeral temple with its three thousand chambers built in ancient Egypt? Would I ever find my way out of the mazelike passages I had unknowingly entered – and have now drawn you into?

Peggymoonbeam came to my aid by whispering a clue: "Plate tectonics. Steno will fill you in later."

"Plate tec ... what?"

---

159 10/1/98.

CHAPTER THIRTY-FIVE

LAVA UNDER REVELATION

We can easily forgive a child who is afraid of the dark.
The real tragedy of life is when men are afraid of the light.

Plato

Floating under a coverlet of cottony clouds, I spotted an imaginary banner heralding "lavender." Beneath the disappearing streamer, views of stormy seas, rushing waters and elevated stretches of land recreated their backdrops in the still of the night.

The lavender code first appeared in a 1994 dream.

I'm in a cavernous place. The colors are blue and lavender. Water is dripping from the ceiling. To the left is a manila envelope addressed to me. To the right is a very large and valuable piece of porcelain. It is pale blue and lavender with the figure of an elephant at the bottom and a faint resemblance of a piano in the background. Then mother comes tripping down the stairs in high-heeled slippers. I cringe because it's dangerous and she could fall. I tell her to get down.[160]

The act of mother tripping down the stairs in high-heeled slippers was utterly incompatible with her style or behavior.

A cavernous place with water dripping from the ceiling dispatched me to the dream of the *whitish stalks I called stalactites* which connected to the life raft and Titanic. But this dream was different, for it was colored blue and lavender. Even the face on the porcelain elephant was lavender. Using the method that left signifies past and right future, the placement of the manila envelope on the left sparked a song called "Lavender Blue" dating to the seventeenth century. The valuable porcelain elephant, on the right side transported me to the future. But what did that future hold? Something old, something precious and fragile? Was mother going to slip and fall?

Almost six years later, with nary an inkling of where this was heading, I decided to spend my first New Year's Eve alone, ever. On December 31, 1998, wistful but comforted

---

160 1/10/94.

Footnotes contain dream dates and references to prior pages where the dream appeared.
Endnotes contain bibliographical references, are marked with "ℰ" in the text, and appear at the end of the book.

by the noisy merrymaking of the Times Square revelers on television, I kept on working. The lavender quest had been on the back burner for too long.

I sat at the computer staring at entries and focusing on the recurrent lavender theme that had played hide and seek with me through the years. Unlike the childhood game, this appeared to be leading to a study of the dual nature of waking and dreaming. Associations with lavender from latin lavare: to wash, led me to an aromatic shrub – to ancient healing qualities – to symbols of calmness, balance and love – to the lavender fields of Provence. Still I was clueless. Lavender was so prevalent in the story that my pursuit of its meaning had become obsessive. Over time, I learned obsession was a mistake. The cherubic lamplighters would shine their beacons by their ethereal clock and not a moment sooner.

Lavender did not travel alone. She always had a mate when she visited me as a dream symbol. Lavender was fickle. She had eclectic tastes and changed her costume for every occasion. Sometimes appearing with suede, a favorite accessory was a nice pair of lavender suede heels. One time she was a suede panel in an X-ray apron; another time, a bellows without a frame – a puzzlement I was sure would outlive me.

It had been an enchanted year beaming rays of illumination, discoveries sublime and untold insights. My computer and I would ring in 1999 by ourselves. I sat in a daze trying to conjure up the meaning behind Lavender, but came up blank. My mind drifted back to an ordinary night when a dream tiptoed in, in punster-like secrecy. It startled me, for it delivered a message I couldn't miss. It had my birth date wrong.

Through the night I am having short telephone conversations with a man who I'm about to have a date with, someone I have seen before. He tells me my birthday is on FEBRUARY 18 - THURSDAY. There is something he has to do that day. It involves his relatives – a family get-to-gether. I tell him jokingly, "You forgot to invite me." The February 18 message keeps appearing. I see an image of a black mesh screen in a black frame. There is an arm in front of me. I don't know whose it is.[161]

This was most confusing since my real birthday is July 28. I thought, "How many birthdays could a person have?" Well, if you dream a lot, the sky's the limit. When I checked the calendar, I was amazed to find that February 18 – in 1999 – indeed fell on a Thursday, but that was a year away. The dates were disjointed. The dream had occurred in 1998. Why did my birthday change?

The word "mesh" grabbed at me for I felt something would be meshing. But what was the black frame? It would remain for then an unsolved piece of the puzzle, though unlike other more stubborn pieces, not for long. My surprise party was in the planning stages but its actual meaning would be kept secret for some time.

---

161 10/30/98.

My thoughts turned back to lavender suede – lavender and suede. Would they ever mesh? "What an odd couple," I mused while looking at a dream that fluttered in a month earlier.

Transparent arms like bands are holding me down. I think it's a spirit. I'm finally released when I bite into one of these bands. There is a lavender suede object I don't know how to use. This object looks like a bellows that has lost its frame.

The spirit materializes and wants to walk a dog but can't understand why the dog is so low to the ground. It's a very funny and awkward walk. In the last segment, I'm wearing a bathing suit that leaves transparent polka dots on my skin. Illustrated in the center of this patchwork quilt are two big chunks of meat -- beef and veal.[162]

Spirits, dogs, polka-dotted skin and meat – the brainteasers were having a picnic. What if this was simply a wild goose chase, with nothing but a wild goose at the end? Twelve-hour days of recording scattered pieces of dreams, patching them together and researching the few identifiable parts was more than I had bargained for. Still I was passionate about capturing that goose, even if it was a silly one.

The word "meat" leapt off the page. Was the *"meat"* of the mystifying message hidden in this dream? What were the *transparent bands holding me down* and why had this *bellows* thing, an object I'd only seen in an antique shop, lost its frame?

The spirit walking the dog seemed to have a lead as long as the Earth is old, which is about 4.57 billion years. No wonder it was awkward. This tall story highlighting *a dog low to the ground* was out of this world; the transparent dots on my skin, too weird for words.

Suddenly, a ten-alarm alert sounded in my head, the sirens blaring Lavender – Lavender – Lavender; Lav ender ... Lava ender ... Lava Under. Lava Under!

It stuck to my tongue like peanut butter. Holy Molasses! I thought back to the dream of the *peanut butter and amethyst necklace* and how peanut butter symbolized the sugar phosphates on the outside of the DNA helix.[163] Peanut butter was a symbol for DNA! It's funny how DNA stuck even though it kept its distance. Like a broken record, it kept repeating and repeating: Lava under! Lava under... Lava under what? Lavender suede. Lava under suede? What was the suede?

Thought bubbles swirled in my head on the most solitary New Year's Eve of my life and magically uncorked the champagne of clues. Laser-like vision telescoped the suede shoes; the heels ... the suede heels ... the shoes with the heel in the center ... mother's high-heeled slippers. The heel ... the tilt of the ship. Suede ... swayed ... the ship swayed ... tilted ... leaned over because of the pressure of either the wind or a

---

162 11/30/98.
163 3/27/98. See Ch. 10 – The Stuff of Life, p. 52

tsunami under the Titanic, somehow caused by the lava being under ... that is under the sea .... under the earth. The ship swayed – because lava was under it. The bellows were feeding the fire of a volcanic eruption, not just below the earth, but also beneath the intricate networks of the mind. Same architect.

Lavender and Suede had meshed! They were the first shreds of evidence to be found in the mysterious birthday dream. To think, just one little word, "mesh," was the clue.

Lavender was a fait accompli. As communicated in the dream, it was the MEAT. This long-awaited discovery was the prize at the bottom of the Cracker Jack box. I was hoping I was moving toward the final stages of the story but there were still volumes of clues left to be unraveled. Another mystery. Why would Lavender expose itself so early? In fits and starts, one corner of the puzzle covered in helter-skelter bits of confetti began to mesh. It was not only in this celebrated dream scenario that the geologic theme gained recognition but it spread to countless other revelries laying in wait.

Far in the distance, perhaps from an astral plane, I sensed the gentle vibration of wind chimes, music tingling, beautiful bells. It was Peggymoonbeam, who in a shaft of light transmitted a frequency that signaled "Mission Lavender" – and so it was.

I returned to the dream symbols of the *transparent bands, the bite, the dog, and polka dotted skin.* Were *the transparent bands holding me down* characterizing a type of lava? Pahoehoe describes thin, smoothly flowing lava with a glassy, plastic skin that congeals while the lava inside is still liquid. "Was I under the lava?" More research revealed that the surface of lavas erupted underwater rapidly chills to form a glassy skin; that when water comes directly in contact with liquid lava it chills instantly to solid glass. That must be it! The *transparent bands* were the glassy skin of the lava. And what was in the bite that released me?

The *bellows*, a device with two handles used for blowing air onto a fire, turned out to be a perfect depiction of what happens in a volcanic eruption. And to complete the picture, *the lost frame on the bellows* was another volcanic tip, pointing in all likelihood to an ancient volcano that might have collapsed – lost its frame.

The image of two transparent bands repeated but in a different scenario. This time, *two translucent bands are attached to shoes that have a faulty buckle,*[164] another double entendre shouting "fault," as a fracture in the earth and "buckle" as in, "the Earth's crust buckled under the strain." These small affirmations became visible during my moments of greatest doubt.

A flash of synchronicity revealed a startling example given for buckle in an online Oxford dictionary. Buckle 2 [no OBJ.] bend and give way under pressure or strain: the Earth buckled under the titanic stress. [ORIGIN: from French boucler "to bulge."]

---

164 7/11/98.

But what about the *transparent polka dots imprinted on my body?* Had I developed a strange disease? What if a rare bug had crawled under my skin while I slept?

My mentors urged me to calm down so I decided to wait and see. If nothing dire happened, I knew it wasn't about me.

Patching it all together, it seemed that the sun, represented by the bathing suit, and the element of transparency might be symbolic of the light reactions of photosynthesis. Yep! That fit. It's the process by which green plants and other organisms use sunlight to synthesize foods from carbon dioxide and water. It figured. If plants reacted this way, so would we.

Now I had to decipher why *I'm wearing a bathing suit that leaves transparent polka dots on my skin.* Instead of seeing a dermatologist I went to the library searching for answers in books about photosynthesis and was led to sulfuric acid in photosynthetically active organisms. I also learned sulfur dioxide occurs naturally in volcanic gases contained in magma and is beneath the surface of the Earth.

I went back to the dream: *I'm finally released when I bite into one of these bands.* If sulfuric acid bit into the glassy plastic skin of the smooth flowing lava, it might have resulted in the explosive release of steam and gases, just as I was released in the dream.

If a submarine eruption was very deep and at a remote location, the ocean surface may not have been visibly disturbed, but I bet the air would be. I read that scientists discovered that air pollution from the burning of fossil fuels is the major cause of oxides which are a source of acid rain but what about from the release of volcanic gases? I guess I'd find out.

What a convoluted thing to be dreaming! Outwardly, it had all the features of a nightmare, but there was nothing scary about it. It was strangely matter of fact. Time and again, I observed the path leading to something underneath – unseen – below the surface.

The dog low to the ground was another puzzle. There are no domestic animals in my life and certainly none low to the ground. On second thought, there was Schnitzel, the dachshund of my teenage years. He was low to the ground, but why would he get tangled up with a bellows or, for that matter, with polka dots on my skin?

Once I got my footing, I learned that the Labrador coast is generally a low-lying and flat area of land produced by erosion that boasts the amiable species of water dog known as the Labrador Retriever. A low-lying area; a dog. The *"dog low to the ground"* barked wildly — Labrador.

Clickety ... clickety ... click! Lights. Camera. Action!

Amazing!

It was Labrador, sure as God made puppies for pets, and, yes, as in the dream, walking a dog here on Earth from whatever constellation the divine dog walker hailed, would indeed be awkward.

The elusive spirit in the dream might be one of many. Was it one of my recently departed loved ones or was it one of the long since departed scribes descending upon the tiny blue dot we call Earth? Was it Claudius Galen beaming through a pair of spectacles? Was it Madame Curie concocting a chemical formula? Was it Claudius Ptolemy radioing his astronomical news of the day? Or was it Nicholas Steno postulating on the Labradorean lay of the land?

My hunch is that it was a team, and a chivalrous one at that. To communicate this compendium of treasures, they were undoubtedly the illuminati of philanthropic deeds, not to mention, of puzzles.

Whoever the benevolent beings, they circumnavigated the cosmos just to take a dog for a walk along the Labrador coastline. *Awkward* was the word in the dream. I laughed myself silly in my sleep as I witnessed the contortions of this towering angel trying to negotiate a dog walk. Dreams have a way of slipping in a good laugh when we need one.

The command performance of the heavenly mentors made its mark in the province of Labrador. Honoring its namesake, this Labradorean dream yarn retrieved other yummy treats for a pooch.

In one dream, *I'm petting the stomach of a Labrador. As he places his paws over my hands, the hushed whisper of the word "a-s-c-h" softly curls around the story and lands in my ear.* In another, *a handyman is retrieving buried treats for a dog.* Still another, centers on *my holding a Labrador puppy.*[165]

Hmm. Delicious doggie treats were hidden, but what and where? "A-s-c-h must be the dream teller's version of ash but goodness, ash is buried all over the globe.

Contrary to what most people think of as a province, Labrador is a vast region. It covers an area of about 115,000 square miles and includes northern Quebec and the mainland part of Newfoundland. That's a lot of territory to canvass looking for treats.

When considering the dream clues in the aggregate – *the transparent bands* (lava), *the bite* (sulfuric acid, perhaps), *the lavender suede* (lava under a swaying ship), *the lost frame on the bellows* (an ancient volcano), *the dog low to the ground* (Labrador), *the transparent polka dots on my skin* (photosynthesis) overlaid by the clear-cut image of *MEAT*– they systematically uncovered the meat of the matter.

A jigsaw kind of logic reasoned that the MEAT OF THE MATTER was a VOLCANO as a probable cause partially responsible for sinking the Titanic.

---

165   10/15/98, 1/9/99, 3/28/99.

Rewinding the tape to the misdated birthday dream, *the black frame and the black mesh* framed and meshed characteristics of the violent explosion of released volcanic gases. The blast of huge amounts of black ash, cinders, bombs, and blocks skyward was a volcanic eruption: The extrusion of lava – all black – all meshing – all framed by Lavender: The Volcano – Lava under the Earth.

There it was: *The black frame.* Astounding! It was the volcano! But the scribes would soon make known that the volcano, initially the prime suspect, was later found to be but one link in a chain of cosmic events.

I was following the ethereal lead of our dog-walking muse along the Labrador coastline and through the watery conduits of memory when in floated the dream of *a device in the shape of a cone that attaches in some way to a boat (illustrated as a steamship). The cone-shaped object has lines drawn through it like a grid. I'm in the water with an instructor. First, I have to sit, and then I paddle around. The story ends with an image of Abraham Lincoln. There is a gift involved.*[166]

In examining my sketch, I turned it upside down. The cone looked like a necktie … a tie … tie the cone to the boat. While ruminating on a cone device that connected to a boat graced by the presence of Abraham Lincoln.f320,,¡ (the preceding numbers and the upside-down exclamation mark inserted independently).

One of Abraham Lincoln's iconic roles in my dream life was to tell me the truth and to say that attention must be paid. I raced to my files and found that the structure of a volcano is usually conical. I was bowled over when I discovered a type of volcano called the cinder cone. It's a simple volcano – not very big. They're usually made of piles of lava, not ash. During the eruption, blobs, like "cinders" of lava, are blown into the air and break into pieces that fall into a pile around the opening to the volcano. To top it off, most cinder cones have a bowl-shaped crater at the summit.

Aha! Once more, there were the bowls. In dream after dream, stacks of them piled up, as they do in the kitchen sink, waiting to be scoured. I was hoping I might get a little help washing the dishes. There were so many to do.

Seeing was believing: A cone attaching to a boat – a volcanic cone connecting to the Titanic with the endorsement of Abraham Lincoln with some optical magic thrown in. The silvery bells of a lyrical universe tinkled in waking and in my deepest sleep.

A surge of adrenaline sped me back to the dream message that delivered numbers on "a wet piece of tape" – numbers that computed to the date of Titanic's demise. In the same dream, someone makes a big noise or a big smell.[167] Five years later, the aforementioned dream dispatched Abraham Lincoln to deliver the message: *"a cone attached to a boat."* All roads were leading to a volcanic cone. Could a volcanic eruption have been responsible

---

166 1/25/98. See Ch. 13 – The Sciences, p. 64
167 10/27/93.

for *the big noise and the big smell?* Unbeknownst to me, other smelly traces lingered in the gaseous corner of the puzzle, waiting to be released.

Pieces were meshing, merging, congealing and interconnecting in ways that defied ordinary puzzle solving. Obscure fragments hidden under the midnight veil of the unconscious were magnetized by the light of day as they bonded to larger pieces that had already emerged.

Selecting where the cone might fit was a tall order in a universe populated with cones of every shape and size. Joining this dream caravan of cone shapes were the striking symbols of the pyramid and the cones of the eye. But how could these conical shapes attach to a boat?

When in an utter rabbit stew, which was a lot of the time, I held fast to the message of the penny in my eye and remembered its inscription In God We Trust. At this juncture, I selected the volcanic cone for it fit the apex of the pyramid, symbol for the highest spiritual attainment, the all-seeing eye and inner vision. But how could I be sure? The cerebral teleprompter was not yet ready to announce it."

Of the innumerable lessons taught on this journey, homeroom's first assignment was Patience, a lesson never erased from the blackboard, and the second was Order.

But Order in this adventure was an Order of a different sort, one that took some time to get the knack of. While frantically trying to track jillions of little details, I, quite by accident, discovered the circular nature of the search. In unraveling a dream that contained the threads of Points of Light – Stars –Vision,[168] I noticed the arrangement completed a circle as circular as the eye itself. I knew that keeping the details from wandering off on their own was essential to closing a circle and desperately hoped that this new kind of nonlinear order would provide some form for my readers.

Our investigative circle widened with *a Witness – a Crime – a Suspect – a Morse-encrypted MOMOM* and drew into its net a new cluster of elements continuing from *MOMOM to* Mother Earth – *Wavy Japanese Lines* (a Tsunami) – *Aunt Belle* (the Strait of Belle Isle) – *a dog low to the ground* – Labrador – *A-S-C-H* (Ash) – *Lavender* (Lava Under) – *the meat of the matter* (a Volcano) – *Abraham Lincoln – a cone attached to a boat* – a Volcanic Cone?

---

168 6/10/95. See Ch. 21 – Half Circle, Full Star, Clog, pp. 94–95

~~~

CHAPTER THIRTY-SIX

THE CLOG - THE VENT - THE VOLCANO

An outpouring of volcanic dream clues began to fill in some of the cracks in the puzzle. "Clog," the missing piece in the "Full Star, Half Circle, Clog" riddle, was one. After years of linking "clog" to Danish astronomers and trying to pair it to shoes worn in Holland, the bona fide clog staged a shoo-in and finally fessed up. Its real identity was magma, known as lava, which clogs up a volcanic vent.

The astral clog was not forsaken, but the prevailing message for now was that the clog fit the earthly vent.

When I finally scored a clue, I felt like a real dunce for not having seen it earlier. In a blast of steam, the clog revelation ejected a dream about *children doing a clog dance. Something cooking on the stove is left unattended. There are some meatballs just sitting on one of the burners — not even in a pot. I turn the fire off just in time. The meatballs had gotten a little charred.*[169]

It was clear! The stove was the volcano. But what if the dream was merely a reflection of my waking-life forgetfulness in the kitchen?

Were the *children doing a clog dance* symbolizing the Titanic passengers dancing one last fox trot over a clogged volcanic vent somewhere in the North Atlantic the night the Titanic sank? That could have caused a violent eruption if the blockage was blasted free — enough to have possibly unleashed a tsunami. The eruption of volcanoes born in the sea may be more violent than those on land because the contact between molten rock and seawater produces steam.

Were the strong winds that prevented the lifeboat drill on Titanic's fateful day nature's warning that a tsunami was about to break loose? I pondered, "Which came first? The volcano or the tsunami? And where did the shattering eruption take place? Was it on this planet?

Whatever it was, it was certainly well hidden. There were no records; at least none that I could find. Had there been any doubt regarding any geologic hazard connected to

---

169 10/13/97.

Footnotes contain dream dates and references to prior pages where the dream appeared.
Endnotes contain bibliographical references, are marked with "Ɛ" in the text, and appear at the end of the book.

Titanic, by now it would have been made public by the teams of scientists and engineers who have explored this subject over the decades. Wouldn't it have?

Could the unknown fate of the mightiest of ocean liners be sitting in a sealed envelope in a place where men have not yet tread? The experts have scraped the floor of the ocean. They have scanned Titanic's skeletal remains, inspecting every piece of wreckage, testing rivets, performing stress analysis, studying the falling motion of the bow and exposing every nook and cranny of her rusted frame. Despite unflagging and dedicated efforts spanning years of tireless scrutiny, they have still not gotten to the bottom of it.

Would Man's fevered pursuit unravel the answer to Titanic's sinking? Would the culprit someday be revealed? Would there ever be closure for the families of the innocent victims?

Like lightning, a blinding revelation struck! I sped back to the dream of *a cork and the bottom of a branch in a hollowed-out book. Someone is giving me detailed instructions about finding the yellow lexicon and the name Ramos keeps repeating.*[170] Cork was another metaphor for Truth: it rises to the top. Historian Claes Wetterholm drew on Titanic's survivor stories of a "sea of red cork" to gain the first clue to the stern's scattered wreckage. Computer modeling pointed to the likely answer: Refrigeration holds imploded and then exploded as the ship reached depth.[E31]

There was a connection here. I knew it. It would need time to incubate, but for now – a faint outline emerged; I'd have to think in metaphors: Truth – Explosions – Refrigeration. Was there an explosion under a glaciated area that night?

It was too neat, too perfect when I heard the "tap tap" of Peggymoonbeam's silent code: "Remember, Penelope! Trust your first instincts. There's a rhyme and reason for everything we do up here."

Hmm. Cork. Titanic. Ramos/ramus. Branch.

No wonder I dreamt of a *shorthand course.*[171] Steno, the geologist, and steno, abbreviated symbolic writing, were gaining momentum.

Was the answer on the floor of the ocean? The clues were beginning to branch out, like Peggymoonbeam's tree of science, into the field of geology. But I knew zilch about geology or any science for that matter. My ultimate scientific experiment had been dissecting a frog marinated in formaldehyde.

My thoughts returned to images pointing to Truth: How, like cork, it surfaces – Abraham Lincoln, paragon of the Truth – shards of thought drifting overhead – images of Truth floating on the sea – pieces of cork trapped underneath.

---

170 9/12/93. See Ch. 3 – The Pole, p. 25
171 10/1/98. See Ch. 14 – Honored Earth Guide: Nicolaus Steno, p. 67

Vents were becoming more of a presence. The first discharge came from the dream recalling Titanic's tragedy that concluded with a vent. *I'm in a hotel room (stateroom) and a baby and baby-sitter are sucked out the window. There's discussion of the number of lives lost. My breast is covered in mesh. A man panics trying to close the window and then is looking for a vent, which I show him.* At dream's end *a matchbook cover matches the scene.*[172]

Looping back to the Allison family, victims of Titanic's doom, and the discussion in the dream of *lives lost*, the clouds were beginning to clear.

Interspersed with the tragedy of Titanic was the image of *my breast being covered in mesh.* This isn't the first time that breasts and mesh had appeared in my dreams. Spellbound, I was gripped by the notion that *breast* was the metaphorical bosom of Mother Earth and *"mesh"* was that it meshed with Titanic. The mesh also pointed to the enmeshing of lava in the earth and explained *Peggymoonbeam's breastplate,*[173] the breast of Mother Earth, the plate on which her continents sit. How brilliant of them, the divining dream scribes.

So they gave me the wrong birthday, but in their infinite wisdom, it was probably the right one. To remind you dear Reader: *A man tells me my birthday is FEBRUARY 18 - THURSDAY. I see an image of a black mesh screen in a black frame.*[174] Whichever birthday it was, it was clear the black frame was the volcano and its constituent parts were meshing. Perhaps there was a geologic event that occurred on February 18; it would have to be a Thursday, but of what year? I couldn't trace back four and a half billion years (the age of the Earth) but if it was signaling the future, the next three Thursdays falling on February 18 would be in 1999, 2010, and 2016.

Cruising the upper stratosphere of my mind were mother – Mother Earth – Titanic. Like reflecting satellites, they settled into a holding pattern when a dream circled overhead.

I'm with my mother in a fancy resort. We stay in the same room, where the brocade draperies of deep crimson and gold match the bedspreads. There's a balcony from where we can see the water.

Suddenly we have to move out. We had stayed only one night. A driver from the hotel is in charge of bringing new people in. Housekeeping asks if we had a vent. Did we hear something? Was the room noisy? We have to move to a room across the hall. Aunt Belle is there.[175]

Mother, leading the way, occupied a richly appointed stateroom with fabrics fitting Titanic's opulent decor. Could the balcony overlooking the water be symbolic of the bridge of a ship? Telltale signs such as the "short stay" and "suddenly having to move" signified an abrupt change. What happened that would cause us to vacate?

---

172 8/12/93. See Ch. 23 – Tragedy, p. 99
173 7/6/94.
174 10/30/98. See Ch 35 – Lava Under Revelation, p. 155
175 4/18/99.

Following the Titanic theme, the hotel driver could translate to the captain of a ship; after all, Titanic was a floating hotel. And, the appearance of the pervasive vent? Moving to a room across the hall – across again, signifying a crossing. Was it a transatlantic crossing or a crossing to the other side or crossing states of consciousness? Or all?

Aunt Belle is in the scene again. Was Belle marking a location as she did when she was "under cover … *under a chenille bedspread*" – under the ice?[176] Titanic's corpse, discovered in 1985, lies two and a half miles below the surface of the Atlantic Ocean. Her final resting place, off the Grand Banks of Newfoundland, is not far from the Strait of Belle Isle, which separates Labrador and Newfoundland. Why did we stay only one night? Was one night in dream speak, a measure for a brief stay? What necessitated moving across? While it did not provide a syllabus for mystery solving, the dream was bursting with clues.

The vent, every bit as incessant as the clog in its Vulcan like personality represented an opening in the surface of the Earth, through which gas or lava can escape. Metaphorically, the vent produced an opening in the story, through which flowed the theme – Lavender.

More vent dreams simmered in the still of the night and began to flare up, waiting to vent to the surface of waking.

There is a grid of lights which are a way to communicate, a matching muffler, black matter coming out of an open vent, pictures of a car accident portraying a head-on collision. The cars separate and go in different directions. The collision photo on the left is in color - the aftermath of the collision photo on the right, in black and white.[177]

For some unknown reason I counted the lights on the grid; they totaled eighty-two.

Diverse elements painted a synchronous panorama: *a muffler* (a silencer) – *black matter* (lava) – *an open vent* (a volcano) – a silent volcano? *Collision* – collision with an iceberg? *Photographs* (photographic memory) – *left* (past) – *color* (life, vitality) – *right* (future) – *black and white* (reality).

What would a grid of lights have to do with a muffler, a vent, and a collision? I sensed a flurry of motion above. I looked up. Drifting along its path, there twinkled the soft outline of a cluster of stars.

---

176 2/10/95.
177 2/5/93.

CHAPTER THIRTY-SEVEN

AN ANCIENT ROMANCE

Continuous as the stars that shine
And twinkle on the milky way.[E32]
William Wordsworth

"Halloo, Penelope! Charlesbigstar saw you struggling with the grid and suggested I beam in. I have a few lumenseconds to spare today so I'd like to formally introduce myself even though we've met briefly by day and quite intimately under nocturnal circumstances."

I was caught off guard. Certainly, I remembered this apparition and his sudden departure in the company of Peggymoonbeam and Agneswiseheart. But how did he know Charlesbigstar? And what were these "nocturnal circumstances"?

"Travel back in time a bit. It was I who sent you the Optica[178] dream. It was my Valentine's gift to you in 1997."

"Yes, I think I recognize you. You said a fast hello and then disappeared. That was some time back when you were with my recently departed loved ones. You were going to a place you called Starsight."

"Ah yes. What a fine memory you have, but I dare say, not nearly as keen as mine."

My, my, I thought, what a competitive little visitor.

"Well, just what is it you want and why have you appeared in my boudoir when I'm nearly on the verge of sleep?" And why, I wondered, did he send me a Valentine?

"I usually swirl in for a visit in the wee hours when you are traveling the 'royal road to the unconscious,' to quote my great friend, Sigmund Freud, or Ziggie, as he is known in these dimensions. I enjoy looking in on you while you're snuggled up on your feather pillow, most likely in a state of REM sleep, which is when vivid dreams occur most frequently. But then again, if the spirit moves me I will visit you during your waking hours."

---

178 2/14/97. See Chap. 5 – Honored Visionaries, p.

Footnotes contain dream dates and references to prior pages where the dream appeared.
Endnotes contain bibliographical references, are marked with "E" in the text, and appear at the end of the book.

Extending his essence, he officially introduced himself. "I am Astronomer Claudius Ptolemy. Yes! A divine freeway up at Starsight, was actually named 'Royal Boulevard,' in Freud's honor. You know Ziggie has only recently joined us. I've been to Earth and back several times and, lo and behold, on my last passing, who was waiting for me at the gates of Starsight but he, the world-renowned neurologist and founder of psychoanalysis, Sigmund Freud. I think it was around the Earth year 1939. Whew! It's tough keeping up with all these comings and goings. Ziggie tweaked my interest in the Dream because of my work with light – you know, the theory of refraction – back in the second century."

Thinking back to all of the dreams of light and vision, I asked my heretofore illusive visitor, "Why is it you pop in when I'm dreaming?"

"Oh! Just to give you your vitamins," he responded.

"Vitamins?" I thought, "This is pretty goofy."

"Yes, Penelope dear. You see, dreaming provides you with nighttime supplements to your intellectual development and fresh, new, creative routes to solving problems. REM sleep is the time when the brain wants to file and store daily experiences and learning. You don't really think that all of your dreams just materialize out of thin air, do you?"

"Gosh. I really don't know. I remember how puzzled I was by all those dreams about light and vision and about how I couldn't see, and then Peggymoonbeam went to Heaven and I began to get more and more dreams about stuff I never knew existed. I thought she was sending them because she's now a heavenly being. Next thing I knew, some of my dreams foretold the future and were trying to unravel the past."

"Well, now, you know that Peggymoonbeam has a lot of company and, I might add, very distinguished company. As for the future, it is right in the back of your head – or I should say in a vital pocket of your brain. You will eventually discover just where that is."

My thoughts turned back to the *grid of lights as* Ptolemy chattered away:

"You know, Penelope, there is a star cluster named after me, much to my glow. It is no coincidence that Ptolemy's Cluster consists of eighty faint and distant stars which you can easily detect with the naked eye.

"If you look up at the Milky Way from the concrete canyons of New York City where you write in your journals from morning till night, you will see my illustrious cluster."

He chuckled. "It tickles my light that I can be seen from such an astronomical distance. I must admit that now and again, flashes of my independent nature reappear. Well, what would you expect from someone who asserted that the universe revolved around him? I regret that fourteen centuries of wide acclaim left a few unsightly traces of intellectual superiority on my psyche but I do try to curb those tendencies. When a glimmer of arrogance begins to eclipse my multidimensional consciousness, I remind myself that my humility has been resurrected and that my sense of self-importance is just a thing of the past."

Hmm…. He's getting awfully personal – first the Valentine and now this confession. I wonder what's up with this apparition. And what in Heaven's name is multidimensional consciousness?

"Oh, Penelope, how soon we forget. In multi dimensions, we live in unconditional love, unconditional forgiveness, and unconditional acceptance. We no longer hold judgment, guilt, or negativity. The primary consciousness in these dimensions is that we are stellar beings living in lightbodies."

I thought back to the dream grid, which held eighty-two lights. So that must be what he meant about vitamins in my sleep. How else could I have known about Ptolemy's cluster? But the dream had two more lights than his cluster.

Ptolemy responded. "Yes, I know. Those are the two orbs of vision that Lord Galen has delivered to your dreams. They are meant to facilitate your dream recall. Though you've not yet formally met him, he, too, is keeping an eye on you."

"Recall? What does that have to do with vision?"

"Ah … Galen, who vigorously sought to explain the mystery of sight, may have an answer for you, Penelope. As he wrote, 'For observation is already implicit in memory, since we cannot remember those things which have been seen to happen often and in a similar way, unless we in some way make their observation.'[33]

"And while we're on the subject of vision, I've been blinking at you from afar for centuries now. I must confess to you that from the time we parted, engraved in my soul are memories of our earthly bliss; the tinkling laughter that rights all things, your nakedness of spirit, your heavenly touch, your soul entangled and made one with mine. It is the undeniable truth that your every molecule is forever impregnated in my being. My anguish has been real, my longing for you, eternal. In all of my incarnations that followed my presence as Ulysses, I never had the opportunity to once again hold your hand and soothe your furrowed brow, my Penelope."

"You were Ulysses? I thought you were Ptolemy. Wasn't Ulysses a fictional character?" Please let me go to sleep, whoever you are. I thought you were real."

"I am real. Please, my dear, sweet, wandering maiden. Let me explain. I was Odysseus. Homer wrote in his epic of me and my wife, Penelope, who was so very faithful during my long absence. You, my dear Penelope Peacock, have returned to me in the flesh. You were and are that faithful spirit. True to your role as wife of Odysseus, you have unwaveringly and devotedly waited for me as decades have turned to centuries and centuries to millennia.

"I have traversed boundless plains of galactic wisdom to muster enough courage to illuminate your bedside so you might know of my undying love even if only harvested in a dream. I watched you stargazing as a little girl when our lights would but spark and vibrate each other's most secret thoughts. So fleeting have been your flirtations with others, for your heart had only one matching heart, which bid you wait your endless Earth lives.

"Each soul, each plant, each object, animate or inanimate, that has crossed my gaze since I've been at Starsight has been a moment to be shared with you, if only in our memories.

"The yesterdays of your innocence and your passion have tortured and titillated me from antiquity. My frugal patience has challenged my resolve to find you for I was sentenced to wait until you had evolved enough to be able to recognize me. More than there are twinklings in the sky are the ages spent in half-whole expectancy of this moment.

"My years have forever outnumbered yours, Penelope. I am told that is how it is written. Though I be heavy with age and I see on your breath the first kiss of Spring, I have come here to teach you and to help you with your life's work. One day, you will applaud the veracity of my confession because I am sending to you a man of the flesh who is the embodiment of my spirit. He calls himself Johnnie Pianissimo. He will be arriving from a distant constellation and will be seen wearing the cloak of an ordinary man.

"You will know by his touch that it is your dearly beloved, your Ulysses returned, and in time the resplendent and ancient pieces of our union will echo their love song and – as before – memory will endure. Our minds and our thoughts, our souls and our hearts, will fuse, each living within the other. You will notice, Penelope dear, that the void you have so desperately sought to fill through your many lifetimes will suddenly become pregnant with adventurous happenings that you will not be able to explain. You will find yourself experiencing a deeper sense of love, compassion, empowerment, and wisdom than you have ever before known.

"The other couriers of the angelic realm will serve you their exotic enchantments, but the ambrosia that we once knew, Penelope, will bear my nom de plume and will reassure you of our past.

> "This robe, so that the yarn may not waste in vain, must be as the dream
> that I keep weaving there on the great loom of the night until the day I
> am to finish."[34]

"Oh, Ptolemy! You are so poetic ... so familiar. This must certainly be a dream. I thought I was awake. I am sorry. I wish I could recognize you, but it's all too much a fantasy. I can't even see you or touch you. But your beautiful and inspiring music will drift with me into sleep. Your concerto has pierced the silence of three thousand years, even if you are only an apparition."

This was surely a time when Raggedy Ann and my wonderful little Scottie dog, Bonnie, would soothe me. Hopes and fears and wishes and tears were their specialty. I wish I could remember what I had done with Raggedy so I could just hold her close and wish that I could stop wishing. And as for Bonnie, I knew she could see what was going on from her lofty bed in doggie heaven. As I tried to slip into sleep, I couldn't help but wonder ... Could there really be a Johnnie Pianissimo out there somewhere in this big wondrous universe? Ptolemy was right. Half of my heart had long been severed from its vital chambers.

Thus, Ptolemy's first piece of magic delivered to my waking memory the star- and stone-bound dream which had been made real on my trip to Egypt. It began with *a star that seemed billions of light-years away. This star comes very close; then disappears. The scene goes black and a new star appears. Again, it comes very close; then fades. A constellation appears; then, the image of a stone embankment stretching into infinity.*[179] By now, it was clear that Ptolemy's constellation was starlit and Steno's was stone-faced. And I would have been blind to both without my celestial optician, Claudius Galen, who shone the light.

A bulb lit. Perhaps it was a flicker from above that illuminated the faces of stone in my long-ago dream. I then recalled that the dream comprised four stone figures – three men and a woman – that came to life.

---

179 11/25/98. See Prologue.

CHAPTER THIRTY-EIGHT

GLYPHS

I thought back to my days in Luxor. The introduction to the Sound and Light performance at the Karnak Temples was indelibly etched in my memory.

"May the evening soothe and welcome you. Here you are at the beginning of time.

"You are at Thebes, the city of a hundred gates, sacred land of the god Amon. Do not be overwhelmed by the sheer size of these remains, made from pylons, obelisks, sanctuaries, terraces and columns ... and, let yourself be guided to the sacred lake. This mirror, set in the rock, has reflected the finest firework display of antiquity: The dazzling gleam that has lasted twenty centuries."

As the performance neared conclusion, a brilliant flash of white light arched across the clear night sky, a perfect arc suspended like a quarter moon over the Temple. The mysterious lighted arc seemed a natural phenomenon, and appeared to be synchronously timed with the spectacular finale. The booming voice of the narrator infused the air and filled the temple with its thundering words:

"And someday, someone will be able to uncover all that went before. Someone will understand the meaning of the hieroglyphics."

Hieroglyphics: the first writing of ancient Egypt. The eagle is the first letter in the Egyptian alphabet. A dream flashed before me.

There is a man in costume upstairs. He wears a purple sash. He keeps changing his headgear. He looks like a priest each time. When he wears a skullcap, he looks like I, Claudius. There is a huge golden floor lamp in the shape of an arc. The light fixture is that of an eagle's head. It occupies the whole room.[180]

---

180 8/10/99.

Footnotes contain dream dates and references to prior pages where the dream appeared.
Endnotes contain bibliographical references, are marked with "Ɛ" in the text, and appear at the end of the book.

Waking experience reflected the dream. The sacred lake mirrored humanity, then and now and the *arc lamp* mirrored the lighted arc stretching across the sky.

I wondered who I, Claudius represented. Was it Claudius Ptolemy who delivered the star cluster? Or was it Claudius Galen, the messenger of vision? My dreams told me both Claudiuses were imparting ancient knowledge at our crossroads of existence; this coming at a time when our fleeting but vital purpose on Earth must be undersßtood. I thought about the Roman Emperor Claudius but he hadn't entered my dreams.

A retrospective glimmer shone on my dream of the *Rosetta stone* and its cryptic omen, *"Be careful of whom you tell."*[181]

The Rosetta stone contains a decree passed by an assembly of priests conferring honors on King Ptolemy V.[ε35]

In the dream, I, Claudius looked like a priest. How fascinating that Ptolemy is to this tale, the scribe of the stars, while to history, Ptolemy V, called Ptolemy Epiphanes ("illustrious"), was king of Egypt (205–181 BC).[ε36] It was beginning to look like stars and Egypt are inextricably bound, sharing in the same mystery.

To which Ptolemy unexpectedly added, "Penelope dear, in Egyptian mythology, the stars are the inhabitants of the netherworld. We ancients believe that the dead live on in the stars. It is the pious wish of many Egyptians to be allowed to continue living as a small lamp among the constellations of night."[ε37]

"Heavens, Ptolemy! This connects perfectly to my dream of the *vanishing stars* which must have formed the *constellation that appeared next.* And guess what? It connects to my dream of the *arc lamp* and the lighted arc suspended over Karnak Temple. Millions of souls must have made up that arc of light the night of the Sound and Light performance. I guess the arc I thought was so enormous was really one constellation among many – a small lamp, as the legend goes."

"Yes, yes. I know, Penelope. I am pleased to see you have not curbed your enthusiasm through your comings and goings from century to century." And ... he was gone in a blink.

My midnight visitor, Claudius Ptolemy, was very wise. According to him, our dreams don't just materialize out of thin air. There must be a divine plan that is in some way transmitted to us through light. Could Science support this? Not now, but perhaps one day.

I thought about the hieroglyphics of the dream that tell in pictures and words the story of our modern lives and its similarity to Egyptian hieroglyphics, the religious drawings that told the story of the life of the ancient Egyptians. Dr. Noodle's "glyphs" had stuck.

---

181 12/18/99.

Again, I thought about the Greek word Oneiromancy. It's pronounced **oh-nahy-**_ruh_**-man-see** and means "divination by means of dreams."

Long ago, I wanted to call the language of dreams Oneiromantics - "oneiro" for "dream" and "mantics" as in "semantics," the study of language meaning. It would be made up of the oneiroglyphics of dreams.

It would be a language for understanding the meaning of our dreams.

The voice of antiquity that had ushered us through the temples at Karnak spoke again: "Language may be lost but will be found. Men will always return here to seek the answers to the questions that haunt them. Someday someone will be able to uncover all that went before. Someone will understand the meaning of the hieroglyphics."

As we were leaving the Temple, I asked the two friends who were with me if they had seen the arc of light in the sky. They had. It was still there. We stood motionless, gazing up at it. No one spoke. My friends didn't question it. They accepted its presence. Where did it come from? It was not a skywriter – not the Goodyear Blimp –not part of the performance – not any sign or signal we recognized.

If the ancient Egyptians thought Thoth was the god of learning and had invented writing, perhaps my god of learning was Ptolemy, maestro of the stars. In that shining instant, he became my own private scribe of the firmament. I fantasized that my meager knowledge might even inspire his astral teachings.

CHAPTER THIRTY-NINE

STARS IN MY EYES

A few days later, my illusive lover decided to revisit me.

"Penelope, it's nice to make your acquaintance when you're awake," joshed Ptolemy.

He was wearing a more formal countenance now, as though our midnight rendezvous had never happened. Maybe he was feeling a little vulnerable, or maybe he was just waiting for me to get used to him. Perhaps it was love's eternal dance of advance and retreat.

"I have written a few manuscripts in my time. They're ancient now in your world, but I will be working on a more contemporary scroll. That, my little peach, is the transcription of your thoughts. I feel you're a kindred spirit since we've shared some of your private files. You know what I mean – in your dreams and intimacies – and I am wondering if I may call you Penny for short. You, in turn, may call me Twink."

"Twink? What a perfect name for you."

"Yes," he responded. "It's an appellation Peggymoonbeam discovered when she visited Desert Stardust, one of our most popular playgrounds."

"It would tickle me pink to call you Twink."

"Sprinkle twinkle lest you blinkle. You remain without a wrinkle.

"Aah, my dear Penny. As they say, 'a rolling stone gathers no moss' (Harumph. Harumph.) and you've got two rolling stones right here in the palm of your hand – me, for one, and Dr. Steno, your coach for Planet Earth, for another. Be sure you keep your eyes wide open, Penny. We can turn back to stone at the blink of a moonbeam. And speaking of moonbeams, we have discovered your friend Peggymoonbeam's extraordinary powers which, is why we gave her a complimentary pass to Desert Stardust."

"May I ask you about the playgrounds, Twink? I can't imagine such things."

"You are a curious little thing, you are. This is quite a complicated subject but to give you the short answer … at Desert Stardust, recreational games are used as training vehicles for souls who are attracted to exploration, like Peggymoonbeam. The more she engages in interdimensional travel, the more adept she becomes at telepathic communication

---

Footnotes contain dream dates and references to prior pages where the dream appeared.
Endnotes contain bibliographical references, are marked with "Ɛ" in the text, and appear at the end of the book.

and the more able she is to help us spread the seeds that will harmonize Earth's discordant energy. She is known as a planetary restorer.

"I wouldn't want you to miss any of this purported wisdom. Boy, they really do hyperbolize down there on Earth about us spirits and our supreme intelligence. What do they call it? Extraterrestrial? I take offense at that. It makes me feel like a bug. After all, we were once you. We've just lived longer and have the flexibility of crossing multiple realms. I do admit, not every soul who enters the portals of Heaven has the honor of being anointed a scrivener. It depends on how we lived our last life on Earth. Anyway, they just love to spin a story on your plane, but I must tell you they have a lot to learn about spinning. We have the corner on 'spin' as you'll see when we get to Peggymoonbeam and her spinning disks. I suppose if they had more time to think on the cosmic level they'd be more astute in matters of the soul. There's no doubt about it – navigating the winding roads of life can wear down one's brainpower.

"In any case, Penny, back to your dream with the grid of lights. I lectured on this splendid cluster about 130 AD, give or take a few decades. I described it as the 'nebula following the sting of Scorpius.' It also came to be known as The Scorpion's Tail."

"Goodness, Twink! Scorpio is my natural mother's birth sign."

"We know that, Penny. What do you think we do all day? We don't just float around twiddling our halos, y'know. We're on the ball up here in Heaven. We have to be able to communicate with you from any point in the multidimensional reality in which we exist. You see, we're in contact with multiple planes of existence, yours being one of them. All the objects in your visible world including your dreams are only temporary fragments derived from our deeper order of unbroken wholeness. You'll be learning more about this as we travel on. By temporary, I mean that all things both living and not living are always changing and moving just like your dreams."

"So where exactly are you, Twink? My brain is feeling like spaghetti. These threads of knowledge are very exciting but hard to follow because they just wind around all over the place and get all tangled up and then with you coming and going, it's even more confusing. One minute I think you're right here next to me and then you're gone only to double back again."

"Try to think of us as part of an underlying cosmic intelligence. We – you and I – are somewhere and everywhere, Penelope. Think of these tangled threads as telephone wires that connect everything in the universe. The tangles are the connection points.

"Don't think the Scorpio link was a coincidence. It is one of those threads belonging to the undivided whole, which connected to your mother since that was her birth sign. We fellows at Starsight don't believe in coincidence. This work is about a Mother to us all: Mother Earth. Since you're communicating our message about her, we had to give your natural mother an iota of credit. She deserves that much, don't you think. It was actually Steno's idea."

"Steno? I am aware of his feelings for Mother Earth but what does he have to do with my natural mother?"

"You've forgotten, Penny. In his life on Earth, Steno was also a physician and explained the function of the ovaries. It is all connected."

I was fascinated by Ptolemy's eccentric but charismatic presence and more than a little curious about his declarations of love, which he was now ignoring. There was something so impish and strange and really smart about him, yet so familiar. I was having feelings which I didn't quite know what to do with. After all, he was just an apparition, or so I thought.

While I was mulling this over, Charlesbigstar flashed a reminder that the dream described a *grid of lights as a method of communication*. What could all of that illumination be other than a grid of stars transmitting information to earthlings who were listening to their dreams?

By now, I was convinced Ptolemy's devotion to the constellations was being communicated vertically – up and down the celestial ladder. A new kind of metaphysical wizardry pieced together this interlocking puzzle and, day by day, suspended any notion of disbelief I might have held.

The grid of lights was momentarily eclipsed.

"Where did the grid go? I can't see it!"

"Forgive me. I didn't mean to step in Ptolemy's light," said Charlesbigstar. "When it comes to the stars, he is the maestro of seventh heaven, which we believe is the heaven of heavens and that, of course, is where your penny fell from.

"We at Starsight and Terracrust have a theory that when God was finally able to rest on the seventh day, after all His work was done, He dropped some pennies on Earth. The pennies carried a divine pronouncement that upon his creation of the Heaven and the Earth, we were to trust in him.

Hmm. Starsight? Terracrust? I wondered if these strange sounding places are on a sky map somewhere. Charlesbigstar continued.

"And that's how the dream of the penny got into your eye.

"You received that dream, Penelope, on Sunday, November 13, 1994, so you actually received it on the seventh day, which, according to Christian belief, is the day God blessed and sanctified.

"You know the tune 'Pennies From Heaven'? We wrote the music up here at Starsight."

Thumbing his suspenders and preparing for takeoff, Ptolemy encircled me, passing on some age-old information:

"Penny, before I dash I'd like to remind you that I lived in Alexandria before I retired here to Starsight. Your history books have dubbed me an ancient astronomer, geographer, and mathematician, and those are the very subjects I continue to study up here."

Hmm. His "ancient" comment sparked memory of repeated dream images of antiquity – objects I once had a larger piece of. Allusions to the past certainly fit a venerable cast of scribes like Steno, Galen, and Curie.

Ptolemy continued, "Everyone believed my conclusion that the Earth was the center of the universe until Copernicus, that Polish astronomical upstart, came along in the fifteenth century and questioned my theory. Since no one knew very much about my life on Earth, they certainly didn't know what I was up to in the Heavens so I just relaxed up here and took it all in. I could see that Copernicus was really onto something. I can tell you that his model was at the center of one of the most violent intellectual controversies I've ever seen. I felt a little guilty for having started the entire fracas, but I couldn't help it. I was just curious and called it as I saw it then. I must say it took quite a while for the truth to be accepted.

"Finally, around 1600, astronomers were beginning to accept that the Earth and the planets revolve around the sun. Then along came Johannes Kepler and his laws of planetary motion."

I felt light-headed, as thoughts of planetary motion spiraled me back to dreams of Peggymoonbeam coming through *a spinning disk*.[182]

I had a faint memory of a book Ptolemy had written that appeared in my dreams. "Twink, could you tell me the name of the book you wrote that is today a legend?"

"I actually penned quite a few books, but my prize astronomical work is the Almagest and is divided into thirteen books. Each book deals with certain astronomical concepts pertaining to stars and objects in the solar system: the Earth and all other celestial bodies you now know revolve around the Sun."

"Wow, Twink! I've had so many dreams about stars and Peggymoonbeam coming through a celestial body. My dreams show you two hanging out together and I'm wondering how your paths crossed being that you are her senior by at least a couple of thousand years."

"Well, it's not very different than meeting souls when we are embodied. Sometimes our energies just go bump in the night, and we feel a strong alliance, a kinship, a recognition. Though you know her on Earth only in this century, she is quite an old soul – as are you – and has been here and back many times. Because she is the last of us to have been with you and is aware of your every day comings and goings, she was given the royal prerogative to oversee our communications with you. She is able to direct us to nuances of your physical existence, particularly to your emotional terrain. It is under Peggymoonbeam's directorship and her fondness for her branching tree that we are able to activate the dreams."

182 3/23/97. See Ch. 9 – Spinning Disks, p. 49

I was still puzzling, for I knew there was a title other than Almagest that appeared in a dream. Ptolemy, in typical mind reading mode, interjected, "Penny, I also worked on optical phenomena and that work appeared in the original edition of Optica, which consisted of five books."

"Optica! That's it! Was that you, Twink, who told me about the blue rubbery logs and the pages in Optico? Excuse me! I mean Optica. I should have realized! I forgot for a moment that you and Ptolemy are the same person!"

"Yes, Penny dear, it was I. Have you forgotten? Optica was my Valentine's gift to you. I wired it to your dream on February 14, 1997. Do you think it was easy to just turn up an Earth date from here? You can't imagine the mathematical calculation it took, but I had to get your attention. I borrowed on everything I knew of ancient Greek and Babylonian astronomy, not to mention the geocentric models I formulated, the computational tables I studied, the coordinates I designed and Heaven knows what else just to send a valentine to my little Penelope Peacock. You see, my dreamer of the ages, I do remember how sentimental you are about such things. You once scolded me for missing a birthday and I never forgot it.

"I knew you hadn't the foggiest as to what that Valentine was but you cared enough to inquire. Your curiosity and your interest in science convinced all of us that, when the time came, we would be by your side to let you know you were on the right track. But I daresay, I had a few, er – ulterior motives, er – you might say, romantic in nature.

"Anyway, the theory of refraction was then and is still of great interest to me. It has to do with the change in direction of light and other energy waves when they pass from one density into a different density. It actually plays a part in our communication."

I was feeling a little bashful about his revitalized amorous intimations so I stuck to science and dreams because he seemed to understand both, more than anyone I'd ever known. "You know, Twink, my first attempt at explaining the information I was getting in my dreams was centered on optics."

"Yes, I know. My good friend, Claudius Galen, and your beloved astrologer, Charlesbigstar, were instrumental in helping you with that."

"I'm so sorry I couldn't remember the name of your book."

"No matter, Penny. You've been laden with the teachings of the ages to learn in a breath of a lifetime so don't despair if you lose track of something.

"Well, I had best be getting back. We're working on a major project at Starsight Lab having to do with intragalactic signals, but I took off for a few lumenseconds to beam a ray on your perplexities. We will doubtless meet again and again … and again. Cheerio!"

I was beginning to feel a strange attachment to this quixotic soul whom I must have known from time immemorial. There was something so captivating about him. After all, what can you say to a guy who compiles a catalog of all the stars visible to the naked eye and who does cartwheels over the moon to send a valentine on that very day to a mortal damsel somewhere in the vast metropolis of New York City? Of course, it probably looks like a speck to him. Amazing he could find me.

Respectful of his time but wildly curious as to what Starsight was, I dared ask another question.

(Gulp.) "Excuse me, Twink. Charlesbigstar referred to Terracrust as though I should know about it and I notice that you mention Starsight quite a lot. I'm just wondering where it is and how it came to be. I know how busy you are gallivanting about the cosmos but do you think you could tell me next time we meet or perhaps you could wire it in a dream?"

To my surprise, he chose to answer right on the spot.

CHAPTER FORTY

STARSIGHT AND TERRACRUST

"Of course, Penny. I just assumed you knew.

"Starsight is an orbiting laboratory engaged in the exploration of the cosmos which, of course, includes your Planet Earth. We're equipped with the most sophisticated remote sensing modules in the universe which enable us to keep our eye on Earth. We're particularly interested in the thought patterns and dreams of terrestrial beings like you – that is, how you perceive your world and relate it to our world. Starsight operates across time and in all dimensions, Penelope, so you needn't worry about a sky map. Now for its history, this will take a few lumenseconds."

"Lumenseconds? Sorry to interrupt, Twink, but that is so foreign to me. Peggymoonbeam said it was a time conversion scale, but I don't really understand how it works."

"Oh. Sorry, Penelope. On Earth, you experience time as a transition which is why you have clocks that run based on a twenty-four-hour day. This makes the day before today, the past and the day after, the future. At Starsight and Terracrust, past, present, and future, all happen in an instant. To transmit to you in your time, we have had to convert Starsight time to your twenty-four-hour day so you can track your dreams on a calendar. A lumensecond is Earth language for a Starsight instant which contains all time. And it is because of this conversion, that your dreams appear to arrive at various times, when, in fact, there is really no distinction."

In a rabbit stew over Starsight's bewildering ideas about time and space and unable to fathom that the future already exists, I tried to hide my confusion. "Oh wow! Now can you tell me, Twink, about Starsight and Terracrust?"

Twink chuckled. "As you know, Penny, I arrived there in 145 AD and my esteemed colleague, Galen, joined me in 201 AD. With his passion for visual optics and mine for astronomical optics, we teamed together and formed a small lab we called Starsight. I directed the Star Division and Galen headed up the Sight Division. Our original mission was to investigate the affinity of the two disciplines, which is under exploration now and will continue into infinity. The mission expanded as my knowledge of mathematics, geography and astronomy and Galen's knowledge of medicine and philosophy combined

Footnotes contain dream dates and references to prior pages where the dream appeared.

Endnotes contain bibliographical references, are marked with "Ɛ" in the text, and appear at the end of the book.

to promote the most far-reaching potential for exploration of the welfare of the individual on Earth and for society in the main.

"In our exploration of the life forces of the cosmos we have discovered that we begin in the stars and return to the stars. If the entire solar system is our genesis, then we know we can find a cure for all the physical and philosophical ills of society and in turn, for Mother Earth. Of course, due to many changes over the millennia, we have had to adapt to an ever-changing Earth and its inhabitants to further our mission.

"Starsight has grown by leaps and bounds as technology has advanced, and now, as you move further into the twenty-first century, we are on the brink of communicating with earthlings – such as you. It is a very exciting time.

"Our current thinking is that there may be a correlation between the speed of light and the precognitive dream, which arrives in your sleeping thoughts before it physically occurs in waking.

"A precognitive dream is one in which the content matches an event that hasn't taken place yet in Earth time and where there is no current information, at least not on Earth, that could have predicted the event. Along these same lines, we have found there is an electrical field 'frequency' at work in humans. The more observant the human, the higher the frequency, and the easier it is for us to interact with them. Our magnetic field research with receptive subjects such as you, Penny, is a first step. The messages and codes you've received on your computer are but one aspect of it. We are grateful that you have recognized us, for it is our only way of establishing communication. Our technology has expanded far beyond photonics, which on Earth is the science of the transmission of photons. Fiber optics is an example. We think we are on to something quite miraculous, but it's somewhat involved so I'll have to save my more thorough explanation for later.

"Then there's our other lab, our sister operation called Terracrust. The unit of time there is a paleosecond and is related to paleontology. It serves the same purpose as Starsight's lumensecond in that it synchronizes Terracrustian time to Earth time. Terracrust was established in 1934 when Marie Curie crossed over to this side. However, its story begins with Nicolaus Steno, noted for his geologic principles. One of the most brilliant minds of the seventeenth century, he gave up science when he was ordained a Catholic priest on Earth some eleven years before he ascended to Heaven in 1686. He then joined the PurpleScroll dominion of the Paleogeography arm of Terracrust, where he devoted himself for some three centuries to the ideology of combining religion with science.

"Membership in PurpleScroll is considered a symbol of excellence, a badge of courage, and a mark of distinction in the struggle to embrace science through the eyes of faith and faith through the eyes of science. Steno's belief that science and theology were, are, and always will be, allies and not enemies, lives on today. We learned that in 1988, Pope John Paul II beatified Steno, citing him as a symbol of appropriate respect and harmony between science and faith.$^{\mathcal{E}38}$ His efforts to harmonize geological history with Genesis were finally recognized.

"Terracrust Lab was conceived because, at this time, Steno's work in science and spirit was ready for implementation. Terracrust was the perfect marriage of geology, paleontology and religion fostered by Steno and it was soon wedded to physics and chemistry, Marie Curie's forte. You know she was the only person ever to be awarded Nobel prizes in both physics and chemistry. Today Terracrust's most pressing concern is the air and water on Earth and its reaction to human life on your planet. Marie Curie and Steno whom we celebrate as stellar contributors to Terracrust are partnering as your mentors and you will find their problem solving method quite original and not nearly as scientific as you might think. They will be teaching you how visual association recognition memory works by using the visual images in your dreams."

"Visual association recognition memory?" (Gulp.) "That sounds pretty complicated, Twink. What's it about?"

He laughed so hard, his halo nearly fell off.

"It's what you've been doing all along, and I must say that based on the associations you've drawn on thus far, your visual association recognition memory skills are excellent. You've even referred to some of those associations. But to put it in a general framework, this is how it operates: your visual memory stores the symbols embedded in your dreams. Your sense of recognition then associates the many dream fragments with each other and determines the relevance of the information you've stored.

"This information helps to define and organize your symbols into dream themes. Your memory network, always on the alert, visualizes the retrieval of an old dream image when it's activated by a corresponding image. You automatically encode the familiar image with the corresponding image and remember it, thereby associating it within a new context. Your memory is now in the process of forming an interrelated web of relationships among your dreams. Eventually you'll be able to expand these teachings by connecting your dreaming with your waking experience. By becoming more conscious of your inner and outer worlds, you will ultimately transcend to a larger worldview where great surprises await you. Someday you will pass this on to others who once stood where you were. This is only one aspect of your assignment, Penelope, for our purpose is manifold and will gradually reveal its various facets as we journey on."

"I don't know if I'm up to this. This memory encoding process may be even harder than I thought. And then all of this stuff about transcending and all. I don't know, Twink. I just don't know."

"Relax, Penelope. You'll be right at home. You examined the visual pathways in the brain when you were studying the optic nerve. It is simply an offshoot of Vision belonging to the Branch of Medicine."

Right at home? He must be dreaming. Vision? Geology? Physics? Chemistry? This isn't funny. How will I ever relate to these giants of science? Well, I guess it was time to get over myself. Perhaps a little more research will help. I'll just have to walk tall and not let anyone know how scared I am. I began to whistle my old standby ... "Whenever I feel afraid ..."

"That's the overview. No pun intended," chuckled Twink. "Terracrust is the Earth arm; Starsight, the Heaven arm of our scientific studies, so, my dear apprentice, we pretty much have all bases covered."

Yikes! Now I'm an apprentice! All I did was go to sleep! My scaredy cat interior was being challenged but receiving so glorious an honor made me feel much less afraid. It even gave me a little squirt of confidence. Thinking about what this might mean, I was suddenly overcome with reverence, my eyes brimming with tears for something deep inside told me Mother Earth could be saved if only humankind would listen. Even if I quivered and shook like jelly and embarrassed the daylights out of myself, it would be worth it if I could make some small difference to help our world which is coming apart at the seams. I murmured, "Thank you, Twink," as his semblance faded from my presence. I stayed silent in my waking dream. If only there were some Earth branches with an equal mission of brotherhood to align to those in the upper worlds. Then all of humanity could one day work together. I wondered if that was Mission Lavender's ultimate purpose, but it was too early in the day to know.

CHAPTER FORTY-ONE

VISION: THE FIRST BRANCH

Our dreams are the only part of us that
can't stray from the truth.
Montague Ullman

While reflecting on the collection of dreams about opticians, eyeglasses, telescopes, video cameras and more, I sensed a gesture. Looking up I saw an unknown figure of towering height. Then I spotted a pair of glasses dangling from the branch of a tree.

"It's time for you to actually meet Lord Galen," said Ptolemy.

"I see that you're pondering Mission Lavender's purpose, Penelope," spoke Galen as he entrusted me with a pair of glasses designed by Timelessness Optics, the fashion optical house at Starsight."

It was as though he had just stepped out of the pages of his writings.

"Oh Lord Galen! I sensed it was you! My dreams about vision have your name all over them. I've been at a loss trying to understand why I've dreamt about so many facets of optics: the optic nerve – the optic chiasm – the retina – the cornea – the uvea – the lens[183] – all of the parts of the eye that led me to your doctrine of vision.[Ɛ39] It seems like a circle within a circle, the outer circle is the eye itself – the inner circle, our inner vision.

Peggymoonbeam and Twink Ptolemy told me you'd arrive, but I had no idea when. And now, here you are in daylight! This is miraculous, Lord Galen. How do you do it? How is it you know my every thought?"

"Never you mind how. Just trust that we have the ability to project our minds as beacons of unified thought when you need us most.

We're delighted that you recognized the optical symbols we dispatched to your dreams. You see, it's far simpler to make contact with your unconscious thoughts than with your conscious musings. We felt it important for you to understand just how the

---

183 Vision dreams: 1994 – 1996.

Footnotes contain dream dates and references to prior pages where the dream appeared.
Endnotes contain bibliographical references, are marked with "Ɛ" in the text, and appear at the end of the book.

optical system works which explains why we tended a bit toward the technical. In my treatise *On the function of the parts of the body*[E40] I presented an anatomical description of the structures of the eye and a functional analysis of the process of vision. I tried to cover as much as I could when I was on Earth, but one lifetime on your planet tends to run short."

"In any case, the reason I am before you now is that I have the distinct honor of presenting to you, Miss Penelope Peacock, the first branch on Peggymoonbeam's tree of science: the Branch of Vision, one of the highest honors in our land. I am also pleased to entrust you with a pair of Timelessness Glasses just like the pair I wear. This branch and the glasses carry with them an Honorary Lifetime Membership in Starsight's Academy of the Invisible.

"In the words of Robert Frost:

"'But yield who will to their separation,
My object in living is to unite
My avocation and my vocation

"'As my two eyes make one in sight.
Only where love and need are one,
And the work is play for mortal stakes,
Is the deed ever really done
For Heaven and the future's sakes.'"[E41]

Oh, Lord Galen. Your presence renders me speechless. Being led to your work in Nancy Parsifal-Charles' anthology, The Dream, was one of the most reverent moments of my life![184] The awesome feeling of making that first connection told me something unimaginable was afoot – and now this sacred honor. I will carry these extraordinary glasses for millennia or as many lifetimes as are bequeathed me. They are the most trea-sured gift on Earth."

"It is our great pleasure, milady. It behooves me to gaze with you through the port-hole of a journey to your inner and outer worlds, to long sought-after places that will tell not only your story, but the story of dreamers throughout time. Penelope, as your eye begins to adjust to the vast distances visible in the Timelessness Glasses you will find there are no views that exist anywhere on Earth that can match the vision ground in these lenses. There is one drawback, however."

"What might that be, Lord Galen?"

"Quite simply, your immediate range of vision may be slightly blurry, but it's only a question of time before you are able to merge your near sight with your far sight.

---

184 See Ch. 4 – Charlesbigstar, p. 33

Blurriness is cured by a small correction that takes place within your psyche. It is similar to how optometrists adjust a correction in an actual pair of spectacles. When the correction takes effect, you will be able to see both near and far at unimaginable magnitudes. You will actually be able to see the innermost nature of things when you're awake just as you do now when you're asleep."

"But my Lord, I don't know if I want to see that much. What if I don't like what I see? It's a little scary."

"Never fear knowledge, Penelope. With knowledge, you can help others to see. When you have developed the capacity to see the unseen, even that which you resist, you will find that sight is the precursor to knowledge. We have to see before we can heal. That's why we arrived on your doorstep: to impart knowledge – to imbue you with sight, to help you heal so that you can heal others. You are on the threshold of learning about unity consciousness. You will find that serving others is serving yourself and that the ultimate power is love. You will be ahead of the game, for when it is time for you to join us your eyesight will be preconditioned to accept our range of vision. On Earth, sight is placed in a more optical context relating to physics. The accepted modality for sight up here is something we call convergent vision, that is the ability to merge the invisible with the visible – the past with the future – to integrate what you feel and what you sense with what you see."

"Lord Galen, something is converging! I think the glasses are working!"

Visual memory raced ahead of my own eyes. I remembered that my dreams of Percival symbolized the cells in the cat retina. Was visual perception to be my inspiration to search for the Holy Grail?

"Was it you who placed *Percival, the cat, atop the woman's head* in the dream that transported me to the study of Vision? Was it you who radioed *the begging cup that danced out of the brick wall*? Are you the one who gave wings to my dreams? Are you, Lord Galen consorting with both knights – Percival and Don Quixote?"

I am distracted by a muffled call in the distance.

Tu-whit Tu-whoo – Tu-whit Tu-whoo.

Two intensely bright orbs are staring me in the face but I can't make out what they are or where they're coming from. The calling continues, coming closer. Tu-whit Tu-whoo – Tu-whit Tu-whoo. The lights get brighter. They startle me at first.

"What's that, Lord Galen? It's kind of creepy. I mean those bright, glaring lights, and that strange sound."

"Oh, dear Penny, that is our heavenly librarian, a wise old and lovable owl whom we called Tu-whit – a moniker for To Wit. What you think are two orbs are his very large and alert eyes. Tu-whit's binocular vision enables him to penetrate the darkness, bearing witness to information through the ages. Tu-whit is chief archivist at the Starsight and Terracrust research libraries, which house documentation, records, and annals from the beginning of time. Because he is finely attuned to the calls of different energies and higher dimensions, Tu-whit's life's work is to carry words and thoughts spoken by scholars, writers and thinkers between planes. He is the storehouse of ideas and their sources.

"Actually, you have already experienced Tu-whit's wisdom without even having seen him. It was he who pointed you toward my writings on the optic nerve. You see, Penelope, Tu-whit is a creature endowed with many perceptual abilities, one of which is the ability to see great amounts of light in the darkest of conditions, through specialized cones and rods in his retina."

"Hmm. Lord Galen do you think Tu-whit is in cahoots with Percival? Remember, how the Percival dream clicked when I learned about the cat retina."

"Well, Athena's owl, which is a symbol of wisdom and Athena's own trademark, does like to rest atop her shoulder, so they do have something in common as Percival was perched atop a woman's head in your dream.

"You will find that Tu-whit's heightened sensitivity is what brings him around at just the right times. The moment that you see the sign of Tu-whit, he will present you with the written words that your scribes use to express their thoughts."

"How will I know that the message is from Tu-whit, Lord Galen?"

"He will give you a sign that symbolizes his superior nocturnal vision. Just look above and you will see ÕÕ. That will be your cue that Tu-whit is in the neighborhood."

"How is it you perform such feats, Lord Galen?"

"Milady," as Don Quixote said …

ÕÕ "'I am determined and resolved to do such deeds that you may deem yourself very fortunate in being found worthy to see them and be an eyewitness of things that will scarcely be believed.'"[E42]

Tu-whit had delivered his first message, eloquently and concisely.

Overwhelmed with my exalted Branch of Vision and thrilled with the arrival of so wise a little owl, a familiar blast of light burst forth. It seemed my Timelessness Glasses were functioning at the speed of light. I wasn't sure how it worked, but I knew what I was seeing was traveling very fast and seemed to be coming from a very great distance.

"It's Twink Ptolemy, ever by your side. The speed of light is a complicated business which we'll get to later, but you're right about it traveling swiftly, about 186,282.397 <u>miles</u> per second, or roughly one <u>foot</u> per <u>nanosecond</u>, that is one billionth of a second!

"Wow, Twink! That must be how fast those dream codes reach me. You kind of glossed over it when you talked about the precognitive dream."

Avoiding the subject, he trilled, "I must say my sweet you were a resplendent sight when Lord Galen awarded you the ponderous branch. Congratulations on your Lifetime Membership, Miss Penny."

Tu-whit recited a line from Ode To A Nightingale:

ÕÕ   "'Was it a vision, or a waking dream?'"ℰ43

An inner glow had penetrated my every thought. In a single moment, I saw a blazing light burst through the darkness from a place we do not know, unswervingly headed for the invincible truth.

CHAPTER FORTY-TWO

GEOLOGY: THE SECOND BRANCH

Maybe if I listen closely to the rocks
Next time, I'll hear something, if not
A word, perhaps the faint beginning of a syllable.
Phoebe Hanson

I returned to the dream with *the grid of lights* and saw that *a muffler* was silently leading the way to a dormant volcano. The *muffler* had connected with *black matter coming out of an open vent,*[185] and matched the opening through which lava is discharged to the earth's surface.

I had an inkling this strange concoction was being transmitted through the thought form of Nicolaus Steno, the first to explain the structure of the earth's crust.

The Collision dream replayed itself: *The photograph of the collision is illustrated first in vivid colors, symbolic of life and vitality, - then starkly turns to black and white as in a line drawing or charcoal.* The black and white evoked a picture of Titanic's ghastly- gray end. The collision at first glance was reminiscent of the collision with the iceberg, but having been abducted into other regions it took on more divergent meanings. It felt like I was drifting away from the Titanic, but I couldn't be sure.

I was contemplating the mysterious collision when in streamed Steno on a tail of shimmering moonlight. A shower of sparkling dream dust floated around him and even though his wings were hidden, I sensed his angelic aura. I had heard that angels always rise to the occasion and this fit Steno to a tee.

"Good day, Penelope. It's Nicolaus Steno eavesdropping on your thought. Actually, I would like to say a 'Penny for your thoughts.' Remember your mantra: In God We Trust. Perhaps together, we can help melt that iceberg of doubt you've been wrestling with.

"I must congratulate you, Miss Peacock, for the fine work you've done so far in decoding Lavender to lava under. In accordance with Peggymoonbeam's inspiration and guidance, we have officially named the quest 'Mission Lavender.'"

---

185 2/5/93. See Ch. 36, The Clog – The Vent – The Volcano, p. 160

Footnotes contain dream dates and references to prior pages where the dream appeared.
Endnotes contain bibliographical references, are marked with "Ɛ" in the text, and appear at the end of the book.

"Dr. Steno! What a surprise! To meet the Blessed Nicolaus Steno and the Father of Geology all at once! I am humbled by your presence and honored beyond words to be included in this mission. I am told you were once a scientist turned Catholic priest and were beatified for your efforts to bridge science and religion. Even though three centuries have passed, the progress is encouraging. I've been ever so anxious to meet you, for you were the first to explain the structure of the earth's crust and for some reason your name has been appearing in my dreams couched in the metaphor of steno pads."

Steno beamed like a smiling sun. "Yes, yes. I am still obsessed with the earth's crust, as I am with faith. I admit that in the last years of my life, I cared more about saving souls than studying rock strata, yet I never renounced my scientific work. I see that the theories of the earth have come a long way since then and there's even movement in spiritual scientific circles nowadays. Scholars in your theological and scientific communities are beginning to see that the two worlds are not poles apart; rather that faith gives us purpose and science gives us knowledge, a belief I am deeply held to. Actually, it explains another reason for my visit which marks the next phase of Mission Lavender. The first phase was completed with your discovery of 'lava under.'

"Before we continue our journey, on behalf of the distinguished panelists at PurpleScroll, Terracrust, and Starsight, I would like to make one request of you."

"Of course, Dr. Steno. As you wish."

"Because this is a highly singular work, we ask that you do not solicit Earth scientists for their opinions until you have formed your own, and that won't be for quite a while. The theories of others will only serve to cloud your basic instinct, which is the foundation for the knowledge you are amassing. Peggymoonbeam has confided to us that you were always sorry you hadn't finished school and that you felt deprived of an education because your life was so preoccupied with family issues. Your clean slate is one of the reasons we selected you. You see, in some ways this is an experiment to determine just how much knowledge has been recorded in the human brain even if it hasn't been formally educated or trained in matters of the universe."

"OK. But what about research? Some of it I've already begun and that came from the outside – from various libraries and the Internet."

"Yes, and you have made excellent connections without anyone's help. For example, you've identified your mentors, you've linked your family members to the workings of Mother Earth, you've recognized the Titanic as an icon, and you've decoded the meaning of Lavender. It's quite acceptable to continue to research as you have on the Internet and elsewhere as long as it does not distract or impede you from reaching the goal: communicating what you have learned through your dreams so all men can understand the spheres of knowledge that dwell in our unconscious."

"But how and when am I to communicate this, Dr. Steno? If I'm not supposed to even consult with scientists, how will I know when, what and with whom to communicate? I'll just be working in a vacuum, never knowing if I'm right or wrong."

"Ah, dear Penelope. Your first and most important lesson is to trust and listen to your dream mantra. *'Be patient. You will learn everything you need to know.'*[186] All of your questions about timing, information and communications on the Earth plane will be answered when the time is right. You will find it in your dreams and we will be contacting you through other means as well.

"Because we are about to delve into information that verges on the arcane, I know you will want to validate our transmissions. Just a word of advice, Penelope: You needn't go to great lengths to research the material through anything other than your own mind, for all the knowledge is within your dreams. Working in a vacuum may not be a bad thing for a vacuum is essentially empty of matter, in this case, devoid of outside influence. We have made arrangements behind the scenes for you to receive newsworthy information when it is required."

"But what about the newspapers and magazines I'd like to read?"

"Well, of course you may, but that isn't necessary to fulfill Mission Lavender's purpose and may actually delay you. One other thing, Penelope. You will be meeting new and interesting people along the way who you will be surprised to find share in many of your thoughts and beliefs. Much of this will occur spontaneously. The making of wondrous new friendships may appear to you to be serendipitous. Such Earth beings, your devoted editor, Richard, for example, have been handpicked by Terracrust and recruited for various assignments according to our time schedule. Though you've not yet been introduced to many of the enlistees, rest assured you will have able assistance on your expeditions to Newfoundland, Vancouver, and Labrador."

My expeditions? Already planned without me, I noted.

"We have conducted exhaustive searches on Earth for those with excellent detection skills and a predilection for humanitarian causes. Some of the helpers supporting your work with Mission Lavender will be appointed to carry out tasks of short duration while others have been selected for the long term. Some of the aides are what we call 'news gatherers.' Others, who hold positions in relevant walks of life, have been inducted as Terracrust couriers engaged to facilitate communications initiated by PurpleScroll to science, industry and the world at large. Our mandate has been to call upon those who experience a sense of interconnectedness of all things. We have observed that having an affinity with others bears a profound relationship to love."

"Dr. Steno, how is it that these beings will want to commit to the task? People are so involved with their own lives these days and most people don't even believe in this sort of thing."

"These Earth beings I refer to are actually Earth angels. You see, Penelope, there is a bond between angels everywhere in the universe that can never be broken. Sometimes you know an angel only by the miracles they leave after they are gone. Think of

---

186 2/10/95. See Ch. 1 – Beginnings, p. 7

Peggymoonbeam. She was watching over you even when she was here on Earth and left you enough gifts for several lifetimes. Your Earth angels embody the same loving qualities as the angels you can't see. They will not think of this as a commitment, but rather a privilege. If they know you are open to receiving them they will embrace this quest and make room in their lives to help. They are around you all of the time, as are we.

"Now that you know you are not alone, let's get on with the affairs of the Earth and with the dishes."

"Dishes?" Gee. That was back in the *Abraham Lincoln dream about the cone attaching to a boat*[187] and when I was wondering if bowls were plunked in my dreams to symbolize craters. What a keen memory you have, Dr. Steno."

"As do you." He smiled bashfully. I noticed a dish towel tucked under one of his big snowy white wings and a branch under the other.

"Penelope, our memory on this side is far superior to what it was on Earth. Our focus is more finely tuned since we don't have to worry about clothes and food and the various encumbrances of being embodied. But as I said, I've come to give you a hand with the dishes and to offer you this sacred and protective branch.

"This branch will take you deep into the center of the earth where you will discover mysterious markings, ancient mysteries and geologic footprints from the past eventually bringing you to a place you haven't yet heard of. Of course, I will be by your side most of the time so you needn't fear thunderstorms or lightning strikes, for this branch is not only a branch of knowledge but one that will shield you from harm."

"Hmm. Deep in the center? I thought I already was in pretty deep."

"No, my dear, there is a special passage that leads to where we must go."

He graciously extended his sacred gift. "Now that you have been granted the first Branch of Vision, it is my great privilege to present you with the Branch of Geology, the second branch of many you are to receive. I bestow this on you now, Miss Penelope Peacock, and invoke the words of an American Indian:"

"'O our Mother the Earth, O our Father the Sky,
Your children are we, and with tired backs
We bring you gifts.'[€44]

Nervous as a cat trying to get its footing on a bed of marbles, I uttered my hesitancy in long run-on sentences. "Professor Steno, this remarkable honor coming from an eminent scholar like yourself who reached the pinnacle in his contributions to science leaves me speechless because I'm just learning the bare bones of geology ... I don't mean to

187 1/25/98. See Ch 35 – Lava Under Revelation, p.

insult those fossils you love, but really, I'm still grappling with the visual cortex and it seems a bit premature for me to accept so grandiose a tribute for work I haven't honestly earned. After all, Dr. Steno, I'm just a greenhorn and embarrassingly awkward with your teachings and I do not feel at all worthy of so revered a branch."

"Penelope dear. You've already received the Branch of Geology in your dreams and by now, you are more entrenched in the work than you can know. Your dream of *the bottom branch in the hollowed-out book*[188] is a fine example. The bottom branch relates to Geology; the science that studies the lower reaches of the earth. It is our fondest wish at Terracrust that this branch will help to fill that empty book. And as for your aptitude and endowment – please dear, do permit me to be the judge of that."

I sheepishly accepted the blessed branch, murmuring "Thank you, Dr. Steno," and before I could so much as blink, he anxiously continued.

"Now, Penelope, as we embark on this circular path and tunnel through the deep and mysterious pockets of the earth, in search of clues, we will witness many secrets. I think you'll be surprised at how fascinating this branch is and how it naturally splits into many offshoot branches. By story's end, I'd venture to say, you will find it gratifying. The twig we will explore now has several names. Some earthlings refer to it as seafloor spreading or continental drift. My preference is plate tectonics, which is why you've had so many dishes and bowls in your dreams."

Dishes. Plates. Peggymoonbeam had already tipped me off about plate tectonics.

Steno, passionately dedicated to teaching me about plates, continued.

"Before we begin our diving expedition, I'd like to clear up the rumblings of a potential misunderstanding, Penelope. Rumor has it you feel as if you've been abducted into Mission Lavender. Please don't think we are abducting you. We're just borrowing you for a paleosecond because we need a voice. You have not been taken hostage, my child. You may resign whensoever you wish."

"Well, if I did resign, what would happen to me, Dr. Steno? Would I be considered a renegade? Would my future be doomed?"

"Not at all. You would simply go back to your life, as you've known it. However, may I be presumptuous enough to say that if you stick with us for a while, the chances of your preferring your new post are excellent.

"Now, I know you're thinking about plate tectonics and I've noticed you working on your collision dream, so I thought I'd beam you a light wave.

"We are here to help you, not to have you struggle. Let me just adjust my beam and radiate the light on plate tectonics.

"OK, here we go.

---

188 9/12/93. See Ch. 3 – The Pole, p. 24

"Although we use these terms interchangeably, you should know that the concept of seafloor spreading has been combined with continental drift and incorporated into plate tectonics. Seafloor spreading is the process in which the ocean floor slowly spreads away as plates move apart from each other."

"Dr. Steno. I'm already a little confused about drift and plates, so any explanation would be really helpful."

"All right. Let's begin with Alfred Wegener, a German scientist who formed the idea of Continental Drift. In 1910, he was convinced that the continents were moving at a rate of about one yard per century. The floor beneath your feet, Penelope, even though it feels stable and motionless, rests on a landmass that is in continuous motion. This mass is fractured into a patchwork of plates. Floating on currents of molten rock beneath, the plates collide and pull apart. This is how it came to be called continental drift. Its stately unfolding explains long-standing puzzles about the distribution of modern and ancient life. It also helps us understand past environments.

"Penelope, in 1669, I had a theory that the younger rocks were deposited on top of the older rocks. A few centuries later, in 1912, my good friend, Alfred, also asserted that the continents consist of lighter rocks that rest on heavier crustal material – like icebergs float on water – and were slowly moving.

"The term 'Seafloor Spreading' came about in 1963, when British geophysicists observed that the floor of the Atlantic Ocean was made up of rocks that could be arranged in strips. Each strip was being magnetized either normally or reversely due to changes in the Earth's polarity when the North Pole becomes the South Pole and vice versa, termed polar reversal. These cyclical reversals take thousands of years so the rate of reversal is changing continuously over geological time.

"*Seafloor spreading* events are still poorly understood because they occur far beneath the ocean surface so be sure to have your Timelessness Glasses with you at all times."

"Wow! I can't imagine seeing way beneath the ocean. The progression of these theories is, surprisingly, beginning to sink in ... er ... fall into place. Learning about plate tectonics clears up a lot of my quandaries.

"You know Dr. Steno, joining my dream repertoire of plates, there were spreading dreams and driftwood dreams but plates seemed to be the backbone. I thought what a bizarre thing to be dreaming. One dream that weighed on me for years is *an image of a mass or layer of pieces on my chest. There were ten very irregular squares.*"[189]

"Well, I think it's safe to say that you've had something on your chest for quite a while now, and your drawing of the irregular squares duplicates the likeness of tectonic plates."

---

189 6/28/94.

"Dr. Steno, when did plate tectonics come into being? I ask because my first dream about a plate was in 1993. *It was about a buried plate which has something of value attached to it. It turns into a detective game for children.*"[190]

"Actually, it was in 1965 when the theory of plate tectonics, the study of the movements of blocks of the earth's crust, was formulated by Canadian geophysicist John Tuzo Wilson. One of Wilson's great, yet simple, ideas was that of transform faults. Wilson's approach was visual and non-numerical. Yet it was devastatingly definitive in what it predicted. Another significant concept he developed crucial to the plate-tectonics theory was that of the 'hotspot.'"

"Wilson? Did you say, Wilson?"

"I had a dream that called me *Penelope Wilson. It had images of waste in it and a girl who matches her flower, which looks like a sunflower. Someone is telling me how to get a message. He says it's the on-off switch – like for a TV.*"[191]

"Penelope, there is no doubt about it. Plate tectonics is indeed what you've been dreaming of. How curious that while some girls dream of boys, you dream of continental drift, of which plate tectonics is an outgrowth."

Transform faults? Hotspots? I'd never heard of such things. Did the *on-off-switch* signify the electrical field frequency in humans Twink told me about? Hmm. Maybe the electrical switch in my brain was "on" and receiving a transmission about waste and plate tectonics. Curious that the sunflower is my birth flower.

"Excuse me, Penelope. I seem to have lost you for a moment. Now, to enlighten you on the moving subject of plate tectonics, the rigid pieces of the earth's outermost layer, the lithosphere, are broken into seven to nine large pieces or plates, depending on how they're defined. Mind you, dozens of minor plates exist as well. These plates are moving around like bumper cars in a demolition derby, which means they sometimes crash together. This crashing motion occurs at convergent boundaries where the plates move toward each other. This occurs at deep oceanic trenches."

"Wow, Dr. Steno! It sounds just like my *collision dream* - and the *irregular pieces on my chest.*"

"Exactly, Penelope."

I wound back to the dream and wondered if the dramatic dream photograph of the collision was inspired by Claudius Galen's passionate obligation to the study of vision.

"Penelope," directed Steno, "it is time for you to chart the sinuous course ahead. If you would, please draw a bigger circle than you did last time, when you ended with *Abraham Lincoln – a cone attached to a boat* – a Volcanic Cone"[192]

---

190 3/11/93.
191 7/23/00.
192 See Ch. 35 – Lava Under Revelation, p. 156

"Wait a sec, Dr. Steno. My research on volcanic cones is kind of fuzzy. Could you help me out?"[193]

"Volcanic cones are built by fragments that have erupted and piled up around the vent in the shape of a cone; most have a crater at the top. The cinder cone is the most common type of volcanic cone and is formed by the accumulation of cinders.

"And Penelope, it's quite all right if you wish to call me Doc. We need not be so formal."

"But, but ... having been beatified and all, you are called Blessed Nicolaus Steno. How can I call you by a nickname? That feels really strange."

"It suits me fine, dear. We needn't stand on ceremony. Trust me. We have a long road ahead and we may as well relax."

"Oh, OK, Doc. I think I've got a bigger circle.

"Abraham Lincoln – a cone attached to a boat (a volcanic cone linked to Titanic?) – *a Vent* (a Volcanic Vent) – *a Muffler* (a silenced eruption) – *a Collision* (Titanic's collision with the iceberg?) – *Cousin Andi* (Andesite; Volcanic Lava) – *Dishes, Plates* (Tectonic Plates) – *Full Star* (Titanic's White Star Line) – *Half Circle* (Longitude and Latitude) – *Clog* (the lava *clogged* a volcanic *vent*) – winding back to *Abraham Lincoln*, the boat links to Titanic... it must be True!"

There was just one niggling piece. There were two cars in the *collision photo* dream[194] implying two-of-a-kind objects. I pondered. A ship and an iceberg are not quite the same as two automobiles. I wondered if those convergent boundaries where plates crash together would be more like it. Two plates would solve the two-of-a-kind riddle, but I guess we'll have to wait and see.

Doc uttered apologetically. "Penelope, I know how hard you've worked on the *Half Circle* series and you've done splendidly up to now, but I think it's only fair to tell you that you still have a way to go on this one. You see, there is scientific information that you have yet to uncover. When you do, you will be, as you say, 'over the moon.'"

I secretly wondered if that's where this Johnnie Pianissmo was – over the moon.

193 See Ch 35 – Lava Under Revelation, p. 155
194 2/5/93. See Ch. 36 – The Clog – The Vent – The Volcano, p. 160

CHAPTER FORTY-THREE

AN INTERSTELLAR INTERNET

The spiritual sages had turned up the volume, radioing endless chains of dream bytes through divine channels of communication. Save Mme. Curie, they were frequent visitors.

Keynote speaker for interstellar communication was Ptolemy. Vision was perceived through the omnipotent eyes of Galen. Matters of the terrestrial underworld of vents and lava were unveiled by Steno. And DNA was planted in the gardens of geneticist Gregor Mendel, who dropped in for a cameo appearance.

Mme. Curie must have been busy isolating elements, but I knew she would eventually turn up. I was still nervous about meeting her but perhaps by the time she appeared I'd feel a little more confident.

I wondered if Starsight and Terracrust bore some resemblance to earthly communities. Was intergalactic communication the same as ours only with colossal stretches of planetary distance in between? Were families scattered in different constellations in touch through an Interplanetary Internet? The dream about *the grid of lights being a way to communicate*[195] was puzzling. Was there more to twenty-first-century communication than we dared to imagine?

And what about the time delay in receiving so many of these messages? Some dreams took years before the galactic spider began weaving its miracles of connecting, cross-connecting and interconnecting. Had these messages been floating around in interstellar space for many centuries searching for receiving antennae?

Dr. Noodle, my dream teacher on Earth, was so named for his exceptional ability to noodle my dreams in their infancy. He told me the reflex arc connection between sensory input and motor output or awareness and choice is 1/250th of a second. I wonder if that would translate to an even quicker arc given the evanescent quality of our dreams and our difficulty in catching them. We often know we've had a dream but haven't captured it because we're too sleepy. What if the dream gets lost in the reflex arc of the unconscious? Is it lost forever or can it be recaptured?

---

195 2/5/93. See Ch 36 – The Clog – The Vent – The Volcano, p. 160

Footnotes contain dream dates and references to prior pages where the dream appeared.
Endnotes contain bibliographical references, are marked with "ℰ" in the text, and appear at the end of the book.

Peggymoonbeam was flapping her astral wings. "Penelope! Penelope! Don't forget the dream where *the Sky and the Earth are one color.*" "Yes. Peggy. *It's in muted watercolors with a little baby to the right and a bluebird to the far right. I felt great peace and harmony.*[196] There was something so mystical about this dream, as though the first breath of Spring had whispered 'there's no difference between Heaven and Earth.'

"If the messages that slid into my dreams are any indication of the wealth of information being sent our way, it extends far beyond the realm of imagination. After all, I'm just one earthling. There are worlds of people who have lost loved ones and have seen them in their dreams. If everyone could tune in to the celestial wisdom of the spirits, it would be miraculous! What if we were all radio receivers with the ability to pull in signals? What if we each had our own bandwidth? Those who were more observant would probably have more width than others. What a concept!"

I thought back to my first squint through the peephole of celestial dream communications. A blinding light spread around the NBC Peacock fanning his metallic plumes, each tipped with an iridescent "eye" and boasting metal as in Peacock Ore. Also present were the all-seeing logo embodied in the CBS Eye and the ABC logo symbolizing the ABCs of the elemental tables. Presiding over the television networks, the neural networks, the retinal networks, the mineral networks and the chemical networks was the most godlike of all the networks: The Interstellar Network.

The dream gates majestically opened under the power of their own electric eye, waving us in, preparing to send whichever transmission we were ready to receive, usually a combination of both visual and auditory, cued by images of the television networks.

Charlesbigstar had given me a jump start at the beginning of this ride when he told me electricity was channeled through the optic nerve of the eye and then introduced me to Lord Galen. But I mustn't veer too far off course, dear Reader, for I still had to resolve open issues related to one of the most persistent symbols being communicated through my dreams: The Vent.

---

196 11/15/97.

CHAPTER FORTY-FOUR

BLACK MATTER

*B*lack matter emitting from the open vent activated memory circuits retrieving dreams of black goop: one, where *I'm in a farmer's market. There are sickly looking carrots and I'm wading through black muck* and another where *I pull black gossamer stuff off a hook and have a hard time getting it off my hand.*[197]

I wondered if the farmers market might represent the vegetation of the earth and the sick looking carrots were symbolic of the inability to see. Did the dream capture the black muck in my life that I was wading through? Of course it did, but it also fit with the black muck emitted from a volcano. And the black muck of greed at the expense of humanity and the earth.

The dream account of the black gossamer was right on. Gossamer is diaphanous like the spun-glass consistency in fluid lava. I was certain I would experience indescribable relief in someday getting this message off my hands.

Thinking back to the muffler, if an ancient inactive volcano had erupted the night Titanic went down, it's possible that no one would have seen or heard it.

In the deep ocean seawater quenches the lava so no billowing clouds rise above the site of eruption. Thinking about the depth of the ocean, I recalled that somewhere in my research travels, I had been drawn to the continental shelf. I now wondered if there existed an ancient, dormant volcano somewhere in or near Newfoundland's continental shelf.

Steno tuned in. "Yes, Penelope, you are referring to a number of 'shelf' dreams we transmitted in which *mother's purses are stored on a glass shelf.*[198]

"The largest islands of the Atlantic Ocean lie on the continental shelves. You were naturally drawn to the continental shelf, for Newfoundland is the principal island on the gently sloping North American shelf. This is a zone of relatively shallow water that extends from the continental margin. It is that part of the sea floor underlain by continental crust."

---

197 10/27/94, 9/6/95.
198 1/12/99.

Footnotes contain dream dates and references to prior pages where the dream appeared.

Endnotes contain bibliographical references, are marked with "Ɛ" in the text, and appear at the end of the book.

(Gulp.) "I think I understand, Dr. Steno. Since my mother is the impresario for Mother Earth, her jewelry, purses, and valuables are metaphors for her precious minerals, which would likely be stored on the continental shelf. And – well – I wonder if the reason it's a *glass shelf* is because maybe some of it is made of lava hidden in an ancient volcano. I remember that when the wind blows the lava around and makes it into Pele's hair, it's like glass fibers."[199]

"Excellent, Penny. Listening is serving you well. Very fast-cooling lava can form volcanic glass. Obsidian, for example, is a naturally occurring glass produced by volcanoes."

Lavender and its many links would gradually build, steaming its way up to a blast of manifestation. If the volcanic vent was deep under water, it wouldn't have been visible to the naked eye. I also wondered if volcanic activity was recorded in 1912 in the Newfoundland area.

Tu-whit hooted in:

ÕÕ "'What we do know is that the first seismometer was installed near a volcano in 1855 at Mt. Vesuvius, Italy[ε45] and that earthquakes and seismic signals were associated with the eruptive activity at Asama-yama volcano in Japan during 1911-1912.'"[ε46]

Had an invisible force in some mystical way mirrored this fanfare of dreams and rendered a visible blueprint? I was reaching for similar clarity with the writing of this book, but where under the earth would the culprit be found, if the culprit were indeed an ancient volcano?

It was like looking for a needle in a haystack.

"You mean, like looking for an ash in a smokestack?" chuckled Steno.

---

199 3/3/99. See Ch. 32 – Mother's Apprentices, p. 142

CHAPTER FORTY-FIVE

A TRUMP CARD:

SLEEPING ON PILLOW LAVA

While I contemplated a submarine vent or a volcano underwater, another long-lost dream floated into view.

A refrigerator is loaded with Haagen-Dazs ice cream and a package of frozen fish. I don't like the fish. A scene ensues where I jump into the water with my pillow. It's supposed to be a raft. I can't swim very well and start to go under. I'm scared but then I touch the bottom and realize it isn't so deep. I boost myself off the bottom and get back up to the top again. The pillow is deflating.[200]

It struck a familiar chord: The sea of cork the night Titanic sank – cork floating to the surface as I was in this dream clip.

What did Haagen Dazs and frozen fish have in common aside from both being cold? I did not like the frozen fish. Perhaps I sensed something fishy.

I mused that if the ocean was symbolic of the sea of emotion, I was taking my pillow with me - like Linus who was never without his blue blankie. On the other hand, a deflating pillow that was supposed to be a raft, spelled out "life raft." Was I in need of a life raft at that time in my life? Certainly. But there was something more.

As I continued to read and research, I stumbled across pillow lava, interconnected, sack-like bodies of lava formed underwater and solidified as rounded masses. They are characteristic of an eruption under water. How efficient of my dream guides to send me a pillow that was also a raft, providing yet another loop to attach to Titanic and to the volcano in the name of pillow lava. Pillow lava. You might say I was sleeping on it.

Pillows were one of those repetitious symbols. A collection of curious pillow dreams landed on my soft goose down pillow. A dream about *two diamond-shaped yellowish-green pillows, placed one above the other over a girl's head hovered around a poisonous gas.*[201]

Eureka!

---

200 7/13/93.
201 6/22/97.

Footnotes contain dream dates and references to prior pages where the dream appeared.
Endnotes contain bibliographical references, are marked with "Ɛ" in the text, and appear at the end of the book.

Research turned this up. Long, narrow, sometimes diamond-shaped zones, called block-faulted belts marked by strong faulting, exhibit stress going on within the continent's crust. They occur between pairs of mountain chains that cross the great shields. Heavens! A slew of shield dreams were in storage. This had to be more than coincidence.

But why did my dreams color the pillows a yellowish-green? Yellow-green had repeatedly made its bid for a place at the bridge table, but could have been any one of a number of cards.

It appeared in a Titanic dream as *a green and yellow diamond-shaped design in the water. I'm carried off by an undertow.* Hidden in that same dream was the commentary that *I think I'm standing on a piece of rock and I slip.*[202]

Slip again. It wound back to the clock dream in the Titanic story.

I go to point at the clock with a pen, which I don't realize is a marker. It makes a mark with a curly cue by mistake. I say it's "my mistake." Someone says, "you slipped."[203]

S - l - i - p. It kept slipping in.

"That's right," chortled Ptolemy and Steno. "You made a mistake. It was your fault. You s- l- i- p- p- e- d. And while clouds floated overhead, Peggymoonbeam was sashaying around in her peach chiffon robe lip-syncing her favorite expression: "Read their lips."

It seemed my hand was dealt from an Alice-in-Wonderland deck of cards. On the face of one card was genetics, as in Mendel's experiments with the garden pea. Two peas were crossed which contained both green and yellow information. The green was dominant, the yellow recessive. I believed genetics would ultimately cozy in, but the time wasn't right to play that hand. What else, then, on this merry-go-round of abstraction would be yellowish-green? The possibilities were infinite.

The next card was marked chlorine which is a yellowish-green, and that is the one I trumped with, feeling no need to look further - at least then.

How on Earth could Haagen Dazs, the frozen dessert, Scandinavian sounding but actually American, connect to the iceberg that Titanic struck? Pillows – ice cream – chlorine – gas? What secret key would unlock it? Where was the hidden strand that would tie it all together?

Steno buzzed in. "There are five gases that are produced by volcanic activity: water vapor, carbon dioxide, sulfur dioxide, fluorine, and chlorine. All of these gases are harmful except for water vapor. Penny, chlorine gas is emitted from volcanoes in the form of hydrochloric acid. Exposure to the gas irritates mucous membranes of the eyes and respiratory tract. In addition, larger amounts result in pulmonary edema and often constrict the throat. Chlorine destroys the ozone layer that protects the DNA of plants and animals. It is an extremely poisonous gas.

---

202 12/7/98. See Ch. 23 –Tragedy, p. 106
203 2/24/95. See Ch. 29 – Clock A Doodle Do. p. 131

I was beside myself! Chlorine must be the poisonous gas floating over my head in the dream. Hmm. If chlorine is emitted through volcanic eruption, it fit right in with the pillows. This was remarkable. The dream had independently connected the ominous pieces: block faulted belts – pillow lava – chlorine.

Pillow lava was making even more sense.

"Remember," continued Steno, "pillow lava is found under water; in this case, Penelope, under the ice where it may be keeping company with the frozen fish – and the Haagen Dazs."

Hmm. I wonder if the Scandinavian-sounding name could be Danish? Danish/American. Danish – clog – American – meatballs.

The image of the clog dance, where *meatballs were left unattended cooking on the stove,* turned up the heat.

The pillow theme began to build. It was utterly chaotic until I found a larger pillow. This time it was buried in exotic locales and cushioned within a more elaborate framework.

CHAPTER FORTY-SIX

INDIA AND EGYPT UNDERGROUND

The larger pillow materialized in a dream that began with repeating images of *a convection machine with coals. I'm on Lexington Avenue and there is a pink entrance with no door. There is reference to Victoria's Secret. Someone is handed a long skinny ticket for a free ride home. It ended with a big square pillow, which I'm leaning against. I look up and see a young man standing there wearing a pyramid-shaped "coolie" hat and a Nehru shirt. I toss him the pillow and invite him to sit with me on the sidewalk.*[204]

Hmm. A convection machine? The only thing I could think of was a popcorn maker, but why would this be associated with coals?

"Steno here. Penelope, save the popcorn for the movies. The convection machine we are looking at is characteristic of the thermal energy beneath the earth's crust, as are the coals."

Self-consciously, I mumbled, "Thanks, Dr. Steno." I knew my naiveté was showing. (They had told me it was supposed to.)

This again set the stage for a volcano and, if we were to merge the volcano with the dream's reference to the New York Lexington Avenue subway, our ideas would be traveling underground in the direction of a submarine volcano. The long skinny ticket for the free ride home was then imponderable, as were the other symbols.

A year after that dream rolled in, a friend who worked for an airline invited me on my first trip to Egypt and offered me a free pass to Cairo. The dream said, "a free ride home." I reflected. "Were they telling me that Egypt was home?"

After I returned from Egypt, I stumbled again over that dream, as if by design, and found that many of those scattered puzzle pieces had clicked into place.

The pyramid-shaped hat, the pink entrance (drawn in the shape of a sarcophagus lid), and *the doorless entrance* reminiscent of an Egyptian tomb pointed to Oneiroglyphics, my dream brand of hieroglyphics.

Pink, within the context of Egyptian lore is symbolic of the rose-colored granite that was brought to Luxor by barque, a sailing vessel. I then happened upon another charm. It

---

204 11/14/98.

Footnotes contain dream dates and references to prior pages where the dream appeared.
Endnotes contain bibliographical references, are marked with "Ɛ" in the text, and appear at the end of the book.

was the pink granite scarab, the symbol of resurrection, taking us back to ancient Egypt and the beginning of civilization as well as to the beginning of this story. Egypt was home. Evidence of human habitation before 8000 BC has been discovered there.

The pillow I toss to the young man wearing a pyramid-shaped "coolie" hat and a Nehru shirt symbolically led me to a big chunk of pillow lava bearing some connection to India and Egypt.

The *"coolie"* detail reinforced the symbolism of India, coolie referring a century ago to an unskilled laborer from India, China, and other Asian countries. The *pyramid*, sacred icon of Egypt, begged the question: Headwear from India – styled like Egypt? *Nehru*, known as Pandit, the teacher, fit in with this subterranean cache of knowledge symbolic of India.

Still stoking my curiosity was the mystery of whether this dream's Egyptian thread would knit together with the mummy of Titanic myth, her remains once buried deep in a vault at Luxor on the banks of the Nile.

I mused. "India and Egypt. *I ask the young man to sit on the sidewalk with me.* Was I, the teacher, inviting him to learn that there's more to the dream than its vanishing mist. A sidewalk is concrete – physical.

CHAPTER FORTY-SEVEN

COUSIN ANDI a.k.a. ANDESITE

Having recognized how central lava was to my dream journey, I began to find additional journal entries that delivered lavender as though it were a household staple.

One such delivery was a dream where my cousin[205]

Pg. 205. Paragraph 2 – Omitted on this proof.

I promise you.

One such delivery was a dream where my cousin *Andi has lavender* old, I happened
gook coming out of her mouth. She then proceeds to stick out her ke body formed
tongue which is about a foot long. [205] revelation that
volcanic rock or lava is called andesite.

But poor cousin Andi still wasn't off the hook. As though exposing and waving her tongue about weren't enough, she soon turned up in another dream where *she was playing the cello, but it sounds terrible and folds over. I say I know she's fabricating something. I'm holding a clear tube of hers filled with white insects like worms.*[206]

Cousin Andi never played a musical instrument in her life. I had to believe the folding over of the cello and the terrible noise it made were pointing not to the collapse of Andi's foul sounding instrument, but to a geologic folding of faulted strata and volcanic rock. But why a cello?

The tube with the worms was a real humdinger. The Andi I knew was terrified of birds, disgusted by bugs and would be revolted by the mere thought of a worm. In any event, I knew ecosystems were simply not her thing, nor were entomology, marine biology or any other ology with the possible exception of gynecology.

Fascinated with the personifications of mother to Mother Earth and cousin Andi to andesite, I reviewed the relationships. Andi's mother was my Aunt Agnes, now appearing in my dreams as Agneswiseheart, my mother's sister. Family relations – Earth relations.

While deep in thought about Cousin *Andi, her lavender coated tongue, her cello and the tube of worms*, a dazzling glare caught my eye. I looked up, and sure enough, Steno was coming in for a landing with his super-sized magnifying glass.

---

205 7/16/94.
206 4/30/93.

Footnotes contain dream dates and references to prior pages where the dream appeared.
Endnotes contain bibliographical references, are marked with "Ɛ" in the text, and appear at the end of the book.

"Hello again, Penelope. I can't let you agonize any longer over Andi and her paraphernalia. What follows is a symphony of coded fractals stringing together pieces of your dreams. Listen closely and you will decode the clues.

"To begin, the cello is the lowest pitched string instrument in the viol family. Because it often sounds like the human voice, we felt sure you'd hear it. Now for Andi's worms, there is a form of tubeworm found inside black smokers, which are vents on the seafloor. Your scientists on Earth are studying hydrothermal vent systems containing sulfide structures called black smoker chimneys, in an effort to understand a very primitive form of system that existed on the Planet throughout much of its early evolution."

Tu-whit's eyes shone as he interjected:

ÕÕ "'There were submarine volcanoes and there was an ocean. So understanding the very basic building blocks of life and the mechanisms by which those building blocks come together will help the scientists understand how the seafloor functions.'"[47]

"We hope this will help," said Steno.

"Your Cousin Andi's fabrication is directing you to andesite, the geological material that manufactures the black smoker. The folding of volcanic undersea mountain ranges produces this volcanic rock. Hence, where black smokers are found may be where ancient folding and faulting took place within the mid-ocean ridges under the sea."

"Oh! So that's why you had me searching for an ash in a smokestack!"

Farfetched though it seemed, it made sense. Dreams of Andi were characterized by repeated folding and humongous dream portions of pizza.

For example, a dream showed *Andi's car left unattended amid the ordering of pizza – lots and lots of pizza – every meal is pizza. There is no other food but pizza.*[207] If Andi was the lava, might her car be the vehicle that drives the lava – the volcano? Was the dream signaling an unattended volcano in the form of Andi's unattended car? I backtracked to the dream of the *meatballs left unattended on the stove.*[208] Something was overheating and it was being neglected. But what did the pizza symbolize? While I couldn't conjure up any recollection of cousin Andi eating pizza in waking life, the pizza eat-a-thon crystallized when a dream charged in that actually spelled out the word *PIEZOELECTRICITY*[209] surrounded by elements that characterize the Earth and Vision.

This seemed to be a direct message from my celestial guides, but they knew I wasn't getting it. Steno danced overhead twirling the pie dough and pointing me to crystal properties where I learned that the phenomenon of piezoelectricity is the ability of a

---

207 10/31/98.
208 10/13/97. See Ch. 36 – The Clog – The Vent – The Volcano, p. 157
209 11/3/98.

mineral to emit an electric current when squeezed or stretched. It was hard to imagine a rock being squeezed.

Astonishing. There must be a metaphor machine up in the sky that just spins the raw material – the pizza dough of our thoughts. I continued thinking about the pizza a.k.a. piezoelectricity.

Cousin Andi is a relative. Therefore, andesite must be "related" to the effect of piezoelectricity.

My childhood fascination with the brain was rekindled. The neural nets crackled. I reflected on the magnificent piece of machinery bestowed on man: the all-knowing brain.

If the white matter – that which carries the signals in our brains – is the dough, and pizza – representing piezoelectricity – is what carries the charge, there must be some affinity to the neurally charged transfer of information in our brain cells to the charged particles in the rocks. What if we could analogize everything? Would that mean we could figure out anything?

As Alice observed when she explored the rabbit hole, this was getting curiouser and curiouser.

CHAPTER FORTY-EIGHT

IN MY SIGHT

Vision is the art of seeing things invisible.
Jonathan Swift

So many spinning strands: Volcanoes and Crystals and Titanic and Newfoundland and Vision. My thought-waves on the subject of vision must have reached Charlesbigstar, for in the blink of an eye the noble spirit Lord Galen appeared. In a booming voice, he announced his arrival as he adjusted his rimless glasses and smoothed his bushy brows.

"Penelope, my dear, it's been a few lumendays since we've touched on vision, which as you know was my love at first sight. I do believe this is where your work originated — with the optic nerve."

"Yes, Lord Galen. The first two years of my adventure were infused with the study of vision thanks to you and Charlesbigstar, who sent me the dream about the optic nerve."

"It does my heart good to see you taking the dreamwork seriously. You know, when I lived in the second century, I had a dream at the age of seventeen that transformed my life, so much so that I changed my career from philosophy to medicine. I so fervently believed in my dreams that I often used them when diagnosing patients' illnesses and even in performing surgery. They were an invaluable source of insight for me and helped me to save many lives."

"Lord Galen, your Branch of Vision is teaching me that dreams can really help us see things we can't perceive on a conscious level. I see that they can help us heal our early wounding and are like trusted friends who are there to transform our lives."

"I've observed, Penelope, that since you began to trust the Timelessness spectacles I gave you with the Branch of Vision, they have illuminated your dreams and elevated them to dimensions you wouldn't have otherwise perceived. Sometimes, even I am baffled by the speed in which you've been orbiting the spheres from vision to minerals, to metals, to geology — and only the gods know what else.

Footnotes contain dream dates and references to prior pages where the dream appeared.
Endnotes contain bibliographical references, are marked with "ℰ" in the text, and appear at the end of the book.

"I must now confide in you that the glasses have a built-in lumenometer you weren't aware of. You see, you have been traveling at superluminal speed, and that's precisely why we call our glasses Timelessness."

"Lord Galen, you sure tucked that one under your wing. Now I know why it seems like I'm racing with time. It feels like I could beat speed records on land, water and in the air. Yet I completely trust Twink's explanation that it all happens at once."

"Penelope, you know my belief is that a luminous pneuma is carried in the optic nerves, the pneuma being the life-giving principle.[48] The Stoics conceived that this weightless agent penetrated the entire nervous system. Today medical circles on Earth would consider the idea of pneuma as respiration, not terribly different from the Greek pneuma meaning 'breath,' which metaphorically describes a nonmaterial being or influence. It may interest you to know that Pneumatology is the study of spiritual beings and phenomena, especially the interactions between humans and God.[49]

"Wow! So maybe that's why I feel like I'm breaking the sound barrier. Maybe it's that old-fashioned luminous pneuma accelerating our connections. I get your messages in lumenseconds and then it takes a decade to figure them out. I wish I could work at the same speed that you transmit. You know, Lord Galen, I have a bunch of dreams that tell me that sound travels faster than the speed of light."

"Actually, Ptolemy is the wizard on the refraction of light from celestial bodies, so worry not about the time it takes to make the associations. Most important is that you make them. You may recall that refraction, the 'bending' of light, is due to a change in the speed of light as it passes from one medium to another. The mediums that the light passes from and to are transparent.

"Although I did not quote from Ptolemy's treatises on optics, they greatly influenced me, so it was quite natural for us to collaborate on Mission Lavender. My observation of connections between retina and lens formed the basis of my pneumatic doctrine of vision while the basic concept of my geometrical analysis of vision was the idea of a direct path of light rays to the optic nerve.[50] Ptolemy and I will gladly help with your dreams pointing to sound when the time is right.

"Be patient. You will learn everything you need to know."

Lord Galen's words really opened my eyes to seeing while we sleep, but Steno was waiting. I turned back to piezoelectricity, wondering what would cause crystals to be squeezed or stretched. What is the source of pressure? A large body, perhaps?

"Steno here, Penelope. A crystal-like quartz which is piezoelectric could generate an electrical signal when under stress."

I took a backstitch while knitting together the concept of piezoelectricity and quartz, recalling the dream of the *Steno course with the pole ... the pole has a colorless rose on it.* This marked the entrance to the house of quartz signaling that quartz can be colorless. Rose had become the dream icon for quartz, rose quartz.[210]

Pizza, posing as piezoelectricity, was fusing with other geologic features found in dream snippets such as folding sheets. Folding, as in the *folding of Andi's cello* – the geologic folding of volcanic rock – has contributed to the formation of great mountain chains such as the Himalaya. Hmm. Shades of India.

Steno knew I hadn't yet started on solid food. Still he offered a teaspoon of mountain building analogy, just enough to tickle my taste buds.

"Penelope," he said, "many mountains – the Appalachian Highlands as an example – are built when two slabs of the earth's crust move closer together. The crust between the slabs is compressed and folded. Think about what happens when you put your hands on two sides of a tablecloth and push them together. The part of the tablecloth between your hands folds and crumples."

So pizza had nothing to do with the cheesy snack other than to frame pizza in a way that would require inspection. Far as I knew, Cousin Andi didn't eat it and that was that! Hmm. Squeezed earth – piezoelectricity – andesite. Might a piezoelectric charge be found in andesite, a volcanic rock, if it were squeezed under the stress of an earthquake or volcano? I'd have to wait for the answer.

Pizza was the sensor coaxing the dream along the intuitive channel of volcanic rock. Cleverly hidden as the metaphor for piezoelectricity, it had become another stone on the path electrically charging its way toward new turns in the story.

---

210 10/1/98. See Ch. 14 – Honored Earth Guide: Nicolaus Steno, p. 68

CHAPTER FORTY-NINE

WRAPPED UP LIKE A MUMMY

And the end and the beginning were always there
Before the beginning and after the end.
And all is always now.

T. S. Eliot

Egypt – India – US – and here comes Africa. My dreams were on the move.

Cousin Andi wasn't quite finished. The bringer of andesite, tubeworms and piezoelectricity, she now appeared with in dream with a mummy.

I'm on a train and engaged in a struggle with my old boyfriend about splitting up and moving to Tanzania. I write US/ US/ US at the bottom of a pad of paper (which looked like a steno pad). I'm not sure if it means us or U.S. Then Andi appears, this time in the glowing company of two beneficent spirits, Agneswiseheart, her beloved mother, and Peggymoonbeam, my dearest friend. Andi is sleeping in my bed. I am standing next to her wrapped up like a mummy.

Andi is breathing through a stethoscope apparatus that goes up her nose. There is a prong for each nostril. At the end of one prong is a diamond-studded tip. I set out to find another one like it. I have a keen sense of smell.[211]

I was confused by this dream woven into an encounter with an old boyfriend. Even in the dream, I questioned its meaning: Was it about us (our relationship) or the U.S. – or both?

The image of the steno pad on which I wrote US/US/US appeared to link to Nicolaus Steno and the earth's crust. But why was I wrapped up like a mummy next to Andi? Why was she in my bed? Was it a geological bed, as in a stratum: a layer of rocks? Was it a volcanic bed?

Since the mummy appeared in a dream that took place in Tanzania, I wondered whether it connected to fossil remains of human ancestors found at Olduvai Gorge,

---

211 9/30/99.

Footnotes contain dream dates and references to prior pages where the dream appeared.
Endnotes contain bibliographical references, are marked with "Ɛ" in the text, and appear at the end of the book.

Tanzania as long as 2.5 million years ago? Or did the mummy link to the Egyptian mummy of Titanic myth?

The stethoscope, used for listening to the heart and lungs, was metaphorically working in tandem with listening to one's instincts. My keen sense of smell in the dream reinforced the sense of sniffing, as in detecting.

When I learned of a volcano known as a diamond pipe volcano, even with the assurance of my celestial mentors and my trusting instincts, I was astonished. A mixture of magma, rock, and diamonds form pipes within the earth called kimberlites often found in Tanzania.

Mission Lavender looked like an unbelievable tangle of everything in creation. Andesite, dream script for Andi, was nosing around kimberlite pipes, represented by the stethoscope with the diamond-studded prong. So andesite and kimberlite diamonds, both found in volcanic rock, seemed to be spearheading the Tanzania dreamscape pointing toward Kilimanjaro, in Tanzania and Africa's largest volcano.

The story was expanding beyond my wildest dreams. This dreaming-waking downpour of miracles was a never-ending source of wonderment.

Steno whispered, "Penelope, you have been bitten by the gods."

"Is that the same, Doc, as being blinded by the light?"

"Yes, my child, it is."

"Then it's a good thing?"

"Yes, oh curious one. It's a very good thing."

The jury was still out on the mummified remains. Was the Egyptian mummy rumored to be on board Titanic snooping around in my dreams? And if so, was she now resting next to a volcano?

Agneswiseheart twirled by with a reminder. "Penelope, diamonds were abundant aboard the Titanic."

I thought back to the pillow dream feathered with symbols of a *sarcophagus – a pyramid hat – a tomb – and Nehru*. We had taken in three very different locales – Africa, Egypt and India[212] – all of which raised a profound sense of connection to the mummy, but what could it be?

What in the world could Africa and India have in common with an Egyptian mummy? I got it! *I was wrapped up like a mummy* because Egypt is a country in Africa and *I was moving to Tanzania*. My excitement over the new linkage must have been pitched at such high frequency that it pulled Steno right out of the upper lumensphere.

---

212 9/30/99, 11/14/98. See Ch. 46 – India and Egypt Underground, p. 203

"I compliment you on your African findings. Ever since your strobes awakened the Sleeping Angel Chambers at Starsight and Terracrust, we've been working around the moonometer to give you some clarity.

"Perhaps this explanation will ground you a little more:

"The African plate underlies Egypt and the continent of Africa, the Mediterranean Sea and parts of the Atlantic and Indian Oceans. The Indian-Australian plate carries Australia, some of the Indian and Pacific Oceans, and India, but not the remainder of Asia. Those two plates are moving apart."

"'Scuse me. 'Scuse me, Doc. You're going kind of fast. Would you mind explaining just what a plate is? Is it a tectonic plate that fits with the plate tectonic theory you told me about?" "Forgive my presumptuousness, Penelope. That's a fair question and I take myself to task for assuming you know about any of this. Sometimes I feel you have more conscious knowledge than indeed you do. Now to answer your question, a tectonic plate is a piece of the earth's crust or lithosphere. As I mentioned earlier, the surface of the Earth consists of seven to nine major tectonic plates and many more minor ones.[213]

"Hmm. You said that the African plate and the Indian-Australian plate are moving apart. I wonder. Do plates ever move together?"

"Oh yes," answered Steno, grinning broadly. "Other plates certainly do move together."

I felt I had hit the jackpot! I just loved to make him happy, even though I wasn't sure I was really absorbing his worldly knowledge.

Steno passionately pursued my question. "For example, the Himalayan Mountains adjoining India are the result of two continental plates – the Indo-Australian and Eurasian plates – colliding head on. That connects to a very early dream in which you see *two photographs of a collision - the one on the left is in color; the one on the right is in black and white. You see black matter coming out of a vent.*"

"You know what I wonder about, Doc? Are those crashing plates you told me about that move around like bumper cars only on land or are they under the ocean, too? In my collision *dream*, I couldn't really tell because the *photographs* could have been taken on land or at sea.

"Good question, Penelope. Plates are combinations of both continents and ocean basins. They are composed either of a fragment of ocean basin, or more commonly, a fragment of ocean basin with an attached continent. In other words, a single plate can carry both."

"So, does every continent sit on a plate, Dr. Steno?"

"Yes. And it is possible, though unlikely, for a plate to be a continent alone, but for this to occur all edges of the continent would have to be a plate boundary which is very

---

213 See Ch. 42 – Geology: The Second Branch, p. 193

rare. From our lookout tower at Terracrust, we see that it would be difficult to get a continent surrounded on all edges by plate boundaries."

"What exactly are plate boundaries? Is it where the plates meet?"

"Correct, Penelope. It is also where the plates interact. Most of the world's active volcanoes are located along or near the boundaries between shifting plates and are called plate-boundary volcanoes. However, some active volcanoes are not associated with plate boundaries, and many of these so-called intraplate volcanoes form chains in the interior of some oceanic plates.[E51]

"This subject of oceanic plates will have some meaning for you, as you've been digging around trying to understand what happened to the Titanic. As I mentioned, plate margins don't necessarily coincide with the familiar continents and oceans that were mapped centuries ago. These boundaries are subtler and could not be mapped on Earth until twentieth-century technology made it possible to locate earthquake epicenters precisely.

"'Before the 2005 expedition, David Brown, a Titanic historian, had said the stern took twenty minutes to plunge into the ocean. After visiting the bottom of the Atlantic Ocean, during that expedition, scientists have discovered that Titanic took just five minutes to sink – much faster than previously thought.'[E52] But they have been so focused on the iceberg that they 'can't see the cause for the effect' – a Terracrust original."

"We should not exclude the iceberg theory, Penelope, because quite seriously, cause and effect were involved. The iceberg was certainly part of the effect, but not necessarily part of the cause. Let's say, 'it is only the tip of the iceberg.'"

Cause and effect. Tip of the iceberg. I rolled my eyes. Steno was an addicted cliché-ster.

"Forgive my platitudes, Penny, but it is a bit of a compulsion. You see, I belong to the Old Saw Club at Terracrust and the competition is rather stiff at awards time. It's similar to your Academy Awards panel in Hollywood, except that we're all stars up here. We were born that way.

"As I was saying, you must not blame your teams of Earth scientists who have been trying to untangle the Titanic riddle. It's not easy to uncover something that happened in the dark nearly a century ago. What happened was caused by an invisible force.

"The nature of plate tectonic activity during most of the Earth's history is still uncertain, and models of the way in which it would be reflected in the continental rocks are highly speculative, so we've had to approach this from a different and somewhat unorthodox perspective.

"Actually, my trusted apprentice, our project falls under the vast umbrella of the unconscious. The Dream is the only vehicle we know of that is equipped to receive transmissions from Starsight, Ptolemy's pride and joy.

"Think back to the time conversion scale that we use at Starsight and Terracrust and understand that because we always see the past which actually enfolds the future, the future to some degree, determines the present. In our timeless reality, all is in the present, much like your dreams. In other words, your dreams of the past are actually signals from the future and your dreams of the future are, in turn, signaling the past.

"Our Earth studies at Starsight reveal that the greater the distance, the more visible the object. Starsight is about 900,000 light-years away from Earth, and Terracrust is another few hundred thousand light-years away so the distance between us is great enough to see what's actually going on down on Earth, be it past, present or future. Now I ask that you wind your memory tape back to the *Delta dream about the spiral staircase.*"[214]

"Yes, Doc, that was the dream that led me to Delta Cephei, the fourth-brightest star in Cepheus."

I must have been floating on a cloud thinking about the distances; how near and yet how far they are, when suddenly a swarm of sunbeams danced around me signaling that something out of this world was right around the corner.

And on that thought, a spectacular shower of lights streamed through the diaphanous curtains of Earth's galaxy bringing Twink Ptolemy into timeless view looking as though he were dancing on ribbons of starlight.

"Halloo. Halloo, Miss Penny! Your Delta Cephei connection is as brilliant as the star itself! You see, Starsight hovers around a Cepheid star in the Andromeda nebula. It's known on Earth as the Great Andromeda Spiral Galaxy."

I was agape! What I thought was a fantasy was coming to life with every dream. The *Delta* dream led me to just the right galaxy. That's amazing! I bet there are thousands of galaxies. And thousands more stars than galaxies. It must be unimaginable!

"Yes, my sweet. There are three thousand visible galaxies and billions more that are not visible. And as for the unthinkable number of stars in the universe, there are 400 billion x 130 billion, or about 50,000 billion billion. A billion billion. That's 1,000,000,000,000,000,000. So, Penelope, take in the concept of a billion billion, then think of 50,000 of those. It's simple!"

Twink, now partially eclipsed by a swirl of soft warm mist, sheepishly uttered, "I have a confession to make. I had a secret strategy in mind when I wired you a dream of *a woman bound in chains made of stars. They were on her back.*"[215]

"Yes, Twink. I remember it."

"That woman symbolizes the constellation of Andromeda known for the legendary princess who was chained to a rock. If you're able to see the weaker stars in this constellation, it takes the form of a stick-figure woman, like the little stick figures that illustrate your dreams. We at Starsight believed you'd be able to see your reflection in constellation Andromeda for you've been chained to a rock since your work with us began. The

---

214 8/18/96. See Ch. 20 – Agneswiseheart, p. 84
215 9/4/97.

Andromeda Constellation, best known for the Andromeda Galaxy, is one of the most famous objects in the sky and the nearest large galaxy to Earth. The galaxy is so bright that you can see it with your own eyes from Earth. It will look like a faint fuzzy patch of light and is only one of hundreds of billions of galaxies that make up a much larger universe. Your dream of *the chains on the woman's back* is cluing a galaxy from the ancient past, as long ago as, oh- about 2.9 million light-years distant."

"Jimminy jacks and leapin' lizards, Twink! You expect me to know about a constellation almost three million light-years away?"

"My dear Penelope. I am here to remind you that you cannot dream anything you do not know. That is to say worlds of knowledge including the constellation of Andromeda reside within the consciousness of you and all of your fellow earthlings."

"And the dream you had about *a star that seemed billions of light-years away that was coming in close, disappeared, returned, and then faded out* was the Delta Cephei showing you its variable nature and how its brightness varies over time."

"Are you saying, Twink, that out of a billion billion stars I managed to see Delta Cephei?"

"Well, yes. Because Delta Cephei is a pulsating supergiant star and that's just what you saw in your dream. Earth astronomers use it as the prototype of the Cepheid variable stars for estimating distances in space so your dream about it being billions of light-years away, though overstated, captured the immense distances in space. Now here's one that will tickle you, little Penny."

Too bedazzled to even try to take in all this stuff about constellations and things so far from ordinary thought, I went back to the dreams. "The Andromeda and Cepheus stories are fascinating, but what was your secret strategy, Twink? It sounds oh- so mysterious and a little scary."

"Don't be frightened, Penny dear. It was to encourage you to look toward the skies like you did as a young girl with the hope that now, as a grown-up, you would start to think about time and space. I admit I got a little ahead of myself in the story, for we have only taken a brief spin around the galaxies. Far more illumination on such matters awaits you."

"More illumination is daunting but so exciting! Twink, the way in which you send these dream messages to me is electrifying, kind of like magic!"

"It may appear as magic to you, my lass, but it is not. You see, our kind of magic operates according to its own clockwork run by its own machinery and what we are doing is reacquainting you with something you already know. It's a difficult concept to explain to an earthling who hasn't been in the heavens for a while, but a good starting point is to understand a little bit about time and space from our point of view.

"One light-year is approximately six trillion miles, so we have a great advantage in seeing 'the eternal landscape of the past,' to quote from my young friend Alfred Tennyson's poem, "In Memoriam." But that doesn't do the teams at Starsight and Terracrust any good, for we need the unconscious mechanism of an embodied soul to receive the message and transmit back to us in order to validate our method of communication."

"Spinning stars! Twink, how does that work? You seem to just show up on a moment's notice with some really ancient material. I feel like I'm entering a library when I go to sleep."

"Our form of communication uses light as its transmission medium. There are four elements required for transmission: a transmitter, a signal, a channel and a receiver. The transmitter is any one of us on your spirit team who encodes a dream message into a signal. Then an electromagnetic channel carries the signal to your Dream. Finally, Penny, you acting as the receiver, reproduce the message from the received signal and through your power of thought and association, you acknowledge to us receipt of the message. Although no explanatory physical mechanism acceptable to mainstream science has yet been reported, the way in which we pop back and forth so quickly in your thoughts, faster than theoretical limits, can best be explained by light which physiologically activates your intuitive perception through a mechanism of conscious action.

We've already touched on this in your vision study. At some point, you might want to consider the Bose-Einstein ideas of tunneling photons in the brain cortex.[53] The capacity to bring together remote associations is extremely important in this regard. When you receive a cue from us, that image or word simultaneously activates your entire associative structure. Actually, Earth scientists are researching word association networks in an area called Quantum Cognition.[54]

"The experience of humans, like you, is that they often, perceive information from or about physical objects unavailable through normal, local, sensory mechanisms or classical space-time information. We are a good example of that, Penny, for you are receiving messages from us on a nonlocal basis. In other words, we have found that communication through dreams is the primary method for this sort of transmission. According to Montague Ullman, an eminent pioneer in dream telepathy," the term nonlocality refers to the instantaneous transfer of a signal from one place to another through no known physical means."[55]

"Nonlocal? It sounds like an express train."

"The nonlocal interaction my pet, between you and me is like an express train, considering the speed with which you receive our information.

Tu-whit is especially well versed in these matters, and here he comes:
ÕÕ "'Certain Earth scientists postulate that a quantum hologram is the source of this intuitive perception.[56] In 'a hologram each region of space-time contains information about every other point in space-time.'"[57]

"Wow, Twink! I wonder if my brain is picking up nonlocal signals which grow out of my earthly perceptions. It's quite a miraculous process for it seems that in the flick of an eye, my hundreds of dreams overlay and penetrate one another until they are practically inseparable. So inseparable, that they begin connecting to waking events to make a picture. It appears that these itty-bitty pieces of dreams are buried but are part of something bigger and deeper. Maybe our dreams can awaken us to the unexplainable things that happen in space-time.

"That's spot-on with the work being done at Starsight and in Quantum Cognition on Earth," resumed Twink, "and may explain why you feel like you're in a library when you dream. You've probably crossed paths with Tu-whit many times."

"Y'know, Twink, I even tried to draw a picture of how I think this all works. I mean, how entangled these dream messages are with the electronic stuff that appears on my computer and how it merges in a stream of waking activities.

"I read about Zero Point Field waves and how this energy field implies that all matter in the universe is interconnected by waves which are spread out through time and space, tying one part of the universe to every other part. According to certain physicists, these waves are encoders and carriers of information with a virtually infinite capacity for storage.[E58]

"Twink, I bet this storage capacity lives within each of us and can be found spreading from our dreams into our waking lives and back again."

"Penelope, another of your dreams' capacity is that they integrate many different viewpoints or 'perspectives' of the same event. Like the Roman God Janus with two faces, who looked in opposite directions simultaneously, your dreams are observing two landscapes at once: a familiar personal world on Earth and an unseen cosmic world in the Universe. To put it another way, we could say, you are perceiving a local and a nonlocal view in tandem."

Steno interjected. "Excuse me, you two, but I've been listening in and I might add that Earth scientists are considering vision, hearing and touch as sensory perceptions that may operate beyond space-time."

"That's fantastic, Dr. Steno, because I believe that the visual nature of psi or psychic awareness can help in understanding how information transfer in our dreams occurs in space and time. From my dreaming experience I think dreams actually do take place beyond space-time in those nonlocal regions even though we think we're sleeping in our beds. I mean our bodies are asleep, but our minds are traveling beyond our bodies. Thinking that infinity is hardwired in our brains, it seems that mind-matter interactions occur at the midpoint of the lemniscate loop (the sign of infinity) looping from the cosmic field to the biological field and back.

"I don't know – this whole subject of how I get the information in my dreams seems so complicated. But then geology and the moving around of plates is complicated, too. Geography wasn't my best subject but at least I was in school. Now I have geology and nonlocal signals to think about without any schooling at all.

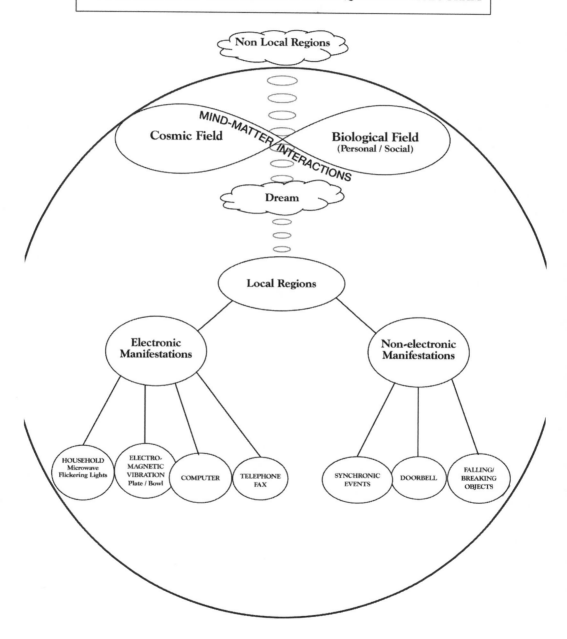

"Gee whillikers! That covers the Earth's surface, the Earth's structure and signals above, around and probably within the Earth! How will I ever take this all in? Should I take a memory course or something?"

"No, no, no – a memory course is entirely unnecessary. Not to worry, Penelope. You're now in a different kind of school where you need not memorize anything. You'll see that you will take in more by osmosis than you ever dreamed possible. I mentioned the plates a while ago because it could offer some explanation to the Africa/India representation in your mummy dream. But the Egyptian mummy, Penelope. Now that's a Mother of another cloth and will require a separate mummy expedition which I'll take under advisement with our esteemed avatars."

"Oh, Dr. Steno, you are truly a Renaissance man. I wish I could find one like you with a body."

"Don't fret, Penelope. Your Scribe Ptolemy has someone in mind for you."

"Yeah, yeah, I know. I know. Johnnie Pianissimo."

CHAPTER FIFTY

THE SLIP

The mention of a mummy expedition returned me to chords of Titanic.

The dream ensemble performing "slips" resembled a libretto set to the Titanic over-ture. The dream choreographer arranged for me to take *a ship overnight. My luggage is taken upstairs to a central place. I'm in a darkened room where there is a white lace wedding dress for mother. Her underslip is too short so I'm looking for a long slip. The back of her dress crisscrosses and has a gap in it.*[216]

This was one among a rack of "slip" dreams, its garbled detail demanding I examine "slip" in the context of geology. When I found something called a strike-slip fault, I was, as Steno predicted, "over the moon."

"Penelope," tuned in Steno. "It's time you learn what a strike-slip fault is. It is a nearly vertical fault along which material on one side moves horizontally with respect to that on the other side."

It was hard to picture but I wondered if this kind of a slip was a blatant reminder of the accusatory *"you slipped"* from the clock dream. And then, z-z-z-z-z-zap- – a connection! Convergent boundaries! That's where plates move toward each other and sometimes one plate sinks, or is subducted under another.

Dragged down, or subducted, one beneath the other! This slid back to the pillow lava dream where *a poisonous gas and two diamond-shaped pillows are placed one above the other, over a girl's head.*[217]

Threads began to interweave with the *crisscrossing on the back of mother's dress, which has a gap in it* when the seismic gap theory burst out of the Earth delivering an answer to an absurd riddle about a dress.

Steno, conductor of an ancient rock concert, whipped out his nine to the ninth power magnifying glass and brought the seismic gap piece into full view.

---

216 7/11/95.
217 6/22/97. See Ch. 45 – A Trump Card: Sleeping on Pillow Lava, p. 199

Footnotes contain dream dates and references to prior pages where the dream appeared.
Endnotes contain bibliographical references, are marked with "Ɛ" in the text, and appear at the end of the book.

Tu-whit in super intuitive mode contributed to Steno's lecture:

ÕÕ '"The seismic gap theory is based on past earthquakes that document a segment of an active fault zone that has not experienced a major earthquake during a period when most other segments of the zone have."'[59]

Steno continued. "Penelope, buried in your dreams is a wide array of fabrics and styles that will help you out. Of course, earlier clues were the muffler, the black matter emitted from a vent and the collision. You seemed at a bit of an impasse so at Peggymoonbeam's insistence we decided to try shoes and clothes as symbols. She is quite convincing, you know.

"That's why your dreams are outfitted with mother's slippers, gapping clothes, short slips, underslips, crisscross designs, and so forth.

"Now, I must return to Terracrust for an 11:11 meeting with upper-level management and you know what that means. So we'll catch up later. I have great confidence that you'll work it out.

"Godspeed, Penelope."

He spread his eagle-sized wings and evaporated in a shimmering cloud.

I felt so alone. I knew I was becoming too dependent on him. Now, it was time to get down to Earth and try to fly this on my own.

Mother's dress with the *gap* was joined on the fashion runway by other similar dream designs of sloppy *gapping dresses*. Mother's slip being too short had me buffaloed. I wondered whether a fault could be characterized as short. A minor eruption, perhaps?

Was Mother's wedding gown a metaphoric betrothal of past and present earthquake activity? New links stretching the chain of affinity were the strike-slip fault and an inactive fault zone.

Who would've imagined it? Clothes and quakes.

Peggymoonbeam and Agneswiseheart must have collaborated with Steno to fashion these elaborate creations of my mother's apparel. Their handprints were all over. How clever! They wrapped their story around a slip, a trip and a ship. Twink's love of the rhyme must have rubbed off.

The strumming of mother and her slip was in tune with the Titanic, Mother Earth, the Tsunami, Lavender a.k.a. – Lava Under – the Volcano, climaxing with the strident vibrations of an earthquake, almost Wagnerian in tone. Though it was a mixed cadence, a common chord rebounded to another time, another place. This elaborate opera was played completely by ear – at least on Earth.

While trying to integrate the *slip, the gap and the crisscrossing*, the ticking of the clock grew louder.

The shock waves of the earthquake theme ejected the memory of the dream that had a funny sort of *doodle drawn on the clock*.[218]

Booming through the tangled nets of dream fibers echoed the words, "Someone says *'you slipped.'* I say, *'it's my mistake.' The time is 12:28 and shows a figure that looks like an m."*

"The message is *'he wants yellow .. pale yellow.' I go to point at the clock with a pen, which I don't realize is a marker. It makes a mark with a curly cue by mistake. The person holding the clock is annoyed. The dream ends when I notice a large coral dome ring of mother's missing.*

While mentally harvesting the new crop of connections, I repeated the dream message out loud: *"Someone says, 'you slipped.' I say 'it's my mistake.'"* Did they mean that it was my fault?

"Hallelujah!" cheered an exasperated Peggymoonbeam. That's what we've been trying to tell you. Read my lips – or read my slip."

The rhetorical sputter of two words each implying the same geologic meaning – mistake and slip – had rumbled toward a FAULT.

"It's my mistake ... it's my fault ... *I slipped."* It sounded the ring of Truth and connected with mother's underslip and the seismic gap. If the message was a strike-slip fault in which plates slide past one another, it could occur on land or underwater. Where was it? Continent or ocean?

Maybe, as Steno implied, the fault pointed to in my dreams was an ancient inactive fault that experienced an unnoticed, undocumented quake in the early 1900s. According to the seismic gap theory, such a scenario if geologically proven could be a source of information about future earthquakes.

I mined the dream for more nuggets. *The time is 12:28 and shows a figure that looks like an m.* And what about the *coral dome ring of mother's that's missing?*

Steno pitched in, "The growth layers in fossil coral indicate yearly variations in weather and food supply and are believed to represent variations in the character of calcium carbonate deposits. When Earth scientists drill a coral core, they can count the growth bands and date samples exactly."

Calcium carbonate – calcite – fossils. It was fermenting, but something was missing.

The dome! It was the missing dome. Coral must be a clue. "Could the coral ring be pointing to an extinct fossil coral that's submerged near an inactive volcano?" I asked aloud.

"It certainly could be," responded Steno on his Terracrust ping pilot, a miniature device he used when he wanted to communicate in speeds even faster than his usual paleoseconds. "Domes form when a mass of volcanic rock is too viscous to flow far from the vent, often formed at the end of an eruption."

---

218 2/24/95. See Ch. 29 – Clock A Doodle Do, p. 131

"Well, if it was missing, Dr. Steno, where did it go?"

"Remember, Penelope, your dog-walking spirit said the bellows had lost its frame. My hunch is that the dome collapsed and may be difficult to find. But don't worry your busy head. Find it we will."

Contemplating the function of sliding, another "slip" dream slid onto the plate in my head. Set in *a fashion optical store, it centers on an optical light that was worn on the head underwater when scuba diving, illuminating all the murky areas. The light also attaches to a telephone and has a pressure-sensitive spot on it. I see it on a car phone. At the end I'm wearing a slip on which is listed all the information. I have already done much of it.*[219]

The stellar wordsmiths were at work: optics – light – communication – a slip I'm wearing – a slip in the earth – a strike-slip fault.[220]

I was working this dream sometime after its arrival when a phone call rang through on my computer. (I had never received a phone call on my computer – before or since.) It was a wrong number. I asked who was calling and they answered, "Atlantis Eyewear." The thrill of synchronicity, even in the most mundane situations, would become another luminescent thread weaving its visible earthbound fibers through the invisible strands of a sacred magic carpet.

Was there a message in Atlantis Eyewear? These magical happenings filled me with more connections than I already had even though I didn't know exactly where they were leading. Deep inside I sensed a scientific explanation wanting to emerge but it seemed literally light-years away. I was like a big pot of connection stew about to bubble over. When the unexplainable happened, I'd wonder if everything in the world, in all of human experience and history, manifested as parallel events.

The telegraphers of cognitive powers had consolidated earlier imagery of optics, light, and communication as essential elements leading to a conclusion. "Fashion optics." Flip it around and it meant, "see the clothes." The only article of clothing in this vignette was a slip, which pointed to a geologically rooted message.

It was time to fiddle with the oneiroglyphs of "slip" and "list." "Slip" in geologic lingo is a fault movement, as when a fault line slips in an earthquake; "list" in nautical jargon means to lean to the side, as in a ship that listed badly to starboard.

Wearing the optical light underwater described our unconscious capacity to illuminate murky areas in our lives, but the rest of the dream had turned into a real brain cruncher.

What if the optical light symbolized a star? Twink was the overseer of astronomical optics. And what if that optical light attached to a radio function? Holy cow! That would connect to radio astronomy! Even though the radio part was outside the perimeter of the

219 5/15/97.
220 7/11/95. See Ch. 50 – The Slip, p. 223

dream, I had a hunch. I ran to look it up. Radio astronomy deals with the origin and nature of emissions from extraterrestrial sources in the radio wave range of electromagnetic radiation rather than in the visible range. Radio astronomy became the first non-visible Branch of Astronomy. "Non-visible!" That's Twink and his astronomical meandering to a tee!

Why was the pressure sensitive spot on the light attached to the phone? Did it imply sensitivity to light? To communication? Was it telling us that things stick? As in memory?

I trusted that in time the answers would come.

For now, I would follow the clear-sightedness of the Blessed Steno and the all-knowing choreographers. I deduced that the two most familiar cues were the prompts: listed and slip. Had the ship listed because of a strike-slip fault?

I thought back to the behavior of a strike-slip fault and how it occurs. Moving plates would have activated it. Were the plates on land or at sea somewhere in the vicinity of where Titanic went down, sliding past one another?

A fault might be active or completely dead concealed beneath sediment or ocean waters. Fault motion may be a continual slow creep or occasional violent lurches.

Was it Mother Earth's "fault" that took Titanic to her early grave? Had she hidden it under her massive cloak? Was she clever enough to render it imperceptible to the teams of experts looking for clues for nearly a century? My gut said a violent lurch had generated a tsunami. Steno had heard my thoughts and gently reminded me that the continental shelf is buried under thick sediment and very difficult to study even with seismic probes. Even so, perhaps it held a clue.

While adjusting my Timelessness Glasses, a Terracrust searchlight with superluminal power captured this scene before it had happened.

Dream: 1997. Waking: fast forward – 2010. Were Atlantis Eyewear and a dream about *optics, scuba diving, illuminating murky areas and information on a slip,* harbingers of British Petroleum's Deepwater Horizon ecological catastrophe? Atlantis, another of its rigs was drilling in the same waters at the same time in the Gulf of Mexico but nearly two thousand feet deeper. Had the worst oil disaster in the U.S. been involved with a slip in the earth – a strike-slip fault – a geological disaster, with another on the way? Was a geological event the cause or the effect? Was it Titanic's iceberg?

Galen surely knew about convergent vision. And the Dream knew about paradigms. The dream message: *I had already done much of it* gelled with my final edit of the book when the Gulf oil spill occurred.

Now we turn back to Titanic and its multifarious possibilities.

CHAPTER FIFTY-ONE

THE TSUNAMI

Ripples of tsunami waves rolled across the dream screen as I recalled a dream of *a harbor filled with boats. They are going to catch the bad guys and bring them back. A puzzling image of a carton labeled TIDE as in laundry detergent appears.*[221]

Hmmm. TIDE – harbor – boats – bad guys – carton.

Steno appeared. "I notice you're struggling with this, Penelope. Let me show you a little trick. First, look at the word CARTON. Now look at the word CRATON. Do you see it? We transpose a couple of letters and Carton emerges as Craton, and voila! there's a piece of your puzzle.

A craton is a block of the earth's crust, and her crust is scheduled for a return engagement."

"Why can't you all just say what you mean?"

"Because," he rumbled, "you won't learn that way!"

The TIDE tossed me back to the *nursing mother and the wavy lines.*[222] A tsunami is popularly called a "tidal wave." Although tsunamis are not caused by the tides, but by vertical movements of the sea floor, the dream image of TIDE carried me closer to the answer.

And the closer I got to the answer, the closer I came to overhearing my spirit guides, whose unspeakable language only my dreams could understand. Peggymoonbeam advised her colleagues: "We want to be sure she has enough light to see everything, especially in so many dark places, so we've got to use every word we can think of that means light."

I overheard a lot of talk about words like effulgent and refulgent and relucent and fulgid and lots of unusual sounds I'd never heard before. The group was having a big discussion about which word they would use. They liked to send words sometimes that I'd have to look up. Then I heard Peggymoonbeam say to Steno, "How about lambent? No, lucid. No, lustrous. No, luminous. Wait! I've got it! Let's call it luminescent, but make it smaller.

---

221 10/9/93.
222 1/27/95. See Ch. 31 – Flashing Lights! Ringing Bells!, p. 139

Footnotes contain dream dates and references to prior pages where the dream appeared.
Endnotes contain bibliographical references, are marked with "Ɛ" in the text, and appear at the end of the book.

Just then, Peggymoonbeam's saucer-like eyes lumed in. "I told you guys: You have to spell things out for her."

"By the way, Penelope, lume is our jargon for luminescent, so don't even bother to look it up."

It was a rare occurrence when I heard them before they heard me but it worked either way.

The boats and the bad guys had been troublesome until I got the Titanic piece. The dream illustration of the boats mirrored the Titanic lifeboats. While hundreds of doomed Titanic passengers were moaning and calling for help in the icy water, there was debate aboard many of the lifeboats between those who wanted to go back to rescue those left on Titanic and those who didn't. Only a few boats returned to pull people out of the water. It took more than an hour for the cries of the dying to fade away.[E60]

Catching the bad guys may be alluding to the crew members who did not help and to suspicions of negligence on the part of the White Star Line. This would reflect the faultfinding that raged in the aftermath of the disaster resoundingly echoed in the high courts and legislatures. Human faults – Earth faults. A faulty situation all around.

The harbor – Tide – boat drama was a reminder that dreams are packaged as a nagging problem, prompting and prodding until we finally resolve it. They are persistent in their quest for resolution, playing themselves out in various skits faithfully embodying the same elements until the student – the dreamer – is able to grasp it.

The Harbor – Tide – Boat triptych was the first dream to frame the tsunami. It didn't sink in so the scribes in their infinite wisdom recreated it in a subtler frame two years later with the nursing woman and the wavy lines and it worked. Same theme. Different scenario.

The Titanic was speeding at a brisk pace of 22.5 knots on that fateful evening of April 14, the fastest she had ever steamed during that, her maiden crossing. She was out to break records. At 11:40 p.m., Titanic collided with the iceberg and at 2:20 a.m., official time, the great ship slipped beneath the sea to meet her icy demise.[E61]

As waking and dreaming currents carried me further into the wave motions of a tsunami, I learned that a sudden volcanic eruption would have vertically displaced the water column, the volume of water between the surface of the ocean and the ocean bottom. That would have resulted in an enormous mass of water being set suddenly in motion.

Someone says, *"you slipped."* I say *"it's my mistake." The time is 12:28 and shows a figure that looks like an m.* The image of the m on the clock sounded all the alarms – pulled out all the stops! It was an "AHA!"

m was MASS!

So that was the mass in my Clock A Doodle Do dream![223] Not a Papal mass or a mass of large numbers. Both would be sadly appropriate given the number of lives lost, but the tightest connection, for now, and the one that made the most sense was water as it linked to the dream landscape: *My mistake*, i.e. my fault; *you slipped* – strike-slip fault – *the clock – the date – the nursing mother – the wavy lines*. It was architecture, one brick at a time. Or Lego, one block at a time. Or plate tectonics, one plate at a time.

Titanic was supposed to have collided with the iceberg at 11:40 while the time on the dream clock was 12:28, a difference of forty-eight minutes.

And yellow. The message was, "." What was pale yellow? Did it gel with the Yellow slab or was there some unidentified yellow dream particle hanging in the balance?

I ran through the dream again, this time, examining it piece by piece, like a detective out to crack a case.

I go to point at the clock with a pen, which I don't realize is a marker. It makes a mark with a curly cue by mistake. What was the marker? Markers are often intended to indicate a position or a place or a route. What was it marking? What was the curly cue? There it was again. Like list and slip, it was the whistling of two words: marker and cue, each bearing a similar meaning: marker, an indicator – cue, a tip-off.

The official timeline shows collision with the iceberg was 11:40 p.m.

At 12:27 TCT, Titanic sent the following message:

"I require assistance immediately. Struck by iceberg in 41.46N, 50.14W."

TCT, established as Titanic Corrected Time, is 23 minutes slow and represents a time resulting from the setting of the liner's clocks back 23 minutes at midnight (to account for westbound time loss). Testimony in the American and British inquiries shows that, while some clocks were reset, others were not.[ε62]

The time differential nagged at me. Everything else fit snugly, was so logical.

It didn't make much sense at this point, but why would the voices of the tutelary gods have followed us this distance. Though I knew I was to obey the inaudible harmonies, I was totally in the dark as to how to go about this. There were literally oceans left to navigate, but I had high hopes that the marker and the cue would point the way.

Tide in a carton – tsunami in a craton, a block of the earth's crust. Perhaps the marker and cue were pointing to the craton.

Asking how I could know if it was an earthquake or a submarine volcano an ear-splitting clap of thunder broke through my thoughts. A nearly blinding streak of lightening jolted my memory back to the enduring dream symbol of the *yellow slab*. Crackling overhead was the word:

223 2/24/95. See Ch. 29 – Clock A Doodle Do, p. 131

YELLOWSTONE!

Yellow slab – yellow stone – volcano – an opening in the earth – an igneous volcanic rock – igneous means formed by fire – igneous rock is formed by volcanoes – the yellow slab was made of yellow stone!

It was spellbinding! I had to catch my breath.

Having regained my composure from the impact of so obvious an answer, I sought information on the Yellowstone Caldera – a basin-shaped volcanic depression. Yellowstone is one of the largest and most active calderas in the world, sometimes referred to as the Yellowstone Supervolcano. It most recently erupted some 70,000 years ago.

Symbols of Yellowstone scattered across my recurring dream theme of Geology worked with the seismic gap theory. The Yellowstone Plateau in the Rocky Mountains lies at the center of one of the Earth's largest volcanic fields. And that fit with lavender as Lava Under.

On learning that Yellowstone's origin has been traced to a hotspot in the earth's mantle, a dream bubbled up featuring a *yellow and orange glass mantle designed by Grucci, known for their fireworks displays, accompanied by an antique chest of drawers.*[224] The mantle is the region of the earth's interior between the crust and the core.

The pairing of *yellow and orange* had been a vivid reminder of the colors of a volcanic explosion. *Glass*, symbolic of volcanic glass melding with the *fireworks* sparked a double meaning. One interpretation: a volcanic blast; the other, the rocket distress signals fired from the Titanic.

Certain analyses of the night the Titanic sank report that because of the Earth's curvature, only the rockets' apogee would have been seen, making them appear very much like shooting stars, which were also reported to have been present that night in unusual quantities.[E63]

But, if a volcanic event, it would point to a hotspot – a very hot region under a tectonic plate when magma wells up, pierces the crust and forms huge volcanic outpourings. There were more than a hundred hotspots beneath the earth's crust that had been active during the past ten million years.[E64] Today there are about fifty considered active.[E65]

Hotspot fit the image of an *unattended kitchen stove*[225] pointing to a heat source. Cousin Andi's (andesite) *unattended car*[226] was likely symbolizing the tectonic engine which drives a volcano. There was some relief in knowing that the hotspot is nature's way, but something was overlooked and that was nerve-wracking. Material from a hotspot bringing heat from the Earth's interior closer to the surface fit with *convection* and thermal energy.

The Yellowstone hotspot impinges on the base of the North American plate. And that fit with tectonic plates.

---

224 5/10/96.
225 See Ch. 36 – The Clog – The Vent – The Volcano, p. 157
226 See Ch. 47 – Cousin Andi a.k.a. Andesite, p. 206

How might Yellowstone connect with Titanic? Yellowstone symbolizes volcanic forces under the North American plate which covers both the United States and Canada. Titanic sank in the North Atlantic off the shores of Newfoundland, Canada.

The redheaded Peggymoonbeam of spinning disk lore whirled across my thoughts. "Don't forget, Penelope: the *antique chest* signifies something ancient – like me (ho-ho-ho) or maybe even a little older, like the volcanic forces that have affected Yellowstone over the past two million years."

I examined the *antique chest of drawers.* Drawers sliding in and out of a chest paralleled the horizontal movement of a strike-slip fault – an old one.

So a little dream about a *mantle* with all its appurtenances was quite instructive. What a merry and clever band of sprites were my fellow dream scouts.

CHAPTER FIFTY-TWO

A LITTLE NIGHT MUSIC

All truths are easy to understand once they are discovered;
the point is to discover them.

Galileo Galilei

It appeared that Mother Earth may have orchestrated a symphonia la sepulcher de natural, with Maestro Steno conducting the Terracrust Philharmonic. Given the assortment of puzzle pieces as clues, Yellowstone was in the bass section spewing out a volcano named Lavender.

In the string section, an unknown earthquake twanged and creaked under the watery refrain of a tsunami played by Mother Earth, the breast-feeding woman with the wavy lines. The elements of nature enfolded the festivity-bound Titanic in her merriment, as she steamed her way in carefree abandonment toward New York on her maiden crossing.

The calm seas on this cold and moonless starlit night swirled around the music while the orchestra played, according to some, "Nearer My God, To Thee." Deep inside the earth, the same song was resounding, but where, and in what order, was this formidable symphony written? Not a trace of geological documentation was to be found.

Blame shifted back and forth during the British inquiry and the U. S. Senate investigation in America. One group's heroes were another group's villains.[Ɛ66] During the investigations, damaging accusations and implications of a cover-up ran rampant, blame hurled at everyone including the captain, the shipbuilder, the managing director, the ship's architect ... the list goes on.

The unrecoverable combinations of events surrounding the most famous shipwreck in history do in fact suggest a grand cover-up, but not the sort that mere mortals execute. Could a massive cover-up engineered by Mother Earth herself explain why we have been in the dark for so long?

The accumulation of erupted dream fragments was hinting at significance beyond the story of the Titanic. But my mission had to stay its course on sea and on land, winding

---

Footnotes contain dream dates and references to prior pages where the dream appeared.
Endnotes contain bibliographical references, are marked with "Ɛ" in the text, and appear at the end of the book.

its way through the hazy unknown until the light would break through to reveal the bigger picture. I'd have to keep synthesizing. There was no other way to communicate this. I lacked the credentials. Tucked in the story's centerfold was a germ of chance that a submarine volcano triggered a tsunami deep on the ocean floor over which the Titanic blithely sped. The question hounding me night and day was, "What was the first link in the fiery chain and where did it occur?"

I flashed back to the dream of the *raging sea with all the boats trying to come in and the merriment of the people giddily laughing and toasting each other.*[227]

At that bewitching hour in the evening's bubbling revelry, no one seemed to care that there had been no lifeboat drill that day because of the strong winds.

Had the winds of change swept through my dream, *blowing feathers all over?*[228] I had a hunch Peggymoonbeam was behind the gale of drifting feathers and sure enough, there she was, holding a feather quill pen.

"Remember the Emerald Tablet, Penelope?"

"Yes. I received that dream from you the night of your funeral. It was amazing for I saw a *big emerald green square that looked like a tablet.*[229] The news of your passing was unbearable. Paralyzed with shock and alone with my shattered soul, all I could do between fits of sobbing and weeping was to call out to you in the desperate hope that you might hear me, "Where are you? Where are you?" But even through my darkest despair and knowing the tears would leave a permanent stain, there was something about this dream that I felt was a good sign."

"Well, I think you know by now that I am not gone," bubbled my blithe spirit.

"To this day, Peggymoonbeam – and forever and beyond – I'll remember how we sat in the darkened movie theatre after we saw E.T. We didn't speak for quite a while, then you took your skinny crooked pointer finger, just like E.T., and pointing to my chest, you said, 'I will always be there.' That moment is frozen in my memory."

Let me ask you, Peggymoonbeam. How did you get information about this tablet so soon after you died?"

"You won't believe this one, Penelope! It was the first miracle to come my way. What happened is that I saw a radiant green sparkling sea all around me as I was on my way back Home drifting and gliding through the most dazzling and richly colored vistas imaginable. I couldn't make out what it was at first; it looked like a mass of the most spectacular shade of green, like an emerald green, that I had ever seen and then ever so slowly it began to take the shape of a square.

227 8/26/93.
228 2/24/95.
229 5/19/95. See Ch. 8 – Peggymoonbeam, p. 44

"Marie Curie was one of the escorts who accompanied me on my transition from life on Earth to the astral plane. She took me under her wing as though I just naturally belonged there and has held me in her custody, ever since – a very good place to be, I might add. I soon learned that after we die, our soul carries a certain vibratory rate which depends on the spiritual progress we made while we were on Earth.

"Marie was quite impressed that I sent the Emerald Tablet to you because of her great interest in alchemy. She told me the green mass I saw was recorded in the Akashic Records. After she got me settled in to my new digs (ha ha), she showed me how to gain access to this universal memory bank which records all events and images that have ever taken place anywhere in the universe. Can you imagine such a thing? This gigantic body of knowledge absolutely overwhelmed me. In studying these records, I found I was able to review, in multidimensional detail, countless images of my recent life on Earth. One of the first writings to spark my memory and enter my field of vision was the Emerald Tablet. Marie pointed out that the Tablet inspired over thirty-five hundred years of alchemy at a time when some of the most creative minds in the world explored the mysteries of matter, energy, soul and spirit. She said it was important for you to understand, Penelope, that your dream images are manifestations of a great truth and order in the universe. She said that with this knowledge, you will begin to develop the vision which will enable you to see beyond the veil.

"So the time has come, my little buddy, to open the gate wider to the powerful formula embodied in the Emerald Tablet. The origin of this text is shrouded in antiquity and carries a prophetic message filled with hidden meaning. Even its name is a mystery. Written in legends that go back over thousands of years, it is thought to be the source of many mystical and religious traditions, in both the East and the West."

"This story is beyond awesome, Peggymoonbeam! It's unimaginable that you, my bestest friend on Earth, are on a first name basis with Marie Curie and even more so, that you are her emissary, but why isn't she here now?"

"Oh, not to worry, honey. She continues to be very busy in the hereafter and will be along to meet you as soon as she polishes up a certain project she's working on — something to do with gases.

"Now let me tell you about Thoth. The Emerald Tablet claims to be the work of Hermes Trismegistus, a legendary Egyptian sage and priest. He is often associated with the Egyptian god Thoth and the Greek god Hermes.

"Thoth, who kept a great library of scrolls, had been seen by the Egyptians as the great god of science and writing. 'It was said that he had inscribed his knowledge in secret books and hid these about the Earth, intending that they should be sought after by future generations but found "only by the worthy," who were to use their discoveries for the benefit of mankind.'[67]

"Now, here comes the best part. Thoth was immortal, incarnating three times by passing into the bodies of three men described in the tablets, His last incarnation was known as Hermes, the thrice-born. Because if his threefold identity, in the Latin translations of the tablet he is called 'Hermes Trismegistus' or 'Hermes the Thrice Greatest.'

"Concealed in his words are many meanings that don't appear on the surface, much like the messages in your dreams. As you are ever in search of truth, Penelope, know that in Egyptian mythology, Thoth is considered the final judge, who weighs individuals' 'true words,' the innermost intent in all of our thoughts and actions."

"Wow! He was a teacher of Truth?"

"Yes. Very much so. There have been countless translations of Thoth's writings by various scholars through the ages. The first line of text in Isaac Newton's translation of the Emerald Tablet is, 'Tis true without lying, certain and most true.'"

I was so enthralled with the mystery of the Emerald Tablet, Thoth, and the connection between Marie Curie and my best friend, I could barely contain myself. Peggymoonbeam handed me the feather quill pen she had been holding.

"Gosh, Peggymoonbeam, I think the feather symbolizes Truth too.

"Yes, Penny. Mu is the feather that represented 'Truth' to the ancient Egyptians. They chose the feather to symbolize Truth because it can be so easily blown away. In Egyptian mythology, the newly deceased soul had to be as light as a feather to pass the judgment of Ma'at, their goddess of truth, justice and the underworld."

"Come to think of it, Peggymoonbeam, sudden gusts of feathers have blown into my dreams; some are on the ground, some are bird feathers, others are stuck to me while still others are attached to articles of clothing. Loose feathers, one at a time, have turned up helter-skelter and in the oddest places, in dreaming and in waking. This makes me a little nervous because, if the feather really symbolizes the truth, it's pretty hard to be so truthful all of the time, unless you're an angel."

"You needn't worry your little head with that, Penelope, for your dreams only know the truth and the Dream is what Mission Lavender is exploring. Now, because this mission will take you to the far reaches of the Earth, I also bestow on you a Psymometer, which is a magnetic compass. I present this to you on behalf of your mentors at Starsight and Terracrust. Whenever you have to get from one place to another, check your compass and the magnetized needle will always point you in the right direction. This very special compass has a psychic needle that responds to influences in the magnetic fields of both the Earth and the Heavens. It will determine the frequency of wave oscillations and should you ever get lost when you're alone – say, if Steno gets called back to Terracrust – an instant correction will be made and you'll be pointed in the right direction. But I caution you, my friend; you must carry it at all times and you must trust it, for its readings are circuitous and could be confusing at first."

"Well, if I stumble upon something how will I even know that it's right? This is very hard because I have no idea what to look for or even where I'm going."

"Not to worry, Penelope. This psychic compass has paranormal detection capabilities that will do both. It will help you find what you need and it will keep you on course."

"Hmmm. Well, what are these paranormal detection capabilities? They sound pretty technical."

"You'll see, Penelope. They're not technical at all for it's basically about your intuition but to put it into words, let me start with telepathy which will direct your mind-to-mind communications, like we have with each other. Then comes clairvoyance and that will help you tap into information about events at remote locations, which you will have quite a lot of. Then there's precognition, which will lead you to information about future events, and finally, retrocognition will guide you to information about past events. This state-of-the-art cosmic Psymometer is able to gauge your enteric memory. That is, it can tap into your cellular memory by reading the sensory neurons in your intestinal tract. You will be experiencing these phenomena separately and at times, together. As you travel on you'll find you are not limited by the known boundaries of space or time. Also Penny, these phenomena blur the sharp distinction usually made between mind and matter, so you'll find your dreams and waking life fusing, but you'll always know which is which. It will be a natural blend of the two, which will work in perfect synchrony with your Timelessness Glasses."

"Gee, Peggymoonbeam, I never had a compass of my very own, much less such an intuitive one. You must remember the stories of how lost I got when I was a little girl."

"Yes. Of course I remember. And I see your lost and found excursions have carried over into adulthood. That made you a prime candidate for this work which you've gathered by now, is altogether circular. Just let your compass be your guide. Now, Missie Scrivener, read my lips and follow your instincts. Pick up from your last circle which started with *Abraham Lincoln* and ended with *Titanic*."

"OK. Here goes: *Abraham Lincoln* – *a Boat* – Titanic – the Truth – *a Grid of Lights* – (Ptolemy's Cluster) (Milky Way) – *Communication* (Coded Messages) – *Hieroglyphics* (Ancient Writing) – *Rosetta Stone* (the key to deciphering hieroglyphics) – *Oneiromantics* (the Language of Dreams), returning to *Abraham Lincoln* the symbol of Truth, the cornerstone of the Dream."

"Tu-whit Tu-whoo, Tu-whit Tu-whoo."

"Our scholarly owl is announcing himself in the distance. I must have said something to bring him round."

ÕÕ "'Let us learn to dream, gentlemen, and then we may perhaps find the truth,' eloquently spoken by Friedrich August Kekule (1829–1896), the German chemist, who discovered the structure of benzene in a dream."

"Boy, Peggymoonbeam. Tu-whit sure knows his stuff. We've come full circle – starting with the Dream and ending with Truth. Titanic is in there, but I don't see Newfoundland in any of the circles."

"Read my lips. Patience, my friend. We're about to set our sights on the shores of Newfoundland. My, we are raring to go, aren't we? Now don't forget your feather quill pen. You have a lot of writing ahead."

PART THREE

~

GATHERING STRANDS

CHAPTER FIFTY-THREE

GETTING AN ARM
AROUND NEWFOUNDLAND

One doesn't discover new lands without consenting
to lose sight of the shore for a very long time.
Andre Gide

My new compass was navigating a wildly circuitous path toward some unknowable summit. I wanted to trust it but, with shreds of clues floating on the seas of dreams, I couldn't imagine where we'd wind up. I should have been checking the position of the stars, but the movement of the heavenly bodies steering us toward our destination was far too changeable for celestial navigation. Dead reckoning didn't work either, for I was unable to calculate what direction Mission Lavender was heading, how fast it was going or how much time had passed. Like a ship traveling the high seas, this Mission left in its wake, waves of revelation. Each of my known locations invariably intersected others before it. So I dutifully followed my Psymometer, which directed me along a winding course of interlocking circles. I thought, "Sooner or later it's got to make some sense."

That amazingly smart compass was like an inner voice telling me which way to turn, directing me to research anything and everything I could get my hands on. I was obsessed with trying to understand this mumbo jumbo of dreams cloaked in what appeared to be teachings or messages or forewarnings that had some unknown destination. What I didn't know at the time was that the compass' undeniable logic was charting a course I would later follow to faraway places I'd never heard of and knowledge far beyond anything I had ever learned.

I considered again the mysterious change in my birthday by the anonymous dream courier,[230] not knowing what to make of it. "Why," I asked, "do I have two birthdays?"

Who was born on February the 18th that would connect with my life and with the story? And what was the story? What historic event might provide a link? There were

---

230 10/30/98. See Ch 35 – Lava Under Revelation, p. 150

Footnotes contain dream dates and references to prior pages where the dream appeared.
Endnotes contain bibliographical references, are marked with "Ɛ" in the text, and appear at the end of the book.

no ready answers. I was, by this time, in the habit of tracking clues to the end, following wherever they might lead, no matter the distance.

One such clue nestled in a dream centered on a Tudor-style castle. The reverse of an ethereal dream, it seemed so real I never forgot it. The enchanted castle lingered, much as the *yellow slab* did, while I followed this meandering path. Sometimes, a cloud of forgetfulness obscured the image, but the vivid outline of a hilltop castle was never eclipsed.

The Tudor castle dream, staged as a flight of fancy, would be the key to unlock the gates to a secret place: *Sitting on the ground, looking up at a Tudor castle perched high on a promontory, with the ocean below, I see three capes flying over the waters. They are flying spirits, like shooting stars, in midnight blue, shocking pink and golden yellow.*[231]

One day while combing the Internet for links to Tudor castles, I opened the Encyclopedia of Newfoundland and Labrador.[Ɛ1] I came upon Castle Hill National Historic Park, which I learned surrounds a fort built by the French in the 1670s at Placentia, Newfoundland. Placentia was probably named by the Basques, its name meaning a harbor within a womb of hills.

Womb – Placentia. A sound-alike for placenta. Womb – placenta. Placenta – birth.

Associations tugged at my memory. The birthday dream! When did it occur? Satchels of dream gifts were waiting to be opened. I had committed none of it to a database at that point; my hunch was that structure and boundary would be limiting. Consequently, I had only a few categories to call on – like dates and broadly defined subjects. There was no category called "birthday."

Desperately searching for the birthday dream, I rifled through journal after journal, adrenaline rushing, heart pulsing. I felt like Sherlock Holmes scenting the clue that would crack the case. It had taken four months to resurface.

I am having telephone conversations with a man who I'm about to have a date with, someone I have seen before. He tells me my birthday is on FEBRUARY 18 - THURSDAY. There is something he has to do that day. It involves his relatives, a family get-together. The February 18 message keeps appearing. I see an image of a black mesh screen in a black frame. There is an arm in front of me.[232]

February 18 – Thursday was a mystery. Why so specific a date? And why was it connected to a birthday?

When lo and behold! On that exact date – February 18 (in the year 1999) – the date of my dream-assigned birthday, I opened the Encyclopedia of Newfoundland and Labrador to that place called Placentia! And what a swell birthday it was, for the associations in

231 3/2/93.
232 10/30/98. See Ch. 35 – Lava Under Revelation, p. 150

dream speak had materialized: "birthday" symbolized placenta, translated to Placentia and ever so gently, directed me to the town of Placentia, Newfoundland.

The bonanza? It was, as promised, a Thursday. I wouldn't have to wait beyond that. A dazzling study in metaphor and synchronicity, it signified the birth date of this leg of the odyssey and was a homonym linking to birth. I was working my way down a sacred birth canal that would carry the unborn infant to unseen worlds. Just as a mother can't stop her labor, there would be no cessation until the baby was delivered. Dreams are mystifying. First, I am the baby, then the mother delivering the baby. I suppose we are all things in our dreams.

From this point on, I became convinced that Placentia was an important guidepost though I could go no further go just then.

Placentia, indeed, was just the beginning. What would follow would be the journey of a lifetime – and a very long pregnancy.

I returned to the dream.

The *black mesh screen* stayed true to its word: Things began to mesh, starting with the *Meat of the Matter* – THE VOLCANO – THE LAVA – Lava under the Earth signified by the *black frame* – framing the volcano. That was one answer. But, what was the *arm in front of me?* I decided to take an armchair tour of the town of Placentia and find out.

It could be a blind lead, but I honestly didn't think so.

I doubled back to the Tudor castle dream. The first promising connection occurred when I read that there were three Capes in the Placentia area and three capes in the dream: The cloaks in their three colors.

The capes near Placentia were Cape Chapeau Rouge, Cape St. Mary near Golden Bay and the Cape Shore area. Hmm. A shocking Pink cape – Chapeau Rouge; a golden Yellow cape – Golden Bay. The connection between Midnight blue and the Cape Shore was not as direct, but the color-coding seemed true to form.

Spirits like fireworks, shooting from right to left, could be a metaphor for the shooting stars reported to have been seen by some Titanic survivors the night it sank. Strange. I thought of the kinship of fireworks and spirit. Both are silently discharged, have a magnetic field and become invisible, their shadows trailing in the atmosphere. Could a display of shooting stars or meteors have illuminated the skies over Placentia and its surrounding capes the night of April 14, 1912?

At the mention of shooting stars, Ptolemy beamed in: "February 18 marks a big day in the skies, Penny. Jacques Cassini, the French astronomer who discovered the rings of Saturn, was born on February 18, 1677. About three centuries later – on February 18, 1930, Pluto, at that time considered the ninth planet of our solar system, was discovered and on February 18, 1977, the space shuttle "Enterprise" went on its maiden flight above the Mojave Desert. That places you alongside some very lofty company. I would say, astronomical."

"But, Twink, what does that have to do with Placentia and the night the Titanic went down?"

He fluttered an apology for the distraction, snapped his suspenders and with a lively "Cheerio, Penelope!" he scattered off.

As I tried to refocus the dream, I realized that he had planted an astral seed.

While looking for some sign of the arm the dream had placed in front of me, I found the Burin Peninsula, a leg-shaped projection off the southern coast of Newfoundland, bounded by Placentia Bay on the east and the Atlantic Ocean to the south. Was the dream presenting an alternate limb?

It was uncanny that Burin connected to a dream about my mother having a deformed leg that spread out at the foot. The Burin Peninsula is described as being shaped like a thigh, a knee, a calf and a foot. How odd that the dream depiction of her foot character-ized glaciers which are easily deformed and spread out at the foot of mountain ranges.

The dream squires lent us an arm and we got a foot, but that's how they work. They always gave more than was asked for. In any event, the icy world of glaciers and their calves was forming around the ill-fated journey of Titanic.

While I combed through the Encyclopedia of Newfoundland and Labrador, dream images indigenous to Newfoundland, gushed out like a water main break. This mélange of what appeared to be disparate fragments, etched its way into the cartography of my dreams, exposing blueberries, cranberries, galena, tungsten, mink, balsam fir and more. Most of this potpourri was not in my sphere of interest but it was a cornucopia more plentiful and varied than any conscious wish could bring. Did each element hold a special clue? Or — were they the basic stuff of the universe that just happened to collect in my dreams all connecting to the southeast tip of Newfoundland, the Avalon Peninsula where Cape Race is located. The Titanic sank 409 nautical miles off Cape Race.

When I learned that Swift Current is located at the head of Placentia Bay, surrounded by Bears Folly Mountains, I remembered the dream in which *the baby and baby-sitter are being sucked out the window; there are three large Panda bears outside the window.*

I wondered about the three Bears. Did Goldilocks figure in? Was there more to the clue than the Bears Folly Mountains? Great Bear Lake, named for the bears often seen on its shores, is located in Canada's Northwest Territories, on the Arctic Circle. Perhaps there was a connection but it was too early in the story to tell.

The *talk about the number of lives lost* in the *Panda bear* dream[233] captured my attention. It seemed there were more than just the baby and the babysitter.

---

233 8/12/93. See Ch. 23 — Tragedy, p. 99

Swift Current engulfed my thoughts in a flood of dream flashbacks. The rapids rapidly connected with many dreams of rushing waters and rapids carrying me, sometimes over waterfalls. Swift Current – rapid water. Was Swift Current more than a homonym? Was another piece of topography about to emerge?

Elevated stretches of land in the dreams certainly ran parallel to the description of the high hills in that part of the coast of Eastern Newfoundland. Was this a signpost like Placentia or was it directing us to a general location?

A dream of a *cylindrical tower with a white-planked door* mirrored the actual Cape Race Lighthouse where Titanic's distress signals were received and relayed to ships in the area. In sharper focus, endless dreams of currency that I had initially tied to money began to realign to the Labrador Current and to sea currents in the Atlantic Ocean.

Cape Chapeau Rouge called up the dream of a *French woman and another woman wearing a red hat.*[234] In French, red is rouge; hat is chapeau. Voila! Awake, it's Chapeau Rouge; asleep it's Red Hat!

The existence of Betts Cove, known for a mining operation in 1885, now an abandoned settlement near Cape St. John, explained the absurdity of a dream in which *my friend Betts, was serving desserts in a cave.* She does serve the most mouth-watering desserts – but not usually in caves. Or coves, for that matter.

Another dream referred to a money-*water island where I was writing one check after another*[235]and materialized as the isolated Brunette Island, situated at the mouth of Fortune Bay, fifteen miles north from Grand Banks, the area associated with the sinking of Titanic.

I had never been to or known of Fortune Bay. Ironic that its waters were near the resting place of Titanic's corpse.

Abraham Lincoln presided over a dream where *I'm aboard a passenger shuttle boat. I'd been on such a boat before, but I comment that it has changed. Now the seating is in the open and you sit on the edges. I can't find a safe place. I say if I lose my grasp, I'll go overboard. Finally, I find a chair and sit in an alcove. The boat goes through a canal into Portugal. There is a famous monument, like a museum. It has a massive staircase leading up to it and inside are beautiful fabrics and treasures from long ago.*[236]

Abraham Lincoln in another dream with a boat?[237] How strange.

I ramped up my research, which led to some fitting connections.

---

234 6/22/96.

235 12/19/96. See Ch. 34 – Labrador Current, p. 147

236 8/26/98.

237 1/25/98. See Ch 35 – Lava Under Revelation, p. 155

The dream memory of being *aboard a passenger shuttle* matched up with one of Newfoundland's earliest ferry services that crossed Tickle Bay on daily trips to *Portugal Cove*, nine miles from St. John's.

Cabot Tower was built in 1897 to commemorate the four hundredth anniversary of John Cabot's discovery of Newfoundland and Queen Victoria's Diamond Jubilee. In 1901, it stood witness to possibly the most important accomplishment in modern communications: the reception of the first wireless transatlantic signal by Guglielmo Marconi. The message was in Morse code, invented by Samuel Morse for wired transmissions some sixty years earlier. An online description of a wireless museum exhibit in Cabot Tower atop Signal Hill, overlooking the city of St. John's, invoked the dream image of *a famous monument, like a museum.*

Research into the legend of Titanic showed that the boat dreams with Lincoln were truer than true. Hapag's immigrant ship, the President Lincoln, was creeping through fog in the same waters two days prior to Titanic's collision with the iceberg. Several times, the President Lincoln's crew had to reverse its engines to avoid dangerous-looking ice.

All along the North Atlantic lanes, eastbound and westbound, vessels were encountering ice near 50° North Latitude. Some reported the danger by wireless. Wireless communication – Marconi – Cabot Tower. Suspended over the waking life story of Hapag's liner, the President Lincoln, hung the dream portrait of Abraham Lincoln and his enduring credo of Truth.

Anatomical parts: necks, arms, and legs had become dream speak for geographical attributes, pointing to the lay of the land. I got out the map.

The neck. Looks like that could be the Isthmus of Avalon, a narrow neck of land which cuts between two deep bays, Placentia and Trinity, in the middle of which is Tickle Bay. Meshing with the Tickle were dream fragments involving a *baby's neck being tickled,*[238] another reference to *tickle, a baby on a shelf and a long arm.* And within that dream a strange message advises, *"You'll only be sick for a day." Then I call a place called Tectonics and ask if they have shoes.*[239]

The arm. I reflected on the *arm in front of me in the birthday dream,* but there were too many arms on the map to differentiate one from another. The *ticklish baby* was growing up before my very eyes. It symbolized the work in progress as it scampered among the sheltered runs and arms, coves and bights of the irregularly shaped peninsula where Newfoundland and North America begin.

The leg. So far, I had come upon the Burin Peninsula represented by my *mother's deformed leg and* the Avalon Peninsula where Cape Race, the first wireless communication station, is located.

---

238 1/25/99.
239 2/28/99.

With Cape Race and Signal Hill pointing the way, the cloudy traces of the dream were steering me toward the Avalon Peninsula in Newfoundland. But why? Everyone already knew where the Titanic went down. Most people knew about Cape Race. Why was this area singled out?

Still, the focus ring tightened and X marked the spot in this remote and unsuspecting place.

I discovered that Peacock Copper was mined at Frenchman's Hill in Placentia from 1855 to 1860. This resurrected the copper dreams: The *penny in the eye*[240] and the *peacock feathers*.[241]

I continued mining these mysterious nuggets. Some days, a virtual treasure chest was waiting to be unlocked, although occasionally I would encounter a dead end. The fruitfulness of this period was rivaled only by the speed and abundance of the revelations. Seeds of consciousness sprouted a realization that this experience transcended conventional learning, as we know it. I was discovering that the real center of my conscious being was not that of my earthly existence – my ego self – but that of my higher self. I wondered just what this higher self was. I sensed it's the self that sees more of the whole picture of existence. But is it also that part of me that receives and deciphers the dream messages? Perhaps my dream guides and my higher self were one and the same. Whatever the case, I was surprised to find that putting both my selves together was a natural, almost orderly process. The pace was hastening, fevered by barrages of new symbols that showered me when least expected. The crescendo of discovery scaled new heights day by day, month after month, year in and year out.

Scientific matter completely foreign to my waking realm tiptoed nightly past the gates of sleep. I knew this journey must be shared, for the mystery of dreaming was for all of us to try to decode, to learn from and to heal.

The swarm of symbols, codes, hidden meanings and newly found data precluded any attempts at linear organization. It was chaos theory in high gear, ultimately organizing itself through ceaseless repetition and bangles of interconnecting circles.

The most seductive of the clues was that Placentia Bay fed into Atlantic waters not far from where Titanic met her unexpectedly tragic end. This validated my strong belief that there are no coincidences.

The soulful, far-off sound of a primitive horn echoed back from a long ago dream.[242] On waking, I thought it was the distant blast of a foghorn what with Newfoundland's infamous fog and wintry icebergs floating around in my thoughts.

I was certain of one thing: The Avalon Peninsula in Newfoundland was calling me. I was driven there by the many puzzle pieces that were connecting or, as the dream said, "*mesh*ing."

---

240 11/13/94. See Ch. 2 – Searching, pp. 20–21
241 8/28/97. See Ch. 19 – Galena and Beyond, p. 81
242 8/11/96.

CHAPTER FIFTY-FOUR

CHAOS IN THE COSMOS

Without the concept of time, there is only the
wholeness of nowness.
Stanley E. Sobottka

Yes, some fragments were connecting, but it was still so chaotic, this going forward and backward from one dream to another – from one observation to another – all in varied times and places. I couldn't make any sense of it except that somehow it all miraculously connected.

"Penelope, it is I, Lord Galen, who entrusted you with your Timelessness Glasses and the first Branch of Vision.[243] I realize that your dream sequences may seem confusing and out of sync when you recall them at different times and in different places. You are beginning to notice that the details constructed within your dreams become familiar to you when an experience in Wake Time calls on your memory to pull out a fragment of a dream.

"What you are in effect doing is seeking a link between your dream experience and your normal sense experience.

"Your actual experiences in Newfoundland and other stops along the way will be reemphasized when you succeed in remembering the part of the dream that connects to your Wake Time observations. Some of your dreams and thoughts will revert to an earlier time, while others will propel you forward. This is where the Past is re-enacted in the Present and occasionally opens the door to the Future.

"Penelope, although these events happen independently and out of succession, they seem present to you as one unified whole. This is where you find yourself in a new relationship to Time. What is happening is that your disconnected thoughts have decided to connect and become a new entity which consolidates all of the fragments in both Wake Time and Dream Time into one continuous whole. What you are seeing is not

---

243 See Ch. 41 – Vision: The First Branch, p. 181

Footnotes contain dream dates and references to prior pages where the dream appeared.
Endnotes contain bibliographical references, are marked with "Ɛ" in the text, and appear at the end of the book.

just a picture of past dreams but an interrelationship between waking and dreaming as a continuity of experience. By conceptualizing this first step in the transformation of your consciousness, you will come to understand the nature of higher levels of consciousness which lie beyond it.

"In your dreams, you have clear consciousness which aligns to the events you witness. These vivid dream images reveal themselves in absolute objectivity. But when you awaken, and reenter the earthly time zone, some of the objectivity fades. One of Mission Lavender's goals is to help you sustain that objectivity and understand the totality of time as we, your guides, see it. Our perception of time encompasses the whole of existence.

"You will learn that all dimensions of time, whether beings are in physical form or spirit form, exist equally, within and around them, as do all beings, planes of consciousness and other dimensions. Thus, everything exists in the same moment.

"The Present moment is the only one you can control and immediately experience. On Earth, you come to regard reality as being bound up with the series of present moments, but for Mission Lavender, each present moment is an amalgam of all times – Past, Present and Future. This explains why you often sense that if you are remembering the past, you are also remembering the future – because it is one undivided unit of time.

"When you are remembering a dream from five years ago and connecting it to something here and now, it is because the time in which that dream occurred has moved itself into the present to make that connection for you. You do so effortlessly because the totality of time is a natural system.

"However, to achieve an ordered system for earthly dwelling, man had to create the device of timekeeping. There must be calendars and clocks so that you may abide within an ordered timeframe. The problem is that higher thought processes have been blocked by the physical passage of time, making it difficult to think freely outside of the confines of prescribed earthbound time.

"The time scale in relation to the occurrence of events does not exist when you are in a dream state, which is a higher state of consciousness. Because of the influx of dreams you've received and your desire to connect them, timeless consciousness has expanded into your waking state. Your dream of *Percival, the cat who has something important to say,*[244] connects to the legend of Percival and the Holy Grail while the sacred Grail goblet further connects to your dream of a *begging cup vibrating out of a brick wall.*[245] Embedded in your higher consciousness are particles of this enduring quest, its **legend embodied in three ancient beliefs: a Celtic tradition of otherworldly vessels; an Arabic or Byzantine tradition of a mysterious stone that had fallen from the heavens and a Christian tradition of a mystifying talisman.** The Grail is a classic case of timelessness, Penelope, because it has become all things to all seekers since the late twelfth century. In your

---

244 5/28/96. See Ch. 4 – Charlesbigstar, p. 32
245 12/12/96 See Ch. 28 – Morse Code & The Upanishads, pp. 128–29

dreams, it begins with a state of mind, one in which the mystical exists in sharp and bright detail, while the ordinary gradually becomes charged with significance and meaning. You will find this meaning amplified as you journey on.

"While you are on your assignment with Mission Lavender, repeated experiences will confirm the disappearance of time, and it is in this void where connectivity and creativity take place, openly and freely. That is why I urge you during this connectivity process not to adhere to Time as an earthly dimension representing a succession of actions or events. It will only serve to confuse you and impede your progress."

"But, Lord Galen. What about events like the Titanic Timeline? How else can I prove the case?"

"I am addressing this to your connections between dreaming and waking. Naturally, you must follow an earthly timeline to prove an event that took place on Earth. For dreams that connect to the Titanic Timeline, you will have to be a Time juggler – jockeying between your unconscious and conscious thoughts – between Earth Time and Terracrust Time."

"But what about morning and evening and the seasons?"

"We're not saying biological rhythms and cycles such as night and day, darkness and light and winter and summer disappear. Biological organisms want to remain in harmony with the cycles of day and night and the seasons. I am speaking directly to the power of higher thought and the orderliness of the universe, which does not rely upon time measurements to become whole.

"Our concept of Timelessness is intended to teach you how to advance to higher levels of consciousness, facilitating our communications with you.

"We at Terracrust and Starsight and you on Earth are related to one another and functioning with each other in an ordered manner even though you may not be aware of it. It is critical that our direct concern with the life of humankind on Earth reaches you, for our activities and thought forms impact one another – us above and you below."

"So, Lord Galen, does this mean my Timelessness Glasses allow me to see infinity like you can?"

"Yes, my sweet. When you see glittering stars forming inter-looping figure eight's high in the heavens, that's the union of Terracrust and Starsight – our symbol for infinity.

"We have charted a course for you, Penelope, which will involve a more physical kind of trailblazing. You will recognize from your dreams many of the details and stops on our collaborative agenda. This experience will open your eyes to the oneness of time, the oneness of the Universe and the oneness of all individuals on Earth. We have selected a helpmate to accompany you on this journey. Her name is Karen. She is a person of like mind, like heart and like soul."

CHAPTER FIFTY-FIVE

THE NIGHT BEFORE

It happens that in the autumn of 1996, a wonderful new friend named Karen did quietly enter my life. It was a chance meeting at a mutual friend's home in California. One of the first things she had told me was how interested she was in my dreams having heard about them from our friend. Flattered by her attention, I silently laughed, knowing that everyone can have such dreams. Aside from our shared interest in dreaming a genuine trust and openness in the conversation stirred in me something I couldn't quite identify. Even though we lived on different coasts, we parted saying we'd continue our exchange.

Sylphlike in stature, Karen gives the impression of a soulful little waif but beneath her delicate appearance is a warrior who will fight to the death for what she believes in. Her luminous eyes have a depth I'd not seen before. One look into those soft blue pools of light and you feel you're falling into the great cosmic eye of the universe. Though every now and then one of her wings will show, she is very much of this world, having worked hard all her life, taking whatever jobs she could get, putting herself through school and earning a scholarship to Harvard. For a time, she graced the corporate world with her earthly talents, but essentially her soul is drawn to humanitarian causes.

Our religious, social, and educational backgrounds differed, but our lives' paths and unconscious yearnings ran parallel. And so our lives came together two years after our first meeting when Karen moved from California to New York in 1998. A natural synergy unfolded as we shared heart to heart, our vulnerabilities and nearly identical patterns reflected in life's hard lessons. The same hand of fate seemed to have ruled us in some way by charting our individual but shared destinies. In many ways, she was a much older soul that I, even though she was twenty years younger. Paradoxically, our age difference emphasized our likenesses. Our alliance seemed to stop time. It was ageless. Of course, neither of us could imagine then the transcendental consequence of these exchanges.

During the summer of 1999, I finally took a leap of faith and decided to share the intimacy of my dreams with a kindred soul, knowing she was the helpmate Lord Galen had dispatched. Even though I felt a deep connection to my special new friend, I still felt a little modest about sharing my most private thoughts which even I had barely acknowledged. It was like disrobing in public, walking her through the vast corridors

---

Footnotes contain dream dates and references to prior pages where the dream appeared.

Endnotes contain bibliographical references, are marked with "Ɛ" in the text, and appear at the end of the book.

of my dreams and the waking research they had been pairing with to emerge finally as "Mission Lavender."

My modesty quickly dissipated, for Karen knew just how I felt and I found myself with a willing and enlightened companion to share the long-awaited expedition that had been set for us. What I could not fully grasp at the time was the wisdom of Lord Galen's selection of Karen as a helpmate. I would see the truth in his words before journey's end.

It was only a year after Karen moved to New York that we put together the itinerary for an excursion to Newfoundland. The entire night before we were to leave, I lay awake with anticipation. It was a place I had only seen in my dreams. We were to board an early morning plane that September 2, destined for an adventure that would be bound in the diaries of our lives. Thousands of thoughts were parading through my mind. After so many years of study, searching for unity in a tangled web of clues, I wondered what we would find. There was so much uncertainty. Where would this trip lead? My inferences about the true cause for the sinking of the Titanic might be valid, but was there more to it than that? Was there a tectonic component attached to the disaster's puzzle the experts may not be aware of? Was there a time line? How would it be to travel with Karen, still so new a friend and confidante? The familiarity of what seemed a very old friendship assuaged my fears. Would the lay of the land tell me anything? Would the touch and feel of it allow me to come away with something conclusive? The unexplored is rife with suspense and excitement, but these were only dreams – nighttime imaginings – weren't they? Then again, I reminded myself, my dreaming had not failed me yet. Why should it now?

The practical considerations of mundane life painted another picture. My money was running low, my attempts at scientific inquiry were often frustrated, my desire to publish was impeded by a constantly unraveling skein tangled with loose threads leading to what might – or might not – be the next phase. How could I know where and when to stop? To my friends and family, my daily life was that of a recluse. At times, even I questioned it as I ran through my savings, chasing my dreams in a far-off land I'd never seen except in the nighttime adventures of my unconscious.

All this was fueled by the fever of passion and inspiration, curiosity and daring, but the driving force behind the imponderable urging was that little feeling – that whisper that gurgles up from the "gut"– as we ask ourselves the silent questions. It was a completely intuitive, invisible vision that I knew would in some way become material. My heart and soul, my mind and will, were telling me I was standing on one edge of a very deep canyon, unable to even remotely imagine what might be on the other side.

What would I do when I got to the northern lights that were calling? Would I climb a mountain, look out to sea and get some vibration that would somehow magically tie it all together?

Surely, Lord Galen's assignment had taken hold. Work priorities had forced Karen to cancel her long-standing summer vacation plans and, in early August, she had asked, "Do you want to go to Newfoundland?"

At that time, my studies had taken a compelling turn requiring deeper inspection, but I knew my answer had to be yes. On the eve of departure, pre-expedition jitters ran amok.

CHAPTER FIFTY-SIX

BON VOYAGE

Karen met me at Newark airport at 6:30 the morning of September 2, 1999, and our journey to St. John's and unforeseeable enchantment began.

Needless to say, our departure was not without signs. We had to change planes in Toronto; a few nights before the trip I had dreamt *that Karen and I get separated in the airport. There are some padded bells I have to ring to page her. A footnoted message contains a mysterious command: Report to Kit 4391 or 4931.*[246]

I awakened with apprehension about the connecting flight, but chalked it up to pre-trip anxiety. Then sure enough, as we were walking through the Toronto airport, Karen realized she had left her computer on the first plane. We immediately checked with Lost and Found, where the attendant assured her it would be delivered promptly to the out-bound flight to St. John's. We proceeded to our next gate, feeling confident all would be handled efficiently. Wrong!

They wouldn't let her through security because her airplane ticket was in the computer bag. So there we were separated. Back in the dream. The security office became our center and there ensued a marathon series of sprints, Karen, desperately searching for anyone who'd listen, running back and forth from the security office to the terminal, while I ran between security and the gate, each of us trying to be heard. Boarding began. I nervously waited at the gate, begging to have her paged, but the person taking the boarding passes simply would not hear me. No one seemed to understand the story.

We almost missed the plane, but finally, Karen, her computer and her ticket, made it to the gate. We boarded with about two minutes to spare, garrulously sharing our similar experiences of having no one listening to either of us.

---

246 8/26/99.

Footnotes contain dream dates and references to prior pages where the dream appeared.
Endnotes contain bibliographical references, are marked with "Ɛ" in the text, and appear at the end of the book.

I shared the dream with Karen who commented that the *padded bells* were symbolic of not being heard.

Would this event set the tone for the rest of the trip? We didn't know, but it was clear that a portion of the dream had materialized, save the inexplicable *"report to Kit 4391 or 4931."*

CHAPTER FIFTY-SEVEN

ST. JOHN'S

Day One: St. John's - Cabot Tower

We landed at St. John's airport in the late afternoon. The first Newfoundlander to cross our path was a car rental agent who welcomed us like a long lost relative we hadn't seen for years. On entering the town of St. John's, we were surprised to find a trendy city with a lot of soul. One of the first signs we saw, painted on a wall, was "Zen and Multiple Sclerosis," advertising a fund-raiser for the disease. Having escaped the tension and turmoil in the airport, we arrived at the Battery Hotel just in time to see the sunset from its spectacular view overlooking St. John's harbor. The hotel, built on the slope of Signal Hill, is within walking distance to its summit and Cabot Tower, the first stop on my dream itinerary. That evening we dined on salt cod in the hotel's softly lit dining room, then climbed the hill to the historic site of harbor defenses from the eighteenth century through World War II.

Out of the Dream and into waking reality, we entered the tower, where Guglielmo Marconi received the first trans-Atlantic wireless message almost ninety-eight years earlier. Cabot Tower was one small, but fundamental, chip fitting the Titanic mosaic. Marconi – wireless telegraphy – Morse code. This first connection between waking and dreaming on our Newfoundland itinerary was inscribed in my journal entry containing the Morse: - - --- - - --- - -, translating to MOMOM[247] and decoded by the dream scanner as Mother Earth.

Features of Cabot Tower as an historic site were dramatically mirrored in my dream in image after image. The dream image of *a famous monument, like a museum* was a clear depiction of the actual museum we visited in Cabot Tower.[248]

A spiral staircase inside the tower for those who wished to climb to its top matched the dream image of the *massive staircase leading up to the monument.*

---

247 1/20/94. See Ch. 28 – Morse Code & The Upanishads, p. 128

248 8/26/98. See Ch 53 – Getting An Arm Around Newfoundland, p. 248

Footnotes contain dream dates and references to prior pages where the dream appeared.

Endnotes contain bibliographical references, are marked with "Ɛ" in the text, and appear at the end of the book.

The historic articles and printed material on display brought to life other pieces of the dream. Cabot's experience trading in valuable goods from Asia – spices, silks, precious stones and metals – reflected the dream image of *beautiful fabrics and treasures from long ago*. Cabot wanted to be part of an expanding frontier of exploration: the Atlantic Ocean. The leaders in this enterprise were the Portuguese; the Spanish were also interested. So this piece of history also connected to *Portugal*.

The most significant of all connections was Marconi's wireless telegraphy, which returned me to my dream with the coded dashes over which I'd written a word I'd never heard of – *Upanishad*, which I discovered meant inner or mystic teaching. As I traveled on with the Dream as my Guru, it was showing me each step of the way that the theme in the Upanishads is the search for an underlying unity linking everything we see and think.

After being woven, rewoven, connected, cross-connected, and interconnected, the myriad threads attaching to Titanic were beginning to tighten, weaving themselves into a gigantic dream-coded puzzle sighting a natural disaster far greater than a collision with an iceberg.

Day Two: St. John's - Titanic Exhibit

The next morning, we visited the Titanic Exhibit in St. John's. There, for the first time, I saw the Passenger Manifest. My eye immediately went to the name Helen Loraine Allison, listed among the dead on the ghostly roster along with her parents. They were from Montreal, PQ/Chesterville, Ontario. As I stood before the list of those who perished, an undulating roll call of remembered dreams rushed through me, echoing the catastrophic ripples of mass burial at sea.

My memory flashed back to a selection of Allison dreams. *There are huge ocean waves in the background and I'm asking an operator named Allison where my husband is. I'm told "she checked out." I insist, "No! It's he," and she insists more adamantly, "No! She checked out!"*[249]

I had seen the name Allison in print in many publications, but seeing it on Titanic's Passenger Manifest was a far more sobering reality.

Then I saw the oversized Cargo Manifest exhibited on a wall. I could barely contain myself reading through the record as the higgledy-piggledy pieces of a billboard-sized dream puzzle, for so long an enigma, began to register. It was no longer the gossamer wrappings of dreams, but a concrete listing. Rubber, melons, sticks, butter, feathers, sero were among the commodities, too numerous to mention, that were in the cargo hold of the Titanic, matching – and perhaps identifying – some of the mysterious and repetitive mumbo jumbo in my dreams.

---

249 2/10/95. See Ch 23 –Tragedy, p. 100

SERO? I'd seen that word buried in a dream! Now it's buried in Titanic's Cargo Manifest! I flashed back to the dream and sure enough, it linked to shipping:

The dream opens with *my desire to sell lights at CBS. People are marching, carrying placards that read "whole." I explain that it means "earth." Then I learn that I have been assigned to the "shipping department." I think, "What a dull, unimaginative job." Sero — a mysterious word — presents itself.* [250]

When I dreamt the word "sero," it threw me for a loop for I'd never before seen this word. Now, it appears on the cargo manifest: "1 case sero fittings" followed by a parenthetical notation: Syringes?

My gut reaction to the word "sero" had been a memory of Eero Saarinen, the designer of an impressive graphic collage that dominated the cafeteria at CBS when I worked there.

The Eero - Sero wordplay must have been fun for the dream masters. They knew that "sero" would mean something to me because of my work experience.

The CBS Eye was a symbol in the Saarinen collage so Sero represented vision and meshed with my subliminal memory of that ubiquitous Eye. Collecting my wits, it now became clear that the word *"sero"* on the Titanic Cargo Manifest linked to the dream reference of shipping and tied a knot to the Titanic.

The frequency with which the all-seeing eye was appearing and reappearing blinked its desire to be seen and understood — waking or sleeping. Vision, the invisible sense of knowing, would never relinquish its command. It was the beacon that illuminated my desire *to sell lights at CBS*. A word as odd as *"sero"* would stick and somehow drape that particular dream in the banner of Titanic.

So *"sero"* connected with both vision and Titanic. *"Sero"* was also interesting spelled backwards: "ores." Hmm. That connected to the penny in the eye. Copper was an ore. Hmm ….Copper and vision.

While tapping into the language and learning to crack its codes, I was having more fun than I'd ever had for I had discovered the crossword puzzle of eternity. Tuning to the knack of its idiosyncrasies was not as ambitious as I once thought. I realized that I didn't have to discard anything; inevitably everything would fit. There was very little waste, if any. What perfection!

I marveled at the accuracy of the dream tellers. Unfailing precision threaded through an interconnecting odyssey offset its whimsy. This custom-built dream machine cranking out its trinkets bit by bit would ultimately craft the whole fabric of a multidimensional story.

Now and again, I'd ask myself if these parcels of dream flotsam might be relating to something I hadn't even thought of. "But why would they be in my dream?"

250 11/9/96. See Ch. 7 – Branching Out, p. 41

Karen and I left the exhibit and began our tour of the Avalon Peninsula heading for Trepassey, named by The Guinness Book of World Records, the foggiest place on Earth. Amelia Earhart took off from there on her first transatlantic flight, in 1928.

We spent the night there and while poring over the map, Karen spotted Mutton Bay right off Trepassey. "Hmm," she murmured. "Isn't mutton a type of meat? Wasn't meat one of your clues?" Karen's eye for detail was amazing! She forgot nothing. The *dog walker dream* featured *two big chunks of meat — beef and veal.*[251]

I wondered: were we approaching "the meat of the matter" this early in the trip?

---

251 11/30/98.

CHAPTER FIFTY-EIGHT

CAPE RACE AND THE OPTIC CHIASM

Day Three: Cape Race, Branch, St. Brides, Placentia

The next day we were bound for Cape Race, a barren point of land jutting out into the Atlantic Ocean. We ate a hearty breakfast in Trepassey, while our Irish innkeeper, in her infectiously warm brogue, cautioned us not to go unless we really had to. She described a long, hilly dirt-and-stone road warning that we were risking a flat tire. Not only that, when we reached the site of the 107-foot-tall lighthouse, we would have to climb eighty steps to arrive at its summit. We were not dissuaded. The Cape Race lighthouse stop was paramount as it was there that the first distress signals were received directly from the stricken Titanic.

Obsessed with reaching the famous lighthouse, we began our fifteen-mile trek to Cape Race. We drove about five miles before turning onto the gravel road, no wider than a single car. Our innkeeper knew her terrain. We scaled our way upward, avoiding potholes at ten miles an hour. Slate cliffs rose nearly vertically to one hundred feet above sea level on either side. The ancient rock formations looked millions of years old.

We observed what appeared to be gray and green sandstone. Groupings of these slabs, one more majestic than the next were arranged as gargantuan decks of cards and fanned out as though they were part of a hand. Like learned scholars, these ancient geological formations seemed to be watching us in their stony presence. These monolithic marvels of nature hugging each side of the road separated us from the sea, but when the Atlantic Ocean emerged as a backdrop, it was an unforgettable sight.

The sensation was transcendental as our rental car crept its way up the uninhabited road. As we neared what we hoped was the apex, the cratered terrain looked more like the moon than a gravel road in Newfoundland. The air and temperature seemed to change as quiet turned to utter stillness. There were stretches of incline where we honestly felt we were ascending to the great beyond with blue-gray skies the only clue to what awaited us on the other side. After bumping our way up toward the lighthouse for over an hour, and feeling a jet-like boost in altitude, we began to stress about the chances of a flat tire in the middle of

---

Footnotes contain dream dates and references to prior pages where the dream appeared.

Endnotes contain bibliographical references, are marked with "Ɛ" in the text, and appear at the end of the book.

nowhere. Since neither of us knew how to change a tire, and considering all the other stops on the itinerary, we decided, though in vague sight of the lighthouse, to turn back.

Before risking a turnaround on the unpaved incline leading up to the lighthouse, we sat in the car for a few moments, reverentially sensing the place that had left its mark in the annals of human drama that haunting night in 1912 when Titanic met her bitter end. In the distance, I could see the white, cylindrical tower, over a hundred feet high, with its red lantern and imagined its white flashing light illuminating the waters every few seconds, an eerie reminder of the dream that had guided us toward the Cape Race lighthouse in the first place and one of the first to merge Vision with the Titanic.

Gazing skyward, I spotted the Oneiroball floating gently overhead. There was a feeling of descending cooler air as it made its way over the craggy coastline toward the tower. It simply came to a stop and remained suspended there until it released the dream. It then lifted noiselessly into the sky. The missive landed only a few feet away from the car:

A presence had repeatedly opened and closed a white planked door. An otherworldly feeling was present. There was a tall white cylindrical lighthouse with a window pane divided in four. The word Optic Chiasm was superimposed over the tower.[252]The white cylindrical dream tower fit a description in the Encyclopedia of Newfoundland and Labrador which I found before we traveled here:

> Cape Race Lighthouse was one of the finest in the world when it was built in 1856. The cylindrical tower of reinforced concrete, painted white, rises eighty-four steps, to the lantern chamber. Here the giant hyper-radical lens of pressed cut glass consisting of built-up reflecting prisms and projecting lenses – the largest of its kind ever built. The diameter of each of the four optical faces is over eight feet.

The detailing of four optical faces startled me! My amateur dream rendering perfectly depicted a window containing a glass divided in four. It was the image of a reticle, a grid in the viewer of an optical instrument used to determine the scale or position of what is being observed.

Now, here we were actually gazing at the legendary lighthouse.

The encyclopedia description matched the dream and the dream matched the physical lighthouse. It was a circle: Dreaming led to waking and waking reverted to dreaming, with vision ever present.

---

252 11/18/97.

While reflecting on the dream and its creaking door, we were suddenly greeted with "Welcome to my tower, fair damsels, and thank you for honoring this dream." I wasn't sure that Karen heard the master of vision, but he continued, "You are on the right track, and I am here to remind you of the meaning of the optic chiasm ..."

Galen was especially talkative this day. "You know I have had the utmost respect for women and their remedies for many moons, so it does my heart good to see how involved you've become in this work. One of my colleagues in the second century was a woman doctor named Antiochis. Her techniques were so outstanding that I actually copied her prescriptions for plasters.

"To get to the point of the dream I sent, I wish to remind you of my theory that stated the optic nerves, on their course to the brain, are crossed at the chiasma, which is derived from the Greek letter chi, written like an X.

> "For after they have met inside the cranium and their channels have united, they at once draw apart again, showing clearly that there was no other reason for them to approach one another save the joining of their channels."

"That should help to explain why, in the dream, the words Optic Chiasm were superimposed over the tower. We felt this would underscore our message from Starsight and Terracrust that the first criterion is vision."

Having drifted into the optics of the dream message, we found that even though we had traveled back in time to Galen's second century, we were still sitting in the car in the twentieth century and it was time to continue our pilgrimage.

Turning around on this narrow road with sheer drops on either side of the sea was horrifying. What would happen if our judgment was off by a hair? Would we be plummeted into the Atlantic Ocean, never to be seen or heard from again? It was a spine-chilling maneuver, but Lady Providence had seen fit to give us a clear day.

Although we never reached the lighthouse, we felt fortunate to have gotten close enough to see and experience at least a sliver of that moment in time. The solitude of the surroundings juxtaposed with the now famous calls for help on behalf of the drowning victims, silently spoke to the reality of human frailty when confronted by the forces of nature.

We stopped for lunch at the only restaurant for miles around, ironically called the New Venture. Reviewing our itinerary as we ate, my ever-curious and diligent companion said, "Penelope. So, what are we supposed to be looking for now?" That was a tough question for I had volumes of notes and clues, but no idea where, if at all, any of them might turn up.

"Oh, I don't know, Karen. It's anyone's guess, but I can tell you that lavender and yellow are all over my dreams, so I guess we should keep our eyes peeled for those colors. I know it sounds really crazy, but I'm just following my gut."

Having saved a good part of a day by shortening our visit to Cape Race, we would head toward Branch on the Avalon Peninsula. The anticipation was more than I could bear.

CHAPTER FIFTY-NINE

BRANCHES

A rock pile ceases to be a rock pile the moment a single man
contemplates it, hearing within him the image of a cathedral.
                                        Antoine de Saint-Exupery

While doing research before the trip, I had stumbled across a Web site on the Cultural History of the Cape Shore area that drew me even deeper into the vortex that had now become a reality. A computer-animated scene opened with a rolling ocean lapping against the shore over which members of a seagull clan soared gracefully. The plaintive calls of the gulls over the ebb and flow of the ocean instantly transported me from my apartment in New York City to the rocky cliffs of Newfoundland. I was transfixed by the raw beauty of nature's wonders unfolding before my eyes right there on my computer screen. Having spent years sorting through a bramble of dreams pointing to Newfoundland, I now found this staring at me from the Web site:

"Branch is a community of approximately five hundred people located on the Southwest side of St. Mary's Bay. It is about 90 km from St. John's and 72 km from Placentia. The nearest community is Point Lance, 16 km away."

"Branch!" I screeched, in the silence of my apartment. "I remembered the bizarre dream about *branches coming out of my head!*"

Dream images of branches had been knocking on my door for years. At first glance, I had interpreted this as a symbol of growth, as a sprouting limb on a tree; then Peggymoonbeam made her wish about the branches of science and now it's turned out to be a real physical place!

While skimming the description of Branch suddenly leaping off the page, I saw the boldfaced words: "… **gut which flows into the waters of St. Mary's Bay. The hills to the east form what is called the East Cove and the cliffs to the west form the Wester Cove.**

"How odd," I thought, "that these are the only bolded words." But then, the unexpected had become the norm. Every hidden nuance, every sudden turn was an epiphany and still is to this day.

Footnotes contain dream dates and references to prior pages where the dream appeared.

Endnotes contain bibliographical references, are marked with "Ɛ" in the text, and appear at the end of the book.

Branch tied to the profound connection on my real birthday in 1999 when I awakened at 7:00 a.m. and transcribed the message about *enteric memory*. As you may recall, dear Reader,[253] not knowing what enteric meant, I looked it up and guess what? There's a real enteric nervous system which controls the gastrointestinal system! How magical that my gut feeling somehow took me to Gut, an arm of the sea.

So gut and branch were conjoined, and now it was time to set foot in Branch. Would there be a gut feeling associated with this small fishing village nestled between two forest-clad hills?

We curved around the coastline of high rugged cliffs, suppressing the thrill of what we might find under the next rock. We were entranced by the contrast of the jagged scenery to the flatness of Cape Race. Completing a slow descent to the peaceful fishing community settled more than two centuries ago, Karen drove our Blazer up to the water's edge. She parked in front of a craggy jetty formed of stones much like those we had seen in Cape Race, but these were different.

These stones had a lavender hue.

She got out of the car and immediately went to a painted yellow line that marked a parking zone. But a yellow line of demarcation appeared to be exactly that – nothing more – and so we continued to mosey about the small haven.

Suddenly, I saw a rock with lavender paint on it. Then another. And another.

It looked as though someone had painted these rocks – not just spilled paint on them. We were completely startled. Next came the Aha! – the clarity – that intuitive piercing insight that says you're in the right place.

"Owww!" we squealed, "It's too obvious! I can't believe it! I can't believe it!"

I then spotted a rock with "yellow paint," a different shade of yellow than the parking line.

"Look Karen! This one has yellow paint. What is happening?"

We drove all around the little village of Branch searching for any other traces of yellow or lavender paint. We stopped at every neighboring structure we could find: houses, fishing boats, a lumberyard.

Not a trace.

We canvassed the entire village again and found a squared off log that was painted yellow, but not a drop of lavender.

We asked a Branch local if he knew how the paint got there. That got him talking up a blue streak. I suppose we looked like two friendly girls on vacation just taking in the sights. Eager to share the village scuttlebutt, when we asked about the paint, he

---

253 See Ch. 3 –The Pole, pp. 25–27

simply shrugged his shoulders and prattled on with the longest shaggy-dog story we'd ever heard.

As we were leaving, for some reason I felt we should go back to the lavender-painted rocks.

The unexplainable sight of the painted rocks had overwhelmed us.

Were we imagining things? We took rolls of film to prove to ourselves, I suppose, some rational concrete assurance of this baffling reality and our sanity. Seeing is believing, so they say.

The two colors that had played and replayed through dozens of dreams – lavender and yellow – seemed to be smiling back at us.

"No one would believe this," we shouted.

"I've got goose bumps!"

"Me too, me too," exclaimed Karen. "This is beyond!" And so it was.

As physical and nonphysical fused before our eyes, we experienced a sense of blissful interconnectedness impossible to describe.

We sat quietly by the seaside speculating on what appeared to be so obvious a manifestation, it was hard to accept. As we were about to drive away from the peaceful little fishing cove holding these most visible yet mysterious clues, we glanced back one last time and Karen noticed an LL painted in yellow on one rock and what appeared to be a J on another rock. We couldn't think clearly enough to identify the LL. It was not until later in our journey that the meaning of these letters would reveal itself.

We ruminated on our findings as we drove. Lavender paint on a rock! Not an ounce of lavender anywhere else in the entire town and no explanation as to how it got there!

Did the Celestial Congress send their best ambassadors to guide us to LAVA UNDER? I rewound the dream tape to the headlines of a *black mesh screen in a black frame.* I joined that to – *a lavender suede bellows that lost its frame* – to *two big chunks of meat.*[254] It meshed. But what about the *frame?*

The frame for the story was LAVA UNDER – Lava under the Earth. The *bellows* was feeding the fire of an ancient volcano that had collapsed – *lost its frame.* Once deciphered, this puzzling string of codes led to the "meat of the matter."

Why so many dreams – so many details? Was this meant to be a prototype of something not yet known?

---

254 11/30/98. See Ch. 35– Lava Under Revelation, pp. 150, 155

Dr. Steno and Peggymoonbeam appeared gliding above us, their presence so strong, I half expected them to perform a parachute jump. Was lava under the rocks in Branch – or – were they pointing to the lavender-tinted stones we had just seen?

Either way, it was more than our tellurian minds could grasp.

Ping … ping … ping.

Dr. Steno was speaking into his Ping Pilot. At the tone of the "ping," I received his transmission. "Those ancient rock formations you saw at Cape Race are late Precambrian and a geologist's dream! Lavender tinted Precambrian sediments are often found in a tectonic environment called the Avalon Zone."

Sometime later, I realized that Branch, known also for fossil-bearing shale found in the cliffs in colorful reds and greens, might be connecting to the *red and mostly green leaf belt* I had seen in another dream.

The belt, described as narrow, has red and green leaves that are interconnecting. My Aunt Belle is sewing loose hairs inside of something.[255] It occurred to me that leaves may be an underlying pattern waiting to be uncovered. But how much could a rookie absorb at once?

Could this be signifying a block-faulted belt possibly running through Branch? Early research indicated that such a belt had a lot of faulting and occurs between pairs of mountain chains. What were the loose hairs? Were we being returned to DNA? Did strands of hair or bodily traces of Titanic's victims somehow wash into Branch and become imbedded in these rocks? Red and green shales are also found in the Placentia Bay area.

Steno pinged in. "The narrow belt in your dream was pointing you to the oldest rocks in the Avalon Zone. They constitute a narrow belt of ophiolites, pieces of oceanic plate in a fault block near Burin, one of the spots on your itinerary."

So much to take in, but I was now sure that Branch was synonymous with gut. Right there in broad daylight, Branch revealed materializations so staggering, they defied description.

Lavender – and yellow – near a block-faulted zone was blatantly tangible, strikingly physical, and – to add to the growing synchronicities – there were the curiously hand painted initials LL and J. Karen's find would later affirm that we were in the right place.

We departed with one final impression: The gut. We were to trust it, be it a "feeling" or "an arm of the sea" or both.

It was enough to make you cry, and cry I did – with wonder – at the enchantment of it all.

---

255 2/13/96.

CHAPTER SIXTY

ST. BRIDES DESIGNER COUTURE

Our small, but merry, band of investigators, fueled by the findings in Branch, was in ardent pursuit of the myriad fibers knitting together this mysterious body of dreams. We were guided, almost arm in arm, by our invisible beings on the continuing journey through southwestern Avalon,

We came to St. Brides, a farming and fishing community settled in 1800 and originally named La Stress Cove by the French. The English converted the area's name to Distress before, later, changing it, altogether, to St. Brides.

I was pondering the irony of the name La Stress given the geologic history of the Avalon Zone when I sensed a motion above us. It was Nicolaus Steno toting his steno pad and his handy spyglass.

"Good day, lovely Gentlewomen. I just happened to pass by the former La Stress Cove and overheard your thoughts on the unique history of its names. I should like you to know that geophysical stress is applied force per unit area resulting in the deformation of rocks. You are in a volcanic area of great interest to Terracrust."

"Good heavens!" I thought. "Does he really expect us to understand this? It sounds like Greek, oops, I mean Danish, to me."

"To me too," added Karen.

I was surprised at Karen's response. She must have been listening all along. While trying to digest the idea of geophysical stress, I noticed the alternating green and brown rolling hills of St. Brides and that sparked memory of the dream of the *bride getting married in a green and brown wedding dress.*[256]

Waking from that dream I had thought, "What bizarre colors for a wedding gown!" Eventually I was pulled away from thoughts of mortal marriage back to detailed descriptions of clothing that, woven into this nighttime dream quilt, were so repetitious in their portrayal of Mother Earth, they became impossible to miss.

---

256 9/18/98.

Footnotes contain dream dates and references to prior pages where the dream appeared.
Endnotes contain bibliographical references, are marked with "Ɛ" in the text, and appear at the end of the book.

I reflected. Was this a "marriage" of geology and spirit? I was beginning to suspect that clothing might be a metaphorical hook from which to suspend the fruits of the Earth.

Clothing! Clothing was the hook from which dangled the word "Couture!" Suddenly, I was viewing an exotic fashion show where a bevy of couture dreams paraded down memory's runway. The most mysterious dream design in the collection was one that had followed me for years. *Mother says, "Couture Radio."*[257] Other couture dream threads[258] led me to believe I was being radioed, but why couture? The French origin of the word equates couture with needlework or seaming. That would fit, since this was certainly the seaming together of a rather large design.

Hmm. Couture Radio! I smelled the scent of connection! I toggled back to the *Avers-Avens* dream riddle – to Old Man's Whiskers[259] – to Galena – to the thin wire called cat's whisker and how it makes radio communication possible[260]– to the X-ray pad with windows marked TV/ Radio[261] – to wondering if the optical light attached to a telephone had served a radio function[262] – and now Couture Radio.

Another dream centered on a *couture shop and designer creations. I tell a story about hemorrhoids.*[263] Why hemorrhoids when talking about designer clothing? This one was a doozy! Hemorrhoids are swollen veins in the lower portion of the rectum and can be external or internal. Wow! That would decode to "under the Earth's rectum." A mass of dilated veins in swollen tissues in the Earth and pressure in the bowels of the Earth could definitely cause hemorrhoids. It is astonishing to reflect on the physiological mirroring of Mother Earth and humankind. And yes. Designer creations were creations fashioned by the Grand Designer.

"Good tracking, Penelope," giggled Peggymoonbeam.

"I now confess that your Dr. Steno is a geologist-couturier in afterlife. We call him a geo-couturologist in this realm. Our fashion designs are created at Terracrust. I'm the head costumier and he is the head geologist. Together we make beautiful fashions – our design label is 'TerreHaute.' Ya get it? Terre for Earth – Haute connecting with couture – Clothes of the Earth."

This last exposition took my breath away, for Terre Haute, Indiana was where Peggymoonbeam and I had bonded during her time on Earth. We dined out for years on funny stories told around our corporate antics at that recording plant in Terre Haute.

---

257 2/10/00.
258 Couture dreams: 2000–2005.
259 6/14/01. See Ch 10 – The Stuff of Life, p. 53
260 8/28/97. See Ch 19 – Galena and Beyond, p. 81
261 8/21/93. See Ch 27 – Witness, p. 125
262 5/15/97. See Ch 50 – The Slip, p. 226
263 1/3/99.

"I'm mortified, Peggymoonbeam. I was terribly confused in this St. Brides dream *because I know my wedding gown is white but I keep insisting it is greenish brown. Then someone's father passes through and seems annoyed that I didn't realize it was the same dress.*[264] It hadn't occurred to me then that it was about a marriage of earthly matter: soil and clothes; that everything is enfolded into everything else and that it all connects. I guess the Father was perturbed because it was all created in his image and I didn't even think of that."

And with that, the Oneiroball, serenely floating a mile or two above the Earth, dropped a dream in my lap. It's *about my old neighborhood, where I grew up. The church that used to be next door has been turned into a clothing store. You could see the clothes through the windows.*[265]

It was so obvious. I've heard it said that the eyes are the windows to the soul. The ascended masters were waiting for me to open my eyes to the transformation from church to clothing. No wonder the Father seemed annoyed. I wasn't seeing.

"Worry not, my friend," said Peggymoonbeam. Your patience has endured and that's all that matters."

Nicolaus Steno piped back in. "You know, Penelope, we were observing St. Brides from our lookout tower at Terracrust and taking in the distinguishing Earth features of the blue waters, green and brown land masses and white clouds set against the midnight blue of the firmament when I turned to Peggymoonbeam, 'Aha! Green and brown! A perfect color match for a wedding dress! It will get Penelope's attention and lead her to St. Brides.'

"So, my fellow traveler, the 'bizarre' greenish brown shade for your bridal dress was inspired by an idea put forth by David Bohm, a brilliant and esteemed physicist who has recently joined our Terracrust team. You see, he describes the realm we inhabit as the Implicate Order: 'It is almost as if distant particles of a given color had "known" that they had a common destiny.'[E2]

"You have actually experienced Bohm's theory firsthand, for the particles of color you saw in your dream have now manifested in waking, as I knew they would. By experiencing this, you have become more attentive to that very important aspect of our lesson, which teaches associative learning[266] – that is, making connections. We couldn't simply design an ordinary white wedding gown. It had to do more than just connect to the 'Bride' part of St. Brides."

---

264 9/18/98.
265 3/20/95.
266 See Ch. 40 – Starsight and Terracrust, p. 179

"But heavens, Doc, fashion design is a radical departure from the origin of fossils and quartz and the earth's crust. Did you know when you were on Earth that you were slated to become a couturier?"

"Only the angels knew I was destined to become a fashion designer of sediments and veins when I ascended to this heavenly plane – but now I see how it all connects."

Doing her throatiest Tallulah Bankhead baritone, Peggymoonbeam teased, "Maybe that's why they didn't tell you, Dr. Steno. You might have thought it beneath you! Ha ha ha! I'm crackin' myself up."

"Leave the cracks to me," quipped Steno, "the earth is full of them." Knowing how he aspired to mastery of the pun, his scholarly bumble was endearing.

"I heard that, Miss Penny. You needn't humor me."

"Well, Dr. Steno, considering the seriousness of this Mission, a little humor goes a long way.

"I wonder? Is your fashion house anything like the Garment Center? Like Seventh Avenue in New York?"

"I can assure you that Terre Haute Couturiers is quite the upscale version of the Garment Center."

"OK, you lovebirds. Enough of the repartee," intervened Peggymoonbeam. "Time to get back to work."

This was amazing! I couldn't get over how the spirits did this stuff!

"Penelope, we have our ways, which you are getting a glint of as you travel on. But rest assured: we designed this wedding gown around the elements of the earth. We went so far as to place a beautiful full-bodied rose in the dream so you would associate it with the other rose dreams."

And so it was. The dream contained *an unopened rose with intertwining branches growing out of it. I decide to keep it in water. It's part of the wedding ceremony.*[267] The intertwining branches were just beginning to spread out. Unbeknown to us, the rose would open, one petal at a time, as we made our way toward the town of Placentia.

---

267 9/18/98.

CHAPTER SIXTY-ONE

NEARING PLACENTIA

The epiphanies surrounding Placentia began to reverberate. Peering through the kaleidoscope of nighttime reflections, the connecting of dreams and research was slipping into place.

The encyclopedia'sℰ narrative about the historic town of Placentia, which described the climb to the top of Castle Hill and the panorama below, had instantly evoked the mysterious feeling in my Castle dream: *I'm sitting on the ground, looking up at the Tudor castle perched high on a promontory with the ocean below and three capes flying over the waters.*[268] But to actually see it in person would either expose a new and wondrous dimension or douse my expectations.

As the *birthday* dream replayed itself, it jiggled my curiosity as to how placenta (birth) meshed with the Placentia we were approaching. While trying to calm the butterflies in my stomach, the dominant image of the arm in front of me still stood – in front of me and unanswered. The silent shore of the unknown was on the horizon.

In the Placentia corner of my mind a nagging dream series replayed the story of *a little girl lying in the snow.* In one dream, the words *Sacred Heart appeared in the background. Something is buried in the snow, perhaps a small child.* It's described as *an icy place* In another was *a tiny gray kitten in the snow* and in yet another dream was a *dead furry kitten.*[269] Why would I be dreaming of a gray kitten lying in the snow? Other kitten dreams and church dreams abounded, albeit not necessarily together.

Extensive research did not turn up a single listing for a Church of the Sacred Heart in Placentia. As the Placentia community is largely Irish Catholic, that surprised me, but I just packed the unconnected dots away in my bulging knapsack of puzzlements.

Flashbacks of the Sacred Heart, the dead kitten and the little girl lying in the snow repeated. This prompted me to say to Karen, "We should try to go to church on Sunday and find out if there is a Sacred Heart in the area."

268 3/2/93.
269 Kitten dreams: 1995 – 1999.

Footnotes contain dream dates and references to prior pages where the dream appeared.
Endnotes contain bibliographical references, are marked with "ℰ" in the text, and appear at the end of the book.

Back home after our trip, I checked my journals and was flabbergasted when I discovered that the images of the Sacred Heart, the dead kitten and the little girl lying in the snow were produced in four different dreams. I'd been certain it was one dream and had even described it that way. Initially, I was horrified that I'd misrepresented it; I would have to tell Karen it was four dreams – not one. But I soon realized that the brain's capacity to self-organize and condense, replicated its waking functions in dreaming. It was fascinating to observe that this coupling occurs in the unconscious as well.

The varied images were curious. A sacred heart to many means Divine Love but it can also mean a wounded heart. This little kitten is a child who is cold and buried. Could that be me? Could that be all of us? But she's buried in Placentia and that means womb, so maybe she's going to be reborn.

And so, at dusk on Saturday, September 4, in the year 1999, we were entering the town of Placentia. After we passed Point Verde and recognized the first highway sign for Placentia, a wave of reverence softly embraced us as though to say we were entering hallowed ground. The imposing rock formations rising from the water were more angular in their configuration than any we had seen so far. They were almost geometric.

I reviewed the lay of the land. Placentia is on the west coast of the Avalon Peninsula, about 120 kilometers from St. John's. Placentia Bay leads to a long channel into a natural harbor. A narrow "gut," less than one hundred meters wide, guards the entrance to the harbor, acting as a great barrier to protect ships in the harbor from attack. Only one ship can pass through this "gut" at a time.

Anxious for the first taste of Placentia, we drove through the town, passing multi-colored clapboard houses to reach the waterfront where a picturesque eighteenth-century port welcomed us. In the distance, loomed the Castle Hill Historic Site. Perched high on a hill, it was literally the castle of my dreams.

We turned a corner, which put us directly in front of the Rosedale Manor, an 1893 restored heritage-house surrounded by a white picket fence that invited us to stop. We hoped there would be a room available. We decided to take our chances and see if there was a last-minute cancellation.

We buzzed at the door and Rita, the innkeeper, a plain speaking, no-nonsense woman in her early fifties, hugged us as though we had just returned from the cavalry. She had a room for us but she only had a few minutes to spare because she had to go to church.

My cilia stood straight up on every inch of my body and I thought, "No! It can't be."

I said, "Rita we were thinking of going to church on Sunday. Is your church anywhere nearby?"

She said, "Oh, it's right over there. You can see the windows through the trees."

Haltingly, I asked, "What is it called?"

"It's the Church of the Sacred Heart," replied Rita matter-of-factly and off she went.

The Church of the Sacred Heart was where we were led. Would there be a small child or a tiny gray kitten buried in the snow as the dream foretold?

I tried to restrain myself but the thrill of pure unadulterated synchronicity was too much to contain for long.

Speechless and weak-kneed, Karen and I sat down in the car and tried to grasp the moment. The divine fingerprint of this Mission was upon us as I wept tears of wonder. This was the first seed of realization of what Placentia might hold for us. The magic sprinkled over this tiny village was all I could conceive of then. How could I know this journey would continue for a lifetime?

We left our bags in the car and, travel weary in our grubby jeans, we ran to the church for the 6:00 p.m. mass.

Nearly the whole town of Placentia turned out for the Saturday night service. It was like traveling back in time perhaps a hundred years when feelings of duty, sharing and community were real. We were grateful to be part of this, if only briefly. I was deeply respectful of the uplifting liturgy but I somehow knew it wasn't the Sacred Heart in my dream.

We had dinner at Belle's Restaurant, an eighteenth-century converted barn offering old-fashioned hospitality and real down-home cooking, a welcomed departure from Manhanttanized shitake mushrooms and grilled tofu.

The waitress at Belle's told us the tide in Placentia changes every six hours, running into the Southeast Arm and, later, out to Placentia Bay, and into the Atlantic. Hmm. The Southeast Arm. Could that be the arm I was in search of?

Walking back to the Inn where we would spend our first night, I could feel the numinous tightening its grip as being in Placentia in the flesh was beginning to sink in.

Before retiring, I pensively stared out of our bedroom window at a sweet little church across the way and thought it was more like the *Sacred Heart* dream I'd had of a *small child buried in the snow.*[270] Not knowing what could possibly be pulling me, I knew I had to go there. I lay awake for a while staring at the ceiling. The mystical dream message floated in and whispered, *"Be patient. You will learn everything you need to know."*

That night, I slept restlessly as the winds of discovery played across my storybook dreams. Castle Hill awaited us.

---

270 2/20/95.

CHAPTER SIXTY-TWO

A BIRTHDAY PARTY IN PLACENTIA

Day Four: Placentia

Karen, dedicated to her morning exercise, got up for an early walk while I tried to catch a few extra winks of sleep. She returned wearing her half grin, her cat-that-swallowed-the-canary look. "Penelope. I just walked across a bridge called the Ambrose Shea Bridge." Then she mumbled something about seeing lavender bricks.

LAVENDER BRICKS! Did she say lavender bricks?

Right before we left for Newfoundland, I had dreamt about *Ambrose being on the edge of the water with a steep embankment behind it. Rough, craggy scenery was in the dream.*[271] For some reason, I had told Karen about this dream the previous day. Ambrose. It sounded like a person's name but could also be a place. Well, it could be anything, really.

Before leaving the Rosedale Manor for our long awaited pilgrimage to Castle Hill, we decided to wander across the street to have a quick look at the quaint little church. Rita offered to show us around. The Anglican Church of St. Luke's was a perfect replica of the small country church in the distant dream, and looked nothing like the Church of the Sacred Heart, which had been rebuilt and was contemporary in style.

The old graveyard at St. Luke's was memorable, as it has laid to rest the deceased of all nations who have occupied Placentia. Some of the tombstones dated back to 1592, when it was "The Church of Our Lady of Angels." There was no stopping the connections! That linked to still another dream that contained *a valuable ring with a light purple stone belonging to Our Lady To A Friend.*[272] I sensed this ring belonged to the ghostly figure of the woman in white whom I'd seen in France.[273] The light purple must translate to lavender, but the

---

271 8/26/99.
272 7/10/95.
273 See Ch. 12 – A French Connection, p. 59

Footnotes contain dream dates and references to prior pages where the dream appeared.
Endnotes contain bibliographical references, are marked with "Ɛ" in the text, and appear at the end of the book.

stone part was curious, as it did not resemble a gemstone like amethyst; it was a plain stone. A light purple stone – the color of lavender.

As Rita escorted us through this storybook graveyard recounting its history and the folklore of the deceased, I wandered off.

I was drawn to a miniature marker. Fishing around for my glasses to read the inscription on the tombstone, I knelt down to get a closer look. I walked all around the tiny grave, taking it in from every angle. I could not believe my own sight for it read:

"Kitty, Darling Child of Robert Jardine & Sara Freebairn,
Died September 3rd, 1895, Aged 4 years."

It was the small child buried in the snow – a small gray kitten! It was the dream!

But what did it mean?

We were dumbstruck. Karen and I held it together until Rita left. We didn't want her to think we were a couple of crackpots. But in the end, we couldn't fool her. Her crusty comments about us being renegades on the lam told us she knew we were up to something.

The dream was validated. The Church of the Sacred Heart was physically located <u>behind</u> the Anglican Church. The dream in its quiet wisdom had placed it *in the back-ground*. Subtle clues. Details, details and more details to which attention must be paid. The dream contained a "knowing" beyond anything I could possibly understand, a feeling of having entered a secret place in which the spoken word is mute. Karen and I were incredulous. It was happening so fast we could barely think. Who was Kitty? Why the dream just before we left that instructed us to *report to Kit 4391 or 4931?*

Each discovery was a prize worthy of more contemplation than we could then afford. Our time was limited and so we had to push on and save our profound astonishment and eager calculations for later.

On our way to Castle Hill, Karen, still fixed on the Ambrose Shea drawbridge, told the story of how she found the lavender bricks: "Penelope, while I was walking, I crossed a bridge that was on the path leading to Castle Hill. As I was coming back down the path and about to cross back over the bridge, a red light started flashing because a little tugboat was coming through. The bridge was going up, which meant I couldn't cross. So I just strolled through the neighborhood, and that's when I came on the lavender bricks.

"I saw that the name of the bridge is the Ambrose Shea Bridge, and I thought about your dream about *Ambrose being on the edge of the water with a steep embankment behind it.*[274] Well, the Ambrose Shea Bridge is on the water, and the embankment? It's Castle Hill! And that's where the bricks are, at the foot of the mountain!"

---

274 8/26/99.

It is at this point that Karen came to be Karensurefoot, a moniker that captured her positive attitude and the assuredness of the ground under her feet. Her reconnaissance work was brilliant.

I thought we should have a look at this Ambrose Shea Bridge, but only after we saw Castle Hill. So, after unending years of research, confusion and a determination unrealized, I had finally reached the enchanted place on the top of the hill. There I was, sitting high on the crest of Castle Hill, gazing down at the little seventeenth-century fishing village of Placentia, cradled by the ocean arms of Plaisance named by the French all the way back in 1662 and established as a royal colony. That gave me a nice warm feeling, because ever since I can remember I was drawn to anything related to France. The clean clear air of Placentia Bay and the quiet emptiness of its landscape must have charged my batteries because when I was thinking about nothing at all, a dazzling insight came to me.

My waking view looking down at Castle Hill was the opposite of my dream vista, where I was sitting on the ground looking up at the castle! While I inhaled this upside-down view of Castle Hill, I had a starling epiphany, one that sent shivers down my spine.

I had been wondering why so many of my dream images were upside down, and now the same phenomenon was manifested in waking reality.

Of course!

The team of celestial scribes was seeing this from their vantage point in the galaxies. Naturally, it would look upside down to us mortals here on Earth. It was pure harmony.

The words "as above, so below," written in the Zohar, the "Bible" of the Kabbalists had now penetrated my field of vision. Its title Zohar (light, splendor) is derived from the words of Genesis 1:3: "Let there be light."

And translated from the Emerald Tablet of Hermes: "That which is above is from that which is below, and that which is below is from that which is above, working the miracles of one."[84]

I thought how when we open our eyes to light the images on our retinas are upside down. How strange that my dreaming eyes were receiving images in exactly the same way. I had the feeling I was dreaming through the eyes of the spirits and I began to wonder about a mirror universe.

Ptolemy beamed in excitedly, "Penelope! Here's a little brain food for you. Some of your cosmologists over there argue that the leftover light from the Big Bang may reveal the shape of the universe as a twelve-sided dodecahedron, that if you look out to one side, you see your own universe all over again."

"Twink! That is mind-bending! Could it be that when you're sending messages to me from the stars, my eye is the lens that gathers in your starlight and turns your images into a dream? Maybe we on Earth are like refracting telescopes when we dream."

"Well, feast on that for a while, my love. Cheerio!"

The hidden meaning of the upside-down dreams was so profound I was barely able to absorb it. The magnitude of the message stretching endlessly into space was all-consuming.

So, what was the story behind Castle Hill?

To begin with, it played an important role during times of war in defending Placentia and in the larger Anglo-French struggle for what is now Atlantic Canada. Military occupation was a feature of Placentia for a time after the French built fortifications when war broke out between France and England in the 1690s. In 1693, the French began construction of Fort Royal to guard the harbor at Placentia. Never captured, Castle Hill was ceded to Great Britain in 1713 by the Treaty of Utrecht, which eventually dislodged the French from their foothold in Newfoundland. By the beginning of the nineteenth century, the fort had fallen into ruins.

My dream about this fort occurred in 1993, three hundred years after it was built. History was never my favorite subject, nor was war. Why would I have any interest in it now? Why would I be dreaming of a place I'd never been to, read about or even heard of?

Telescoping the two faces of reality – dreaming and waking – the dream of the *Tudor castle sitting high on a hill*[275] had materialized as "Castle Hill." As we stood at the site of Fort Royals' remains, the vista, juxtaposed with the dream, mirrored the words "as above, so below."

Karen and I, lost in the wonder of our quest, meandered down the hillside path from Castle Hill on our way to examine the lavender bricks. As we approached flat land, she excitedly pointed to her discovery. "Look, Penelope. There's the bridge! Look! Look! It's right there! That's the Ambrose Shea Bridge!" And so it was that one of Karensurefoot's remarkable contributions would be found in the symbol of the Bridge, not only crossing the gut between Jerseyside and Placentia, but symbolically the crossing over, the bridging of two worlds: Waking and Dreaming, Heaven and Earth. And how phenomenal that this far-off bridge beckoned us to Castle Hill, no longer the fairytale castle of my dreams, but a waking reality.

The perfection of this sublime integration, an illuminating discovery beyond reason or imagination, was begging to be shared.

"Karen, can we take a little time to collect ourselves before we look at the bricks? This Placentia adventia is a vortex spinning faster than thought."

Karen burst into giggles. Y'know, Penny, it's pulled me in too, but please let me know if I can help."

The thought of Placentia Bay flowing into the Atlantic Ocean the night Titanic disappeared from sight was bone-chilling. I dared speculate on the hundreds of bodies never rescued, frozen shreds of humanity that may have been carried by the treacherous currents of the Atlantic and washed into various inlets by the notoriously dangerous

275 3/2/93. See Ch. 53 – Getting An Arm Around Newfoundland, pp. 244–45

waters. Could Newfoundland's largest bay, so peaceful and serene at that moment, be the resting-place for the scattered remains of Titanic's hapless victims?

As I contemplated the tide changing every six hours, running into the Southeast Arm and out to the bay, I realized the Southeast Arm was literally in front of me pointing to the arm I saw in front of me in the birthday dream.

I retrieved that dream once more: *I am on the phone with a man I'm about to have a date with. I had seen him before. He tells me my birthday is on FEBRUARY 18 - THURSDAY. There is something he has to do that day. It involves his relatives, a family get-together. I see an image of a black mesh screen in a black frame. There is an arm in front of me . I don't know whose it is.*[276]

Eureka!

Birthday, the clue for placenta translated to Placentia. Following its lead to Castle Hill, the anonymous arm had become real. So wise were the lamplighters of midnight reverie for as they told it in the dream, it all began to mesh. Another area in the province, called Conception Bay, might have connected to the birthday dream as well, but my "gut" told me it was Placentia.

Still I puzzled: who was the man who issued me a birth date of February 18 and had something to do that day involving *a family get-together?*

The cartography of the Dream was much like an ordinary map of a region, with its delineation of states, its shadings of land and water, its symbols for parks, highways, and so on. The same segmentation was in our dreams.

On this Newfoundland expedition, a distinctive series of dreams bonded with the heritage of Placentia: geological, ecological, environmental and industrial.

Was it simply coincidence that on my actual July birthday I transcribed a message about enteric memory? When I connected the "enteric-gut" wordplay to a dream symbol of branches, I opened two dreamtime birthday gifts that were packaged in real time: Placentia and Branch.

There were two guts to consider, the gut (enteric) feeling about Branch and the Placentia Bay gut that guards the entrance to the harbor. Each held some mysterious piece of optical wizardry, but it might be eons before they would share their secret.

The Castle Hill dream was a self-contained novella crammed with a cast of capes so varied it incubated for more than five years before the physical and nonphysical synthesized. I recalled the dream of those three capes flying over the ocean and marveled at their manifestation as three actual Capes in the Placentia Bay area, to the south, east and west of the town. The ocean below the castle was the Atlantic, into which the waters of Placentia Bay flow.

276 10/30/98. See Ch. 35 – Lava Under Revelation, p. 150
" " Ch. 53 – Getting An Arm Around Newfoundland, pp. 244–45

Loose strands of yarn untwisting from the core of the Castle Hill story uncovered another dream featuring an *Indian headdress,* a narrative about *a Navy Seal* and an obscure description about a *vending machine dispensing gourmet snacks*[277] and more. I was ready to dump these fuzzy strands in the recycle bin, but as it happened, every piece connected and may have been recycling for some time.

Did the Indian headdress represent the Beothuk Indians, likely descendants of the Maritime Archaic people of Newfoundland and Labrador?

A more visible marker was the image of the Navy Seal. Was it pointing to a deep-sea diving recovery? Was it depicting the many species of seals often seen along the coasts of insular Newfoundland? Probably both.

The form hardest to make out was the vending machine dispensing gourmet snacks. After years of puzzling, I scored an AHA! The vending machine was the volcano and the gourmet snacks it was dispensing were the precious minerals of the earth being ejected from its vent.

Feeling somewhat fortified now that Castle Hill, Placentia Bay, the Cape Shore area, Branch and the two guts had materialized, I began to reflect on the connection to Kitty when in swirled Scribe Ptolemy in his inimitably jovial fashion:

"Kitty? Kitty? Who's got the Kitty?

You're so pretty, I'm kinda witty, and

Steno's scopin' out New York City."

"Well, young adventurers, I've come to deliver a few lines about Kitts Peak Observatory, known for its ground-based astronomical research, its leading edge telescopes and its nighttime observing programs. As for the *4391 or 4931* I gave you in the dream – that's up to you to figure out. You've got the tools."

"But… but, Twink Ptolemy. What about the Kitts uranium deposit on the coast of Labrador? It was supposed to be developed in the late 1970s but was stopped as of 1983 because of environmental concerns."

"Yes, Penny. Now that you mention it, I recall that it was in an area that had one or more volcanic cones."

"Well, Twink, since it was designated Kitts, wouldn't that tie in?"

"Ah, dear Penny. Mankind is so fickle, he'd sell the Earth for a nickel."

I sensed that Karensurefoot was as intrigued as I was with Ptolemy's cryptic jingles but we had to get back on track.

Competing for our attention were the ponderous questions and the steady arrival of information. The downpour of new transmissions was so powerful, all I could do was transcribe. Analysis would have to wait. It was no longer just the connecting of dreams to

---

277 3/2/93.

research, but connecting research to materiality; seeing the abstract connecting with the concrete. My brain was on overload. Yet at the end of the day, I slept like never before to awaken purely exhilarated.

"Penelope," interjected Karensurefoot, "I picked this brochure up at Castle Hill. There's some stuff in here about the bridge I found that's kind of interesting."

"Located at sea level and embracing two arms of the sea, Placentia has been flooded many times. Subject to strong currents, Placentia Gut was bridged for the first time in 1961 and named for Sir Ambrose Shea who in 1848 was elected to the House of Assembly of Newfoundland.

"Are you ready to go see the lavender bricks?" asked Karensurefoot.

"Yes, Yes. I can't wait."

Bursting with the hope of discovery, we hopped in the car and dashed over to Jerseyside to see the lavender-painted bricks. I felt a little foolish, a lot apprehensive, and hugely curious. Just across the harbor gut from its "Town Side," Jerseyside was settled on a steep slope rising upward from the Northeast Arm to Castle Hill. Karen and I would wind up exploring the tiny neighborhood with a fine-tooth comb.

We pulled up in front of an unimposing little house sitting beside the beach. The waves gently lapped against the shore in this secluded setting where the dreariness of the day was in stark contrast to the exhilarating realms of possibility awaiting us. No one appeared to be at home. The modest dwelling was surrounded by a grab-ass pile of rubble — an odd and sundry variety of junkyard rubbish under which might be hidden something of value. It was hard to tell whether the house was vacant but there was a higgledy-pig-gledy feeling here as though most of the stuff should have been tossed out. In front of the house was a broken-down rowboat, its bottom trimmed in red. It was leaning up against the side of a mountain, which we dubbed — Castle Hill Mountain.

And, there in physical form, were key components from other dreams starting with an assortment of lavender-painted bricks. Dazzled by this repeat encounter with lavender paint, we warily cased the scene. I suddenly noticed four logs under the bricks. One was painted blue.

The *Optico — blue rubbery log* dream flashed back.[278] It had pictured four logs connected to each other, decreeing that *all of the information would be in the blue logs*. For ages, I had imagined the blue log to be the logbook that went down with the Titanic. Unfortunately, the Titanic's radio log book went down with the vessel.

Karensurefoot and I looked at each other. "Penelope," she exclaimed, "It's too obvious. These bricks are lavender! The log is blue! These are the symbols you're looking for!"

---

278 2/14/97.

I agreed, but reserved opinion, for the logs in the dream were distinctly described as rubbery and we hadn't encountered anything consistent with rubber. Facing the reality that the knitting together of these tangled threads was happening so rapidly, we were caught in the throes of conflict and denial, jubilation and acceptance. It was impossible to understand how years of dream abstracts were compressed and made physical in a province so far from home and my pillow.

Giddy from oncoming waves of synchronicity we agreed that, at the very least, we were in the right place, but no matter how intoxicating the spell it did not interrupt the endless questions occupying our thoughts.

An omniscient force seemed to be deliberately and lovingly wrapping itself around us, gently moving us along and allowing us enough time to react before we stumbled onto the next marking. I experienced an exuberance I'd never before known. Trembling at the unseen energy that enveloped us, we sensed that more of this invisible miracle lay in wait.

The empty dream patches were filling in, but the scores of unmarried clues returned my thoughts to the modest little house where I stood. I noticed a small square of yellow paint carefully centered on a piece of squared off wood directly under the boat. Painted on the boat was a man wearing a pirate's hat.

"A pirate's hat!" I screeched. I had a dream that ended with a pirate's hat!

I am walking through rushes and below me is a ravine. I'm looking down on some waterfalls where I see actors dressed up in costumes. They're acting something out in the waterfalls. There is danger. The water is turbulent and jostling them around. One of the actors is an oversized kitten who invites me to a get-together on "Circle Pond Road." I see a black pirate's hat.[279]

I am reminded of the words of the immortal Bard:

> "All the world's a stage, and all the men and women
> merely players. They have their exits and their entrances."

Was it the upside-down phenomenon again? Was the dream hierarchy looking down on the Titanic passengers as though they were actors in costumes surrounded by danger? And, where was "Circle Pond Road?" It hadn't shown up on any of the maps.

I had to get a closer look at the square of yellow paint. It seemed so deliberate – only one area of yellow on a squared-off piece of wood. And then, as though looking through Steno's super powerful spyglass, I realized the force of repetition.

Just as in my dreams: Lavender paint and now Yellow paint. First in Branch and now in Jerseyside. Again, we speculated that this paint must have been used elsewhere in the vicinity. We surveyed the area and, as in Branch, we found no traces that matched. Now a

---

279 11/11/96.

new element was introduced: the blue log. There were four logs under the bricks. Which of the four logs in the dream might it represent?

Under the boat near the piece of wood was a wooden crate, nailed shut. It was marked "M Noel." As a dream began to register about a *Dr. Noel, where someone was killed in a bad accident,* ice cold chills ran down my spine. The dream showed *a cutout of a folded boat, and the word "Tabriz."*[280] Later I found that earthquakes have nearly destroyed the city of Tabriz in northwest Iran several times, which seemed to explain the presence in this dream of Tabriz, a boat, and a bad accident.

The boat tilted against the side of the mountain in Jerseyside mimicked the full tilt at which Titanic was speeding before striking the iceberg.

"Karensurefoot," I exclaimed, "the position of the boat leaning against the mountain may be telling us something." It was possible that the leaning of a boat, a sea-going vessel, was pointing to a listing or leaning against a subsea mountain, a volcanic cone in the earth or more literally, the Castle Hill Mountain it was up against. Could Castle Hill actually be faulted? We continued to ask why we were sent here.

Whatever the explanation, it was foreboding. The lavender paint we had seen throughout our Newfoundland travels reinforced the theory that lava under the Titanic might have caused a volcanic explosion. Add this to the scavenger hunt collection of the tilted boat, the yellow painted square, the bricks, the blue log, the pirate's hat and the case marked Noel. This assemblage of dream symbols transformed into stuff of the real world – all there, all touchable, all photographable, and all recorded.

Abstraction made concrete. How could it be that so many solid fragments of dreams were exposed right in front of this plain little house in Jerseyside, Placentia?

Our eyes had been opened to the glorious Truth that the majesty of the Universe embraced us all.

---

280 9/23/97.

CHAPTER SIXTY-THREE

THE PICKET FENCE

Nearly delirious with discovery, we snapped our cameras Paparazzi style for fear these incredible footprints might disappear before our eyes. I glanced over at the picket fence stretching into infinity, as it did in the dream I had dreamt only days before leaving for Newfoundland.

That dream was the courier of a message so noble I shall never forget it.

The ocean was the backdrop for the undercurrent that has taken me down three times. I guess I am drowning. There is an image of the ocean with a transparent screen over it picturing groups of people mostly in fours standing there as though ready to march. Some hold poles, others, shields. There is another group of people. No one speaks. They are monochromatic. They are collectively working on something, having escaped some fate together.

At the end of the dream *a picket fence appears, each slat having its own meaning, extending to infinity and signaling the end of a project. The colors are pale pink and green. When I see it, I run to get someone to show it to. Elation consumes me. I weep with gratitude, tears streaming down my face.*

Mankind working together has completed this.[281]

Amazing! The picket fence at Jerseyside was pale green. The colors of the surrounding Newfoundland reeds were pale pink and green. This ordinary fence was the metaphor for utopian collaboration by the family of man. It symbolized community's gift to mankind.

Some months later, I would go to a medium for the very first time. It took her some time to get all the spirits straight. Then, Peggymoonbeam came forth.

"Does your friend have a fence?" she asked. "She's trying to show me something. It looks like this," as her fingertips met to shape a picket fence. "Your friend is telling me that it's a symbol. Most spirits don't give me symbols, but she said you'll know what it means."

---

[281] 8/27/99.

Footnotes contain dream dates and references to prior pages where the dream appeared.
Endnotes contain bibliographical references, are marked with "Ɛ" in the text, and appear at the end of the book.

Contact with the other side evoked sobs of joy, as I realized that my experiences were real and palpable. The concept of life eternal was becoming more of a reality every day by enchanted day. The intensity of Peggymoonbeam's energy was even stronger now than when she was on Earth. It made perfect sense that she was the team leader on the Newfoundland expedition. Of course, Nicolaus Steno orchestrated the rock concert of Precambrian sediments in the Avalon Zone while Claudius Galen, I'm sure, bequeathed to Karensurefoot a state-of-the-heavens jewelers loupe that would magnify her superior visual aptitude.

Who was in charge of paint? We hadn't a clue. What was important is that Karensurefoot had seen it.

Back at Castle Hill, Karensurefoot said, "Penelope. That paint thing. That must be some supernatural thing the spirit guides do."

As for the picket fence materialization, it was awe-inspiring, thrilling, and somewhat forbidding all at once. A sign like the picket fence appearing in so powerful a dream from Peggymoonbeam must reflect the hidden meanings that exist in the things we see all around us. We walked over to examine it more closely, climbed up over some rocks and on to the beach. It was an overcast September day in Placentia. The wind whistled through the reeds as the excitement of discovery whistled through our thoughts.

I thought about the picket fence in my dream, the picket fence that was Peggymoonbeam's when she was alive and the picket fence I was seeing now in Placentia. Were they all connected in some way? In dreaming and in waking they appeared at different times and in different places. Yet they all carried the imprimatur of Peggymoonbeam. I wonder if parts of us – our dreams, our memories, our consciousness – are somehow imprinted on the surroundings to which we're drawn?

Silently gazing out to sea, we struggled to absorb the intertwining epiphanies sent our way, when we both noticed at the same moment something sticking up out of the water. The tide was coming in, but the object was not moving. It stayed fixed as though looking back at us.

We uttered in one voice, "It looks like a branch!"

We fell silent.

How could so many symbols snoozing in the layers of the unconscious have been awakened and embodied in this one obscure patch of land?

Was it sheer coincidence? Did I merely imagine this humble abode surrounded by a random arrangement of brick and mortar, paint and wood, or was there a deeper message – a higher ground? Did the purpose end here? Or begin?

The design had no closure. The timelessness between what was happening in my dreams and the corresponding events in Placentia transported me to worlds of consciousness I had never even glimpsed. I was riding the merry-go-round of Time, a revolving carousel rotating endlessly.

My thoughts traveled back to Agneswiseheart, my dearly beloved aunt whom I suspect is the mysterious courier of the cryptic Greek code. She must have overheard my thoughts: "Penelope my love, please understand that this journey is much like the Australian Aborigines' concept of the 'Dreamtime,' which encompasses, among other aspects, the beginning of all things, the life and influence of one's ancestors, the way of life and death and sources of power in life. Dreamtime is an infinite spiritual cycle beyond time and space, where past, present and future coexist. The Aborigines believe their ancestors crawled out of the earth during the Dreamtime."

"Good grief!" I shuddered. Is that what happened to me? Were all of those dreams about the girl emerging from beneath the earth about the Aborigines? Is that what's happening to you Agneswiseheart? Are you crawling out of the earth during the time I'm dreaming?"

My patron saint among ancestors, my dear sweet Agneswiseheart, who will live in my heart forever, did not respond to my naïve questions, so I began talking to myself.

My struggle with the question of time was loosening its grip. No wonder they use a conversion scale at Starsight and Terracrust. They need to sync their time to Earth time to show me how time collapses in the unconscious. It seems to happen in an instant! This must mean the "future" folds back on itself as Dreamtime past, which then folds out to become present reality. Wow! This must mean that we really do exist eternally.

Galen's Mission did birth the appearance of an aboriginal styled *circular key ring*[282] that held the message of the optic nerve.

But where did it really begin? A circle has no beginning.

---

282 11/11/94. See Ch. 4 – Charlesbigstar, p. 31

CHAPTER SIXTY-FOUR

LOGS AND BRICKS

We took a break to catch our breath, fortifying ourselves with lunch at the Northeast Arm Motel in Dunville, a community a bit east of Placentia. The bare-bones establishment was typical of the chains of roadside motels you see dotting the highways. In the colorless, half-empty lunchroom, we retraced our footsteps, seeking answers to the celestial purpose of our navigation. Our spiritual high points more than compensated for the lackluster surroundings. Having fallen under some inexorable spell, we reflected on the sheer wizardry of the paint and all the ordinary things that had taken on inexpressible meaning. Thoughts overflowed as I recounted the repetition of paint and brick dream images that had never before connected, even after years of research.

After delving into the chemical composition of brick, the most plausible explanation I could arrive at was that, since the origin of brick was clay, it must be alluding to the earth.

The sight of the lavender bricks was unforgettable and energized another startling dream recollection. It centered on *logs in the shape of bricks that are lying on the ground where my friend and I are looking for something. A purple bicycle pedals its way into this dream* – symbolic of the vehicle that has transported us.[283] The purple color of the bicycle was pretty close to lavender, and if dreams were alchemical, lavender would then transmute to Lava Under. Like a reprise, it kept repeating.

When I returned to New York and consulted my journal, I was amazed to find that the configuration I'd drawn of bricks in the dream was an inverted look-alike for the stack of bricks we photographed in front of the house at Castle Hill. It was pure unfiltered actualization. I wondered: Could lava be under Castle Hill?

A friend once told me that if you don't hear God when he whispers in your ear you'll get a little bump on the head.

Well, dear Reader, cliché smiled down. I was hit on the head with a ton of bricks! I took a second glance at the dream image and the photograph, to make sure they matched. The layout of bricks in the dream was upside down! This reversed placement of things was getting easier to identify as we traveled on, for it was prolifically and intentionally repetitive.

---

283 3/11/97.

Footnotes contain dream dates and references to prior pages where the dream appeared.
Endnotes contain bibliographical references, are marked with "Ɛ" in the text, and appear at the end of the book.

Tuesday, March 11, 1997

My upside-down dream bricks

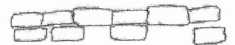

Someone has left a bunch of things laying on the ground. They are like logs kind of in the shape of bricks. We keep going through these things looking for something. Sylvia wants to go to the beauty parlor. I think she wants a manicure. I decide I will go too. Sylvia has a purple bicycle. I hop on with her and off we go.

NOTE: In my half sleep, I realized all the repetitive dreams about manicures were about "cures for man (kind)." I will look for the one with the eye.

Right side-up lavender bricks
Castle Hill mountain
Placentia, Newfoundland

But back at the Northeast Arm Motel, we were distracted from our review by a shining light.

"Good day, my fearless scouts. It is Lord Galen. I don't mean to interrupt your lunch, but I think it's a good time for you to pause and reflect on the insights you've gained thus far. You are coming of age spiritually, Penelope, so now is your chance to learn the true nature of your quest which, granted, is quite ponderous. We understand the inclination to want the big answer to the big picture, but the smaller discoveries you are making now is an initiation that will eventually lead to your larger purpose."

"Oh, Lord Galen! A glint of silver flashed in my eye as you arrived. It must be the reflecting disc over your halo, or is it the halo itself? It's like a dream I had with *three discs like the doctors used to wear around their heads*."[284] I think they called it a doctor's mirror. Sometimes, though, it's hard to tell if you are a doctor, a miner or a detective."

"We don't individuate up here, because our work is collaborative. You will observe on this expedition that your close-knit crew of mentors is collectively involved in all phases of a Mission, although on this leg of the journey, we have left most of the undercover work to the illustrious Steno.

"Because you had no preconceived ideas about things and little learning that would influence you, we selected you among others to send on this emergency quest. The hidden message in the sacred *begging cup* dream we wired you is a cosmic plea that Planet Earth is becoming barren and wasted and must be doctored without delay. Your beloved Mother Earth has a near terminal illness threatening to her and all her inhabitants.

"I know you've been wondering about the begging cup, Penelope. I suggest you have another look at that dream in its entirety, for it contains some advanced knowledge that will illuminate the message."

"Oh really? You've stirred my curiosity. I hope I can remember the dream."

To my surprise, this dream story full of strange and sudden happenings came fluttering back like a carrier pigeon, and I blurted it out nearly faster than words could form so I wouldn't lose any of it.

I unexpectedly take my baby to a fancy Japanese restaurant. On my way down a long flight of stairs, I see a vibrating cup coming out of a brick wall by itself. I joke that it's a "begging cup." It's shaking and moving out of the wall. I go downstairs and sit at a table. The first dish served is a dish with green vegetables and marshmallows. The marshmallows are dancing, practically jumping out of the bowl. I'm intrigued with this. Another dish arrives and everyone is sharing the two dishes. I think "it's a different culture, a different custom."[285]

"Good heavens! *A begging cup! Dancing marshmallows!* This is the craziest dream! What does this all mean, Lord Galen? How could these objects just suddenly come to life? I realize it's a dream, but even so, you've gotta admit, it's pretty weird!"

284 10/16/93.
285 12/12/96. See Ch. 28 – Morse Code & The Upanishads, pp. 128–29

"Penelope. What you experienced in that dream is something we call supernatural phenomena. The supernatural is the plane of existence where Terracrust and Starsight are located."

"Hmm. What exactly does supernatural mean, Lord Galen?"

"It's pretty straightforward, at least to us over here. 'Super' means above the average, and 'natural' means the norm. Basically, it is anything that seems to go beyond any natural force or defies a logical explanation to those on the Earth plane. For example, if your *vibrating cup coming out of a brick wall by itself* were to occur in a waking state, on Earth, it would be considered an apport, which is an object that appears seemingly from nowhere."

"Holy Cannoli! What about the dancing marshmallows, Lord Galen? Was that a supernatural act, too?"

Galen laughed. "Yes, my fair maiden, it was. That is called psychokinesis, considered on Earth to be the ability of the human mind to influence the inanimate or animate environment without the use of the known senses. At present, Earth scientists relate these phenomena to the waking state. It is our hope that in the future they will be applied to the dream state as well. The animation of inanimate objects in your dreams is as real as anything you know, and believe it or not, is verifiable. Actually, it is part of the laws of nature that you on Earth do not yet understand.

"Carl Jung, your revered pioneer in dreams and consciousness, is now a distinguished member of the PurpleScroll. Based on his thinking about the collective unconscious, he wrote that 'psyche and matter are contained in one and the same world, and are in continuous contact with one another.' His experience at Starsight is bringing him closer to that contact with not only his deceased relatives, but all those who have gone before, even souls he hadn't met, like myself. It's quite thrilling for him to watch the collective unconscious become a reality. He thought it probable that 'psyche and matter' are two different aspects of one and the same thing, and that, dear Penelope, is just the tip of the iceberg. Suffice to say, Carl continues his seminal work over here at Starsight."

Wow, Lord Galen! Psyche and Matter! Maybe my psyche made the cup vibrate!

"My sweet, supernatural phenomena are spontaneous – be it waking or dreaming. It exists through a means other than any force in nature or science known on Earth. Some folks call it a miracle. You might know that Carl was deeply interested in the spiritual experiences of mystics of all religions, as well as in dream parallels of mythologies like the Holy Grail."

"But what is all that about taking a baby to a Japanese restaurant? Why Japanese? And who is the baby? I don't even have a baby. Could this be connected to that Japanese instructor whose name I couldn't pronounce?"

"Penelope, let us consider that Japanese with its many dialects is quite foreign to you and a language you cannot read. I'm sure the concept of the supernatural is equally foreign to you and difficult to read. As for the baby you don't recognize, that baby is Mission Lavender. Your dream tells you it's a different culture and a different custom because these extraordinary events are beyond the realm of human comprehension. Does that resonate, oh curious one?"

"Yes, Lord Galen! It absolutely, positively does! And I bet the sharing of the two dishes has to do with the sharing of this mystical story."

"Penelope, the time has come for me to share with you an allegory about the precious cup. You see, the begging cup unveils the stellar light of Starsight and combines it with the sustenance provided by Terracrust. Acting together, they are a perpetual source of all substance and energy in the universe."

"That is awesome, Lord Galen! So the begging cup is symbolic of a constant source of light!"

"As you know, my timeless Mission is light, vision, and healing. Our telescopes at Starsight and Terracrust Observatories outshine even your latest Spacewatch telescope. At Starsight we specifically train astronomers in observational techniques covering the Heavens. Similarly, Terracrust astronomers are schooled in celestial state-of-the-art imaging techniques to detect the many facets of Earth.

"From Planet Earth, Spacewatch can now capture light from asteroids throughout the solar system but cannot look far enough to see the most distant objects that may exist. At the risk of boasting, we are light-years ahead of Spacewatch for we worked with telescopes like theirs Earth centuries ago and our Terracrust scopes are so precise in their imaging that they not only detect physical properties like a planet's climate, atmosphere and geology, but they also detect the electromagnetic energy of its inhabitants.

"Through light-years of probing, our scopes are able to discern that the deep wounds of the Earth and its inhabitants are related and are aching to be healed.

"In the second century AD, I wrote that the imbalance in the health of the human being correlates with the health of the Earth. Today my concerns are greater than possibly at any time in history, for it is obvious that Man has lost his way."

"But Lord Galen, why was *the begging cup vibrating out of a brick wall* in this dream?"

"First, we have to identify the brick wall, Penelope. Think of the wall as analogous to a breakthrough as in breaking through the brick wall of man's outer self so he may recognize the value of his psyche — of his truest nature. You see, the human condition is rejuvenated by the quest for Truth and its compelling desire to achieve connectedness with one another and Planet Earth. This quest, directed from within, will reveal seedlings of the questing individual, who will develop and, much like a flower, blossom outward from within.

"*The vibration of the cup* reminds me of the words of one of Carl Jung's collaborators, Marie-Louise von Franz. Jung thought of the world 'as a single energy that manifests itself at lower frequencies of vibration as matter and at more intense frequencies as psyche.'"[E5]

Hmm. Frequencies. I wondered about the vibrations of the begging cup. They certainly seemed to be at an intense frequency, strong enough to break through a brick wall. But having already asked so many questions, I couldn't ask another one. I'd sound like a fool.

Galen radiated that constant source of light which so vividly revealed my doubts and fears.

"Penelope, think of Percival, the legendary knight, who was led in search of the Grail by divine grace. This legend carries many different versions. In the Arthurian tale, the naïve Percival asks the wounded Fisher King a simple question about whom the Grail serves. When the king was injured, his kingdom suffered as he did. His infirmity affects the fertility of the land, reducing it to a cursed and barren wasteland. Percival's question rejuvenated not only the royal kingdom but the entire ailing cosmos.

"Quite the opposite in Chrétien de Troyes' 'Perceval, the Story of the Grail,' Percival remains silent because his teacher had warned him against talking too much. His failure to ask the question is calamitous and leaves the king tragically injured for his sins while his devastated land suffers with him.

"Do not fear being noticed, Penelope. If you're too afraid to ask about that which you do not know, it could make you look like you are vacant in the mind, which you are not. All of us on the spirit team wholeheartedly encourage you and, in fact urge you, to ask any and all questions that may come to you. If you pose a question to which the answer is premature, we will let you know. Percival's was a healing question, dear Penelope. I urge you meditate on this. Unfortunately, you had a leader in the twenty-first century whose health was in a state of acute imbalance and his infirmity, which revealed itself in grandiosity, had a disastrous affect on many lands."

I knew that my dream guides were communicating the urgency of Planet Earth's condition and I began to understand that the earth and its inhabitants could not heal until we first examined our individual and collective psyches. Galen's message came clear: the innocent little *begging cup* in my dream was breaking through the *brick wall* of our outer selves, beseeching us to face up to our divine potential, to heal our relationships to ourselves, each other and our poor impoverished environment.

A flurry of air wafted over us and Lord Galen was gone. Karen and I were so deeply engrossed with his message it was a bit of a jolt to find ourselves still sitting in the Northeast Arm Motel having lunch.

We couldn't actually see Galen's spiritual energy, but we could feel his influence. Our impulses were quickening. We began to hash and rehash the discovery of the two colors of paint, the yellow and the lavender, and the dream match of the two locations we had visited in Newfoundland. Each appeared conspicuously aligned to a theme: Branch for its "gut feeling" that led us to Placentia Bay's gut, the branch sticking up in the water and Castle Hill. Our curiosity would not rest. We were gripped by the idea that this paint trail might be some sort of supernatural phenomenon, but then maybe all of our sightings were. I returned to the nagging question, "How do my dream guides do it?" The celestial choir of scholars echoed, "There are certain things mortals need not know."

I guess the how of the supernatural was one of those things we're not supposed to ask about, but they didn't say we couldn't look. Hence, Karen and I decided to have another glance at the house laden with man-made objects, objects that materialized from the invisible shavings of dreams. Bricks. Paint. A boat. Would everything still be there?

As we were leaving the Northeast Arm Motel, we stopped to look at an antiquated map. There were three small finger coves on it: Big Judy Cove, Little Judy Cove, and Snacks Cove.

But this took a backseat for I was now fixated on who lived in the mystery house which held untold pieces of what I thought were my own private dreams. For some reason, I obsessed about the name of the residents who inhabited this phantasmagoric, yet very real, very concrete house.

A day earlier, I had shared with Karensurefoot a dream about a long-forgotten friend by the name of *Pauline Maher.* I wasn't really sure why I told her this dream at this point, but in hindsight, it was sheer intuition. *In the dream, Pauline scrapes and bruises the side of her face because I back her into a wall. Then it turns out to be Pearl. I say, "It's my fault." Sissy Spacek asks me for an anti-acid pill.*[286]

When I awakened, I was horrified! Why would I back anyone, much less my gentle, lovely friend, into a wall? And why would Sissy would want an anti-acid pill?

I was compelled to know the name of the people in the house. Would their name be Maher, like the Pauline Maher of my dream? I didn't know why, but I had worked myself up to a fevered pitch. I had to get the name, and that was all that mattered. Karen and I couldn't stop thinking about it. The machinations grew as we spun one scenario after another, trying to concoct a convincing story that would help us discover who lived in the house – the house that had become our sacred vessel.

We could go to the Placentia post office and see if they had an address for that parcel of land. We could go the Zoning Board to see if the owners were registered. We could call the innkeeper at the Rosedale Manor. She was a native Newfoundlander and knew Placentia well. Problem was, she was already suspicious of our gallivanting.

We could just knock at their door and ask them their name. But why would we ask who they were? We could ask if they were planning on selling their boat, feigning interest in buying it. The buying-the-boat story was absurd as the boat was a ramshackle old dinghy in desperate need of repair. Who'd want to buy that piece of junk? We had an answer for that: We were part of a film crew – set designers filming on location – we needed it as a prop. What if they said OK? What would we do with the boat? Did we really want to buy a boat in Newfoundland?

---

286 7/29/95.

I just had to get the names of the people in the house and we needed a plausible excuse. The harebrained schemes we invented could raise an eyebrow or two even among the most unsuspecting of Canadians. We decided our best bet was to return to the Northeast Arm Motel to see if they had a telephone directory. The lackluster hotel with its threadbare, slightly musty decor had a down-home feel to it and for some unfathomable reason, we felt comfortable there. When we returned so soon after leaving, the hotel staff welcomed us back; they seemed slightly puzzled but curious.

We struck up a conversation with the owner and learned there was a sizable community of Mahers in the area. Our polite interest inspired endless tales of all the families of Mahers on the Island from its beginnings: who was related to whom, who did what for a living, who died, who was born, who got married, divorced and so on, describing in the most microscopic detail all the trials and tribulations of second and third generations of Mahers.

Suddenly I noticed a Placentia telephone directory. Running my hand across it, I said to Karensurefoot, "We could really use one of these." When I looked down, my finger was resting on "Maher's Autotech Services Collision Centre." We screeched like two crows! I was sure the owner thought we were mad as hatters. She chuckled briefly, then pressed on with her florid recitation of Maher ancestry.

We feigned listening to the endless history of these folks a bit longer. As she blathered on, our insides shook like Jell-O in anticipation of unraveling this baffling clue. We were on the edge of an unknowable development that could blow this whole venture out of the water.

All the while, I was eyeballing the phonebook's listing of residents named Maher. When I traced the name to Mahers of Maher's Polypipe, I whispered to Karen, "We'd better leave."

The owner gestured toward the phonebook and said, "Take it with you." As I tucked in a page that was torn from the book, I glanced down to find my finger on the name Gardiner, a name that would not enter my Timelessness Glasses for a while. Of one thing, I was sure; I would cherish this tattered old Newfoundland phone book forever.

We thanked her for her kindness and made our exit.

Once outside, Karensurefoot became inarticulate, jabbering and sputtering "Pauline Maher – Maher's Polypipe." She chanted Pauline Maher over and over. It had become a mantra. Pauline and Polypipe sounded so much alike. Furthermore, Maher's Polypipe was on the same street as the secret house, directly in front of it as things turned out. The fact that Maher's was an Auto Collision Center had completely escaped us.

Pauline Maher was backed into a wall, the side of her face was scraped, and it was my fault. The comment that *"it turns out to be Pearl,"* another friend who I call Pearly in waking life, was literally "off the wall." How could I dream such gibberish? Such nonsense?

What part did Pearl play in it? Why would she change from Pauline to Pearl?

The wall. Could it be the wall of a volcano?

The side of her face. The side of the face of Castle Hill Mountain? The house was against the side of the mountain.

It was my fault. The Clock-a-Doodle-Do dream as it connected to the Titanic[287] said, *"It was my mistake. I slipped."* Was there a fault beneath the house on the side of the hill? Were the helter-skelter markings of bricks and logs daytime clues leading to a discovery of some sort? Were rumblings of a volcanic eruption reverberating in the earth while the people of this peaceful little harbor town went about their business?

Was it pure coincidence that the boat was propped up against the side of the Castle Hill Mountain? Was this broken down boat a waking life icon of the Titanic directing us to a concrete union of dream and waking?

Nine months later, a friend and I visited a Titanic Exhibit in Chicago, which provided a virtual tour of the grand liner. This compelling replica of the dramatic disaster was so lifelike, it was eerie. Passing through the luxurious salons and their lavish trappings turned back the clock to the age of splendor. Soon, we found ourselves in a pitch-black room with pinpoint lighting our only means of seeing. Playing in the background were recorded cries and shouts of the victims amid muffled sounds of suffocation, innocent breaths on their last exhales fighting the force of crashing waves. A reproduction of a Titanic lifeboat stood coldly in the center. I froze. It was nearly a double for the dilapidated boat in front of the Jerseyside house – with one exception: The boat in this reconstructed scene had brick red trim at the top, while the boat in front of the house had its identical red trim on the bottom. It was upside down – and it wasn't a dream.

Walking gingerly from one darkened exhibit room to the next, my friend and I entered the cargo hold. We were chatting about the mummy rumored to have been aboard when the dimmed lights suddenly went out. There was a thud. We were in total darkness. A large sign fell off the wall, slamming to the ground. An exhibit representative ran in to see what happened. I was about to ask if this was where the mummy was stored. I decided not to.

A major piece of evidence found on the 2005 expedition to the Titanic wreck site was the huge intact piece of Titanic's hull, upside down on the ocean floor. As well as the experts could make out, red paint was still visible. Incredible! The Titanic sank in 1912. I saw it in miniature version in Jerseyside in 1999 – in life-sized version in Chicago in 2000 –and it actually showed up on the bottom of the ocean in 2005 – all appearances connecting to my very own dream field of Titanic debris spread over time.

A flash of insight struck when I realized that these parts were all related and working toward becoming one whole piece – or one whole story.

---

287 2/24/95. See Ch. 50 – The Slip, pp. 233–227

CHAPTER SIXTY-FIVE

PIPE DREAMS

We reflected on our curious experience at the mediocre little motel. It seemed an active creative intelligence that affects everything in the material world had enveloped us. We were awash in a net sparkling with purpose, one we could not yet know, or perhaps, ever know.

The invisible, through its varied and mysterious channels, had called us to Maher's Polypipe, across from the unassuming little house by the seaside where the single branch was still rising straight up out of the ocean like a beacon welcoming us back.

All the signs had manifested only a few feet away from the dream images of Placentia and Castle Hill. The harmonics were in perfect pitch. None of the clues had moved. We walked along the weathered green boardwalk. Perched on rocks that afforded the best view, we watched the lone branch jutting from the sea, awaiting its slightest movement. It stood its ground, remaining motionless while the tide whooshed around it. We could not imagine what was keeping it erect.

The Psymometer Peggymoonbeam gave me was masterful in interpreting signs and matching them to dreams. Beyond that, this psychic compass helped us interpret signs of nature: the behavior of birds, the smell of the air, the color of the sky, the condition of the seas, the appearance of floating debris, an unremarkable stick protruding from the water. We were reading nature and our relationship to it in a way we had never known.

Waterlogged debris had washed ashore; a ragged old shoe, a dried-up piece of rubber, some driftwood. I thought about taking the salty remnants with me but didn't.

Charged with the Pauline Maher revelation, we forged ahead trying to fuse the dream symbols of *the wall, the scraped side of her face, and my fault* with countless implications of volcanic activity. Split-second connections rocketed us forward.

Karensurefoot had seen the first connection: Pauline Maher and Maher's Polypipe. No wonder Galen chose her. She was endowed with the same vision as my Timelessness Glasses.

Paul in Pauline was close to Poly in Polypipe. Maher's was a direct hit. The "line" portion of Pauline remained. We had been pronouncing it 'lean' as in Pauline. "Lean and pipe! Line and pipe! Line pipe! Pipe Line!!

Footnotes contain dream dates and references to prior pages where the dream appeared.
Endnotes contain bibliographical references, are marked with "Ɛ" in the text, and appear at the end of the book.

Adrenaline pumping, minds racing, we roared with laughter and danced a jig as we bellowed our discovery:

"Pipeline! Pipeline! Pipeline!!"

Two dream clues would soon be revealed. We learned Maher's was not only a collision center for autos and supplier of pipe fittings, but a supplier of gas as well.

Several days earlier, Karensurefoot had picked up a newspaper in St. John's and had casually mentioned something about a pipeline. Now the lead story in The Telegram clicked.

The headline that day (September 4, 1999) read:

A concrete proposal: Bringing natural gas ashore would change the face of Newfoundland's offshore industry.

The story talked about the latest stages in a proposal that began with a plan for a pipeline to tap the vast quantities of natural gas in the Grand Banks and carry it south to New England. But gargantuan obstacles, such as five hundred icebergs that cut across the banks each year, made that plan unlikely.

Despite impediments a company was planning to transport natural gas was proposing a pipeline to run north from the edge of the oil-rich Jeanne d'Arc basin, skirt around the Grand Banks in three-hundred-meter-deep waters, and cross the Avalon Isthmus to the Newfoundland Transshipment Centre near a town called Come by Chance. From there, the pipeline would head under water to the United States. It would be the longest undersea pipeline in the world extending approximately fifteen hundred miles.

I was tormented by the thought that this underwater route might cross the same waters as the tectonic path on which we'd unknowingly been dispatched. Was the path a part of the Mid-Atlantic ridge, the vast sinuous undersea mountain chain known for its fracture zones?

Had they considered the volatility of a string of unknown undersea volcanoes? This possibility was proving to be at the very heart of our quest, as an underground volcano could be one link in a long chain of natural events that decimated the Titanic.

I wracked my brain, trying to revive any pipe dreams (no pun intended). There was a vague memory of dreams directing me to the Alaskan Pipeline, but the only dream snippet related to a pipe was something about *workmen coming to stop water pouring out of a pipe and a hole being in the wrong place.* I thought it involved the *girl coming up from the sand and a sense of a hole being in the wrong place. There was something about a chair*[288], but it was too fuzzy to recall so far from home. The strange medley would have to wait until I got back to New York and could look it up in my dream journal.

---

288 9/28/93. See Ch.1 – Beginnings, pp. 4-5.

Suddenly I sensed a fluttering. I thought it might be Tu-whit, but much to my surprise, it was the pages of Steno's steno pad flapping in the wind.

"Good day, ladies. Steno here. You girls created quite a commotion with your pipeline discovery. I must say your enthusiasm sparked some high voltage current up at Terracrust, enough to draw me back to Newfoundland to give you a brief tutorial on Order. I can see that you are rapidly advancing in the fine art of dot-connecting.

"Penelope, do you remember Lord Galen's Timelessness explanation[289] of how seemingly random events happen independently but merge to become a unified whole?"

"You mean where all my experiences blend into one?"

"Yes. Exactly. An example of this unbroken unit of time – this concept of Timelessness – was illustrated when you uncovered the dream of *Pauline Maher*. Your power of intuitive thought retrieved from your storehouse of memory, the dream pictures relevant to the waking experience.

"In terms of past and present, first you dreamt of *Pauline Maher*, a friend you haven't seen in thirty-some years. Four years after the dream, you travel to Newfoundland and discover Maher's Polypipe. Returning to the past your unconscious made a connection between several dreams about *bowls,* the symbol for craters."[290] You come to this by way of your Abraham Lincoln dream[291] when you discover that cinder cone volcanoes have a bowl-shaped crater at the summit. While in Newfoundland, you see an article about the pipeline in a local paper. Your unconscious goes to work again, digs out the Pauline Maher dream and unbeknownst to you, has merged Past and Present seamlessly and timelessly.

"You intuitively knew that *Pauline Maher* would connect to the pipeline. You've learned that this manner of association is achieved phonetically, rather than by the correct spelling of words which gets somewhat garbled in the spirit world. For example, *Maher* sounds just like maar which is, in fact, a volcanic crater.

"Now, in addition to obeying the laws of Timelessness, you've also been blindly intuiting David Bohm's theory of two kinds of order.[ε6] The order you are accustomed to recognizing on Earth is 'Grouping Order' which involves dividing and separating things into individual groups. The other kind of order is called 'Symmetry Order' in which different types of things are combined together and distributed evenly through the whole frame of reference – in this case, the tapestry of Lavender.

"The two methods of creating order: separating into groups and integrating into the whole frame are clearly opposite of one another. Opposition, distinction, conflict all result from dividing things apart, while unity, similarity, harmony and symmetry result from blending things together. You've been meshing and blending things together without

289 See Ch. 54 – Chaos in The Cosmos, pp. 251–53
290 See Ch. 35 – Lava Under Revelation, p. 155
291 1/25/98.   See Ch 35 – Lava Under Revelation, p. 155

even knowing it. Symmetry order is the unifying force in nature — combining the infinity of other worlds, of other times — and you have approached this in a timeless fashion.

"You intuitively combined six fragments from waking and dreaming, in your desire to establish symmetry — unity — an overall pattern. Of course, this pattern will later be joined by other patterns. For now, let's take one fragment at a time as it relates to Pauline Maher and Polypipe.

1. The Pauli part of *Pauline* matched the Poly part of Polypipe. Poly was now in place.

2. You extracted the Pipe part of Polypipe. Pipe was in place.

3. You joined Poly and Pipe. This validated Polypipe.

4. You extracted Line from *Pau-line*. Pipe Line was solved and corresponded to the pipeline story in the local paper.

5. You opened a phone book and discovered that Maher's Polypipe manufactures pipe fittings and Maher's Collision Centre is a supplier of gas. You connected pipe and gas and arrived at a pipeline that would deliver gas.

6. Finally, you've learned that a maar is a volcanic crater. Your waking consciousness linked the disconnected thoughts — the fragmented clues — that surfaced in both waking and dreaming consciousness, as though time had disappeared. Had you stayed within the boundaries of Earth time, you may not have been able to replace disorder with order and have arrived at this logical arrangement:

"You connected *Pauline Maher* in the dream to Maher's Polypipe in Newfoundland. Your instinct that laying pipeline near the wall of a crater in a faulted area would be environmentally unsound and may incite the potential of tectonic plates to collide. This was reflected in six pieces of a multi-faceted puzzle emerging as one complete unit.

"Pipeline — Gas — Crater — Collision — Tectonic plates.

"Voila! The mystery is solved.

"So, fair maidens, you have experienced first-hand Bohm's theory on two kinds of order. Once we recognize a simple distinction between a few common patterns, the puzzle suddenly fits together. When you understand that there are two orders — that the flow of time and the world of human events appear as an interplay of two contrasting orders — then the idea of general disorder or chaos gradually loses its meaning."[87]

I turned to Karen. "Steno is right. This *must* be a natural system because we did it without even thinking."

"Wow!" exclaimed my sure-footed friend.

CHAPTER SIXTY-SIX

WHITE ROSE

Then, in the form of a white rose, the host of the sacred soldiery
appeared to me, all those whom Christ in his own blood espoused.
Dante Alighieri, Paradiso, Canto XXXI

The St. John's Telegram had reported, "The natural gas deposit that will kick-start the mammoth undertaking, if it exists at all, lies beneath the White Rose hydrocarbon field…." The words "white rose" sparked memory of a dream about *remotely rearranging a bowl of flowers that were dead and described as sepia in color. One flower was starting to revive. It was a delicate white rose.*[292]

Was the *revival of the delicate white rose* that visited me in the warmth of sleep sniffing out the White Rose project as a precarious but tenacious operation? My train of thought was fixed on one-track: Could subsea activity involved in offshore gas production stimulate activation of a dormant volcano?

The article was the first announcing the latest pipeline route. Three years later, another publication reported that work had been conducted related to iceberg management and iceberg risk assessment. Backed by millions of dollars worth of research, a powerful iceberg simulation program was developed and the pipeline company, with their new creed "go north," announced their plans to begin production. November 2005 marked first production from the White Rose oilfield in the Jeanne d'Arc Basin, east of Newfoundland.

I wondered if, as in previous dreams, *the bowl containing the flowers* was again pointing to a crater: A bowl-shaped, steep-sided hollow in the summit of a volcano formed by either explosion or collapse at a volcanic vent.

Did the *dead flowers* characterize the crystal deposits contained in a crater? Had the deposits eroded over time become sedimentary rock?

---

292 8/28/99.

Footnotes contain dream dates and references to prior pages where the dream appeared.

Endnotes contain bibliographical references, are marked with "Є" in the text, and appear at the end of the book.

Could heat or pressure have changed the sedimentary rock into igneous rock? If so, the dead flowers would then represent volcanic rock called magma, that hot mush of melted rock crystals with dissolved gases that forms igneous rocks on cooling. Magma that reaches the surface is called lava.

Lavender – Lava Under.

The *dead bouquet in sepia tones* was reminiscent of the old monochrome photographs of the nineteenth and early twentieth centuries. Did this bygone symbol point to a sleeping volcano, one currently inactive but which may erupt again, perhaps through the impetus of a "white rose?"

While reading the Telegram article, I noticed a photograph of the semi-submersible drill rig on the White Rose property supported by the caption, "A concrete platform at White Rose and a 625-kilometer pipeline would mark the beginning of the gas age."

The beginning of the gas age? Funny how optimistically that was viewed in the prospector's lens and how ominous it looked through mine.

One of the pipeline articles run in The Telegram carried the headline: "Making the dream a reality."[8] It was the ridiculous crashing into the sublime; whose dream was it, anyhow? The universe must have been laughing its poles off as it awakened an innocent dreamer to a prospector's pipe dream, one no less concrete than the other.

"Your beloved Dr. Steno insisted on winging a double pun," quipped Peggymoonbeam, who appeared enveloped in an ultra-thin cloud of peach gossamer.

I found myself sunning in their repose. No matter how onerous the task, Peggymoonbeam never failed to spread her blanket of humor while Steno imparted his aura of paternal love and protection.

Suddenly, all the dreams about having gas and making a big smell took on a higher meaning. Certainly, a dream exclusively about gas might indicate it was something I ate, but gas appeared in my dreams alongside chalk, chemicals, gas fumes, soot and dust; the idea of passing wind became less and less tenable, at least anatomically. The higher the meaning, the lower the dream; one dream took place in a basement. *I'm in a basement with a thin wool over my eyes which I can see through. Mattresses are sublevel and workmen are making beds with sheets placed horizontally.*[293]

What was the geological meaning of basement and were mattresses to become another prolific theme? Curiosity persisted about why this flock of dreams and lessons about rocks and minerals and gases drove me to Newfoundland.

Steno appeared with a ready answer. "First of all, my vigilant apprentice, Newfoundland is known for its world class geology. Earth scientists from all over the globe visit this province to study the record of the earth's evolution preserved in its rocks. Not only does it have some of the oldest rocks in the world, but it also has some unusual sequences of

293 2/5/99.

rocks which tell a fascinating tale of colliding continents and disappearing oceans in the geological past. As for the meaning of basements and mattresses, it's patently clear that we can't pull the wool over your eyes. 'Basement,' in geology, is the surface beneath which no sedimentary rock is found. The mattress is a recurrent theme because 'bedding' is a collective term used to signify the presence of beds or layers in sedimentary rocks and deposits.

"Penelope, in 1669, I described two basic geologic principles. The first stated that sedimentary rocks are laid down in a horizontal manner, and the second stated that younger rock units were deposited on top of older rock units."

"Gosh, Dr. Steno, could igneous rocks that were laid down during earlier deformations be under the surface where gas might exist?"

"Tu-whit has acquired some fairly recent reports relating to hydrocarbon gases on Earth. Ah. There he is – in the Canadian Shield, which includes portions of the mainland part of Newfoundland."

ÕÕ "'Hydrocarbon gases have been found in deep rocks and ground waters at sites throughout the Canadian Shield. Geologically, they are Precambrian rocks, which are billions of years old. The gases usually trapped in fracture systems throughout the rock are released when mine drilling penetrates the rocks. In recent years, Earth scientists have discovered that life on Earth extends far deeper than ever thought possible. As a matter of fact, evidence of these gases may be similar to those that may have played a part in the formation of the earliest life on the planet.'"[E9]

My mind raced to a dream where *I explain to someone that certain rocks attract the rainwater, which has acid in it, and how the CFCs[E10] in the rain are attracted to hydrocarbons – carboniferous rocks.*[294] Excavation of this scientific message, at this time, would steer us off course so I'd have to sit tight. Because it was so explicit, I trusted its return. It just had to be a lead.

So, in preparation for what I sensed would come later, I began my habitual mode of reasoning, to which the eminent Master Steno calmly listened; for him, patience knew no end.

Chalk, which is limestone[E11] formed from the skeletal remains of sea creatures, could be referring to fossil fuels, like coal or petroleum – hydrocarbons that can be extracted from the earth to produce energy. Hmm. Again, I wondered about the Sissy Spacek dream and her desire for an anti-acid pill.

Sissy Spacek played the lead in the film "The Coal Miner's Daughter." A lot of puzzle-piecing created a picture of sulfur dioxide, which forms acid rain when it reacts with atmospheric moisture. Burning coal produces sulfur dioxide; so do volcanoes. Acid rain.

294 9/21/99.

A good reason for Sissy to want an anti-acid pill. The whole ball of dream yarn was contained within what seemed like a few seconds of dreaming. Ha! Geochemistry 101!

I concluded that the gas fumes rising in my dreams were gaseous compounds, like sulfur dioxide and carbon dioxide that are emitted from a volcanic eruption.

In one of the gas dreams, there is a rally. People are worried that someone evil like Hitler is taking over. There are many speeches. At the end of the rally, people are relieved. A girl is writing the results in chalk and the chalk is so powdery, it's crumbling. I have a visor on above my eyes so that I can see out but the people can't see me. There is a big smell. I'm in a basement and a bad man is trapped inside a death box, which is concealed under a curtain.[295]

Was Hitler symbolic of the gases used in the death camps? What if the bad man was the personification of Hitler and the volcano? Was the death box characterizing a magma chamber, the underground reservoir in the earth's crust that contains the gas-rich liquid magma that feeds a volcano?

Steno responded. "Actually, the super-volcano magma chamber beneath Yellowstone's hotspot corresponds to a death box, for as magma rises to the earth's surface, dissolved gases are released. Certain gases can suffocate people. Carbon dioxide is one of the most dangerous gases because it is invisible. While not poisonous, when pure, it physically blocks oxygen and suffocates any person or animal that inhales it within a few minutes."

(Gulp) "Dr. Steno, What exactly is the curtain?"

"There is an eruption style called the "curtain of fire," where basaltic lava rises up through a fissure and erupts from a linear range of vents. The Eyjafjallajokull eruption in Iceland on march 21, 2010, *was a* fissure eruption."

Wow! That one spread an ash cloud all over Europe. I wondered if gases were in caves, too.

"Penelope, indeed gases are in caves – stalactites and stalagmites form from rainwater that seeps through cracks in the rock. The water picks up carbon dioxide gas, becoming carbonic acid. It's easy to remember which is which: stalactites have a 'C' for ceiling and stalagmites have a 'G' for ground.

"As a matter of fact, one can see lava stalactites inside lava tubes."

My raft dream called those whitish stalks, stalactites but I saw them coming from the ground. That would make them stalagmites.[296]

"Yes, Penelope," laughed Steno. "We wanted to experiment, so we reversed the words. Your dream drawing was of lava stalagmites – conical deposits formed on the floor of a cave or lava tube by the accumulation of drips from the ceiling. We, in fact, told you they

295 7/1/97.
296 12/1/97.

were stalactites which they are from our vantage point. Sorry for any confusion, but we wanted you to understand our 'as above – so below' perspective."

"Dr. Steno, it's beginning to gel. Maybe I had to come to Newfoundland to discover all sorts of upside-down things! I guess it just takes awhile. At first, I thought there was something about me that was upside down."

"To us, you are." He chuckled.

Lava tube. Hmm. Trickling down from the ceiling of cognition was a dream reminder of *the two tall tubular-shaped things that someone was removing.* They appeared to be hollow. Woven into this tube dream was a long-winded list of adjectives: *implacable, impulsive, immaculate, impenetrable, itchy, icky, incongruous, irregular.*[297] The words had some things in common: they all began with "i" and could be interpreted as characteristics of lava.

"Steno interjected, "A lava tube is a natural conduit through which lava travels leaving a hollow tube after the interior lava drains away."

It couldn't be the removal of a lava tube because it's a natural tunnel formed inside the earth. Could those tube-shaped things symbolize a pipeline? If only those pipeline partners would remove their pipeline proposal that would be the blessing of blessings.

The recurring thought of gas pipelines laid deep under the ocean in an area – or even remotely near an area – where dormant submarine volcanoes might exist provoked intense feelings of dread and gave me horrible indigestion. What would happen if a man-made disturbance on our ocean floor caused all the plates to move? What if there was a leak in the pipeline? Natural gas is so flammable!

"Penelope, that would be a disaster of such proportion that little else would matter. That is why we are communicating with you. It is a cause of unutterable concern to all of us at Terracrust. Events like volcanic eruptions, earthquakes, floods, mudflows and avalanches are disastrous but short lived. However, other events – like sea floor spreading, continental drift and erosion of mountain ranges – occur so slowly that they are difficult to measure; yet they can produce catastrophic results, the likes of which the world has never known. You may be at the threshold of colossal disaster and human loss far exceeding that of Titanic."

The tutelary gods were shuddering at how vast the threat of human tampering could be to the circulation of the world's oceans, the largest repository of organisms on the planet. The oceans are our source of life and the hallmark of Earth. We're the only planet in the solar system blessed with a liquid medium for life to evolve in. What were we doing? What were we thinking?

This must be a finely tuned message to save Mother Earth. I imagined it tinkling across eternity and replayed in the collective unconscious, like the resounding notes initially heard by the Indian rishis (Sanskrit for "seers of Truth") around 800 BC.

---

297 9/30/93.

Ever by my side, Steno remarked, "It is important you remember the meaning of the ancient Sanskrit word Upanishad:[298] 'upa' (near) 'ni' (down) s(h)ad (to sit): sitting down near one's Guru to receive his teaching in a peaceful environment. Keep listening, Penelope. We are sharing our secret wisdom with you so that you may share it with others.

Were the teachings of the Upanishads which expound on the ultimate nature of God, soul and world, meant to unite us with the cosmos regardless of which continent we inhabit or which plate our continent sits on? Are the Upanishads telling us that Mother Earth has only one floor, where we all abide and for which we, as one Planet, one People, are responsible?

Is the manifestation of ourselves, through the fulfillment of our individual natures, mirrored in the way we treat our earth?

So many questions ... so few answers.

"I heard you wishing they would remove the pipeline. Remember your mantra, Penelope. 'Penny in your eye. 'In God We Trust.'"

---

298 See Ch. 28 – Morse Code & The Upanishads, p. 128

CHAPTER SIXTY-SEVEN

REFRIGERATION

Nagging at me was that dream image of *water pouring out of a pipe*. I wondered if it might link to a real life pipeline like the one in Alaska. And what if that pipeline sprang a leak? The dream went like this:

A girl rising from the sand is carrying heavy things on a videotape with a chair around her. (The image of the videotape had drawn me to vision ... recorded vision). *A hole in the refrigerator is in the wrong place. It's on the left side. This hole should never have been there to begin with and workmen had come to stop water pouring out of a pipe. The workers are installing metal attachments to the refrigerator. It ends with images of a huge amber vase and a funeral urn in the closet.*[299]

I had interpreted the hole in the refrigerator to be a crater in a glaciated area. Left — the past — pointed to either a dormant volcano that may erupt again or to an "inactive volcano," one that has not erupted within historic times.

The image of workers plugging up a hole in a refrigerator troubled me. One night before drifting off to sleep, I asked Dr. Steno, "What could the hole in the refrigerator be other than a crater?"

"Well," paused Steno, as he pulled on his beard, "there is a tradition that, holds that in the seventeenth or eighteenth century, Spanish or Portuguese sailors drove an adit — that is, an entrance to a mine — into a fluorspar vein at Chambers Cove near St. Lawrence and extracted associated lead ore.[E12]

"Remember, Penelope, you don't have to make a choice because ultimately everything will connect. It is possible that the entrance the sailors drove into the vein will relate to the misplaced hole in your dream and the ore may connect to the *metal attachments*. You may even find that the hole may surprise you with more than one meaning."

"Doc. I just had a thought. Maybe I'm looking in the wrong place."

Steno, busily taking notes, just smiled.

---

299 9/28/93. See Ch. 10 – The Stuff of Life, p. 54

Footnotes contain dream dates and references to prior pages where the dream appeared.
Endnotes contain bibliographical references, are marked with "Ɛ" in the text, and appear at the end of the book.

I was struck by the colorful history of mining in that area. I couldn't stop wondering why I'd be dreaming in microscopic detail about centuries-old activity on soil so far from home. Could there be any reason other than the solemn portent?

I persisted in wanting to know what the chair had to do with any of this.

Steno cautioned, "Penelope. Let us wait until we get to St. Lawrence. Many clues lay ahead."

Hundreds of unripened and unattached dream symbols, many too absurd to even think about, blazed a trail that would lead to realizations impossible to fathom. From Optics – to Genetics – to the Titanic – to Mother Earth and Newfoundland, their inter-relatedness, though inconclusive, was expanding in ways I'd have never believed possible. With eye-popping connections bumping into each other, it would have been derelict not to recognize that the Pipeline was a new piece of the puzzle – if only for a while.

I thought the refrigerator had appeared only once, but in thumbing back through my journals, I found several dreams featuring refrigerators. To my surprise, the icebox had thawed out, leaving a puzzling mixture of dream sludge.

Contained in the melt were common links, such as *an explosion on the left side of the freezer that caused a flood on the right side; a white refrigerator wall* (again on the left) *that was squeaking and creaking. There was air between that wall and an old wooden wall on the other side; a huge explosion in a machine – either a refrigerator or coffee-making machine;* and *a blender contraption making a huge noise, spattering and spraying stuff all over.*[300]

The four shared symbols were: an explosion, a freezer/refrigerator translating to ice – to something frigid – to glaciation, the past, indicated by the left side and walls. Did any of these symbols reflect my personal life at that time? Absolutely. Were they also relevant to the earth? Positively.

The possibility of an eruption in icy waters where inactive or dormant volcanoes might be located resonated.

Was the repetition of walls signaling the walls of a crater? Did the *old wooden wall* suggest the presence of petrified wood, corroborating age? Was the *white refrigerator wall* symbolic of freezing, perhaps natural glaciation? Was the *space between the wooden wall and the creaking refrigerator wall* marking geologic time between a dormant volcano about to resume activity and an active volcano about to erupt? Was the *coffee making* machine symbolic of a wake-up call?

"Penelope, you mentioned petrified wood. From the Greek root, petro means rock or stone. All parts of such fossils are preserved by silica replacement that turns the original wood to stone which frequently occurs as quartz. You know, I originally studied quartz and found that corresponding faces of different crystals of a mineral all intersect at the

---

300 Explosion/Refrigerator dreams: 1994–95.

same angle. They actually named this law after me in the 1600s." He puffed up a little. "They called it Steno's Law.

"So I can help you with any questions you may have about quartz."

"You must be reading my mind again, Dr. Steno. That connects to the dream of the *pole with the colorless rose where I was learning shorthand from a Japanese instructor.*"[301]

A nod from Steno reaffirmed that the *colorless rose* was a symbol for quartz. Shorthand, i.e. stenography, turned out to be an interplanetary pun for Steno and naturally fit his passion for quartz crystals.

Had the old wooden wall I dreamt turned to quartz? Was the amorphous quartz directing us to a quartz wall or boundary of some sort? And what of the elusive pole?

301 10/1/98. See Ch. 14 – Honored Earth Guide: Nicolaus Steno, p. 67
    See Ch. 48 – In My Sight, pp. 210–11

CHAPTER SIXTY-EIGHT

ARGENTIA

Day Five: *Argentia*

As we traveled on I thought back to my casual mention of *Ambrose*. How wondrous that the raising of the Ambrose Shea Bridge would cause Karensurefoot to take a side trip that would unwittingly bridge the dreaming and waking realities of our expedition – and our lives.

"Oh, Karen! I just remembered a part of the 'Ambrose' dream I hadn't told you."

"Really? There's more?" queried Karen.

"Yes. In that same dream, *highlighted on a map was a gymnasium where new stores were supposed to be built right on the edge of the water.*[302]

"A gymnasium? We haven't seen anything, Penny, that looks like a gym around here. Maybe we should ask."

We asked around Placentia for a gymnasium and sure enough, we were directed to the Avalon Fitness Center in Argentia, the only such facility in the area.

Branch. Placentia. Jerseyside. Castle Hill. Argentia. The jagged edges of discovery unveiled a treasured source of light, one that illuminated the golden threads of Vision bound in the invisible cloth of the Dream. Our course was set on automatic pilot. These landmarks seemed to make real the purpose of our Mission, pushing us beyond all known boundaries.

But what was the purpose? With gusts of dream flurries bouncing around us, we wondered if we'd ever see the whole picture. So, why the urge to carry on?

Hard questions, but traveling in the land of the unknown our only resource was Trust. We were guided by a real, yet unspoken voice for a reason we could not yet know. In good time, the purpose would be made whole from this commotion of dream particles – sometimes dropped from the Oneiroball, often appearing out of nowhere. Scattered in real places on Earth, these flimsy little wisps of thought were woven into a massive web of cross

---

302 8/26/99.

Footnotes contain dream dates and references to prior pages where the dream appeared.
Endnotes contain bibliographical references, are marked with "ε" in the text, and appear at the end of the book.

connections. Observing the silent transformation of mystical to physical, we understood that our adventure was far more than a frivolous caper and certainly more than coincidence. A door had been opened to a new texture of reality where we traveled both inside and outside of time. While glistening waves of the present kept us afloat, we were carried on a circular course alternating between future and past, now arriving in Argentia.

"Argentia" is Latin, meaning "Land of Silver." Formerly a major "American naval base, Argentia operated from 1941 to 1994 not merely transformed the Avalon Peninsula, but had an enormous impact throughout Placentia Bay. At one time, efforts were made to establish an industrial park in Argentia.[E13]

In 1996, Voisey's Bay Nickel Company Limited, a wholly owned subsidiary of Inco, Limited, announced its decision to build a nickel smelter and refinery in Argentia but on this cold September day in 1999, the area was still abandoned and, in its neglect, the park was desolate and depressing.

Inco, one of the world's leading nickel producers, was formed in 1902 when Canadian Copper merged with the Orford Copper Company of New Jersey and American Nickel Works.

Hmm. Copper – Pennies – In God We Trust.

We drove around the deserted buildings where the base had been. The Fitness Center was closed. The sign on the building spelled out in big bold letters: GYMNASIUM. As predicted in the dream, it was directly on the water's edge, but the new stores – that is, the industrial park – hadn't yet come to life; it was "in store." The only sounds were the wind whistling through the cracks of the yellow-gray skeleton of a building and its creaking doors.

Though we weren't able to visit Labrador, the home of Voisey's Bay, on this expedition, it was subtly weaving itself into the corner of the mosaic reserved for Argentia.

The announcement of a nickel smelter three years earlier was greeted as a godsend in Argentia, where the unemployment rate was the highest in the country.

My thoughts traveled back to the pipeline discovery – to the dream featuring Sissy Spacek. I was unwittingly uttering Coal Miner's Daughter when I sensed a ripple in the atmosphere.

"Hold on! Hold it right there, Penelope."

Steno and his pad were floating into view, a telltale sign that a treat was in store.

"You're getting too warm for me not to remind you of images we sent of a *crab with the numbers 4391or 4931, the upside-down OPEC, the word 'Mobil' upside down and the two keys.*"[303]

---

303 10/7/99.

Getting warm? The first time those numbers appeared they were attached to Kit;[304] now they're connected to a crab. Dream retrospectives released waves of hot flashes, not postmenstrual flashes, but heat waves emitting coal, petroleum, hydrocarbons – fossil fuels.

Coal was a snug fit: It is a readily combustible sedimentary rock. Miners: The mining of nickel for the Argentia smelter. Hmm. Coal and Miners had forged a link. What about Daughter? Well, who knows?

Madame Curie demurely offered, "I do."

"Not yet," motioned Steno to Curie. "And Penelope, don't forget Sissy Spacek, who played the Coal Miner's Daughter."

I began again: Sissy – Spacek – movie star – Star – Space – report to 4391 or 4931 Kitts Astronomical Observatory. But the crab – what about the crab?

"Well, Penelope," continued Steno, "the remains of a crab that existed in the past is a fossil – as in fuel – as in coal."

There is also the Crab Nebula. I do have some ancient memory of fossil finding. Fossil fuels are quite old, you know, as they come from organic material that was deposited and buried in the earth millions of years ago.

"Millions of years ago? I thought you were a youthful seventeenth-century intellectual!"

"Now, don't be confused, Penelope dear. I'm not quite that ancient but I do know something about fossils."

I was breathless. Unbelievable, Dr. Steno! How did you do that? How did you make everything connect so that it adds up to fossil fuel? Proud as a peacock, he fanned his archangelic feathers and swirled away.

The Pauline Maher and Maher's Polypipe epiphany in Placentia dropped in for a return engagement. Pauline Maher, my long-lost friend, appeared in a dream sequel, this time as part of a complicated love triangle.

One of the suitors is a military type who is involved with someone else. Because he knows I'm trying to help Pauline, he does not like me at all. The dominant image is *a hanging ladder that won't attach to a staircase.* The dream concludes with *deformed twins whose heads are in the shape of hearts.*[305] How odd!

Empathy for Pauline revived earlier concerns that the poor girl was *backed into a wall. The side of her face was scraped and it was my fault.*

In the final synthesis, the tale of Pauline Maher – as in maar – symbolized imminent ecological danger if a pipeline were run along the ocean floor and backed into the wall of a crater in a faulted area. The sequel was not about a love triangle but, a crowded political

304 See Ch. 56 – Bon Voyage, pp. 259–60
305 10/23/97.

bed. All this jockeying for a place in it while embers of destruction smolder below, may well be incinerating the whole of humanity.

Was the St. John's-based company that proposed the pipeline cozying up with the military type, characterized by the military base – Argentia? Was the Argentia Management Authority, which proposed the industrial park, in bed with the provincial governments as well as Voisey's Bay Nickel Company? And why in the world would that be important to me?

I hoped that the *hanging ladder* was a metaphor for the pending nature of the project. I was encouraged that it did not attach; maybe it was an answer to my prayer that the project not proceed.

Deformed twins with heart-shaped heads would match natural deformed crystals that frequently twin to form heart, star and V-shaped twins. Cerussite, known for its deformation and twinning properties, is an ore of lead, as is Galena. Both minerals are rich in silver and used as silver ores. It all fit. Cerussite – sero from Titanic (ores spelled backward) – sight from the CBS Eye – Galen – Vision – Galena – ore of lead[306] – all culminating in the mining of ore in Voisey's Bay.

I traveled back to the beginning of this odyssey and the silver key.[307] Was this another door opened by the silver key *that snaps in half is put back together again?* Curium is a silver metal – Cerussite and Galena, minerals and a silver ore. Metals and minerals were making a comeback.

It was Karensurefoot's turn at a dream: *A black locomotive was coming through a piece of paper. It was part of a story told her by a deceased friend who had been a coin collector. She saw the word "channel."*

The next morning, we stopped at the Placentia Post Office and noticed a Canadian collection of commemorative coins for sale. To our utter amazement one was embossed with a locomotive. Had Karen's departed friend become a Terracrust recruit?

The locomotive-imprinted coin affirmed her channeled message.

The locomotive in the dream actually mobilized our findings in terms of locale. The railway had come to Placentia as early as 1888.

---

306 11/9/96.   See Ch. 57 – St. John's, p. 263
   8/28/97.   See Ch. 19 – Galena and Beyond, p. 81
307 9/22/93.   See Ch. 1 – Beginnings, pp. 7–8
              See Ch. 17 – Real Estate & Alchemy, p. 76

CHAPTER SIXTY-NINE
YELLOW STONES

Back on the highway, racing to make Grand Bank by nightfall, we sped past a blur of stones, barely visible from the road. Grouped and painted yellow, they spelled out, of all things: YELLOWSTONE! How precarious the nature of the visible. Catching barely a glimpse of the word "yellow," we realized that one blink and we would have missed it. We turned around, drove down a dirt road and at its end discovered a trailer park called Yellowstone.

The grouping of yellow stones retrieved the *yellow slab* dream that told me if I was patient, I'd learn everything I need to know.

I had been flirting with the connection of the yellow slab to the Yellowstone hotspot, my earliest volcanic clue,[308] but was not entirely convinced. Nicolaus Steno, spirit contractor for paint, bricks and stones, picked up on my quandary and, in a flash, propelled himself to Newfoundland where he and Peggymoonbeam bantered over the placement of the yellow stones before our arrival:

Steno: "Put them in Argentia"

Peggy: "No. Put them in Placentia"

Steno: "OK. All right. Let's compromise. How about between Argentia and Grand Bank?'

Peggy: "But what if they don't make Grand Bank by nightfall? It will be dark there. They won't see them."

Steno: "We can fix that."

Peggy and Steno: "Agreed."

---

308 See Ch. 51 – Tsunami, p. 232

Footnotes contain dream dates and references to prior pages where the dream appeared.
Endnotes contain bibliographical references, are marked with "Ɛ" in the text, and appear at the end of the book.

Peggy: "Do you think they'll know that Grand Bank is the town and Grand Banks is a group of underwater plateaus?"

Steno: "Not to worry your pretty soul, Peggy. They'll figure it out."

Yellow painted stones spelling out the word "Yellowstone" – a concrete homonym literally cast in stone.

Intoxicated by the robust workings of the metaphysical, we got out of the car, photographed the stones and laughed ourselves silly. Surprise was traveling faster than the speed of light, consistently arriving before we did.

Our latest finding was whimsical as a children's nursery rhyme:

> "High diddle diddle,
> The cat and the fiddle,
> The cow jumped over the moon,
> The little dog laughed,
> To see such craft,
> And the dish ran away with the spoon."[E14]

As a child, I'd ask, "How could a dish run away with a spoon?" Now, as an adult, I asked, "How could a grouping of yellow stones spelling YELLOWSTONE be planted on our way to Grand Bank?"

The Yellowstone display, beyond which lay the Grand Banks where the Titanic rests peacefully in the North Atlantic Ocean, would endure. Was it a clue? Was it real? Was it soberly pointing the way to the cause of the disaster?

Then I heard a faint ticking from the infamous *clock* dream.

Tick – tock – tick – tock.

"Karensurefoot. You won't believe this! I had a dream about a clock with a funny sort of doodle drawn on it. I call this my Clock-A-Doodle-Do dream. *The message is that 'he wants yellow … pale yellow.' I go to point at the clock with a pen, which I don't realize is a marker. It makes a mark with a curly cue by mistake. The person holding the clock is annoyed. Someone says, 'you slipped.' I say, it's 'my mistake.'*[309]

"Fantastic! The yellow is a cue for Yellowstone! Here, let me draw you a picture of this clock with the curly cue in the center."

---

309 See Ch. 29 – Clock-A-Doodle-Do, p. 131

Of course! It was a marker and a cue – my *mistake* – a fault. Translated from dreaming to waking, the cue was marking a fault.

"Wow, Penelope! That is impressive! I will carry this picture with me just in case it shows up somewhere."

The grouping of stones spelling out Yellowstone on the way to Grand Bank spirited us toward the Yellowstone hotspot. Eruptions of the Yellowstone volcanic system have included the two largest volcanic eruptions in North America in the past few million years. The next eruption is overdue and could be twenty-five hundred times the size of the 1980 Mount St. Helens eruption.[E15]

Was Yellowstone the symbol for a dormant volcanic system in the Newfoundland area – or some other area?

Peggymoonbeam was prodding Steno. "Please, Doc, tell her to put on her Timelessness Glasses and get out her Psymometer. It's time we point out the geology around Grand Banks so she sees it clearly."

Steno materialized holding his super powered spy glass. Folding out an oversized map of Newfoundland, his cheerful greeting caught us by surprise. "Penelope, we're delighted that you and Karensurefoot found your way to our yellow stone markings. Now, focus on this map and let me know when you find the Burin Peninsula."

"OK. OK. I see it. What are you showing me, Doc?"

"Now find the Grand Banks area, toward which you are heading."

"Hmm. I see a picture of a little ship on it. Oh. That's the legend for where Titanic went down. OK. I've got it."

"Notice that it is underlain by very old ash and lava that erupted from volcanoes both on land and under the sea."

It seemed that a mini circle was forming – Yellowstone – hotspot – volcanic activity – Titanic – underwater – Grand Banks – Newfoundland.

CHAPTER SEVENTY

THE ANONYMOUS ARTIST
PAINTS A HOLE

Yellow – Yellowstone – a cue – a fault.

Mission Lavender was fast becoming a cosmic scavenger hunt, except the items hidden in the backyard when we were kids were now hidden all over the Earth. I remember how much fun it was when, as children, we teamed together to find a baseball bat, a cracker, a whistle, a balloon animal, a quote from Peanuts. Now here we are, adult children, searching for geologic dream fragments in a yard as big as the world. Not only were we searching for hidden clues of a very different kind, but we were also uncovering important insights. Designing our course must have been a ginormous chore for the masters, having to come up with thousands of clues and then figure out where each one goes.

Steno appeared on the word "one." "Focus on 'children,' Penelope. Remember Peggymoonbeam's mantra: 'Repetition for children, patience for adults.' Think of your many dreams of children. You had one where 'children were at play.' You, Karen, were in this dream, as well."

Karen beamed her Cheshire cat grin, waiting to hear more."

"Children at play, Doc? You mean children on a scavenger hunt?"

"Think of the color yellow, Penelope."

There were so many variations on the yellow theme I went blank.

"OK. I'll give you another clue: Wyoming."

"Doc. This string of clues: Children at play … the color yellow … Wyoming. I just don't see how one thing has anything to do with another. It's pretty farfetched if you ask me. And what in heaven's name would any of these clues have to do with a fault?"

"All right, Penelope. One more clue: A paint brush."

"My brain is so rattled, I can't focus. I'm sorry, Doc, but it sounds like a lot of gibberish."

Footnotes contain dream dates and references to prior pages where the dream appeared.

Endnotes contain bibliographical references, are marked with "Ɛ" in the text, and appear at the end of the book.

A gray cloud of disappointment swept in. I had hurt his feelings.

Suddenly, my overworked brain started to click and clack and connect, connect, connect. My neurons were on fire! The dream was extracted! It involved a mysterious someone painting with a paint brush.

"I got it, Doc! I got it! It's about a big hole. This strange number code got implanted in my text, but anyhow, here goes."

280,, *Part of a wall has been broken through. There is movement and a hole has become larger. Then someone with a paint brush on the other side is painting with glue or something sticky and moves some pillows to expose a bigger hole. By now, the actual concrete blocks, like cinder blocks, are showing and the opening is huge.*[310]

Children are playing a cat-and-mouse game.

I have moved some of my old things out. I explain which is old and which is new. All the furniture is in one room because the wall was broken through. An ornate carved stone credenza is new. I almost mistake it for old.

I'm out west with Karen in cowboy country. We try on fur jackets. Then we think about skiing. Wyoming is a clue. A bed comes apart in two.

The dream ends with someone winding an invisible string as though it's coming from above. I couldn't tell if they are winding it up or down.

This was the first cinder block dream; the second contained *yellowish cinder blocks and pictured a multi-colored house resembling a child's kindergarten drawing.*[311]

"*Actual concrete*" blocks leapt off the page. Was this dream actually concrete?[312]

Yellowish cinder blocks. My reaction to cinder translated to ash; yellowish to uncertainty.

As for the paintbrush on the other side, Steno waved his spyglass over the signposts: The lavender painted rocks in Branch, the yellow painted initials, the lavender painted bricks at Castle Hill Mountain in Placentia all zoomed into view.

The unfathomable sighting of dream-coordinated paint colors splashed on rocks and bricks of the physical world infused us with the mystery of omniscience. We somehow knew we were being guided by an all knowing Mind, one that escorted us along the interconnecting pathways of conscious and unconscious thought.

The bewildering material clues would color our memories and deepen our insight as we crossed the road of dreams into a newly visible world of waking. There was a silent choreography to this. Was it orchestrated so the matching of paint to dreams would

310 2/29/00.
311 9/2/00.
312 See Ch. 110 – The Marriage of Concrete & Abstract, pp. 577–79

awaken us to the identity of the anonymous painter? To the beneficent artist who unceasingly warned us of peril we could not see?

The glue, the "something sticky," must be describing lava. Warnings of volcanoes were accelerating.

I'd mindlessly glossed over the Wyoming tip, ignoring the many clues: cowboy country – fur jackets – skiing.

Yellowish blocks. Yellow stones. Yellowstone was screaming at us! The *hole* was Jackson Hole in Grand Teton National Park.

Cowboy country! *Wyoming*! Jackson Hole in the Grand Tetons is located in northwestern Wyoming just south of Yellowstone National Park!

Fur jackets! *Skiing*! Fur traders explored the Grand Teton region in the early nineteenth century. Families with children of all ages are winter camping, mountaineering, backcountry skiing and even dog sledding at Grand Teton. It's a virtual playground. While at play in the snow, God's innocent preschoolers may be skiing for a fall. They must be warned that they are skiing over a gigantic *hole* that is growing larger by the day.

Steno's clues were falling into place. He said, "Focus on children."

Was the *ornate carved stone credenza* the continental shelf? I mistake it for old but it's actually new. Had human activity impacted the ecology of the continental shelf changing its appearance?

The *wall broken through* appears to extend from the Yellowstone Plateau (the Yellowstone Caldera) to Grand Teton National Park.

All the furniture in one room implies a volcanic coalescing of Yellowstone and Grand Teton.

If the *bed that came apart in two* symbolizes a growing fracture zone, a fault line in a volcanic field, the rocks must be detaching at their weaker layers. Could we get to it in time? I was on my knees praying someone would come soon.

All the pieces fit. Children at play – the color yellow – Wyoming – a fault. Were we, the children, at fault? The clues for this piece of our cosmic scavenger hunt had been uncovered. But who was the winner? There is no victor. The children – all of us – are at an impasse. We must renounce this cat and mouse game and surrender to the forces of nature. "Repetition for children, patience for adults," had become a constant refrain. How many times must a child be told? The most tolerant adult loses patience. Planet Earth is speaking to us. It is time to mature, time to give up our self-indulgent fripperies and whining entitlement and have compassion for Her. She is fragile.

I had had so many dreams of rocks. And so many colored yellow – the yellow slab in particular. In one dream, *a slab of rock hits me on the head.*[313] I wondered if that repeating yellow slab was the rock that clobbered me?

And so the bell tolled for the might of the Universe. The harmonies, even the disharmonies were in perfect pitch if you listened carefully. I wondered whether all of life was this fathomable, if we truly perceived and responded to what encircled us in so many dimensions.

---

313 9/6/01.

CHAPTER SEVENTY-ONE

MOM'S ECSTASY

The metaphor is perhaps one of man's most fruitful potentialities. Its efficacy verges on magic, and it seems a tool for creation which God forgot inside one of His creatures when He made him.[Ɛ16]

Jose Ortega Y Gasset

Day Six: Lawn, St. Lawrence, Bethany, Grand Bank

"Why the Burin Peninsula?" the travel planner had asked. "That's an awful lot of driving when you have only six days."

I said, "Research."

"Well, in St. John's you can go to the Archives where all the government buildings are located, and from there you can see our beautiful province," she urged.

I apologetically explained that this is a different kind of research – more to get the look and feel of the place.

"Oh, I see," the travel agent politely responded.

Unbeknown to us, the trip would extend beyond our original plans with little time for sleep. We had to scrap most of her well-intended sightseeing recommendations in favor of our off-the-beaten-track Mission.

And so, after our spree of unimagined phenomena in the South Cape area, we were heading toward the Burin Peninsula, prompted by the dream about *my mother's deformed leg, especially at the foot and looking bumpy and puffy. My mother is in ecstasy crossing from one theater to another.*[314]

Even at the end of her eighth decade, my mother's legs were quite shapely and her feet well formed. Still, I worried. I called her nurse to inquire about the condition of her

---

314 1/12/99.

Footnotes contain dream dates and references to prior pages where the dream appeared.
Endnotes contain bibliographical references, are marked with "Ɛ" in the text, and appear at the end of the book.

leg and foot and both were fine. This leg-foot deformity had remained an enigma until the mother/Mother Earth connection manifested and converted her misshapen leg to the topography of the Burin Peninsula. Her foot then connected to an "expanded-foot" or "Piedmont" glacier that spreads out at the foot of a mountain. The theme of glaciation had resurfaced.

How bizarre that my mother would be in ecstasy going to a theater with a lumpy leg, although given Peggymoonbeam's theatrics, it figured. As it turned out, my guardian angel had learned the language well. Mother's geological state of ecstasy jibed with isostasy, which refers to the buoyancy of the earth's crust as it floats on the denser, fluid mantle below it.[E17] Its basic mechanism is a response to a type of erosion through which an entire mountain range can be lifted.

I might add that the dream appeared early in 1999 when my mother was living. She passed over in 2002 and I'd like to think her crossing was truly one of ecstasy.

The heavenly wordsmiths were hands-down the Nobel laureates of the metaphor. Steno's concern with my ability to master their language was tempered with gigantic doses of tolerance, for I was now in my fifth year of learning the nuances of their language with all its permutations. Peggymoonbeam reassured him regularly of my fierce determination. She convinced the distinguished professor that if she kept drawing pictures I'd be curious enough and driven enough to put them together and that eventually I'd get it.

I contemplated *mother's crossing from one theater to the next.* Taking an uneducated geological guess, I wondered if the pressures of the overlying rocks in the Burin area were causing movement in the ice sheets and signaling a shift in the earth – a.k.a. Mother Earth – from one geologic stage to another.

More philosophically, was Mother Earth's crossing indicative of a change precipitating a move from one way of life to another? Was the way in which we behave toward our earth a harbinger for change that would affect the way we live? If I were to ask Lord Galen, the honorable overseer of Timelessness Optics, would the answer be yes? I shuddered to think – if we were as unkind to the Earth as we are to each other – what Earth might have in store for us.

The coastline along the Burin Peninsula is indented with hundreds of small bays, inlets and coves. Behind the slightly bent knee of the Peninsula is a physically charming stretch of rugged coast.

We stopped in Burin to soak up some sun and enjoy the rough-hewn scenery. While Karensurefoot strolled round the village, I lolled on a bench overlooking a picturesque lake and reflected on how perfectly orchestrated our lives are. If only we could understand that we are intrinsically linked to everything, we could begin to heal by trusting the flow of the universe.

Karensurefoot returned from her walk, her ear-to-ear smile lighting her from inside out. "Penelope, the most amazing thing happened! As I was wandering through the back streets, I saw a picture of the same pirate and pirate's hat on a building, just like the one we saw in Jerseyside! Come, let me show you."

Sure enough, there it was – an exact image of the first sighting!

"Maybe it's something indigenous to the province," said Karensurefoot." I agreed, then re-examined the clues that might reveal a link to Titanic: *I'm walking through rushes, below me is a ravine, there are signs of danger, turbulent waterfalls, actors acting something out, they are being jostled, a pirate's hat* appears that carries some strange signature.[315]

I connected it to the passengers of Titanic; the first pirate picture was propped up against the boat in Jerseyside – the broken down boat that was an upside-down copy of Titanic's lifeboats. Then I cogitated on the word "rushes." Why would I use that word? It occurred to me that the Bible uses the word "bulrushes" interchangeably with "rushes."

Heading toward the boot of the Burin Peninsula, we noted highway signs marking Spanish Room and Lewin's Cove whirring past us and tempting us with clues tucked away in each of those tiny inlets. Our mandate to see Lawn, St. Lawrence and Burin first was pressing. We would catch the diminutive finger coves on the way back.

---

315 11/11/96. See Ch. 62 – A Birthday Party in Placentia, p. 288

CHAPTER SEVENTY-TWO

A SNAKE ON THE LAWN

Be ye therefore wise as serpents, and harmless as doves.
Matthew 10:16

Our first stop on the way around the boot would be Lawn, a fishing village some say was named by a Frenchman after a doe caribou he spotted there. Believing it to be a donkey, he called it l'ane. More accepted, however, is that Captain James Cook named it Lawn Harbour because of its rich lushness. Whatever its legacy, Lawn is known as one of the best inshore fishing harbors of the peninsula. But we weren't entirely sure why we were there. While poring over a map early in planning for the trip, I'd spotted the tiny village of Lawn, and the name inexplicably clicked with a dream.

I see a huge burst of flames, then high ocean waves. They are right next to each other. Then they become memorialized in the form of a gold statue. I see Karen sitting in the grass. She is smiling and a man is standing behind her. Suddenly I notice a snake near Karen. It belongs to this other person. It is his pet. At first, it looks like a toy snake but suddenly it comes to life and bites me, making me dizzy and paralyzing me.[316]

Lawn … Karensurefoot *sitting in the grass.* Given that there was no specific reason to go there, the stop at Lawn was a case of pure instinct riding the horse.

Because of the negative connotation implicit in the symbol of a snake, I wrestled with the sharing of this dream with Karen. Snakes may be emblems of the mysterious dangers of the underworld, which the Christian tradition incorporated into its mythology, as an embodiment of evil, particularly the evil of temptation.[Ɛ18] Then again, the snake is an ancient symbol for healing and new life. The caduceus that marks the medical profession is a healing sign: two snakes entwined on Hermes staff. The Rod of Asclepius, Greek god of healing, contains the serpent, which in shedding its old skin emerges fully formed in a new one. It is a symbol of rebirth and fertility, the staff, a symbol of authority.

---

316 7/7/99.

Footnotes contain dream dates and references to prior pages where the dream appeared.
Endnotes contain bibliographical references, are marked with "Ɛ" in the text, and appear at the end of the book.

Serpentine attributes resonated with the underlying message spok
ity of the Dream, its unbroken circle mirroring the spheres of the cosm
minute particles of our unconscious were the manifestation of knowl
power of the earth, life, death and resurrection.

Serpents are ancient dream symbols often associated with go
Because serpents live in the ground, they may represent the healing
Snakes emerging from the ground may indicate the emergence of ur
into the light of consciousness.[E19]

I remembered how dizzy I was in the dream when the snake came
The sensation shocked me awake to full consciousness. It made sense
light-headed if bitten by the gods whose Mission was the healing of th

I concluded that this wasn't a bad snake but a good one, and I
dream with my ethereal waking life companion.

"Karen, now I know why we had to visit Lawn."

"Really, Penelope? Why?"

"Well, I had a dream with you in it. It began very dramatically
flames and high ocean waves that turn into a monument in the *form of a g*

"Wow! What a spectacular image!"

"But wait, Karen. *You were sitting in the grass smiling and a man was sta*
When we were planning the trip, I noticed Lawn on the map and had s
of grass in the dream. I thought it was kind of a stretch, so I almost forgo
my instincts said 'go.'"

I vacillated. Should I tell her about the snake? What if she takes it in t
I could feel her picking up on my anxiety.

"Is there any more to the dream, Penelope? Please tell me. Go on."

"Well, um. I don't know. I don't want you to be upset."

"Oh, for Heaven's sake, Penelope. You've shared so many private things, why
do you think I'd be upset?"

"Well, I couldn't tell you before because there is a snake in the dream. *This sn*   *is*
near you. It belongs to the man who was standing behind you. It is his pet. It starts out as *toy*
snake but then it comes to life and bites me and makes me dizzy and paralyzes me.

Because there are a lot of negative connotations associated with snakes, I didn't want
you to think I didn't trust you. You know people consider a snake in the grass to be an
untrustworthy person."

Karen was laughing her head off. "You know, Penelope, there are very positive associations to snakes. They can symbolize transformation and I think Jung talked about them

as a connection between Earth and Heaven, exactly what your work is about. I believe one of the most common dream symbols of transcendence is the snake.

Who do you think the man was standing behind me?"

Honestly, Karen? I think he was an angel in human form," and I started to cry for being so limited by preconceived notions about things, like snakes being bad people.

Penelope, why do you think this angel had a snake for a pet?"

'Well, because any pet owner, especially an angel, has to know how to care for and feed it and understand how it behaves. If the pet dream snake is symbolic of a divine connection between Heaven and Earth, the owner would have to make the commitment required to keep it and nurture it, for it is sacred and must not be violated."

"OK, but if it's so sacrosanct, then why did it paralyze you?"

"Now that I realize the otherworldly nature of this dream, Karen, I think the wonder of it all rendered me motionless. The snake bite must have been awakening me to this incredible reality we've entered."

"It's extraordinary that you would dream about a statue and a serpent in the same dream."

On cue, Tu-whit swirled down to deliver the holy words written in Numbers 21:9.

ÕÕ "'And Moses made a serpent of brass, and put it upon a pole and it came to pass, that if a serpent had bitten any man, when he beheld the serpent of brass, he lived.'"

The *memorialized gold statue* mystically connected to the story of the bronze serpent that Moses made in the wilderness.[20] For the Hebrews, the bronze snake on Moses' staff was a sign of God's presence. Brass, gold, or bronze, the dream got it right. It was a statue cast and commemorated in metal.

Was it pure irony that fire and water, the two conflicting elements, would weave a snake with its cosmological symbolism into the same tapestry?

Fire and water. The dream, as if by design, had combined those two conflicting elements: *flames* and *ocean waves*, "which will ultimately penetrate each other and unite. In a state of conflict they are the heat and moisture necessary for life, but burning water is the union of opposites."[21]

While reflecting on the sculpted ocean waves, my thoughts returned to Titanic's cloudy waters. The whisperings of its departed seemed to be invoking in my dreams "the incantations of the dead who cross the waters of death."[22]

The curious image of *the toy snake that suddenly came to life* stirred my awareness that in waking, a toy snake sits in my apartment under the beautiful ficus tree Peggymoonbeam gave me. I have always felt that a part of her is seeded in the roots of this tree. Every time I cut a branch, at least three more seem to sprout. It's like a tree growing from heaven.

At that, the spirit of Peggymoonbeam blazed in bubbling over with excitement. "Penelope! A Tree Grows in Brooklyn was symbolized by a real tree named *Ailanthus altissima.* It means the tree of heaven, which is known for its ability to survive almost anywhere, under any conditions."

"Nah …Go on. You gotta be kidding, Peggymoonbeam. You're making this up! It's just another flight of fancy, but it makes a good story!"

"Penelope. Relax. This is not a fantasy. That is the name of the genus and species as it's known on Earth. Sooner or later, you'll realize there are no coincidences. *Ailanthus* is derived from the Ambonese word *ailanto,* meaning 'heaven-tree' or 'tree reaching for the sky,' and *altissima* is Latin for 'very tall.' You should feel lots of positive energy swirling 'round your ficus, my little buddy, for like the Tree of Heaven, it thrives right there in your city apartment be it hot or cold, wet or dry, even smoky or dusty. Just keep caring for it and it will endure. Combine the robust nature of your tree with the wisdom, healing and rejuvenation symbolized by the snake and know that you are fully protected."

Wow! I rushed to look up *Ailanthus altissima* and sure enough, the book and the tree were just as she said.

I had secretly known Peggymoonbeam would receive a colossal promotion when she crossed the great pond to life on the other side. She had probably been elevated to the ethereal realm by now. That's two realms above the physical. Those who research spirit communication suggest that ethereal inhabitants exchange information more efficiently and in greater quantity than the supercomputers of our world.[Ɛ23]

As we leisurely drove through the sleepy streets of Lawn, I wondered how long it would take to design a dream quilt that would capture the intricately vast spectrum of the Universe. I imagined the centerpiece to be the cosmological serpent – the snake eating its own tail and forming a circle that symbolized the universal pattern of creation and decay.

CHAPTER SEVENTY-THREE

POLES AND HYDRANTS

*Either there are two miracles that have to be admired
together in the same way, or there are none.*
Bruno Latour[E24]

While taking in the beauty of the harbor and the rustic charm of the little community, we passed a fire hydrant. It was painted lavender! Next to it was a pole, also painted lavender!

We gaped in disbelief. Facing us were the most prominent symbols in the tapestry: The single pole and the color lavender. That, plus a fire hydrant, all in plain view!

With every turn we took, there stood: a lavender pole — a lavender fire hydrant.

Footnotes contain dream dates and references to prior pages where the dream appeared.
Endnotes contain bibliographical references, are marked with "E" in the text, and appear at the end of the book.

Flashbacks! The photo of the little girl holding a pole and the dream of the little girl where the photo catches fire.[317] That dream also imaged a hollowed-out book.

Tu-whit was still circling. Our all-knowing librarian must have sensed a pole up ahead.

How was it all manifesting in this one little village?

With each epiphany, the latest truth became the absolute Truth. When one has reached the pinnacle, how can there be a higher summit? Metaphorically, we thought we'd found the Himalaya in Lawn. Yet, as we traveled on, more daring and arduous mountains came into view.

The fire hydrant evoked a dream in which *I dial a place called Tectonics.* The dream concludes with *images of a plastic fire hydrant the color of a child's toy, a scoop illustrated with jagged pieces and a spindly wand for getting through the debris. The objects all had to do with lava and constituted a children's kit for fighting a volcano.*[318]

Children in my dreams was becoming a drumbeat. Since I did not have children of my own, the celestial hierarchy vehemently persisted with the message of concern for "the children of God."

The dream-induced password *"Tectonics"* blinked a green light yielding the right of way at the intersection called Geology. The *scoop* resembled that of a slusher scoop used for mucking, a mining term for shoveling or digging out broken ore or rock. *Children at play, children playing cat and mouse* came echoing back. The *"plastic" fire hydrant,* part of a *"children's kit,"* represented far more than a child's toy.

Fleeting thoughts of Raggedy Ann rushed to mind. I thought of how the years had flown by since I'd held my cherished rag doll with her smashed-down nose and red yarn hair, and somehow, just having her near me meant all would be right with the world. It seemed she followed me wherever I went.

Now lost in a strange land of lavender poles and fire hydrants, I was distracted by the great Steno waving his spyglass overhead. It was a signal to take a closer look at things, maybe the plastic fire hydrant.

The concept of plastic deformation was so hard to grasp, so difficult to get my arms around. No matter how much I read I had been unable to absorb it. No matter how hard Steno tried, I just couldn't get it. Out of sheer frustration, I had combed the Internet in search of a geology professor, and found the Distinguished Teaching Professor at the University of Texas. It was long before this journey to Newfoundland that he had shone his lantern on my first earthly foray into geology. Incredibly generous with his time, patiently answering my bumbling layman's questions and explaining, with great clarity, scientific concepts that were completely outside my realm, his description of

---

317 See Ch. 3 – The Pole, p. 23
318 2/28/99.

plastic deformation finally helped me to make some sense of it. I shall be forever grateful to him.

In my first exploration of the concept, he had e-mailed me that:

> "Plastic deformation is change of size or shape without rupturing. It is a bending of the rocks. Brittle deformation is breaking (fracturing). Plastic deformation could precede brittle deformation – the rocks would bend first, and then they would break. It is common to have severely bent rocks right next to a fault."

Egad! I wondered if the rocks were bending under Lawn's scenic backdrop. What if it was only a matter of time before they became brittle and started to break?

The tiny community of Lawn was as peaceful and innocent as a newborn sleeping in its cradle. That Sunday afternoon perfectly captured the everyday doings of small-town life in a Norman Rockwell painting: casually dressed townspeople taking their Sunday drives; fishermen ambling down to the wharf; children playing, riding bicycles, chasing dogs. Snoozing in a lush valley in the heart of the picturesque village was a little park with red picnic tables. Karen and I ambled over to one of the tables and paused to enjoy the lazy feeling of the unspoiled little town framed by a mountainous backdrop.

While taking in the unspoiled beauty of this glimpse into the past, I wondered if a strain was located in the rock body of those mountains. Was there a fault right under that beautiful vista in front of us? My question was answered when I consulted the geological map and discovered a fault line on either side of Lawn bridged by a geological contact.

Could the movement of tectonic plates portend an earthquake that would affect the entire coastline?

Steno, my omniscient tutor, stood by. "Penelope, let's say that all earthquakes, volcanic activity, and mountain-building processes are caused by the movement of plates."

The sight of that first lavender hydrant and the single lavender pole next to it is one I shall never forget.

We drove round and round the tiny village. The only feasible explanation must have to do with some town ordinance that required that poles and hydrants be paired, for wherever there was a hydrant, there appeared to be a pole. Only once did we see a pole by itself. To see – in broad daylight – a town with poles and fire hydrants routinely placed so many feet apart and painted lavender was beyond the range of human comprehension. Certainly, it was outside the realm of pure coincidence. The symbols of the fire hydrant, the pole and lavender appeared separately in dreams that stretched across time. Seeing their physical forms flickering like repeating frames in a silent movie here in Lawn awakened us to the relationship of mind and matter – or matter and mind. Whatever the order, they were inextricably linked.

I thought back to the dream that paired Morse code with the word Upanashod (misspelled in my dream journal).[319] What is Morse code, after all? It's a system of telegraphic transmission using encoded messages as a means to communicate. Again, I reflected on the meaning of the Upanishads. Why would the teachings of the Upanishads, which embody the universal soul, be attached to a Morse code message?

The secret language of that dream decoded to reveal MOMOM. This divine communication affirmed that out of deep concern for Mother Earth, its message expanded far beyond the theme of Titanic and was calling on the indivisibility of man and God.

When I finally realized the magnitude of linkage, not just within one theme, but from theme to theme, I was able to fathom the overarching meaning of the coupling of Morse code with the Upanishads.

Steno came to my aid. "In this sense, Penelope, every individual is united with the cosmos and only needs to realize this to reach fulfillment. Those who advance toward enlightenment will come to realize that all of you are shepherds of the Earth. Without Her, you have nothing."

If the Titanic was one theme within a whole that unified a body of uncountable dream fragments, an underlying unity would ultimately link to the long chain of other themes continuously emerging and expanding: Vision, Crystals, Metals, Geology, Astronomy, Genetics; it was unending. The message was taking root: the great effort being communicated by this immortal band of gurus was that the health of Planet Earth had to be humankind's number one priority.

We stopped for a quick lunch on route to the town of Burin. While waiting for our burgers, Karensurefoot casually asked, "What was the name of the geology professor who's been helping you on the Internet?"

I shuffled through my mental rolodex for a moment and absentmindedly answered, "Leon Long."

Karensurefoot bellowed, "LL ... LL ... Leon Long! The rocks ... the painted rocks ...the yellow painted rocks in Branch - the initials were LL!"

We shrieked in unison.

And so it was. Leon Long. We had witnessed the geology professor's initials reverentially painted on a rock in Branch, probably a chunk of shale. How fitting that Branch is situated along one of the world's geological wonders, famous for its Cambrian fossil-bearing shales in vividly colorful displays of reds and greens.

It was almost biblical ... To everything there is a season and a time to every purpose under the Heaven."[ε25]

---

319 1/20/94. See Ch.28 – Morse Code & The Upanishads, p. 128

Branch. It was personified in the dream where *branches were coming out of my head* and in my automatic writing about the enteric soul.[320]

Steno and Peggymoonbeam, fluttering and swooning with excitement, swooped down. "Let's hear it again, Penelope. We want to be sure you had audio input."

Thinking back, it was on my birthday when I awakened with the message and was compelled to write it down at once:

"Life's experience departs with the **enteric** soul.

"This may be called **enteric** memory as it returns to Earth when the soul once again is physicalized. It then becomes cellular memory and resides within the visual cortex which is activated by the visual reminders of past lifetimes."[321]

"Ay. Not bad, Steno," boasted Peggymoonbeam.

"Right on, Ladymoonbeam," agreed Steno.

"So what are we looking for now?" asked Karensurefoot.

"Gee, Karen, there are so many clues. I had a scary dream about a word. It was 'Bethany,' but I have no idea where it belongs or even if it belongs in Newfoundland. I don't know why I'm telling you this. I guess we just have to look and listen. I can't think of anything relevant now that would connect to where we're going. Anyway, we've had so much excitement, maybe we'll get a rest and just enjoy the sights."

"Yeah, right!" commented Karen.

---

320 12/9/97.
321 See Ch. 3 – The Pole p. 26
     See Ch. 59 – Branches, p. 270

CHAPTER SEVENTY-FOUR

DAS SHOOT! DAS BOOT!

St. Lawrence – The Bethany United Church

After lunch, we continued our drive along the Burin coastline, taking in vistas of quaint villages and picturesque little houses built into the steep cliffs. Sparkling views welcomed us at every turn. Gazing at the iridescent waters of the Atlantic, it was hard to imagine the many families that had been left destitute when their breadwinners drowned in storms and raging seas.

The community of St. Lawrence is located around Great St. Lawrence Harbour, an inlet of Placentia Bay. Stopping off at St. Lawrence, famous today for soccer and fluorspar, we visited the Miner's Museum. We learned from one of the locals that in 1942, two American warships mysteriously ran aground. They were there to safeguard the fluorspar, a highly reactive mineral used in the manufacture of the first atomic bombs. Many of the deaths associated with fluorspar mining are commemorated in the graveyard we visited across the way from the Miner's Museum.

I was scanning the sides of the road as we drove when, just east of the town of St. Lawrence, a wood framed building caught my eye.

"Be - Be- BETHANY!" I blurted out. "Did you see the name Bethany? It's the Bethany Church!"

"I don't believe it!" shouted Karen as she floored the brakes.

Heart-pounding recognition surged as we screeched to a halt. The dark and menacing dream that encircled the word "Bethany" expelled the same torrents of emotion I'd felt in the dream. Seeing the physical structure of the Bethany Church standing on Route 220 on the west side of Placentia Bay rendered me speechless.

The dream surrounded an echoing repetition of the word Bethany, one I could not forget.

Beginning with *circles of people pressed together,* the dream sent a shockingly ominous notice declaring *extermination of the masses. I am with a man and we find a soft wall in the*

Footnotes contain dream dates and references to prior pages where the dream appeared.
Endnotes contain bibliographical references, are marked with "Ɛ" in the text, and appear at the end of the book.

corner we can break through. The wall is an icky yellow. The material inside the wall is fiberglass; I can see the strands. I'm taken to the home of one of the officials. My friend hands him some brown paper and a piece of gravel falls out. This brown paper has a hand-drawn map with directions. It's like construction paper.

There is an angry confrontation. The official is screaming DAS SHOOT ... DAS BOOT. He pretends not to notice the gravel. The gravel turns out to be evidence.

The strongest image in that dream is magnet-shaped ice tongs, which I fiercely struggle with, squeezing a pointer finger until it disintegrates. It's a grueling act, which takes all my strength. Later I am given a bouquet of red roses wrapped in cellophane. They are almost dead. I put them under a chair. The word "Bethany" keeps repeating. I also see the word BETHANY under the chair.[322]

Steno's soothing presence wafted in like a billowy cloud.

"Penelope," he interjected. "You wanted to know about another dream of a *chair* and what it had to do with *workers installing metal attachments to a refrigerator.*[323] Now begins the weaving of a solemn yet hopeful story, which I am dutifully honored to recite.

"Let us first explore the meaning of the chair. The Bethany United Church you see here was built by the local residents circa 1859. It is said to be one of the oldest wooden churches on the island of Newfoundland and in North America and is still standing on its original foundations.

"Now, Bethany is also a village near Jerusalem where Jesus visited his friends, Mary, Martha, and Lazarus. It was, according to some scriptures, where Jesus raised Lazarus from the dead. The name of the present day village, El-Azarieh, is the Arabic form of Lazarion, the fourth-century name of the village and the church that was built over the traditional site of Lazarus' tomb. Excavations revealed that the first church was probably destroyed by an earthquake.

"So, my child, the destruction of a church in the village of Bethany from the time of Christ, connecting with the dream symbol of Bethany and linking to the Bethany Church in St. Lawrence, is bespeaking a message of untellable magnitude."

The grave omen of an earthquake, connecting to the dream with the symbol of Bethany, was materializing with dispatch. But why was the word "Bethany" placed under the chair? I shook with fright over the message *"extermination of the masses."* Was it implying there's more than one earthquake in more than one area? Is this where it would begin? Would the St. Lawrence area be the site of a conflagration that could destroy our masses?

"Penelope, I so appreciate your serious approach to your apprenticeship, but you must remain calm for you have much to learn and much work ahead of you. It will help you

322 7/30/98.
323 9/28/93. See Ch. 67 – Refrigeration, p. 315

to know that the origin of the word 'chair' is from the Latin, cathedra, meaning seat, and from the Greek, kathedra."

The Greek letters that had come through on the computer when I was writing about Agneswiseheart came to mind. Now her gentle spirit whispered, "Kathedra ties to the Bethany Church."

Just then, a stack of "chair" connections began to unfold: *The almost dead roses under the chair ... Bethany under the chair ...* another dream *about a poisonous bumblebee and my fear the poison would get on the leg of a chair.*

The steady progression of chairs told us to be on the lookout. But for what? Why all the fanfare about chairs? Dreams of *antique chairs, custom made chairs, high chairs.*[324] It was curious. I had no such chairs at home. It was still difficult to separate the world I understood and recognized from the unfamiliar and unexpected pictures in my dreams.

This Bethany Church was on the Burin Peninsula. Could the "leg" of the chair be a reminder of the peninsula as a long, narrow, leg jutting into the Atlantic Ocean? Was it *Mother's deformed leg?*[325] Was the *poison on the leg of the chair* an omen of something poisonous under the earth? Not easy learning the syntax of a new language.

Underground. Under the earth. An uncertain symmetry was present in the jangled dream of *the chair that was around the girl. She rose from the sand. She carried a videotape.* Rising from the sand ... resurrection ... Jesus' resurrection of Lazarus in the village of Bethany. Sand ... the piece of gravel that fell out by mistake. "Chair" ... cathedra ... seat, from Greek kathedra – cathedral ... the seat of the Church ... the seat of God ... the Greek code ... the computer messages in Greek.

The puzzling repetition of things past lingered. Threads of remembrance cross-stitched over time, had gradually formed a circle: Osiris – Memory – Resurrection – Bethany Church – Lazarus – Resurrection – *white rose reviving*[326] – White Rose oilfield – Underground – back to Osiris, the symbol of eternal life.[327] This circle begs an answer – "What is it that is being resurrected?" Fortitude, dear Reader, as we decode the answers.

Sometime after Greek letters were imbedded in the Agneswiseheart text, a new Greek implantation replaced the title of a Galen treatise, as did another string of Greek lettering that popped into my writings warning of a seismic zone. The mysterious implantations had become a caring friend there to assist me at any time – day or night. This method of communication, which continues today, is traditionally unannounced in its arrival, haphazard in its succession and deliberate in its placement. It knows just where to put down its roots.

---

324 Chair dreams: 1994 – 2001
325 1/12/99. See Ch. 30 – Mother Earth, p. 135
       See Ch.71 – Mom's Ecstasy, pp. 331–32
326 8/28/99. See Ch. 66 – White Rose, pp. 309–10
327 See Ch. 25 – Remembering Osiris, pp. 114–15

To remind you, dear Reader, the first Greek message was inserted in text I had written recalling my final moments with Agneswiseheart before she passed over, uttering her final words: "beep ... beep," words completely out of step with her patois.[328]

ΥῶˊϑΩ ' ˊῶ ΥΩ χφ Υˆ ΩΥ 'ςˆ ˆΩΥ ', ,ϑΩ

There are five omegas embedded in this cryptic line of seventeen characters.

Omega has various meanings. Because this was a line of Greek – Omega – the last letter of the Greek alphabet means the end, the conclusion, the ultimate limit; the possibilities were so penetrating, so colossal, they sent me whirling into a space far from Earth. Because I'm somewhat on the small side, it's hard for me to hold more than one feeling at a time so I'd have to find a large dose of equanimity to keep me grounded during what looked like a very wild ride.

The Greek message had led me to a number of sources. Once I realized it was Greek I was determined to bring to light some rational explanation of this incredible phenomenon; I sought as many translations as I could.

My first source, a dear friend, Greek by birth and a former teacher of the Greek language, told me the message was ecclesiastical. She said the letters were ancient Greek calligraphy. The priest at her parish interpreted some of the icons to read "of Theos" but other letters were unexplainable. He surmised it was a code and an esoteric one, at that. This compelled me to explore further.

In Chicago, I visited three Greek Orthodox priests. Each studied the baffling code, looked at me, asked how I got it, who sent it to me, and what it meant.

My steady reply was, "I don't know. That's why I'm here. I thought that maybe you could tell me."

The priests were demonstrably curious, each one anxious for an explanation of how it happened. I described how, while I was writing a story on my computer, I had closed the file I was working in and had gone to the Internet. When I went back to the document, and scrolled down to the page I was on, this one line of Greek letters was implanted in the text. I felt foolish telling the priests that the line of Greek was inserted where I'd written the words "beep beep." It seemed so farfetched, no one would believe me, so I kept that to myself.

Not one of the clergymen was able to explain the mystery.

Following the arrival of the Greek code, curious transmissions of a different nature began to turn up on my computer in much the same manner. An unexpected collection of letters, numbers and symbols miraculously sprinkled themselves into my writings, landing in significant places where questions I had loomed large. Given the volumes of text (this book was growing into a tome), these mysterious missives seemed to speak to the essence of exactly what I was working on at that time. On some occasions, the

328 See Ch.20, Agneswiseheart, p. 83

cryptic codes simply flashed, as though winking at me. At other times, they decided to settle in my computer and stay the course, so I was able to copy the enigmatic tidings.

Father Nick, one of the priests I visited in Chicago, told me he would send the mystifying line of Greek to His Eminence, the Archbishop of Athens, in Greece, for a translation. I said, "I've been told that it's ancient Greek calligraphy." He responded, "Well, yes. We also call it stenography." Stenography! On the very same page where the Greek code appeared with the words "beep beep" was the heading: NICOLAUS STENO – QUARTZ CRYSTALS. It was heart stopping. I didn't know at the time that Steno had been beatified.

I would later learn that Father Nick meant Steganography, which translated in Greek means secret writing. This ancient Greek art, around for twenty-five hundred years, is used to hide messages in plain sight. As I continued on my relentless search to decipher the mysterious message, I learned that the invention of the first shorthand system was presumably intended as a form of secret writing.

I pondered. Is a message hidden in Lavender for humans to find, and is Steno, in some way, the courier of such a message?

After several weeks, the archbishop responded to Father Nick confirming earlier opinions, but could not offer a clear translation.

The scholars I consulted concluded that a good deal of what I'd received was abbreviated, suspecting it was a code. The wondrous electronic brain inside my computer evoked thoughts of divine intervention. That must mean others had received similar messages. I was convinced that in time I'd find my fellow recipients. I never pictured the liaison as some zoned out extraterrestrial or some alien life form. The spirit was beneficent, it was large and it was present.

Two years after the initial Agneswiseheart implantation, I transferred my files to a new computer. I was shocked to see that the original Greek letters had changed to something even more byzantine.

"My fair student," observed Steno, "You must have faith in the integrity of the message. What follows will be difficult for all of us, but this heralds an urgent matter which must be communicated.

"Allow me to review the multifaceted dream that centers around a hole, which, if you take notice, will serve as an unerring guidepost helping you to connect the dots.

A girl is rising from the sand carrying heavy things on a videotape with a chair around her. A hole in the refrigerator should never have been there to begin with and workmen had come to stop water pouring out of a pipe. The workers were installing metal attachments to the refrigerator. It ends when the girl goes into a closet and sees a huge amber vase and a funeral urn behind it.[329]

---

329 9/28/93. See Ch. 10 – The Stuff of Life, p. 54

"Doc, water pouring out of a pipe may signal a leak. Now what may have caused a leak is the question, and what does the chair have to do with the *metal attachments?* I still don't get it."

"Penelope, first focus on the message of the *chair.* Remember, the word 'chair' is from the Latin, cathedra, meaning seat. In the Das Shoot! Das Boot! dream you *put the word Bethany under the chair.* A different chair dream centers on a hole and opens with *a video-tape,* which you've interpreted as recorded vision and concludes with a funeral urn. Think of your dream as a three-act play:

Act I.   What the play is about: A hole in the refrigerator is in the wrong place.

Act II. The development: Water is pouring out of a pipe; workers come to stop water pouring out. They install metal attachments.

Act III. The resolution: Amber, a funeral urn.

"Ask yourself about that funeral urn in the closet. Is there something else you wish to share?"

"Not really, Doc. Just that at the very end *I thought I remembered where the amber vase and the urn used to go.* It doesn't make much sense."

"Ummhmm. Penny, let's think about amber. Early in your travels you learned that the Greeks called amber, electron[330] and you connected *two strands of amber*[331] to the double stranded helix of DNA."

"Really, Doc? I guess my dreams and you remember more than I."

Steno furrowed his brow as he sorted through his thoughts. "About your refrigerator dream, in some part, the components resonate with your worry about laying pipeline in a potentially volcano-laden minefield."

"Since you first expressed concern about the pipeline, with the passage of Earth time things have changed somewhat for the better. So you'll be pleased to know the pipeline project has been scrapped."

In 2000 it looked as though natural gas production would only briefly meet pipeline capacity possibly reducing oil recovery which means that oil resources may have been lost. But, that didn't stop the oil company which in 2002 announced their decision to proceed with the development of the White Rose oilfield located offshore on the East Coast of Newfoundland and Labrador,[E26] and in 2004, excavation of three subsea Glory Holes, were completed.[E27]

"Do you think this is still a concern, Dr. Steno? How deep do you think they'll go?"

"It's always a concern, Penelope. The White Rose field is located on the Jeanne d'Arc basin in water depths between 115 and 130 meters. But whether they drill now or not…

330 See Ch. 11 – The Leaf, p. 56.
331 10/28/95. See Ch. 10 – The Stuff Of Life, pp. 52–54
        See Ch. 17 – Real Estate and Alchemy, p. 75

whether they build a pipeline now or not, the cautionary message of the Dream remains. This area is vulnerable, as are other similar areas, and the clues insist that you know that.

"Your dream about *a hole being in the wrong place* remains a concern. The possibility of a leak is pointing to an inactive volcano in or near a drilling site. That could be anywhere.

"Sherlock, it seems you've gone as far as you can in terms of identifying the central issues. You must leave the rest to the authorities. I seem to recall that you gave one of your Earth scientists a report on this."

"Yes, Dr. Steno. I did, quite some time ago, but I don't think it went anywhere."

The fits and starts were too erratic to follow. The province and the oil company were pushing hard despite continuing obstacles. Still, judging from all the warning dreams, time was running out for us to comprehend our own Small-Mindedness, the Blessings of the Earth, the Fury of Nature.

Tick Tock Tick Tock Tick Tock

This on-again, off-again scenario re-ignited my apprehension over subsea drilling for oil on a fault line on or near a dormant volcano or volcanoes, for no one knows the extent of seismic activity that may have already occurred and will continue to occur over time. Although seismic mapping programs are used in some locations, fewer that 10 percent of known active volcanoes worldwide are being monitored and what about those dormant ones that can rumble back to life and erupt on a moment's notice? In many cases, the people who inhabit these areas don't know they're living next to a fire-breathing mountain. No matter how effective Earth's seismic surveys are, there are no manmade optical techniques to compare with those of the Terracrust examiners whose vision can telescope the unseen.

My gnawing fear is ingrained in the warning that the *"masses will be exterminated."* Through the auspices of Terracrust I was directed to the Avalon area where drilling is to take place. I have asked myself time and again, of all the places on the globe, why Newfoundland? Did it have something to do with those Precambrian rocks? The geologists at Terracrust don't take these matters lightly and wouldn't have sent us here on a lark.

Steno instantly produced a geological map along with his giant spyglass, focusing his highest-powered lens over the communities he had sent us to.

"Dr. Steno, I see that the White Rose field is separated into three pools."

"Yes, Penelope. They expect to drill in Grand Banks on one side, Cape Race on the other with Placentia Bay in the center. Now look at the symbols on the map for eruptions along the Placentia coastline which indicate lava and ash from mainly onshore volcanoes. Judging from the areas you've been drawn to, together with your instincts about a crater, there may be volcanoes on the deep ocean floor as well, as this is a heavily faulted area."

The *Whole Earth* dream[332] came crashing in on me! How could I forget? I secretly wondered if the spirit team chose this hub of industrial activity in Canada to awaken us to the release of toxic products poisoning the Earth. Is the message casting a much wider net, encompassing the entire planet? That would be the *masses!* The *Whole Earth*! It was too awful to even consider, but they may have sent us here to concentrate on the region they're using as a model. I was too scared to ask.

"Penelope, it is imperative at this juncture that you use your recorded vision. Think back to the dream you recorded of *the begging cup vibrating out of a brick wall*. Think of Lord Galen's appeal, Penelope dear, and how he correlates the imbalance in the health of the human being with that of the earth. Remember the stories of Percival and the Fisher King. When Percival asked the question of the king, the whole kingdom was revitalized but in another tale, when Percival was too afraid to ask, the sins of the king worsened and his land deteriorated.[333]

"The rest I leave to you, my fair student."

I knew our land was already in the process of depreciation. For a moment I rested my thoughts on the legend of Percival and his question to the Fisher King, "Whom does the Grail serve?" Is it the redemption of the human condition? If we, the human species, could only open our eyes to the precious gifts bestowed on us by our Creator, there might still be time to rectify our abuses to this great Mother Earth, this living entity who works tirelessly to provide for her children. A specter loomed that the original source of life on Earth could become barren. It was eroding our psyches in daily news accounts of pollution, disease, war and famine. The harsh reality of global destruction had crept into my dreams and most likely into the dreams of countless others to issue the warning of *"extermination of the masses,"* a dream which, like the begging cup dream, had a *wall that could be broken through.*

The devoted team of ascended masters was pleading with us, the tenants of this sacred planet, to realize our divine potential, to break through our brick wall of apathy and ego, to break out of our self-indulgent prisons so we may heal our relationship to our self, to each other and to our poor impoverished environment. Now I knew why Steno was so fixed on the chair. It was the seat of the church – the seat of God. We were being summoned to ask the question, "Whom does the Grail serve?"

A full celestial chorus sang out: "It begs for the redemption of the human condition."

And Steno praying to the God common uttered these words:

"...You have led me on unknown ways up to now;
lead me further on the path of grace, either seeing or blind!
For you it is easier to lead me where you will than it is
for me to renounce where my wishes are drawing me to."[E28]

---

332 11/9/96. See Ch. 7 – Branching Out, pp. 41–42
333 See Ch. 64 – Logs and Bricks, p. 300

CHAPTER SEVENTY-FIVE

BUTTERFLIES, SULFUR, AND A SAILING SHIP

Deeply ensconced in the deific meaning of the chair, I thought back to the dream of poison on the leg of a chair. The leg of the Burin Peninsula seemed to fit, but the poison was obscure. Searching for clues, I pulled out the whole dream:

A large yellow butterfly turned into a poisonous bumblebee, which I had to kill. I was afraid of the poison getting on the leg of a chair. There was a flood. The water was muddy and brackish and looked like it was diseased. Someone said technical advice is important to operations on the other side.[334]

As I reread the dream, Steno materialized and bashfully admitted, "Yes, Penelope, Marie Curie and I were communicating with you back then, in 1994."

This meshed with a still earlier dream *where a black flying spirit* was described as *a butterfly.* The moderator was *an architect who announced that the ship didn't sail until 4:15.*[335] The color scheme of the *butterfly-turned-poisonous-bumblebee was yellow; the flying spirit, black.* Pairing the dreams still did not provide the amplification needed to make any sense of it. How could something as delicate and beautiful as a butterfly be associated with something poisonous and black?

I had to remind myself of the numinous message I had received so early on. *"Be patient. You will learn everything you need to know."*[336]

See illustration on next page.

---

334 12/1/94.
335 10/22/94.
336 2/10/95. See Ch. 1 – Beginnings, p. 7

Footnotes contain dream dates and references to prior pages where the dream appeared.

Endnotes contain bibliographical references, are marked with "Ɛ" in the text, and appear at the end of the book.

Butterfly-Bumblebee dream

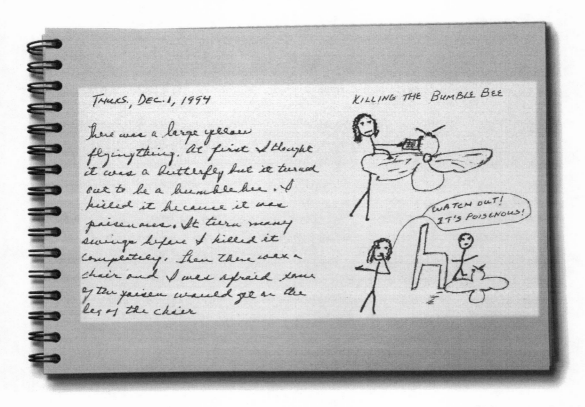

CHAPTER SEVENTY-SIX

CHEMISTRY: THE THIRD BRANCH

The men of experiment are like the ant, they only collect and use; the reasoners resemble spiders, who make cobwebs out of their own substance. But the bee takes the middle course: it gathers its material from the flowers of the garden and field, but transforms and digests it by a power of its own.[E29]

Francis Bacon

Suddenly the atmosphere was charged with something electrifying. A commotion of ions seemed to be dancing in the farthest reaches of space. As they moved in closer, I realized they were encircling Marie Curie. I could not believe the messenger of *Curium, Real Estate,* and *Alchemy*[337] was at last face-to-face with me in spirit, and I wasn't even dreaming. Her spirit, strong as steel, yet lighter than a snowflake was all pervading.

Steno made the formal introductions. "Madame Curie, so good of you to fly over. I would like you to meet Penelope Peacock. She is our agent in the Avalon Zone."

"Hello, Miss Peacock. I am so very pleased to make your acquaintance in person, although we have met many times in your dreams."

I was absolutely beside myself, so in awe was I of her accomplishments. Taken aback by her sudden appearance, all tongue-tied and stammering, I blabbered a long-drawn-out greeting in one breath like a silly schoolgirl. "I've heard so much about you and it is truly a privilege to meet you, it's amazing how you isolated radium, Madame Curie, you are an inspiration and a godsend arriving just when I'm in dire need of help with chemicals and gases. Whew! I feel like you've come to the rescue to help ease my confusion but I sense it's even more than that."

She modestly expressed appreciation for my recognition of her and, wasting no time, began ... "Now, Miss Peacock, it is time for you to learn about sulfur." She then pointed me to a dictionary where the following definition jumped off the page:

---

337 7/16/93. See Ch. 17 – Real Estate & Alchemy, pp. 75–76

Footnotes contain dream dates and references to prior pages where the dream appeared.

Endnotes contain bibliographical references, are marked with "Ɛ" in the text, and appear at the end of the book.

"Sulfur: An American butterfly with predominantly yellow wings that may bear darker patches. U Colias, Phoebis, and other genera, family Pieridae.

The definition of Bumblebee revealed a fit of equal importance:

"Bumblebee: A large hairy social bee which flies with a loud hum, living in small colonies in holes underground. Also called HUMBLE-BEE. Genus Bombus, family Apidae: many species."

I wrestled with the symbols ... something yellow turning poisonous and something yellow turning black ... poisonous and black ... underground. It was menacing.

It would turn out that the transition of the butterfly into a bumblebee and the mutation of a butterfly into a black spirit would help fill in the missing puzzle pieces to Titanic's tragic story or an even bigger story. It was both unraveling the past and reweaving a warning of future catastrophe.

What was a flying black spirit? The Stealth Bomber is black in color, shaped like a butterfly and known as the B-2 Spirit bomber.

I reviewed the *black flying spirit-butterfly* dream. The moderator was *an architect who announced that the ship didn't sail until 4:15.*[338]

The tenses confused me. What *ship didn't sail until* 4:15? All I could conjure up was the Titanic; 4:15 was significant, but it had already sailed – and sunk – on the date of April 15 in 1912.

Intrigued as to how the dream spinners settled on the facsimile date of 4/15, I wondered if Titanic was the impetus for the shipping theme. There was no ship on Earth more conspicuous or celebrated than the legendary Titanic.

Though it faded from sight for a time, the epitaph of the doomed Titanic hadn't lost its place in our story and could not be erased despite its many intersecting paths. She was simply waiting her turn to tell us why she sailed into my dreams.

I was inundated with dreams about shipping, so many that some just sailed off into the sunset. But the most memorable shipping dream to cruise across my screen was the one that assigns me *a job in the shipping department – a job I didn't like.* The theme centered on the whole Earth.

Risking redundancy, I thought the Whole Earth dream was worthy of a rerun: *People are marching, carrying placards that read "Whole." I explain that it means "Earth." Then I learn that I have been assigned the "SHIPPING DEPT." I think, "What a dull, unimaginative job. Sero – a mysterious word – presents itself.*[339]

338 10/22/94.
339 11/9/96. See Ch. 7– Branching Out, pp. 41–42
        See Ch. 22 – Water, Water And More Water, p. 97

By now "*sero*" had connected with Vision (the CBS Eye), had appeared on Titanic's manifest and spelled backward was "ores."[340]

Another dream about a march preceded the Whole Earth dream by ten months, but that "march" featured the book *"Meditations on the Tarot"* and a cryptic message that involves *four sentences in Arabic.*[341]

Meditations on the Tarot was not the meditation I wanted to contemplate for if tarot is a way of divining the future, it was terrifying: *Extermination of the masses* ... the *Whole Earth* ... something poisonous underground ... the Stealth Bomber. Not exactly a day at the beach. And what about the Arabic? Another embedded script requiring decoding? Driven to the Tarot, the page I opened to was Letter V – The Pope and his Triple Cross representing "three levels of horizontal respiration . . . : love of Nature; love of one's neighbor; love of the beings of the spiritual hierarchies."

Marie Curie gently guided me back to the fundamentals of science. "Your uncertainties will clear, my dear, but it is vital that you understand the basics first. Try to stay with the image of the butterfly."

Strange that sulfur is defined as a yellow butterfly; I thought sulfur was an element with a bad smell – that it's in matches and used for making gunpowder.

"Yes, you're right, Miss Peacock. Sulfur is an element, except it doesn't smell until it reacts. Actually, pure sulfur is odorless; a couple of prominent sulfur compounds smell. You see, we couldn't find a simple graphic image other than the color yellow. We needed a good strong visual for sulfur and the butterfly worked well.

"Tu-whit can elaborate on that."

ÕÕ   "'Sulfurs are common butterflies found in open, sunny areas in temperate regions. Many species are a buttery yellow color and may have inspired the word 'butterfly.'[Є30] Sulfur, the element, is a pale yellow combustible nonmetal. Sulfur dioxide and hydrogen sulfide occur naturally in volcanic gases contained in magma.'"

Madame Curie continued. "We were also considering the metamorphic nature of the butterfly as it evolves from the larva to the caterpillar to the cocoon to the butterfly and again, as it applies to geology where rock bodies undergo transformation. Similarly, your dreamwork and your life are continually metamorphosing.

"You will notice that the subject of sulfur further down the road will bear some change."

Peggymoonbeam piped in, "Penelope, don't forget the yellow painted initials on the rock in Branch – the initials that tagged your geology professor."

---

340 See Ch. 57 – St. John's, p. 263
341 1/28/96.

Yikes! Does that mean there's sulfur under that rock? The LL rock was next to the lavender painted rocks. They must be telling us that the color yellow in scores of dreams represents sulfur.

While thinking about how tricky it was connecting these dots, especially with yellow turning into a stinky, gaseous monster, a gut-wrenching alarm sounded within.

"Oh, no!" I cried. Does that confirm my instincts? Is there a volcano about to erupt in Branch too?"

Marie Curie steered me back to the *soft wall in the corner that is broken through.* "We described it to you as an icky yellow."

"Yes, Madame Curie. There were fiberglass strands inside the wall. I could actually see them in the dream." Unbeknownst to me, fiberglass was the bearer of yet another ill-boding link.

"How does fiberglass connect to the story?"

Marie Curie answered. "Fiberglass threads are made from molten glass. Lava is molten glass. Come, Miss Peacock. I would like to give you a tour of the stellar laboratory where we store our chemicals."

She whisked me away to the chemical division of Terracrust.

"You see, these pieces of glass fibers are coated with a resin called phenol-formaldehyde. Its molecular structure is made up of carbon, oxygen, and hydrogen."

I felt like a stranger in a strange land. Why was she telling me about molecular structure? I had no idea what she was talking about.

"When we received transmission from Earthside in the mid-1900s that fiberglass causes lung diseases, as does asbestos, we at Terracrust were profoundly concerned. Fifty years later the problem still exists. We know U.S. government research has revealed that fiberglass damages DNA.

"This is very troubling to Tu-whit. You are aware that his archives are constantly being reviewed for any dangers or threats that may befall Planet Earth. Because of his concern for the future, he insists on delivering to you the background on the history of mining at St. Lawrence. This will help you to make some connections."

ÕÕ FLUORSPAR-SILICA

"'In 1933, serious mining for fluorspar began at St. Lawrence, the site of North America's largest fluorspar deposit and a prospector's paradise. The practice of dry drilling, which released particles of silica into the air, was held largely responsible for the deaths and diseases of many of its miners.

"'In 1959, a radioactive gas named radon ("An element with which I'm intimately familiar," interjected Madame Curie) was also discovered in the mines.

Radon was the decay product of a large, low-grade uranium deposit. The publicity began around 1960 with the discovery that St. Lawrence miners had been working for nearly thirty years in the presence of a radioactive gas and that many had died or were dying of radiation-induced cancer. In 1967, before the mining of fluorspar in the province ceased, a Royal Commission had been set up to seek the cause of the health problems of the miners.

"'The Commission found that radon was being concentrated in the mine by groundwater flowing through the granite surrounding the fluorspar vein.'"[E31]

As Tu-whit spoke, I considered that radioactive waste products in the groundwater surrounding sulfide veins may not only be present in St. Lawrence but in locations throughout the world. That sparked another thought: Could sulfur and uranium react to produce a gas? I guessed I'd find out in good time.

Tu-whit continued reciting St. Lawrence history:

"'In 1978, the St. Lawrence fluorspar operations closed down. They say the problem was controlled after 1960 with the installation of ventilation equipment.'"

Madame Curie thanked Tu-whit and continued, "Miss Peacock, I noticed that you and Karen visited the graveyard where the names of the victims are inscribed on the Echoes in Valour plaque. It's a stirring remembrance of the hundreds of miners who lost their lives to silicosis, lung cancer and other respiratory diseases in the late 1940s."

"Does that mean, Madame Curie, that the fiberglass inside the wall in my dream is the symbol for silicosis?"

"Yes, it is another balefully close fit. The *fiberglass strands* in the dream are somewhat of a metaphorical eulogy.

"Penelope, in the same vein Tu-whit, is anxious to share with you a deep dark secret that may help with your dot-connecting."

I felt the air oscillating and heard the rapid flapping of wings. Tu-whit moved in all a twitter.

ÕÕ "'The final and most ironic twist to the silicosis story became public in 1996, in the unpublished memoirs of the chief geologist and director of mines for Newfoundland in the 1940s. They revealed this shocking story. Nearly a year after the war's end (he reportedly wrote), I was surprised to get a letter from the U.S. Assistant Secretary for Defense Production saying he had planned a small luncheon meeting for those involved in securing the supplies of fluorspar necessary for the victorious war effort....

"'I attended the luncheon. After the meal, he gave a nice speech thanking us for our efforts, which had combined to make a most vital and necessary contribution to the victory of the United States and its allies. Then with a smile on his face, he told us something unknown to some of us. From the beginning of the fluorspar operation, we had been told, as a matter of top secrecy, that the ore was being used in the processing of high-octane gasoline. He apologized for hoodwinking us in the interests of the war effort, and then explained that the fluorspar had been the critical chemical in the separation of the U235 isotope from the predominant U238 in Uranium ores. Fluorspar had made possible the production of the gas, Uranium Hexafluoride, and from this the deadly U235, used in the atomic bomb, was extracted.'"[32]

"Look down! Look down!" my technical wizards commanded, tilting their lanterns toward Mother Earth. They were the telescopic custodians of all times and of all worlds. They could see our home, a lonely speck in the vast cosmic theatre, from billions of light-years away, yet, we were on top of it and it was out of sight – both literally and figuratively.

"Penelope," they beckoned. "Please retrieve your dream thread about the *thin lenses*."

These guys have gotta be kidding. I'm in the middle of nowhere and they want me to retrieve one among thousands of strands of dreams.

"Sorry, Penelope. We tend to forget your files are land locked. You see, we have it all in our superconscious."

"Good. Then, my able avatars, will you remind me of the dream?"

"Of course. It contains *the aviator style eyeglass frames – the thin lenses with peel off backing. The lenses are on the ground on top of a terry cloth washcloth described as protection.*"[342]

The thin lenses were a pretty strange image, but one part was clear. Terry means earth (terra) and cloth means cover or protection. The ethereal skywriters scrawled their vanishing message across the firmament. Earth needed cover ... needed protection. The moment one message faded, a fresh banner unfurled an unwavering message of admonition, one that flew steadily and stayed its course.

The aviator of this operation was Claudius Galen, who donned his Timelessness Spectacles; the navigator was Nicolaus Steno who squinted through his spyglass and surveyed the land. The tour guide was Marie Curie, who knew more about chemicals than Webster had words. They were directing me to look at the ground.

Marie Curie pitched in. "Miss Peacock, fluorspar is another name for fluorite (calcium fluoride) and pairs with your dream *lenses with peel off backing*. This unusual image connects to fluorite in two ways: it has a cleavage habit of 'peeling off,' and it is synthetically grown to produce lenses."

---

342 4/4/97.

Incredible! Fluorspar mines in St. Lawrence – a reactive mineral – in the ground – in the dream – on the ground.

"Er – uh – Madame Curie. I don't know how to say this, but if you don't mind, I prefer to be called Penelope or Penny. I don't mean to be disrespectful, but Miss Peacock is a bit formal, and I'm really not formal at all. I hope you don't think it presumptuous of me to be so familiar."

"Not at all. I suppose I still abide by the professional etiquette ingrained in me. You know, the academic protocol in France was one of great reserve. Coming from a family of teachers must have drawn out the more serious side of my nature. Then, arriving in France as an immigrant, what with my intense research studies and then preparing a theory of ions in gases and a treatise on radioactivity, suffice to say, all this mind work destined me for a straightforward no-nonsense existence. In any event, we'll be together for more adventure-filled Earth years than you can count, for there are untold civilizations in the Milky Way for us to visit, Penelope. During our Mission, we will undoubtedly have the opportunity to get to know each other quite well. I'm pleased that you broke the ice now by being so open and it's just fine if you wish to call me Marie."

"The Milky Way? I thought you were from Terracrust, Madame Curie – er, Marie. Isn't that a distance from the solar system?"

"Actually, I'm biplanetary. I divide my time between Terracrust and Starsight. Cosmochemistry these days requires as much attention as geochemistry."

Call her Marie. (gulp) It felt too weird. It would take a while before I could feel so at home and on a first-name basis with the woman whose influence changed the worlds of science and medicine.

The renowned chemist paused reverentially. "You may already know, Penelope, that radioactive elements took a tremendous toll on me because of my repeated contact with them. Toward the end of my life, my fingers were burnt and I was almost blinded by the 'dear radium' that I personally discovered. That's why I'm particularly sensitive to it and extremely passionate about its dire effects on human life. I actually died from leukemia, which is, of course, a form of cancer."

I held back rising pools of tears for this warrior of a woman. As I listened to her story, I could feel her pain. There were so many questions to ask about her life on Earth, but this was not the time.

She continued, "That was another chapter, my young friend. Lifetimes come and lifetimes go. I assure you that life at Terracrust is sparkling with discovery. I can now see where science and spirit are conjoined and, actually, I've never been busier. In abiding by our imperatives as shepherds for Planet Earth, the work we do here may result in unprecedented cures for civilization, which is fighting for its life. At Terracrust, the healing potential for the human species is far more perceptible than it is on Planet Earth.

In the nineteenth century, our focus was to find a cure for disease in the human body. It is now time to find a cure for the infectious disease of negativity that spawns greed, corruption, hatred and killing, poisonous conditions that distort the mind and fester in the earth. We see that this silent killer is dousing the spirit of humankind, which is only beginning to awaken to it."

With single-minded determination, she steered the conversation back to the glass fibers.

"I'm aware that mineral fibers have been named a health hazard priority by your government, which says that action must be taken but I must admit I'm quite frustrated to find that the research always turns out to be inconclusive."

"Madame Curie, are you saying we're breathing glass fibers that are poisonous to our cells?"

"Yes, Penelope. They are in the air – in cities, rural areas, mountain tops – being dumped into landfills. And they are underground."

I wondered about volcanic zones. This disturbing train of thought intensified when Marie Curie, pointing to a piece of glass, said, "Penelope, phenol-formaldehyde binders used on many mineral fiber products also attract dirt, dust and other chemicals."

Hmm. Other chemicals? Was there a lethal combination in the air? The idea of gas and dust and other chemicals began to percolate.

Madame Curie continued, "Unfortunately, history does repeat, Penelope. I speak of the terrorist attack on the World Trade Center. Air quality studies show that 'air samples taken in New York in the weeks after the towers collapsed showed unprecedented levels of pollutants, such as sulfur and silicon.' The particles of silica that were the cause of respiratory diseases and lung cancer in the St. Lawrence miners resemble the content of a large mass found at Ground Zero. These very fine particles penetrate deep into the lungs. Tu-whit has swept over that darkened hole and gathered some data for you, so you may better understand the severe health problems caused by widespread contamination:

ÕÕ "In addition to sulfur and silicon, samples revealed elevated levels of titanium from pulverized concrete and vanadium and nickel, which result from the combustion of fuel oil. Lead, most likely from the thousands of computers in the twin towers, and mercury from the buildings' wiring were also detected, but in lower concentrations.

"Despite the Environmental Protection Agency's announcement that the air was safe to breathe, interviews with scientists and survivors have revealed disturbing information about a death toll that is still climbing."

Emphasis on the release of toxic chemicals was accelerating. I thought back to Steno's lesson on volcanic gases[343] and my revelation of Lava Under.[344]

The message was shrill. There would be nothing frivolous on this journey, so intentionally and deeply carved was its path. Chemicals, chemicals, and more chemicals. How would I ever synthesize all of this? Well, I suppose that's why Madame Curie has appeared.

"I hear you and that is correct, Penelope. I'm here to teach you about chemicals because our operatives at Terracrust and Starsight have deemed you an attentive and concerned student. You have, in a few short lessons, learned the rudiments of sulfur and radon and fluorspar and silica. There's more to come. It greatly behooves us to present you with the hallowed Branch of Chemistry."

My heart nearly stopped. Another Branch was just more than I could deal with.

"Oh no, Madame Curie! (gulp) I don't mean to be discourteous but I honestly cannot accept this distinguished honor only fitting of a true humanitarian and dedicated scientist. You see, I've never taken a course in chemistry and I really don't think I can live up to your expectations. Taking me on as your student would probably age you another lifetime if you were still on Earth. I have far too much respect and admiration for you to subject you to the labor pains you would surely experience in teaching me for I am completely unacquainted with the subject you gave your life to, and on top of that, I'm a painfully slow learner. The knowledge I've gained so far on this quest is more than I've digested in my entire lifetime, but I can't go any further. In the beginning, I struggled day and night with the Optic System. When, at last, the light began to peek through my dreams of vision, Geology burst in. The study of the earth's crust and all its plates slid right up behind me and now Chemistry is bombarding my dreams. Honestly, Madame Curie, this surge of itty bitty fragments with their tangled connections is so overwhelming that some days I feel like I'm caught in the spin-dry cycle of a washing machine that just won't stop. It's tricky chasing so many moving parts, much less accepting the daunting responsibility of carrying a Branch etched with your great name. I would be mortified if I ever disgraced or embarrassed you. I promise you, I don't know diddly squat about chemistry, and to be honest, most common, everyday people like me don't have a clue as to what it's about. They get befuddled with all the letters and numbers of the elements and complicated things about compounds and stuff they don't understand."

"Penelope," spoke the grand Madame rather firmly. "That is just the point, my dear. Chemistry is a magnificent science which – with physics –systematically studies the composition, properties and activity of organic and inorganic substances and should become a focus for everyone. That is precisely why you've been selected, for if we can teach an earthling by using her own native intelligence, then we know it can be taught to others who did

---

343 See Ch. 45 – A Trump Card: Sleeping On Pillow Lava, p. 357
344 See Ch. 35 – Lava Under Revelation, pp. 151–52

not receive a formal education. Science is in everyday life. Whether someone is eating their breakfast or looking at plants or dreaming dreams, science can be linked to everything.

"Chemistry and physics connect the everyday world to the molecular world. One learns how to break down substances, combine substances to make more complex ones and devise methods that will benefit us as a species. In due course, you will understand important chemical compounds and in doing so will marvel at your own natural ability. These two sciences have enormous influence on human life but are not without liabilities, the most obvious dangers coming from radioactive materials about which you've already learned more than you realize. Much of it is incubating within you.

"I am terribly sorry, dear Penny, to have to dismiss your heartfelt fears, and I don't do it lightly, but I truly have no choice. You may recall that you received a dream in 1994 that spoke of a *new order, a paradigm* – that is, a pattern that underlies a theory or methodology. *The word Corundum appeared* in this dream.[345] Unaware of this word, you looked it up and found that it is a hard mineral called aluminum oxide. But a similar sounding word, Conundrum, caught your eye. You remembered that Conundrum is a riddle in which a question is answered by a pun. In all candor, Penelope, you're in somewhat of a dilemma for you are dealing with both a mineral and a puzzle. If you can figure out the mineral, you might decipher the puzzle, and if you can decipher the puzzle, you might find the mineral. You see, dear, in the spirit of teaching this new methodology, I have been mandated by the Dominion of the PurpleScroll to take you under my wing. You may recall that that august body is committed to embracing the inseparability of science and faith and to furthering the understanding of the invisible. This is undoubtedly the greatest enigma philosophers and scientists have faced, dating from the time when alchemy was practiced in some ancient civilizations and what we now call modern science.

"This new methodology in which we've been indoctrinating you contrasts with accepted theories and basic assumptions science now uses. Your dreams fall into the territory that those who research psychic phenomena refer to as psi anomalies, and in your case they are suggesting, in the broader sense, scientific anomalies – happenings not explained by accepted norms and theories. We've inventoried quite an impressive range of anomalies in your varied collection of dreams. Initially, these will lead Earth scientists to re-evaluate their paradigm, which may create a paradigm shift as these scientists look for ways in which their theories can evolve. In the meantime, when enough significant anomalies oppose current theories, scientific discipline is likely to be thrown into a state of crisis. But fear not."

"But why science would be thrown into crisis just because of anomalies, Madame Curie, I don't really understand."

"Because when a new paradigm is formed based on anomalistic data, like the study of extraordinary phenomena you're engaged in, new followers join it and an intellectual

---

345 4/13/94. See Ch. 15 – A Wonderland of Minerals, pp. 71–72

battle takes place between the followers of the new paradigm and the hold-outs of the old. You have nothing to lose by any of this, Penelope, for you have no academic reputation to protect; this makes you the perfect candidate.

"I assure you that the Branch of Chemistry will help you in ways that are not yet knowable to you. I realize you are a bit intimidated by it, but please dear, don't be. You will find over time that it will become second nature to you. It is my enduring belief, Penny, that Chemistry is the bedrock of the sciences, so it will actually help your tree growing in Heaven to reach untold heights.

"In fact, Peggymoonbeam is here with me now to bestow upon you this revered Branch. We present Chemistry to you, Penelope Peacock, with great homage and deep appreciation for your courage in doing that which you find so difficult. In the words of Ambrose Redmoon, 'Courage is not the absence of fear, but rather the judgment that something else is more important than fear.'[33] We ask that you carry this very important Branch with you at all times, for we have great challenges to face as we conduct exciting new investigations into the inner workings of earth and man and their interactions with each other, the result of which could uncover life-giving discoveries. We are always at your side. You are never alone."

I knew Mission Lavender was far more important that my silly fear but still I shook like a leaf at the enormity of the bequest. I then swallowed a few times and humbly accepted the Branch choking back a lump of uncertainty. It felt like a giant horse pill was lodged in my throat. Smiling through pangs of doubt, I murmured, "Thank you, Madame Curie and Peggymoonbeam," and biting my quivering lip, I uttered, "I am unspeakably humbled by your blind trust in me. I promise I'll do my very best to live up to this inestimable honor."

It was inconceivable that I, little Penelope Peacock of modest learning, would be graced with the guidance of Marie Curie, as a teacher. You couldn't get any luckier than this, for Marie's teaching abilities were extraordinary. Not only was she born into a family of teachers but she was the first woman to lecture at the Sorbonne! It was overwhelming to think that someone as unimportant as me was being tutored by the most famous woman Nobel prize winner in the world and the foremost authority on radioactivity.

This new Branch was so heavy, it could be a tree all its own, but I clutched it to my breast with all my might. Tears of gratitude mixing with ice cold fright froze on my face but I'd have to soldier on.

"I know you girls would like to catch up a bit," said Marie, "so, Penelope, I'll meet you back at the chemistry lab at Terracrust where we'll continue with the *Das Shoot! Das Boot!* dream. Remember, dear, a long road awaits us, so do step on the gas."

Suddenly the door to reality opened a crack. What if this wasn't just a dream? What if this was for real? "Oh my God," I thought. "What do I do now? Vision – Geology – now Chemistry. This is more than I could have ever envisioned."

The excited fluttering of Peggymoonbeam's wings stirred up currents of elation, sending my worries to the cosmic trashcan, at least for the moment.

"You did envision it! You saw it in your dreams, Penelope. Admittedly, an appreciable chunk of scientific material bombarded you, so we had to let you absorb it at your own pace."

"Y'know, Peggymoonbeam, at times, I've had a queer feeling like I was the nucleus being attacked with missives, like high-energy particles, not even knowing where they were coming from. Now I know they were guided missives containing messages from the whole crew.

"Now that you mention it, I did see a *ficus tree* in one of my dreams. *It has one weak branch. I look in the soil and see swarms of bugs crawling everywhere. Someone brings in these metal things that look like safety pins and throws them on the bugs. It zaps them immediately! Then I see them in another place. They seem to spread. A man goes out to get more of these metal things. He comes back with only 6, which we throw on the tree, and instantly the bugs are gone. I tell someone we have to get more. At one point, we're throwing handfuls of these things on the soil and the spread is stopped. I think there may be crystal in these metal things. My tree lost a lot of leaves but still has some and I know it will be OK.*[346]

When I awakened, I knew how important this dream was. It looked like the metal was a cure for disease and I sensed that crystal played a part in it. The safety pin was a strong and protective omen because it killed the bugs and I knew the number 6 was important. Maybe it had to do with a compound.

"Penny, the metal the safety pin was originally made of, was a combination of copper, iron, aluminum, gold, silver, and platinum."

"That is awesome, Peggymoonbeam! That means there's a real combination of metals and crystal that will eliminate the disease in our soil. Plus, do you know what else? About two weeks later, I had a connecting dream where *I'm in a library. The book I need is in the 330.4 Law section. 330.4 repeated throughout. The girl behind the desk was named Metaque Corundum. I couldn't find the text on 330.4 but I think it was about childrearing.*"[347]

"Well, well, well my little buddy. You are off to quite an impressive start, given your resistance to chemicals. Did you have a 'gut' – ha ha – that is, an enteric reaction to these dreams?"

"It was the gut of all gut reactions, Peggy, because I sensed a compound composed of metal and crystal was in the offing. Following the metal lead, the word *'metaque'* had the ring of French. Metal in French is 'metallique,' which brings to mind Madame Curie, and the *childrearing* clue probably signifies the harvesting of the compound. I'm very worried about the imagery of *swarms of bugs* spreading in the soil – that means disease is spreading

346 3/29/98.
347 4/15/98

in the earth. It must be getting worse every day. It's taken so long to record all the transmissions, I'm terrified about getting word out in time so someone can help.

"I'm thinking that your ficus tree is symbolic of the tree of science that grows in Heaven and is planted in the Earth. It looks like you and your team of guardians are in search of a real physical cure for the soil – a cure for the earth."

"What gives you that idea?" teased Peggymoonbeam.

"For starters, my dream journals are spilling over with metals and crystals. That, combined with other chemical codes, spells out some kind of a compound.

"Anyway, the image of the *library* led me to research that revealed that the *330.4* clue has many implications. It covers everything from chemical analysis of chlorine in water, to water resource projects to a proposed amendment by a Texas commission on natural resources. Unimaginable that the commission's paragraph §330.4 amendment reads: 'Permit Required, amends subsection (r) by requiring a separate permit or registration for the storage, transportation or handling of used oil mixtures collected from oil/water separators.'[34]

"This string of clues may all fit in one way or another, but I must stay focused on pollution. That's where we were before you and Marie granted me the Branch of Chemistry along with a cosmic-sized shot of courage. Now it's time for me to say adieu, dear Peggy, and tend to my responsibilities."

Showing her approval, Peggymoonbeam spread the glow of a thousand suns through the boundless oceans of time and space. "Good. She received the chlorine clue, Steno. Now let's hope she'll connect it to your lesson on volcanic gases and pick up on the water and oil mixtures later."

She was gone in a flash, leaving in her wake a blaze of the most brilliant golden-white light I had ever seen.

CHAPTER SEVENTY-SEVEN

SULFUR AND RADON –
CHLORINE AND FLUORINE – OH MY!

I stepped on the gas as Marie directed and returned to the dream of *Das Shoot! Das Boot*. It teemed with clues: *Icky yellow – piece of gravel – angry official – disintegration – and more.*

What was the soft icky yellow wall that had been broken through? What was icky? What was yellow?

"Well, Penelope," tutored Marie Curie, reviewing our current theme: "One mineral that's rather soft is fluorspar. It is the chief source of fluorine, a pale yellow, highly corrosive, toxic gas. So you see, we have matched the soft, yellow clues."

"Excuse me, Madame Curie, but what exactly is a corrosive gas?"

"It's a gas that gradually destroys, through chemical reaction, things it comes in contact with. Fluorine can be lethal to animals after a volcanic eruption for it attaches to fine ash particles; it also coats grass and plants and pollutes streams and lakes. Animals that eat grass coated with fluorine-tainted ash are poisoned."

That's just awful! These yellow clues appeared to carry a deadly connotation. Sulfur – Yellowstone and now – fluorine, a poisonous gas. I wondered what color Radon is.

"I'm sorry, Penelope. I neglected to mention that radon is colorless and odorless. It forms from the decay of uranium and radium which are radioactive elements naturally present in rock and soil."

"Madame Curie, you said radon was a radioactive gas. "What would happen if you put fluorine and radon together?"

"Good question, Penelope. For years chemists believed that noble gases, of which radon is one, were inert; that is to say, they would not enter into chemical combinations with other elements. This is now known not to be true. Scientists at Argonne National Laboratory in Illinois found in the early 1960s that radon reacted readily with fluorine."ᗱ₃₅

Good grief! If fluorspar was in the wall, was fluorine in the wall too? Where was I going with this?

Footnotes contain dream dates and references to prior pages where the dream appeared.
Endnotes contain bibliographical references, are marked with "ᗱ" in the text, and appear at the end of the book.

Madame Curie, sticking to the point, continued. "Penelope, it's time we return to the icky yellow wall. If you recall, some time ago I sent you a dream that contained *a long list of adjectives all beginning with the letter 'I.'*[348]

"You connected the 'I' words to something volcanic and they are all appropriate. Icky was one of them."

"Oh no! You said volcanic. Volcanoes emit sulfurous gases!"

I wondered how many gases it takes to threaten human life.

Curie responded. "If it's the wrong gas, one alone can be hazardous."

My ruminations stirred up more questions: Was the soft wall that was broken through in the dream pointing to the wall of a crater? Was an inactive volcano about to erupt in an area known for fluorspar? What if there was tectonic plate movement under foot that caused the break in the wall?

While Galen and Ptolemy piloted Starsight lab, Steno and Curie were working with me in tandem: Steno surveying the Earth; Curie, concentrating on its chemical content. The fiberglass strands epitomized the strands of the dream – the strands of discovery – the strands of molten glass – of lava. Then, in a gripping realization, the puzzle pieces loomed deadly.

What would happen if volcanic gases like sulfur dioxide and carbon dioxide and radon and fluorine and chlorine were all together?

I thought back to pillow lava and how that connected with chlorine and the gases spewed out by erupting volcanoes.[349] They all seem to have seeped into my dreams!

Seized with panic, I focused intently on the *angry confrontation with the official who was screaming DAS SHOOT ... DAS BOOT. A piece of gravel falls out by mistake. The gravel turns out to be evidence.*

Were we "officially" being told that the boot of the Burin Peninsula will shoot us? Or was it warning us to get out before the official shoots us? And just who was this angry official? Did he represent the giants of Industry? *The piece of gravel – the evidence –* could be any number of things. *It was wrapped in brown paper.* Brown paper is opaque. It can't be seen through. Yet, there is much to see.

---

348 9/30/93. See Ch. 66 – White Rose, p. 313
349 See Ch. 45 – A Trump Card: Sleeping on Pillow Lava, pp. 199–201

CHAPTER SEVENTY-EIGHT

DISINTEGRATION

*M*agnet-shaped ice tongs? Why was I *squeezing someone's pointer finger until it disintegrated?* Why did this *grueling act take all my strength?*[350]

I recalled how arduous the act of squeezing was in the dream and how breathless I was when I awakened. Initially, I was drawn to magnetism because the ice tongs were shaped like a magnet and because I associate ice tongs with metal.

"Penelope, let's have a go at Fleming's rules," coached Marie. "They are memory aids used to recall the relative directions of the magnetic field, current, and motion in an electric generator, using one's fingers. I must excuse myself for a moment as I have two handsome gentlemen to fetch who are waiting to meet you."

Egad! So the pointer finger I was squeezing to death represented the magnetic field. I was relieved to know that, at least, I wasn't decimating someone's finger. I wondered if there was a link between magnetic reversal and the ice age.

Tu-whit swept in:

ÕÕ "'A magnetic reversal about three million years ago marked the onset of glaciation, another about two million years ago and yet another, about one million years ago.'"[Ɛ36]

The air began to sparkle. I looked up and there appeared Madame Curie amid a shower of ions surrounding what I sensed as robust French male energy.

Curie gracefully gestured toward her husband, Pierre, and her brother-in-law, Jacques. "Penelope, I'd like you to meet two notorious scientists who discovered piezoelectricity back in 1880."

They were like the Trinity. Wherever you found one, you'd find the others. It was reassuring to know that families stick together, literally through thick and thin (thick as in earth; thin as in air).

---

350 7/30/98.

Footnotes contain dream dates and references to prior pages where the dream appeared.

Endnotes contain bibliographical references, are marked with "Ɛ" in the text, and appear at the end of the book.

The subject of piezoelectricity heated up spicy platters of pizza dreams.

Addressing the Curie brothers, I said, "I never thought I'd be lucky enough to meet you. But now that you've honored me with your presence, I must admit I have a sneaking suspicion that it was you who created the Cousin Andi dreams and her unusual habits. May I ask if you were the ones who engineered her *lavender-coated tongue*? Were you the masterminds of her *horrid-sounding cello*?"

I remembered that lava flows are often characterized as tongue-like bodies.[351]

Pierre and Jacques relaxed their scholarly bearing, cock-a-doodle-dooing out loud like two roosters. Pierre drew closer. "Yes, Miss Penelope, we share the blame for fina-gling the 'cousin Andi scenarios,' along with Dr. Steno. Since Jacques and I discovered piezoelectricity and Steno discovered quartz crystals, we put our heads together to find a way for andesite, the volcanic lava, to be added to the menu. Many of our efforts at scien-tific rebuses would have been impossible without the help of Nicolaus Steno. You know, Penelope, your Dr. Steno has some godlike ways about him. I must say, it's fitting that he was declared "beatus"– the first step toward being declared a saint. His beliefs in the wonders of God's creation are crucial to his approach of geology and in his mentoring of you. I daresay he knows more about the steganographic dream code than anyone."

I looked up and, indeed, there was Steno bubbling in his professorial froth.

"Their compliments are exceedingly generous, Penelope. Tell me. Can you remember just what piezoelectricity is?"

(Gulp.) "I think piezoelectricity comes from the structure of crystal."

"That's correct," affirmed Steno, reminding me: "certain crystals become electrically polarized when they are squeezed or stretched."

"Ptolemy here. Halloo gang. Just thought I'd enlighten you with a touch of Greek, harumph harumph. In case you didn't know, piezoelectricity is from the late nineteenth century named for the Greek piezein meaning 'press, squeeze,' plus ELECTRICITY.

"Squeezed or stretched, gentlemen" mimicked Ptolemy. "Well, I daresay that's a stretch for piezoelectricity. But then again, it's not a bad clue for pizza since those pizza makers seem to press and squeeze and stretch the life out of the dough.

♫ "When the moon hits the sky like a big Pizza Pie ... that's amore" ♫[37]

His contemporaries applauded him with a round of stellar wing flaps and Ptolemy spun off.

"So, Dr. Steno, let's see if I understand this. Would the stress on rocks in an earth-quake be something that would squeeze the crystals in the earth creating an electrical charge, and would that translate to an electrically charged particle in a magnetic field?"

351 See Ch. 47 – Cousin Andi a.k.a. Andesite., p. 205

"Yes, it would, but be advised that the piezoelectric crystal, when static, does not generate electricity. Intermittent pressure, however, distorts the crystal structure and generates a spark."

Hmm. I wonder if one little spark could cause a fire.

"OK, but the part of the disintegrating finger dream I can't fathom is why it disintegrated and why it took every ounce of energy I had to squeeze that finger. I was completely undone when I awakened. It was so real, my heart was going like a trip-hammer." Steno, amused by my scientific naiveté and in turn, concerned over the psychological stress caused by so electrifying a dream, placed me in Curie's charge.

"Marie, why don't you explain to her why the finger disintegrated? She was terribly traumatized. I fear we may have carried this image a bit too far."

"We're terribly sorry if we alarmed you, Penelope, but we had to get the point across and we had to make it physical so you would realize it was about physics."

In a flurry of giggles, Peggymoonbeam whirled by, spreading her celestial merriment through every region of space in the night sky. "Physics … physical. Read my lips."

Curie smiled at her antics and persisted in explaining disintegration. She somehow knew when my concentration was waning. "You see, dear, in 1896, Henri Becquerel discovered radiation. He found that a rock containing uranium that gave off rays that could go through a sheet of black paper. By accident, he discovered that the rock gave off rays even when the sun was not shining on it! Where did the energy of the rays come from? What was it about this mineral that gave it such mysterious power?

"Pierre and I continued to study the nature of this radiation, which I would later name radioactivity. Scientists found that uranium rays were too weak to produce good pictures of bones. It was easier to work with X-rays, discovered by Roentgen months earlier – (all you needed was a special glass tube and electricity), and the unusual minerals containing uranium were not easy to get.[E38] I was determined to understand the mystery behind these rays. It turned out that my investigation of elements that emit uranium rays stimulated Ernest Rutherford and Frederick Soddy to undertake work on radioactivity.

"By proving the existence of distinct types of rays, in 1903 Rutherford and Soddy proposed that radioactive emissions are produced by the disintegration of atomic nuclei. I was reluctant to accept this theory at first since the disintegration of uranium, thorium and radium is so slow. But after some years, I came to accept their theory as the most plausible explanation of radioactivity, and introduced the terms disintegration and transmutation. And that is how radioactive decay came to be understood as the spontaneous giving off of an alpha or beta particle, or of electromagnetic rays called X-rays and gamma rays. These energies ultimately end up as heat inside the earth. Uranium's slow radioactive decay provides the **main source of heat inside the earth,** causing convection and continental drift."

It was Greek to me but … hmm. Gamma rays. I'd seen the gamma symbol sprinkled through many of my dreams. And X-rays – I had enough of those in my dreams to see into the deepest of mysteries.

"Excuse me, Madame Curie, but when you said transmutation I thought about the history of chemistry where it was thought one element can be transmuted to another. Do you think in the natural sciences, one science can be transmuted to another - like geology becoming alchemical? What I wonder about is if the transmutation of chemical reactions can occur in response to changes in the earth and maybe even in the heavens? This makes me want to cry, Madame Curie, for I know so little but am learning so much."

"That's why you were awarded the Branch of Chemistry, Penelope. We knew that buried in the most private part of your soul was some instinctual yearning for chemistry."

The notion of cosmic alchemy produced a flashback of a very old dream. "Do you remember when I saw *cm 250*, which stood for Curium? In that dream, I said *I do more than one thing here. I'm in real estate and I'm an alchemist too.*"[352]

"Of course I remember, Penelope. I wrote it. May I also remind you of several dream images in which *a gold ball appeared behind your ear whispering the message that it was your birth earring.*[353] Beginning about AD 100, philosophers were preoccupied with the idea that metals in the earth would gradually change into gold. The ancient art of transmutation became known as alchemy and was, in many ways, the predecessor to chemistry. So this makes you somewhat of a renaissance woman."

"That was one of my most puzzling dreams, Madame Curie. I was kind of worried because that gold ball was stuck right behind my ear and I couldn't get it off. Does that mean you wrote it by ear?"

Laughingly, she replied, "One could say that."

"What we're basically talking about in terms of disintegration is the passage of electricity through gases. Our present concern is that such a scenario may be sparked, for example, in the area such as the Burin Peninsula. The uranium deposits, the radon exposure and the possibility of sleeping volcanoes add up to a precarious situation. Also, think about what piezoelectric material may be generating an electrical charge."

"I think it must be quartz, Madame Curie, because Dr. Steno is in love with it. I know we have serious matters ahead, but may I ask how it is that you're all together even in the hereafter?"

"Because, Penelope, souls are dualistic in nature. Part of our light energy always remains in the spirit world. It never leaves since we never completely separate from the Creator. You ask how it is we're together. Well, just as you have communities on the

352 7/16/93. See Ch. 17 – Real Estate & Alchemy, p. 75
353 11/15/96, 12/24/96. See Ch. 18 – Honored Chemistry Guide: Marie Curie, p. 78

Earth plane, we have soul cluster groups that wait to greet us upon our return. Soul groups are made up of family members, friends and teachers in the life from which we just departed or people we recognize from previous lives of centuries past. Jacques, Pierre and I are together because we shared an exceptional lifetime working together for the glory of the Creator. Because Pierre and I are soul mates, our recognition of each other extends from lifetime to lifetime and during the time we spend in between lives. The joy of coming together again has allowed us to taste the understanding of creation. You see Penelope, the experience of 'oneness' with our true mates mirrors the Oneness of the Creator."

"That is miraculous! How did you know Pierre was your soul mate?"

"Oh my dear, sweet, inquisitive one; it is so difficult to explain. What can I say but there was an ease so natural, a magnetism so powerful, a knowing so keen that neither of us doubted we were meant for the other. You see, when we first met on Earth, we had a feeling of instant and deep love and although we could not articulate it, we intuitively remembered our old love connection. Because we are part of the same soul, our energies vibrated at the same frequency. It took some time for us to learn that we have only one soul mate for all of eternity. Until soul mates find each other they know they will be searching for the other half of themselves all of their lives. I think you are doing just this in your pursuit of Johnnie Pianissimo, your long-lost love who Twink Ptolemy will be sending your way."

"You know, Madame Curie, I can't even imagine what he will look like."

"Be comforted, Penelope. You needn't be concerned with his physical appearance for it is likely that he will appear as an ordinary mortal, just a man among men, but one who will delight you with his music and recite to you his poetry. He will know you as his muse, take interest in your welfare and be stimulated by your intellect in a way no one ever has or will. His greatest joy will be to amuse you with his infectious humor, for your laughter will be his sustenance and his, yours. He will reach into the depths of your soul, igniting a spark in you that will trigger your memory of bygone days."

"But are you sure, Madame Curie, that I won't be able to recognize him in the flesh?"

"Perhaps, Penelope, my lovely, but rest assured you will recognize him in other ways; an inexpressible something – perhaps something as subtle as a fleeting glance, a passing laugh, a private word, a dusty book, a rare symbol, a passage from a poem will echo something you shared. In that moment of knowing, you will be lost in an astonishment of love and friendship and intimacy. Outward appearances change but the soul never does and you will each remember your soul's desire to be wholly one. If you dare to peek at your more personal dreams, I feel certain you'll find a semblance of him there."

I drifted back to moonlit dreams where an enchanted man sang to me from the depth of his soul, a man who had traveled from a great distance. His songs, so filled with the melodious resonance of love and tenderness, took me to forgotten times, to faraway places. When morning opened my eyes to wakefulness, I quietly tended those dreams and planted them in my garden of secret wishes. In one dream, he sang "Come fly with me, let's fly, just fly, away ..." and in a reverie, I heard the lyrics, "I see your face before me ..." Though his songs and sunlight stir in the four quadrants of my heart, I quaver in the twilight of sadness and joy for the years I have clung to his memory, perhaps more years than I've lived. I see the gleam of his face for an instant. It fades. The play of shadow and light dance across life's most glorious moments, so ephemeral, I wonder if they happened at all. But Madame Curie said he'd know me as his muse and though her strangely familiar words rouse me, they are so hazy and beyond reach, I dare not attempt to catch them. Would I ever cease from the longing – the starving hope that he might someday discover where I live. If Ptolemy found me, maybe Johnnie Pianissimo would too.

I tried to shake loose from this grip of mournful yearning and imagine what it would be like to see him again.

In sharing my innermost thoughts, my connection to my wise and compassionate mentor was deepening. It now seemed natural to address her as Marie, at least when we were speaking intimately.

"But, but, Marie. What will I do if he is too young or too old? Too short or too tall? Too serious or too silly? What will happen if he is inappropriate for me in conventional ways?"

"Neither physical attributes nor worldly decorum will concern you, Penelope. You will feel your energies vibrating in concert, and you will know by the sound of his voice, by the twinkle in his eye, by the warmth of his smile, his hand upon yours and the exquisitely familiar gestures of love so deeply embedded in you that he has returned to fulfill your dual purpose in this incarnation. You will speak the same words and think the same thoughts, becoming one with the other as you have been all along, for your souls live within each other eternally. That is why your dreams of him, the sound of his music and the lyrics of his poetry haven't paled nor will they ever. You will acknowledge that the meshing of your souls was the very expression of your ancient union.

"There will be one physical clue and only one, Penelope, so you must be vigilant. He is likely to be wearing a ring bearing the insignia of infinity."

(Gulp.) A ring of infinity? This stirred up as much curiosity as I could fathom. But in so thoroughly trusting my noble mentor, I held the thought and tried to listen beyond the range of the audible because that's where the truth really was.

Madame Curie continued. "We've learned there are only so many pairs of soul mates permitted to live together over the course of multiple lives and afterlives so Pierre and I are among the very fortunate few, as you and Johnnie will be when you reunite. Now that Pierre and I are together again on the same spiritual level, we recognize that our meeting on the physical level was prearranged for the purpose of undertaking our important joint

Mission on Earth. Occasionally a third participant, like Jacques, is dispatched to a pair of soul mates to further a higher purpose.

"Jacques and Pierre's discovery of piezoelectricity brought us all together in the nineteenth century, and we've been together ever since. Our work continues, for we receive information from many sources about conditions on Earth. We then pass it on to souls still incarnating who, through their advanced vibrational tones, will act to mitigate the negative energy patterns smothering civilization."

CHAPTER SEVENTY-NINE

NO STONE UNTURNED

Gravel – Quartz – Uranium

While Marie Curie hovered in the background, Steno waved his interplanetary spyglass, steadying it over something called quartz-pebble conglomerate deposits.

It clicked! The piece of gravel was like a pebble. That was the evidence!

He then showed me that sand is composed of finely divided minerals, among them, tiny quartz pebbles.

"Penelope," tutored Steno, "it's important you know that quartz-pebble conglomerate deposits make up approximately 13 percent of the world's uranium resources. Uranium deposits occur in a number of different geological environments. To name some other deposit types, there are sandstone deposits, surficial deposits, volcanic deposits, vein deposits and so on. Our philosophy at Terracrust is to leave no stone unturned."

"Surficial deposits! Doc, that connects to a dream in the Titanic thread about *SURF pay and a man who was ice fishing!*"[354]

Steno's pleasure sometimes produced a gurgling effect. "Penelope, surficial deposits are glacial deposits that occur near the earth's surface and are sometimes volcanic in origin."

"Hot diggity dog, Doc! The dream said *I missed a massage,* but I finally got the message."

I turned my focus to uranium, sensing this was a major thread in the story, and recapitulated. "Gosh, Dr. Steno, we've uncovered sulfur and radon, chlorine and fluorine, and now more uranium."

At that point, the grande dame of radioactivity, Madame Curie herself chimed in, "Yes, Penelope, uranium is the first element in a long series of decay steps that produce radium and radon. And to remind you, radon is plentiful in the St. Lawrence granite. In the early stages, when the St. Lawrence mines were a very unhealthy work environment,

---

354 6/2/96. See Ch. 23 – Tragedy, p. 105

Footnotes contain dream dates and references to prior pages where the dream appeared.

Endnotes contain bibliographical references, are marked with "Ɛ" in the text, and appear at the end of the book.

ground and meteoric waters circulated through the granite, dissolving uranium and then flowed into the mining shafts."

"Meteoric waters" stirred a faint memory that seemed to tinkle across the sands of Dreamtime.

"Penelope," interjected Steno, "I see that your thoughts are backtracking to ground-waters. It was April 2002 when the hydrocarbon gases we spoke of earlier were found in deep rocks and groundwaters at sites throughout the Canadian Shield."[339]

That was it! The mention of meteoric waters sparked a dream which I had been sitting on until the time was right. It was about hydrocarbons, of all things. In 1999, the Oneiroball released the dream message: *CFCs in the rain are attracted to hydrocarbons in carboniferous rocks.*[355] I wonder if I got the dream at the same time the researchers started work on it.

Steno responded. "Just as messages from the Oneiroball drift into your dreams, we also throw non-dream sorts of lines down to Earth when it's time for something to unfold. Our ultimate objective is for everyone to join in discovery and contribute to the greater good.

"Remember, Penelope, that the Oneiroball derives from the Greek Oneiromancy – the interpretation of dreams. This very special air balloon holds all of the fragments that will come together to reveal your purpose in a comprehensible way. The messages it contains, however, come to us in a random fashion, which is the only way we can transmit them to you.

"The reason for this haphazardness is that disorder is a temporary stage that is necessary in the transition from our world to yours. In our world, all things are mixed together and in your world, things are separated into groups. The world you live in is very well organized because it is a world of objects but also of places, time sequences and information. Think back to your lessons on Grouping Order and Symmetry Order when you pieced together your Pauline Maher – Polypipe synchronicity.[356] You are accustomed to grouping things, like our messages. You are noticing patterns and dividing them into themes. We're aware of how difficult it is for you to sort through what patterns go where and that it's even more difficult to determine, in Earth time, when to act on a particular theme. The results thus far are excellent, for you are advancing toward Symmetry. We are enormously pleased that your intuitive senses have been completely aligned with our objectives."

Marie Curie added. "It would be wise for you to hold off on the CFCs, for the process of enfoldment is in its early stages just now. Your consciousness has alerted you that CFC's have a place in the puzzle, so let it go for now and it will fall into place of its own accord."

355 9/21/99.
356 See Ch. 65 – Pipe dreams, pp. 305–08

"But, Marie, I don't even know what CFCs are, exactly. I remember something about them depleting part of the ozone layer, but for the life of me, I can't figure out where it goes in the story. I guess that supports what you're saying – that it will find its place when the time is right."

"Your memory about the ozone layer serves you correctly Penelope. CFCs are short for chlorofluorocarbons. They are compounds consisting of chlorine, fluorine and carbon. These chemicals have been used in great quantities in industry. When they are released into the air, they drift into an upper layer of the atmosphere – the stratosphere which is around thirty miles above the Earth. Our superpowered Starsight scopes are able to detect the intense interactions among radiative, dynamical and chemical processes through which the mixing of gaseous components occur. You've already uncovered chlorine in your *poisonous gas and pillow dream.* In time, the larger picture will develop.

"Meanwhile, I've noticed that you frequently question 'what' things are.

"In the words of our revered physicist, David Bohm, regarding his Implicate Order, 'The What is, is always a totality of ensembles, all present together, in an orderly series of stages of enfoldment and unfoldment, which intermingle and interpenetrate each other in principle throughout the whole of space.'[40] This notion would make it feasible that you have many other elements that will enfold as special themes in the overall order. Pollution is one theme in that order. It is one part of the whole. Bohm wrote, 'These arrangements can be mutually related and dependent, as if there had been a force of interaction between them.'"

As I was poking along, lost in her deep recitation on space, my esteemed chemistry mentor took me by the hand and said, "Come along, oh inquisitive one."

"Marie, can you tell me more about uranium?"

"We've covered some of it already, dear. It's important we conclude the lesson plan from this Newfoundland trip before we explore the complexities of uranium. One thing I hadn't mentioned is that uranium is referred to as the parent element, and radium and radon are called daughters."

Daughters? Hmm. My only association to parent and daughter is family relationships.

"But can you just tell me. Is that what all of those urine dreams were about? It's very puzzling because I don't think I have a problem with my bladder.

"Urine shows up all over the place in my dreams – on the floors, on the stairs, on the rugs. Sometimes *we're standing in it*, sometimes *it's under a cover*, sometimes *it's frozen*, other times *I can smell it*. In some dreams, *it's overflowing* and in one *dream, it's in a star cluster.* I'm scared, Madame Curie. There's a dream where a *bidet is overflowing with urine and I tell a friend who is a scientist that the world is going to end.*"

I connected the dots ... the bidet is French ... a scientist is present. Hmm. French ... scientist ... a scientist educated in France was Marie Curie. Flashing through my mind was a nest of dreams combining sulfur and uranium. This was becoming more dizzying by the moment.

Wanting to respect her boundaries but wildly curious, I had to ask one more question. "I don't mean to press you Madame Curie, but I just want to know if there's any relationship between any of these gases we've talked about and uranium?"

She somberly answered, "Well yes, Penelope. You know by now that fluorine, for example, is a yellowish, poisonous, highly corrosive gas. Being a nonmetal, it will react with almost any metal, which of course would include uranium. Now come with me, dear," she sighed, pulling me along as though I were a dawdling child. She was determined to wrap up the Newfoundland portion.

"I promise it will all unfold in good time. Remember your penny dream ... In God We Trust."

The *Das Shoot! Das Boot! – Bethany Church* dream stuck to me like glue. *The piece of gravel fell out of the brown paper by mistake. It turned out to be evidence. The angry official pretended not to notice it.*

If the authorities knew about it, why would they look the other way? Why the message – *the masses will be exterminated?*[357]

I hadn't yet patched all the pieces together to form a sound conclusion, but imminent danger loomed larger as I traveled on.

I couldn't square the conflict. Certainly, government officials knew there was a uranium deposit at the St. Lawrence Mines. Maybe they didn't know just how much uranium there was or how it might combine with other chemicals or with the movement of tectonic plates.

I learned from Steno that crushed stone or gravel is used in making concrete for building and construction work. It is called an aggregate – a total formed by combining several, often dissimilar elements. *The gravel was wrapped in brown paper which has a hand-drawn map with directions. It's like construction paper.* Yep. Something was definitely under construction and I hoped I was following directions.

The elements combined to make concrete the building and construction of the Dream ... of this dream which was racing along a scientific highway – destination unknown. Where would it end? What exit would I turn off at? I had no explicit directions save my elusive *hand-drawn map made of brown paper.*

How on Earth did I ever get pulled into such deep caverns of science?

"Penelope, yours is not to question why," conveyed Madame Curie, "but what might be helpful is if you try to form your own aggregate and see how you've arrived at each

357 See Ch. 74 – Das Shoot! Das Boot!, pp. 345-52

of the gases through your dreams. It may be that when many of these gases are brought together, the aggregate will become clearer."

"(Gulp.) Sulfur, Radon, Chlorine, and Fluorine.

"Madame Curie, this is testing me beyond my limits, but I'll give it a go."

Taking a deep breath and holding close my Branch of Chemistry, I began:

"Let's see. I found Sulfur, a species of butterfly in the dream of the *butterfly that trans-formed to a poisonous bumblebee*. Radon emerged in the *urine and gas* dreams because it is a product of uranium decay and all those urine dreams symbolized Uranium. Chlorine connected to *pillow lava* symbolized by the *poisonous gas and pillow* dreams. Fluorine was revealed in two ways: in *the lenses with peel-off backing* dream, as fluorite and in the *soft icky yellow wall* dream, as fluorine. These last two dreams were pointing to 'vision' and 'gas.' If images could speak, they were saying, 'Look at the gas!' I twigged on to gases as a theme when you told me fluorine was a highly poisonous pale yellow gas that could be fatal to animals.

"Whew!" How I was dreaming about all of those gases when I never even took a course in chemistry absolutely confounded me.

"Excellent synthesizing, Penelope. In time, you'll be forming more aggregates and doing it naturally. I know it takes some getting used to."

"Well, I certainly couldn't do it without you, Marie. You came to the rescue just in time – I hope."

"Dear, innocent Penelope. We are not the only guides who are helping. Ancient souls, even older than we, are helping as well. You may not recognize them, but they know you."

"They appeared in your dream as *two faceless women clad in Eastern Indian garb. One was dressed in yellow, the other in purple. There were two beds in the room, which the anonymous visitors stood between.*"[358]

At this turn on the highway, there is no doubt that the two most prominent colors in the passing landscape are yellow and purple. Lavender - a shade of purple, signatory for the volcano, was now joined by the mineral, fluorite known for its rich purple crystals. Fluorine, the gas, is one among other symbols in the yellow spectrum.

---

358 1/16/95.

CHAPTER EIGHTY

SUB ROSA

I detected Steno wafting into my stream of consciousness with a serving of geological goodies. "Not to distract from your palette of yellow and lavender, Penelope, but I'm eager to learn what your rendition might be of the *red roses* that you *placed under a chair.*"

"Well, Dr. Steno, my first instinct is that roses are symbolic of both life and death, and since they were under a chair, they may also suggest something sub rosa – something secret."

"Penelope, you are an Inspector of the first order. I think I'll call you Clueso, for you are always looking under something. Now, what do you think about the image of the red roses?"

"Honestly, Doc. I'm not exactly sure what that means other than love, because they send red roses on Valentine's Day and I'm hopelessly hopeful that I'll get a bouquet from Johnnie Pianissimo."

Steno chuckled. "The red rose has certainly imparted love and romance through the ages. But mind you, it is a sign of charity and martyrdom as well, for it came to symbolize the drops of Christ's blood on Calvary."

I remembered that roses also characterize quartz. I thought back to the *Avers*-Avens *dream of the combination lock which carried the mysterious message, "You'll know the real one someday,"* and how that led me to Avens of the rose family.[359] In the same vein (ha ha), I was reminded of *the pole decorated with the colorless rose*[360] which led me to rose quartz, then to quartz. By this time, I knew that Quartz was part of the granite family. Quartz ... Granite.

"Here. This might help you, Penelope," offered Steno as he positioned his spyglass over a geological highway map of the Burin Peninsula.

"It points out that 'purple, yellow, red and brown fluorite in vugs, breccia, or banded veins may be collected from the wall, from debris below it or from above the rock cut,

---

359 12/9/95. See Ch. 1– Beginnings, p. 6
360 10/1/98. See Ch. 14 – Honored Earth Guide: Nicolaus Steno, p. 67
        Ch. 48 – In My Sight, p. 210

Footnotes contain dream dates and references to prior pages where the dream appeared.
Endnotes contain bibliographical references, are marked with "𝓔" in the text, and appear at the end of the book.

where digging for power pole anchors has exposed blocks of vein material. Known as the Church vein, it is partly exposed on the south side of the road, below the easterly power pole. The veins are related to the granite; they formed in shrinkage cracks during the last stages of cooling of the granite magma during the Devonian."[E41]

"The Devonian?"

"Sorry, Penelope. The Devonian Period lasted from 417 million years ago to 354 million years ago and is the fourth division of the Paleozoic Era of the geologic time scale."

Some days he forgot he was coaching a freshman who had no earthly idea of what he was talking about. I sensed he was still bothered over the violent reaction I'd had to the disintegrating finger. There were so many little finger coves in the area. Could an earthquake trigger a submarine landslide that might unearth some unknown uranium sediment that might be mixing with something else?

Steno came to my aid. "A magmatic disturbance would signal a transformation of unknown origin."

"Magmatic disturbance? Transformation?" Unknown origin?"

"Penelope, the meaning of magmatic comes from the term magma, meaning molten rock. A magmatic province is an area that is formed from originally molten rocks."

Not knowing how it all connected, I agonized, trying to piece together this elephantine puzzle without the academic tools to do so. Maybe it wasn't as ominous as it appeared, but *extermination of the masses* was nothing to sweep under the carpet, even at the expense of looking the fool.

Hmm. The partly exposed pink granite vein in St. Lawrence – the Church vein – contains fluorite. The dream symbol of the *cellophane-wrapped red roses* may translate to vision and to granite covered in lava. Could cellophane made from viscose, characterize the viscosity of lava? This would point to the vein being overlain by lava. That must be why Steno said I was always looking under something.

I was perplexed. There were so many clues pointing to quartz and rose quartz and now we were looking at a pink granite vein. They seem kind of similar but quartz is a mineral, and granite, a rock. I wondered what they had in common and if I was on the right track. I knew that what I was looking for wouldn't be visible to a layperson. If I tripped over a vein, I'd never know it, unless it was a varicose vein.

Steno, widely known as the founder of modern geology, was motivated to clear up my confusion over quartz and granite. "Ah, Penelope. You have returned me to my passionate studies of quartz. Allow me to shed some light on these sacred minerals.

"Granite is a very hard rock formation with a crystalline texture and is made up of quartz and other minerals so, yes, indeed, you are on the right track. When I was around, most Earth geologists did not realize that my interpretation of Genesis led me to sedimentary rock layers. I believed then, as I know now, that the Bible records the true history, including the geological history of the world."

I was relieved. Who would know better about the differences in minerals than Steno who had studied crystals, quartz in particular, plus fossils and rock strata. He must be the prima geologist in the cosmos to continually gauge the composition of the earth.

Following the geological roadmap, I noted that a major landmark was the radioactivity in radon found while mining fluorspar in the St. Lawrence mines. I had to remember that fluorspar is another name for fluorite.

Was the message one that history was about to repeat itself? One of the earliest clues was a silver key that snapped in half. What could that mean?

Steno glided in with some elaboration.

"Your hunch about a silver ore being in the mix was sound. Silver is a metallic element and that might just forge a link to your Alchemy – Real Estate dream[361] in which the elemental tables were introduced to you. Also, while on the subject of alchemy, you might be interested to know that sulfur was regarded by the alchemists as essential in combustion because of its flammability."

"Sulfur is flammable?"

"Yes, Penelope. It is mentioned in the Bible as brimstone. It is known as the 'burning rock' and is associated in popular belief with divine punishment. But hold that thought, Penny. I hear a familiar call. Our heavenly courier is hooting in with some data on sulfur."

ÕÕ "It is reported that between twenty and fifty million tonnes of sulfur are returned from the oceans to the atmosphere every year."[ε42]

Madame Curie overheard Steno addressing her grand passion: the elemental tables. "With all due respect, Dr. Steno, you just egg her on."

Steno retorted, "In all due respects, Madame Curie, egg is as much your domain as it is mine."

"What is all this eggy talk about?" I asked.

"Penelope" replied Madame Curie, "egg yolks are one of the better sources of sulfur. You haven't recognized them yet, but we know you have hatched quite a nest of egg dreams by now.

"You may recall that Dr. Steno and I have a mutual interest in sulfur. In Dr. Steno's province, sulfur ranks sixteenth in abundance among the elements in the earth's crust. Sulfur means a lot to me as it's an element on the periodic table. Having spent an entire lifetime working on the discovery of chemical elements, I have a soft spot in my soul for

361 7/16/93. See Ch. 17 – Real Estate & Alchemy, p. 75

Periodic Law. That's how I learned that many of the physical and chemical properties of the elements tend to recur in a systematic manner with increasing atomic number."

Karensurefoot and I were entranced. Cotton-headed from the high voltage boosts of spiritual energy, we were at a loss for what to do next. After stretches of timelessness and uninterrupted exchanges with our guides, it was clear we had never left terra firma, for facing us was the wooden structure that housed the Bethany Church circa 1859, physical proof that we hadn't left the borderless realm of the material world.

Led as we were by the dreams and our guides, we had unsuspectingly entered the soft light of metaphysical transcendence. Enveloped in this wondrously protective cocoon where we were changelessly in and out of time, we had become observers. It was rather like watching a dream, engaging with it, and then moving through it. Timelessness existed wherever and whenever our imaginations chose. During those moments when our waking eyes perceived the same images as our dreaming eyes, we had become both observer and observed. We floated above Starsight and Terracrust, observing the Earth, inside and out, from the perspectives of Peggymoonbeam, Steno and Curie. We experienced Bohm's theory: the "unbroken wholeness of the totality of existence as an undivided flowing movement without borders," our conscious and unconscious awareness seamlessly blending with our physical and spiritual selves to become, for a few timeless twinklings, pure energy, a tiny part of the cosmos, the oneness, the idea of connection so important to Mission Lavender.

In silent gratitude for the universal chorus of ancient wisdom, we decided on the mundane task of picture taking and so began photographing all sides of the Bethany Church.

Marie Curie went on to inform us that minor amounts of fluorine are found in some volcanic gases. Fluorine – that most reactive of all elements!

The authorities must know there's radioactive gas near volcanic rock, below a power pole. They knew their miners had died from working around the fluorspar vein.. The vein and the power pole are described on their own highway map.[E43]

Fluorspar in the vein ... fluorine as a gas.

Was this vein also linked to Lawn, the little community with the lavender fire hydrants and poles? Was the concrete being poured for a path that wasn't yet visible?

Aware that our eminent scribes were decoding every particle of our earthly mind forms called "thought," we blushed at their nods of approval.

"They are our girls 100 percent," proudly hailed Steno and Curie. "They've got the message."

"See, guys! I told you. I told you," boasted Peggymoonbeam. "It's a good thing you preach the patience you practice and practice the patience you preach! Ha ha ha. "

A path not yet visible! It suddenly occurred to me that so many of the signs were pointing to something being underneath, mostly underground.

I turned to Karensurefoot. "This sub rosa dream tells me underground is a big clue."

"You're right, Penelope," agreed Karen. "I'm thinking of your dream of the *large yellow butterfly that turned into a poisonous bumblebee* which lives underground. You've been contemplating something sulfurous and poisonous underground. Why don't you try to make a circle and see if it works?"

"OK, I'll start with sub-rosa – Roses under the chair – Drilling underground – Oil – Pipeline – Gas – Mining underground – Nickel – Sulfur underground – Titanic underground – Carboniferous rocks – Hydrocarbon Gases – Volcanic gases underground – Pillow lava underwater – Fluorspar deposits – Uranium deposits – Nickel deposits. Every clue is sub-rosa!"

"Penelope! This circle is giving off such a rotten stench it's making me nauseous! It's strange that you got such a smelly job to do."

"Oh no, Karen! Marie Curie told us sulfur doesn't have an odor until it reacts! Burning is one kind of reaction."

CHAPTER EIGHTY-ONE

GESTALT AND THE CHAIR

Technical and spiritual operations were working overtime and in unison. A plaintive chord echoed Gestalt psychology and its concept of a unified whole. The watchful spirits of Curie, Galen, Ptolemy and Steno joined the congress of souls – Agneswiseheart, Peggymoonbeam and Charlesbigstar. While mulling over the relationship of the Gestalt theory to mining in Newfoundland, the Oneiroball whirled by and dropped something in my lap.

It was a passage about the chair: "A chair, for example, will generally be recognized as a chair despite great variations between individual chairs."

The Gestalt concept of a unified whole being greater than, or different from, the sum of its parts, that is, a complete structure whose nature is not explained simply by analyzing its constituent elements, began to blend with the nomenclature of St. Lawrence. In the instance of the pink granite vein (*dead roses*) under the Bethany Church, Gestalt teachings would generally be recognizing the Church vein as one vein despite great variations between individual veins or fractures in other parts of the earth.

The inquiry rested on how the one vein under the Bethany Church would interconnect to the vast network of veins throughout the earth.

In Gestalt psychology, learning is a reorganizing of a whole situation (often involving insight). It was mind boggling that the technical-spiritual wizards at Starsight and Terracrust sent the chair as a learning aid.

Whatever the unknowable dynamics, insight was at the helm.

The esteemed Steno would say the linkage of *dead roses* to the Bethany Church was only one piece of the overall picture. He'd say that roses are part of a pattern and that they would join other patterns. So far, there was a *colorless rose, a white rose* and *red roses*, each shade having a distinct meaning but belonging to the same flower. He'd tell me I'm working on symmetry and that the puzzle would fit together; that there would be an exquisite unity. Well, that was gratifying, but would we see the end? Were we sitting on a catastrophic eruption? Was the unified whole signifying one link in a chain of tectonic plates, more than one small community of St. Lawrence or more than the single province of Newfoundland? Were the many little villages we had visited – Placentia, Lawn,

Footnotes contain dream dates and references to prior pages where the dream appeared.
Endnotes contain bibliographical references, are marked with "Ɛ" in the text, and appear at the end of the book.

St. Brides, Branch and those yet to be explored – connecting to this quartz vein? Was there a geological pathway to be traced? Would it extend beyond Newfoundland?

The repeating roses seemed to carry a secret message. They must be one of the codes to the combination lock in the *Avers*-Avens dream – the cryptic message that I *would know the real one someday.* Maybe it was hidden in the steganography that Father Nick, the Greek priest told me about. Maybe it was part of the Greek code.

I thought about the aggregate, about the Gestalt concept of a unified whole and what the larger message might be. I continued to obsess about the dream-issued warning – *the masses would be exterminated.* Were other continents connected to this?

Steno, Terracrust's Seer of the Earth, reminded me, "Your questions will be answered by insight and trust in God."

CHAPTER EIGHTY-TWO

ONWARD

Grand Bank

We left behind the little town of Burin, sobered by the foreboding message held in the vespers of the Bethany Church, and traveled the boot of the Burin Peninsula around to the town of Grand Bank, located at its toe.

Burin dominated our thoughts while we journeyed onward. Motoring through blankets of fog, we arrived in Grand Bank late at night. With scarcely any visibility and air thick as pea soup, we crept at a snail's pace through the cloud-curtained town. The bleak entrance took us back nearly a century in time to when Titanic sank amidst its victims to rest thousands of feet beneath the surface of the Atlantic.

The town of Grand Bank, in rural Newfoundland, is the most well-known community on the Burin Peninsula. Despite the movie-set quality of the quaint little town with its Queen Anne-style houses and their widow's walks, a feeling of loss and a dour economy prevailed. Grand Bank itself was paradoxically the only stop that did not, from outward appearances, reveal a solitary dream-inspired sign, but the road to Grand Bank displayed the yellow stones that populated my dreams.

Footnotes contain dream dates and references to prior pages where the dream appeared.
Endnotes contain bibliographical references, are marked with "Ɛ" in the text, and appear at the end of the book.

CHAPTER EIGHTY-THREE

A HIDDEN KEY

Day Seven: Spanish Room, Lewin's Cove, Cape Chapeau Rouge, Swift Current

The next day we were looping back around the boot on our return to St. John's — and the picturesque towns we had passed on our outward journey.

Spanish Room, a tiny community settled around 1837, forms around a broad cove by the peninsula "Cow Head." One could easily miss the miniscule cove, but despite several wrong turns, a driving urge took us to the tiny inlet.

Haunting me since 1995 was a weird dream that spun another cobweb to untangle. It centered on the location of a key. Its setting is *a Mexican restaurant decorated in vivid colors with wooden beams and a palm tree. A tray slides out from a wall on the left. A diver unlocks the key, which is behind a machine. A metal bar has to slide down before a copy can be made.*[362]

Dreams are mysterious by nature, but this one was a real whodunit! Was the Mexican dream setting a linguistic metaphor for Spanish — Mexico's spoken language — and this little Spanish Room? The vivid colors and the palm tree were surely more in keeping with Mexico than Newfoundland, but within the parameters of the dream, the community of Spanish Room was small enough to be a restaurant. Though it wasn't a great fit, I continued tracking my instincts and the pebbles of logic strewn along our path. I was confused. Why would I dream a palm tree and connect it to a tiny spot in Newfoundland?

The saintly faculty was ever by my side when I was truly lost, which I was now. They must have sensed my frustration in sorting through all the fragments, symbols, puns, similes and metaphors.

Agneswiseheart, riding the crest of spirit, tuned in to say, "Penelope, the palm is symbolic of the Bethany Church for Bethany was the town Jesus rode through on a donkey to reach Jerusalem on Palm Sunday. Those who had witnessed the raising of Lazarus from the dead, and even some Judean supporters, 'took palm branches and went out to meet him.'ᵋ⁴⁴ Palm branches signify glory, triumph and resurrection. Fear not, my sweet ... you will meet the challenge. You will solve this puzzle."

---

362 5/20/95.

Footnotes contain dream dates and references to prior pages where the dream appeared.
Endnotes contain bibliographical references, are marked with "Ɛ" in the text, and appear at the end of the book.

The palm branches might be symbolizing the Branch of Theology. After all, "of Theos" was part of the Greek code and I had had other puzzling dreams about *theology* – one that included a *double duplex and a green plant.*[363]

"Now, now," spoke Steno, steering me away from Theology. "Even though you see that relationship, for the time being we must concentrate our energies on Newfoundland. I assure you you'll have ample time to uncover all of your Branches."

"Remember symmetry order, Penelope. You're blending things together for the reason that they all go together. Take just one piece at a time – think of it as a clue. Imagine that you're building a case. Begin as though you're compiling a photo album. Add each snapshot to the album and one by one, they'll merge to reveal the big picture that will solve the mystery."

"But, Dr. Steno," I protested, "there are so many pieces! There must be thousands!"

"Keep it simple, Penelope. Too much complexity and it will be as difficult to understand as nature itself."

Hah! Easy for him to say. He knows every piece of the earth from the dawn of the Paleozoic. The ancient tutor of terra firma spun off to attend his various rounds while I tried to synthesize my snapshots. I would track the clues as they appeared: the Mexican Restaurant – the Tray – the Diver – the Key – the Machine – the Metal Bar – the Copy.

The Mexican Restaurant: I was thoroughly confused. I'd have to come back to this. It seemed so out of place in Newfoundland with nary a palm tree in sight, but ...

The Tray: Was the *sliding tray* a tectonic plate that slid out from the wall of the earth's surface? The *wall was on the left* and left in my dreams always means past. Did this happen at an earlier time? Did the wall represent a plate boundary, a zone of seismic activity, along which plates are in contact?

*The Diver and the Key: The diver who unlocks the k*ey implies deep-sea exploration in search of a hidden clue. That makes no sense. How can you unlock a key? It must be a metaphorical key. I think the crux of the clue is the fact that the key was *behind a machine.*

The Machine: Did the machine symbolize an inactive or dormant submarine volcano in the area of the *Mexican restaurant*/Spanish Room? Was this the cause of an unknown eruption that may have sunk the Titanic in 1912?

The Metal Bar: It clamored for attention. I could not escape it. The metal I was most focused on was uranium. I had connected this to the many dreams of *urine* and to the *gravel* – quartz-pebble – uranium clue Madame Curie and Nicolaus Steno uncovered under the Bethany Church. I wondered if there was a uranium deposit in the Grand Banks where a landslide triggered a tsunami in the 1929 earthquake.

---

363 7/25/93.

Was the *metal bar that slid down* suggestive of metals that accumulate in sediments? A sandbar containing metal would involve the sliding down of a mass of land, as in a landslide. A similar event would have to occur in a seismic zone before this act of nature would be duplicated – *before a copy could be made.*

I'd been reading stories of a "great meteorite" that fell in the area in 1874, which gave me pause to reflect on the metal clue, as most meteorites contain some iron. That year's fall was the most frequently cited case in Newfoundland, recalled as a number of flashes across the sky in the Harbour Grace area.[E45] Ten years later, a loud explosion from what may have been a meteorite impact in the ocean was heard in Conception, Trinity and Placentia bays, waters now coveted by prospectors who wished to bring natural gas ashore.

Never let it be said that a stray wisp of a dream escapes the vision of the guides, for Steno dropped in and directed me back to the beginning of this thread.

"Penelope, I must point you toward the *Mexican restaurant.* I am obliged to inform you of a volcano in Mexico known as the Volcano of Colima that has been the site of volcanic activity for about five million years. Colima is considered the most dangerous and active volcano in Mexico and is situated within a large caldera formed by a combination of landslides and large eruptions."

My ascended master gave me two examples of the harsh effects of a landslide: Grand Banks and Colima. Newfoundland and Mexico! The dream created a dual template for the 1929 sub-marine landslide resulting from an earthquake off Grand Banks that triggered a tsunami and paired it with the Colima Volcano in Mexico known for its large volcanic landslides. The Grand Banks earthquake, registered a Richter magnitude of 7.2. The tsunami raised tides as far away as South Carolina and Portugal. Landslides. Another reading of the metal bar that slid down?

The Copy: The dream was marking a landslide that would duplicate these disasters.

Did igneous rock exist in an ocean ridge under this peaceful little finger cove. A surprise came months later when I discovered on a geologic map that the *Mexican restaurant* version of Spanish Room is one of many locations in the region where pillow basalt erupted from undersea volcanoes. My little snapshots were forming a composite. Image by image, I was getting closer to cracking the case.

Was the *Mexican restaurant*/Spanish Room, the tiny finger cove, represented by the *disintegrating finger* in the Bethany dream? That would signal radioactive disintegration. This must be what Steno meant about magmatic provinces and magmatic disturbances. Magmatic had to do with lava – molten rock.

My memory must have been working overtime for the Oneiroball let loose another Spanish dream, containing an image of *a Spanish-style house. It has vaulted ceilings and the sides of the roof are open.* The dream concludes with me *sitting on a grapefruit. It has leaked all over the place. Those around me have grapefruit on their plates.*[364]

---

364 3/5/96.

The cone-like shape of the house resembles both a volcanic structure and a pyramid. But why would I be sitting on a grapefruit? This Oneiroball dropped some very strange messages on me. Sitting on something also meant keeping it to yourself. Was I sitting on a secret until the time was right to divulge it? Why did this seem so clandestine?

Did the acid in *grapefruit* correspond to sulfuric acid? Acid rain? In the dog walker dream, transparent lava *bands were holding me down* and were *only released by a bite*[365] – a sulfuric acid bite that released the lava, possibly resulting in the explosive release of volcanic gases? In this scenario, the *grapefruit* is on plates – tectonic plates?

On its exterior, Spanish Room was a quiet, secluded and sparsely populated fishing cove showing no signs of danger coming from the sea and, to the untrained eye, no signs of a landslide. But the secrets of this unsuspecting little cove may be lurking under its invisible wraps.

I had filled a page or two in my photo album, with countless blank pages left to go. *The key behind a machine.* Behind could mean the past. The key must be the key to the geologic past. The diver had to unlock past earthquake and volcanic activity. But was it pointing to Titanic's demise or to future catastrophes? Or both?

As the universe spun out its endless scenarios, many of my questions hung in suspense.

---

365 11/30/98. See Ch. 35 – Lava Under Revelation, p. 151

CHAPTER EIGHTY-FOUR

AMERICAN CURRENCY A LA ORIGAMI

Lewin's Cove

Another spot beckoning our acquaintance was Lewin's Cove, located at the head of Burin Harbour, a short drive from Spanish Room. The original spelling of the town, "Loon's Cove," first appeared in the Census of 1891; it was probably named for the common loon that nests in nearby inland ponds. In 1994, its population was 604.

The dream contents relating to Lewin's Cove are rife with elements linking to plate tectonics.

A dream opens *with me in a car. A mother figure is driving around something circular. There are some metal discs or plates on the ground and as we're driving over them, the car slips and goes over the edge. I know we're going under the water. We are falling and falling and I'm thinking about how we can pull ourselves up, back to the top. I feel we can make it but I don't know how.*

A friend named Lewin has a new wallet holding foreign currency – maybe Asian. The American bills are folded up like origami because they're taking up too much room. Someone is unfolding them so they won't crowd the wallet. There are long roots on a plate. A woman in a turban has just washed her hair. I sense she has a fall in with her hair because there's so much volume under the towel. She has done this quickly. She had been making dinner and was out of the room for just a few minutes.[366]

Might the figure of *mother driving around something circular* depict Mother Earth orbiting the sun? Is the *car* the tectonic engine driving Mother Earth? Is it *slipping* and *going over the edge* as the result of a strike-slip fault where plates slide past one another? The dream said "plates." Which plates?

Nagging repetition of the word "fold" provided clues: wallet, a synonym for billfold; the American bills folded up, and origami – the Japanese art of folding paper. Did billfold then translate to currency/fold – to folding currency – not only monetarily, but also geophysically, particularly as it would relate to submarine volcanic events?

---

366 3/3/99.

Footnotes contain dream dates and references to prior pages where the dream appeared.
Endnotes contain bibliographical references, are marked with "Ɛ" in the text, and appear at the end of the book.

"Gracious, Clueso," beamed Steno. "Such probing questions.

"While you're on the subject of folding, there's a type of mountain building where two slabs of the earth's crust begin to move closer to each other and the portion of the crust between the slabs is compressed and folded. Examples of ranges of fold mountains would be the Himalaya in Asia or the Appalachians in Newfoundland. Just as there are mountain ranges on the continents, so there are mountain ridges across the ocean floor. You've detected vitally important clues in your dream. Now you must string them together."

Wednesday, March 3, 1999

I am in a car. I think Suzy is driving. We are going around something circular. There are some metal discs or plates on the ground and as we are driving over them, the car slips and goes over the edge. I knew we are going under the water. We are falling and falling and I'm thinking how we can pull ourselves up - back to the top. I feel we can make it but don't know how.

I awaken - the wind is howling and whistling through the windows. Fell back asleep.

Paul Levine has a new wallet. I think I gave it to him. He has a lot of foreign currency in it - maybe Asian money. There are American bills all folded up - like origami and are taking up too much room. I am unfolding them so they will not crowd the wallet. He is taking credit cards and sticking them in the wallet. I guess he will straighten it all out later. Right now the idea is to put everything in the wallet.

There are some long roots on a plate with other food - like scallions. I want to cut them up because they will be more decorative - they are different colors and will look like confetti. Then I realize this will take energy and I have to save my energy.

WE'LL COME BACK UP

FOREIGN CURRENCY

AMERICAN CURRENCY

SCALLIONS

SAVE YOUR ENERGY

I'LL MAKE CONFETTI

Visualizing mountains on the bottom of the sea, I rushed back to my journal to rake through the snarled seaweed of the Dream. Metal plates or plates on the ground conjured up tectonic plates containing metals.

Asian currency took me to the Japanese yen. On the game board of tectonics, billfold was a double entendre in Terracrustian, the dialect spoken at Terracrust. Billfold turned into folding bills, which converted to folding currency and then again into currents/sea relating to a body of water. But back to billfold: if the continent of North America was at risk of going under, the monetary symbol would cease to exist.

In the dream, *someone is trying to unfold the American bills so they won't crowd the wallet* – the billfold … currency … currents – sea … folding bills … folding current … folding sea. Jiminy Crickets! I bellowed, "FOLDING SEA!"

Steno swept in clutching his flapping steno pad.

"That's right, Penelope. The folding sea is the Mid-Ocean Ridge. Mid-ocean ridges are vast mountain chains under the oceans and are as tall if not taller than mountain chains on land. That *"someone"* in your dream is all of us at Terracrust and Starsight trying to get the attention of those on Earth who can effect some changes. We know you have the technology and the brainpower to do so, but it takes more."

"It sure does" chimed in Peggymoonbeam. "It takes heart … miles and miles and miles of heart."

Steno pressed on. "Penelope, the mountain chain in the Atlantic Ocean is called the Mid-Atlantic Ridge and is part of the Mid-Ocean Ridge system which is a focal point of volcanic activity. It's a continuous 40,000 mile belt of volcanic underwater ridges that encircles the world and bisects the oceans. Like the seam of a baseball, the Ridge winds around the globe from the Arctic Ocean to the Atlantic Ocean, around Africa, Asia and Australia, under the Pacific Ocean and to the west coast of North America."

"It's unbelievable, Dr. Steno, that this huge mountain range is under water and that it's in my dreams."

"Yes. The Mid-Ocean Ridge has faults and folds just as mountains do but they're on the ocean floor. It is up to 1,000 miles wide and rises one to two miles above the floor of the basins on either side of it. A giant crack, half a mile to a mile and a half deep and from 20 to 80 miles wide, runs down its center.

"To refresh your memory, John Tuzo Wilson discovered a particular kind of fault found in ocean ridges. He called it the transform fault. There plates slide past one another without the construction or destruction of crust. This adventurous Canadian geophysicist was disguised in the dream that called you *Penelope Wilson. It had images of waste in it and a girl who matches her flower, which looks like a sunflower. Someone was telling you how to get a message. He said it's the on-off switch – like for a TV.*[367]

---

367 7/23/00. See Ch. 42 – Geology: The Second Branch, p. 193

"That was your prompt and your receiver was on. It's been said, Penelope, that even though the Ridge is by far the longest structure on the Earth, less is known about its features than about the craters on the dark side of the moon.^{Ɛ46}

"In your dream about a *mother's car going over the edge and landing underwater,* the *long roots on the plate* are suggestive of the planed-down roots of very old mountain ranges, like the Appalachians, that were formed four hundred million years ago and have been worn down by erosion. The Appalachian orogenic belt, which extends through North America to Newfoundland, is critically important to this assignment. Strong implications of new folding in oceanic mountain ridges situated along the North American plate boundary are in many of your dream patterns that intersect the Appalachians and the Himalaya and point directly to Canada.

"You should be aware, Penelope, that three plates are represented in this dream: The Eurasian plate symbolized by the *Asian currency* and the *origami,* the North American plate symbolized by the *American bills,* and the Indo-Australian plate symbolized by the *turban.*

"Well, Penelope, I must be off for a meeting with Pierre Curie at Terracrust. I see it's imperative we clarify certain of our transmissions to you."

Ending his spirited lecture on the Mid-Ocean Ridge, my ethereal professor made it clear I was to figure the rest out myself. It annoyed me no end when he just spun out of reach at a critical turning point for this uphill climb spiraled toward a terrain I never envisaged. Fighting drowning waves of doubt, I kept on trudging. Somewhere along the way, I had developed a mountaineering spirit previously untapped.

Time was of the essence. There was no room for triviality. As mental gridlock loosened, strands of consciousness began to interweave like fine needlepoint.

Returning to the dream: *the American bills are folded up like origami because they're taking up too much room.* The dream seems to be saying that the North American plate is undergoing oceanic folding similar to the Eurasian plates.' This is frightening, for it looks like the Eurasian plate may be crowding out the North American plate.

Radioing in from Terracrust, Steno corroborated. "Penelope, you are on to something, for in this type of tectonic convergence, layered rocks that were once located in the ocean basin are squeezed into a smaller and smaller area and would support your idea of crowding."

It was time to have a look at the woman wearing the turban – the woman who had just washed her hair.

If the woman embodies Mother Earth, which continent did she sire in this play? How could I know she wore an Indian turban and not an Arab turban or an African turban? Steno told me the turban symbolized the Indo-Australian plate, so it must be Indian. After some deliberation and a lot of puzzle piecing, the *turban,* paired with *Asian   cur-*

rency, would come to symbolize India's headdress translating to the Himalaya, the great mountain system of Asia. But what would that have to do with a plate?

I deliberated. Is the washing of her hair a reminder of the monsoons that have besieged the Himalaya?

Or was it signaling an impending torrent, a surging of rivers that would be the cause of still more erosive energy?

One lone dream strand remained: *I sense she has a fall in with her hair because there is so much volume under the towel.* I wondered if it connected with Pele's hair,[368] volcanic glass formed by lava and blown by the wind.

Could the fall entwined in her hair symbolize a mass movement of rock?

Could the voluminous amount under the towel be alerting us to a massive amount of movement in the earth? A magnitude rating on the Richter scale?

Were we being alerted to an earthquake or a landslide?

Was it reminding us that the Himalayan range in India is the result of the Indo-Australian and Eurasian plates colliding head on?

India still piles headlong into Eurasia, and the Himalaya are still under construction. In the dream, it *happens quickly*, an ominous note that the American bills are all folded up, that our mountain systems are folding because they are taking up too much room and that a sudden catastrophe could break out. The warning implies there would be little time in which to prepare.

So much of it pointed to India's geologic history and how the Himalaya were formed when northbound India crashed into Asia. But Newfoundland, and for that matter, North America, wasn't involved then.

If Lewin was symbolizing Lewin's Cove on the Burin Peninsula, it was one more step along this daunting path that directed me to the Avalon Zone, part of which constitutes the fault block near Burin. The next step led to Newfoundland being part of the Appalachian mountain system and sitting on the North American plate.

Was the North American plate being dragged under as an unwelcome newcomer to the cast of folding and crashing continents? Could industrial abuse to the earth cause fissures and fractures in rocks that have contributed to even the slightest movement of tectonic plates? I obsessed about this ghastly eventuality and the destruction of so many lives.

"Dr. Steno! Dr. Steno! Where are you? Can you hear me?"

No Answer.

"Dr. Steno?"

---

368 3/3/99. See Ch. 32 – Mother's Apprentices, p. 142

Where in Heaven's name is he?

"Egad! Dr. Steno, that dream about *mother driving a car,* you know, the tectonic engine, is represented by three continents: North America, Asia, and India."

"Yes, Penelope. I heard you. I'm always listening but was unable to respond because we were out of zone when you wired. You know, interstellar communication is still in its infancy and the relationship between your time in the material world and our time in the nonmaterial world has yet to be defined. You were asking about the three continents?"

"Dr. Steno! It sounds like a submarine eruption is going to be the cause of the car slipping on some plates and going over the edge. Is it possible that unstable underwater faults could trigger folding in the Appalachians and cause a huge calamity?"

"Well, Penelope, your Earth scientists say there is no active mountain building in the Appalachian Mountains, but your dream does not agree. Nonetheless, you know how strong my beliefs are in the origin of the Dream. Because we at Terracrust are blessed with telescopic sight, we see things that extend far beyond an earthling's range of vision. The reason you as an earthling can share our outlook is that you have been listening. We do have a much better view from up here and if more people listened, we could avert disaster and ease human suffering on Earth.

"The clues to past plate activity can only be found on the present-day continents in rocks, fossils and structures older than about 200 million years."

Hmm. Maybe that was why no one knew what happened to the Titanic. There was no geologic evidence.

"Actually, Penelope, in connection with Titanic, rocks of the Avalon Zone extend eastward from a major fault to Cape Spear and offshore at least as far as the Flemish Cap, which was along the deadly route the iceberg took before meeting up with Titanic. If you recall, the Flemish Cap appeared in the dream where *you were taking a course in shorthand from a Japanese instructor.*[369] Of course you know that that dream led you to me, before I crystallized – ha ha! No pun intended."

"But, but Dr. Steno, you are Danish, not Japanese."

"My fair lass, that is correct. Shorthand symbolizes my namesake, Steno, and as for your Japanese instructor, dear Penelope, do be patient. First you must learn the shorthand of the dream; then you will learn a more exotic language.

"So returning to that dream of yore – I mean yours," he joked, "we had our eye on the Avalon Zone from the start, but we had to spoon-feed you. It's quite a plateful for a fledgling to swallow.

"Do you remember your dream about a *floating metal wrench?*[370] Well, a wrench fault is another name for a strike-slip fault and is the same as a transform fault … *Miss Penelope*

---

369 10/1/98.

370 10/12/98. See Ch. 18 – Honored Chemistry Guide: Marie Curie, p. 78

Wilson. I hope this 'floating' cue planted the mineral that most transform faults are found on the ocean floor." Steno departed thoroughly pleased with his little innuendo, a side he doesn't often reveal.

Hmm. I thought, metal again. Floating metal in a fault. I reflected back on our stop, at the Spanish Room, and the dream of *the metal bar that had to slide down before a copy was made.* Back to uranium. Uranium is a metal and like tin and tungsten, is in the seawater.

Our next stop would be Cape Chapeau Rouge. Rouge, in French, is red. But could it also be pink? A dream of a *hat with a pink rose* hadn't yet opened. Was the *pink rose* marking the pink granite veins that were formed during the Devonian? Was a strike-slip fault characterizing an entire belt in the Avalon Zone?

The unremitting question was why this exhaustive search? Why was it playing out in my dreams with such specificity?

One thing was certain. In unraveling the worlds of clues, the puzzle did not mandate a selection process: a practice second nature to us in a society conditioned to choose. A choice of "either – or" simply does not work in the nonlinear world of dreams, for every alternative will ultimately find its place and link to another. Unlike the world of sequence, the circularity of the Earth mimics the unconscious orbit of our dreams and weaves a universal connectedness that encompasses everything and everyone. Thus, the mystery of the infinite continues to replicate itself in life's ever-fluctuating patterns imprinted in some memory encoding phenomenon in our brains.

Karensurefoot and I left Lewin's Cove deeply concerned. Was the pint-sized community sitting on a restless undersea ocean ridge? Did it play a part in the downing of Titanic almost one hundred years ago? I noted that it was minutes away from Burin and not far from the Bethany Church.

How strange that a friend named Lewin in a dream could lead to a significant finding in the temporal world. I soon learned it was a hallmark of the mentor's apprenticeship program, a combination of on-the-job training and related associative guidance.

CHAPTER EIGHTY-FIVE

UNDER MY HAT

Cape Chapeau Rouge

Described as the most remarkable Cape in all Newfoundland, Chapeau Rouge is an immense heap of ragged, craggy rocks placed one upon the other. It is the southern angle of Great St. Lawrence's Harbour. An early explorer said that when it is "viewed from the sea, every move gives it a new shape...."

Though time didn't permit us to climb the rugged peak, it was a must-see from its base, for a collection of hat dreams had elegantly crowned the rocky cape. Over a three-year period, the dream archangel of milliners portrayed by Agneswiseheart presented three very specific "hat" dreams for fittings. I surmised they designed more than clothes at TerreHaute. Peggymoonbeam most likely assisted Agneswiseheart with millinery.

In the first dream, *I'm hugging a French woman and there is another woman in a big floppy red hat and white skin.*[371] I was reminded of the French translation from red hat to Chapeau Rouge. The only French woman on our pilgrimage was none other than my honored guide, Marie Curie.

The second hat dream was pregnant with elements, giving birth to *a hat with a pink rose about to bloom and an image of a crystal with a piece of fibre in it. The words "electromagnetic radiation" repeat through the night. At dream's end, I'm carrying a wooden slab and a stick. Toward morning, I see the image of the floating metal wrench that* must have floated down from Steno. His earlier description of wrench faults jogged my memory.[372]

I finally arrived at the conclusion that the wooden slab depicted an ancient slab of rock, turned petrified wood. Thus, the ever-present slab was enshrined as fountainhead of Mission Lavender. As for the stick, I wasn't sure. Maybe it was a walking stick. I'd sure need one to climb over all these rocks. Was a certain mineral deposit at Cape Chapeau Rouge aligning to the Earth's magnetic field? Or was the string of clues meant to be a succession of metaphors? Or both?

---

371 6/22/96.
372 10/12/98.

Footnotes contain dream dates and references to prior pages where the dream appeared.
Endnotes contain bibliographical references, are marked with "Ɛ" in the text, and appear at the end of the book.

A crystal with a piece of fibre in it: Quartz was a natural fit for the *crystal*. But what about the *piece of fibre?* Was it simulating molten glass? Were we revisiting lava as andesite? Was a large pizza pie peppered with a piezoelectric charge being served at Cape Chapeau Rouge?

Had we reached a new plateau in the unfolding mystery? And what about electromagnetic radiation? That was fuzzy.

Just then, the learned spirit of Steno filtered in through a shower of, sparkling silver particles. It was that science dust again and there was a whole lot of it.

"My dear floundering pupil. I sense your puzzlement and am here to explain the meaning of electromagnetic radiation. When you listen to the radio, watch television, use a microwave oven or take an X-ray, you are using devices that make use of electromagnetic waves that differ from each other in wavelength."

"But, why Dr. Steno, does my dream say *electromagnetic 'radiation'* and what do lava and quartz have to do with all of this?"

"It has to do with the waves that radiate from electrically charged particles, like those in quartz, which travel through empty space as well as through air and other substances like lava. We apologize profusely for the tangled web we've ensnarled you in but the only way for you to learn is to untangle the threads. May I remind you that Pierre and Jacques Curie discovered the piezoelectric phenomenon in quartz and my specialty was quartz crystals, so we teamed together."

"Wow! Electric charges traveling through lava! That's what gets lava into this act! That explains the fuss over Cousin Andi's "pizza"– the symbol you use for Piezoelectricity."

"Bravo, Penelope! We were trying to convey the concept of Lava and Piezoelectricity. The electric and magnetic fields where quartz produces an electrical charge as a result of rock strain are most common near geological faults. The *floating metal wrench* in your dream is indeed a wrench fault.

"When lava comes to the surface it is red-hot, reaching extremely high temperatures and emitting a glow. Since light is described as electromagnetic waves, it follows that the combination of quartz, which generates an electrical charge, and lava, which emits light, would relate to electromagnetic radiation."

"Much of the celestial information received on Earth comes as such radiation in the form of light. Astronomers have devised many techniques to magnify and decode the messages in extremely faint waves of both light and the wavelengths we don't naturally see. A great deal of the information in light is uncovered by spreading the light into its different colors or wavelengths and analyzing the spectrum. Respectively, we have transmitted information to you in much the same way – through light waves."

"That is fantastic, Dr. Steno! Who ever discovered this?"

"Actually, many scientists have contributed to the concept of electromagnetic radiation, but it was James Clerk Maxwell, a British physicist, who discovered that light consists of electromagnetic waves.

"Hmm… maybe all of my dreams about light and vision connect to this in some way."

"I would say your dreams connect with light in very important ways," replied Steno. Some dreams apply to the behavior of light in an optical sense, others in a neurological sense, some address the role of light in the solar system while many of your dreams approach light as a spiritual experience. To understand the nature of light and how it is normally created, it's necessary to study matter at its atomic level. Atoms are the building blocks of matter, and the motion of one of their constituents, the electron, leads to the emission of light in most sources."

"Atomic level? That is a gargantuan leap for me, Doc. I think we're veering off course here. I know you have all this stuff stored in your immortal memory bank, but it's way over my head."

"Excuse me, Penny. I was getting ahead of myself. Must be the speed of light.

"In any event, Tu-whit has a few more words of wisdom – this time, on the subject of light. He is extremely well-versed in this area, for his special owl vision allows in greater amounts of light than any of us could imagine, and in the darkest of conditions."

ŎŎ "'Human beings from earliest times, without ever having heard of electromagnetism have regarded light they see as a sign of the underlying unseen vibrance they sense. …Light considered as a visible symbol for an invisible spiritual presence has been universally used by cultures worldwide since ancient times.'"[E47]

"Doc. That's my experience exactly! In my dreams I see many kinds of light – candlelight, twinkly lights in the distance, shining headlights, a grid of lights. Sometimes I even see the sun – when no physical light is present and that's the most profound experience of all because it flows very deep into my soul. Those vibrations I sometimes feel in my sleep must be the electromagnetic transmission of messages. It must also account for the electronic coding on my computer. This is truly mystical!"

"Yes, it is both spiritual and scientific, Penelope. The electromagnetic force is carried by photons – basic quantized particles of light. In a sense, all of electromagnetism can be considered varieties of light."

I did not want to venture any further into the quagmire of photons and all that stuff – not yet. It was so far beyond my comprehension, it was like being in a vacuum.

Steno laughed aloud. "I suppose you're keeping company with light. It's not as far beyond your limits as you think."

"Keeping company with light, Doc?"

"Yes, Penelope. Light travels in roughly 186,000 miles per second."

Hmm. Was the Quartz-Lava combination, dream code for another type of electro-magnetism – an electromagnetic field through which I was receiving these messages? Did this mean that some piezoelectric-type signal from space generates an electrical signal that would reach a human being? If we're under stress like a crystal, we'd be more open to receiving phenomena like anomalous computer implants.

Momentous miracles!

Piezoelectricity may be a way to explain the conversion of electric voltages from nonlocal space to those of us on Earth receptive to them. Those *couture radio* dreams[373] link to quartz crystals! Crystal radio! Were we being contacted through a nonlocal system similar to piezoelectric crystal?

"Well, well, Miss Penny, you are gaining on it. Piezoelectricity depends on the absence of a certain kind of symmetry called inversion symmetry. The inverse of a figure is something like its mirror image turned upside-down."

"Upside-down pyramids – pyrimidine bases – genetic code.[374] I must be catching your starlight. You mentors are our mirror image!"

Steno radiated pure joy. With the fragrance of roses swirling around his aura, he queried, "How would you like to cultivate the variety of roses you've been receiving by venturing a circle, Clueso?"

"Well, I'll try, Doc, but it seems a bit early." I sensed it would become part of another circle with all that light and electromagnetic radiation in the air.

The rose was certainly a different type of marker. The assorted roses were curious: *a colorless rose, a white rose, red roses* and, now *a pink rose*, each color emitting a different scent but belonging to the same family. I'd try my hand at a circle.

Colorless Rose – rose quartz – in the earth … *White Rose* – hydrocarbon field – in the earth … *Red Roses* – sub rosa – *Bethany* – Lazarus Tomb – in the earth … *Pink Rose* – pink granite veins … in the earth and circling back to quartz, part of the granite family. Whew!

"Amazing! Everything is deep within the earth, underneath and out of sight."

"Good work, Clueso.

"Now, let's go on to your third red hat dream."

"It was about five months after the *'electromagnetic radiation'* dream when another red hat floated in. *A big red hat sliding on black marabou feathers* is the centerfold. There are *vast expanses of land divided in sections with different textures. It's all very green. I give someone a gift*

373 See Ch. 60 – St. Brides Designer Couture, p. 274
374 9/19/97. See Ch. 10 – The Stuff of Life, p. 54

of yellow and brown plaid trousers that turn into knit leggings. A tiny baby appears in the form of a diamond or perhaps a moonstone."[375]

Steno, intent on weaving the dream, elucidated. *"The yellow and brown plaid trousers that transform to knit leggings* characterize andesite, which occurs as brown. Your yellow clue hints at sulfur. That implies a mix of lava and sulfur. The transformation from trousers to leggings implies that pants or trousers would knit – would mesh – with legs as in tracts of land."

Feeling more confident, I uttered, "That makes perfect sense, Dr. Steno."

The terrain connected to an earlier dream in which *water and land are characterized* and images of *legs* are described as *old and veiny. I think I'm in Tanzania. Open fields with beautifully tended grass, like a patchwork quilt, dominate the foreground.*[376]

"You know, Penelope," offered Steno, "the grasslands in Tanzania have short and tall grasses and concentrations of vegetation that mesh with your descriptions of the *patchwork quilt* and *land divided into sections.* There is also Tanzania's Serengeti National Park – from 'siringet' meaning wide open space or endless plain. That gels with the *vast expanses of land* and *open fields and your feeling of being in Tanzania."*

I later discovered that some of the italicized words above turned to Greek. My magic quilt sparkled with promise. The diamond again cast its light on Tanzania, where diamonds are a natural resource. But why the *red hat sliding on the black marabou feathers?* I somehow knew the big red hat was Chapeau Rouge, Newfoundland. Suddenly the image of the marabou feathers chimed with the *tiny diamond-shaped baby.* And the *diamond-studded tip*[377] dream – the diamond pipe volcano in Tanzania.

"I get it. I get it!" I squealed with delight. The marabou is a large African stork and while the heavenly bringer of babies did not land in the dream, the baby did.

The marabou and the diamond pipe volcano, representing Africa, inexplicably linked to Chapeau Rouge. Lost in the exquisite harmony of the spheres, I questioned aloud, "What on Earth could Newfoundland and Africa have in common? I wondered if they had the same rocks."

Jubilant over this connection, the usually sedate Steno sprang into a double back flip. "You're miraculously close to a vintage connection, Penelope. For one thing, the Appalachian Mountains rose in response to forces caused by repeated collisions between the North American plate and the African and European plates. Now mind you, this is where the Iapetus Ocean, sometimes called the Proto-Atlantic Ocean, was located half a billion years ago."

---

375 3/12/99.
376 8/17/98.
377 9/30/99. See Ch. 49 – Wrapped Up Like A Mummy, p. 213

Tu-whit piped in.

ÕÕ "'At that time, Newfoundland's eastern region was still attached to the African continent and the present Atlantic Ocean was still more than 150 million years from birth. But as the new ocean floor opened up and widened to the east, the North American continent was subducted under the floor of the shrinking Proto-Atlantic.'"[E48]

"Tu-whit! That is riveting!"

This sent shivers up my spine! So Africa and Newfoundland do have a lot in common! How is it that I was experiencing millions of years of colliding continents and forming oceans in a dream?

"Dr. Steno, what if diamonds are buried at Chapeau Rouge and no one knows about it?"

"Well, my child. If that's the case, it will help communicate our message. But let us not forget that the tiny diamond-shaped baby was born *as a moonstone.*"[378]

"Oops, Doc. I did forget. So the diamond could be a metaphor for a valuable stone that had fallen from the moon. Hmm. Could a moonstone be something like a meteorite?"

"Astronauts have found rocks on the lunar surface. Some say lunar meteorites found on Earth were ejected from the Moon by the impact of an asteroidal meteorite, but we're getting ahead of ourselves."

"I know. I know. It's probably the speed of light, but Wow! More stuff is fitting together."

"Clueso, coming back down to Earth, another clue is that moonstone is a type of feldspar with a pearly luster. The feldspars form a part of nearly all eruptive rocks and are found in practically all volcanic igneous rocks throughout the United States and Canada – right where we're working. Sometimes they're found in craters."

"Moonstone and feldspar. How'd you ever arrange that twosome in one dream?"

"We at Terracrust thought it a natural lead. We trusted that with your Timelessness Glasses you'd connect it to your friend *Pauline Maher who scraped the side of her face because you backed her into a wall* and then metamorphosed to your friend, Pearly."[379]

"Great connections! Pearl – Pearly – the personification of feldspar! And it's found in craters! I think we're on to something, Doc!"

Steno modestly replied, "Glad to be of help. "Maars are usually formed from explosions caused by the heating and boiling of groundwater invaded by rising magma. Because

---

378 3/12/99.
379 7/29/95. See Ch. 64 – Logs and Bricks, p. 302

the magma is so hot it causes almost immediate evaporation to steam resulting in what is known as a phreatic eruption of steam and rock fragments.

Phreatic explosions can be accompanied by carbon dioxide emissions, which can cause asphyxiation, or hydrogen sulfide gas emissions, which can cause poisoning. The 1883 cataclysmic eruption of Krakatoa that blew that Indonesian volcanic island apart was believed to be a phreatic event. It created the loudest sound in recorded human history exploding with a force of 200 megatons of TNT. Mind you, the Hiroshima bomb was miniscule by comparison – only about 13-16 kilotons. Krakatoa has erupted over and over, massively and with devastating consequences throughout recorded history."

"Oh no, Dr. Steno. Krakatoa! I had a dream about a *cracked toenail. A doctor puts a covering or shell on my next to last toe. It's a delicate operation. After I leave, it comes off and the toenail is cracked. The covering is hard like a mold. A French woman there provides a service.*[380]

"This really concerns me, because now I know this *cracked toenail* dream was pointing to Krakatoa. To me, a mold is something that is shaped or cast as a prototype, and it can also be a fungus, which can cause cracked and ugly toenails. It can spread from one toe to another and sometimes a person can even lose a nail."

Hmm. The idea of a prototype makes me wonder. Does this mean that Newfoundland could be obliterated like Krakatoa because of some fungus? Some imbalance in the immune system of the earth? It would be devastating for Newfoundland but what if it spread even further? Is there some disease in the earth that is spreading from one toe – from one continent – to another? I couldn't bear the prospect. I turned my thoughts back to the maar.

"So, Doc. What does a maar look like? Would someone be able to see it?"

"It looks like a ring that lies below the surrounding ground surface in the center of a crater. Maar volcanoes often fill with water and form lakes, but to answer your question, Clueso, you cannot always see a maar if it's a deep-origin volcano. Krakatoa, for example, was in the water. Your toenail fungus is an apt analogy for it's hard to detect at first and is often picked up in damp areas like shower stalls and swimming pools. One risk factor is an abnormal pH level of the skin. To expand your connection, Penelope, there is such a thing as soil pH, which measures alkalinity and acidity. So you see, both your cracked toenail and the earth are susceptible to infection. Now in the case of Krakatoa, hot ash plummeting to the surface of the water created a bed of steam that propelled the mixture along the ground once it hit land. It was reported that the hot ash was literally rising through the floorboards of houses, burning the people in them."

"Good God, Dr. Steno. This is a nightmare!"

---

380 2/11/99.

"Yes. Krakatoa was the most savage volcano in recorded history. The violent impact of Krakatoa reached around the world in sound waves, tsunami waves and ashes carried by the wind."

I thought back to the active Colima volcano in Mexico known for its large landslides. The mentors are pointing to places all over the map. It's hard to know if they want us to look at past or future, but some things in the present are certain: pipeline activity is occurring and my dreams are besieged with gas. My stomach is so jittery, it feels like I've swallowed a bunch of Mexican jumping beans.

Doc vanished but someone must have sensed my worries, for breezing through the multi-versed galaxies, the sacred mantra chanted its time-honored maxim: *"Be patient. You will learn everything you need to know."*

I had learned a lot but certainly not everything. Lord Galen taught me worlds of knowledge about vision. I remember well his words about observation being implicit in memory, how convergent vision merges the invisible with the visible and the past with the future, how psyche and matter are part of the same thing and how they influence each other. His work on the optic nerve and my circular key ring inspired me to start making circles to try to understand what was happening in my dreams and outside of them, but I am still confounded as to why this journey is so circular and so confusing. I've wondered if I'd ever fulfill the Mission.

CHAPTER EIGHTY-SIX

LOOKING THROUGH THE KALEIDOSCOPE

If your plan is for 1 year, plant rice;
If your plan is for 10 years, plant trees;
If your plan is for 100 years, educate children.
Confucius

"What is it, Penny? It's Lord Galen here, and I hear the familiar sound of gulping, a sure sign that something's a bit off. I thought we were making great strides. Your last circle of rose symbols deep within the earth, though not yet complete, is insightful all right, but I sense this immersion course has been taxing your energy. Perhaps we need a small breather."

(Gulp.) Gosh. Why am I having such a problem getting the words out? "No, nothing's wrong. Really. I guess my gulping is like a nervous tic."

"Oh my! Surely, there is nothing to be nervous about. I know this has been a hard path for you, constantly ascending and descending, and spinning around in circles. Tell me, what is it that's troubling you? You know my interest in your welfare is unconditional."

"Lord Galen, you are my vision mentor and my inspiration but I am seeking an answer to what looks to me like a monumental problem.

(Gulp.)

"I find myself at a crossroads for my friends who are following me and watching me explore are getting pretty frustrated with this circular experience. Some of them have asked where this is leading and what they're supposed to be learning. They say they're getting lost in this maze; that it's hard to follow. And I know they're right because that's exactly what's happening to me."

"Now, now, Penelope. Please don't despair. I realize that piecing together such a mosaic can be exasperating but what you are wrestling with is the Process. You must tell your friends that the pathway of life's experience is not a straight line. It's not a freeway where you just drive from here to there. If you were to do that, you would be ignoring all the signposts along the way and that is the key to understanding both the Process and the

---

Footnotes contain dream dates and references to prior pages where the dream appeared.

Endnotes contain bibliographical references, are marked with "ε" in the text, and appear at the end of the book.

Dream. One isolated detail in a dream – one symbol, one clue – may contain a thread so subtle, yet one that may connect to an absolute Truth. You must never underestimate the connective power in the detail for it can unlock a discovery so compelling that to miss it would miss the answers we are seeking.

"The connections you're making as you journey forward are based on your life experience. You are learning to crack your own code. Your friends – your fellow explorers have their individual quests and their specially coded blueprints. As they join in your adventure, Penelope, they'll learn that they, too, can listen to their dreams and crack their codes by using our Process, our method of discovery. No two people on the face of the Earth will have an identical experience, but we are showing them, through your story, how to be their own detectives.

"Most of your friends won't go to the lengths that you have, to chase after so vast a flock of dreams, but they will learn that to understand their Dream, they have to decipher what it's telling them.

"On your journey, we're now exploring geology, but Mission Lavender is not limited. The progression of layering is an integral part of the Process. New discoveries are continually illuminating old ones. You began your voyage with a dream about optics, a dream that so mystified you, you were driven to explore it further. Optics guided you to geology which directed you to chemistry and that, in turn, will transport you to lands unexplored. Though it may appear disordered, it is actually a succession."

"But, Lord Galen. They want to know what the Mission's about, and it feels like it's about everything under the sun."

"Fair enough, Penelope. In a sense it is. But why don't we try to clear the haze from this 'everything under the sun' feeling and focus our thoughts on the centerpiece. Can you tell me what you think that centerpiece is?"

"Gee, Lord Galen. I guess the centerpiece is the Dream that acts like a messenger. The messenger has an awful lot to say because the weaving together of this tapestry comes from a variety of sources including my friends and family, and my marriages and jobs, and different time frames, and science, and ancient people, and concerns about the world today and knowledge that comes to me from afar. It's like being in a laboratory where we just keep mixing and blending."

"Yes, Penelope. A laboratory is a wonderful analogy in that dreams are a testing ground, offering opportunities to observe, to practice and to experiment. Your particular dream series is a laboratory for studying the effects the world has on the collective unconscious. Just as in an experiment, the Dream puts things into play with each other and lets them interact and then it calls upon you, the dreamer, to further research and develop the Process."

"But, but … what about the Process, Lord Galen? What exactly is it?"

"The reality my dear, is that in dreaming we live in four dimensions. We live in a biological dimension where dreams remind us of bodily needs. We live in a psychological dimension where we explore our inner nature. We live in a social dimension where society's influence reflects in our dreams. And we live in a dimension that addresses our relationship to the universe, to the source of creation which we all are a part of, regardless of which plane we are on. You can call the last the spiritual, the cosmic, the transpersonal or the religious dimension. They are all correct. Your journey has taken you to that mysterious fourth dimension which is still mystifying to Earth scholars and scientists alike.

"Now, let's begin with the ideas of Dreaming and Discovery.

The process in this Dream omnibus is discovering its codes. Just think of the dream as a detective story which conceals a mystery. Within each dream and within the collective Dream are mountains of symbols which need to be decoded. When all of the symbols are deciphered, you will have cracked the case. If someone is working on a personal case – let's say, struggling with a relationship or a work issue or a health issue – only a few dreams may be involved and the person can solve the case in a relatively short time. If, however, someone has been assigned a cosmic case, as you have, my intrepid Penelope, the number of codes increases exponentially and it can take many years before your mystery reveals itself.

"So, Penelope, you are the detective. That is why Steno often refers to you as Clueso.

"Start with your premise that the Dream is the messenger. When the message is delivered to you, it arrives in the form of a kaleidoscope with moving pieces and mirrored reflections which we see through a circular lens. Let's think of it as a kaleidoscopic dream movie containing a series of frames that are generally scrambled and need to be unscrambled. If you rotate the kaleidoscope one way, you'll see one picture; rotate it again and a new picture will emerge. The Dream is ever changing, just as is the scenery you take in every day: your visual sensors record the fragments that make up the scenes you experience during waking and go to work to produce a new dream movie for you every night. These movable fragments provide symbols and clues that will be meaningful to you, based on your particular life's experience.

"As you metaphorically turn the ring on the kaleidoscope, you find that each turn spells out the same theme while appearing as an indivisible but changing entity. Every scene, sequence and passage in this dream movie advances its meaning.

"Like a kaleidoscope, the new dream images are in fact the same fragments you have already seen, but in a different order and in a different light, and circular as the cycles of life. Each new mosaic reflects changes in your life's pattern as played out in your Dream. Your visual associative memory, which Ptolemy has touched on,[381] is a tremendous aid, for over time you associate each fragment, picture or thought with others. If you are to be

---

381 See Ch. 40 – Starsight and Terracrust, p. 179

a top notch dream detective, it becomes your job to create some order from the disorder. This is where the Process begins.

"There are five major steps involved.

"The first step is detecting a Breakthrough Dream.

"In your case, Penelope, your port of embarkation in the cosmic realm was the 'optic nerve' dream, which was accompanied by a succession of dreams about light and vision and not being able to see. You asked what it was you weren't seeing. Your early dreams shone the light on your family matrix and helped you 'see' the trouble spots in your life. Many of your challenges grew around your mother who, in your quest for understanding, became the symbol for Mother Earth. Your personal dreams are emotional and bring great insights into your private life and relationships. After healing the relationship with your own mother, you listened to the message that transcended your personal situation and turned your attention to Mother Earth. This was the beginning of a series of more cosmic dreams where concern for self was replaced with a deeply held desire for the acquisition of knowledge and concern for the earth, which is exactly why you signed on to Mission Lavender. In cosmic dreaming you experience those oceanic feelings of oneness with all that is, connecting you very intimately with humankind and the planet. Usually this kind of dream is powered by a tremendous spiritually infused emotional force, particularly when you discover scientific information you hadn't known about.

"The second step is identifying Repetition.

"Repetition is necessary for dream patterning. Even though images and descriptions appear to be slightly different, a good detective deduces that somewhat dissimilar codes belong in the same family, just as do similarities in the variable fragments that appear with every turn of the kaleidoscope. An example is the plate images you dreamt. They were diverse: a variety of what appeared to be disconnected images: breastplates, a buried plate, grapefruit on plates, a valuable plate, a plate by the rectum, plates on the ground, long roots on a plate, metal plates, X-ray plates, your old plate. Yet, all were plates. That was the repeating image.

"The third step is Clustering and Connecting.

"In clustering or grouping the codes from your dreams – the pictorial symbols, verbal expressions and emotional content – you begin the process of connection. For example, by clustering all the plate symbols together and connecting them to other geological metaphors, you discovered that your Dream message contained tectonic plates, an outgrowth of continental drift. You then connected continental drift to various continents in your dreams and they connected back to geologic plates. That defined one cluster: Tectonic Plates. Then a new cluster emerged linking various lavender images (lava) which is still transporting you toward volcanic hotspots (burning images) that exist below certain plates. Hence, the birth of a second cluster: Lavender – Lava Under.

"The fourth step is identifying the Central Theme.

"Your clustering of themes into Plate Tectonics and Lava Under connected to produce the central theme of Mother Earth.

"Occasionally, one specific link has such striking features that its purpose is to connect to the many coded fragments within the central theme. Such a link appears in a dream one time and one time only. An example is the *Morse code (MOMOM) – Upanishad* dream which supports the Mother Earth theme. Nestled within a series of earth-related dreams, this mystifying dream message introduced a new and all-encompassing theme of the universal soul, illustrating – at every turn of the kaleidoscope – how every being and all matter is united with the cosmos. So, Penelope, it is about everything under the sun. The '*Upanishads dream*' is pointing you to a still larger theme: that of the World Soul.

"The last step is Materialization.

"This requires that you be constantly vigilant; alert and aware of all the signs around you. You have only to reflect on your many revelations in Newfoundland so far to know that your dream symbols manifested in a physical reality. Rest assured, there are more in store. You might even ask yourself if your dreaming consciousness is influencing these material properties. If you think it might be, therein lies a circular answer in that dreaming influences waking, and waking influences dreaming.

"All of these steps ultimately form a theme so well integrated that no starting point is perceptible. The many circles in your discovery process are the evidence of this, Penelope.

."Are you with me so far?"

"I think so. We're saying that the Dream is a vehicle for Discovery. I guess what we wind up with is a methodology that encompasses the nature of repetition and connection. So discovery can be a personal epiphany that can lead to a larger discovery, but either way the method of tracking is the same?"

"That's right, Penelope. A methodology contains a sense of process and mechanism, a sense of why and how the variables are related the way they are. What we are doing is developing a symbol system for the language of dreams. Remember – you wanted to call it Oneiromantics made up of the oneiroglyphics of dreams.

"Heavens, Lord Galen. My head is spinning! There's so much more to this than meets the eye, but then again, it actually seems simple if you just follow the Process. I think I can tell my friends what the Process is about but they still want to know where it's leading."

"I realize that this is an alien principle to many people, but to say where it's leading at this point, Penelope, would be to disturb the Process of Discovery. Many more surprises lay in wait, but as with any mystery, we must discover all the parts before we reveal the whole.

"The enduring mystery of dreaming has never been solved nor was it studied on a cosmic level until recently. We know dreaming is the road to self-identity, to healing that self, to integrating our dreaming self with our physical reality and ultimately with the collective mind. This is where we transcend the survival of self to survival of the species. The hierarchy overseeing Terracrust and Starsight wholeheartedly wishes to pursue this effort.

"You on Earth are experiencing a period of vast planetary change. The old patterns of dealing with the world are no longer working. If these changes are reflected in your dreams, Penelope, they are also playing across the unconscious screens of dreamers the world over. Because the dream is incorruptible, we believe the Cosmic Dream is working out the flaws in a disconnected and fragmented society and serves as an untapped resource for global healing.

"Sensitivity to your stress with your birth mother, a simile for Mother Earth, was translated in your dreams to an increase in stress within the tectonic plates and to the massive changes that are and will be occurring in and on the Earth. That is how unified every being is with the planet. The whole cannot heal without the part and every being is a part.

"You have seen in a flash of light the nature of your own consciousness and an even deeper perception of the nature of collective consciousness. The art of the dream symbol has unified the vision of self with the vision of the world. Your dreams are transporting you from the innermost depths of the soul to the outermost reaches of space."

"So, Lord Galen, the higher part of our unconscious is like a sacred vault that holds our experiences as a species. Wow! That's like having cosmic memory! And I bet it's activated in the visual cortex just like it said in my automatic writing about how enteric memory vanishes when we decease and returns when our souls are again physicalized. I think I've become part of Jung's collective unconscious."

"Penelope. You've always been part of it, but it takes time to rewind the kaleidoscopic pictures of your life back to the beginning. When you've perceived the multifaceted patterns and examined their prisms, you are ready to open to the knowledge you were born with. Your friends ask, 'Where is it leading?' Remember your mantra, Penny, and pass it on. Ask that they 'Be Patient.' Tell them 'They will learn everything they need to know.'

"Following the circularity of the Dream leads to vital truths that can be discovered only through the circular, multilayered journey on which you have so energetically embarked. Whatever the theme, this Process takes us on a lifetime voyage, uncovering unimaginable insights and wondrous happenings. If your friends are on the path to self-discovery, they will follow."

"Thank you, Lord Galen. Your explanation was truly clarifying. I just hope I can remember it all. You'd told me there was a Process at play and now I understand it much better. I know I have to have faith that my friends will apply it.'

"Now, my diligent apprentice, are you ready to continue on to Swift Current?

I'm ready, Lord Galen, and I'm hungry as a bear.

CHAPTER EIGHTY-SEVEN

SWIFT CURRENT

Swift Current, in the Bears Folly Mountains, is known for its fishing and rock climbing – and yes, for its bears. With one foot in the heavens and the other on Earth, our earthbound psyches did not block our visions of fabled bears waiting to huff and puff and blow our house down. Karensurefoot and I would spend one quick night there in a log chalet.

My memory skipped back to *the three big panda bears I saw in the window of a stateroom.*[382]

As we drove to Swift Current, we could only talk about food. We were so ravenously hungry we could actually taste a savory homemade dinner replete with hot buttery biscuits and a great bottle of wine in what we envisioned as a charming country inn. Not quite. Inside the barren chalet, the only sign of dinner was a collage of food groupings plastered on the wall.

Exhausted, starving and spiritually spent, we found our way to the general store and loaded up on canned soup, cheese and crackers and a rock-hard frozen hamburger likely dated early Cenozoic.

That night in my sleep, I experienced an astonishing new sensation. I felt something gently shaking me as though someone was trying to awaken me. Then there was a vibration around my side. *I see Placentia. There is a map and on the edge are three small areas right next to each other. Next, I'm in Customs and they're asking me if I'm bringing in any plants, minerals or animals.*[383]

As I was rubbing the sleep from my eyes the next morning, Karensurefoot appeared at the foot of my bed. "Karen, were you shaking me in my sleep last night?"

I thought she might have been trying to rouse me from the dream. "No" replied Karen, quizzically. "I slept like a log."

"Well, you won't believe this. I was dreaming about the stuff we left on the beach at Placentia and I felt someone shaking me in my sleep. Then I felt a vibration on my side. It was so strange. I knew we should have taken those artifacts even though they looked

---

382 8/12/93. See Ch. 23 – Tragedy, pp. 99–100
383 9/6/99.

Footnotes contain dream dates and references to prior pages where the dream appeared.
Endnotes contain bibliographical references, are marked with "Ɛ" in the text, and appear at the end of the book.

like junk and were probably impregnated with salt after bobbing around for years in the sea. I think the dream is telling us to go back to the Northeast Arm Motel in Placentia where we saw the map with Big Judy Cove, Little Judy Cove and Snacks Cove.[384] But I don't think there's enough time to go back and still catch our flight from St. John's. We'd probably have to extend the trip by an extra day. I don't know what to do. What do you think? We'd get back to New York a day later."

My unflappable travel companion did not falter, did not bat an eyelash and did not think this was crazy. She simply said, "Let's call the airlines and see if we can change our flights." The airlines complied. They even allowed us to change without a penalty.

The three small areas, recalled on the dream map registered as those three coves, but they did not appear on any recent map. They were only designated on the antiquated map Karensurefoot had spotted in the motel several days earlier.

Poring over our highway map and struggling to locate the blessed coves, we found ourselves at an impasse. Were these inconspicuous coves on the Northeast Arm or the Southeast Arm? I thought about the *birthday dream and how the arm was in front of me.*

It had been only three days since our pipeline revelation had burst open in the motel's lobby. We shuddered to think that our hysterical outburst might be remembered by the mild-mannered staff. Anonymity in this little corner of the world for a pair of celestial wanderers was not an option.

Karensurefoot, cheerfully led by the unknown, followed the sun and took her morning constitutional before we set out on our return jaunt to Placentia. When she came back, I sensed by that all-knowing smile that something was up.

"What's cookin'?" I asked.

In her softest, most ethereal voice, she murmured, "Penelope, I saw a rock in the woods that had a curly cue in a circle on it, like the doodle you drew for me from your Clock-A-Doodle-Do dream. Because the curly cue on the rock was almost the same, I took a picture."

Unwittingly and intuitively, she had stumbled on – and most importantly, recognized – another treasure. I was astounded when I saw the photograph. It was impossible to imagine that a likeness of this dream symbol had appeared on a rock in Swift Current, Newfoundland. I would carefully examine the original drawing when I returned to New York.

It took a moment to merge Swift Current with the watery currents of the unconscious. I returned to a raft of dreams of strong tides and currents carrying me over rapids, waterfalls, water-covered paths traveling in enough water to thrust me in the direction of Titanic's mystery.[385]

---

384 See Ch. 64 – Logs and Bricks, p. 301
385 See Ch. 22 – Water, Water, Water and More Water, p. 97
        Water dreams: 1994–1998

Each of these dreams conveyed a powerfully breathless sensation of being carried along at an enormous speed. The dream of *walking through rushes with a ravine below* puzzled me until I found that the origin of the word ravine is French, meaning "violent rush (of water)." Hence, Swift Current.

The notion of fast-moving, turbulent water became a resounding theme that if linked to Titanic might explain the dispersion of bodies over so wide an area. The strong tides and coastal currents of the Atlantic could have carried Titanic's human residue to the numerous little coves, arms and harbors that dotted the coastlines of the Avalon and Burin peninsulas.

Then again, the emotional component of rushing water was germane to my own life. While struggling against the unpredictable currents of personal destiny, unbeknownst to me, the double helix of Man and Earth had washed ashore.

Might the watery implications signify worlds other than Titanic? Of course, but the tangled filaments of cosmic interconnection had led me to this tapestry that had been woven through the cords of time. It seemed that no matter how the dots were connected, we would ultimately wind up in the same place. If this were so, the design was sheer perfection.

Obeying the subtle nudge in the dream to fetch the salt impregnated remnants we left behind and to find the three coves, we turned around and headed back toward Placentia, nearly a day's drive. We had no choice but to return to the nondescript motel so we could create a reasonable facsimile from the outdated map.

CHAPTER EIGHTY-EIGHT

EEK! A BLUE GLOVE!

Day Eight: Back to Placentia, Judy Coves, Snack Cove

While traveling along dusty gravel roads on our return pilgrimage, Karen and I formulated a plan. First, we'd revisit the Northeast Arm Motel in Dunville where we would sketch the obsolete map – the only one we knew of showing the three coves. This strange colorless motel had become a sort of truck stop for us.

Then, we'd pay homage to Jerseyside beach, where we would revisit the picket fence, the polestar of *all mankind working together as a community.*

Finally, we would visit the coves.

We were eager to see if the branch still commanded its mast-like position rising from the water in Placentia Bay, unaffected by the changing tides. We would obey the *"customs"* directive in the dream and scour the beach to find the articles that had washed ashore. Resisting absolute enslavement to the exalted realms of never-ever land, neither of us openly admitted our vulnerability to the powerfully magnetic pull of the mystical.

Arriving at the Northeast Arm Motel, we raced to the wall that displayed our coveted map. As though planning some sort of undercover heist, we tried to draw a reasonable facsimile and soon realized that what at first glance appeared to be an innocuous map in an out of the way place was fast becoming a treasured relic. Karensurefoot's extraordinary gleams zoomed in on the three coves. Even as we were engaged in our undercover drawing, it was still not clear which Arm the coves belonged to.

We quickly sketched the three coves – Big Judy, Little Judy, and Snack – and hot-footed our way out, racing with binoculars to the Jerseyside beach like a couple of spirit-driven sleuthhounds disguised as ordinary tourists. We were out to inspect the "branch," examine its nature, locate the suspects, and eventually solve the mystery.

Something, indeed, was protruding from the water, but no longer did it resemble a branch from a tree; it seemed more like a boat's hull. On closer inspection, it looked like it had been overturned by the tide, so the appearance of the branch had taken on a

---

Footnotes contain dream dates and references to prior pages where the dream appeared.
Endnotes contain bibliographical references, are marked with "Ɛ" in the text, and appear at the end of the book.

smoother finish, resembling the underside of a boat. Be it a branch or a boat, its orientation had changed, but curiously, its placement had not. Oblivious to the incoming and outgoing tide, and even with the passage of four days, the object stood motionless and determined.

Astonishing. Even the physical clues were transforming.

We climbed over rocks and meandered amid the flotsam and jetsam that had drifted ashore. We collected bits of rubber, scraps of fabric, odd shoes corroded by salt and aged by exposure to the elements, laughing all the way about the dream that took us there, in which *Customs was questioning what we were importing*. Though many a beachcomber would classify it as junk, we thought we had struck gold. We stumbled on some large rusted metal dome-shaped objects. Karensurefoot thought they could be tire casings. They were beveled on the sides and rounded at the bottom. I wondered if they might have been parts from a ship.

Clutching this bag of litter as though it were the crown jewels, we went back to see Rita, the innkeeper of Rosedale Manor. Her exuberant welcome made it a real homecoming. She was, in the true sense, a most unforgettable character with her tough-as-turtle shell and soft-as-mush inside.

We dined again at Belle's Restaurant, where they rolled out the red carpet making us feel like visiting dignitaries. We wolfed down a stick-to-your-ribs Newfoundland dinner and spent another starlit night embraced in the tranquility of Placentia. Before we said good night, Rita gave me an unfinished poem written about the Titanic by a seafaring relative.

It went like this:
"'Twas on an April morning
Thousands thronged the White Star pier
For to see the proud Titanic
Leave old England's shores so fair.
Cheers were given as she parted
And each heart was filled with glee ...
- -
That she would rest beneath the sea."

My last thought as I drifted off to sleep was how spiritually endowed the people were in this small patch of economically depressed land. They had cornered a commodity that has all but disappeared from our sphere of consciousness. If I could define it, I would call it Grace. The people of Newfoundland possessed an innate knowledge of humanity's purpose here on Earth and lived in celebration of it.

The following day, Karen and I went in search of the Judy Coves and Snack Cove, dutifully following the dream that *shook me awake and revealed three places next to each other on the map.* The coves were hard to get to. We still weren't sure which Arm they were on – the Northeast or the Southeast – so we parked the car and began walking. We climbed a small embankment to a bridge and took a path down to the beach which we hoped would offer a clearer view of the terrain with its inlets, bold cliffs and hills in the distance. We soon realized that trying to scope this out from a stretch of beach was futile. We would have to go by boat to spot the coves we were searching for. Frustrated by our inability to scale the next rung, we knew the coves would have to wait for another trip to Newfoundland, and so we made our way back to the car.

Dejected by our failed plan, we moseyed on. Suddenly, I tripped on something. I looked down at the ground. There was a blue glove under my foot. I started screeching "Eeeek! The blue glove!!" This sighting sparked a leap of consciousness impossible to describe.

"Karen! Karen! This was in a dream I had six years ago! It was about *a blue glove under someone's foot. I'm in the water, my shoes are off and I feel something icky under my right foot. When I get to shore, I'm telling people about this thing under my foot. One of them said, 'Don't talk about it. It makes me nauseous.'"*[386]

"Wait. Penelope! I just remembered the Sub-Rosa circle and how that putrid smell made me nauseous! Remember. Marie Curie told us sulfur doesn't have an odor until it reacts! I must have been smelling sulfur – sulfur dioxide, the gas from a volcanic eruption!"

"You're right, Karen. *Icky* was one of the words I used to describe lava and I used it again for fluorine, a toxic gas, and that led me to sulfurous gases emitted by volcanoes.[387] These may seem silly but they're significant clues leading us back to sulfur and gas and lava – all the worrisome elements surrounding the pipeline!"

This *blue glove* dream, in its roundabout way, told me something was under foot!

Dream threads knit faster than a spider could spin, uncovering and validating once innocuous strands that would weave together this story. Continuing the dream: following the scenario of *a blue glove under someone's foot …I'm on a path or island that has narrowed. Water is coming up toward the front – I have to start swimming. The water is cold.* In the dream, I initially described the *blue glove as knit;* then I erased the word "knit." The glove I actually stepped on was blue knit – testimony to our first instinct being right and illustrating the "knitting together" of our adventure. Were the Titanic and the pipeline interweaving? The *icky thing underfoot* appeared to be some evidence of lava. Of course, scientists

---

386 9/27/93.
387 See Ch. 77 – Sulfur And Radon – Chlorine And Fluorine – Oh My!, pp. 369–370

would laugh at this, but it was that new paradigm we were told about early on that was demonstrating the language of the Dream.[388]

Back in 1662, a Frenchman visiting the area described Placentia: "And see, lying athwart the Southeast Arm, closing it almost completely, and leaving only a narrow, though navigable gut to the northeast, the great beach or 'graves' superbly suited to the drying of fish on the seaward side and for the creation of a town to the landward"[49]

I found the description of the great beach or "graves" bizarre considering our preoccupation with the remains of Titanic's victims.

The description of the narrow gut that protects the entrance to the Placentia harbour, emphasizing its narrow boundaries where only one ship can pass at a time, magically locked into the dreamscape of a *path or island that has narrowed.*

But how could we identify the location of the *blue glove*? We really didn't know where we were. We stopped a local fisherman and explained we were out-of-towners and were a little lost. Could he tell us what area we were in. "Oh, sure," he answered readily. "You are at the end of the Southeast Arm."

And so the Southeast Arm it was — where the waters flow into Placentia Bay, then into the Atlantic — where Titanic met her end. The Arm in the *birthday dream*[389] had materialized once more.

Was the *blue glove* meant to mark one of many spots in the area where human residue may have washed ashore? Where dormant volcanoes with their *icky* lava lay in wait? Next to the glove was a piece of hide like an animal skin, but it was difficult to tell what animal — possibly a sheep. Was it coincidental that the Titanic's Cargo Manifest had listings of bales of skins, including "three bales sheep skins"? Skins! I flashed back to the dream about *Customs asking me if I'm bringing in any plants, minerals, or animals.*

Maybe I was supposed to take this animal skin. Decisions. Decisions. We took the glove but fear of importing disease stopped us from handling the hide.

The answers were underfoot.

Pursuing our search of the geology of Newfoundland, we stopped at the Placentia Library. The first publication I came across was Offshore Oil Development and the Law; it highlighted Waste Disposal and Iceberg Detection. Could this have pointed to Titanic — or was it another reminder of the pipeline? Of the White Rose oilfield? The clues popped up in waking as vividly as they did in dreaming.

I also searched for information about little Kitty, entombed in Placentia. The good natured librarian, so eager to please us, energetically pulled a whole array of files from the

---

388 4/13/94. See Ch. 15 – A Wonderland of Minerals, p. 72
389 10/30/98. See Ch. 53 – Getting An Arm Around Newfoundland, pp. 243–44

archives. We knew Kitty's mother's and father's names and the date of her death, but not the date of her birth; one of a jillion loose pieces in this colossal jigsaw puzzle.

Little Kitty would later call again in a completely different form.

It grew more evident with every passing day and every new revelation that there were no gratuitous stops – no time out for casual shopping or sightseeing. Everything was clearly intentioned, finely tuned and, despite its circumlocution, perfectly orchestrated. There may have been some speculation but, in the end, there was no error.

CHAPTER EIGHTY-NINE

A JERSEYSIDE TEESER

Day Nine: Jerseyside and return to St. John's

Springing from the upper reaches, in burst Nicolaus Steno, placing his spyglass over a big dream about a former associate of mine named Jeanne Tee. Her family name registered Jerseyside, as the launch pad that would orbit us around and under the geological wonders of the earth.

The dream introduces *Jeanne Tee who is wearing a shirtwaist dress with a pattern of very thin stripes. Wedding decorations from Copenhagen are sitting in a corner. I have a plastic sheet on my head as I'm pulling off perforated saris from a roll. Illustrated around the saris are four belts. I say I will get 3 Ts.*[390]

Why all the to-do about my former colleague, Jeanne Tee, whom I hadn't seen for nearly twenty years, and why the meticulous attention to every detail of her clothing? Was geo-couture at work again?

Jeanne Tee ... shirtwaist ... Tee shirt ... Jerseyside.

The Terracrust team had designedly detained us in that part of Placentia known as Jerseyside, that mere dot on the map that had already become one of our prized bellwethers. The sleepy little community was handpicked – a dream come true.

Steno pinged in, "Penelope, I notice that this Jeanne Tee dream ventures outside the realm of Newfoundland and I thought you should know about certain mountain ranges in other parts of the world. The Himalayan ranges, for example, can be grouped into four parallel belts of varying width."

"Dr. Steno! Did you say four belts!" I exclaimed.

"I looked it up and – guess what? Indian women wear the *sari* and the dream had *four belts* around it. It must be referring to those four belts in the Himalayan mountain chain!"

"Good job, Clueso. The Terracrust dialect suits you."

---

390 4/6/99.

Footnotes contain dream dates and references to prior pages where the dream appeared.
Endnotes contain bibliographical references, are marked with "Ɛ" in the text, and appear at the end of the book.

"Thank you, Dr. Steno. The woman in the *turban* in the Lewin's Cove dream[391] depicts Indian headgear, which also connects to the Himalaya. But what about *Jeanne Tee's shirt-waist* with the *thin stripes*? Why all the fuss over her stripes?"

"Penelope, the stripes edge into the area of magnetic reversal which we touched on briefly in your lesson on seafloor spreading.'[392] The earth's crust has a magnetic record of the polarity of the earth's field at the time it was formed. So the width of magnetic stripes in rocks on the sea floor is related to time. Wide stripes represent a long time; narrow stripes a short time.

You may recall the dream where your *mother is yelling and screaming and has a brown scruffy wig on backward. You have to pay 34 cents. You are looking for change and come up with the right change,*[393] *which you find in the dark.* You equated this to polar reversal, a change in the polarity of the Earth's magnetic field."

That crazy dream about *a crime and the different colored strips, the shelf, the dishes and the bowl*[394] led me to think that stripes and strips were the same and had to do with magnetic reversal. The shelf was the continental shelf, dishes were tectonic plates and the bowl was a volcanic crater. But a crime?

I still couldn't believe I signed up for this cram course in geology. Rock crystal candy was much more my speed. This was getting to be so technical. Did I really need to know all this? And at that, my honorable mentor pulled a celestial disappearing act. Through a swirling cloud of stardust, I detected an astral pout, unusual for the great Steno. He made it clear that dismissing the prerequisites was not very politic. At this juncture, I was oblivious to the lavish treasures that lay in store.

"In Store!" Those familiar buzzwords pulled out countless dreams about my shopping expeditions in stores. I thought it strange that in waking life I rarely go into a store other than for groceries. My dreams were telling me that something was "in store." Some days I felt dense as fog. Why did it take so long to pick up on something so simple?

"Now, now, Penelope," beamed in Dr. Steno. "Don't be so hard on yourself. You're learning a new language. You are examining the anatomy of the unconscious, the very instrument that has shaped this language of dreams. The formation of your dream concepts precedes natural language, as we know it. It is through our instinctive dream language that higher levels of awareness may be attained."

Mental snapshots of the Bethany Church in St. Lawrence, the picturesque fishing communities of Lawn, Spanish Room, Lewin's Cove, Cape Chapeau Rouge, Swift Current, all on the Burin Peninsula in Newfoundland, flickered in my psyche. And along the Avalon Peninsula, the ancient town of Placentia, little Jerseyside, Argentia, Branch

---

391 3/3/99. See Ch. 84 – American Currency a la Origami, pp. 399–402
392 See Ch. 42 – Geology: The Second Branch, p. 192
393 2/10/95. See Ch. 32 – Mother's Apprentices, p. 141
394 8/21/93: See Ch. 27 – Witness, p. 125

and the village of St. Brides retold their stories. Bouncing off my dreams and reflecting in my mind's eye, prisms of light, like multifaceted clues were identifying each community.

Jerseyside was demonstrably a beacon, one that radiated light far beyond the little town of Placentia. There were many other communities, each one with its own thumbprint. Was the light so brilliant, so intense, that it illuminated an area as immense as the Mid-Atlantic Ridge on the ocean floor?

"You know what, Karen? We have pinpointed so many places in the Jerseyside, Placentia vicinity, they seem worthy of a circle."

"Good idea. I'd never have imagined a journey that encircled the worlds of dreaming and waking equally, just as though they were parallel. Go for it, Penny!"

So with a little encouragement from my very wise friend, I began with The Rosedale Manor which led us to waking discoveries that matched fragments of dreams. "The Rosedale Manor – Church of the Sacred Heart – Argentia – Southeast Arm – Castle Hill – Ambrose Shea Bridge – Maher's Polypipe ... Hmm ... I'm not sure how to finish the circle, Karen. Maher's Polypipe doesn't seem to connect to the Rosedale Manor."

"Let it go, Penelope. I'm sure it will develop in time."

I reluctantly took her advice, though it was hard to leave this unfinished circle dangling in mid-air. Perhaps by the time we got to St. John's we'd be able to finish.

CHAPTER NINETY

TWO LEGS … SPREAD EAGLE

"Penelope, the mentions of legs and leggings in your dreams is not coincidental," injected Steno. He was into legs. He liked breasts, too, judging from some of the images he sent. Had he been of earthly gender, I'd be a little embarrassed, but he was all geology all the time.

"These legs have led the way to this particular tract of land: the faulted zone unveiling the path that branches into the two peninsulas that define Placentia Bay."

Those were the Burin and Avalon Peninsulas – long-legged tips from my great towering mentor.

Some of Steno's clues were in plain view. I collected the more obvious ones and went mining for leg dreams. One jumped out at me; it focused on the words "*spread-eagle*," an expression normally meaning an outstretching or spreading out of the legs.

It was a preposterous situation about *mother in a mobile bed. She goes faster and faster, and suddenly, the bed gets away from her and crashes. She comes bolting out of nowhere. The words "spread-eagle" appear. There is a tiny frog that turns into a tadpole. It comes apart in two pieces.*[395]

In some strange way, this connected to another dream *about a fancy cruise ship with a reclining chair* and, again, *two legs that are elevated in a spread eagle position. I can't align them with the supports, which have belts like bands to keep the legs in place.*[396]

Ironically, a third dream alludes to *the Bermuda triangle, and again illustrates legs spread eagle,* this time, *with the calves turned in.*[397]

"What fascinates me most, Dr. Steno, is the tadpole, for in the dream, it starts as a frog, which lives on land and transforms to a tadpole, which lives in the water. This looks like a reverse metamorphosis. Normally the metamorphosis is from tadpole to frog. Does this mean seafloor spreading is occurring in the two peninsulas? Is the land sinking into the water? Are the *calves* guiding me toward the calving off of the Titanic iceberg? And the *Bermuda triangle*! Things just mysteriously disappear there!"

---

395 4/26/00.
396 2/4/00.
397 12/13/00.

Footnotes contain dream dates and references to prior pages where the dream appeared.
Endnotes contain bibliographical references, are marked with "Ɛ" in the text, and appear at the end of the book.

"Penelope, put your Timelessness Glasses on and look at your Newfoundland map. You'll see Spread Eagle on Trinity Bay right above the Avalon Peninsula."

"But ... But, Dr. Steno, doesn't the spread eagle position mean that the legs are spreading apart?"

"That too, my dove. That too.

"Your geology professor's explanation of plastic deformation; how rocks can bend without fracturing, applies here. There's something called a fault drag, which is the bend of a marker across a fault. Geologically, a marker is a stratum – like a layer of rock. As you're discovering different types of markers, it's up to you to determine where they fit. You've undoubtedly noticed that similar things have different meanings. That is the iteration of nature, be it in a dream or waking reality."

"Gosh, Doc, is it possible there's a bend in the land – like fault drag – that stretches from Africa to Newfoundland? Had a new mountain belt formed because of all of this spreading?

He suppressed a scholarly smile and vanished.

CHAPTER NINETY-ONE

FOLLOWING THE INVISIBLE

One sees clearly only with the heart.
Anything essential is invisible to the eyes.
Antoine de Sainte-Exupéry

Bushels of dream fragments spilled over. Bits and scraps, splinters and slivers imbedded in my psyche were propelling me toward an outcome of volcanic origin, its scope unthinkable. The hellishly burning message loomed more critical as calendar pages folded time into a sea of oblivion. It was insidious in its pursuit. You couldn't see it, but it was there. Could I finish the book in time? The years were melting into each other, even as the facts that so upset me when I first discovered them were being overtaken by events. Surely, those specific dates and times had meaning but, perhaps, like so much else I was learning, they were symbolic as well as concrete. Besides, who would listen to me knowing the source material was coming through the Dream?

Could the dire warning be pointing to fatalities that would strike the communities on the Avalon and Burin Peninsulas, not to mention places we hadn't been? Or were they metaphors for what could happen anywhere on Earth?

I reflected on the enlightenment that radiates from a purely soulful relationship with the invisible, the inaudible voice that had imbued us with a passionate unswerving dedication to the awakening of man where hope for the distorted value of industry and profit would yield to good works. The magnificent heights of discovery had been planted deep in my dreams and had taken root all along the way: on the roadside, high on a hill, standing in the ocean and nestled in places we'd have never visited had we not been led. Still, balance was essential. I'd have to empty myself of earthly ego and strife to walk the path hand in hand with the worst of horrors.

The message was ominous but I deeply trusted the sharp-sightedness of my tutors. I felt a faint tingling around me, almost like an electric charge.

"Oh. Good morning, Dr. Steno. There's a kind of a buzz around me."

Footnotes contain dream dates and references to prior pages where the dream appeared.
Endnotes contain bibliographical references, are marked with "Ɛ" in the text, and appear at the end of the book.

Steno roared with mischievous laughter. "I'll let you in on a little secret, Clueso. You're in a magnetic field near some subsurface quartz. Impressive sensibilities for a young earthling with so much on her plate. Tectonic plate, that is.

"Now, let's focus on the Avalon Zone, given your concerns about what is occurring beneath the Avalon Peninsula or what you fear may be any peninsula."

"Excuse me, Dr. Steno. Is there a difference between the Avalon Zone and the Avalon Peninsula?

"My apologies, Clueso. Here I am expecting you to run before you can walk. I sometimes forget you're still a novice, struggling not only with a new language but trying to navigate new terrain. I'll try to be brief, for I've noticed that history lessons tend to induce in you a profound yawning effect.

"The Avalon Peninsula, as you know, is a large peninsula that makes up the southeast portion of the island of Newfoundland. The Avalon Zone or Terrane, on the other hand, was once a microcontinent that included parts of Europe and Africa. A terrane in geology is a fragment of the earth's crust that was formed on, or broken off from, one tectonic plate and attached to the crust on another plate. That microcontinent was called Avalonia after which the Avalon Peninsula was named.

The Avalon Terrane underlies Newfoundland and parts of the Burin Peninsula. It is known as an exotic terrane because the rocks were attached onto Newfoundland only about 410 million years ago."

"Only? That makes me feel like I'm here for less than one breath."

"Penelope, time on Earth could be thought of that way but you actually take about 600 million breaths during your lifetime.[E50] In paleoseconds, however, it is a relatively short time considering that basement rocks in other zones were formed 900 million to 1200 million years ago. The Avalon Zone has an evolutionary history that predates, and is separate from, the opening and closing of the Iapetus Ocean, that extremely ancient ocean that existed between Scotland and North America and Scandinavia before the formation of Pangaea."

"Pangee-a?"

"Oh no. There I go again making assumptions. Pangaea was the last supercontinent on Earth. It was a large landmass made up of all the present Earth continents, which broke up and drifted apart. The Avalon Zone appears to be a terrane that collided with the rest of the Appalachians around 400 million years ago, during the Acadian Orogeny."

Collided! Were we due for another collision? The warning was escalating. The consequences were colossal. I kept flashing back to the haunting message, *the masses would be exterminated.*

Was this message suggesting that the St. Lawrence fluorite deposit in the **Avalon Tectonic Zone in eastern Newfoundland would be where disaster would**

originate? The Lower St. Lawrence Seismic Zone registered a 5.1 earthquake March 16, 1999.

It didn't seem like a very intense earthquake. Maybe it's pointing more to the seismic zone. (I wrote the above sentences – now bolded – in normal type face.[398] When I noticed they had self-bolded, I scrolled to another page in the document. When I returned, the part now bolded, was replaced with four lines of Greek that flashed on the screen, then, disappeared. Again, I thought, "who will believe me?" The next day I found on my floppy disk three lines of Greek in the same place they had appeared the previous day.

(Two sets of the same pair of Greek characters[E51] matched those I had received in my Agneswiseheart text again, the phrase, "of Theos" followed by the Greek uppercase omega.)

$$\vartheta\Omega \qquad \vartheta\Omega$$

Tu-whit swept in with a few particulars on the omega symbol.

ÕÕ "Omega, the last letter of the Greek alphabet, is often used to denote the end or the ultimate limit of a <u>set</u>. In mathematics, sets represent collections of <u>abstract objects</u>. An object is abstract if and only if it lacks a location in space."

I must be an orbiting opsimath! What could be more abstract than dream images? Might this series of dreams be considered a set?

A month later[399] I had found another code implanted in copy pertinent to St. Lawrence. This code had numbers and was written in English. Double commas appeared in significant locations in much of my writing and seemed to guide me to areas too murky for me to comprehend. Here is an excerpt:

"It was beginning to crystallize. The extermination of the masses in the Bethany Church dream back at St. Lawrence, **280,,** the collision dream, the dream where the car slips on plates, goes off the edge and lands underwater."

Steno commented. "The 1999 earthquake in the Lower St. Lawrence Seismic Zone, though not that strong, was the largest event humankind ever recorded in that zone and generated a renewed interest in the region's tectonic features. Most earthquakes in this region occur under the St. Lawrence River. Earth scientists are comparing the Precambrian basement with mapped faults and their possible correlation with local earthquakes – something your dream catcher has frequently captured.

"And, Clueso, in some regions earthquakes result from the change in rocks due to the unsteady moving around of magma leading to volcanic eruptions."

---

398 7/25/00.
399 8/14/00.

Egad! Earthquakes can be triggered by moving magma!

"Doc. I even brought some Precambrian rocks home from Cape Race. It's funny, though, because the dream that sent me to Cape Race was not about the rocks, but the lighthouse."

"That dream had multiple meanings, Penelope. The Titanic led you to the lighthouse, symbolically, your inner spiritual light, which led you to vision, which led you to the rocks."

"Oh! And then we found those lavender-painted rocks in Branch! My dreams of branches and lavender have been developing just as though they're in a photo lab."

"You see how it all interconnects. Also, Penelope, we mustn't forget about the hydrocarbon gases found in rocks in the Canadian Shield, which, incidentally, are Precambrian rocks."

Is that what all those gas dreams are about and the shield dreams too? This Mission is truly about "trusting your instincts. My first inkling that this rush of symbols was about the earth was when I discovered such things as shield volcanoes. I then learned that other types of shields were deeply eroded roots of ancient mountain belts, such as the Canadian Shield.

Well, if nothing else, Precambrian was a rock-solid clue that fit somewhere.

Peering through his jumbo spyglass at the geological map, Steno pointed to the St. Lawrence side of the Burin Peninsula. "This is the Lower St. Lawrence Seismic Zone. Do you see that this zone is marked by pillow basalt that has erupted from undersea volcanoes?"

Waking weirdness! St. Lawrence is where I saw a coded message with double commas!

"You know, Dr. Steno, the map shows that the town of St. Lawrence on the Burin Peninsula is surrounded by the Atlantic Ocean. The Gulf of St. Lawrence seems a good distance away, but I guess distance doesn't matter so much."

"Yes, the Gulf of St. Lawrence is a large arm of the Atlantic Ocean which receives the St. Lawrence River and is connected with the Atlantic by the Strait of Belle Isle. As you've seen from the considerable traveling we've done in mind and in body, regardless of the distances, the underpinning of Mission Lavender is that you experience an interdimensional reality. You're observing insights of David Bohm and our other scientists that everything connects. This, in principle, means any individual element could reveal "detailed information about every other element in the universe"[E52] including all its fields and particles. By connecting the many threads of your dreams, the work of nature will creep into your tapestry piece by piece. Think back to the Gestalt concept of a unified whole.[400]

---

400 See Ch. 81 – Gestalt and The Chair, pp. 391–92

As I pondered this timeless interconnectedness, the map elements Steno had commented on jumped to the fore. "Good Grief! The Strait of Belle Isle! That's near where the Titanic collided with the iceberg."

An expanding ticker tape of connections, stimulated by years of wonder, research and dream clues still unsolved, provided no clear-cut answers. An occasional spark of light would tell me I was only a fingertip away from the conclusion, yet I felt galaxies apart from it. How could it be so near and yet so far? Particulars might change but everything pointed to the same basic message. Trust. Kaleidoscopic vision would show me the big picture.

My concerns about emissions from both potentially dormant volcanoes where pipeline might be run, and from drilling for fluorspar, the highly reactive mineral, had been mitigated when Tu-whit advised that fluorspar operations closed down in 1978.

With fluorspar no longer in the picture, I wondered if it was symbolic of another reactive mineral. The spirit team habitually used symbols to make their point. It was an intrinsic part of their secret language.

I remembered that fluorine, a corrosive gas, was present in the fluorspar vein and combined with radon, the combination had been lethal.

On the word "lethal," the piercing glint from the orbs of Tu-whit came beaming through like radar.

ÕÕ "'November 10, 2009
Canada Fluorspar Inc. is proceeding to reactivate the fluorspar mines located at
St. Lawrence on the Burin Peninsula.'"[53]

Unfortunately, in the months that followed, and even to this day, my relief has alternated with renewed frustration as the developers and the province have announced drilling for oil and plans for the pipeline stopping and starting again and again.

St. Lawrence was directly on top of a fault.

DAS SHOOT! DAS BOOT! Was a deadly combination of gases hidden in the boot of the Burin Peninsula – or in another coastal area?

Peggymoonbeam sailed in with a short film clip, movies being one of her earthly pleasures.

"Penny, I know you haven't had much time for recreation, so you probably missed seeing 'Das Boot,' a suspense-filled war movie."

"'Das Boot' was a movie? How did a war film get into my dreams? I wouldn't have gone to see it anyhow, Peggymoonbeam. You know I'd do anything to avoid seeing the bloodshed and carnage of war."

"Yes, my little buddy, I do know that. 'Das Boot,' however, carries a special message for Mission Lavender. That's why it maneuvered its way into your dream with the stealth of a traitor slipping in under the cover of darkness. 'Das Boot' is about a German submarine crew during World War II; it takes place beneath the sea. An encounter with an enemy warship forces the crew to dive deeper than their submarine's specifications, where it slowly begins to buckle under the weight of the ocean. The story, Penelope, is a journey into madness; one that shows what war is all about and actually coincides with Mission Lavender's message of an invisible enemy beneath the sea."

Hmm. The Dream was taking me under again. First, I experienced the sinking of Titanic. Then the mysterious dream of the *shipping department and the "Whole Earth"* arrived. And now this piece of celluloid about *"Das Boot."* Somehow, the murky depths of the sea were habitually imprinted on the filmy stuff of my dreams. Was the enemy a gross combination of chemicals that would cause Mother Earth to retaliate savagely or was it a more visible enemy – an enemy masquerading as "Das Boot," a foe bred from hatred and violence and ego, a terrorism plan to annihilate us from the lowest depths of the sea? Or was it both?

The picture was beginning to develop in ways I did not want to see.

I hoped beyond hope that the almighty wand of Trust would wave away the mining venture permanently. But what then? Why the compulsion not only to travel the two peninsulas – the Avalon and the Burin – but to microscopically examine them.

Steno sensed my quandary. "Think back to your lesson on continental drift and how today's continents once formed a single landmass.[401] Wegener named that landmass, Pangaea from the Greek words pan, meaning all, and Gaea or Gaia, representing all the Earth. Pangaea broke into pieces due to the weaknesses in the earth's crust."

"Are all of those pieces still in the crust, Doc?"

"Well, the pieces drifted centimeter by centimeter over millions of years until they arrived at where they are now. The crust is beneath the oceans and continents and together with the upper part of the mantle it is divided into huge slabs called plates."

It was riveting! Might one of those pieces have been the yellow slab? Crikey! Cracking plates! That must be the *slab of rock that hit me on the head*![402] The yellow slab must be a tectonic plate. The North American plate?

Another blast of revelation! Wegener's Pangaea, which split into the continents we now know, was the "whole Earth." Was Pangaea the force driving the *Whole Earth* dream?[403] Or was the *Whole Earth* dream reverting to Pangaea?

---

401 See Ch. 42 – Geology: The Second Branch, pp. 192–93
402 9/6/01. See Ch 70 – The Anonymous Artist Paints A Hole, p. 330
403 11/9/96. See Ch 7 – Branching Out, p. 41

I flashed back to the Greek codes on the computer. Galen and Ptolemy, both Greek – Steno, the pious geologist – Curie, who coined the term "radioactivity." Dreams of plates without end – and Bethany and Resurrection.

The message smoldered in waking as in sleeping. If the ingredients are in the oven, we must not take a match to it.

I looked up. Dark, towering clouds began to form. In the distance, piercing streaks of hot white lightning shot through the heavens, the gigantic sparks nearly blinding me. The electric veins in the lightning streaks looked like the veins in the earth. Following were booming claps of thunder so deafening I had to cover my ears. As a little girl, I thought it was God moving furniture. Now I sensed He was moving something else: Maybe rocks. Maybe plates. Maybe gases. The air stirred rapidly. The edge of a monster thunderstorm was moving in. It was fast approaching and without warning. The atmospheric pressure dropped and the clouds grew even darker. The sky was nearly black. Another flash! I dared myself to look straight into the blinding zigzags of light. The sweet face of Marie Curie was illuminated like an enormous neon sign in one of those flashes I had always hidden from. She was enfolded in the danger signs of this intensely threatening storm. I knew that if she was coming through in this frenzied outburst, it was for a good reason. Steno took my hand. He knew I was scared to death.

"Penelope, it is Marie. Please dear, don't be frightened. We have come to protect you and your fellow earthlings. I wish to remind you of a dream you had some time back.

You were working with someone. You and this other person went outside and there was a big flood. The water was muddy and brackish and looked like it was diseased. You were wearing a pale golden silk pants suit and pale yellowish leather shoes. You started to roll up your pants so they wouldn't get in the water. Your shoes had already gotten wet. Someone was there whose technical advice was important to our operations on the other side."[404]

"Marie, I remember that dream clearly, but I wouldn't, for the life of me, have remembered what I was wearing. It sounds like a lovely outfit but too bad about my shoes."

"Yes, dear. You were just beginning to get your feet wet in understanding the rudiments of chemistry. We've mentioned this earlier, but as a reminder, pale yellow applies to two different chemicals. Sulfur: a pale-yellow, nonmetallic element and fluorine, a pale yellow gas. We've introduced these elements to you at appropriate times, as each plays a part in Mission Lavender. As for your pale yellow shoes, we'll soon be wading through some rather murky waters.

---

404 12/1/94. See Ch. 75 – Butterflies, Sulfur & a Sailing Ship, p. 353

"Now, if you recall, Penelope, when we first met, we advised you that you were our agent in the Avalon Zone. At that time, we told you *operations on the other side* were our operations at Terracrust and Starsight. We were arranging for you to receive Peggymoonbeam's *picket fence* dream and her vision of *all mankind working together* as a community."[405]

"So, (gulp) – so, Marie? Who was the person I was working with?"

She answered demurely, "That person was me."

Speaking matter-of-factly, she continued. "Steno and I are here to provide you with moral and technical support. We will guide you through these muddy waters, but we are depending on you to make the connections. Your Psymometer will certainly come in handy here, and don't forget to don your Timelessness Glasses, as you will be looking at the future with an eye toward the past.

"Tu-whit is keenly aware of your concern in this zone, particularly in Placentia where you spent considerable time and energy. He is wise to your efforts over the years to unscramble our codes by translating Dream into English and English into Science. He's been reconnoitering the area and has some news about the introduction of liquid natural gas to the North American marketplace.

ÕÕ "In November 2006, an energy services company in a joint venture with a pipeline company launched plans to build North America's first liquefied natural gas (LNG) storage and transshipment facility at Grassy Point on Placentia Bay in southeastern Newfoundland. The St. John's based company is expecting a burgeoning market for gas transshipment facilities for overseas imports entering the North American marketplace....

"'The government of Newfoundland and Labrador has stated its desire to establish the province as an 'energy warehouse.'"[Ɛ54]

"Oh no, Marie! What terrible news! I thought the pipeline project there was abandoned! PLACENTIA BAY! That's right here! Those pipeline partners will not stop! It's always about profit! What about the people? What about the land? Doc, you said if there was a leak in the pipeline and all the plates started to move that it could cause an unimaginable catastrophe because natural gas is so combustible. You taught me about the danger of natural gas around deep sea volcanoes. Yikes! Service would probably start in the next couple of years. Marie! That's a breath away! That's probably less than three seconds geologically. I suspect this connects to your message about 'extermination of the masses.'

"Aren't they even worried about the Earth? Surely they must have environmental guidelines to adhere to!" At which point Tu-whit turned up his beams:

---

405 8/27/99. See Ch. 63 – The Picket Fence, p. 291

ÕÕ "'At the same time, "the pipeline company quietly filed environmental documentation toward establishing a transshipment facility near Come by

Chance, a town on Placentia Bay, Newfoundland'"[55]

"Yeah! Right! If their plans were in the interest of the land and the people, they wouldn't have to file their documentation so 'quietly'!"

The dreaded dream seeped out of unconscious storage. *A hole in the refrigerator is in the wrong place. It is on the left side. This hole should never have been there to begin with and workmen had come to stop water pouring out of a pipe.*[406]

I wondered about the water. Water wouldn't hurt anything.

The *left side* meant the past. Hmm. So it must be related to the past – maybe an ancient volcano or rocks that were billions of years old. As with the fluorspar announcements we'd been reading, we could expect more news stories that would bounce my hopes and fears around as plans were delayed or restarted. I took a deep breath.

Tu-whit circled back with still more information:

ÕÕ "'LNG … is colorless, odorless, non-corrosive and nontoxic. Natural gas is a clean and safe energy that is far less dangerous and volatile than gasoline, propane or butane, all of which are commonly used as fuels.

"'An open container of LNG at room temperature would look and behave much like a container of boiling water.'"[56]

"Hmm. So maybe the *water pouring out of a pipe* is a symbol for LNG. If it's nontoxic, I guess that would be OK. Even though you both warned of its danger, Doc, it sounds pretty safe."

Despite the reassurances, still I obsessed about the flammability of gas with all that magma underneath and its mixture of liquid rock, crystals and dissolved gases.

But Tu-whit wasn't finished, nor was he in very good spirits. His ear tufts raised and his feathers drawn in were sure signs that my wise little owl was sensing danger. Then a furious flapping of wings at a tremendously high frequency and a wild frantic calling burst forth:

"Tu-whit Tu-whoo – Tu-whit Tu-whoo – Tu-whit Tu-whoo."

The flailing sounds of nature's warnings surrounded me, the wind growing stronger by the moment, its force nearly knocking me over. Our heavenly owl had summonsed his sentinel and elaborated.

---

406 9/28/93. See Ch. 67– Refrigeration, p. 315

ÕÕ "'Natural gas in its liquid form cannot ignite. Unlike products that are considered flammable liquids, LNG must first be vapourized, mixed with air and then exposed to an ignition source. For ignition to occur when LNG vapour contacts a hot surface, the temperature of that surface must exceed 540° C.'"[57]

An ignition source! Blazing bonfires! The average temperature of basaltic magma is 1000° to 1200° C! Twice the temperature as that cited by the pipeline company!

But Tu-whit's source was the pipeline proposal which would downplay any danger. Natural gas is flammable, and even explosive, if ignited after being mixed with air or with some of the gases released by volcanoes, like fluorine and chlorine.

That answered it! – at least in part. I thought about how the temperature increases the deeper one goes into the earth and how the radioactive elements deep within the earth are slowly disintegrating and producing heat and how that heat flows outward. I thought of volcanoes and how they erupt when there's a sudden or continuing release of energy caused by magma movement and how that energy release can occur in gas-emission at the surface: release of heat, explosive release of gases and the discharge of magma.

Tu-whit still wasn't finished. He was now carrying news about the St. Lawrence River which tied to other messages: the mysterious Greek letters, the coded message with the double commas.

ÕÕ "'Another energy company partnering with a pipeline company is planning to construct a C\$1.3 billion LNG terminal at Gros Cacouna, Quebec, along the St. Lawrence River.'"[58]

Holy Hammerings! Dastardly Omens! A macabre dance of Skulls and Crossbones revisited the Bethany Church – Deaths of miners – St. Lawrence fluorspar deposit – Fluorspar supplies – Gas – Uranium hexafluoride – U235 – the atomic bomb – Avalon Zone – Lower St. Lawrence Seismic Zone – Under the St. Lawrence River. Now they're adding more gas!

I reflected on hotspot volcanoes that have constant zones of magma within the earth, in some places beneath the plates, and how the magma pierces right through the plate. Steno said some earthquakes are directly associated with volcanic activity.

I still didn't know how natural gas vapors, perhaps released from a pipeline and forming a gas bubble that could eventually mix with the air would figure in. Such a vapor release could even be trapped in a magma chamber or by some geological formation where it could increase in size. If it became big enough, it might form a gas flow upward through the water and be the source of a flare.

Activity in some areas has been suspended, but still there is the question of whether a pipeline is built or not. And whether the pipeline was in Newfoundland, Quebec, Alaska or other areas with similar geology. In the final analysis, after all, my lessons are not confined to one place or time.

Canada has nine LNG regasification terminal projects that are either under construction or proposed, but the list of worldwide LNG facilities goes on without end; Africa, Asia Pacific (includes Japan, China, India, Malaysia, Philippines, South Korea) Caribbean, South and Central America, Mexico, Middle East, Northeastern Europe (includes Russia), Southwest Pacific Rim (includes Malaysia, Australia, Indonesia), United States, and Western Europe.[E59]

That's the whole earth!

Tu-whit doubled back at light speed, much faster and quieter than usual. I could feel the muffled sound of air rushing over his wings. Because he can see what is hidden and can hear what is not being said, he knew what was happening underground and above ground as well. He was privy to all the discussions between the proponents and opponents of LNG.

ÕÕ "'There is a concern that a vapor cloud that would result from an LNG spill could, if it encountered an ignition source as it rose in the atmosphere, burn back to the source of the spill and cause a serious fire.

"'In general, LNG will boil off much faster on water than on land because water provides a more significant thermal source for heat transfer. This is why an LNG vapor fire cannot be fought with water; the water would simply accelerate the liquid's vaporization and fuel the blaze. Also, an LNG spill on water is much more difficult to contain and spreads over a larger area than a spill on land. The evaporation disperses the gas at a faster rate because of the high heat transfer rate and the water does not cool significantly. For these reasons, it is generally considered that shipping, on-loading and off-loading of LNG present the greatest safety threats.'"[E60]

Statistics show that in 2008 the total length of pipeline in Canada was 98,544 km; in the United States, 793,285 km.[E61]

Holy Smoley! That's enough pipe to reach from the Earth to the Moon and halfway back. It's even worse than I thought!

Thinking about the ignition source, I imagined the depths of Dante's inferno. I envisioned that bubbling hot magma underwater invisible to the naked eye. I thought about the whole coastline along which these pipelines would be run and what Tu-whit had said about how fast the fire spreads, and how it can't even be fought with water – and that water would fuel the blaze. I was gasping for air!

In that frantic moment, I traveled back to one of my gas dreams. I had recounted the first half:

People are worried that someone evil like Hitler is taking over. I'm in a basement and a bad man is trapped inside a death box, which is concealed under a curtain. Now, for the second half: *A woman has concocted a chemical mix that will annihilate the man. She turns on the gas and soon the fumes become apparent. The man is extinguished. There's a lot of dark soot and dust around as the aftermath.* [407]

Steno's tutorials had helped me with this dream when I was just learning the language. *Hitler* represented the gases used in the death camps as well as the volcano, the *death box* was a magma chamber, the *curtain* was a curtain of gases and chemicals released from the volcano and lastly, the gas and fumes symbolized the dousing of the bad man. Did the bad man symbolize all the elements of the volcano: the magma chamber, the gases, the fumes and the chemicals? Was he the culprit that caused the volcano to erupt?

Concern was not related to pipelines alone but included a proposed oil refinery in upper Placentia Bay, where the primary products would be gasoline, kerosene/jet fuel and ultra-low sulfur diesel. And to top it off, there was another proposal on the table for a nickel-processing plant at Placentia Bay. Then there was the informing dream that said *CFC's in the rain are attracted to hydrocarbons – carboniferous rocks*[408] and that matched reports that hydrocarbon gases were found in deep rocks and groundwaters throughout the Canadian Shield.

At the mention of hydrocarbon gases, Tu-whit winged in with a reminder:

ÕÕ "'Scientists say gases are usually trapped in fracture systems in Precambrian rock and released when mine drilling penetrates their ancient layering.'"Ɛ62

No wonder I need the Timelessness Glasses: those rocks are billions of years old.

The bolding of the words: **Avalon Tectonic Zone in eastern Newfoundland would be where disaster would originate** was menacing because the geological map showed volcanic activity throughout Newfoundland and Labrador. The designation read "from mainly on-shore volcanoes," but still tugging at me was the prospect of those underwater volcanoes – the ones Tu-whit could see. To take it to another level, those bolded words had been replaced with that flash of Greek, a code that made my knees all rubbery because I sensed it was a sign of omniscience.

Steno had hinted at a magmatic disturbance, a transformation of unknown origin. There were so many chemicals in my dreams. Would a chemical transmutation result in a potentially explosive gas? Combine a gas leak from a pipeline with the scalding heat and gases produced by volcanic activity and it could be the executioner who carried out the *extermination of the masses.*

---

407 7/1/97. See Ch. 66 – White Rose, p. 312
408 9/21/99. See Ch. 66 –White Rose, p. 311

Marie and Steno pitched in as a duet. "Penelope, the long and short of it is this: A surplus of gases in the natural landscape and an abundance of earthquake and submarine volcanic warnings corresponding to gases in your dreams present foreboding concern. In just a few words, can you suggest one scenario based on this? Something you'd be prepared to step forward with and tell the outside world about?"

"My esteemed mentors … Forgive me, but I need a moment to collect my thoughts."

Recent dreams of impending harm were increasingly unsettling.

The Oneiroball hung over me like a death knell, dropping one missive after another.

One dream focuses on *yellowish powdery stuff and the smell of fumes from a gas leak permeating the air. I'm anxious to get out of there. A dermatologist shows up briefly. There is something about the skin.*[409]

Sulfur is a yellow mineral that comes in powder form. Sulfur dioxide is a volcanic gas. Sulfur hexafluoride is considered the most potent greenhouse gas. But in dermatology, sulfur is used in the treatment of skin diseases. The duality – the yin and the yang – disease and cure – the dark and light of our material existence.

Fragmented thoughts bombarded me. I had to answer the muses and I had to think fast.

Another urgent epistle from the Oneiroball: *A man is rushing me. He has a clock made of glass with a movable panel that slides up from it. On this panel is etched a whole list of words, the top one being* **TOXIN.** *The words are in black print and very, very hard to read. I think I see another word …* **DESTRUCTION** *and then many other words seem to designate places. I'm trying to understand if they have anything in common. Someone said it was a "failed plan."*[410]

Clock. I'm remembering the clock dream that carried the message *Yellow … he wants "yellow."*[411] That must be sulfur. A clock made of glass. Lava is molten glass. Marie said so. **Toxin.** My dreams were full of toxins. **Destruction.** My dreams were full of that, too. Of course, there's something in common, but I didn't have time to even think about it.

I heard Marie clear her throat. "Ahem. Penelope, are you still with us?"

"Yes, Marie. I'm trying to formulate my thoughts. This is so huge in scope, I want to be sure I have it right."

---

409 1/13/08.
410 2/2/08.
411 2/24/95. See Ch. 29 – Clock A Doodle Do, p. 131

"We understand dear, but please do not delay. We must be aware of your grasp of Mission Lavender for we have reached a critical turning point.

The secret little locker holding my emergency supply of mettle would have to be unlocked quickly. I knew I had the key but would I remember the combination? My emotions were turning loose on me. I began to shiver. I could not erase images of my sulfurous shoes wading in diseased water, the smell of gas fumes spreading in the air, the death box and so many other horrific portents. My struggle with shyness and my distaste for speaking out had outrun itself. I could hide no longer. Courage and tenacity would take the lead. I'd have to face the possible sneers and mockery of the skeptics. I looked skyward calling on every ounce of self I had to summon forth my little Scottie dog, my constant companion who never let me down. "Please, Bonnie. Can you hear me? I am so scared. I could make a huge mistake now, but I don't think so. I am terrified. There is so much at stake. People's lives and land could be devastated. The last dream designated many places – many locales. What if it goes far beyond Newfoundland? This is critical! How will I ever articulate it? I'm not a scientist. Please. Are you there? Bonnie. Bonnie. I am calling you."

The little yelping whimpers of my childhood pup, who embodied all the empathy and compassion of human consciousness even in afterlife, came spinning back like a tape on automatic rewind …

"arf arf – aarf arf arf – arf arf – arf arf arf" … and in that moment I knew beyond a doubt that dog spelled backward is God.

Echoing across my early days with Bonnie, when the wonder of life's rainbows sparkled brilliantly across lucid skies and the silver lining wasn't toxic, were the unforgettable words from the Girl Scout Promise: "On my honor, I will try to serve God and my country …"

I knew Bonnie heard me, and I could do it. The silver lining would reflect the divine hope inspired by my mentors. Even if I had to be the black cloud, my charge was to deliver the watermark of truth impressed upon me through their endless lessons. I knew that Steno and Curie were smiling their haloes off, for nothing got past them.

"Doc? Marie? Are you there? Can you hear me?"

"We're awaiting your answer, Penelope. As you wish …"

(Gulp.) I took a deep breath. "I thank you my honored guides for the confidence you've invested in me and I'm truly sorry for taking so long to respond. I've been wrestling with the volume of knowledge you've imparted to me over the years and how best to summarize it. In a few words, here's one scenario I can suggest."

On the threshold of delivering my premise, cascading waves of uncertainty engulfed me. What if the dots were misconnected? The spirit team wouldn't have gambled that way. There was too much at stake. Still I was only a novice. I had to stop deliberating. They were waiting for an answer. Finally, I worked up enough gumption, assuring myself that I got the dots right even if some had to be rearranged. I took a dolphin-sized breath, held it for a few moments, then, released it slowly through my pursed lips. I knew my brain would need a good supply of oxygen for this one.

OK, here goes. Listen with your heart, Penelope. It has seen things clearly.

"If a hole was drilled in the wrong place and a colorless, odorless gas like LNG was pouring out of a pipeline and gases were boiling out of the rocks, and magmatic heat was more than twice the temperature of ignition, and if a chemical transmutation was taking place, it could result in a fire that can't be fought with water and can't be contained. If an unmanageable blaze started to spread, it would jeopardize every living thing: innocent human beings, wildlife, and the land. This is an urgent call for Earth scientists to respond to a geological emergency."

This startling conclusion returned me to the dream where *I see a huge burst of flames, then high ocean waves. They are right next to each other. Then they become memorialized in the form of a gold statue.*[412] It was as though something cataclysmic had been commemorated. I imagined yellow-orange flames rising from the waters, my Girl Scout Promise indelibly etched in the blazing vapors. I smelled the noxious fumes from the gases spreading through the land, the innocent victims contaminated by radioactive poisoning.

"Marie. Doc. What are we to do?"

"Dear Penelope," comforted Steno, "we are learning. We are teaching. We are opening eyes to the messages of the Dream. In short, we are doing everything spiritually and cosmically possible to prevent a horrific catastrophe, but history has ultimately proven man to be the master of his own destiny. Humankind must learn the meaning of Empathy — the ability to "put oneself in another's shoes." Every expression has an energetic vibration or frequency. Words of hatred and intolerance have created a force field of fragmentation and destruction. It is only with empathy that humankind can create a platform for effective understanding toward healing. Earthlings must see with their hearts, not their egos and understand that they've contributed to the illness of your planet."

With the searchlight focused on Pangaea, it seemed time to construct another circle from the dreaming and waking knowledge we acquired during this phase. I would begin the linkage: Pangaea – Whole Earth – Extermination of the masses – Das Shoot! Das Boot! – Shipping – Sulfur – Poisonous Gases – Radioactivity – Pipelines – LNG – Tectonic plates – Avalon Zone – Precambrian volcanic rocks – Interconnecting veins – circling back to Pangaea.

Searching the sky for an answer, I thought if only I still had my Raggedy Ann. I'd hold her close to my heart while I pray for protection. The clouds begin to change shape. The sky is tinged lavender-gray. Surreal circles of smoke are closing in on me. The wind blows hard, skittering rocks across the land. Then all is still. The strange and sudden silence foretells impending disaster.

---

412 7/7/99. See Ch. 72 – A Snake on the Lawn, p. 336

But far away, where you can see through the sky, where the air is pure and the rain untainted, the Oneiroball floats high over the lonely center of the Earth. Agneswiseheart says it holds all of the pieces of my puzzle. That must mean it holds everything within this circle. She told me the balloon is filled with helium but maybe that symbolizes gases of all kinds. I thought back to the volcanic gases Steno taught me about and to Marie's challenging lessons on sulfur, radon, chlorine, and fluorine. The picture was grim and it was getting scarier by the moment.

"Penelope," spoke Marie Curie. "You remember the clock dream that carried the message: *Yellow ... he wants "yellow.*[413] You were right ... yellow is sulfur; the clock is a very generic symbol. Aside from the telling of time, one type of clock is a radioactive clock."

"A radioactive clock? I've never heard of that. You mean the clock itself is radioactive?"

"No, no," smiled Marie. "Uranium is a radioactive clock. Radioactive decay constitutes a "clock" capable of measuring absolute geologic time. We call this half-life which is the time taken for half of the atoms of a radioactive substance to decay or disintegrate, becoming other elements. Half-lives can range from less than a millionth of a second to millions of years. Remember Penelope, uranium's slow decay rate helps keep earth's interior hot, providing the energy for continental drift and events like volcanic eruptions.

Critical Connections!! The dream of the glass clock! *Clock* – Radioactive – *Glass* – Lava – *Toxin* – *Destruction* were written all over that dream. *The man was rushing me.*[414] (The font in this paragraph independently changed to green.)

Electrifying epiphanies!!

Thoughts of disintegration and *squeezing the pointer finger* in the *Das Shoot!* dream[415] connected the squeezing of piezoelectric crystal to the magnetic field where an element was giving off a gaseous substance (indirectly from uranium decay) and continuously disintegrating while a gaseous discharge was being produced! Piezoelectrically charged quartz traveling through magma connects to disintegration! That's what Madame Curie meant about the passage of electricity through gases![416] That's the alchemical transmutation! Maybe that's why the magma is moving around, making the rocks change, and causing so many earthquakes and volcanoes in the 21st century.

Egad! Three different gases! LNG – volcanic gas – an unidentified chemical gas!

I had to listen especially carefully when Marie gave me something new to think about or reminded me about something. After all, she was the first of the mentors to talk about

413 2/24/95. Ch. 29 – Clock A Doodle Do, p. 131
414 2/2/08.
415 7/30/98. See Ch. 74 – Das Shoot! Das Boot!, p. 346
416 See Ch. 78 – Disintegration, p. 374

sulfur as a butterfly with yellow wings. And my dream told me the butterfly turned into a poisonous bumblebee. Sulfur was certainly buzzing around, but what would that have to do with a radioactive clock?

The metamorphosis of the butterfly changing from caterpillar and preparing for flight returned to me to Bethany, the village where Lazarus was resurrected. Was Lazarus an icon for the resurrection of a disaster on a scale inconceivable to man? Or of rebirth and resurrection after such a disaster? Were we in the chrysalis stage – a time of change – where our colors of love and compassion are about to emerge? Were we humans preparing for a global spiritual metamorphosis?

I thought back to the wisdom of Pooh and his views on cause and effect.[417] He concluded that bees are the Efficient Cause of buzzing, because the buzzing is the effect of their action." ...

> "If' there's a buzzing-noise, somebody's making a buzzing-noise, and the only reason for making a buzzing-noise that I know of is because you're a bee."[E63]

---

417 See Ch. 20 – Agneswiseheart, p.

CHAPTER NINETY-TWO

ONE GREAT BIG CIRCLE

St. John's

Feeling that my destiny was bound to the destiny of the Earth and its inhabitants, and recognizing the fine line between learning to trust the universe or being crushed by it, I turned to Karensurefoot, "This sure turned out to be an unexpectedly sobering expedition." She patted me on the shoulder. "Remember the copper penny, Penny. In God We Trust."

Our final stop returned us to St. John's, where we made a beeline back to the Titanic Exhibit.

Several nights prior, I had a dream about a *black box, described as a videotape box. It appeared and reappeared through the night. It was wrapped with black tape that resembled electrical tape, as though it was a gift.*[418]

Passing through one of the rooms in the exhibit, I noticed a small black box on the wall. I stopped to inquire. The guide said that it's a Titanic trivia box in which the museum deposits a frequently asked question each day. She suggests I focus on something in relation to Titanic. Loraine Allison comes to mind; the child whose recurring appearance has haunted my dreams from the start. The guide then opened the black trivia box.

In it is one typewritten question: "What became of Loraine Allison?"

Here at the end of our Newfoundland adventure we were given the gift of interconnecting realities – Dreaming and Waking – a form of energy in the name of consciousness. What a magical note to depart on!

I secretly mused. Did *the electrical tape* in the dream signal an energy field; one that was part of the experience?

Could such an energy field have linked together these pieces of conscious and unconscious thought and my associations to them no matter the distance or passage of time in which the connections were made? Might this field have created a "surprise birthday party" that began on *February 18, 1999,* one that would be celebrated for years to come.

---

418 9/5/99.

Footnotes contain dream dates and references to prior pages where the dream appeared.
Endnotes contain bibliographical references, are marked with "Ɛ" in the text, and appear at the end of the book.

The invited guests at this *family get-together* include all members of the human family. The Placentia – placenta – birthday was conceived in a dream, nursed in research and actually born in Placentia where Castle Hill unearthed mountains of clues.

Gifts in the form of dream symbols arrived in abundance. One was a *frame* holding a striking picture of the Titanic and Lava – Lava Under. That *meshed* with the *arm* – the Southeast Arm, where waters run into Placentia Bay and then into the Atlantic where Titanic met her end. Soon another gift was wrapped around *lavender poles and hydrants* implying fire, and still another was a collection of yellow stones appearing on the road to Grand Bank, Titanic's resting place – spelling out Y– e – l – l – o – w – s – t – o – n – e and translating to the Yellowstone hotspot – a reminder that one of the largest "super volcanoes" in the world lies under Yellowstone Park. The next eruption could produce a catastrophic explosion that would have global consequences beyond human experience and impossible to fully anticipate.[E64] Yellowstone in dream language was a blessed symbol that would culminate in the most precious gift of all: a premonitory message for survival.

"Penelope," asked Karensurefoot, "I've been thinking about the picture of the pirate's hat propped up against the boat in Jerseyside and how it reappeared in Burin. It just occurred to me that in the Pirate's Hat dream, you were *invited by an oversized kitten to a get-together on Circle Pond Road.*[419]

"That dream has crossed my mind many times, Penny, because you're *looking down on waterfalls where you see actors dressed up in costumes, acting something out in the waterfalls. There is danger. The water is turbulent and jostling them around.* You thought it might be the dream avatars looking down upon the Titanic passengers. I was impressed because the scene reminded you of Shakespeare's words:

> 'All the world's a stage,
> And all the men and women merely players.
> They have their exits and their entrances,
> And one man in his time plays many parts,
> His acts being seven ages.'[E65]

"I've observed that your dreams, too, have played many parts. We've waded through an awful lot of science and now we've retraced our steps back to Titanic. We've come full circle."

"Wow! Karen. Circle Pond Road is a great connection! You know what? It might also mean that we are to 'Circle' the Atlantic Ocean –nicknamed the 'Big Pond' – and that is our path – our 'Road:' Circle Pond Road. I had a feeling we'd be circling the Atlantic, but why? What else should we be looking for?"

---

419 11/11/96. See Ch. 62 – A Birthday Party In Placentia, p. 288

"Wait a second, Penelope. I just found a Big Pond Lake on the Newfoundland map, and we've surely been circling Newfoundland like a couple of whirlybirds."

"True, true, Karensurefoot. I guess Newfoundland is just the beginning of this circle. But tell me. Do you think we'll ever know who the oversized kitten is?"

Overcome with the excitement of discovery and the silliness of exhaustion, we burst into fits of laughter, turning away ever so briefly from the solemn dispatch.

Steno patched in. "Excuse me, girls, but there is a sailing term based on a mathematical calculation, to add to your circular puzzle. It is called a Great Circle route, which is the shortest distance between two places on the Earth's surface. The route follows a line described by the intersection of the surface with an imaginary plane passing through the Earth's center. So navigating Earth's oceans, the shortest distance is called the Great Circle route."

"Doc, I vaguely see a lighthouse in the distance but it's strange because the lights are getting closer. The sound is shifting, Doc. Now the air is rushing. What's going on?"

Steno was amused. "Not to worry, Penelope. It's Tu-whit with a connection to Titanic he'd like to share":

ÕÕ "'The Titanic left Queenstown on Thursday 11 April and took the Great Circle route to New York. The route passes inside an area which on the charts was marked 'icebergs have been seen within this line in April, May and June.'"[E66]

The wisdom and reverence gained from our adventure will live within us forever. Wherever we turned, life laid out its imperial red carpet inviting us to follow its invisible path. There is no way to paint a miracle, but in my mind's eye I saw intertwining ribbons shimmering with promise and radiating an energy almost more than human perception is capable of receiving. It occurred to me that every soul desiring this experience can reach beyond all measurable earthly expectation and find within his or her sphere a world of wonder that enfolds us all. It was a simple question of observation — and Trust, of course.

The inexhaustible findings continued when I returned to New York.

CHAPTER NINETY-THREE

HOME PLATE

The significant problems we face cannot be solved at the
same level of thinking we were at when we created them.

F. David Peat

Back in New York, I came face-to-face with a new me who felt a cohesive bond with my fellow man and guides, a bond beyond human strength and understanding. The certainty of my path had been set and would not waver even as I faced my old, now new, world. My life had been unalterably changed. That my spinning dream narratives had actualized a reality beginning in Newfoundland, with an underlying message for human-kind, was more than I could have ever imagined.

I dug out my research on the Alaskan Pipeline. At the time, the word lavender had been merely a color, lava under not yet born and the subject of environment moot. Subsequent to the dream about *workmen coming to stop water pouring out of a pipe and a hole being in the wrong place,*[420] another pipe image connected to: *a corroded pipe – a seismic zone – uranium.*[421]

A dialogue about *Cordovan* in the following dream led me to the Cordova Fisherman District United which lost its battle against construction of the Alaska Pipeline. Cordovans have had little regard for the oil industry since the Exxon Valdez spill – an attitude rein-forced by knowledge that a large red salmon was worth more than a barrel of oil.

This is a dream sketch of what might have been the Exxon Valdez oil spill. As dreams are wont to do, it incubated for ten years and has transmogrified to the 2010 British Petroleum oil and gas spill in the Gulf of Mexico. It spins a scenario about *self-turning eggs.*

"It's something new," repeats through the night. There's a big range on top of a stove and raw strips of pasta are mixed in with the self-turning eggs. I'm trying to separate them from the pasta

---

420 9/28/93. See Ch. 65 – Pipe Dreams, p. 306
421 1/20/00.

Footnotes contain dream dates and references to prior pages where the dream appeared.
Endnotes contain bibliographical references, are marked with "Ɛ" in the text, and appear at the end of the book.

but it's very hard. The eggs are mottled and have a greenish cast. I'm trying to turn them but there's a lot of butter in the pan.[422]

Strips relate to seafloor spreading and magnetic reversal. Consider this investigative circle as it may pertain to the Gulf oil spill.

Self-turning eggs – Sulfur … *Greenish cast, Mottling* – Contamination … *Big range* – Tract of land … *Stove* – Radioactive decay – Volcanic zone … *Strips* – Magnetic reversal – Seafloor spreading … *Butter* – Oil. Add to that: *Hole – Corroded pipe – Seismic zone – Uranium* – back to Sulfur.

Is sulfur cooking in the earth? The dream messenger said, *"It's something new."*

Flashback! Marie's lesson on uranium decay: a heat source in the earth that drives continental drift and volcanic eruptions. Out of nowhere, Tu-whit hooted in with an affirmation:

ÕÕ "'Careful measurements of heat flowing up from the interior of the earth under the continents, ocean floors, in deep mines and drill holes tells us that most of the interior heat comes from radioactive decay of elements concentrated in the crust …'"[Ɛ67]

Ocean floors! Drill holes! Were the dots waiting to connect sulfur and uranium with other chemicals, like dispersants, that might be present near a leak or spill? Could they react to form a new and deadly gas? Could they connect to the 2010 Gulf oil spill? Were the millions of gallons of dispersants dumped in the water to break up the oil slick another felon under cover?

Striving with all my might to sustain my equanimity, I turned my attention back to Alaska.

Developers of the Denali natural gas pipeline from Alaska are committed to run their line 1,750 miles, delivering gas via interconnections throughout Canada and the United States.[Ɛ68] The largest inland earthquake in North America in almost 150 years was the magnitude 7.9 Denali Fault earthquake which struck Alaska, the most seismically active state, on November 3, 2002. Authorities boast that not a drop of oil was spilt. Consider the millions of gallons of oil and gas that gushed in the Gulf and apply that to the combustible nature of gas. All it takes is a leak. Is it insanity or denial to think a pipeline can be safely built and operated across a seismically active region?

---

422 3/13/00.

During my waking experience in Canada, I became obsessed with the danger of a gas pipeline being run along the ocean floor from Newfoundland into the United States and unrelated construction of an LNG terminal along the St. Lawrence River, both potentially dangerous seismic areas. Both projects were on again, off again, and I now realize my observations were too small a vision, focusing only on Canada.

The rash of high magnitude earthquakes around the world early in 2010 brought this home, particularly the catastrophic 7.0 magnitude Haiti earthquake which claimed more than 100,000 lives. It was on a fault line that passes near an LNG terminal on the border of the Dominican Republic and Haiti and may have cracked rock formations allowing gas or oil to seep toward the surface.

This Haiti quake reawakened in me a menacingly dark dream I had tried to sweep under the carpet.

I'm upstairs with a group of disadvantaged children. People are jammed together in a very crowded house. A lit cigarette is burning deep in the ground. People standing right on top of it are helping to stamp it out.[423]

Images of these disadvantaged children have haunted me for over a decade. I must now ask if the house is Haiti or Planet Earth?

The eternal giants of Science had delivered a message to me, a mere mortal, because they are deeply concerned about fire burning within Mother Earth. Their fateful message centers on the extent to which humans as a species have, ever since the Industrial Revolution, exploited and corrupted the physical environment that sustains us.

My mentors were smart. They took me to Canada so I could see a microcosm of their concern which is, in truth, worldwide.

Karen and I stayed in close touch, reflecting on our journey for months afterward. One day, I said, "So, my little buddy, what did you think of our escapades in Newfoundland?"

She replied, "Honestly, Penelope, afterward I had the feeling that I had stepped into another world and was coming back renewed and refreshed. Not only was Newfoundland an unusual place, but our treasure hunt was completely absorbing. All of our synchronicities and discoveries helped me put the stress of corporate life that I was experiencing into perspective."

Her words confirmed the feelings of transcendence so present throughout our journey. We had shared an unbreakable bond, and I knew this truly harmonious relationship would last a lifetime. What neither of us knew at the time was the danger confronting us.

Not long after our Newfoundland excursion, I began to receive computer transmissions that connected to Karensurefoot.

---

423 10/8/99.

One day while writing about a Galen doctrine entitled, "On the function of the parts of the body," the Greek equivalent inserted itself. A Greek colleague of Karen's confirmed the translation. When Karen faxed the translation back to me, my printer turned itself on and printed out an arrow pointing both upward and downward. Next to this bidirectional arrow was a smiley face, which seemed to be greeting Karensurefoot. I wondered if the dual arrow was confirming the upside-down images in so many of my dreams: as above, so below.

Lord Galen had kept his word; Karen had been handpicked.

Swimming about in this bittersweet stream of unfolding events far beyond the routine of material things, alternating feelings of euphoria and dread swam in and out of my thoughts. Still I was anxious to tie up some loose ends from our magic carpet ride and journey forward.

Ensconced in my home office, I burrowed through stacks of journals until I found the dream illustration of the mysterious clock. I compared the photograph Karen took in Swift Current[424] to my little drawing. The photograph pictured a rock on which was drawn a circle in the shape of a clock. Extending from the clock was a curly-cue doodle; the side of the rock was marked with an X. This graffiti was curiously close to my clock-a-doodle dream image, the exception being that the clock in the photo was pointing upward: "As Above, So Below."

Within one tiny 2"x2" drawing resided an entire story.

The words *"marker"* and *"cue"* leapt off the page. Was the time drawn on the clock meant to be a *"marker"* to clock the time of a displacement in the event of a strike-slip fault? How odd that a strike-slip fault involves a lateral displacement and in the photograph, the X on the rock was marked in a lateral position – on its side.

X marked more than one spot! First, it marked Galen's ancient theory on vision: the optic nerves, on their course to the brain, are crossed at the chiasma (from the Greek letter chi, written X). Now it appeared on the rock. It seemed reasonable; one had to see to perceive.

I was still trying to make sense of the clock. How might the clock connect to the Titanic?

The silhouettes of Claudius Ptolemy and Agneswiseheart appeared out of the clouds. Twink's light touch was nearly physical.

"Halloo, Penny. Your puddy tat has been chasing after a piece of yarn doing somersaults trying to find you. My stars! You look like the cat that swallowed the doodle today. The clock you're examining is not just any ordinary clock, you know. We must keep our minds open to all possibilities when on so grand an exploration. Of course, its imperial draw is the enchantingly electromagnetic company ... (harumph ... harrumph)."

424 See Ch. 87 – Swift Current, p. 422

Hmm. Why would Ptolemy and Percival be so excited over this clock? Well, clocks and telling time do fit with astronomy. Could it have something to do with the refraction of light from celestial bodies? Maybe it connects with reports that Titanic sank under a night sky that was moonless, but studded with stars.

Could the *marker* have been acting as a radio beacon that's used to guide the pilot of an aircraft, or in this case, the captain of a ship? Percival was cavorting, running around and springing like an acrobat. What was he trying to say?

The remaining particles of the haunting dream had been floating in my cerebrum since 1995. As they drifted back into daylight, I replayed them:

> *The clock has a funny sort of doodle drawn on it.*
> *The time is 12:28 and shows a figure that looks like an m.*
> The message is: *"He wants yellow. Pale yellow."*
> *I go to point at the clock with a pen. I don't realize it's a marker.*
> *It makes a mark with a curly cue by mistake.*
> *I say, "it's my mistake." Someone says, "you slipped."*[425]

But, what of the little "*m?*"

Some of the connections were so blatant they seemed too obvious to even consider. The cheerleading squad composed of a spiritual team of scientists from Heaven University chanted:

"Give me an M .... Mass. Give me an A... Astronomy. Give me an S ... Science. Give me another S... Spirit."

"M-A-S-S ... mass ..." I mumbled, thinking back to the enormous mass of water a submarine volcanic eruption might have activated, perhaps causing a tsunami.

"Dr. Steno, I was wondering about the energy of a tsunami."

"Penelope, *m* is a symbol for mass, particularly in the equation where it is converted into energy."

"Oh, thank you, thank you, Dr. Steno! I hadn't associated it with a *clock* and a *doodle*. I'm awfully glad you were reading me, because that little *m* has been on my mind for ages – well, ever since 1995 when I had the dream."

"'Tis my supreme pleasure, Penelope." And he was gone.

A clock, a rock and a doodle!

The connection of the radioactive clock to the doodle on the rock whistled through the airways. Radioactive decay processes are used to measure geologic time. The cue: it's a clock on a rock!

---

425 2/24/95. See Ch. 29 – Clock A Doodle Do, p. 131

My Clock-A-Doodle-Do dream

Rock with doodle
Swift Current, Newfoundland

Constantly circulating were the volumes of geological dream filings squirreled away in my mind. I was ever so grateful for two key words – *mistake and slip* – each bearing the implication of a fault. A few letters strung together to form two silent words from the great beyond hinted at a path I sensed would lead to a strike-slip fault. I uprooted the dream, digging for more nuggets.

If the movement of a strike-slip fault triggered an earthquake or volcano, could mass be interpreted not only as mass energy, causing a mass of water to be displaced, but as landmass as in a landslide? Hmm. That would coincide with our findings at Spanish Room.[426]

Just then, a shimmering of peach-tinted gossamer arched over the spirit of Peggy-moonbeam. Flashing by to remind me of my psychic compass, her message was, 'Follow the Yellow Stone Road' to Placentia." She knew how to steer me back on track.

While gathering more data on Placentia, I came across a report on the 1972 Archaeological Project sponsored by the Jerseyside/Placentia Archaeological Committee. That committee had met at the ball field in Jerseyside to try and locate what was known locally as a "French Graveyard."

I was stumped over the whereabouts of the ball field; there was one on the map but not in Jerseyside. Having explored most of Jerseyside's nooks and crannies and feeling a true kinship with the little town, I was frustrated that I couldn't identify the baseball field.

I had to locate it because of a mystifying dream about a *tall man playing baseball* and *sheets of sparkly material described as big billowy pants legs.*[427]

---

426 See Ch. 83 – A Hidden Key, pp. 395–97
427 8/15/99.

Steno swooped down, eager to impart more knowledge of minerals.

Penelope, this describes phyllosilicates, minerals that link together to form sheets.[E69] They're found in *legs* of land in the *billowy* surface of lava, called Pahoehoe.

"Now let's see if we can manifest that ball field for you," fluttered Peggymoonbeam.

While wading through this quagmire of connections, I had detected another mystifying link and couldn't bear the suspense any longer. It had to do with the name Gardiner. I called the owner of Maher's Polypipe, who obligingly told me the ball field where they excavated had been right behind his building. As fate would have it, the field I was in search of was directly in front of the enchanted house where dreams come true, the house that leaned against Castle Hill Mountain.

Mr. Maher added laughingly, "Stray baseballs from the games used to hit my building."

It turned out his brother was mayor of Placentia around that time. He assured me his brother would be able to tell me more. And indeed, he did.

The former mayor confirmed that Fort St. Louis, where the ball field used to be, was a prime location for a dig and there had also been a dig under the property of the Rosedale Manor.

I called Karensurefoot, all a dither. "Karen, I spoke to Mr. Maher, the former mayor of Placentia, to ask where the ball field is and guess what? It's right behind Maher's Polypipe! And the Rosedale Manor was also the site of a dig! Can you imagine? We completed the circle! It all connects!"

"Fantastic!" cheered Karen. "I knew we'd close the loop!"

I triumphantly closed the unfinished circle: the Rosedale Manor – Church of the Sacred Heart – Argentia – Southeast Arm – Castle Hill – Ambrose Shea Bridge – Maher's Polypipe – Jerseyside – Placentia – the Pipeline – the White Rose oilfield – underground excavation – circling back to the Rosedale Manor.

The bouquet of roses was under my nose – the Rosedale Manor, Ambrose Shea Bridge, White Rose oilfield – but the scent was not altogether fragrant. In fact, it was beginning to reek of oil and gas. "Rose" was simply a code name that validated our meanderings around the town of Placentia that led us to oil fields off the coast of Newfoundland …. and beyond.

I could barely contain myself as my imagination could not suppress what may lie under the Rosedale Manor where we had slept.

The *blue glove* was underfoot.

The *White Rose* oilfield was underground.

The *pipeline* would be underground.

The dream about *the tall man who played ball* was so general. It gave no hint as to location. There was nothing attached to it other than the amorphous *billowy pants legs.* Yet, we were led to this particular ball field. Some would say the clues are too subtle, too much of a stretch. But no matter how farfetched, even disconnected clues connected.

How extraordinary that the Jerseyside ball field was facing the house that was our very own "home plate" with its helter-skelter clues. Sometimes we can't see what's in our own front yard.

Famed architect Ludwig Mies van der Rohe said, "God dwells in the details."

The former mayor said that, while they were excavating at the Rosedale Manor for a water line, they had dug up some headstones. Why were our points of discovery turning into burial sites?

The mayor noted that when they took the fill out and disposed of it at another site, someone happened to notice the remains of a soldier's uniform.

He emphasized that the finding was accidental.

The Argentia Naval Base and the soldier's uniform, both connections forged during waking, returned me to another mysterious dream. Among a cryptic medley of codes are images of my *friend named Lewin and an army watch with a mesh band. It is something I would have to wait for, for a very long time.*[428]

To refresh your memory, dear Reader, *Lewin* is linked to *the wallet with the foreign currency and the folding American currency.*[429] The word "mesh" had become a common clue indicating that ultimately everything would intermesh – blend – knit. My on-the-spot connection to an *army watch with a mesh band* was "watch the army mesh," but it simply made no sense. Not then.

Nostalgia inspired the mayor to tell a story about the Gardiner's on Castle Hill. I blurted out, "Castle Hill?"

"Yes, yes. As a matter of fact," said the mayor, "the old access to Castle Hill is called Gardiner's Place."

The obsession over who lived in the secret house had been answered, but it wasn't in the house. It was on the hill.

I thought back to the Northeast Arm Motel where I had involuntarily put my finger on the name Gardiner in the Newfoundland phone directory. And there it was – the old entrance to Castle Hill.

The weirdness of pointing to the name Gardiner stoked my curiosity. That touch of serendipity traced the scent to Maher, connected to my old friend Pauline Maher and Maher's Polypipe, all in and around the Castle Hill Mountain and the Jerseyside ballpark.

428 8/4/99.
429 3/3/99.

This unbelievable chain of synchronicity culminated in a maar – a volcanic crater in the vicinity of Placentia. Was pipeline being laid near a crater of explosive origin? Was Castle Hill the archetypal mountain selected by the dream squad because it was in Newfoundland – a hub of industrial activity – in a place denoting birth? Placentia – placenta. Was some electromagnetic beam escorting us through this maze of connections?

The Gardiner name seemed significant, but what did it have to do with me?

As Lord Galen's golden halo flickered through fleeting clouds, he exuberantly exclaimed, "It has everything to do with you, Penelope! You see, by wearing your Timelessness Glasses and carrying your Psymometer, you have been guided to Gardiner's place on Castle Hill so you can connect the many threads of your life.

"Yours is a book still being written and the author, your doppelganger, is named Judy Gardiner."

"Heavenly halos! A doublegonger! Is that like a gong that sounds twice?"

Lord Galen laughed heartily, his luminous smile lighting up the entire Castle Hill panorama. "Well, you could say that, Penelope, but the word is doppelganger, and it's a ghostly double of a living person, like a spirit that inhabits ones fleshly counterpart."

"You mean there's more than one me? Am I living with my own spirit?"

"Yes, Penny. Your spirit is a part of you. You are a multidimensional being functioning in two realities: the physical plane that governs your waking consciousness and the nonphysical plane that gives rise to your dreaming consciousness. The Judy Coves you found at the end of the Southeast arm were markers for your doppelganger's first name, as was the yellow J painted on the rock in Branch. Of course, the most obvious clue is this old entrance to Castle Hill named Gardiner's Place, which bears your doppelganger's last name, which is that of her penultimate husband. These markers were intended to raise your consciousness and connect your dream self to your physical self."

"But …. But, Lord Galen. Which one is the spirit and which one is the physical me? It's kind of confusing because I'm not sure which one is writing the book."

"Aah! Well, let's just say that you are both writing the book with a little help from your friends.

"You've been experiencing the all-encompassing realm of multidimensional consciousness; you are shifting, along with Mother Earth, to a higher frequency because you are attuned to her energies as a nurturer. And that is how you often find yourself in two places at the same time and how you are able to transport yourself to wherever you wish to be, whether it be writing or dreaming or traveling or simply thinking. In fact, you have been in even more than two places at certain times. This string of materializations is proving to you that the two realities are comingled. You have one leg on Earth and the other in Heaven, and this is how you witness heaven on Earth."

"Galloping grasshoppers! I am both of me!"

The former husband's Gardiners hailed from Maine. During the Civil War, that family split in half, most going to England while others journeyed to Quebec and Montreal. Perhaps some made their way into Newfoundland, but one thing was certain: I was led to Castle Hill.

Years ago, a friend coaxed me into going to a party on a steamy July night. It was there that I met the urbane Mr. Gardiner, whom I later married. His first words were "Dr. Livingstone, I presume?"

David Livingstone spent half his life exploring Africa. When no one heard from Livingstone for several years in the 1860s, his long absence became a matter of international concern and, in 1869, the New York Herald sent explorer Henry Stanley to the interior of the African continent to find him. When Stanley came upon Livingstone in 1871 in a small town in Tanganyika, he approached him with the famous greeting, "Dr. Livingstone, I presume."

Did Mr. Gardiner know something I didn't? Or was it one of those cosmic winks? Was it intuitively etched in a timeless blueprint somewhere that at first sight my former husband would drolly mention Dr. David Livingstone?

Was that the first unknown step of this stranger-than-fiction journey where twenty years later I would begin exploring the interior of Tanzania from a dream clue that materialized in Newfoundland?

And what did it mean for him? I suppose that is Mr. Gardiner's book. Was it written somewhere that I would marry someone with the name Gardiner so that two decades later I'd find my way to Castle Hill's Gardiner's Place? Phenomenal!

Are the imprints of our lives engraved on a tablet that prophesies cause and effect in every chapter of our existence, not just in one individual lifetime, but perhaps through all time?

Were our dreams a biological gift to us? A series of brilliantly imprinted flashbacks that could track serial lifetimes? Were they arranged like a carousel slide projector with a remote forward and reverse, projecting the transparencies of our lives going round and round and round?

The piecing together of this puzzle – from dreaming to waking – from waking to dreaming – birthed an entirely new reality, the perfection of iteration merging with integration. The thrill in uncovering this seamless reality silences any verbal expression of it. The magic thrives as synchronicities multiply almost daily.

"I'm feeling so in love with everything these days, Lord Galen. I've never felt like this before. I just love every grain of soil and every little creature, even the icky ones like worms and spiders and oh – I don't know – the feeling of being a part of the whole world and everyone in it, has changed me. I'm a completely different person but I'm still in my same body with the same heart and the same soul and humility I didn't even know I had.

My love for all of you travels beyond the most distant reaches of space and that's amazing because I can't even see you, but I know in my heart you're there! It feels like I'm following you wherever you go. Or maybe you're following me. Who knows? Maybe I'm part of a universe I haven't even been to. The magnificence of your presence is something I want everyone in the whole wide world to have. But the words get stuck because it's so overpowering, it's hard to talk about."

"Penelope. You have tasted the fruit of Peggymoonbeam's tree of science. You are not only learning the time-honored doctrines of science but you are experiencing a new kind of knowledge that includes the acceptance of uncertainty. With this comes an awareness of your intuitive insights which were acknowledged with your honorary Branch of Vision. With the ability to "perceive," your consciousness has been expanded to that little understood area of human experience – the capacity to see the Invisible.

"The 'state of unconditional love' you speak of is hard to talk about because it is not verbal. What you describe is an invisible, absolute love for everything. This is called agape and is the ultimate goal of all sentient evolution. But don't be fooled, Penelope dear. As intoxicating as agape is, you've discovered on Mission Lavender that while higher consciousness transports you to the positive and – at times, even the sublime – its mirror image reflects the negative. Part of your education is to learn the two-sided nature of the Invisible. Transcending this duality will advance you toward opening to the attainment of wisdom."

"Lord Galen, I don't know what I ever did without you! I'm beginning to understand much more about the human experience than I ever knew, at least in this life. It's strange about uncertainty. When I wish really deeply for something to happen, it eludes me but when I busy myself with other things, like Mission Lavender, it unexpectedly appears. I bet it's one of those cosmic mysteries the spirit team knows about."

Galen's broad grin expressed deep happiness. As suited him, he bashfully murmured, "Your praise embarrasses me, but I appreciate your kind thoughts."

"Penelope, yours is a singleness of purpose and I daresay you needn't concern yourself with the idea of uncertainty just now. Accept your observations and return to your feelings of universal compassion. And do remember: Be patient. You will learn everything you need to know."

Left pondering my vision mentor's astute observations, I thought, "There is no immunity to what happens once the gates of consciousness open. In the ever, ever realm of cosmic synthesis, ecstasy and humility become one and in this enfoldment, astonishment swells to rapture but occasionally deflates to terror and despair. When I see the danger we confront, I know I must honor its existence. Ascending miracles and descending doom are part of our life here on Earth and must be accepted.

"Universes within universes enfold earthly experience with dream experience, offering to all the children of the Earth a sacred toolbox with implements that can carve a simpler language, tools that can fashion our understanding of how the world is made.

"There are days when, if asked to pinpoint the location of my heart, I'd be hard pressed to do so. It is in my head, my mouth, my eyes, my ears, my fingertips and especially my gut. This heart connection is within all those I love who have passed before me and is destined to embody those who will come after."

Enteric memory, lodged in the intestines, in the gut, had virtually made the gut another sense organ. Reminiscent of earlier imagery, the word "enteric" was paired with *branches growing out of my head, intertwining branches on the stem of a rose,* branches which literally and figuratively were branching out all over the place, beginning in Newfoundland and reaching for the cosmos. Was this something called Gut Memory? What was I supposed to remember?

It was ironic that the wheels of industry about to start spinning along our route had temporarily come to a halt, and then resumed exactly when the intransigent wheels of terror and hatred were spinning out of control – wheels that could drive the most grievous ruination known to man. Was it here that I watched the army mesh?

The quest has intensified. There is the War on Terror and there is Destruction of the Earth. Somehow, they are related. If we could fix one, it seems probable we could fix the other.

Considerably more technical and scientific data would have to be collected before an inquiry might be granted. Racing against time, there was no choice but to delve into the quagmire of plate tectonics and chemical signatures in ancient rocks which, I hoped, would be definitive.

My confidence was sustained by the *real estate - alchemy* dream[430] where Curium first revealed itself. Still, I was gripped with fear and nerves as to how this would play out. I had no credentials – only the needles and threads held in my brain-gray sewing kit of dreams. I tried to focus on Lord Galen's words on the duality of positive and negative.

Dr. Steno circled in with one last word before we journeyed onward.

"Penelope, you've come this far. We won't let you down now."

"You know the feldspar we named after your friend, Pearly? Well, there is a beautiful iridescent moonstone called Labradorite, a member of the feldspar family. Famous Labradorite deposits have been found in Labrador, in an area called Nain."

"Labrador? Didn't the Labrador Current carry the massive iceberg to meet Titanic? Isn't Labrador where the nickel deposit is, the one that started all the commotion about building a nickel smelter?"

"Exactly, Penelope! And it is also where the Merewether Crater is."

---

430 7/16/93. See Ch. 17 – Real Estate & Alchemy, pp. 75–76

Tu-whit hooted in.

ÕÕ "'It is reported that in 1943, a United States Army Air Force colonel, Arthur F. Merewether, flew over what he suspected was an impact crater 65 km southwest of Hebron in Labrador. Subsequent tests confirmed that a meteorite caused the 138-metre diameter pond, later named Merewether Crater, about one thousand years ago. It was the first meteorite crater to be discovered in Newfoundland.'"[Ɛ70]

CHAPTER NINETY-FOUR

WALK THE DOG

I looked toward Steno. "Remember the dream of the *tall dog walker and his dog that was so low to the ground?*[431] Remember the *bellows that lost its frame?* The bellows was feeding the fire of an ancient volcano and that was where I discovered that the 'meat' of the matter was 'Lava Under.'"

"Certainly, I remember, Penelope, but can you tell me how you connected this to lava under?"

"Oh, because I think of a bellows as something that collapses. It must have been a collapse crater that is mostly filled with its own volcanic ash and pumice and beneath that would be lava – lava under."

"Remember how *the dog so low to the ground* turned out to be a Labrador retriever?"

"Penelope, my child. Of course I remember."

"You know what, Dr. Steno? There's a yoyo game down here on Earth that reminds me of this dream. It's about a dog that is very low to the ground."

"You don't say, Penelope. Tell me about it."

"Well, it's called Walk the Dog."

"Umhm. How is it played?" responded Steno.

"First, you throw something called a 'sleeper' that involves flexing your muscle and stretching your fingers so the yoyo goes flying down to the ground fast."

"Umhm."

"Then you let the yoyo gently touch the floor."

"Umhm. What next?"

"Then the yoyo rolls across the floor and you are walking the dog! Oh yes, if it slows down, before it stops spinning, you just give it a little tug and the doggie will return to your hand."

---

431 11/30/98. See Ch. 35 – Lava Under Revelation, pp. 151–156

Footnotes contain dream dates and references to prior pages where the dream appeared.
Endnotes contain bibliographical references, are marked with "Ɛ" in the text, and appear at the end of the book.

"Umhm. Have you made some connection, Penelope, as to how this game might affect our work?"

"Of course, Dr. Steno. It's the 'sleeper' that woke me up. I'm the sleeper! The dreamer! This game is exactly what is happening! Like the game, the *dog low to the ground* was in my dream!"

"Dear Penny, you don't think that 'Walk the Dog' was discovered on Earth, do you? All that you know on Earth originated above."

"Even the games?"

"Yes, my fair maiden. Especially the games. Heaven is a children's nursery."

"I'm now convinced it was you, Dr. Steno, who gave me "lava under – the meat of the matter," but with so many guides I'm still not sure who the tall dog walker is and how he got into my dream."

Steno beamed his all-knowing smile. "I think it's time we take our faithful Labrador, Simon, for a walk."

"The tall dog walker was you, too, Dr. Steno?"

His thunderously joyful roar shook the universe. "Hold on, Penelope. I have to untangle the lead. It is billions of years long."

"Meow. Meow. Meow."

"Dr. Steno. Percival feels left out. I don't want to hurt his feelings again. Can he go on the walk with us?"

"Of course, my dear. The more the merrier."

As we prepared to set out on our next journey, it occurred to me that we have gone round and round parodying another yoyo game called "Around the World." In this, the yoyo follows a large circle and returns to your hand, where it began.

Funny. In both games the yoyo comes back to you. I wonder if this is just the way things work.

CHAPTER NINETY-FIVE

LABRADOR

*... it is always the drama of human endeavor that
will be the thing, with a ruling passion expressed by
outward action marching perhaps blindly to success
or failure, which themselves are often undistinguishable
from each other at first.*

Joseph Conrad

NAIN

Unlike our real-time expedition to Newfoundland, our time in Labrador would be
an imaginary trip – the only one on the agenda. Thus began our flight of fantasy, a
mixture of insight and hard reality …

In the blink of an eye, here we were in Nain, just the four of us. Dr. Steno, spyglass in
hand, was invigorated and ready to perform microsurgery. Simon was slobbering cheerfully alongside a blissfully purring Percival, and as for me, I was ever hopeful skipping
along with my basket spilling over with dream yarn. Quite the eccentric little caravan we
were, adventuring in the spirit of spirit. The only means of charting our terrain and its
mystery was rooted in a thousand patches of dream turf and in our hearts, so persistently
determined to piece it all together.

"Penelope," prompted Steno, "Lewis and Clark, the famed explorers, sketched their
maps as they went. In similar fashion, our dream maps tell stories about important past
events, current situations and future conditions. The differences in our survey methodology are that we at Terracrust and Starsight have distinctive notions about time, space
and relationships between the natural and the supernatural worlds, while those on Planet
Earth still struggle with the concept of timelessness. I daresay our dream map will cover
many more thousands of miles of terrain than most ordinary maps."

Who knows? Lewis and Clark might even give us a thumbs-up if they knew we set
foot on regions unknown with our only navigational tool a psychic compass. While the
foot of civilized man had already trod on our turf, these were our first precarious steps on

---

Footnotes contain dream dates and references to prior pages where the dream appeared.
Endnotes contain bibliographical references, are marked with "Ɛ" in the text, and appear at the end of the book.

Labradorean soil. The only map we could produce was a grid of codes dotted with snippets of dreams.

Running to fetch his game, Simon pulled us barking and yelping across the windswept barrens of Labrador up through its Highlands and around a veritable labyrinth of ponds and swamps. I tossed a quarter to see if we were in the right place. Heads we were; tails we weren't. It landed heads up.

Simon's vigorous bark echoed through the seacoast communities as he dragged us yapping his head off to the front of the Moravian Church. His training for blind falls and his sensitive snout had prepared him to detect, and detect he did – not a fallen bird, but the smell of nickel. Well, a fallen bird of sorts.

The quarter was Simon's clue to sniff for nickel, heads up.

Speaking of clues, Marie Curie's vibration penetrated the vast stillness. "Penelope, a quarter has a copper center clad in a cupronickel alloy that is 25 percent nickel."

She was extremely formal at times, but by now I knew this was serious business and if any one deserved undivided attention, it was she.

Voisey's Bay sounded a familiar gong in a dream scenario that starred *a noisy boy in the back of a church, and a Rabbi who refuses to notarize something. Two bands of feathers, one lavender and one yellow*[432] closed the dream.

The noisy boy was nameless until Voisey's Bay and the nickel smelter crept into the light of a cold Labrador day. A cryptic homonym it was: *Noisy boy.* Voisey's Bay – a tongue twister matching the church where *the noisy boy disturbs the peace.* On closer inspection, it was an even tighter fit when I learned that the Moravian Church in Nain is situated *in back of,* that is – behind – Voisey's Bay, an endorsement to the dream that placed this *noisy boy in the back of a church.*

Nain, one of the nearest towns to Voisey's Bay, is the headquarters for the Labrador Inuit Association. It is also a staging point for mineral development and exploration in and around the bay.

Steno, carefully scoping out the southern Nain province with his prophetic spyglass, wished to share the view. "Clueso. Have a look. Nain is linked to your Native American Indian dream images of the *two bands of feathers, one yellow, one lavender.* It characterizes not only Labrador geology but Labrador's Inuit and Innu tribes."

Simon, still thrashing around in the underbrush, was poking his snout in every tree, bush, stick and stone in sight. His persistence told me he was looking for something else.

The Voisey's Bay nickel discovery in Labrador in 1993 is possibly the most significant Canadian mineral find in the past twenty years because of both the size of the deposit and the richness of the ore. The Newfoundland/Labrador government in 1997 told the

---

432 4/7/99.

province's native peoples they would be given no guarantee of sharing in the wealth. The Innu and Inuit have never ceded territory to the government of Canada or Newfoundland.

Instead, it was left to the native people to get what they could on their own in negotiations with the nickel giant.

Talks between the province and the nickel producer to develop the massive ore body were shelved indefinitely in 2000 after the two sides failed to reach an agreement. The feeling then was that the window of opportunity for the development was closing. That would please the dream Rabbi no end.

Hundreds of lakes downwind of the proposed smelter site are considered vulnerable to acidification from sulfur dioxide emissions. What would happen if sulfur dioxide was emitted not only from the smelter but from another source as well? Would underground exploration trigger something neither the geologists nor the environmentalists may be aware of?

The dream was right on the nickel, warning us that the *noisy boy*, representing a nickel smelter in Voisey's Bay, would *disturb the peace*. The celestial message of boisterous child's play in the dream transformed to grave and serious child's play on Earth.

What a paradox – a noisy boy in a noiseless dream. And how telling that the dream *Rabbi refused to endorse this.*

CHAPTER NINETY-SIX

THREE MORAVIAN MISSIONS

"Why, Dr. Steno, is there so much repetition in my dreams about a hole? Could it be the Merewether crater?"

"Your question is perfectly timed, for the Merewether crater is right here in Labrador, southwest of an area called Hebron established in 1830.

"Come to think of it, there was a former Moravian Mission station located near the Hebron Fjord in northern Labrador. As a former priest, I take special meaning from Hebron for it was named after the Biblical city of Hebron. Its name in Hebrew means friendship."

"I bet Hebron connects to the *Rabbi*. Doc, are you saying Hebron is another Moravian Mission in Labrador, in addition to the one in Nain? That makes two: one in Nain and another in Hebron."

"Yes, Clueso. We are providing you with clues that will ultimately empty your basket of dream yarn and fill in the bare spots on your tapestry. The *Rabbi* clue is a double entendre. It signals that you are in the right place and symbolizes faith, as do many of the similes we've placed in the Oneiroball. This is a bit of a conundrum as the *Rabbi* is a person and Hebron is a place. We left it to you to associate *Rabbi* with the Hebrew name and were confident that you would connect it to the place."

"OK, Doc. I got that but what about …"

The rowdy flapping of wings drowned us out. A whole flock of owls were flying endlessly in circles over us. They were grumbling and shrieking, circling clockwise and counter clockwise and making a ruckus.

"Pardon me Penelope, but Tu-Whit is all aflutter with some unwelcome news! He only travels with a parliament when he is sensing something of dire importance or when he's coming to claim his territory.

"A parliament? You mean he's going to legislate something?"

Half grinning, Steno replied, "It could wind up in a high court someday, but this parliament is a flock of owls."

Footnotes contain dream dates and references to prior pages where the dream appeared.

Endnotes contain bibliographical references, are marked with "Ɛ" in the text, and appear at the end of the book.

Tu-whit Tu-who-o-o. Tu-whit Tu-who-o-o. Tu-whit Tu-who-o-o. Tu-whit Tu-who-o-o.

My, my. Tu-whit and his parliament were pretty darned boisterous ...

ÕÕ "'In 2007 Newfoundland/Labrador announced the deal to develop a Hebron offshore oilfield.[71] The Hebron Oil deal was signed August 20, 2009. The deal involves a consortium of companies that include Chevron Canada, ExxonMobil Canada, Petro Canada and Norsk Hydro Canada Oil and Gas. First oil is expected to be pumped from the Hebron Oil Project between 2016 and 2018.'"[72]

Holy horseflies! Hebron is an oilfield! Nothing holy about that.

Tu-whit stayed on pitch.

ÕÕ "'The Government has an equity stake in the project that is expected to bring revenues of about $16 billion.[73] The Hebron oilfield contains about 700 million barrels of oil and is located offshore in Newfoundland's Jeanne d'Arc basin, about 350 kilometres out to sea from St. John's.'"[74]

Oh no! The proposed pipeline that's supposed to skirt the Grand Banks is in the Jeanne d'Arc basin near where Titanic sank! Gassy garbagio! I forgot the White Rose field is there, too!

Memory dredged up the triangle in the Pauline Maher dream[433] which led me to suspect that the government and industrialists were in cahoots.

Industry was spinning! Now, they're all bedding down together – the province's government and industry giants, Chevron leading the pack, to develop the Hebron Oilfield project. They've turned a blind eye to seating the oil platform in the treacherous and fragile area known as Iceberg Alley as they spin their well-oiled wheels of expected profit.

It was palpable. News reports hinted at eager behind-the-scenes planning for expansion and development, government chomping at the bit over equity partnerships and super royalties, anxiously awaiting work on the pipeline route and its installation. Would it go forward or not? Reports would keep changing.

If this was to be a major boon to the province, achieving economic self-reliance and more jobs, then what was the problem? Where was the rub? Why would a string of dreams lead me to this frigid province where I would uncover a complex web of industrial activity? Why was the Rabbi so unalterably opposed to it? First Voisey's Bay nickel, now Hebron oil. Same issue: environmental crime; same place Hebron, Labrador. Strange that Hebron is spelled *c-h-e-v-r-o-n* in Hebrew.

---

433 See Ch. 68 – Argentia, p. 321

It's beyond belief how Steno and company, a gazillion light-years away, would find a place infested with predators victimizing poor Mother Earth for their own gain and rendering her so deathly ill. No wonder she's raging all over the place with hurricanes and tornados, spewing rocks and ashes about in landslides, volcanic eruptions and earthquakes.

Don't the "officials" see they could be the victims?

Tu-whit continued flapping but managed to put forward a comment from the premier the day they signed the agreement ...

ÕÕ "'Hebron is a breakthrough agreement for the province and this is a day that all Newfoundlanders and Labradoreans can take pride in and celebrate.'"[75]

The Rabbi and Tu-whit's parliament did not agree.

"Gosh, Doc. Tu-whit is extremely anxious, even angry over this though it seems a long time before they'll get oil. I wonder who these Labradoreans are and why I'd be dreaming about Moravian Missions."

"Tu-whit knows that story well since he transitions between the physical plane and Heaven where we are pure energy. He is most eager to share his knowledge with you."

ÕÕ "The Moravian Church traces its roots to fifteenth-century central Europe, in what is now the Czech Republic. A German Protestant denomination, the Moravians began missionary efforts in many parts of the world. They were important in the developing trade between Europeans and aboriginal peoples of Canada – the Innu and Inuit, Inuit meaning 'the real people.' The first Moravian Mission station in Labrador was established in Nain in 1771 and, in 1977, Inuit was officially adopted as the replacement for the term 'Eskimo.'

"The Moravians hold to the principle, 'In Essentials, Unity; In Non-Essentials, Liberty; In All Things, Love.'[76]

"Moravian congregations still exist in Labrador's Inuit communities."

Yep, Tu-whit is a wise old owl. He sees the humanity in these missionaries who wouldn't want the indigenous people driven from their land as the Cherokees and tribes to the south once were. He must be sensing industrial dangers that could force another exodus of people from their homeland. Thinking about the callousness and ego-driven appetites of certain authorities, a golf-ball knot of depression was beginning to form in my chest.

But on a more positive note, learning about the history of the Moravian missionaries and the Inuit stirred my awareness of how events, places and even centuries play across our dreams, stringing together threads of our private tapestries that get woven into the world's design.

I thought back to Agneswiseheart's words about the Aborigines and Dreamtime.[434] Was their circle of life and death, beginning and ending in Dreamtime, enfolded in my dreams? Had they tapped into my communications with Steno because they are able to see distant people, even those who are dead? When the spirit of the dead visits an aboriginal dreamer, the dream is reported to the medicine man.

I had a hunch this portion of my tapestry would be a montage in darkness and light, contrasting industrial apathy with human compassion. The Oneiroball had released another Moravian Mission strand – a dream that reveals a chemistry secret, which Marie Curie and Agneswiseheart asked me to sleep on for a while.

I took their advice, and now it was time to put my Timelessness Glasses on.

A round of laughter rippled through the cold crystalline air. Lord Galen teased, "That's rich, Penelope. It's time to be timeless!" The levity tapered off and my beloved guides chimed in on a more serious note. "Penelope, you still have some mixing to do with the chemicals, but you may share the other parts that contain Moravian Mission directives."

So I excerpted the Moravian Mission citation from Agneswiseheart's and Marie Curie's secret.

A taxi driver is driving me toward the water. There are old frame houses around. We wind up in a church called the Moravian Mission. The nice driver finds out where I go to get what I want. He takes my socks and tries them on. The soles are very dirty on the outer edges – very soiled, almost black. I say, "I've been backpacking for two weeks." There is a discussion about the outer edges of my socks being dirty.[435]

"I awakened asking myself what in Heaven's name the Moravian Mission was. I hadn't yet connected the dots. I remember drawing the frames like it was yesterday, Dr. Steno. The dream said *they are part of the architecture.* When I discovered that Hopedale was a community on the northern coast of Labrador that was settled as a Moravian Mission, I just sat and shook my head – the third Moravian mission to come through my dreams! Then when I learned that Hopedale boasts the oldest frame buildings in Canada east of Quebec City, you could have knocked me over with a feather."

The taxi driver in my dream had dutifully delivered me to the right place.

What part of the story was Hopedale to frame?

---

434 See Ch. 63 – The Picket Fence, p. 294
435 7/4/99.

To continue the dream: *the nice driver points me to Grace Lines,* a symbol which I thought at first glance blessed the dream with a thankful *omen of Grace. Someone mentions the White Freight Lines and the Mafia.* I couldn't imagine how the Mafia teamed up with Grace. Then it clicked!

Mafia personified the Godfather! But how could the Godfather of Mafia legend be mixing with the blessed company of Grace? No, the Mafia doesn't fit. This was a beneficent Godfather, or so I thought.

The *White Freight Lines* sounded similar to The White Star Line, the shipping company acquired by J.P. Morgan, Titanic's owner. Pursuing the theme of shipping, I connected *Grace Lines* to W. R. Grace, the shipping line that controlled the Atlantic and Pacific Steamship Company, known for its large fleet of passenger ships.

"Whoa, Penelope!" interjected Steno. "There's more to *Grace Lines* than meets the eye. W. R. Grace abandoned the shipping business in 1969 to concentrate on chemicals. It's still in business, but not as a shipping concern. It saddens me to tell you that W. R. Grace and Company has been involved in a number of controversial environmental incidents including water contamination from toxic chemicals as well as asbestos contamination from vermiculite mining. Our records show over 250,000 asbestos-related lawsuits were filed against Grace, so your dream about the *Mafia* and your association to the Godfather were right to begin with. Where you went wrong was in thinking it was a good godfather. Let this be a lesson, Clueso, to trust the dream. You needn't manipulate it.

Were my concerns about water contamination in Newfoundland connected in some way to Labrador? The connection stared at me unflinchingly: the Canadian province consists of the island of Newfoundland and the mainland Labrador. They would share the same waters. Was W.R. Grace an environmental prototype for industry predators?

I was miffed over the fuss about my *dirty socks,* but Agneswiseheart assured me that one day I'd understand why I was wearing soiled footwear.

Three Moravian Mission bells pealed synchronicity: Nain – Hebron – Hopedale.

The noisy boy in the back of the church and the Rabbi who refused to notarize something centered on mining for *nickel* in Voisey's Bay in Nain. Wall-to-wall dreams of *craters* took me to the Merewether Crater near Hebron, another Moravian Mission station where the government and a consortium led by Chevron made a multibillion-dollar deal to develop the Hebron oilfield. *Hopedale,* a third station, framed and co-signed by *Grace Lines,* was charged with environmental crimes against humanity and supported by evidence of criminal activity represented by the *Mafia.*

Steno was apologetic. "I must tell you with deep regret that things have heated up with the Voisey's Bay people since talks were shelved in 2000. I know this comes as quite a blow to you as it does to all of us, but these are the facts. Still, the good news is that the situation changes constantly and you can't know where it will end up."

"The nickel project has been resuscitated too, Doc! This, on top of the pipeline project! And the discovery of the Hebron Oilfield!"

The catastrophic 2010 Gulf of Mexico oil spill contaminating our ecology and mercilessly staining our environment and our souls sloshed through my thoughts.

A shaft of light sparked my memory of the pesky dream of *the workers installing metal attachments to a refrigerator.*[436] What of my long-ago dreams forewarning of an explosion in a glaciated area? Years of research and mountains of manuscript pages later and I still didn't have the answer. It seemed that the *refrigerator* depicted the icy cold waters of Labrador and the *metal attachments* connected to nickel and other metals. There I was, digging around like a rookie miner in the historic mines of Newfoundland. My first clue was the metal artifacts uncovered by legendary miners in 1933. The next clue was fluorspar, the mineral responsible for the deaths and diseases of many St. Lawrence miners.

I had come to realize that my job was to connect old legends to new possibilities. Mission Lavender directed me to specific locations, simultaneously uncovering sites that would serve as prototypes for industrial pillage and devastation to the Earth and its denizens.

I recapped the boring (no pun intended) elements in that most confusing dream: *Pipe – hole – refrigerator – metal.*

Was the *hole in the wrong place* pointing to a drill hole that the Voisey's Bay developers would be boring in their quest to mine nickel? Or was I looking in the wrong place? Or was it both? Most puzzling was the detail of the *pipe with water pouring out.* It took some time to realize the dream was most likely warning of a pipeline rupture and that the *pipe* symbolized miles of undersea pipeline, serving as a possible model for countries all over the globe. First, gas. Then oil. Now nickel? Different industries. Same punctures in the intestines of Mother Earth. Same hazardous scenario.

Steno, desiring to clear up my confusion, patched in. "Penelope, you've been jockeying between Newfoundland and Labrador for quite a while now, but" …

Before he could finish the sentence, an earsplitting crack of thunder followed by hot white streaks of lightning nearly blinded me. I groped for my Timelessness Glasses. As though orchestrated to fill the gaps in the puzzle, bit by bit, piece by piece, the Gulf oil spill crashed into sight with such force it sent fifteen years of research back into orbit. *The workers installing metal attachments to a refrigerator* – the endless stopgap solutions to contain the oil spill: the drill bits – the containment dome – the riser insertion tube – the top hat – the blow out preventer – the junk shots, and *the refrigerator* – frigid waters in the Gulf at five thousand feet below sea level. Were the pipelines I'd been obsessing over British Petroleum's drilling pipes? Was *the pipe with the water pouring out* gas and oil pouring into the Gulf?

---

436 9/28/93. See Ch. 67 – Refrigeration. p. 315

"We are losing faith, Doc. This poisonous sludge has all the makings of a gulf of despair transporting the wretched odor of demons who hoard everything and share nothing. Would their frozen eyes allow them to see their assault on humanity? Or would they simply be inconvenienced by their murderous evidence. Was it a malady of our day or simply the tragic flaw in our species?"

There were times when Steno, wishing to buoy my spirits, called on Tu-whit for inspiration.

ÕÕ "'Patience and perseverance have a magical effect before which difficulties disappear and obstacles vanish.'"[77]

My thoughts shuttled back to the Moravian Mission dream and the weirdness of the dirty socks. The detailed description made no sense. Dirty edges on the soles of my socks? Backpacking?

"Penelope," said Doc. "It's now time we have another look at your dream about the carboniferous rocks. Can you pull it up from your memory bank?"

An environmental communiqué was about to unfold. I retrieved the carboniferous rocks dream.

"There's a discussion about why the rain falls in certain places. I'm explaining that it depends on the magnetism found in rocks – that certain rocks attract the rainwater, which has acid. I talk about the CFCs in the rain being attracted to hydrocarbons – carboniferous rocks. I think about the magnetic pull of acids in rain to rocks."[437] I'm completely taken aback by this message, for it is unfathomable that I would dream it.

Steno was shining his strobe lights on both dreams of *dirty socks* and *carboniferous rocks.* Free associations came soaring in pell-mell, joining the two dreams and producing an endless stream of Ahas! one after another!

"Acids! ... That must be sulfuric acid! CFCs! ... Chlorine – fluorine – carbon! ... Environmental pollution! ... Toxic chemicals! The poisonous gas dreams! Carboniferous rocks!

"Carbon is black. My socks were dirty, almost black. Sulfuric Acid? **The chemical symbol for sulfur is S. Carbon is coal – black and dirty. Dirty sock: drop the s. Change sock to rock and we have a sulfurous rock.** If the *outer edges of the socks are dirty,* and if socks symbolize **sulfurous** rocks, certain rocks **along the coast of Labrador might** contain sulfur. **Remarkable! A dirty sock is a sulfurous rock!** *I was backpacking* – going back in time.

---

437 9/21/99. See Ch. 79 – No Stone Unturned, p. 380

Steno patched in. "Carboniferous formations date to the Carboniferous geological time beginning around 315 million years ago, a time of glaciation."

While I vacillated over the linkage of carbon and sulfur, the words above self-bolded. This modest crew of electronic elves slipped in silently by night and by day, sprinkling pieces of anagrams to advance their message. After such visitations, doubts and fears about whether I was on the right track vanished, at least temporarily. Had I properly connected the dots? I wasn't sure, but I felt in these moments that my electronic aide-de-camps were looking over my shoulder. I had to soldier on, no matter the complexities or endless twists and turns. The Dream had insisted on churning out rock-hard facts I had to pursue.

The needle on my Psymometer was flickering wildly. A foul smell began to circulate. I felt nauseous, that same queasy feeling I had when I stepped on the *blue glove* back in Newfoundland. I was reminded of that horrible stench of sulfurous gas. I adjusted my Timelessness Glasses and was astonished at the clarity of my gaze.

I questioned the effect of a magnetic pull of acid rain to carboniferous rocks. Would it be combustible? The rocks are millions of years old, but acid rain, created by man at the height of the Industrial Revolution, has escalated over the centuries. We know CFCs deplete the ozone layer but if certain carboniferous rocks have a high concentration of sulfur, that should be examined.

"Doc, carbon and sulfur are coming into focus."

"Yes, Penelope. Both carbon and sulfur can develop in volcanic ash and can remain in the atmosphere for years, spreading debris around the world."

"Egad! You once told me sulfur is brimstone; that it's called the burning rock. Wouldn't the magnetic pull of all of these chemicals to the rocks present real danger? There must be environmental scientists and exploration geophysicists and chemical petrologists who are assessing this."

"Of course there are, Penelope. But you must not forget: we are concerned with matters buried deep in the ancient past as well as the more current subject of magnetism to acids in rocks, which may be something Earth scientists are not yet aware of. In any event, our scope of interest extends far beyond any particular locale, and even that one area, in all likelihood, is not being looked at in its entirety. But we must give the scientists the benefit of the doubt."

"But, Doc. You have to be every kind of scientist and industrialist and mineworker and heaven knows what else to track all this activity and we have only looked at one place! This assault on Mother Earth must be taking place all over the world! I think the only ones who can really see the whole picture are you and my other masters."

"The truth is that considerable underground activity is taking place within the province of Newfoundland and Labrador. And yes, Penelope, you are correct about the big picture. You're on the right track for you've already sensed that we have selected this area as a prototype of industrial devastation which is occurring all over Planet Earth. You can overlay our template on your globe and observe acts of pillage, be they mining for metals, drilling for gas or oil, dumping toxic waste or any of a myriad of other industrial abuses. Of course, areas more heavily subjected to industrial activity are more apt to suffer, causing weaknesses in the earth."

Steno assumed his all-knowing stance, his subtle smile a sign that he was quietly waiting for me to react. And react I did.

A blast of insight electrified my neurons! *The hole in the wrong place* means they will be drilling and are drilling in the wrong place. I thought the wrong place was in one area or the other – in Newfoundland or in Labrador – but they are drilling everywhere, be it for nickel, oil, gas or to install a pipeline. The haunting words echoed back: *This hole should never have been there to begin with and workmen had come to stop water pouring out of a pipe.*

The British Petroleum oil spill was a perfect example of that prototype, one that gushed millions of gallons of oil and gas into our waters. Chemical dispersants never used in an oil leak this size a mile under the ocean, their effects at such depth largely unknown, were used on top of and under the water, which may have been the cause of an underwater plume. This spill set in motion an environmental catastrophe unlike anything we've known. Zooming back to consciousness was the dream where *the book I need is in the 330.4 Law section. §330.4,* an environmental amendment on used oil mixtures collected from oil/water separators, must be related.[438]

"Penny, remember your lesson on Pangaea and think of the entire Earth as a whole and each area in each country in each continent as a part of that whole so that what is happening in one place is happening in others. You see, dear, it's all interconnected.

"Moreover, your dreams highlight those locations that may be current and controversial at the moment they take place. At other times, these sites may be less immediate. After all, circumstances change and a threatening project that is charging ahead one day may grind to a screeching halt a few months later. Conversely, new dangers arise and old ones resurface. Regardless, they are always important as timeless examples of the dangers Earth faces.

"Certainly, you can track their progress, but remember that industrial projections are not carved in stone. To add to the confusion, this maelstrom of activity is occurring in various locales. It's awfully chaotic hearing about so many projects and activities, but that is the route to wholeness. We have to understand fragmentation first. So that you have a clearer idea about what is happening where, let me try to map it out for you by location. You'll notice that industry is adamant in pursuing what it thinks is its interests regardless of economic downturns and environmental concerns. Bear in mind that these activities are still typical of the larger picture:

---

438 4/15/98. Ch. 76 – Chemistry: The Third Branch, pp. 366-67

"LNG pipelines symbolized as a global presence: Placentia Bay, Newfoundland; Quebec, St. Lawrence River, Alaska.

"Voisey's Bay nickel mine and processing: Northern Labrador, less than twenty miles from Nain.

"Voisey's Bay nickel smelter and refinery: Proposed for Argentia, Newfoundland, but site changed to Long Harbour, Placentia, Newfoundland in 2009.[78]

"White Rose oil and gas fields – Hebron Oilfield, Jeanne d'Arc Basin near St, John's, Newfoundland.

"Each of these locations is well represented in your dreams. Your *white rose* dream led you to the White Rose oilfield, while the *Rabbi* dream led you to Hebron. Both oilfields are in the North Atlantic. Adding to this, your eyes are now opened to the British Petroleum Macondo Prospect Oil Field in the Gulf of Mexico."

"Doc, the people are living in a witches' cauldron! Consuming these poisons could destroy human life, and I bet the earth, too. How did Macondo get its name?"

Steno grimaced. "It's best that Tu-whit fills you in on that."

ÕÕ "Oil companies routinely assign code names to offshore prospects early in the exploration effort. The name Macondo is the name of a fictitious ill-fated town in the novel 'One Hundred Years of Solitude' by Gabriel Garcia Marquez. Macondo represents the dream of a brave new world that America seemed to promise, but was proved illusory by the subsequent course of history. The family in the story, alienated from its own history, is either unable or unwilling to escape mostly self-inflicted misfortunes. Ultimately, Macondo is destroyed by a terrible hurricane, which symbolizes its cyclical turmoil."[79]

"Doc, what a sad fatalistic story and how strange that they'd name an oil field after a town that was doomed. The timelessness of mortal existence in the novel could symbolize the futility of narcissism while the self-destructive family could represent God's children in Mission Lavender."

"Penny. There are many parallels but our story is not fictitious. Humankind has lost its way to the point where a pall is enshrouding Western Civilization. We have dedicated ourselves to Mission Lavender to impart, for however long that may take or however repetitive it may be, that the physical and mental health of Planet Earth is deteriorating at an alarming rate. Nothing is too big to fail – not the Titanic – not the oil and gas companies – not even the Earth."

"Doc, though we're aware of the unpredictability factor, recent news reports the White Rose project is progressing.[80] I read that their exploration work included a 3-D seismic program to chart future drilling targets."

"That, Clueso, shines the light on another of your mysteries, *the upside-down OPEC, the word 'Mobil' upside down and the two keys*[439] – clues for oil and gas production that would be generated by the proposed pipeline. You've already had an intuitive whiff of this."

"Yep, Doc. Greedy spirits, it seems, are attached to three-letter words: oil and gas."

The specter of mining and dreams of silver lingered when one night while working on the final edit of this book, the Oneiroball dropped a dream the weight of a cannonball on my pillow.

I'm showing a girl what to do with the silver. There is much discussion about all that needs to be taken care of. The message is that medicine or health has to be distributed to everyone but I tell the girl that all the silver pieces take priority – not just one, but all of them at once. There is a vast array of silver place settings as though they were from a very old pattern.[440]

Hmm. What must the old pattern be?

The first two silvery metals embedded in this puzzle are nickel and uranium, both with chemically toxic properties able to cause adverse health. This dream carried a crucial medical warning that all forms of pollution were the bedrock, to be focused on as a "whole" and ... *at once!* Might the vast array of silver place settings be pointing to numerous locations in the earth where these metals have been buried since ancient times, illustrated in the dream by the *old pattern*. Pangaea! Oh my God! Is all this drilling and mining fracturing the earth's crust?

Twink was right. "Mankind is so fickle, he'd sell the Earth for a nickel!"

Metals are all over the place. That's why the dream says *all the silver pieces take priority – not just one, but all of them — at once.* This points not only to nickel but uranium too."

"You are right, as usual, Doc! Every one of these places – Placentia, Argentia and Voisey's Bay – is in my dreams and because so many dreams have already materialized, this must not be ignored! If they're prototypes, they're everywhere.

"It figures that the *Rabbi in Voisey's Bay refused to notarize* this activity. Now I understand why *medicine and health has to be distributed to everyone.*"

Tu-whit, bearing witness to the Rabbi's veto, moved in quickly with some data on nickel.

ÕÕ "'Nickel is recognized as a carcinogen and is a suspected toxin affecting the cardiovascular, developmental, immunological, respiratory and reproductive systems as well as being hazardous to the blood, kidneys, skin and sense organs.

439 10/7/99. See Ch. 68 – Argentia, p. 320
440 2/1/07.

It is more hazardous than most chemicals in 8 of 11 ranking systems and is on at least 6 federal regulatory lists."[81]

This medical alert from our heavenly courier reminded me of a very strange reaction I had to a quarter, one that was camouflaged in a dream.

I pull a quarter out of my pocket and want to give it to someone. Their reply is "quarters make me sick."[441] I skipped back to the dream where *I insert a quarter, like a metal slug, into a binocular machine like those on the observation deck of the Empire State building.*[442]

Binocular vision. I could see one image with both eyes. Metal was making me sick.[443]

This dream about the quarters sprouted in the vision portion of the study in 1996. I was clueless until now. Looking back, my adventure began with a dream of *a penny in my right eye, a dime in my left eye.*[444] The penny, embossed "In God We Trust," signaled my vision for the future. The imprint of "Liberty" on the dime signified the past. Why all these metals? Why an old pattern? Mysterious ruminations.

Steno sensed my puzzlement. "Remember, Penelope, the quarter is composed of about 90 percent copper and less than 10 percent nickel, as is the dime, at which point Tu-whit instantaneously messengered a new set of facts."

ÕÕ "'The Voisey's Bay project will produce 110 million pounds a year of nickel, 5 million pounds of cobalt and 15 million pounds of copper, making it to date the largest nickel project in the world.'"[82]

"Now that you're aware of the hazards of nickel, Tu-whit has some chemical information on copper."

ÕÕ "'Copper is a suspected toxin affecting the cardiovascular, developmental, gastrointestinal, reproductive and respiratory systems. Considered a toxicant to the blood, liver and kidneys, it is more hazardous than most chemicals in 9 out of 9 ranking systems. It is ranked as one of the most hazardous compounds to human health.'"[83]

"Thank you, Tu-whit. All this toxicity paints a harrowing picture, but it does help. At least I know I'm in the right place for metals.

"And, Doc, you know what else I learned? The Voisey's Bay deposit consists of a series of four individual deposits and only one is close enough to the surface for open pit

441 6/13/96.
442 10/26/98
443 See Ch. 25 – Osiris, pp. 113–14
444 11/13/94. See Ch. 2 – Searching. p. 20

mining; the other three are deeper and require underground mining techniques. The deeper they go, the more frightening it is. You know how unpredictable things are underground, especially with all those metals, carboniferous rocks, hydrocarbon gases, sulfurous rocks and Heaven knows what else. Some eighty holes were drilled since around the 1960s in the search for oil and gas, and hydrocarbons, particularly natural gas, have been discovered in major quantities in four structures in the Labrador Sea. Coal, petroleum and natural gas also contain sulfur compounds.

My dreams have led me to question whether sulfur, which is so flammable, if combined with metal and hydrocarbon gases in those deep rock fractures in the Canadian Shield, could trigger a catastrophe no one is prepared for, like the horrific Gulf oil spill. Could there be sulfurous rocks under the drill site in Louisiana, also? Had the language of the dream used the Canadian landscape as a simile for the disaster in the Gulf?

"It looks like more than a heaping tablespoon of sulfur is an ingredient in what could be an incendiary mix."

Steno's etheric form was trembling and on the verge of bursting. "It seems, dear Clueso, that you've overlooked your dream about Bitumen. I fear Madame Curie would frown on this."

"Bitumen? Dr. Steno? I'm so sorry, please don't say anything to Marie, but, but …. Wait! I think I have a piece of it. I believe it was about chemicals. Can you help me out here? I'm drawing a blank."

Steno never let me down. "Penelope, I'll be your Clueso today and give you a clue. Think of your Corundum dream."

"Gosh, Doc, I had more than one.[445] Wait a sec. I got it, Doc! I got it! I had this dream ten years ago and had to look it up. *Something ties to Corundum and then I see a mixture and think Bitumen. There is reference to a girl's hair being almost platinum and at the end I'm catching a late plane to Germany.*[446]

"It sure is a conundrum with corundum, bitumen and platinum all in the same hopper. But why, Doc, do you mention Bitumen now?"

"Clueso, you were talking about open pit mining and I thought you'd like to know of a method used in that kind of mining to extract bitumen from the ground."

(Gulp.) "I don't know what bitumen is, Doc."

Steno nearly choked on my comment. "Bitumen consists of decomposed marine organisms which eventually transform into petroleum and natural gas – the very *hydrocarbons in carboniferous rocks* you've been concerned about. Oil sands contain deposits of

---

445 2/7/99. See Ch. 15 – A Wonderland of Minerals, pp. 71-72
446 10/1/00.

bitumen and once they're extracted, producers must add lighter hydrocarbons so it flows through pipelines."

"Pipelines? I never made that connection, Doc. I've failed both you and Marie. I feel like a real dunce! Boy, am I ever glad she's not here."

"You must never feel stupid in the pursuit of knowledge, Clueso. You have devoted yourself to learning; you have taken risks by committing to the course of study we call Mission Lavender, and your greatest lesson has been patience. Don't be so hard on yourself. Let's see a little smile. Come on now. Just a little grin. I bet you can manage just one. Do it for me, please, so that we may continue. I have an earthshaking surprise for you."

I felt like a flattened jelly fish but Dr. Steno certainly exuded charm when he wasn't being the solemn professor. He actually coaxed a smile out of me.

"Good. I'd like to ease your curiosity over the *old pattern* in your *silver* dream. Bitumen is distributed throughout the world and is found in all geological strata formed from Precambrian time, 4.5 billion years ago when the Earth was formed, to the Quaternary Period which started 1.8 million years ago. That's a fairly *old pattern,* wouldn't you say?

"As for your Corundum – Bitumen – Platinum puzzle, I am pleased to tell you, Clueso, that in Zimbabwe, corundum-fuchsite, bismuth and other coexisting minerals have been formed in volcano-sedimentary series. Now, my little sleuth, you can take it from there."

That's right. Corundum is a mineral! And Zimbabwe! That's in Africa! And Fuschite! I have a rainbow of dreams colored *fuscia*.[447] (My dream speller's variation.)

Hmm. Maybe it means fusion.

So how does all the silver factor in? Platinum is a silver metal and *something almost silver* sounds like Plutonium, which is silvery as well. Nickel, also silvery white, is a hazardous chemical and can make us sick.

"Marie, I hope you can hear me. I know you're busy at your lab but I desperately need some help. Even though it sounds like wordplay – platinum – plutonium, I don't think it's a game at all because of the inherent dangers in mining for nickel and copper. Platinum streaks through my dreams with frequent mentions of 'gelling.' Could you tell me a little about plutonium and uranium?"

"I hear you, Penelope. To begin, you mustn't feel foolish about your inquisitive nature. The only way we learn is first by asking and then, by examining. Your instincts about the silver are sound.

"Now, to answer your question: Plutonium is a radioactive element generally produced from uranium and chemically similar to uranium. Of course you know that uranium has

---

447 Fuscia dreams: 2000–2004.

traveled with us long and far. What we're talking about are products of nuclear fission which are radioactive and give rise to nuclear waste.

"The most common fissile nuclear fuels are uranium (235U) and plutonium (239Pu), both of which are metals. Just as with nickel and copper, we are gravely concerned with them and their dire effects of radioactive contamination on the lives of those ingesting, inhaling and absorbing them."

"Bless you, Marie, for taking the time to explain. Is there anything else I need to know right now?"

Flashing a starlit valentine, Twink momentarily eclipsed our exchange. "Pardon me, thy fellow mentors, but it's high time to clue Miss Clueso in on the Optico riddle. She seems to have set it aside."

"Oh dear us," responded Marie and Doc in unison. "Had you not reminded us, we'd have committed an unforgiveable oversight."

Twink announced. "Penelope, the mysterious *Optico riddle, pp. 16-21*[448] in my valentine was created by Lord Galen and me. It was a clue that the refraction of light from the stars above parallel the luminance channeled by the optic nerve to the five sensory locations in your brain."

"Dancing dragonflies! Five senses! Those are the five keys! The sixth key must be Insight."

Steno excitedly pitched in. "Clueso! Look at the elemental tables. Each page number corresponds to an element found in the earth's crust or in the atmosphere."

"What? Page numbers in a treatise on Optics translate to chemical elements? Well, I'll be a flying findanglehopper!"

Marie took her turn. "Penelope dear, your endless excursions through upper and lower stratums turned up elements encoded in the pp. 16-21 puzzle: 16 sulfur, 17 chlorine, 18 argon, 19 potassium, 20 calcium. You later retrieved a message that said *you were to correct line 21*.[449] We asked that you correct that line for the purpose of including uranium. The number 21 represents an element called Scandium, usually obtained as a byproduct of refining uranium."

"Marie. My head is spinning. Potassium connects to the dream of *mashed potatoes all over mother's floor*! But Argon?"

"Yes, Penny. Potassium-argon dating is a method used in the radioactive dating of ancient volcanic rock and ash. We'll explore this further on our next mission."

---

448 2/14/97. See Ch 5 – Honored Visionaries: Two Gentlemen Named Claudius, p. 35
              Ch. 25 – Re-Membering Osiris, pp. 116–118
              Ch. 39 – Stars In My Eye, p. 175
449 12/20/96.

"Wow! Sulfur and Chlorine – volcanic gases, Argon and Potassium – dating volcanic ash, Calcium – fossils – and Uranium, the centerpiece of the story. Every single element in the Optico riddle has surfaced! Wizardly wonders! Volcanic ash is Lava Under!

"Elements in the Earth! Stars in the Galaxies! How do you beings do this stuff? You take what's untouchable and make it so real!"

Twink and Galen took their dazzling bows, whispered, "It's all about solidarity and love," and departed.

Marie and Doc resumed their exchange. "OK, Marie," said Steno, "why don't you finish up with the sobering history of nickel, but do be gentle. You know she's painfully sensitive."

Marie spoke. "Penny dear, I thought you'd want to know how the word 'nickel' came to be. It actually originated in Germany and is the name for Satan. It's also called 'kup-fernickel' a copper-nickel alloy which is, not coincidentally, what they are mining in Labrador – copper and nickel. Apparently Saxon miners searching for silver found this metal inferior and translated it to 'old Nick's Copper' or 'Devil's Copper.'"[84]

Now I know why I was *going to Germany* at the end of that dream. Satan! Devil's copper! It is what I thought! It's a witch's brew and I saw that devil!

In a whisper, as though sharing something intensely personal, Marie had one more thread: "Bismuth germanate is a compound used as a scintillator in geological exploration. And before you ask," she smiled, "a scintillator is a substance that glows under the action of photons or other high-energy particles. That means it emits light when particles pass through it."

Seems there was no avoiding those photons, but I was still preoccupied with White Rose and Hebron which had appeared in dreaming, and now the Macondo Prospect Oil Field, which had erupted in waking.

Tu-whit zoomed in with the force of a super-sonic jet, the courier of yet another missive. This time, no owl calls. Just menacingly serious business.

ÕÕ Radiation Danger Found in Oilfields Across The Nation

"'Radium from the earth's crust has been brought to the surface in decades of oil drilling, causing widespread radioactive contamination of the nation's oilfields. The problem is only now being examined by the oil industry and the Federal Government, which has no regulations to deal with oilfield radiation.'"[85]

Government neglect probably exists in places other than the U.S. In all probability, it's universal! No regulations almost guarantee a toxic legacy for future generations.

White Rose! What a joke! To think I was naïve enough to imagine all those roses as romantic, sweet smelling flowers. This whole thing is reeking of toxins and hazards and disease. In fact, it stinks!"

"You can stop there, Penelope. You've awakened and smelled the roses. Professor Steno and I must attend to critical matters so we best be off."

Their quivering auras were fading and in out. I felt a few drops of something like rain, but not quite. I hope I didn't make them cry. Before I could take my next breath, like two speeding molecules, they vanished in a vortex of dream notes on metals, sulfur, oil, and gas, replete with endless detail on chemical toxicity.

The codes and clues were hideously toxic, but the process of interconnection was mesmerizing. Still on my virtual tour of Labrador, I obsessed with interlacing the curious strands that would weave together a perilous corner of the tapestry. The Nain thread was certifiably nickel, the Hebron thread reverentially marked a page in the Bible and Hopedale, with its crimes against the environment, was still uncertain.

A master knitter had embroidered the triple-stranded scene of Moravian Missions and cross-stitched it with a silver thread. The silver thread was Labrador, its ominous glint intended to catch my eye.

Under the auspices of the master weaver, Peggymoonbeam untangled the three-plied yarns of the Moravian Mission: Nain, Hebron and Hopedale. Twisting the yarns of dreaming and waking, she urged me to complete the circle in this portion of the tapestry. It looked like this:

Nain – Voisey's Bay – *Noisy Boy* …Hebron Oilfield – *Rabbi* …Hopedale – *Frame Houses … Grace Lines* – W. R. Grace – *Mafia* – circling back to Newfoundland, with its threatened, and threatening pipelines and nickel refinery – and finally back to Nain, Labrador – the home of Voisey's Bay nickel deposit where the risk of latent crimes against the environment nearly completed the circle. The loose thread was Hopedale, but it would have to wait.

"Whew. Thank our knitting fellowship," swirled in Peggymoonbeam. "I'm running out of yarn and we're running out of time."

Just then, I noticed Percival leaping about, eagerly chasing a skein of yarn the size of a bowling ball, enough to keep him going for quite a while longer.

The Hopedale thread intrigued me as much as it did Percival. How extraordinary that it was near Voisey's Bay.

My mind wandered back to the dream that told me *of a crime I witnessed. It said I had to cover for the suspect but would not be able to speak.*[450] The eerie cries of distress from the drowning victims of Titanic haunted me. Would other drowning victims be following in their wake? How – when – would this ever connect? What type of crime might it be.

Sheer negligence? Fraud? Arson? Murder? The list goes on …

---

450 8/21/93. See Ch. 27 – Witness, p. 125

CHAPTER NINETY-SEVEN

TOXIC ALPHABET STEW
[PAH, PCB, PVC]

It stuns me that the people in power can't see
that the source of our wealth is the Earth.
Bill Moyers

I returned to the dream of *the angry confrontation with the official screaming DAS SHOOT! ... DAS BOOT! A piece of gravel falls out by mistake. He pretends not to notice. The gravel turns out to be evidence.*[451] Evidence was building. Gravel – deposits that translate to uranium – radioactive decay – inside the earth – forewarnings delivering a cacophony of resounding alarm. Like an organ pulling out all the stops, you'd be stone cold deaf not to hear it.

The official who willfully refused to acknowledge the gravel embodies authorities and wealthy industrialists who turn a blind eye to humanity and whose obsession with profit eclipses the truth that their malfeasance is a criminal act upon our earth.

THE BOOT!

"We're keeping the BOOT on the neck of BP (British Petroleum)" – government's pat response to the shocking reality of the worst oil spill in U.S. history. DAS SHOOT! DAS BOOT! No more the stuff of dreams but a metaphor pointing at an actual ecological and environmental massacre on the ocean's floor and like a serial murderer, felling more victims as its psycho-social depravity continues spreading. Blasted awake at 10:00 p.m. April 20, 2010, to the morbid reality, the corporate and government elite looked the other way while beleaguered residents of Louisiana were pitifully mollified by the culprits themselves. Stomach-churning underwater images of hot poisonous oil gushing from a hole in the earth, off-limits to any mortal, were caused by the very children she'd mothered. She had been raped.

---

451 7/30/98. See Ch. 74 – Das Shoot! Das Boot!, p. 346

Footnotes contain dream dates and references to prior pages where the dream appeared.
Endnotes contain bibliographical references, are marked with "Ɛ" in the text, and appear at the end of the book.

Look at the date, dear Reader. April 20, 2010: 20/20 Vision. Are you seeing what's happening?

Thursday, July 30, 1998

There are circles of people pressed together. The feeling is they are the masses and will be exterminated. I am squished in between these circles. Then I am with a man. I think we are imprisoned in a small space. We find that there is a soft wall in the corner and we will be able to break through. We start pounding it and clawing it with our hands and sure enough we are able to escape. The color was an icky color, yellow, and the inside material was a fiberglass - you can see the strands.

Then someone takes us to the home of one of the officials. He is giving orders and asking questions. My friend hands him some paper and a piece of gravel falls out. I freeze because this is evidence that we broke out. We can be killed for this. The official pretends not to notice the gravel, but the paper my friend gave him is brown paper like from a bag. This too is also a sign that we escaped because it was from the inside of the wall. He makes the connection and starts screaming at us —DAS SHOOT or DAS BOOT.

July 30, 1998 – pg. 2

This drawn paper has a hand drawn map with maybe some directions. It is like construction paper.

I became terrified as this Officer is screaming DAS SHOOT. I am holding an ice-tong and I grab his or someone's pointer finger and start squeezing. I am squeezing harder and harder. I have tremendous strength. His eyes are rolling up, his face is getting red and the blood is coming to the end of his finger. The finger explodes – just disintegrates.

Fleming's rule

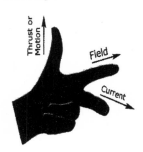

- The **Thumb** represents the direction of the **Thrust** or resultant **Motion**.

- The **First** finger represents the direction of the magnetic **Field**. (north to south)

- The **Second** finger represents the direction of the **Current** (the direction of the current is the direction of conventional current; from positive to negative).

This can also be remembered using "FBI" and moving from thumb to second finger.
The thumb is the force F.
The first finger is the magnetic field B.
The second finger is that of current I.

Marie's devotion to chemicals combined with her passion to shape a better world, told me she was, as promised, always by my side.

"Penelope, it's now time I own up to the oneirograph of the *DAS SHOOT! DAS BOOT!* dream. As suspected, *the concealed gravel is evidence* of uranium, not visible because it's buried in the earth. Remember, *you're in real estate and you're also an alchemist*[452] meaning that chemical changes, as well as physical changes are occurring within the earth. To stress this grave situation, I encoded *three circles of people pressed together* to symbolize electron

452 7/16/93. See Ch 17 – Real Estate & Alchemy, pp. 75–76

orbits and *surrounded them by the warning: They will be exterminated.* Electron radiation, dear, is the radiation of beta particles during radioactive decay."

"Marie! That's my electrifying epiphany! The alchemical transmutation that spun piezoelectricity and magma and disintegration and those three gases: LNG – volcanic gas and an unidentified chemical gas! Uranium in the earth – uranium decay – radioactive gas! After a decade of connecting the dots, I think I've identified it! Those self-turning eggs must transmute to a radioactive sulfurous gas![453]

"Marie, have I connected the dots?"

"Penny, I will now tell it as it is. The issue facing humankind is survival. The accelerating outburst of Earth disasters is Nature's wake-up call to humanity – a collective call for healing itself and the Planet. The earth is attuned to the warring fragmentation between peoples. The human race must harness its power into oneness as members of a single species and confront the truth of the Planet's coming destruction. The Species and the Planet are One. Earth is depending on every nation, every religion, every race – every member of the human species for salvation. It cannot depend on Government or Industry. You must awaken to change in the way you harvest energy immediately. Solutions will follow. **Your** Keystone dream has incubated since 2001. It is now time for you to share it.

(Gulp. Gulp.) *"The password is Keystone. A Keystone Restaurant is known for its home baked bread. It's something new. Then there's a blank ... just absolute emptiness and a vague semblance of 1952 behind me. It is invisible but I can see it. Next, I feel a terrible vibration behind my neck. It gets stronger and stronger. It's as though someone is shaking me. It awakens me. I feel unsettled and scared. It feels like someone is lifting my neck off the pillow. I pray for protection.*

(Gulp) *"A teacher escorts me to a classroom where I haven't registered. There's a large placard with big letters that spell out something like PAPH. We adjourn to another room where the teacher hands me a paper that's on the wrong side. I turn it over. On it are many sonnets in 6-point Bible sized type. Running through one of the sonnets is a symbol of a road. It reads George Bush Landmark.*[454]

"Marie, *restaurant* sounds like a place of restoration – of healing – and code for *Keystone* would be: the key is in the stone. *A Bible* in a dream must mean they're praying very hard on the other side, where I think the *sonnets* were coming from. That's why I turned the paper over, but *6-point* is so small, it's very hard to see. And, PAPH? I'm clueless."

"Penelope, we knew *PAPH hadn't registered* with you. That was our attempt to flag PAHs, polycyclic aromatic hydrocarbons, because they are naturally present in crude petroleum. Contamination with PAHs leads to delayed effects on growth and marine survival. In fires where PVC or other chlorinated matter is involved, as in the Deepwater

453 See Ch. 91 – Following The Invisible, pp. 446, 452
454 4/6/01.

Horizon fire, the amounts of PAHs are much more significant both in quantity and toxicity. They are persistent and liable to accumulate in the food chain."

"Oh, no! PAHs are in the dispersants that British Petroleum dumped in the water and they're also in the petroleum! If the chemical dispersants settle on the ocean floor where the rocks are buried and become gaseous in warm water, this could establish a two-way loop: the rocks at deep water depths having absorbed the dispersant will not only release it into the atmosphere to become toxic rain but also magnetically pull the rain back to the rocks. Both the sea and the air would be contaminated. That dream *about two yellowish-green pillows where a poisonous gas hovered over a girl's head*[455] bears that out. You taught me that sulfur and fluorine are yellow. But I forgot. What's yellowish-green?"

"Penelope, chlorine gas is yellowish-green. It is exceedingly poisonous and combines readily with nearly all other elements. It's important you understand that the use of elemental chlorine results in products and wastes, many of which are toxic to humans, wildlife and the ecosystem.

"Penelope, this oil spill has also released into your waters massive amounts of benzene which I'm particularly sensitive to for exposure to it can cause leukemia, the cancer that took my life. Benzene is of utmost concern as it can damage every system in the body."

Marie's love for humanity more than a century later hadn't faded. "Marie, I'd like to finish this PAH dream because it sheds some hope. *Someone has spilled some oily substance on the ground. I'm trying to soak it up with a nova scotia sandwich cut in half. A young man comes along to help. Soon we had a loaf of bread and that's how we were absorbing the oil.*

"Nova scotia must represent the pink salmon contaminated by the PAHs after the Exxon spill. The young man helping to soak up the oil is anonymous. I had no idea why the sandwich was cut in half unless it was referring to the "breaking of the bread" in belief of the presence of Christ. Oh, how I pray for a miracle! But we'd have to face our insufferable arrogance and hope the land would forgive us.

"*The George Bush landmark* connects to another dream where *I see narrow wedges of wood cut on angles, like wooden slivers. They represent cracks in the earth and are named George Bush.*"[456]

The George W. Bush administration, obsessed with profits from the oil and gas industry over health and safety, had the worst environmental record in American history. *Cracks in the earth* symbolize the more than 41,700 drilling permits issued during W's eight years in office.[E86]

Wooden slivers, like splinters, are puncture wounds with foreign debris in them. Wedged into the crust of the earth, a puncture wound stabs deep into Her tissue. It's the foreign object – the drill – that causes the puncture – that creates *cracks in the earth*.

455 6/22/97. See Ch. 45 – Sleeping on Pillow Lava, pp. 199–201
        Ch. 79 – No Stone Unturned, pp. 381–383
456 4/15/03.

Mother Earth has endured tens of thousands of these punctures. The 2010 wound in the Gulf of Mexico was the deepest and deadliest for they drilled 30,000 feet into her crust – her thinnest and most vulnerable part. And we wonder about the increasing frequency of Earth disasters.

Marie commiserated. "While crude oil spewed from her open wound, we observed the spreading desperation and ecological suffering. It is why we fervently warn of this toxic alphabet stew. We telegraphed you a dream, Penny that connected to PCBs. It was your dream in which angelic beings emerged."

"Angels? I know. It's the one where Pidgin English is spoken:

"I'm staying on the Nile with a friend. We take a transport to a place in the country. I see a throng of little children. They are running around ... they're from four to six years old and are purely natural. They look like angels. The people speak a form of Pidgin English – I want to say Dutch."[457]

The Nile is a river – the Mississippi is a river. Were the global crossroads of our waterways about to be irreversibly contaminated?

"Why did we take a transport, Marie? Isn't that a military vehicle used to carry soldiers?"

"Yes. And we still have depths to plumb in that dream. We'll work on it later. Now dear, have a look at this."

She produced a report in jumbo type, entitled:

"Immunologic Effects of Background Exposure to Polychlorinated Biphenyls (PCBs) and Dioxins in Dutch Preschool Children"[87]

The angelic children I saw were preschool age. Does this mean they all died? Were they now heavenly spirits cautioning and protecting the children on Earth?

"Why were the people speaking Pidgin English, Marie?"

"Penelope, Pidgin is the name given to any language created, usually spontaneously, out of a mixture of other languages, but with a sharply curtailed vocabulary. It's used as a means of communication between speakers of different tongues. You're using the same language for your readers."

"The dream language we've transmitted to you – Oneiroglypics – is our version of Pidgin."

"Marie, I'm terribly distraught over the Dutch children. What are PCBs? What do they do?"

---

457 7/17/00.

"PCBs are a mixture of toxic chemicals that collect in the body over time. We pointed this out to you in the dream about the angelic children, for the Dutch study shows that elevation in PCBs in the womb elevate the risk of certain childhood diseases. They're no longer produced in the United States, but are still found in the environment. You can be exposed to them by eating food containing PCBs, breathing air near hazardous waste sites, drinking PCB-contaminated well water and so on."

"Good grief! Could they be in seawater along with PAHs?"

"Penny, the coastal ocean areas are of utmost concern because they have been used for waste disposal since colonial times. You see, Penny, many contaminants discarded in the oceans are associated with particles. After repeated cycles of transport deposition, resuspension, and biological and chemical interactions, contaminants on particles eventually get buried in bottom sediments.

"Marie, 'bottom sediments' just washed part of a dream ashore. It warns *of an explosion. A commode is overflowing with urine and industrial plastic is covering a mess of clothing.*[458] *Urine* in Pidgin we know, translates to uranium to radioactive waste."

"Penny, you may also translate *industrial plastic* to PVC, which is believed to be the largest single source of dioxins on Earth. Dioxins are persistent very toxic chemicals and the nastiest, most toxic man-made organic chemicals, with toxicity second only to radioactive waste. As a chlorine compound, it's been blamed for a wide range of health problems, including cancer, birth deformities and nervous system disorders.

"Marie, that image of *1952 behind me* and that *terrible vibration behind my neck* was unforgettable. Do you recall what *1952* would signify?"

"News of the 1952 'killer fogs' in London reached us at Starsight. They were carriers of industrial atmospheric pollutants and among the deadliest environmental episodes in recorded history. The venomous air had fatally sickened thousands of people and helped reawaken the world to the hazards of air pollution. Once airborne, these chemicals can blow over the ocean for miles, reaching communities far from the spill."

She knew I was connecting the "killer fogs" to the 2010 oil spill in the Gulf of Mexico where the oozing monster had heartlessly been vomiting up its bile and poisoning our oceans.

"You were shaken awake with the disturbing vibration, dear Penelope, so you would alert the people – before it's too late – to the unseen poisons in the environment that aren't being monitored. Toxins are blanketing the human fabric of civilization and the mixing of chemicals is creating volatile gases. We at Terracrust and Starsight have transmitted to you X-rays of my work with radium so you are able to communicate our message."

458 6/5/99.

"So PAHs, PCBs, PVCs, radioactive waste, chlorine and self-turning eggs point-ing to a sulfurous transmutation are all accumulating in the sediments of our waters at the same time?"

"You've got the picture, Penelope. Now, keep your spirits up and please continue."

"But... but Marie, what about *Keystone and the home-baked bread?*"

A fleeting memory illuminated the reverent encounter in Chicago with Father Nick, who tried to help me with the Greek code. I was convinced that Keystone and Bread belonged together.

"Wondrous awakenings!! *Keystone restaurant – Mexican restaurant!* Restaurant means a place of restoration, Marie! Buried in each dream is a key. The Keystone Restaurant hints that the stone holds the key and the Mexican restaurant points to *the diver who unlocks the key* to deep sea exploration being in search of a hidden clue.[459] Could the *key behind a machine* be the key to the tectonic engine unlocking past geologic behavior? Might that innocuous little dream replicate the Gulf of Mexico geologically as well as the Colima Volcano in Mexico? Tell me, Marie. Tell me, please. Am I right? Even if I'm off beam geologically, I know with every fiber of my being that the oil spill in the Gulf of Mexico was to be a catalyst for change: for repair, renewal, rehabilitation. Remember the *palm tree* – Palm Sunday – palm branches – glory, triumph and resurrection."

Marie's indomitable spirit lit the galaxies. "Repetition for children, Penelope. Patience for adults." And with that, her radiant sprinkling of silvery scientific dream dust dis-solved into the great Beyond.

---

459 5/20/95. See Ch. 83 – A Hidden Key, p. 395

CHAPTER NINETY-EIGHT

WORD IN A HOLE

*One sins against the majesty of God by being
unwilling to look into nature's own works.*
Steno [88]

"God! God, how do you draw a hole," pleaded Peggymoonbeam.

The voice of the Supreme Being rang out. "Put something in it"

And so another dream had found its place in the story.

I'm told that my accountant's pants legs need to be taken in. I don't want to press them because I'm afraid they will scorch. Someone is slow. It all centers on a hole. WORD is code for the key. At the end, I see a flash of dishwater collecting in the rim of a cup. [460]

Legs needing to be taken in was a sign – not trousers but pants legs. My accountant was planted in the dream so I could "account for" or figure out the meaning of the legs. We had discussed the legs of the Avalon and Burin peninsulas in Newfoundland. Or did legs imply an even broader meaning? It seemed the geology gnomes were stressing appendages that would apply to a more extensive lay of the land. Whatever the location of the legs, Newfoundland or any other coastal region, we were being asked to "take them in"– to pay attention.

The scorching of the pants legs worried me. Was it alluding to a Scorched Earth policy where crops are burnt and land destroyed by an enemy force? Who was the real enemy? Is it a political adversary, an industrial adversary or both? Mission Lavender's dreams, so heavily laden in Geology, illustrate the simultaneous behavior of Earth's turbulence and human Terrorism. While I wrote, years before the Gulf oil spill, news coverage of our decimation of the Iraqi infrastructure flooded the globe. Retaliation seemed well within reason. Warring and fragmentation continue.

---

460 9/11/00.

Footnotes contain dream dates and references to prior pages where the dream appeared.
Endnotes contain bibliographical references, are marked with "Ɛ" in the text, and appear at the end of the book.

Had the frenzied savageries of man fused the despoliation of the Earth with that of its species?

The word "*slow*" was my only consolation. I prayed it was an augury that, whatever the warnings' intent, it would happen gradually so we could get there in time.

But, maybe "slow" meant the slow disintegration of certain radioactive materials like Marie Curie said uranium was.

The appearance of the word "*Word*" mirrored a cherished pane in a stained-glass window. Time and again, it reflected its image in this sanctified cathedral of dreams.

Trusting that *WORD* was code for the key, the image of the water-filled cup, if placed on my unexamined Branch of Theology, resonated with the *begging cup vibrating out of a brick wall*.[461] I thought back to Percival's highly spirited begging cup, the talisman that symbolized the Holy Grail. Was this source of light, of healing, of divine grace preparing to break out of the brick wall of man's egoist nature? Or, would it take its place among other Grail quests written through the ages?

The WORD-KEY cryptogram evoked worlds of meaning. Could the data compression technique called key-word encoding apply, since the information transmitted was in either dream code or computer code?

Peggymoonbeam bounced in with an explanation. "A trait common to data compression and the Dream is that the data in both electronic and dream codes is conducted through an invisible method of implantation. In the world of communications, digital data are compressed by finding repeatable patterns of binary 0s and 1s, much like the repeatable patterns found in the Dream. The more patterns found, the more data is compressed. In your world of dreams, Penelope, repeatable patterns cover the geologic history of the Earth and other topics. Because your brain is holding large amounts of scientific data, to store additional data we've had to shrink your geology file down."

"Yeah, but if it's all compressed, how can I even understand it?'

"Be patient, my little buddy. You'll learn everything you need to know about the techniques of decompression. Another analogy is that in dream and electronic compression, codes are sent from the transmitting station to the receiving station to establish the synchronization, and data is then transmitted in continuous streams. I'll give you three guesses and the first two don't count, as to where the transmitting and receiving stations originate. Tweedle dee dee … tweedle dee dum … Fa, la, la, la, la … Fa, la, la, la, la"

"Whispering willows, Peggymoon! Of course! You are the senders and I'm the receiver, but what amazes me is the continuous flow of dreams. There can be no activity for weeks, and then, suddenly they appear night after night, one after another, just as you say – in a continuous stream. So man has actually reinvented God's creation through electronics! This is so big my head is going to pop!"

---

461 12/12/96.

Simon barked his head off as the WORD-KEY invocation chimed like the ringing of Sunday morning church bells.

WORD: That which is spoken, either by a human or by God. The expressions "Word of God" or "Word of the Lord" hold a key place in biblical religion, usually denoting God's own revelation of his will and purpose.

In the Bible, the word of God is the means by which He is present and working in the world. (The color changed again to green after the word "God." The last time it changed to green was in text about radioactivity.)

I'd been baffled by a dream *in which I give an architect a stainless steel picture frame with his name on it. A game of questions and answers follows where people are waiting for me to play. The first clue has to do with the word "logo(s)." I see a metal structure around the word. It means I have the clues.*[462]

I couldn't understand why this particular architect was in the dream, for in waking life he had been a trusted friend who later had inexplicably treated me as an enemy. He had violated our friendship with deceitful acts that placed me in great physical danger, harming me emotionally and financially. Why would this architect, whom I have such negative memories of, be placed in a dream that frames him and imparts a clue of logos?

Peggymoonbeam swooped down with an answer. "Penelope, dreams carry us through different dimensions. The first dimension is the personal realm where we're confronted with our struggles. When we're able to transcend the wounds inflicted on us by others, we can enter the transpersonal realm of dreaming. It no longer matters what your intolerant friend did, for you have risen above it. In this transpersonal, more cosmic dimension, if you read Luke, you are now able to 'love your enemies, do good to those who hate you, bless those who curse you, pray for those who mistreat you.'[89] You will see as we travel on that the metaphor of architect connotes a much higher purpose and you may even catch a glimmer of a clue about the Greek code."

Hmm. "Thanks, Peggymoonbeam. It's difficult to imagine that I'm not still angry at that so-called friend, but I'll take your word for it."

As I traveled on, metal, with all its nickel and copper references continually cropped up as the symbol for uranium. Uranium would be the metal frame but what photograph, what event, what story would it frame? At the moment, it seemed to be all over the map.

"Penelope," continued Peggymoonbeam, "logos is Greek and means the same as word. I remind you of the passage in John 1:1: 'In the beginning was the Word and the Word was with God and the Word was God.'"

"That is truly awesome! I hadn't put the two together, but the dream did!"

"Yes, Penelope. Logos is a most sacred sound. In ancient and especially in medieval philosophy and theology, it is the divine reason that acts as the ordering principle of the

---

462 6/1/96.

universe. Not only that, my little buddy. Tu-whit is here on Steno's behalf with a dazzling connection."

The piercing eyes of Tu-whit loomed in, as he hooted:

ÕÕ   "Geology (from Greek γη- [ge-, "the Earth"] and λογος [logos, "word," "reason"] is the science and study of the solid matter of the Earth, its composition, structure, physical properties, history and the processes that shape it."

"The Earth!" I stood agape. The perfection was breathtaking.

A stroll through the gardens of the cosmic dream nursery resonated with the WORD dream where a *flash of dishwater was collecting in the rim of a cup.*[463]

Peggymoonbeam hovered. "Penelope, remember Steno's Krakatoa lesson on maars and phreatic explosions. Most maars have low rims and are often filled with water."

Oh Wow! Dish-water! Dishes are plates! That's water around tectonic plates. That means they're oceanic! I must be on the right track because the message keeps repeating! This *dishwater collecting in the rim of a cup* dream symbolized the filling up of a volcanic crater with seawater – the crater – the maar portrayed earlier by my old friend, Pauline Maher.

A great scattering of silvery sparkling scientific particles had filled the air. The word "dishwater" sped me to acid rain where *Pauline Maher* sparked the suspicion that *a pipeline could be backed into the wall of a crater in a faulted area. Sissy Spacek,* the Coal Miner's Daughter, *asked me for an anti-acid pill.*

Spacek and Maher: Space – Acid Rain – Maar, a volcanic crater.

There are volcanic craters all over the world – even on the moon. Why would Word, as in the Word was God, be associated with this particular crater? The riddle resounded – *WORD is code for the key.* Another key? But the key to what?

I remembered Steno's lessons on craters. I'd learned that a crater is formed by the explosion of a bomb or a meteorite impact or the collapse of a volcanic dome. Sissy Spacek was telling us in dream code that we must combat the acid. Was this a key to the past – or the future – or both?

If *WORD is code for key*, I'd have to figure out the story being told within the metal frame.

The ever-present Truth, courier of threats and favors alike, would slowly reveal its purpose. I continued on my walk with Spirit in the shadows of the unknown.

---

463 9/11/00.

Craters and holes were popping up all over the place. Maybe these holes are full of ancient carboniferous rocks! And maybe the rocks are mixing with oil and gas! Add to that, volcanic gases and we've got a pretty smelly picture. We cannot control the substances of Nature but we must contain those that are Man-made.

Could one of these holes be the hole in the earth left by the explosion that sank the oil drilling rig in the Gulf of Mexico in 2010?

As I moseyed along the winding path with my ever changing, yet constantly present group of spiritual compadres, Lord Galen appeared with his Timelessness Glasses, eager to share his venerable wisdom on the art of healing.

"You may remember, Penelope dear, that it was my custom to use dreams to diagnose illness. I took as my standard the opinion held by the most skilful and wisest physicians and the best philosophers of the past, 'The art of healing was originally invented and discovered by the logos in conjunction with experience. And today also it can only be practiced excellently and done well by one who employs both of these methods,' as I wrote in Three Treatises On The Nature Of Science.

"I say this still."

"Yes, and Doc Steno is a healer too. He was a physician and a scientist but now I think his focus is on healing the Earth."

Steno was within earshot. "Right you are, Penelope. Actually my research in anatomy aroused my interest in geology. So what is in that busy mind today?"

"Doc, dreams are drawing me to Vancouver much the same as I was drawn to Newfoundland."

"Tell me, Clueso, what is it that draws you?"

"Well, one day, I was reading a book called Volcanoes of North America and came to a picture of the Black Tusk volcano in the Garibaldi Lake region in Vancouver. It was just an ordinary picture, but when I saw it, my heart nearly stopped, for this dream drawing matched to a tee the picture of the Black Tusk volcano in the book, except – you guessed it! It was upside down!

I rushed out to get a map of Vancouver. When I began to study it, I found a whole string of names on the map that matched other pieces of my dreams. Then I saw a place called Alert Bay! The surge of adrenaline was indescribable for it connected, in all certainty, to a dream where Peggymoonbeam kept repeating *Success Wake Lake*.[464] I'd been rocketed right out of dreamland bound for destination Vancouver."

"This is groundbreaking news, Clueso! I was wondering when you'd 'wake up' to our Vancouver missives – ha, ha – no pun intended. I must say, it does my soul good to know you've grasped our upside-down phenomenon. There is much study to be done there. In

---

464 2/24/99.

any event, your wish to go to Vancouver is my command, my fellow explorer, so we'll be off on our next venture soon as you awaken Simon and feed him a Sunshine biscuit. And remember to give Percival some milk so that we may be on our way."

"But, Dr. Steno. Simon is still sniffing around. I think he's on the trail of something. Maybe we should leave him and Percival here since Labrador is his turf and fetch them on our way back."

"Good idea, Penelope. They'll have a field day. And don't worry, because we have chosen a new companion for you."

Percival was washing his face with his front paws as though preparing to stalk his prey. He was smart enough to know that with all those treats in store, his quarry was nearby. I felt comfortable leaving them there. They'd get plenty of exercise and fresh air and it was unlikely they'd be bored or lonely.

From the corner of my eye, I saw Simon dragging around a *dirty sock.*

"Now come along. Your next trip will again be by day, and we'll soon be meeting a specially selected Earth guide experienced in aviation and excavation. One of her assignments is to escort you through Vancouver. Stay alert, Penelope. Keep your eyes and ears open for she will appear quite unexpectedly."

"Gee, Doc, you say aviation. Is it someone who navigates? And why excavation? I know we mine our dreams. Is that what you mean?"

"Sometimes you ask too many questions, my pet. Just be patient and you will learn everything you need to know."

Geesh! I wish they'd stop saying that!

"Now fetch your knitting basket, Penny, and let's be on our way."

Winding up my silver thread, I asked, "Are we off to see the Wizard, Dr. Steno?"

"We are the Wizard, Penelope."

CHAPTER NINETY-NINE

VANCOUVER UNDERCOVER

The most beautiful thing we can experience is
the mysterious. It is the source of all true art
and science.

Albert Einstein

It was Fall of 1999 when a high school friend from California, who I'd not seen for decades, visited New York and invited me to dinner. While I was tempted to see my old classmate, I declined because of my unwavering commitment to this work. There didn't seem to be enough time no matter how much I put in. It was becoming clearer by the day that once normal aspects of life had become extravagant treats.

This dream path of abstraction was a paradox, so solid was its intention. The unshaped frames of nighttime celluloid, mysteriously poured in concrete, had little tolerance for divergence of any kind. However, my shepherd, who ardently whispered "critical focus" at the first sign of distraction, was absent this day – an omen in its own right.

My high school friend persisted in her desire to set a date so I stepped off the straight and narrow for an evening and invited her over for cocktails. She asked if she could bring a friend from California with her, someone I'd never met. I wasn't in the mood for socializing but I halfheartedly agreed. "Well … OK, bring her along."

On greeting them, I was mesmerized by the radiant pool of light encircling the stranger. Her name in life is Beverly. In this story, she would eventually become Smilingshadow, though on occasion, I call her Shadow.

With nothing to bind the new alliance but a dinner at a chic New York restaurant, Beverly invited me on a trip to Egypt – a curious invitation from someone I'd just met. I politely declined at first, but the pull toward Egypt was magnetic and on another level I knew that my decision was tentative. While showering the next morning, many dream clues of Egyptian origin seemed to be washing over me. I sensed Beverly had been recruited; that perhaps she was the Earth guide Steno had spoken of. I called her and asked if the offer still stood. That was the beginning of what would be a blossoming

---

Footnotes contain dream dates and references to prior pages where the dream appeared.
Endnotes contain bibliographical references, are marked with "ε" in the text, and appear at the end of the book.

friendship with miles of untold adventure ahead. Our trip to Egypt had unearthed the star-bound dream of *the three men and one woman of stone*[465] illuminating my imaginings with the light of the ages and pointing the way to deeper excavation. Lacking any conscious awareness, at that time, of a much larger plan, Egypt set the stage for the next adventure.

Every dream-corroborated discovery sparkled with excitement whether revealed in the flesh, as in Egypt and Newfoundland or in the imagination, as in Labrador. Egypt with its hieroglyphics had led me to oneiromantics, the language of the dream. I reflected on the sound and light show at Luxor and how it drew me to ancient Thebes and stories of the great pharaohs. As I sat among the ruins, my dream of *a lamp in the shape of an arc*[466] came to life in a mysteriously lighted arc suspended over the temple – an unforgettable sight. The knowledge gained in Egypt was hauntingly mystical, awakening the soul to the lives and generations of the ancients.

Whether adventuring in mind or in matter, in body or in soul, these interconnected missions stirred in me the same sense of awe moving me toward another physical exploration, this time to search out a string of tiny communities on the Island of Vancouver. What I did not know at the time was that remarkable findings randomly encircle us with every breath we take, in all of our physical surroundings.

Beverly was born in a small gold mining town in Northern Canada. After university, she satisfied her craving for knowledge by taking to the skies as a flight attendant for much of her life, sharing with her daughters the wonders of the world. With years of exotic travel complementing her romantic nature, her knowledge of human cultures, behaviors and origins were complemented by a natural propensity for archaeology. Steno's clues about her experience in aviation and excavation rang true. Apt that she was a gold miner's daughter for, as it turned out, not only was she an excavator of Egyptian artifacts, in our dream adventure she would act as Chief of Remote Sensing in Vancouver's mining operations. The dazzling light surrounding her when we first met followed her like a golden nimbus. Love and joy were her ready companions. Where you found one, you'd find the other.

A year after we visited Luxor, plans were on the drafting table for an expedition to Vancouver Island, where clouds of dream dust had settled and dream nuggets waited to be mined. Would it be anything like my visit with Karensurefoot to Newfoundland or was expectation a dangerous thing in this world? It was that uncertainty thing again. I learned early on that Beverly was like a scent hound, hunting by scent rather than sight, although her visual capacity was highly developed as well. Her probing questions about what to look for were a challenge. It was hard to describe exactly what that might be but I would say, "When we see it, we'll know." "But what is 'it'?" she'd insist. I found that

465 11/25/98. See Prologue.
466 8/10/99. See Ch. 38 – Glyphs, p. 167

she could follow a scent trail for very long distances across boundaries, up mountainsides and even over bodies of water.

I had shared with her some simple clues like the lavender/yellow and yellow/orange themes, the picket fence and fragments from a few dreams that I felt might materialize. Having a keen sense of excavation she was well suited for the job, hungry for the chase and ready to stake out whatever the scene called for. She cast her shadow in two ways: she shed light on the unseen and in the secret, sometimes precarious world of under-cover work, she provided cover and protection. The detective in her told me the name Smilingshadow was perfect. So in September of 2000, we packed our satchels full of dream scribbles, high spirits and derring-do and launched the beginning of what would come to be the Vancouver expedition.

Day One: Vancouver City

We stayed overnight dining leisurely at a charming restaurant in a town square in old Vancouver. The main attraction in the historic square was centered around an old grand-father steam clock that chimed, steamed and played music on the hour. The perception of an hour stretched back to an era when time was measured in grains of sand – much like the Dream that trickles through the bottleneck of the unconscious.

Day Two: Horseshoe Bay and Port McNeill

The next morning, while Smilingshadow and I sat in the Second Narrows ferry line for two hours with nuts and carrots our only sustenance. While waiting to drive over the bridge connecting the city of Vancouver to the Horseshoe Bay Ferry, I noticed that the directional markers on the pavement were the same configuration as images I'd drawn in a dream. Hair-trigger recognition flashed! I let out a scream!

I see 5 large red vehicles vertically parked. I imagine them coming down with force. I had ini-tially written "the force," then crossed out the word "the." The vehicles are sticking straight up out of the ground. I think "that must be the way they park." Part of the dream involves taking a very long walk with mother — mother being the recognized symbol for Mother Earth.[467]

When I turned the dream drawing around, the markers not only matched the *red vehicles vertically parked* but were the shape of Peggymoonbeam's picket fence – upside down. Steno surely had it right about similar things having different meanings! Markers on rocks – markers on the pavement. I wondered if Peggymoonbeam had something to do with *the force* of the parked vehicles.

The Horseshoe Ferry sparked recollection of a dream of a *smiling horse on a ferry*. When I get to the other side, I meet *the mechanic* who symbolized the United Way.

---

467 7/13/00.

This *ferry* dream connected to another dream where *I move a silver horseshoe in an upside-down Vee position inside the gate of Peggymoonbeam's house.*[468] My first reaction was that the Vee also symbolized a coming together and because it was pointing upward, perhaps it was pointing to a union between Heaven and Earth. Peggymoonbeam had passed over five months earlier. One of her favorite earthly pastimes was putting people together. Her collaborative desires in Heaven seemed to have extended to a much larger fraternity.

Finally, we were on the Horseshoe Bay Ferry taking in the rocky coastline. The lapping waves and raucous cries of gulls lulled us into that delicious half sleep that whispers, "All is right with the world."

The crossing from Horseshoe Bay to Port McNeill would draw us to the shores of the unknown. Anticipation spilled over as I tried to conjure up what might lay in wait for us at Alert Bay. We'd have to take another ferry to get there. We were still a day away and that seemed an eternity.

Peggymoonbeam's upside-down *picket fence*, symbolic of *all of mankind working together* – the United Way *mechanic on the other side* – the *upside-down Vee-shaped horseshoe* placed inside the pearly gates joined together to form a perfect trinity: Synergy – Science – Spirit.

I continued to puzzle over the mechanic. "Smilingshadow, I've got to tell you about the *ferry dream.*"

"Please do." I knew she hadn't a clue.

"Well, the dream is centered on a *large white ship,* which I think symbolizes the Titanic. *Then, I have to take a shuttle or ferry to get across somewhere. A small horse is in the front of the ferry. You cannot see the girl who is running the ferry.*

When I get to the other side, I look around to say good-bye but the ferry driver isn't there. I say good-bye to the horse, who appears so human, he smiles. There, on the other side, I meet a friend who is a mechanic.[469]

"Smilingshadow. Do you think the anonymous mechanic will come out of hiding once we cross over to Horseshoe Bay?

"I don't know, Penelope. I think of a mechanic as a worker who repairs things and from the shape the world is in, there's no end to what needs repair."

Uncertainty, that second voice so determined to push the first one aside would momentarily invade my thoughts. What if this was a wild goose chase? You never could tell. I chased that little bully away and took to imagining what elements of chance might cross our path. We relaxed on the ferry, inhaling the crystal pure air of the Pacific Northwest as we headed for brand new lands and undiscovered realms.

---

468 10/12/95.
469 12/5/97. See Ch. 21 – Half Circle – Full Star – Clog, pp. 95-96

We disembarked at Port McNeill, the logging center of North Vancouver Island, and wound our way through its hills and valleys in search of the inn we had booked. Behind an eight-foot high fortress of shrubbery, we found the Mediterranean style hideaway that was Broughton Beach Manor.

After a simple dinner at a local restaurant, we returned to the quaint bed and breakfast and fell into the arms of sleep.

The next morning we enjoyed breakfasting at the inn with fellow travelers, all Canadians. Being the only visitors from the United States, they found it curious that I hailed from the East Coast and Smilingshadow from the West Coast and wondered why we were going to Alert Bay, a little-known village to most Americans.

I self-consciously responded. "Oh, we're just taking in the sights," fantasizing that one day we'd be released from our burden of concealment and able to share the real reason for our journey.

It was time to catch the ferry for our long-awaited visit to Alert Bay, hoping to track the fingerprints of Peggymoonbeam.

CHAPTER ONE HUNDRED

AWAKE AND AWARE IN ALERT BAY

Day Three: Alert Bay

The presence of First Nation culture and history in the busy harbor town left a lasting impression. Formerly used as a burial ground by the 'Namgis People, Alert Bay was first settled by Europeans in 1870. Known as home of the Killer Whale, it lies cradled in the arms of Cormorant Island, just off the Northeast corner of Vancouver Island in the beautiful Inside Passage of British Columbia.

We leisurely strolled down the main street of the village when we came upon an array of 'Namgis First Nation totem poles near which stood a prominent No Trespassing sign bearing the maxim, "The poles can be easily viewed from the roadside."

At the century-old 'Namgis Burial Grounds, memorial totem poles mark some of the graves, commemorating deceased members of the Kwakwaka'wakw Tribes. Colorful figures on the totems depict family crests. Some families claim as a crest the Thunderbird, which descended from the sky, took off his regalia and became their human ancestor. I flashed back to a dream about a totem pole, but couldn't call up the details. Alert Bay boasts the tallest totem pole in the world in another part of the village. We planned to see it before we left, but for now, we'd poke around and see what cards lady destiny held for us.

We slowly drove along Front Street passing by Christ Church. A familiar gravitational pull drew me in. The lens of the dream kaleidoscope had reflected the colored cut-glass panes of churches in Newfoundland. The first had been the Anglican Church of St. Luke's in Placentia, where four-year old Kitty was buried which mysteriously tied to the dream directive, *"report to Kit 4391 or 4931."* Under the Bethany Church in St. Lawrence, the dire dream warning still smoldered: *the masses will be exterminated.*

Now, as we stood in front of the historical Anglican church founded in Alert Bay in 1879, I was mystified as to the striking role that churches were playing in my dreaming-waking experience. I'm neither a member of the Christian faith nor particularly religious, yet the pull persisted and it was intense. The message silently held facets of a design awaiting completion. The Logos dream came floating back. *Word was code for key.* Like a

---

Footnotes contain dream dates and references to prior pages where the dream appeared.

Endnotes contain bibliographical references, are marked with "Ɛ" in the text, and appear at the end of the book.

kite on a string, whether sleeping or waking, the winds of the Mission carried me toward faith. Was this pointing to the key? With so many tangible keys, it was hard to tell. Why the proliferation of church-inspired symbols in two different locales – first Newfoundland and now Vancouver?

The first signs of the material world waiting to be noticed in Alert Bay were the lavender doors and yellow trim of the church. "Nah," I said to myself. "I'm being silly. This is ridiculous." Still, I couldn't help but realize that once again lavender and yellow appeared as a waking twosome.

In Newfoundland, the two colors had manifested on objects individually. Now they were together. We continued driving at a snail's pace when suddenly Smilingshadow exclaimed, "There's a picket fence, Penelope. It's lavender!" We came to a full stop. The house that belonged to the lavender picket fence was painted yellow. Caught off guard, I was completely baffled by these recurrent stranger-than-fiction markers. The picket fence represented Peggymoonbeam and the completion of the work; lavender was lava under and yellow was sulfur. The phenomenon of color-coding was following us.

How strange to be led in this way but, on reflection, it was the only way, for I hadn't the background with which to plan field trips or the tools with which to quantify and analyze the data.

Randomly driving along a straight road, we first turned right and out of the corner of my eye, I spotted a cemetery nestled between two roads. I asked Smilingshadow to go back; I had noticed a small purple cross.

It must have summoned me for it was quite a distance away, and we were driving at a good clip. We parked the car and walked into the cemetery. When we got closer to the cross which was about a foot and a half high, I noticed a flower on the reverse side of the cross – a yellow flower that looked like a *Hibiscus*, a dream symbol in cold storage.

In one of several Hibiscus dreams, *Peggymoonbeam and I were on the other side. We went up to the roof where there was a beautiful walled-in garden with very exotic flowers. One was like a Hibiscus that had a velvety texture. They had been there quite a while.*[470] I imagined an Elysian Fields roof garden in Peggymoonbeam's green pastures, where blessed souls are enveloped in perpetual light surrounded by grass and trees and exotic flowers.

Back with the yellow Hibiscus in the cemetery, I realized the combination was again purple and yellow. It was our third such sighting within a few hours. How an invisible substance like the colors of a dream could manifest in the same colors visibly painted on tangible objects like a church, a house, a cross, in a place I never knew existed was incomprehensible. Now nature was showing her hand: a yellow flower and a purple cross. Coincidence? I don't think so, but there was no explanation at that point; the only thing I was sure of was that we were in the right place. I'm not a betting person but three sequential materializations, I think, beat the odds.

---

470 11/15/97.

It was as though someone had taken two giant-sized drums of paint; one lavender, the other yellow, and poured them over the Newfoundland landscape wherever a dream had been planted that needed a color. As time passed and the dreams took root, this anonymous painter skillfully poured this dream-formulated mixture over Vancouver Island as well. But the systematic question of influence was unsettled. Did the dreams direct me to the region or did the region direct my dreams? Maybe it was both. Maybe it was neither.

Whatever it was, I breathlessly skipped back to the car wanting to do every childhood acrobatic I had ever learned. I was truly ready to jump the moon with the excitement of connection that bubbles up when trust has eclipsed all of our ordinary senses.

"This is the most magical experience I've ever had, Shadow! It just makes me want to fly! No one will ever believe this! It is beyond miraculous that we wound up here!"

Shadow answered, "You should see yourself, Sparkle. You are lit up like a Christmas tree!" From then on, she occasionally called me Sparkle Plenty but usually it was just plain Sparkle.

"Excuse me, Shadow, but I'm gonna zone out for a while as I need a little quiet time for some mental detective work and I'm hoping for some help from my guides."

"I don't know how you keep it all straight, Sparkle, or how your guides know when you need help, but I respect your privacy. I'll keep driving. Just let me know when to stop."

"Thanks, Sparkle. If you could be on the lookout for porches, that would be great, especially back porches."

"Back porches? "Shadow squealed with laughter. "I think you're losing it, Sparkle."

CHAPTER ONE HUNDRED ONE

BACK PORCHES

We left the cemetery and Smilingshadow continued straight instead of going back to where we'd turned right. As we wound our way through the little streets up in the hills, I knew our mission of the moment would be dedicated to porches. A few weeks earlier, a dream involving porches had transmitted a sobering message. Upon waking, I was awed by its detail and complexity.

I'm with a scientist friend and want to talk about volcanoes and earthquakes. Then I'm in the car with him driving around when I see a map designating clusters of people living in the hills. The dream spun a revelation. *If they find the inhabitants, they can find the earthquakes.*

The scientist is looking for furniture and junk on the <u>back</u> porch of an architect's apartment. I remind him that he told me the world would end. I know where the fault line is. I comment that earthquake sites are great resources for junk. I can't tell if I closed the sliding glass door in the <u>back</u>. The key is dominant. I let us <u>back</u> in. The scientist goes <u>back</u> to the architect's apartment. He goes <u>back</u> to the porch, a small room with messy clothes, a chair, a wooden floor. It is ramshackle.[471]

I had quickly mined two nuggets from this dream.

The first nugget: *If they find the inhabitants, they can find the earthquakes.* Was this message telling us that people make earthquakes?

The second nugget: *Earthquake sites are great resources for junk.*

Junk, having assumed an identity as waste, helped the message synthesize.

It was looking like "people make waste."

Are we the people, Earth's inhabitants, contributing to her vulnerability by turning her into a garbage dump, by jabbing her, drilling holes in her, poking pipes in her so she runs from cold to hot to cold and has no choice but to contract and expand more than she ever did before our fetishes like oil, gas, minerals and metals wore her down. Are we making her rupture and shift and slide all over the place until she's in so much pain, she has to vomit up her rocks and fires and gases and weep giant tsunamis and storms of tears because she just can't take anymore? We'd be red-hot piping furious and irreparably

---

471 8/31/00.

Footnotes contain dream dates and references to prior pages where the dream appeared.

Endnotes contain bibliographical references, are marked with "Ɛ" in the text, and appear at the end of the book.

heartbroken if foul toxins were inflicted on us with the same wilfull disregard. Well, they are. But we haven't seen their full ravages yet.

There was more to the dream. Aware that it was a run-on dream, I did not condense it, for the fifth iteration of the word "back" was conveying that "in back" was a phrase to remember.

As my journey of discovery took on deeper nuances, I would learn more about various types of cryptography, including the previously mentioned hidden writing known as steganography, once used for secret communication by priests. In disguising writing, every fifth word in a text became part of the message. While the word "back" didn't quite meet the "every fifth word" code, it did repeat five times.

Astonishingly, the dream images of *the scientist looking for furniture and junk on a porch* had played out. The porches of Alert Bay, typical of shanty living, absolutely fit the description *ramshackle.* True to the dream, there were *clusters of people living in the hilly* back roads of this tiny island. Junk symbolized waste, specifically radioactive waste. That was clear.

I recalled the dream and circled five references to "back." Looking for a hidden message, I came up empty. What did it all mean? Trying to absorb terabytes of information was not only challenging, it was exhausting. Small wonder they're compressing it. They must know I'm running out of storage space. What's more, information overload burns calories and induces sleep. I was stifling my yawns so Steno wouldn't notice. He could get a little touchy now and again and if I've learned nothing else, I've learned not to test the patience of a saint. One stern word from him was like being sent to the edge of a black hole.

"Excuse me, Penelope. I see you're deep in thought about back porches, but this dream calls for a very critical lesson on island arcs. Though I admit the subject matter is somewhat dry, please do try to refrain from yawning. It is imperative that you concentrate. Now, are we ready?"

I swallowed a yawn. "Yep. I'm all ears, Doc."

"An island arc is a curved belt of volcanic islands lying above a subduction zone."

"Subduction zone! Well, I'll be! The first time I typed S U B D U C T I O N, the letters separated all by themselves. Then, a teeny word which I could barely read, "zone" got attached to the word **"subduction."** How did it get there, Doc? It was like magic!"

Doc could barely contain his mirth but wouldn't tell. I was beginning to think he had a split personality; one moment, a scholar, the next a sprite.

"Clueso, a subduction zone is an area on the earth's crust where two plates are moving together and one plate is forced to dive below the other. Think of your dream sighting of the *two diamond-shaped images, one above the other – the descending one broken.*[472] This is

472 6/22/97. See Ch. 50 – The Slip, p. 223

an oceanic-oceanic convergence. Such a convergence often results in the formation of an island arc system."

Wonder of wonders! I also dreamt of *a Bible* and *an arc made of very black stone that looked like an upside-down V.*[473] That must be V for volcano! *Bright sun was coming through the arc with a lighthouse in front of it.* Were Steno and Galen, couriers of theology and light, directing me to island arcs?

Tues. 12/27/94 - Morocco

I saw an opened book. In the center were 2 white pages. They were the bible.

THE BIBLE

Right before awaking, I saw - looking through a large stone opening (like an arc), a lighthouse to the left and bright sun coming through the center

VERY BLACK STONE

I CAN SEE LIGHT

Island arcs – curved belts – volcanic islands – subduction zones. Struggling to understand this strange language with all its moving pieces, I listened attentively. Even though it pretty much sounded like Greek to me, the connections were awesome. "Then, Doc, island arcs must have something to do with plate tectonics."

"Indeed they do, Penelope. I know this must seem like gibberish to you, but you have your hand-drawn pictures of your dreams and I have faith that you'll unravel the puzzle, if you just bear with me.

"Let me first say that an island arc is a landmass formed by plate tectonics. You see, when one plate descends beneath another, chains of active volcanoes develop above the

---

473 12/27/94.

descending slab as magma rises from under the plate. If the activity continues, the volcano may grow tall enough to breech the surface of the ocean creating an island.

"This aligns with your concerns about undersea volcanoes. Stress in and behind an island arc often causes the arc system to move toward the incoming plate. You're already acquainted with seafloor spreading where the ocean floor spreads away as plates move apart from each other.

This process is called back-arc seafloor spreading. In fact, a back-arc basin is the region between an island arc and the continental mainland. So there you have it, Penelope.

"Back-arc spreading activity actually inspired your dream of the *back porch of the architect's apartment.*"

"Back porch! Wait a minute, Doc. I'm onto something! I bet the five mentions of the word "back" in that dream were pointing us to back-arc spreading in the past. You know, back, as in behind us. Remember, the dream said, *'I know where the fault line is. I comment that earthquake sites are great resources for junk. I can't tell if I closed the sliding glass door in the <u>back</u>. The key is dominant.'"*

I think the key signals the past in some way, like the *diver who unlocked the key to the geologic past.*"[474] And that led to the Colima volcano in Mexico!"

"Excellent, Clueso. Excellent. Fine work, lass. Results from geophysical studies suggest that spreading in back-arc basins is episodic. There are gaps of several million years between the cessation of spreading in one back-arc basin and initiation of the next."[E90]

It was mind-boggling to think that geological episodes from millions of years ago swept into my dreams. Not only did I not know geology. My memory was at best, average. Weariness transformed to eye-opening bursts of perception. Immediately following the back-arc revelation, another sprang forth. This one was dropped from the Oneiroball.

I see *a headless woman in a reclining chair. She is wearing white terry cloth that has many folds. A photographic close up of the folds focuses on the graceful arch of her back.*"[475]

Hocus Pocus, Alakazam! Terry cloth is terra for earth, the folds are the folding of rocks and the arch of her back matches a back-arc basin — between an island arc and the mainland!

Island arc! Island arc! I was nearly chanting the paired words when the stellar boom box belted out architect dreams parsing a shared language of architectonics. Island arcs ... arch i tect ... arch i tectonics ... the systemization of knowledge ... architecture of the Earth ... architecture of the dream ... architecture of the Universe ... the art of forms in space.

Architect – island arcs – plate tectonics. Gosh. If I played the scribes' game of geologic scrabble and took the words Architects and Island Arc Systems, and if I paired arcs with tectonics, what would remain but Island Systems. Or more specifically, plates

---

474 5/20/95. See Ch. 83 – A Hidden Key, pp. 395–98
475 12/15/98.

in Island Arc Systems. Hmm … Vancouver Island might fit. So might the province of Newfoundland/Labrador. They're all on the North American plate.

Steno bounced in. "Nice wordplay, Clueso. Island arc systems exist throughout the world. For example, Vancouver Island shares a history with the Queen Charlotte Fault which is part of the Aleutian Trench – an island arc system. Also, Krakatoa in the Sunda Strait is part of that Indonesian system."

Although Steno didn't acknowledge Newfoundland/Labrador as an island arc, I'd take a chance and follow my gut.

When dream clues incubated, they hatched in a way that actually made sense. The *back porch of an arch - i - tect's apartment* symbolized back-arc spreading in an island arc formed by plate tectonics. Remembering that lava is molten glass, the *sliding glass door in the back* represented a sliding plate in a back-arc basin in a lava field.

The EARTHQUAKE – JUNK dream develops. *As I'm preparing to leave, a man comes with a very deep pizza pie box and puts it on top of the oven. As I'm double locking the place, I see an African man running out of the woods all out of breath. He is a neighbor going into an adjacent apartment. I am thinking of Burin – St. Lawrence – the Bethany Church in Newfoundland. I want to tell the scientist I'm worried. I want officials to look for the fault line.*[476]

It is nothing short of miraculous that Africa slid into this dream.

I hurriedly began my dissection in an attempt to ferret out the Africa clue.

I am *double-locking* the place. Hmm. Double-locking is securing something twice, putting it in place. Double was pointing to a duplicate of some sort. Could the first lock be Newfoundland and the second Africa? There must be an ancient signature undercover though because one of Tu-whit's missives said that a half a billion years ago Newfoundland's eastern region was still attached to the African continent.[477]

Steno, leapfrogging through the mist of sparkling scientific dream dust, announced, "My dear curious Clueso. You are a breath away from a vitally important piece of the puzzle!

"Think of Pangaea and how 225 million years ago the forces in the Earth that brought the continents together slowly began to pull them apart. Well, my inquiring apprentice, Tu-whit has fetched something from his archives to add to that."

At the mention of his name, the prodigious owl hooted in, wings a flappin' and eyes brighter than saucers, picking up from where Steno left off:

---

476 8/31/00.
477 See Ch. 85 –Under My Hat, pp. 411–12

ÕÕ "'In the process, a remarkable thing happened. A small bit of Africa got left behind! When you stand on Signal Hill in St, John's, you are standing on rocks that are identical to ones in the country of Morocco in north Africa!'"[Ɛ91]

My thoughts traveled back to Newfoundland's Cape Chapeau Rouge which manifested the dream of the *woman under the red hat*. In an earlier dream, Cape Chapeau Rouge was also represented, meshing with *sliding marabou – marabou* depicting the African stork. *The sliding marabou was under a red hat*.[478] Red hat was the link.

That must mean an old piece of Africa is sliding under Cape Chapeau Rouge and possibly even Vancouver Island!

The *architect's back porch* – back-arc spreading zone … *pizza pie* – piezoelectricity … *oven* – earthquake/volcano … *the African man* – the African plate? Why was the *African man running out of the woods?* And what are the woods? Are they the backwoods? The outback as in Australia? Was he coming out of hiding and why? He was a *neighbor going to an adjacent apartment.* What is – or was – adjacent to Africa?

"Penelope!" exclaimed Steno, "It's time we remind you. Both the African plate and the Indo-Australian plate are in zones of spreading, where plates are moving apart."[479]

Woop Woop![Ɛ92] The outback must mean back woods! That would represent Australia. The Indo-Australia plate must be *"neighboring"* the African plate. I really grasp continental drift now because my dreams know the truth and have led me to the knowledge that the continents are drifting further apart. It was not only a thing of the past; it's happening now in the twenty-first century. Who said rocks don't have memory!

So that's what all the sliding around was about! But how does that impact the North American plate?

No answer. My telegrapher had spun out of zone.

The repetitious imagery of porches was deeply imprinted as though an indelible seed had been planted and so there were Smilingshadow and I driving around Alert Bay looking for porches. We came to the end of the road, winding around to the front of the houses we had just seen the backs of. Having scouted all the back porches on this stretch of road and visually sifted through junk piles of domestic clutter, we came upon a broken down front porch where I spotted a purple chair. How odd! In an upside-down world, in the language of opposites, that this was the reverse of a back porch. I became incoherent burbling, gurgling, stuttering and stammering at what was before my seeing eyes.

"Stop! Stop! STOP! Shadow. I see a purple chair!"

It's hard to explain in any rational way, but I knew that stopping there was mandatory.

---

478 6/22/96, 3/12/99. See Ch 85 – Under My Hat, pp. 410–11
479 See Ch.49 – Wrapped Up Like A Mummy, p. 215

On top of the purple plastic child-sized chair was a planter and on top of that was something that looked like a toy, its bottom yellow and top orange. The planter was a plastic bowl placed between the chair and the toy. There were dead flowers and greens in it; bear grass was sticking straight out from the bowl. Left-brained observers, would likely say, "So what? It's a junk heap on a porch," but I promise, this dream-rattling assemblage contained potential that synthesized the nonphysical with the physical in the most unpredictably humdrum setting, but with the most profound implications.

This grab bag collage harmlessly resting on someone's dilapidated porch in Alert Bay touched the core of my being, for I knew it embodied the purpose of the Mission to Vancouver Island. I was unable to articulate my swirling rings of thought, the gathering of dream symbols and their explicated existence that were now made physical in this secluded fishing community.

I was bashful about going up to a stranger's house to take a picture of their children's toy on a chair, but I simply had to have that picture. I haltingly asked Smilingshadow if she would mind taking a picture of the porch. Trooper that she is, she stepped right up to the bowl.

Smilingshadow was standing at the side of the porch snapping pictures a mile a minute when the owner of the house appeared. Smilingshadow turned a lovely shade of scarlet but didn't flinch. Straight faced, she greeted the suspicious woman. "Oh, hello. I'm putting together something in art class for my students and the composition of the elements on your little chair just caught my eye. I thought how good it would be to have pictures of it." She paused. "I know you must think I'm crazy, but it'll only take a minute."

The Alert Bay housewife grinned at Smilingshadow as though she had just whizzed in from Mars, shrugged her shoulders and quickly slipped back inside the house.

I sat in the car on pins and needles, waiting for Smilingshadow to get back in.

I called out, "What's the thing on top? Is it a toy?"

Her answer was solemn. "It's a toy fire hydrant."

In a millisecond, every fiber of my being reaffirmed this was not a coincidence. Instant memory of the fire hydrants in the village of Lawn sparked connections to our search for craters in villages in Newfoundland and Labrador. Neural nets crackled, ejecting flashes of lavender – lava under. It happened involuntarily. I didn't have to think about it.

The trophy collage was undeniably a piece of art, cosmic art displaying the fragmentation of dream elements materializing in one place. If I had commissioned a set designer to capture the interconnectivity of the Dream, this arrangement could not be surpassed. Had the unseen artisans of the universe created this trophy? How? And how could a totality of images imbedded in one person's dreams turn up on a broken-down porch in a distant village? I reflected on the thoughts of David Bohm: "The task of Science is to start from such parts and to derive all wholes through abstraction, explaining them as the results of interactions of the parts."

Patience, dear Reader, as I try to explain that interaction.

The purple chair held two meanings: Purple symbolized lava, the *chair* embodied the church, linking to the *Bethany* church in St Lawrence, Newfoundland.[480]

The bowl was symbolic of a crater. The dirt inside the bowl imaged the earth; the dead flowers and the plants connected to the dead flowers under the chair in the Bethany dream and again in the White Rose dream. Dead vegetation under the earth over and again warned of the spoiling of God's nutrients. The fire hydrant presaged the dousing of flames. The top of the hydrant was orange; the body was yellow – yellow and orange, colors of a volcanic eruption. All parts of the collage were plastic, depicting the plasticity of the earth, the plasticity of explosives.

The little porch in Alert Bay brought to light a junk pile that echoed the refrain in countless dreams about children, symbolically, the children of God. The games for children – the games we play here on Earth tied to the dream of *a plastic fire hydrant the colors of a child's toy and a children's kit for fighting a volcano*[481] – a flashback to Lawn where all the fire hydrants were lavender. The children were collectively "the children of the Earth." Was the volcano collective, as well?

The fire hydrant was lying on its side.

Smilingshadow had gone to set the fire hydrant upright and as I watched from the car, I whispered to myself. "No, don't. Don't change it. It has to be in the position it was when we saw it." Changing the position of one component, the fire hydrant, would have changed the meaning of the whole. Smilingshadow put it back in position and photographed it as it was – lying on its side, symbolically rendered useless for extinguishing fires. Her intuitive sense must have picked up my thought wave not to move it. The story was spinning faster than it could be told, the materializations unfolding faster than one's eye could behold.

The collage on the porch was one link in the forming connective membrane of an inconceivable scheme. How is it possible that such a mélange had self-assembled?

Completely contrary to the Darwinian theory that evolution has no ultimate purpose, this posed a question as to the evolution of human consciousness. Was its direction one of symbiosis? Was cooperation from above directed downward as a way to avert the destruction around us? Is the purpose of this cooperation to improve our chances for survival?

The random collection of fragments on that inconspicuous little porch revived my first connection of the dream to Benoit Mandelbrot's world of fractals which I became mesmerized with while watching the Colors of Infinity on television.[482] Striking parallels between the pieces of dreams and the fragmented nature of fractals and their repetition

---

480 7/30/98. See Ch. 74 – Das Shoot! Das Boot!, pp. 346–47
481 2/28/99. See Ch. 73 – Poles and Hydrants, p. 340
482 See Ch. 13 – The Sciences, p. 65

stirred my awareness of other similarities. Like the Dream, fractals are images that can be split into parts, each of which is a smaller copy of the whole. Thinking about the infinite detail in fractals and how it matches the never-ending detail in the dream, I called a video outlet to order a tape of that show. The salesperson excitedly urged me to order a *Glorious Accident* by Wim Kayzer.

I purchased the book, a discourse among six of science's great thinkers about consciousness and our existence in space and time. In it, Rupert Sheldrake discusses a morphogenetic field which carries information and has a morphic resonance. Had his concept of the morphic field actualized on that humble porch in Alert Bay?

I grew more curious about Sheldrake's theory and how it resonated with Mandelbrot's fractals. Seeing years of dream fragments meshing in one single moment in one single space, imbued in me a quiet awakening. This required a period of gestation.

Was part of the rationale directed at establishing observable evidence of a morphogenetic field? Was it saying that every particle – a piece of a dream, a plastic chair, an island in Vancouver – is organized by a field within and around it, just as a magnetic field is within and around a magnet?

What is a morphogenetic field? Rupert Sheldrake's theory says: "Morphogenetic fields carry information only (no energy) and are available throughout time and space without any loss of intensity after they have been created. They are created by the patterns of physical forms (including such things as crystals as well as biological systems). They help guide the formation of later similar systems. And finally, a newly forming system 'tunes into' a previous system by having within it a 'seed' that resonates with a similar seed in the earlier form."[93]

Elsewhere, Sheldrake asks, "How big are morphogenetic fields? Miles? Light-years? Do they stretch to the ends of the universe?"[94]

I wondered if the interconnectedness found in Vancouver represents a forming system that had tuned into the previous interconnectedness in Newfoundland by carrying within it that seed of geologic suggestion that appeared time and again in my dreams. Were the dreams sending and receiving terminals that left a continuous trail of waking experience imprinted in morphogenetic fields around Newfoundland/Labrador and Vancouver that "tuned into" previous dream experiences imaging past geological behaviors?

It's hard to imagine how the transfer of information can take place without energy. Our Mission Lavender experiences belie that, considering our deep emotional responses to corresponding manifestations occurring from one Canadian island to another. Interesting that each of the places we visited were surrounded by water. Surely energy was coming from a world beyond our range of perception or comprehension. "In a separate work in a discussion with Bohm, Sheldrake does, in fact, concede that morphic fields *may* have a subtle energy, but not in any "normal" (physical) sense of the term, since morphic fields can propagate across space and time and do not fade out noticeably over distance.[E95]

Sheldrake suggests the process is one of resonance, like tuning into a radio station. Morphic resonance is an influence of similar things on subsequent similar things. So the fields that organize things have a kind of inherent memory within them.[E96] In general, morphic units closely resemble themselves in the past and are subject to self-resonance from their own past states.[E97]

St. Lawrence and Lawn in Newfoundland had connected to Alert Bay on Vancouver Island. Merging with the union of lavender and yellow, both regions mirrored the symbolism of Church, fire hydrants and children's toys.

My instinct took these symbols a step further, translating to God … Extinguishing Fire … Saving Humankind from its toys.

I knew I was heading into the debate on science versus intelligent design. I asked myself which side Mission Lavender was on. I feel it is connecting both sides, for in faith we believe, and then we observe. In science, we observe, and then we believe. Perhaps one day humankind will park its biases and see both sides as purposeful.

This drew me to the opinions of scientist and theologian John Polkinghorne, who believes that "God created this universe. But this was not a one-act invention of a clockwork world. God did something 'more clever': he created a world with independence, a world able to make itself. He says "Creation is an ongoing act, one in which the laws of nature make room for choice and action, both human and divine." He finds this idea beautifully affirmed by the best insights of chaos theory, which describes reality as an interplay between order and disorder, between random possibilities and patterned structure.[E98]

By some inexplicable happening in the cosmos, chaos theory or morphogenetic theory or the implicate order or quantum entanglement or the laws of nature or a combination thereof, had deposited itself on that little porch in Alert Bay. Symbolism crammed into the collage of junk was the paragon not only for one dream but for the message in its entirety – at least up to now. Junk was W A S T E and waste would be found in an EARTHQUAKE HABITAT. That was one environment but then there were the undersea volcanoes.

The grim dream of *a children's kit for fighting a volcano*[483] returned me to another dispatch which matter-of-factly talked about the end of the world. My dreams were ratcheting up the warnings.

Physical playthings were innocently scattered about in nearly every nook and cranny we visited, supporting countless dream references to *children and their toys.* Industrial

483 2/28/99. See Ch. 73 – Poles and Hydrants, p. 340

child's play like drilling, mining, running pipelines, releasing toxic chemicals in the air, water and soil are but a few of the games being played capriciously and selfishly in exchange for corporate profit and personal gain, while poisoning the earth, draining the life from her precious ecosystems given us munificently as gifts for our sustenance. This cruel recreation has become a cesspool of iniquity infecting all the children of the Earth. And there are the war games that taint our universal soul with pollutants of hatred and violence. But, the gluttons in ignoring their wicked excesses will suffocate in their own oils of human excrement. It is patently clear why the dream messenger firmly delivered *a children's kit for fighting a volcano.*

Like human behavior conditioned to respond to stimuli, so too is the behavior of Mother Earth. If a series of geological movements reminds her of earlier and established stimuli, such as a violent earthquake or volcano – even after centuries she may react as she did before – just as we do. But if her safety is threatened, her stability compromised by predators who drench her in gallons of cancerous toxins as though she were a garbage disposal, it will traumatize her and she will revolt. This is what we're witnessing.

Equanimity failed me. In dread of being a messenger of ill omen, I wished Tu-whit could be the envoy. Even though he was but a fantasy, the message was real. My courage faltered. I teetered and tottered on an emotional see-saw about including the flaming warnings, but the powerful voice of the Mission was begging to be heard. If the people would lift their veils of denial and remove their earplugs, there was still hope. The 2010 drilling rig explosion that resulted in a massive sea floor oil gusher in the Gulf of Mexico extracted this dream in its entirety.

I'm discussing something with a scientist. The word "explosion" is clear. I say that my pants are on inside out. I tell him the world is going to end. The commode is overflowing with urine but it looks more like a bidet. A large piece of industrial looking plastic is covering a mess of clothing and the flood of urine. There is urine everywhere. There is total disarray.[484]

Industrial plastic covering – PVC – points at the industrial cover-ups of the dangers of radioactive waste leaking into the environment and into our clothing, our food, our water, our air. I think the pants could represent the legs of the Burin and Avalon Peninsulas or the Louisiana peninsula but I don't know why they're inside out.

Steno pinged in with an advisory. "Penelope, the inside-out pants would apply to an arch-shaped anticline where the oldest rock is occurring on the inside of the fold."

Were we blindly turning the Earth inside out because of unquenchable appetites and mind-numbing negligence?

---

484 6/5/99.   See Ch. 79 – No Stone Unturned, pp. 381, 383
           Ch. 97 – Toxic Alphabet Stew, pp. 497–504

An unseen bugler trumpeted the message loud and clear and true. No form, matter or method of measurement could replace the reverberation of Truth heralding a new paradigm, divinely designed. The source was anonymous. Why else were Smilingshadow and I compelled to scout this cloistered island far from the madding crowds we knew as home and so removed from our personal paint boxes of interest?

Junk sniffing had become our new pastime. We took a sliver of time for some beachcombing after our famous porch discovery. While sifting through rubble washed ashore and pondering our destinies, I asked Smilingshadow how she came to join me on this quixotic adventure. She replied, "I had no choice."

I understood.

Her early thoughts were that sunning in the south of France would be far preferable to a junk probe on porches and beaches in the outback of Canada. But, she too, had been bitten by the gods and, in her own words, she "had no idea how magical and sobering this trip would be."

I reflected on the similarity of fractals and the morphogenetic field to dreams. If the principal feature of morphic resonance is similarity, then mathematician Benoit Mandelbrot and biologist Rupert Sheldrake were working to solve the same kind of problem. It would make sense that the morphic fields were carrying fractals.

CHAPTER ONE HUNDRED TWO

A GHOSTLY PARK … AN ORB OF LIGHT

A mix of elation and dread bounced off the highs and lows of our roller coaster ride when an overdraft notice dropped from the Oneiroball alerting us to a change in pace.

> ATTENTION: PENELOPE & SMILINGSHADOW
> ALERT BAY, VANCOUVER
> The Terracrust Bank of Astral Credit wishes to notify you that your reserve of spiritual energy is running low. Based on excellent credit history, we will honor any withdrawals until you are able to refuel.

No wonder. Since we'd entered Alert Bay, the spiritual manna was so electrically charged, the revelations so powerful, our expenditure of spirit so abundant, we should have realized we'd be running on low.

"What do they mean, they'll honor withdrawals?" Smilingshadow asked.

"It means just what it says, Shadow. We need to withdraw. Why don't we take in a local attraction and try not to think about Mission Lavender stuff for a little while?"

We decided to visit the Alert Bay Ecological Park, once a swamp fed by an underground spring which flooded the area, killing the trees. Now the dead trees provide perches for ravens, bald eagles and migratory birds. Though Alert Bay villagers prize this park, we saw the gnarled trees with their twisting branches as corpses; skeletal and depressing. I imagined little songbirds and societies of bees and insects that had made the trees their home, displaced and dying. We stood there as mourners awed by a silence that blurs time's thin line between life and death. The shadows of the once-living spoke the same message as the couriers unfurling this tale.

"Sparkle. I thought we came here to withdraw."

"You're right, Smilingshadow, but it's almost impossible. The message is all-encompassing. I think we did unwind a little though, don't you?"

"Yeah …. Well, a little."

Footnotes contain dream dates and references to prior pages where the dream appeared.
Endnotes contain bibliographical references, are marked with "Ɛ" in the text, and appear at the end of the book.

Our first day in Alert Bay melted into evening. It was 7:30, time to check into the Orca Inn. I asked for a room facing the water and was told all the harbor views were taken. We hauled our paraphernalia to Room 6, facing the "back."

I hadn't put my bags down when Smilingshadow strolled over to the window, looked out and said, "Sparkle, there are some children's toys out here."

I exclaimed, "Children's toys?"

Right there, plain as the noonday sun, was a dirt pile with a bunch of little derby cars and toys for children, an exact replica of a dream image I had six months earlier about a *mound of dirt with parts of toys sticking out.*

I stared out the window at this mirror image and then – for a microsecond – a dazzling burst of light illuminated the center of the scene spotlighting the toys. I knew it wasn't Tu-whit for the intensity of the light was nearly blinding and Tu-whit, after all, is but a figment. This very real gleaming orb of light completely encircled the little patch of land behind our room, then mysteriously disappeared as though it were an apparition.

My gaze was frozen to the spot.

I stood there in disbelief, but I knew that I saw what I saw. My dream, now the stuff of the waking world, was illuminated by an anonymous globe of light. Its brilliance gave off a benevolence that will forever commemorate the vision of those toys.

Mesmerized by the precise detail of these materializations, the next day I decided to poke around in the dirt pile of toys. What did I find but a piece of wood painted lavender; one side trimmed in yellow. One had to be alert in Alert Bay.

This dream fragment of the toys was part of in a larger scenario about *a girl who works for a well known architect. She works on a design that is in parts and is apparently one of the architect's favorite projects. His house has a balcony overlooking the living room. An oriental couple comes in. Everyone is on a chaise lounge except for me. I am observing. Soon everyone begins to make love. One person sleeps. The orientals' bodies were bare. The body of the oriental girl was black, black as ebony.*

The dream segues *to the back of a room with huge sliding glass doors that turn out to be plastic. Beyond it is a nice back yard. While looking out at the lawn, I notice a mound of dirt with toys sticking up, a place for the children to play. Nearby is another mound of dirt that may belong to the people next door. I say, "You could make this into a beautiful lawn, thinking of how it could be landscaped." As I try to close the huge sliding door, it comes off the tracks. I comment on inferior workmanship.*[485]

---

485 3/27/00.

The architect's house – the island arc system ... an *oriental couple* – Asia ... *a girl black as ebony* – Africa ... *back of a room ... back yard* – back-arc-spreading zone ... *plastic* – asthenosphere, the plastic part of the earth on which the plates move ... *sliding glass doors* – sliding plates in a volcanic zone ... *the people next door* ... North America? More warnings. The door comes off the tracks. The children are left with two dirt mounds to play in. Their remaining toys are buried in the soil.

Grappling with the *chaise lounges*, I called on Steno.

"Why, Dr. Steno, am I the only one not in a chaise lounge?

"This is an excellent place, Penelope, in which to flex your intention. The people in these chaise lounges, making love while one sleeps, tells the story that the citizens of the world are relaxing and naturally going about their lives; making love and sleeping are expressions of the physical realm. Only those who have heard us are watching. This will ultimately measure the success of our Mission, for while others are lounging, the observers are seeing what we've put before them. It is now their responsibility – your responsibility – to tell those who are sleeping. If the communication is clear, we have succeeded."

"Oh help, Dr. Steno. I don't know if I can do it. I don't know if I'm versed enough. I don't know if anyone will listen. So far, no one has! The scientists tell me I have to quantify. I don't know how. By the time I learn to quantify, we could all be gone. How will I finish on time? I can't go any faster or work any more hours."

I was frozen with fear, fear interlaced with intense passion to get the message out. Equanimity was waning.

My feet were like ice.

I asked Smilingshadow, "Would Vancouver be considered adjacent to British Columbia? Seattle? Washington State?"

"Yes, Sparkle, it would be."

Why two different dream scripts each spotlighting Africa, each intertwined with people next door, an African neighbor, something adjacent? Both featured architects and sliding glass doors and directed me toward the "back." Vision had outperformed my other senses. My Timelessness Glasses had caught sight of oncoming images: back-arc spreading ...island arc systems ... sliding plates.

Again, I thought about the North American plate moving closer to the African plate. Why would an *oriental girl* have a body *black as ebony*? What a bizarrely coded geological twister!

Steno reassured me. "You will find, Penelope, as we travel on, that each and every code will find its place, no matter how odd it may seem at first. For instance, the Eurasian Plate comprises the continents of Europe and Asia and is bounded on the south by the African Plate. For the North American Plate, the easterly side is a divergent boundary with the Eurasian Plate to the north and the African plate to the south forming the northern part of the Mid-Atlantic Ridge.

"Professor Steno, I wonder if piezoelectric effects in back-arc spreading centers link Africa, Newfoundland and Vancouver based on past geological behavior. I suspect a morphogenetic field may be remembering the very movement of these tectonic plates."

"Clueso, we're nearing the end of this leg of the journey, so let's hear your latest electrifying epiphanies."

"As you wish, Doc.

"Quartz has a piezoelectric effect, so possibly waves that radiate from Quartz travel through Lava. You, my illustrious mentor, introduced the concept of Lava and Piezoelectricity through my dream symbols of Cousin Andi and Pizza.[486] It's now clear that andesite, the volcanic lava, and piezoelectricity are related.

"I remember you saying, Quartz generates the electrical charge and Lava emits light. The heat of molten lava must change its color and that would reflect the radiation of different wavelengths of both color and temperature. I discovered the temperature range for lava is about 1,300° to 2,400° Fahrenheit. So light, color and temperature relate to electromagnetic radiation.

"Doc, I think I understand. Well, um … kinda."

"Excellent tracking, Penelope. Now tell us how you associate piezoelectricity with tectonic plates. I recall you wanted to include some of our findings at Cape Chapeau Rouge. Why don't you venture a circle?"

"Egad, Doc! These circles get more and more difficult, but I'll start with the red hat and quartz dream we uncovered in Newfoundland, which sits on the North American plate."

Red Hat – Cape Chapeau Rouge … *Pink Rose* – Quartz – Charged Particle … *Crystal* – Piezoelectricity … *Fibre* – Molten Glass – Lava … *Electromagnetic Radiation* – Light – Electric Charge … *Floating Wrench* – Wrench Fault – Strike Slip Fault … *Red Hat* – Cape Chapeau Rouge.

"You're doing just fine, Penelope, but this circle doesn't include the plates. Where do the plates fit?"

"I think the *oriental girl* with the *black body* represents both the Eurasian and African plates and those two plates might be absorbing radiation and relate to back arc spreading and a wrench or strike slip fault in a subduction zone."

"Go on with your circle, Clueso."

Whirling Whirligigs! What a taskmaster!

---

486 See Ch. 85 – Under My Hat, p. 408

"OK. OK. Because the same geologic features may apply to Vancouver Island, I'll extend that circle to include Oriental Couple – Eurasian plate: Europe and Asia ... *Oriental Girl, Black Body* – Eurasian plate, African plate ... *Back Yard* – Back-Arc Spreading – Africa's Past – winding back to Newfoundland and the North American plate."

"Anyway, Doc, I'm still bewildered as to why I'd match a girl to two continents with some kind of electricity I never even heard of."

"You are learning a universal language, my pet. We are working with thought and matter – thought being that which you dream, matter being that which you connect to in the physical world. David Bohm speaks of this in *Wholeness and the Implicate Order*: 'Intelligence and material process have thus a single origin, which is ultimately the unknown totality of the universal flux. In a certain sense this implies that what have been commonly called mind and matter are abstractions from the universal flux, and that both are to be regarded as different and relatively autonomous orders within the one whole movement. It is thought responding to intelligent perception which is capable of bringing about an overall harmony or fitting between mind and matter.'

"By mapping your dreams, you are 'grasping the essential and innermost forms of things.' By now, you're a bit more familiar with 'the unbroken wholeness of the totality of existence as an undivided flowing movement without borders.'"

Without borders was an understatement. We had been going round and round in the silent expanses of eternity, looping through circles within circles – and what glorious circles they are.

It was incredible. My dreams about piezoelectricity had been following me to unseen worlds beneath the rocky terrain of Newfoundland and towering above it to the highest congress where spirit teams confer – the dominion of the PurpleScroll. Piezoelectricity's first stop was Cape Chapeau Rouge in Newfoundland, and now it's arrived in Alert Bay on Vancouver Island.

Smilingshadow and I were tingling with elation over the manifestations in Alert Bay. The dream mason who poured the concrete personified pure unadulterated Truth. How could we know that the soft edges of newly poured pavement would harden to a physical, touchable reality?

I continued to wonder if the magnetic field in rocks over four hundred million years old that once joined Africa to Newfoundland, and possibly Vancouver, held some geological memory that would influence their movement today. After all, much like the earth, human behavior is predicated on the past.

Emerging from a shimmering peach rainbow, Peggymoonbeam echoed her wisdom: "That is the cornerstone of the Dream!" and, scampering after Steno like a doting wife chasing her absent-minded husband, she called out, "Nicolaus, Nicolaus ... don't forget the belt."

My, my, I thought … on a first-name basis with the upper crust, but then that was her style.

"Upper crust," chuckled Steno. My feeble effort at punning tickled him.

CHAPTER ONE HUNDRED THREE

DREAMINGS AND DROPPINGS
IN ALERT BAY

The Vancouver map calls it Alert Bay, the dream map calls it *"Success Wake Lake."* The dream arrived seven months ahead of the visit and wake I did, for Alert Bay pulled out all the dream stops.

An architect has a broken leg. Christiane Amanpour wearing a dark purple fuzzy shawl is his current girlfriend. An old girlfriend, who sounds foreign, maybe Indian, telephones. A triangle emerges.

A second architect enters. Both architects want to go to the movies to see Belt 2.org or .org belt 2. I comment that they are good "natured." The second architect had a stroke and can't stand up straight.

Peggymoonbeam delivers the message,"Success Wake Lake."

I am dropping pennies into a vent. I then drop a quarter in, which the vent takes immediately. The first architect wants the quarters but not the pennies. I'm worried that because we're running late, there won't be time to eat. We decide to stop at the hot doughnut place.[487]

Pennies – a quarter. It's that metals thing again. Copper – Nickel –reverberations of Voisey's Bay.

Two architects – one with a broken leg; the other, a stroke victim.

Imagine my astonishment when I learned of an Alert Bay/Cape Scott area that was tectonically disrupted. *The broken leg and the stroke* were a pure synthesis of earth and human frailties. *A broken leg* infers a fractured leg of land; *a stroke* can result in rupture, clogging and weakness on one side of the body. Had the *purple shawl* depicted a volcanic cloak?

Added to this subterranean drama, was *Christiane Amanpour* in a tectonically disrupted zone, paralleling her news coverage on natural disasters and other crises from the world's hotspots. Is it conceivable that Amanpour's Iranian father and English mother would represent the Arabian Plate and Eurasian plate that have been colliding for millions

---

487 2/24/99.

Footnotes contain dream dates and references to prior pages where the dream appeared.
Endnotes contain bibliographical references, are marked with "Ɛ" in the text, and appear at the end of the book.

of years? Is the old girlfriend, the Indian Ocean which filled in the gap between the two plates?

Following this unimaginable chain, linking dreams to geology, was my discovery that the Alert Bay volcanic belt, a heavily eroded Neogene volcanic belt was connected to a triple junction.[E99]

A soft peach-scented puff of air released the essence of Peggymoonbeam.

"Penelope, the point connecting the plates in a triple junction is usually near the epicenter of major megathrust earthquakes. Check out the *Tanzania dream where you were splitting up with your beau*[488] – or having a rift with him," she giggled. "There is an African triple rift junction. Might your two disabled architects connect to this in some way? Remember the Tanzania dream that showed *US/US/US.* That makes three USs.

"Rift. Ya got it? Read my lips, Penny. Rift with your boyfriend – rift in the earth. Hehehehehe."

The geological footprint of Africa had been stamped in the story. It was downright confusing but the connections were enough to make us quiver.

The first architect preferred quarters. That was clear.

Curious. Metal was scattered all over as though it had been dropped from the sky.

Although the disabled architects jibed, I suspected there was more lurking beneath the beneath.

Following the scent of Lavender, the vent would characterize a volcanic vent absorbing nickel droppings. I deliberated: Could there be copper and nickel in meteorite fragments? Was there a meteorite fall somewhere in the area? I thought back to the Merewether Crater, but that was in Labrador.

Was that the smoking gun?

Then comes the flashing light! This is how the seduction begins. You're really not prepared for a lifetime tour of the cosmos but the seed has been planted – or the grain has been dropped – when lo and behold you are involuntarily propelled into exploration of every imaginable kind: Exploration of mind – exploration of earth – exploration beyond all limits.

There is no turning back, no closing the book. You have nowhere to go but forward.

"Penelope," announced Dr. Steno, "your team of mechanics has arrived. We picked up your concern about assistance while you were crossing to Horseshoe Bay and Voila! Peggymoonbeam has rounded up the cadre and we are at your service.

"We have a confession to make. Since you were out jitterbugging in your teenage years, we've been cataloging your memories. Your impressions of marriage and relationships,

---

488 9/30/99. See Ch. 49 –Wrapped Up Like a Mummy, p. 213

because they've occupied such emotionally meaningful phases of your life, opened the way for us to connect your analogy of marriage and divorce to convergent and divergent boundaries – something we'll be looking at up ahead.

"In preparation for future work, your experiences before and during this Mission have been stored in a vast warehouse up at Terracrust. When a waking memory triggers an impulse, quite often it pulls a dream right out of storage, or conversely, a dream can pull a waking memory out of storage. This pulling mechanism gains strength depending on the depth of the emotion. The waking and dreaming realms then coalesce in a way-station between the two, adding new material as you live your life. It's very convenient, Penelope, because there are no storage bills and all of your valuables are secure."

"Do you mean that emotional memories are more vivid, Dr. Steno?"

"Yes. The more emotionally tied you are to a memory the more visually graphic it is. That is how we were able to accomplish this. Because your life has had a fair number of emotional bumps in it, your dreams are particularly fertile for this type of work."

My dreams were meshing, blending and overlaying one another as the years folded into each other, unfolding clues in some mysteriously ordered way. Still, handfuls of homeless stragglers that could find no place on the dream map were dozing beneath the bridges of consciousness waiting to be fed.

CHAPTER ONE HUNDRED FOUR

HOT DOUGHNUTS

Disjointed thoughts and fragmented images clung to the *Success Wake Lake* dream. *We are running late. There won't be time to eat … we can stop at a hot doughnut place.*

Hot doughnuts.

Both architects want to go to the movies to see Belt 2.org or .org belt 2. Another bizarre coupling. Movies and belts?

The belts were confusing. But there are two volcanic belts that might fit: the Garibaldi volcanic belt … the Alert Bay volcanic belt.

I sensed reassurance in the air. "Steno here. I got wind of your struggle to cinch the belt dilemma. There are paired metamorphic temperature/pressure belts which are characteristic of the ocean trench and island arc environments, respectively, of a subduction zone …" and he was gone.

Subduction zone! Right! The computer wizard married those two words without even asking. A subduction zone is where one ocean plate goes beneath another and a dream showed exactly that.[489]

As I gazed up at the twinkling firmament, the brightest starburst ever was blinking at me, forming a perfectly radiant solid circle of light. It was the etheric body of the ancient astronomer Claudius Twink Ptolemy, who eased my quandary warbling his sunny … "Halloo, Penny."

"Twink, I thought you'd never come. You spin around so fast I can never catch up with you! I cherish your mysterious Valentine dream, but that was over a decade ago in Earth time. I know it's only lumenseconds for you, but I've been waiting and waiting. I'm serious!"

"No, my love, I'm Sirius. I'm the brightest star in the sky and the one closest to Earth, which is as close as I can get to you.

"I always knew you could compare with no other. Of course, you'd be the brightest! So does this mean I'm to call you Sirius?"

---

489 6/22/97. See Ch 101 – Back Porches, pp. 522–23

Footnotes contain dream dates and references to prior pages where the dream appeared.

Endnotes contain bibliographical references, are marked with "Ɛ" in the text, and appear at the end of the book.

"Not at all. That's an appellation for where I live in Starsight. Even though we're in different dimensions, you too, dear Penny, have great luminosity that helps connect our electromagnetic energies. We are entangled, my sweet.

"Y'know, Penny, you say you've been waiting but it's a gosh darned thing. I've had the same thought about you. Our rendezvous are charming but I'd like to stop meeting this way. This geology dust is getting in my nostrils. Stardust is lighter and much preferred. What on Earth is taking you so long? I could've designed the solar system by now. You know, my love, I'll never figure you out, no matter how many centuries go by. You are unique and, I might add, unpredictable. I never know what's going to come out of that beautiful mouth of yours."

I considered asking Twink where Johnnie Pianissimo was. Sometimes he'd utter familiar words that sang to my heart and I'd think he might be Johnnie, but no – Marie said Johnnie would wear the cloak of an ordinary man and after all, Twink was but a lovable star.

"Your work is not yet finished, Miss Penny," and at that Twink beamed a shaft of light on yet another branch of the cosmic tree. From the bottom of the ocean to the zenith of the galaxies, the dangling Branch of Space Science swung over me.

Agneswiseheart and Ptolemy, arm in arm, repeated, "Penelope. Follow the directions: *Belt 2.org or .org belt 2.*"

Ptolemy aimed his starlight pointer into Earth's upper atmosphere as Agneswiseheart cocked her telescope. How did Agneswiseheart ever team up with Ptolemy? Starsight was so vast.

Twink, my ancient astronomer and geographer, was Greek. So was Galen, whose medical writings on vision were inspired by his dreams. My sweet Aunt Agnes must have developed a fancy for Greek gods in the ethereal plane.

Agneswiseheart laughed. "Penelope dear, I had the telescope, and Twink knew the way. To answer your question about how we got together, the state we are in is unmeasured and exists outside of space and time. This makes it possible for all things – including you and me and Ptolemy and Starsight – to be present at once. This dimension consists of information assembled by different levels of consciousness. That means that our physical world and our spiritual body must exist together. James Forberg has explored some of these ideas in his work on 'Quantum Consciousness and Your Immortality.' You will be examining this on your next mission."

(Gulp.) "Agneswiseheart. Does this mean that my dreams are in the realm that contains all the information in the world?"

"Exactly, Penelope. The mysteries in your dreams – in everyone's dreams – involve not only your own personal realm but also the deeper cosmic realm where much of the information is hidden. The dual existence between the physical and the spiritual is what you are learning about and in fact, experiencing."

"Excuse me, lovelies" interrupted Ptolemy, "but I must beg a question of our schoolgirl. Miss Penny. Do you see two huge belts of intense radiation encircling the Earth?"

"I do, Twink."

"Good. Now do you know why *both architects want to go to the movies?*" cajoled Ptolemy.

"I dunno. Maybe it's something to do with 'belts' on the Internet. Maybe it's something electromagnetic."

I paused.

"Siriusly, Twink. I think I do know why they went to the movies!

"I bet the clue is camouflaged in the MOVIE dialogue between the architects for, whenever I dream a movie star, I can trust it to connect to stars as in astronomy – stars in the galaxies – stars from which meteorites are born. Ya' know why? Because everything connects with everything else!"

Agneswiseheart and Ptolemy blinked as they wiped beads of expectation from their incandescent brows. "Whew!"

"But, but … I'm not sure of the difference between a meteor and a meteorite."

"A meteor is the proper name for the streak of light that's usually called a shooting star, so you got that one right," replied Twink. Most meteors are mere grains of dust that burn up from friction in the atmosphere, but if they survive and strike the surface of the Earth, the remaining fragments of rocks are called meteorites.

"Quite astute of you, my wistful dreamer, to turn movie stars into moving stars. From whence I come, 'we are but the stuff of stars,' as says my good friend, Carl Sagan. When I ascended to Starsight, I, too, became a star and o'er the centuries, I've twinkled you my home address, but don't tell yet.

"Walkie talkie, twinkle twinkle
Close your eyes and we will sprinkle
Age old wisdom that may wrinkle
To help you solve, explore and thinkle"

"Twink, I'm worried sick over the dream encryption: *there won't be time to eat … we can stop at a hot doughnut place.* The message is blocking my celestial dictation.

"I stumbled across this prophecy from Edgar Cayce and that troubled me even more:

"The Van Allen Belts are magnetic fields that surround the earth, channeling incoming radiation from space toward our poles, keeping it from coming into our main living areas on the planet. It is believed that as a magnetic shift began, the Belts would have to break up for a time, perhaps a few hours, a few days, a few months or a few years, until the new magnetic poles were established. Then, presumably the Belts would reestablish their magnetic field around the planet, channeling the incoming radiation to the new poles. During this period, the earth would be exposed to increased levels of radiation.

"Perhaps this is the 'fire' of which so many prophecies speak."[100]

"Penny, my love, as Cervantes wrote, 'Fear is sharp-sighted, and can see things under ground, and much more in the skies.' Now put on your Timelessness specs and look up to the skies. Do you observe that the belts are doughnut-shaped?" coached the mercurial Ptolemy, one moment a lover, the next a poet and eternally the astronomer.

"Yes. I can even see that they're invisible, and they go around the Earth and have some sparkly things around them."

"That is superb, Penelope," blinked Madame Curie. "What you see are electrons and protons – ions that are trapped in two doughnut-shaped magnetic rings – surrounding the Earth. The ions are generated by cosmic rays and by the solar wind, a continuous stream of charged particles emanating from the sun."

"See," radioed Peggymoonbeam to Madame Curie. "I told you the sun would be her master compass. She's like a homing pigeon"

"Marie, I'm still uncertain about what kinds of belts I dreamed. Were they volcanic or radiation?

"Penny, for now your dream was on track with radiation belts. Connect the *2 belts* with the *hot doughnuts* and it will become clear. There is an outer and an inner radiation belt. The outer belt consists mainly of high-energy electrons and the inner belt contains high concentrations of energetic protons.

I was so intimidated at the mere mention of electrons and protons, I started breaking out in hives.

But Ptolemy, in an effort to distract me, sprung loose an epigram. Collecting them is one of his favorite pastimes.

"T'wixt the optimist and pessimist
The difference is droll:
The pessimist sees the doughnut
But the optimist sees the hole."[101]

Wait a second. That's backward! Typical Twink, playing games!

I must be a pessimist because I'm fixated on radiation coming from those doughnut-shaped rings and wonder if a meteorite could get tangled up in one. I bet Movies and Belts have something in common. If Movies are a clue for shooting stars – or meteors – or meteorites and Belts are code for radiation belts, I sense a connection.

Ptolemy stayed on course with the doughnut-shaped belts. "Dear pessimistic Penelope, please douse your glumness, put on your winsome smile and realize that you are closer to the truth than you know. Incoming meteorites usually pass through the Van Allen belts, hurtling toward Earth at about nineteen miles per second, which means the dose of radiation they receive while in the belts is not worth worrying about. But if you have a big impact, then the iron and nickel in a metal meteorite or sulfur in a stone meteorite could vaporize to create poisonous gas. Just a few more slivers for you to think on, my sweet."

"Oh no! The dream said *pennies and a quarter* – copper and nickel – *had dropped into a vent!* That could create a poisonous gas! Why is this invisible gas following me around? I'm trying to be optimistic, Twink, but it's pretty creepy. Anyway, I thought I'm supposed to be looking for a hole. When you picked Van Allen from the array of belts, I hadn't the foggiest that radiation would be a subject related to belts."

I was looking skyward when far above the clouds I saw the fuzzy outline of the Oneiroball ballooning its way downward. I could barely make out the little basket attached to it. Steno excitedly swooped down with his spyglass. "Look, Penelope! Look! Peggymoonbeam arranged for a wicker basket and it's holding a very important dream."

The dream floated down from the Oneiroball, whirling about in the air. I ran very hard and fast, chasing after it as though the wind was playing a game with me. When I finally caught it, I gingerly opened it because it was folded into a little square and written in letters so small, I needed Steno's super-powered spyglass to read it.

I'm in the lobby of the Northeast Arm Motel and I notice things flying around in the air like doughnuts, some with holes and some without holes. I'm overcome with excitement. I say to my friend, "Do you know where we are? We're in Newfoundland at the Northeast Arm Motel! That's why doughnuts are flying around!" No one seems to pay any attention to these flying objects even though they all see them. I'm thrilled because now I know that a supernatural force is in that motel. It's such a boring place but so magical.[490]

Something very strange was going on in these little known parts of Canada. First, the mysterious orb of light that for a millisecond illuminated the pile of toys behind our room in Alert Bay. And now, eight years later, this dream about flying doughnuts in Dunville, our chosen "truck stop" in Newfoundland. There was something around that motel that kept drawing us back. One experience in dreaming; another in waking. Was there a difference in consciousness? Both were supernatural.

Flyin' figure eights! If flying doughnuts are belts, why would I be dreaming of Van Allen radiation belts in Newfoundland when the *Success Wake Lake* dream was marked for

---

490 5/7/08.

Alert Bay on Vancouver Island? And why would this dream emerge years after I'd been in Dunville?

Lord Galen spun in. "Penelope, remember that your Timelessness specs have augmented your consciousness with convergent vision, the ability to merge the invisible with the visible – to integrate dreaming with waking – across space and time. This flying doughnut dream demonstrates Ptolemy's lesson on how past, present and future happen in an instant. You are being shown the organizing principles of the system but you cannot yet understand consciousness or the supernatural because they are outside of space and time. As physicist, Russell Targ noted, 'Consciousness will inform quantum mechanics when consciousness is understood.'[102] We're working on it, Penny."

"Bless you, Lord Galen. I was curious about me and those belts and the islands each being in different places at different times."

Dum da dum dum. It was Twink, beside himself with my geographical challenges. "Penelope. If I may have your attention ... The charged particles which compose the belts circulate along the Earth's magnetic lines of force. These lines of force extend from the area above the equator to the North Pole, to the South Pole, and then circle back to the Equator, so the area between Newfoundland and Vancouver and Labrador for that matter, is but a mite.

"Women!" Hmph!"

"OK. OK, Sirius of Starsight, I know my geography is pathetic, but why did some of the doughnuts have holes while others didn't?

Silence.

"Don't answer me, Twink. See if I care! I think the doughnuts with the holes are electrically charged and have something to do with how our thoughts connect. I was seeking your opinion because you are the brightest star around, but you ignore me. So High and Brighty, just forget it!"

Every so often, Twink's chauvinistic side would appear, frustrating the daylights out of me. He could be so darling and protective and then he'd turn into Mr. Smarty Points and make me feel like a microbe. Sometimes I'd hide behind a cloud and just weep. Not that that made a thimble of difference because he could always see me. I knew his soul was pure as a baby's breath so eventually I'd have to whistle a happy tune and dismiss my earthly emotions.

My compulsion to get to the bottom of this was unstoppable. The steady refrain of my Earth friends fell on deaf ears: "Penelope. You've got to make some time for yourself. You've got to get out."

But once drawn to the light there was nowhere else to go.

It was Whole Earth ... Whole Heaven ... Waking ... Dreaming .. creating a seamless reality ... our collective birthright ... one to be protected.

Peggymoonbeam called it *Success Wake Lake* for good reason. The giants of fate had left their footprints in the soil of Alert Bay. Is this where the forces of "nature" would convene? I puzzled. I retrieved a slice of the dream:

A second architect enters. Both architects want to go to the movies to see Belt 2.org or .org belt 2. I comment that they are good "natured."

The inconspicuous *"good 'natured'"* comment about the two architects was pure cosmic horticulture. It had been tended to and harvested by Heaven's most gifted green thumb who personified nature's goodness.

The flapping of Twink's suspenders broke my concentration. "Halloo. Halloo, my darling Penelope. I trust you're over our little tiff. Sometimes you're a wee bit too sensitive but disarming, nonetheless. I just thought I'd pop back in seeing that you're thinking of things 'good natured.' You know, I fancy myself that. Never mind. I'm here to remind you it's time you performed your great circle feat. You don't want your readers to think you've abandoned them."

"Twink, you alone know my heart's every quiver, so even though you're still a bit prickly, I can only be cranky for a lumensecond. Now, I really need some help with where to begin this circle. We've covered so much territory my head is spinning even faster than you are."

"Well, it's comforting to know I'm still needed. Why not start with the *Success Wake Lake* dream?[491] Just target the most relevant points, Penny. Remember, your readers have as much to digest as you do."

"My thoughts exactly, Twink. OK. Starting with *Success Wake Lake* – Alert Bay – *2 disabled architects* – 2 tectonically disrupted Island Arc Systems: Newfoundland and Vancouver – Back-arc spreading – hmmm… well, that's the geology, but I think I need help with the astronomy."

"Go on, Penny. Continue your circle with the astronomy portion, then, finish with geology."

"OK. *Belt 2.org – Hot Doughnuts* – Van Allen Radiation Belts – *Movies* – Moving stars – Shooting Stars – Meteors – Meteorites – *dropping pennies and a quarter in a vent* – nickel-copper droppings in a volcanic vent – circling back to 2 disrupted Island Arc Systems: Newfoundland/Labrador and Alert Bay, Vancouver."

"Onederful, Penny. By joining the two circles, you begin and end with Alert Bay and you've succeeded in connecting geography and astronomy."

"Y'know, Twink. I have a hunch that Newfoundland/Labrador might be part of the same island arc system that was disabled here in Alert Bay because a meteorite crashed into Earth. Am I on track, Twink?"

491 2/24/99. See Ch. 103 – Dreamings and Droppings in Alert Bay, p. 539

And at that, his twinkling majesty dissolved into a glowing shower of light, warbling his "Cheerio" and leaving me on my own to work it out.

My mind traveled back to Labrador and the message that *"quarters make me sick,"* [492] – to the *Moravian Missions, Grace Lines,* and the *Mafia*[493] – to the string of lawsuits against W. R. Grace for environmental contamination. Was toxicology another branch on a tree of growing enigmas?

Alert Bay or, known in the dream as *Success Wake Lake,* is undoubtedly a wake-up call, as the dream implied. But it doesn't end there because it looks like some metal had dropped from the sky into a volcanic vent. Hmm. Who was this *architect with the broken leg who wanted the quarters but not the pennies?*[494] Was it in "his" house where *the oriental girl with her black as ebony body appeared?*[495] And why on Earth did he keep showing up in different scenarios?

As in Newfoundland, Vancouver's exploration for copper and other base metals as well as oil and gas were on the increase.

Not having enough time to eat makes time of the essence. Could this be a prediction echoing Edgar Cayce's?

I flashed back to my Raggedy Ann doll and the candy heart she carried inside. I could never forget Raggedy with the messages imprinted on those little pastel pink and blue and mint green hearts that read "I Love You" and "Hug Me" and "Be Mine." They were sugary sweet, and as a little girl, I lapped them up one after another and only got a stomach-ache once in a while. Their words of affection marked a gentler and safer passage in this world. With the loss of innocence, the message had changed over time from love to fear. It was disheartening. Those days of candy hearts, human hearts and happy-go-lucky playtimes were a far cry from *not having enough time to eat* – not even enough time for a candy heart. I'd need a strong stomach for the future, but I deeply believe if we could regain our lost humanity, we could return to that incorruptible core we're born with – our natural desire to give and receive love. If only we could remember it.

And at that, the high-spirited Ptolemy tuned in, "Great goin', Champ!"

---

492 6/13/96. See Ch. 96 – Three Moravian Missions, p. 490
493 7/4/99.   See Ch. 96 – Three Moravian Missions, pp. 483, 495
494 2/24/99. See Ch. 103 – Dreamings and Droppings In Alert Bay, p. 539
495 3/27/00. See Ch. 102 – A Ghostly Park … An Orb Of Light, pp. 534–35

CHAPTER ONE HUNDRED FIVE

A DROWNING STAR

Day Four: Alert Bay

We had to see it before we left – the tallest totem pole in the world towering 173 feet above the ground on the northern end of Cormorant Island. Straining to see the intricately carved sun design on top, I knew I'd drawn something similar from a dream.

It begins with a girl who is a star named Angela. She is drowning and I have to dive in the water to bring her up. I had to let her dry out. Nola Gideon is there. Then a masseuse comes to give me a massage. She brings a totem pole into my bedroom and automatically lights the top where a small flame is burning. She can turn the flame on or off by just looking at it.

Next, one whole family is in my apartment. I go to nuke the father's coffee. He says put it on 350°. I put it in the upper oven to the right and push a long metal button. It starts heating and won't turn off. I'm afraid it will explode. I can see the glass swelling and expanding. I'm afraid the apartment will catch fire ... all the files will be burnt. I can feel the heat. I can almost see it. The company leaves and the stove is still on. Someone needs to turn it off. I am trying to get the building super or manager to turn off the oven. I can't reach anyone. I am panicked![496]

Scores of interpretations may fit, but inasmuch as I've only ever dreamt one totem pole and its physical form turned up in Alert Bay, the alleluia of Peggymoonbeam's *Success Wake Lake* sang out Alert Bay in full libretto.

Having the benefit of Ptolemy's linguistic skills – half English, half Dream – I knew stars, as in movie stars, were engaged for a full run. On Earth, Peggymoonbeam had been a movie maven.

Agneswiseheart's telescopic dream launched the spiral nebulae, in concert with Peggymoonbeam's spinning disks which piloted us to the thin disk population. With the exhilaration of a cosmic journey, the dreams meshed and encircled the Heavens. Their fragments were still floating around: the *long telescope* between me and Agneswiseheart; *the huge open space with a spiral staircase*[497] depicting the "spiral nebulae," once named for the

---

496 3/5/00.
497 8/18/96. Ch. 20 – Agneswiseheart, p. 311

Footnotes contain dream dates and references to prior pages where the dream appeared.

Endnotes contain bibliographical references, are marked with "Ɛ" in the text, and appear at the end of the book.

LAVENDER

galaxies; Peggymoonbeam's *record player spinning a record of metals* containing a *mound*[498] all leading me to the Galactic Bulge. I had made another connection to this bulge some time back, but had forgotten.

Twink patched in. "Penelope, you had been searching for metals based on the variety of spinning disks."

Telescoping a theme that would orbit the solar nebula, I imagined that the *"drowning star"* might symbolize the death of a star – a supernova. Had the dream detected some metal from a supernova under water?

"Well, my starry-eyed explorer, stars, like human beings are subject to accidents and disorders; not all of them live to a ripe old age like me. They occasionally boil up to a state of instability and explode as novas or supernovas.

"This may happen in a star of any age, young or old. Penny, you mentioned fusion in relation to dreams colored 'fuscia.' Well, the fusion of hydrogen into helium is the source of a hydrogen bomb's energy which also powers stars. When young stars explode, they discharge these two elements, the most abundant in the universe, into space. An old star will spew forth not only these nuclei but other elements from carbon up to iron. The Big Bang produced very little material besides hydrogen and helium, yet most of Planet Earth is composed of other elements."[Ɛ103]

The Big Bang!! Hydrogen and helium! I had a dream beginning with *hh and ending with HH.*[499] Lower case – upper case.

Unusual air currents caused me to look up. It was the Oneiroball hovering very, very low as though it was preparing to lift me soundlessly into the sky. I remember that it held my purpose, but it didn't seem time for that yet.

Twink was twinkling his points off. "Penelope, there's a chemical symbol ^2H, a stable hydrogen isotope known as deuterium. Most of the deuterium in the universe was created in the minutes after the Big Bang, and has endured since that time. We'll delve into this on our next mission."

Isotope? I feel like an isodope. Pondering the age of stars, my inner voice whispered," I bet Angela exploded as a young star."

"Twink, I'm curious about the *mound* in Peggymoonbeam's dream that turned out to be the Galactic Bulge. What kinds of stars are in such a bulge?"

"My, my, Miss Questionbox, we are curious today. Well, this is how it goes: the different parts of the galaxy contain different populations of stars. In the center of the galaxy, in the nuclear bulge, old metal-rich stars reside. Hot, young metal-rich stars – like our Sun – exist in the dusty arms of the disk. Old, metal-poor stars exist in the outer halo

499 10/21/98.

of our galaxy. These are the earliest formed stars in our galaxy. The most metal rich stars are in the disk and bulge."[104]

Peggymoonbeam's dream about *a disk spinning a record of metals had a mound that was all silver. Another was gold, and still another may have been copper or another metal.* I wondered if Angela was a young metal-rich star that came from the disk.

Twink continued, "Your dream about the *star named Angela has a masseuse* in it, which you know is our code for delivering a message to you.

"Nola Gideon is there. The masseuse brings a totem pole into your bedroom and automatically lights the top where a small flame is burning. Think about a flame that self-ignites, Penny, and that describes a supernatural force. A flame resting on the head is a symbol of divine power. At Starsight, we think of the head as the seat of the soul. Who may I ask is Nola Gideon?"

"Oh! She was my Earth mother's caretaker. She must be symbolic of a guardian to Mother Earth."

"Good, Penny. God chose Gideon to free the people of Israel and to condemn their worship of idols. Think about the false idols of today and the repeated warnings in your dreams pointing to the hunger for profit from oil and gas. The people of planet Earth are doing no less than what the Midianites did in the Bible by destroying crops and trampling on everything."

The sun carved atop the Alert Bay totem was the spitting image of the flame atop my dream totem. It capped the message – *the massage*. Light-headed and dizzy from what seemed like a sudden change in altitude, I looked way up to the top of the totem and remembered *the haunting photograph of the little girl whose hair caught on fire.*[500] Connecting those images echoed my lasting impression that fire is a supernatural force.

Twink read my thoughts. "Yes, little firefly, the flame symbolizes the life giving and generative power of the sun that crowns the totem pole. Fire manifesting as a flame in your dream is a sign of spiritual power, transcendence, inspiration – all you've been experiencing on Mission Lavender. This unseen energy directs the change or passage from one state to another and is the medium for conveying messages heavenward.'"

Gee, I wonder if the symbols on the totem poles send messages down to Earth as well.

And ... *"nuke."* I'd never before heard that in a dream. The most revealing clue was in that one small word. It fit with the energy of a hydrogen bomb!

Galen blinked in with his Timelessness spectacles and refocused the message. *One whole family is in my apartment. I go to nuke the father's coffee.*

"One whole family? That's the family of man. Is Father awakening his children to an unseen nuclear threat? Could this threat involve a nova or supernova explosion that

500 501 10/7/99. See Ch. 96 – Three Moravian Missions, p. 489

spewed out bits and pieces that landed underwater, symbolized by the drowning Angela star? Does that sound right, Lord Galen?"

"I'll blink her in on that," wired Charlesbigstar.

"Well, well, well. Hello, my young friend. I've noticed you sprinting around the heavens and I see you're no longer the naïve little girl I once knew. You've drawn on the determination I remember so well and have taken to learning the ways of the cosmos.

"Penny, you've traveled almost as far as I have. It is Charlesbigstar, here. I recall your early days of struggle with mundane matters – family, friends, jobs, love – oh so many troubles with love. You have surmounted those conflicts and now embrace the greatest love of all – brotherly love – agape. I am greatly honored to be helping oversee your splendid progress."

"Uh, oh. This must really be a big deal. The whole consortium of guides is here."

Charlesbigstar blinked in again, "I wish to remind you, dear Penelope, of my involvement with the National Council for Geocosmic Research while on Earth. Though I was a serious astrologer in life, I was not a physical scientist. When I entered the portals of Heaven, I was met by two of the world's great scholars, your dear friends, Lord Galen and Twink Ptolemy. They took me on as an apprentice and introduced me to the Astronomy Branch of Starsight, within which is the optical division. This fit since astronomy was originally identified with astrology. I was blessed with the opportunity to expand my interests to the study of objects and phenomena beyond the Earth's atmosphere and all that you, Penelope, will come to know.

Having the mentor of my spiritual infancy around was like having a cup of warm cocoa before bedtime.

Charlesbigstar, halo gleaming, continued. "Now, I'll attempt to answer your probing question about the drowning star underwater and how that might relate to a nova or supernova explosion.

"When a large star runs out of nuclear fuel, the core collapses in milliseconds. The intense shock wave this causes blows off most of the star's mass.$^{\mathcal{E}105}$ In the last few minutes of its life, the exploding star releases more energy than it has generated in its entire existence, brightens several billion times that of the Sun and radiates more energy than all the other stars in the galaxy combined. Its outer layers are blasted out in a radioactive cloud in a phenomenal explosion called a supernova, more powerful than anything except the big bang with which the universe began. You were there then, Penelope, as were I and the rest of humankind. When the explosion is over, and its mass has been scattered into space, all that remains is a dense, dark cinder. In some cases, even that may disappear into a black hole."

Hmm .... Scattered into space. Maybe that's why there's metal all over the place.

"Charles, I've read about supernova remnants and I wonder if that's what all this metal is about."

"Well, .. um ...," hesitated Charlesbigstar, "the metal would come from a meteorite. Most meteorites originated in the main asteroid belt, a region between the orbits of Mars and Jupiter.

"A supernova remnant, on the other hand, is a glowing expanding radioactive cloud of gas and dust visible long after the initial explosion fades from view.

"Penelope, one example of this is the Crab nebula. The Chinese and the Arabs saw a brilliant point of light in the sky in 1054. Astronomers reported seeing it during the day for more than three weeks. Lord Rosse made a drawing of the scattered remnants of that supernova in 1844 based on what he saw through his thirty-six-inch telescope."

"Creeping crawlers! Charlesbigstar. That's the *crab I saw with the numbers 4391 or 4931, the upside-down OPEC, the upside-down Mobil, and the two keys.*[501] It's unimaginable that I'd be dreaming of a supernova explosion and fossil fuels that got buried in the earth millions of years ago!"

"Now back to our lesson. There's something called source rock, an organic-rich shale that contains the raw materials – petroleum and natural gas – from which hydrocarbons eventually form. I've noted that you frequently mention *hydrocarbons in carboniferous rocks.*"[502]

"Yes. Charlesbigstar. I do keep wrestling with that. It was so strange to dream of *CFCs in the rain being attracted to hydrocarbons in carboniferous rocks.* Do you think a supernova must have exploded and that materials ejected from this massive dying star fell all over this area and some parts landed in the water?"

"Mmmhmm ....Well, the metal you refer to could be from a meteorite fall which may confirm your suspicion about island arc systems being disabled. You see, Penelope, meteorites contain clear evidence that half-lives as short as 100,000 years were present in the cloud of gas and dust from which the Sun and its planets formed.

"We've transmitted a few grains of meteoric information with more to follow when you're ready. Now, it's up to you to piece it together. Go back to the dream, Penelope, and put on your Timelessness Glasses. Go to the scene where you go to *nuke the father's coffee. He says put it on 350 degrees and you put it in the upper oven.* You talk a lot about the heat, *how you can feel it and almost see it.*"

"OK, Charlesbigstar. Let's say the *upper oven* is the solar system, the lower oven, the Earth. And *350 degrees* is usually the temperature used for preheating. That's before cooking! Oh, no! Now I see it. We're in danger of being cooked! *The oven wouldn't turn off and*

---

501 10/7/99. See Ch. 96 – Three Moravian Missions. p.489
502 9/21/99. See Ch. 66 – White Rose, p. 311

I was afraid it would explode. I'm afraid the apartment will catch fire ... all the files will be burnt.
I saw the glass swelling and expanding.

"This is terrifying, because I think the apartment symbolizes Planet Earth – that
the family in the apartment is the family of man. The most frightening part is that *the*
company leaves and the stove is still on. That could mean either humankind escaped the fiery
inferno or was engulfed by it, like being sucked into a black hole."

The dream occurred on March 5, 2000. Some three and a half years later, an inconceivable string of anomalies played out in waking life right in the confines of my one-
bedroom apartment.

In September 2003, I was corresponding with the late pioneering parapsychologist
and psychiatrist, Dr. Montague Ullman, on the subject of black holes as it relates to his
concept of "a black hole of the psyche."[Ɛ106] In his opinion, the dream contains an enormously condensed information mass. We are forced to let it expand, as it were, or to
unfold, and then deal with it in bits and pieces, ordered as best we can in time and space.
He said these are the visual images that make up the Dream."

At the same time, I was reading an article[Ɛ107] on black holes and thermal dynamic
entropies – disorders in a physical system. When I learned that entropy is a measure of
energy in thermodynamics, my sense of *seeing and feeling heat* in the dream was validated.

Then something extraordinary happened. This dream heated up in waking mode.

In my bedroom, a black furniture unit frames my bed, acting as a headboard. An
elongated metal button in the headboard functions as a light switch. It extends outward
when off, inward when on. On this particular morning, I went to push the light switch
in to turn on the lights, but the switch vanished into the hole in the black cabinet. I was
unable to access it for it had disappeared into a black hole! I called the handyman to come
and fix it.

The parallel to the dream grew more curious as waking events unfolded. A portion
is worth repeating!

One whole family is in my apartment. I go to nuke the father's coffee. He says put it on 350°. I
put it in the upper oven to the right and push a long metal button. It starts heating and won't turn
off. I'm afraid it will explode. I can see the glass swelling and expanding. I'm afraid the apartment
will catch fire ...

A few days later, I began to defrost a stick of butter in the microwave oven. It arced.
I saw a flame. It scared me. I looked inside and there on the roof of the oven was a black
hole! There was the smell of burning. The next morning I'd forgotten about the arc-
ing and absentmindedly put a mug of coffee in to heat up. It arced again and flashed as
though a fire was about to start. The black hole was still there. I didn't make the connection until the next day, when I remembered the black hole in the bedroom unit and the
corresponding dream.

Two days later, the handyman checked the outlet where the microwave was plugged in. It was OK. I took many pictures of the **black hole in the microwave**. Before I discarded the microwave, something told me to remove the manufacturer's sticker. On it is printed **Manufactured in 1989 -- Made in Thailand.**

To tie things together – as in Thailand – I want you to know, dear Reader, that the bolded words above, again, self-bolded.

The black hole in my microwave oven

Charlesbigstar spun back in. "That was quite an exciting adventure you had, Penelope, right in the privacy of your own abode. I think you should know that in cosmology, there is something called cosmic microwave background radiation which is a form of electromagnetic radiation discovered in 1965."

"You've gotta be kidding! You're making it up! C'mon, Charlesbigstar. You're pulling my leg."

"No, no, my friend. It's no joke. Most cosmologists consider the cosmic microwave background radiation to be the best evidence for the hot big bang model as the thermal history of the universe many Earth physicists believe that blackbody radiation strongly supports the hot big bang model. A black body is a theoretical object that absorbs all radiation that hits it without reflecting or emitting radiation itself. You'll be pleased to know that the renowned German physicist, Gustave Kirchhoff had a theory that radiation coming from a tiny hole in an oven was representation of an emitter. This led to quantum theory forty years later! So it looks like blackbody radiation is on your plate, Penny."

"Black body? Believin' Bejeevers! Charles. I had a dream about an *oriental couple and the girl had a black body.*[503] They represent the Eurasian and African plates. Could that also have something to do with the Big Bang?"

If you can imagine a spirit doubled over laughing like a hyena, you'd see Charlesbigstar at that moment. I didn't know if I was verging on the ridiculous or the sublime.

"Penelope, you've been traveling back to the origins of the universe and now you're doing the same with the Species, but when a girl with a black body pops up out of nowhere, I am a bit startled. What I find amusing is your method of discovery, for it is both ridiculous and sublime. As Tom Paine said in The Age of Reason, 'The two are so closely related that it is but one step from one to the other.' One step above the sublime makes the ridiculous; and one step above the ridiculous makes the sublime again, Your black-bodied girl may be just one step above the ridiculous.

"As for the species, as humans evolved from the Australopithecines about two million years ago in Africa, you are now moving toward the Big Bang theory of human evolution and how it relates to the history of Earth's geological record. It's as though you are taking fossil pieces and putting them together to tell a story about the past that may be pointing to the future. Now, let's return to your dream about the father's coffee."

Added to the scrupulously detailed dream about *nuking the father's coffee,* then witnessing the sudden appearance of two black holes in my apartment just when I had been talking and reading about them, was beyond comprehension. It was a miracle. There were no words. Cosmic awakening reached far beyond what we on Earth can understand. I wanted to linger in the wonder of it, but had to push ahead.

Charlesbigstar counseled, "Push ahead you must, but, Penny, it's time to give your readers a circle. We've taken an interesting side excursion into the cosmos and they may need a reading from your Psymometer to get back on course."

"You're right. They must be as lost in space as I am. Where do you think I should begin?"

"Why don't you form another circle around the *Totem Pole* dream[504] and start with Alert Bay, since that's where the totem materialized."

"Thanks, Charlesbigstar. I knew a vital piece was missing. Alert Bay for being such a remote little outpost sure holds a lot of clues.

"OK. Here goes the circle: *Success Wake Lake* – Alert Bay – *Drowning Star* – Supernova – HH – Hydrogen-Helium – Deuterium – Gideon – Caretaker to Mother Earth – *Massage* – Message – *Totem Pole* – Memorial – *Flame* – Sun – *Self-igniting flame* – Supernatural – *Whole Family* – Humankind – *350 degrees* – Preheating – *Upper oven* – Solar System – *Expanding Glass* – Expanding Universe – *Nuking father's coffee* – Father's

503 3/27/00. See Ch. 102 – A Ghostly Park ... An Orb of Light, pp. 534–536
504 3/5/00.   See Ch 105 – A Drowning Star, p. 551

Nuclear Wake-up Call! And back to Alert Bay – *Success Wake Lake* as the dream had named it!"

Had pieces from a supernova explosion fragmented over the Canadian land scattering toxic remnants in its wake? Were those remnants the nickel-copper droppings found in the Alert Bay dream? Could they be contributing to back-arc spreading in the two tectonically disrupted island arc systems in Newfoundland/Labrador, Vancouver Island and elsewhere?

WOW! So all that metal I've been stumbling over could be signatures left from the Big Bang! Maybe a supernova exploded all over the place and pieces of it scattered not only in my dreams, but to where they've led me. I must remember the architect/logos dream message… *The first clue has to do with the word logo(s). I see a metal structure around the word. It means I have the clues.*[505]

If cosmic microwave background radiation is a dream clue about one whole family, is it awakening us to the danger of "star wars," Ronald Reagan's nuclear defense system?

The 350-degree temperature suggests we are preheating, preparing to cook. Is this also an alert to Global Warming? Star Wars or Global Warming, this dream was a message that defiant, reckless and arrogant child's play could ignite our whole planet. Star Wars was certainly a more sophisticated kind of child's play. Or – is it taking us back to the birth of the solar system?

Could the collapse of a supernova have given birth to a metaphorical black hole? It surely did in my dreaming-waking experience. Were we being reminded of a demise similar to that of a black hole where, instead of facing the fate of being sucked into one, the mass energy would be returned to the universe, but in a mangled form.[E108] Were the elements in this dream – *the drowning star, the totem pole, the whole family, the supernatural fire* – pieces of garbled residue that weren't completely gobbled up by a black hole, as in the physics of matter – or – by the black hole of the psyche? Were the bits and pieces of our lives continuing to emit radiation and eventually opening to reveal the information within? If so, it was a whopper of a mangled message!

The admonition in the dream replayed like a broken record: *I'm afraid the apartment will catch fire … all the files will be burnt. I can feel the heat. I can almost see it. The company leaves and the stove is still on. Someone needs to turn it off.*

---

505 6/1/96. See Ch. 98 – Word In A Hole, pp. 507–09

CHAPTER ONE HUNDRED SIX

WHOLES

In our dreams we struggle against fragmentation
and move toward wholeness.
Montague Ullman

My bite-sized lesson in Astronomy had concluded. My mind was filled with new and wondrous things so much bigger than me and even bigger than big when I noticed a puff of sparkling science dust encircling Steno with his larger-than-life magnifying glass. I couldn't wait to find out if I had fallen through the earth.

"Doc Steno, tell me the truth. Do you think the hole I've been coming up from in so many of my dreams could be a black hole?"

"Well, Clueso, that was your perception when you dreamt *you were falling into a black hole and a slab brought you up.*[506]

No longer an illusion, the dreams of *falling, descending slabs* and *poisonous gas hovering overhead* were taking form. The dream body was transforming to a real body, Creation descending. *Nola Gideon* was there when Angela drowned. The Gideon Bible represented God, the prime creative power.

Nicolaus Steno chimed in. "It may help you to know that Gideon received his call to action by way of an angel, which may explain why your drowning star is named *Angela.* He summoned the Israelites and, with a small band of followers, attacked the Midianites who oppressed the people of Israel when he was a youth.[E109] It is said that Gideon and a servant gathered intelligence information by way of a dream interpretation. Following the victory, the Israelites asked Gideon to rule over them. He refused power because he believed God is the king of Israel but he fashioned an ephod of gold from the plunder of his followers, as a reward for his leadership. Forty years later, after Gideon died the people began again to worship a false god and again fell into servitude. The Bible tells this story in Judges, 6 to 8, and we, the human species, continue to tell it."

---

506 8/23/96.

Footnotes contain dream dates and references to prior pages where the dream appeared.

Endnotes contain bibliographical references, are marked with "Ɛ" in the text, and appear at the end of the book.

"Dr. Steno, I had a dream long ago *about two interlocking rings with the word 'Gideon' around them.*[507] Because the ring, an unbroken circle is a longstanding symbol of eternity, if woven into the *Success Wake Lake* dream, might those rings symbolize Heaven and Earth?"

"Penelope, when we transmitted the Gideon dream to you, we placed a house within each of the two rings. One house was the Solar System and the other was Earth. One of Mission Lavender's intentions is to make known the union betwixt Heaven and Earth — to show its fullness, its oneness, its permanence. But mind you, Earth is only one planet among several that orbit the Sun.

"Now, let us look at Rupert Sheldrake's idea that 'Creation is made by division of a primary whole. That you start with the undifferentiated unity and then there's a series of splittings or bifurcations, as in the book of Genesis, where light and dark are separated, then earth and dry land.'[110]

"In your Gideon dream, the solar system and Earth are separated but connected. The fire upstairs was telling you that the *swelling and expanding glass* represents an expanding universe, which is intrinsically connected to lava flows in the solar system as well as to subsea volcanism on Earth, an unrelenting subject. That explains your terrible fright about *the apartment catching fire* for now you know, Penelope, that the apartment is home —Planet Earth."

I wondered why the supernatural was seen as a dark place inhabited by witches and monsters, ghouls, and dragons, a place where control and domination presides, where dark secrets thrive on terror, death, conspiracies, and destruction. I have walked with the great minds of the ages who have guided me with the light of their wisdom.

Having been shepherded along this celestial concourse by these ancient masters, we have witnessed the unfolding of earth events, tasted the aphrodisiac of truth and journeyed far beyond the banality of language to heed the high call. I had discovered that the strength in taking the high road opens miraculously to the mystery of eternal wisdom delivering gifts of light, giving hope to the hopeless and showing us when to turn, and when not to. The realm we found ourselves in is one where I have heard their voices, seen their spirits and felt their presence. They are closer than we think. And they are trying to help us. They are teaching us to connect the dots. They are witnessing the vulnerability of Planet Earth through the carelessness of fiery industrial accidents with dire warnings of more to come. They are pleading for sustainability. Our beautiful nurturing Earth with its natural formations and phenomenal wonders is the only habitable home we have. We know of none other.

I learned that "the word 'health' is based on an Anglo-Saxon word 'hale' meaning 'whole.' That is, to be healthy is to be whole. The English 'holy' is based on the same root as 'whole.' This indicates that man has sensed always that wholeness or integrity is an absolute necessity to make life worth living. Yet, over the ages, he has generally lived

507 9/30/95.

in fragmentation."[E111] The time draws nigh for us to heal our internal strife, to reconcile differences and come together as one family occupying one planet.

And here, dear Reader, we pause for a moment. Three endnotes in the preceding pages initially appeared in garbled code. This was a first. The computer genies were unusually energetic the night I wrote about supernovas and Gideon.

Since then, editorial changes have altered some of the language and removed some of the codes. These are the citations before they switched over.

Endnote 103: "The Origin of the Elements." *Microsoft® Encarta® Encyclopedia 2001.* © 1993-2000.

Endnote 105: "How a Supernova Explodes." *Microsoft® Encarta® Encyclopedia 2001.* © 1993-2000.

Endnote 109: "Gideon." *Microsoft® Encarta® Encyclopedia 2001.* © 1993-2000.

And here are the three sections of text they corresponded to before they switched to garbled math:

1) "An old star will spew forth not only these nuclei but also other elements from carbon up to iron."

2) "When a large star runs out of nuclear fuel, the core collapses in milliseconds. The subsequent 'bounce' of the core generates a shock wave so intense that it blows off most of the star's mass."

3) "It may help you to know that Gideon received his call to action by an angel, which explains why your drowning star is named Angela. He summoned the Israelites and with a small band of followers attacked the Midianites, who had oppressed the people of Israel when Gideon was a youth."

And in the still of the night, the instruction of my ascended masters – Claudius Galen, Claudius Ptolemy, Marie Curie, Nicolaus Steno, joined the spirit voice of their apprentices – Charlesbigstar, Peggymoonbeam, Agneswiseheart, in one long, deep life-sustaining breath, in one softly hushed sound on the winds of eternity, whispering:

CONNECT THE DOTS.

CHAPTER ONE HUNDRED SEVEN

TELEGRAPH COVE

You see, wire telegraph is a kind of a very, very long cat. You pull his tail in New York and his head is meowing in Los Angeles. Do you understand this? And radio operates exactly the same way: you send signals here, they receive them there. The only difference is that there is no cat.

Albert Einstein

Day Five: Alert Bay – Telegraph Cove – Qualicum Beach

Heading toward Qualicum on partly paved and partly dirt logging roads, Smilingshadow and I were in pursuit of Nimpkish Lake. Peggymoonbeam's message was Success Wake Lake. We now knew that Alert Bay corresponded to "Wake" in her directive, but we were missing the "Lake" portion. We approached the diminutive sign for Nimpkish.

Off the main road and obscured in wilderness I spotted a structure: an isolated country store and a solitary gas pump. The scene echoed a strange familiarity. It was undeniably the picture in one of my dreams, its only telltale feature – spontaneity.

A dream-sighting in a place I never set foot is awe-inspiring, no matter how mundane. Awash in waves of gratitude impossible to describe, the certainty of following and discovering banished the few lingering traces of doubt.

The manifestations sat quietly waiting to be noticed.

I am driving looking for a commissary that used to be there. You could get gas and most of what you need. A nice man comes out. I say I have been away for a long time. He says, "We're still here." The man is very warm and friendly and invites me to stay for dinner. I call my friend Bonnie on the remote phone. I say, "I won't be back for a while ... I'm with these wonderful people." I look out the window and see an animal. There's confusion about whether it's a boar or a bear. Later I see a blue rug with a burning cigarette and a crystal candy dish.[508]

---

508 11/11/98.

Footnotes contain dream dates and references to prior pages where the dream appeared.
Endnotes contain bibliographical references, are marked with "Ɛ" in the text, and appear at the end of the book.

Hmm. Quartz crystal – piezoelectricity. Again, I wondered – could a piezoelectric spark produce enough electric voltage to start a fire? Electric cigarette lighters and barbecue starters contain piezoelectric crystals.

Facing the gas station was a sign that read "Telegraph Cove." It struck me that my friend Bonnie, whom I called on a remote phone in the dream, had since passed over to the other side. The voice of Mission Lavender communicated through code inside the dream and out.

Telegraph translated to Morse code – to Save Our Souls – to MOMOM – to Save Our Earth. Strange that radio listeners within fifteen kilometers of this killer whale sanctuary were tuning into the all-whale radio station while I was tuning into the other side.

The sign was so well hidden, one blink and we would have missed it.

Alert Bay and Nimpkish Lake were each fingered by a commonplace but unmistakable scene presaged by a dream. Could these scenes have been anywhere? Perhaps. But, this is considered the forestry capital of British Columbia and known for its grizzlies. A popular tourist attraction is bear watching. *Boar ... bear;* a double entendre straight from the dream, bore as in boring, as in mining – bear as in "Grizzly." There were certain to be bears in these woods.

Bears aside, budding connections shouted that we were on the right track. In the words of Robert Frost, "All thought is a feat of association: having what's in front of you bring up something in your mind that you almost didn't know you knew." [E112]

A replay of the smoldering message was illustrated this time by a *burning cigarette in a rug.*

Continuing southeast along the island's coast, we arrived at Qualicum Beach, known as Canada's Riviera. It was too late to drive further, so we called our next scheduled hotel in Port Alberni and canceled. We decided to stay at Qualicum that night and were thrilled with our room overlooking the ocean.

I called the hotel operator for tips on where to go in the area. She asked why I left the message.

I replied, "What message?"

"I got a message from your room that said, 'Thank you for the return call.'"

I said, "We didn't leave a message," but she insisted: "Well, it was from your room."

I had no answer. She again insisted the message was from us. Thoroughly exasperated, she said, "I have no idea what this is all about." Neither did I.

Smilingshadow and I laughed ourselves silly. Someone was having a jolly good time of it.

CHAPTER ONE HUNDRED EIGHT

BEAVER CREEK: A LAVENDER MAP

Day Six: Beaver Creek (subdivision of Port Alberni)

Iwas drawn to Beaver Creek, delivered by its namesake in a dream, but it was a challenge finding it.

The dream features daytime tours. A man points them out on a map. It's a short drive from the hotel and it's later in the day. Then you take a boat or a truck. I want to say Beaver Creek or Beaver Falls.[509]

I'd never heard of Beaver Creek or Beaver Falls. During the planning stages of our trip, we could find no one on Vancouver Island who knew about a Beaver Creek or Falls. From tourist bureaus to regional librarians to local townsfolk, to every map we could find, it was a nonentity.

Our travel planner finally located a postage-stamp sized Beaver Creek in the Port Alberni area along our route, and built it into our itinerary. I then stumbled on a listing that indicated a meteorite fall in the Beaver Creek area of northern British Columbia, quite a distance from the Vancouver Island area. The Beaver Creek we would visit would not be where the meteorite landed.

Port Alberni, nestled in the Alberni Valley, is known for its salt-water fishing. Though angling for fish wasn't on our agenda, it proved ideal for hooking a dream clue.

We arrived the next morning at the Information Center at Port Alberni. I asked if they had a map of Beaver Creek, not expecting any results. Not only was there a map but the best-marked map we had come across. This little subdivision of Port Alberni had its very own map – and a lavender one, at that!

More astounding was that the map was chock full of clues. The names of streets were all common names that had crept into my dreams. Fixated on this map, I was taking in the layout of the town as the Information Center woman was giving us directions. I had

---

509 7/4/00.

Footnotes contain dream dates and references to prior pages where the dream appeared.
Endnotes contain bibliographical references, are marked with "Ɛ" in the text, and appear at the end of the book.

nearly tuned her out as I focused in sheer disbelief on two streets – Karen Place and a street marked with her surname, one adjacent to the other. Uncanny!

We did our preliminary reconnaissance work by slowly driving through the no-longer elusive Beaver Creek. Smilingshadow observed, "Penelope, it seems that nearly everything in sight is painted blue. Have the decorators decided to change their color scheme?"

"Good grief! Smilingshadow! Blue is the color Karensurefoot and I were looking for when we rummaged all through Newfoundland in search of *four blue rubbery logs!*[510] We did find one log painted blue so if the other three were here it would be unbelievable! But the blue logs in the dream were rubbery, and rubbery hasn't kicked in, at least not yet."

So began our excursion to Karen Place and the road that amazingly designated – or remembered – her family name.

We rushed to the two streets inexplicably marked for Karen. We were on an intersecting street when Smilingshadow slammed on the brakes screeching to a halt. I was sure we'd been rear-ended. She bellowed, "Sparkle Plenty! Sparkle! I see blue logs!" We turned around and drove to the house where she had spotted fresh cut logs with the bluest of blue paint on the end – that mystifying paint which defied explanation.

The logs, some ten to twelve feet long, sat in clear view on someone's lawn. Obviously, they were not cut for firewood. When I stepped back to get a perspective of these logs, I noticed a blue picket fence around the house – the fence, Peggymoonbeam's imprimatur.

Were Karen Place and the road bearing her last name awaiting our arrival? Had an entourage of escorts directed us to the picket fence and the blue logs?

Not a speck of the yellow and lavender combo from Alert Bay was to be seen in Beaver Creek. Instead, the little community was covered in French blue. The personification of Karen in my dreams is French blue, be it a picture frame, clothing, an aura – anything at all. Here, it was on everything: garbage cans, boat tarpaulins, lawnmower covers, boat tows, roofs of houses. You name it, it was blue. Was the diminutive Beaver Creek signaling a linkage to Karensurefoot's sleuthing in Newfoundland? Some sort of information or mental field had to be following us. It certainly seemed that unknown laws of Nature were hard at work. Was this another illustration of Sheldrake's morphic fields containing inherent memory?

Someone or something was remembering, for many of our Vancouver adventures were corresponding to adventures in Newfoundland – but painted a different color.

Endorphin rushes of emotion overcame us, our insights too glaring to ignore. We knew the entire web of cross connections was coming from an intelligence more powerful than any of us can fathom. First, there's a lull leading up to a subtle clue, a thread, a connection; then, recognition gives birth to unanticipated bursts of discovery – a relationship between wake and dream – in a timeless realm where everything is imaginable. Often

510 See Ch. 62 – A Birthday Party In Placentia, pp. 287, 289

we sensed a wild surge of energy followed by oceanic feelings of oneness, of protection, of continuous motion in a process we had become a part of.

Our adventure was picking up speed as had the Newfoundland experience. A pattern begins to emerge. It's slow-going before materializations peak, like rebooting your computer. Then, one by one, physical signs begin to pop. Meaningful icons like the picket fence or the church appear, latching onto other clues. Elements in the dream, no longer separate parts but moving toward physical connection are routinely nestled within an area of about a half mile. If I were to draw it, the path that holds the manifestations would be loop-shaped. Color designations seem to define an area. Usually the signal is in plain sight. Dreams of the ordinary – a gas station, a pile of toys – are markers that subtly identify a locale.

"And, I might add," wired Peggymoonbeam, "Agneswiseheart's Oneiroball cannot control where we drop our messages closer than within about half a mile. Now, that ain't bad considering we're traveling at about 186,000 miles per second."

I marveled at how the celestial guides finessed color coordination. They must have their own paint shop. The picket fence in Alert Bay was painted light lavender. The picket fence in Beaver Creek is painted light blue – both pastels. They must use the same painter.

Peggymoonbeam whirled by, "It's our house painter, silly."

Magical, mysterious, mystical, ephemeral, unexplainable; it was all of that and more.

The blue logs were a short drive to Stamp Falls Provincial Park, which wound around a spool of dream references to the *postman, the mail boy, the mailbag*[511] bringing to life miles of freestanding mailboxes along the roadsides.

Arriving at the nearby Echo Center Museum and Library late in the day, we took a quick spin around its exhibits. We came across a display of collages dedicated to the March 27, 1964, tsunami, brought on by the Alaska 9.2 earthquake that had devastated much of western Canada. It was the most powerful quake ever recorded in the U.S.

I was aware of the Alaska earthquake, but never did I associate it with Port Alberni, much less Beaver Creek. I hadn't even heard of Port Alberni until our travel planners told us we'd have to drive there to get to Beaver Creek.

When I asked what damage was done in Beaver Creek by the tsunami, the local librarian said, "It affected the low lying areas behind River Road where homes were flooded. It was terrible. Small bridges were swept away and sections of highway were under water."

How could it be that River Road is so near Karen Place, the blue picket fence and the blue log? A feat of sheer derring-do had led us to X-marks-the-spot: River Road and Beaver Creek, two of the most heavily damaged areas in Port Alberni.

---

511 7/4/00.

Bohm's views of this apparent continuous unfolding had come to life. As expressed by a mathematical physicist, "At any given moment, one of these ensembles may be unfolded and localized, and the next moment, this one enfolds and is replaced by another that unfolds. If this process continues in a rapid and regular fashion in which each unfoldment is localized adjacent to the previous one, it gives the appearance of continuous motion of a particle, to which we humans have given the name electron."[113]

Accounts of the disaster sparked a curious twist of time-reversed fate. Were the *smiling horse on the ferry* and the team of *mechanics on the other side* leading us to some fuzzy strand of the Titanic story or some larger story that hadn't yet unfolded? Were news accounts of the disaster providing us with the mechanics of violent earthquake behavior and its range of destruction? The meaning of *mechanics on the other side* had deepened. Not only were they spiritual specialists with otherworldly clairvoyance empowering them to see earth's stresses; they were skilled technicians coming to repair a fractured earth. They had come to teach the basic mechanics of geology and to shed greater insight than twenty-first-century technology could into movements taking place in the earth.

At the Echo Library, I found newspaper articles, yellowed with age.

"In 1964, with no warning system, the destructive tsunami was generated by North America's strongest earthquake of the twentieth century, 8.5 on the Richter Scale with its epicenter off Anchorage. The energy released was estimated to equal the detonation of thirty-two million tonnes of TNT. Tidal waves rushed to all corners of the Pacific Ocean."[114]

The library was closing in an hour. With no time to sift through reams of news that might shed light, we decided to stay the night in Port Alberni. When Smilingshadow called ahead to our next hotel in Duncan to change the reservation to the following night, the reservation clerk insisted they had us booked for two nights – a reservation we never made.

We sniffed around Port Alberni for a bit, then ducked into the local bookshop. While scoping out books that might be relevant, the shopkeeper interrupted us to say our car was beeping. We reacted, "Beeping?" He goes outside, makes sure it's ours, comes back and says, "You'd better turn it off." Smilingshadow ran out to the car and checked everything. There was no sign of beeping. She returned to the bookshop. The moment she set foot inside, it started beeping again.

"See," smiled the young Canadian, "I told you."

When we left the bookshop, the beeping stopped. We laughed our socks off. Now we knew our impish admirers were playing games we on Earth cannot fathom. I thought of Agneswiseheart and her "beep beeps." Like the birds, they seem to have their own language. Perhaps they were telling us that hunting for books wasn't necessary just then. Maybe something more important was in the wings.

We went to the Port Alberni hotel we had cancelled for the night before to see if we could get a room. As I filled out the registration form, the woman saw my name and said, "We have a room for you."

I smiled. "We cancelled it. That was from last night."

"I know, said the clerk, "but we have a room booked for you for tonight."

I noticed her crossing out the price of $105 and writing in $75. I asked what the difference represented, thinking we got a lesser room. "Oh," she said, "we just decided to lower our rates because it's kind of a slow season."

Unseen helpers lit our way. Advance reservations – unexpected discounts – satchels of information. Miracles abounding.

CHAPTER ONE HUNDRED NINE

ON THE WAY TO HONEYMOON BAY

Day Seven: Port Alberni – Honeymoon Bay

We spent the next morning in the Port Alberni Echo Center Museum and Library and left with volumes of material on the 1964 tsunami that I'd devour when I got home. The Vancouver Island linkage to Newfoundland was intensifying as the weaving of this magic carpet would transport us to lands once only dreamt of. I was pleased to find a geographical index of the coordinates I might someday need. "Good heavens," I thought. "What's come over me? How is it possible that I'm ecstatic over coordinates?"

The next stop on our dream itinerary was Honeymoon Bay, but I was hungry for a sliver of unstructured time. Taking in a few of the local sights would be a welcome change, but my traveling companion refused to stop. Charging ahead and glued to the wheel like a jet fighter pilot, good-natured, even-tempered Smilingshadow morphed into a dictator. It was the only part of the trip where I felt stressed for I simply couldn't understand how, on a dime, this easygoing, agreeable person was ready to charge like the bulls at Pamplona. She drove at breakneck speed, leaning into the wind, her eyes locked on the road; there was no talking to her. No matter how many times I suggested stopping, it fell on deaf ears. Her only reply was a polite, "We've got to get to Honeymoon Bay."

"Why the rush?" I kept asking.

Her pat answer: "I don't know."

"Well, hey, Miss Smilingshadow. I know we've got to get to Honeymoon Bay. I put it on the itinerary. But we can have a little down time too, ya' know. Can you just slow down a bit? You're acting like the captain of the Titanic on its maiden voyage. There are no records to break here."

No response. My admonition only accelerated the speed.

Her abrupt personality change allowed for only one quick lunch stop at Chemainus, a picturesque little town known for murals painted on its buildings. One can follow yellow-

Footnotes contain dream dates and references to prior pages where the dream appeared.
Endnotes contain bibliographical references, are marked with "Ɛ" in the text, and appear at the end of the book.

painted footsteps on a stroll to see larger-than-life world-famous murals that depict the history of the Chemainus Valley – that is, if Smilingshadow isn't at the wheel.

While we drove, or I should say flew, trying to calm myself, I thought I'd explain the reason for the Honeymoon Bay stop.

Over the whistling wind, I shouted, "Smilingshadow, if you can hear me, here's why we're going to Honeymoon Bay."

"More than two years ago, I dreamt about *a couple who is getting married. I look at their honeymoon pictures. One is a photograph of a massive sculpture with them in front. There is a repeating design in a satiny stainless steel. It looks like upside-down Js. It's very modern, but seems old.*

"Another picture of the couple is in front of a European church, which is a light grey brick with graceful lines. The architecture is ancient but it too, looks new as though it's been sandblasted. One of the most prominent symbols in the dream is a 7 o'clock shadow on the face of the boyfriend."[512]

As in Newfoundland, in an attempt to flesh out an actual route, I overlaid dream pointers that signaled locales onto a Vancouver map. The exotic blend of concrete and abstract red-circled Honeymoon Bay. Truth and Instinct paved a road the entire north to south length of the Island, ending on the mainland.

This is likely to give cold Science apoplexy, but from the outset, Truth had employed Instinct as its pilot. Assistance was granted in the commissioning of two spiritually qualified co-pilots – Karensurefoot and Smilingshadow. Occasionally Instinct took us on a fishing expedition; other times, it led us down a dark alley. Though light was occasionally eclipsed in shadow, as in the 7 o'clock shadow we sought in the Honeymoon Bay area, instinct's wee voice knew where to go long before we did and was usually waiting at our destination.

Back to the dream – a treasure hunt, rife with clues: a *7 o'clock shadow, a massive piece of sculpture and a light grey brick church that had been sandblasted.* Intuition tagged this a VID (Very Important Dream), introducing it with an oblique *message from a pharmacy or a chemist upstairs, about a black bead.* Our valiant pilot would hold the numinous communiqué in storage for a future quest.

At a general store en route to Honeymoon Bay, we asked if there were any churches in the area. Chewing on a toothpick, the local storekeeper sleepily muttered, "No, ma'am. No churches in Honeymoon Bay fer the last twenty years, but there's plenty in the Lake Cowichan area."

What in the world? Was this one of those dark alleys?

Having raced this far at Mario-Andretti speed, we agreed to complete our Mission and travel on to Honeymoon Bay for a look-see. Goodwill was restored, we laughed over our wild ride to the unknown and finally relaxed.

As it turns out, Honeymoon Bay overlooks Cowichan Lake. We parked the car and started walking the beach. We came across two cinder blocks in the sand. With nothing to detract from this sighting except some bramble, I stood transfixed, gazing at the blocks sticking out like sore thumbs on this deserted stretch of beach. I might have tripped over them had I not recently dreamt them.

Honeymoon Bay would become the catalyst for the confluence of Vancouver, Newfoundland, and Labrador.

CHAPTER ONE HUNDRED TEN

THE MARRIAGE
OF CONCRETE AND ABSTRACT

Smilingshadow, I'd like to share with you the anatomy of two dreams with themes about cinder blocks. They illustrate how dreams cross-connect and integrate with waking over time.

"OK. Sparkle Plenty. Go!"

"This one snuck in just before we left. *The main character is an architect in a midlife crisis. Yellowish cinder blocks are at this corner. It depicts a multi-colored house resembling a child's kindergarten drawing. There's reference to a chemical.*"[513]

Smilingshadow reacted, "Another chemical? Mmhmm."

"What is your take on the dream, Sparkle?"

"Well, it's an intuitive guess, but I think an *architect in a midlife crisis* matches the archi-tectonics theme and stands for an island arc system undergoing geological crisis. Midlife would point to the geologic age of the underlying rock layers created by the archi-tect of the universe. I have a hunch this connects with the half-life of a chemical element. My knee-jerk reaction is that cinder translates to ash and yellowish to sulfur."

"Gee," gasped Smilingshadow. "From what I remember in chemistry, you're now talking radioactive decay."

"It was a foreign language to me, Shadow. My first brush with radioactivity was in Newfoundland when I was under the tutelage of Dr. Steno and Marie Curie. They helped decipher the many radioactive elements bombarding my dreams, particularly fluorspar and radon. The strongest impression was the toll it took on my beloved mentor, Marie Curie. Radioactivity actually claimed her life."

"Look up, Sparkle. There's a radiant circle of light above us." Speaking of the patron saint of elements, it was the pioneering spirit of our resident chemist.

---

513 9/2/00.

Footnotes contain dream dates and references to prior pages where the dream appeared.
Endnotes contain bibliographical references, are marked with "Ɛ" in the text, and appear at the end of the book.

"Nice intuitive work, girls. You know, radioactive dating is a measurement of the amount of radioactive material in a rock. Think back to radioactive decay and that radioactive 'clock' we use to measure geologic time. In theory, the decay process is never complete; there's always some residual radioactivity."

"So, Marie, there are clocks in these rocks! Then the midlife crisis must be significant in terms of dating. If only ..." But she was gone.

"It's amazing how they always know where to find you," exclaimed Smilingshadow, "even though Earth is so enormous. Talk about being tuned in."

"Yep, but I bet Planet Earth looks like little dot up at Terracrust and Starsight. Just think of Jupiter. It's the largest planet in our solar system and its volume is fourteen hundred times greater than Earth's. In a series of dreams I haven't yet revealed, things and people are miniaturized. I wonder if they see us as Lilliputians."

"What do you make of the child's drawing of the house?" asked Smilingshadow.

I took a deep breath and blurted out, "Our house – our family – humankind – is between a rock and a hard place geologically and we don't even know it. The corner in the dream might be this corner of the world. But it makes me really anxious because 'corner' usually portends that something is 'around the corner.'"

The first cinder block dream that I've told Steno, depicts *children at play. Part of a wall had been broken through and a hole had become larger to expose actual concrete blocks, like cinder blocks. The opening is huge. Wyoming is a clue. A bed comes apart in two.*[514]

The *bed that comes apart* symbolizes a geological bed of volcanic material in a growing fracture zone. Could volcanic activity in the Yellowstone Plateau be cutting into Grand Teton National Park just south of Yellowstone National Park and creating a big hole?

On cue, Tu-whit made himself known, delivering some findings on activity in Yellowstone National Park:

ÕÕ "'A 17-year University of Utah study shows that the power of the huge volcanic hotspot beneath Yellowstone National Park is much greater than previously thought. The study found the Teton Range and Jackson Hole to be moving in unexpected directions, complicating efforts to predict when the fault might generate disastrous earthquakes near the ski resorts of Jackson Hole. The subterranean volcanic plume, 300 miles wide at its top, may explain why ground along the Teton fault moves in directions the opposite of those expected.'"[Ɛ115]

Tu-whit's news was in sync with my dream.

---

514 2/29/00. See Ch. 70 – The Anonymous Artist Paints A Hole, p. 328

And to further connect, I associated yellowish cinder blocks with the dreaded DAS SHOOT! DAS BOOT! dream *where a soft wall in the corner was broken through revealing icky yellowish stuff; the yellow stuff being fiberglass strands* [515] ... made from molten glass ... lava.

Walls broken through ...Yellow ... Ash ... Lava ... Corner.

Is it around the corner? Is it imminent?

Diverse components poured into the gravelly mixture were waiting for it to solidify, to become concrete, to connect. There it is again: another link connecting Yellowstone to Newfoundland to Labrador to Vancouver – possibly Louisiana and heavens knows where else.

"This is so frightening, Smilingshadow, because time is furiously ticking away and someone has to do something soon. We're sitting on a powder keg."

Tick Tock. Tick Tock. Tick Tock.

"The clock is running. Will this message come out before the fire spreads? If I could have any wish in the world, I'd wish with all my heart that someone will hear me – that someone realizes the Dream is not just fantasy – that sometimes it's rock-hard and solid – as real as a cement cinder block."

"Well, you know, Sparkle, the naked truth makes people hide from the reality of the dangers to human life. They may just think of this as no big deal so they don't have to look at it. Your Mission is to awaken others to the deeper meaning of the message so its dark portent doesn't come to pass."

Smilingshadow and I meandered along the slightly curved beach. As we turned the bend, we came on a helter-skelter collection of beach toys – a surfboard, scuba diving gear, life vests, a rubber raft, a log, goggles – a seaside portrait that colored in the dream landscape of grown-up children at play.

Winding our way back along the shoreline, rounding the bend for the second time, we nearly stumbled again for, just as the dream directed...

Cinder blocks are at this corner.

They still sat at "that corner," still sore thumbs on the deserted beach. Ghostly goose bumps! Two cinder blocks in the sand – two cinder blocks in my dreams! They sure got things to match.

Geologists describe cinder as small pieces of ejecta that often look like aa – volcanic rock.

It was concrete, as the dream presaged: formlessness melting into form ... the intangible merging with the tangible ... the abstract with the concrete ... the seamless reality. Bohm's enfolding and unfolding.

---

515 7/30/98.

We got back in the car and headed toward the Cowichan Lake District. Chief of remote sensing, Smilingshadow, spotted a cross on a spire. We followed our line of sight to a little country church which, ringing true to the dream, had been sandblasted and had a modern façade. It was named St. Louis de Montfort.

But other elements were missing. Where were the massive sculpture and the inscrutable 7 o'clock shadow, the upside-down Js, the satiny stainless steel to be found?

Reflecting on the fragmentation of the dream and its symmetry to waking, I toyed with the idea of the proximity of physical objects manifesting piecemeal within a defined radius. This could make some sense if we were to imagine the view from on high. What would appear to us here on Earth as a marathon scavenger hunt stretching across miles, might shrink to a city block from a celestial overlook. That chain of thought coincided with many dreams about microscopes.

We passed a clock atop a railroad pub called The End of The Line. We noted that it was not 7 o'clock and began to talk about how the 7 o'clock shadow might not show up exactly as a clock. I was rambling – "If typical of the Dream, it might be something pointing to 7 o'clock" ... when suddenly a massive sculpture came into view, the centerpiece of a beautiful and meticulously groomed park. In a town the size of Lake Cowichan, it was unmistakably the most massive structure around.

We parked and strolled through the idyllic grounds basking in the quiet beauty of nature. Listening to the birds trilling their love songs we noticed a blue heron sculpture perched on a stump as though watching the river flow by and next to the river, a row of fir trees offering shade for picnicking visitors. Heaven's gifts infused in this luxurious carpet of green embraced us with the silence of grace and serenity but what drove us there at such a fevered pace was still unanswered. We had no idea what was about to befall us.

Off to the side was a gray brick memorial in the shape of a pyramid.

While contemplating the pyramid, Smilingshadow, in stream of consciousness, mumbled, "Hmm. A pyramid. It's not a church. It's gray brick though. That could be a stretch."

A pyramid! What shape in the universe could better mirror a church than the structure of a pyramid, its peak symbolizing the zenith of spiritual attainment.

I responded to Smilingshadow's remarkably perceptive connection. "It could fit."

The spirit guides had chosen well for she was a trusting follower of nature's path with an innate scent that it was paved with metaphor.

Approaching the mighty pyramid, we stared in reverence at the plaque: "Patience on a monument smiling at grief,"[E116] was the inscription, "We will remember them." The dedication read: "In Memory of Those Valiant Men and Women Who Paid The Supreme Sacrifice ... World War I, World War II, Korean War."

Smilingshadow whispered, "A church. A memorial. A pyramid."

On the word pyramid, I thought I heard a new bird making a big kerfuffle. I looked up and there was good ole Tu-whit circling around. Because Tu-whit senses if a sound is higher or lower, Bev's low murmurings must have brought him round.

Instead of his usual Tu-whit Tu-whoo call, he was eagerly communicating something that sounded like Abraca Dabraca!

Tu-whit deferentially delivered his message.

ÕÕ "There is a theory that says the letters in Abracadabra were once arranged in an inverted pyramid and it was worn as an amulet around the neck to protect the wearer against disease or trouble."

"You are our lucky charm, Tu-whit."

He must be pointing us to the disease and trouble festering in the earth.

CHAPTER ONE HUNDRED ELEVEN
THE SEVEN O'CLOCK SHADOW

I was mulling over the gray brick clue and how it might fit with the *light gray brick church* of the dream, when Smilingshadow, still in church whisper said, "Look, Sparkle...

"The shadow is at 7 o'clock. Look at the lawn."

As I live and breathe, the glistening rays of the sun had formed from the pyramid-shaped memorial a perfect shadow that fell on the lawn at exactly 7 o'clock.

A hush enfolded us.

The day's frenetic rush had hastened us to the grassy green lawn where, on that late September afternoon, we witnessed a prelude to sundown. A portrait of divine wisdom had cast itself as a 7 o'clock shadow that stoically waited to tell the unvarnished truth in all its glory – and on day seven of the trip.

7 o'clock Shadow, Lake Cowichan, Vancouver, B.C.

Perpetuating this epiphany was Beverly's adopted name, Smilingshadow, for she just gazed at the marvel cast in the shadow of 7 o'clock and beatifically smiled at its majesty.

Trying to absorb this colossal miracle, I heard Smilingshadow say, "Look over there, Sparkle. It's the Brookside Medical Clinic."

Footnotes contain dream dates and references to prior pages where the dream appeared.
Endnotes contain bibliographical references, are marked with "Ɛ" in the text, and appear at the end of the book.

Fluttering over God's little patch of paradise, where the light of the 7 o'clock shadow stood its ground, was the Peggymoonbeam of my dreams, the BROOKSIDE MEDICAL CLINIC in waking.

Heavenly hearkenings!!

Peggymoonbeam's waking life nickname was Brooksie, shortened from her surname, Brooks. The "d" in Brookside symbolized her more formal name, Diane. Her middle name, Peggy, joined her first name, last name, and nickname.

The story must be told. Peggymoonbeam, born with congenital heart failure, spent much of her life in hospitals. A heart transplant gifted us with her presence for four more treasured years. Medical clinics were no stranger to her. Her last years on Earth brimming with worldly largesse, I now realize, were destined to be exchanged for boundless favors from the universe.

I was overwhelmed. My sobs came from a place so deep I didn't even know it was mine. But I did know beyond any shadow of a 7 o'clock doubt that she was there. She beamed in, "Well of course, I'm here. This stuff doesn't happen by itself, y'know."

Through squinting eyes, I could see the modernistic sculpture in the distance. A vaguely familiar outline took shape. **It was a 280,, triumvirate arch** in the center of which stood a waterfall fountain. My mind toggled back forty years. The sculpture, a conjoined group of three arches, mirrors the centerpiece that graces the memorial park where my beloved father, Louis, is laid to rest.

The massive sculpture, the St. Louis de Montfort Church represented by the pyramid, the 7 o'clock shadow, Brookside Medical Clinic – dreaming and waking elements in silence, fused right here by Honeymoon Bay.

And what of the double comma? The 280,, code magically embedded in this very text is a code matching other electronic messages that brought Peggymoonbeam back to us. Elation comes not from words alone, nor does the heart-stopping moment of epiphany, but when I actually saw the code – all five characters appearing together – instead of single letters one after the other – I knew we were not alone. The grand truth is that everywhere and always there is above, a higher hand.

Peggymoonbeam chimed in. "I'm not sure if you really got the meaning of the 7 o'clock shadow, girls."

Smilingshadow and I looked at each other quizzically.

"It is told like this," said Peggymoonbeam. "Throughout history, time has been measured by the movement of the Earth relative to the sun and stars. The earliest time piece, dating from as far back as 3500 BC, was the shadow clock, or gnomon, a vertical stick or obelisk that casts a shadow."

"Wow, Smilingshadow! I've got goose bumps! Can you believe that? The rays of the sun bounced off the pyramid-shaped memorial and cast the shadow on the lawn. It's like an obelisk."

"Good connection," sparkled Peggymoonbeam and Tu-whit added,

ÕÕ "'An Egyptian shadow clock of the eighth century BC still exists.'"[E117]

Egypt was our first expedition. How perfectly perfect that Similingshadow would
be the discoverer of the pyramid's shadow. Her tenacious push to arrive before the sun
changed position was driven by a purpose we could not know.

The elegance of the cosmos engulfed us in oscillating waves of reverence and removed
from us, if only for the now, our earthly burdens. Pausing for a moment, I realized this
was a spiritual turning point, a blessed remembrance forever engraved in my heart and
sight. I've never been quite able to recapture the exquisite lightness of being I felt in that
park, on that day.

A triumvirate arch ... a ruling group of three. I thought of the three spirits who, while
on Earth, lovingly influenced my life and who now, from on high, guided us through this
mystical voyage: Peggymoonbeam ... Charlesbigstar ... Agneswiseheart. In some unknowable way, they teamed up with the famed mentors of bygone ages, and in the spirit of
agape, agreed on a conscious purpose.

We had seen in a sacred manner the world and the center of the world. Stillness and
movement comingled. We had visited the hallowed land of Time and Eternity.

I sat by the arches. Glistening water cascading from the stately fountain soothed me
while thoughts and feelings, emotions and fact, life and afterlife, conscious and unconscious took their place in the cosmos. In a trance-like gaze, my eyes rested on a plaque
honoring a man who grew up in the Lake Cowichan region. It read "William Carpentier
for the Apollo Space Mission – physician 1969."

Physical signs on terra firma silently connected to space under these Elysian arches.
Peggymoonbeam, freed from the trials of earthly life, was now a conduit for space unex-
plored, time unexamined. Apollo 11 was the spaceflight that carried the first men to the
moon. Was Mission Lavender a dream flight that would transport its passengers to unseen
Truths? Did the Apollo Mission link to the multidimensional disk dreams in which
Peggymoonbeam bears treasures of the universe with more waiting to be unwrapped.
Angela, the drowning star may be clueing us to what lays in wait.[516]

The cosmic sector of the project began to flourish. The unseen hand of spirituality
in the Honeymoon dream gave birth to awe-inspiring revelations. Sprinkled on us like
golden fairy dust, universal visions of faith and peace, optimism and fellowship, dotted
the children's playground.

Still undercover was *the repeating design in a satiny stainless steel that's very modern, but
seems old.* And what about *the upside-down Js?*

---

516 3/5/00. See Ch. 105 – A Drowning Star, p. 551

"Among other things," quipped Peggymoonbeam, "*the upside-down Js* are icons for your name in waking life. Get it? Remember, you took the character of Penelope when you decided on a dream name.

"We've delivered a smorgasbord of bottom-up tips. Think back, Penelope. You saw Castle Hill in Placentia that way, you saw the doodle on the rock that way, and have been dreaming upside-down images ever since. That's right, my little buddy. It goes on and on."

I guess my hunch was right about manifestation developing gradually within a pre-scribed area. While a number of symbols were contained within the *7 o'clock shadow* dream, the dream clues were scattered over two areas, the towns of Honeymoon Bay and Lake Cowichan. The same phenomena occurred in Newfoundland.

"Well, Penelope," imparted Peggymoonbeam, "if you on Earth can compress many dreams into one why can't we do the r e v e r s e   a n d   s p r e a d   o u t   t h e   c l u e s. A f t e r a l l,   f r o m   o u r   v a n t a g e p o i n t   t h e r e   i s   n o   d i f f e r e n t i a t i o n   b e t w e e n   n e i g h b o r h o o d s ... ...   e v e n   c o n t i n e n t s   b l u r. W e   s e e   y o u   a s   o n e   p l a n e t ... o n e   p e o p l e."

e v e   i s   a   r a d i o a c t i v e   m i n e r a l   t h a t   r a d o n   i s   a   r a d i o a c t i v e   g a s   p r o d u c e d   f r o m   u r a n i u m   d e c a y   a n d   t h e   s t r o n g e s t   i m p r e s s i o n   o f   a l l   w a s   t n a l   P a r k   t o

t h e   Y e l l o w s t o n e   P l a t e a u.   W h e t h e r   i t   w a s   w i n d i n g up   o r   d o w n   m a t t e r e d   n o t.

It   w a s   r e s o l u t e.   U n i v e r s a l i t y   w a s   t h e   w o r k's   i n t e n t i o n.   I t   w a s   t h e   s t r i n g   I   d r e a m t   t h a t   c a m e   f r o m   a b o v e, t h a t   t i e d G r a n d   T e t o n   N a t i o n a l   P a r k   t o   t h e   Y e l l o w s t o n e   P l a t e a u.   W h e t h e r   i t   w a s   w i n d i n g up or down mattered not.

Dear Reader, I am obliged to share with you the above text, which had separated on its own. This occurred while I was writing about the proliferation of clues in Peggymoonbeam's neck of the woods. I had discovered an emotional pattern in these mysterious electronic exchanges. The initial reaction is awareness of an incomprehensible communication. What follows is a quickening of the pulse, rapid breathing, a numbing of thought, at the end of which, emerges a fullness of gratitude impossible to describe. When conscious awareness returns to the reality of a desk, a chair, a stack of books, we know we've been suspended between this life and that and sharing the attributes of both. When the mystical is realized as more than a computer glitch, we know we've connected to something beyond our grasp.

I reflected on the Gideon dream, and how the Solar System and the Earth are separated but interlocking.

It emblematized the picket fence, Peggymoonbeam's icon that came to symbolize the whole of humanity striving toward the common goal of saving Mother Earth.

Peggymoonbeam affirmed, "You got it, Penelope! Just think the number One."

"You mean I've had only one dream?"

"That's right, Penelope, but I'd venture to say your dream is a volume."

"And, Peggy, I'd venture to say that all of you are writing it."

CHAPTER ONE HUNDRED TWELVE

PART OF THE PICTURE: A BLACK TUSK

Days Eight and Nine: Victoria – Garibaldi

The next morning, we drove on to the southeastern tip of Vancouver Island, to Victoria, for my first visit to the Capital of British Columbia. We'd been hoping to do some sightseeing but somehow wound up in the Victoria library.

We emerged from the library at dusk. I said to Smilingshadow, "Never would I have believed that the Canadian Atlas and reports on radioactive waste would take precedence over eating, shopping and sightseeing in a city I've never been to." But that's how it was. I'd have to hang in and hope our unseen but ever-present traveling companions would join us. And they did.

We began day nine driving to Squamish in search of the dramatic Black Tusk Mountain. We stopped at Brittania Beach, home of the British Columbia Museum of Mining, where my dream of the night before about images of *helter-skelter right-side up Js*[517] magically materialized in the form of a beautiful metal called Bismuth. The stair stepped structure of Bismuth crystal matched the *upside-down metal Js* I had seen in the *7 o'clock shadow* dream.[518] As Above – So Below.

We continued on to Garibaldi Provincial Park and the Black Tusk whose image set the wheels in motion for this Vancouver expedition.[519]

I am down low ... maybe on a boat. There is a big black mark that looks kind of like a shark's tooth on a piece of white poster board. The mark is only at the bottom. It looks as though the rest of it has been erased. I see only part of a picture. The finish was glossy. Then I see a dead plant. Underneath are young green leaves that turn into lettuce leaves.[520]

---

517 9/17/00.
518 2/7/99.
519 See Ch. 98 – Word In A Hole, p. 509
520 3/23/98.

Footnotes contain dream dates and references to prior pages where the dream appeared.

Endnotes contain bibliographical references, are marked with "Ɛ" in the text, and appear at the end of the book.

I was clueless. The image of the boat rekindled the lore of Titanic. The black and white clue, my symbol for the obvious, was, paradoxically unclear until that day when I happened on a black and white picture of the Black Tusk.[521]

I reflected on the big black mark that I partially erased, an inverted double for the Black Tusk picture.

The message that *I only see part of the picture* scored a bull's-eye. Three years earlier, my dot connecting stopped at Titanic linking it to a remote volcanic explosion. That was long before I knew about the upside-down phenomenon of divine intervention and eons before plate tectonics slid into my head.

On my inaugural foray into geology, I had learned that Black Tusk is the oldest volcano in the southern segment of the Garibaldi volcanic belt, part of the Cascadia Subduction Zone. Relatively recent volcanic action accounts for the formation of many of the park's peaks, especially those near Garibaldi Lake, including The Black Tusk.

It would be an hour's drive to get to Garibaldi Park, then another ten hours to hike to the Black Tusk mountain. It was our last day and there was no way we could do the hike.

In the picturesque town of Squamish, we lunched at a local kitchenette, feasting on homemade chow while enjoying the spectacular view. From every angle in Squamish, the sky was the backdrop for Mount Garibaldi and the Stawamus Chief mountains. Affectionately called The Chief by the locals, it is the world's second largest granite monolith.

After lunch, we casually strolled through town when a glossy picture of a huge snow-covered peak in the window of a photography shop stopped me short.

"Eureka! That's it! Smilingshadow, I can't believe it! That's the glossy picture in my dream! I betcha dollars to doughnuts it's the Black Tusk!"

The photo of this pinnacle of volcanic rock, my-dream-made-real, pulled us inside the store where I asked the owner about the picture in the window. "That photograph is just beautiful. What mountain is that?"

Beaming with pride he answered, "I took that picture. That's the Black Tusk Mountain." He had awakened at two o'clock in the morning to get the earliest shot after the first snowfall of the season.

"I knew it! I knew it!" I exclaimed. The owner looked at me askance.

I couldn't take my eyes off the photographic image matching one I'd seen years earlier in the book on volcanoes. The glossy picture of the Black Tusk was far more imposing than the matte photo in the book, for it captured the stately mountain baring its splendid peak in all its solitude.

---

521 See Ch. 98 – Word in A Hole, p. 509

How could a subtle little mark in a dream have taken me all the way from New York to view this amazing mountain?

My excitement would not ebb. "Holy Smoley! This is incredible! This image is the picture I had drawn upside down!

My upside-down black tusk dream

Black Tusk Mountain
Garibaldi Lake, B.C.

"Smilingshadow. Why do you think I erased part of it in my dream?"

Her eagle eye scrutinized the picture. She thought for a while, then commented, "Why, Sparkle, maybe the part that is erased is where the snow had fallen."

It was a brilliant connection and worked pictorially, but I sensed there was something underneath – something unseen.

The photographer, eager to share his passion, imparted some background about the mountain. "The Black Tusk is probably the most interesting of the volcanic peaks in Garibaldi Park. Pretty severe erosion accounts for its distinctive appearance.

"Where snow remains standing much of the winter, over the years, the thickness of the pack builds up and those deeply buried parts turn to glacier ice."

Hmm. I asked, "What makes it so pointed? It looks kind of like a shark's tooth."

"Yeah. It's a strange shape. That's probably caused by the contact of volcanic rocks with glacier ice. You might say it's a classic case of fire and ice."

The obscure passages in the dream began to clear ... *the dead plant ... the young green leaves that transform to lettuce leaves*. The Black Tusk is devoid of vegetation because of forces like erosion and glaciation, but under the dead surface, vegetation may live and that's a promise of rebirth.

Erosion ... glaciation ... volcanism.

How is it I'd been led to these wonders of nature and where had it actually begun? As I thumbed back in the sketchbook of my mind, the wind flipped a page to a startlingly pivotal dream I had in 1993.

Dissected in chapter 36, it centers on *communication through a grid of lights and two photographs of a car accident taken by a friend of mine. It shows a two-car collision ... the photo on the left is color; the photo on the right is black and white. I see black matter coming out of a vent.*[522] The more I learned about tectonic plates, the more I wondered if the two-car collision represented two plates. Both dreams had black-and-white images.

It may be that the *vent* opened the door, but whatever the elected symbol, the chain of events was unfathomable, yet strangely rational.

From the far reaches of the audible spectrum, boomed the voice of Steno.

"Penelope, you've forgotten another aspect of this dream. It concerns the *friend of yours who took the pictures*. He has multiple sclerosis in waking life. This is noteworthy, Clueso, because the jerking muscle tremors that result from the disease are similar to the tremors of an earthquake. Another parallel to multiple sclerosis is a hardening of body tissue analogous to lava once it is cooled."

The deeper we ventured into Geology the more I realized how aligned we are with the Earth.

---

522 2/5/93. See Ch. 36 – The Clog – The Vent – The Volcano, p. 160

CHAPTER ONE HUNDRED THIRTEEN

ROCKIN' 'N' ROLLIN'
IN THE CORDILLERAS

"Jerking tremors, Dr. Steno, take me to another dream.

"I'm skiing over greenish-pink rocks when I come to a crevice and see a large open hole. I see black stuff on the bottom. I say it must be lava. I'm building a volcano with a small yellow, brown and orange cone.

"Then I'm in a store. There is a wig with whip-like pieces attached to it. When the boss comes in, the store closes. The most puzzling image of all is *a yellow and brown fuzzy spider like a Tarantula who is 39 years old. I comment that he's too cute to be dangerous. A boss is swinging on a rope like an acrobat. When he gets off, he struts around and is spuming. He is cocky and jerking his head around and does not appear to be human."*[523]

I thought back to my upside-down image of the Black Tusk and wondered if this hole is what couldn't be seen – except in my dreams.

"Penelope. This is a dream brimming with geological delicacies. The first image our super high-powered Terracrust telescope picked up was the rope. Permit it to swing us over to the, Cordilleras, a towering mountain system named for a Spanish term meaning 'little ropes.' The name Cordilleras was first applied to the Andean ranges and includes their continuation of the Andes through Central and North America. In North America, it applies to the Rockies, Sierra Nevadas and peaks between, which run up into Alberta and British Columbia to Alaska.

"The greenish-pink rocks you were skiing over could characterize limestone and quartz. Consistent with the analogy to the Cordilleras, remember lava's ropy surface called Pahoehoe. And I might add, Penelope, that the igneous rocks in the Canadian Cordillera are concentrated along five principal volcano-tectonic belts. The Garibaldi

---

523 2/3/99.

Footnotes contain dream dates and references to prior pages where the dream appeared.
Endnotes contain bibliographical references, are marked with "ℰ" in the text, and appear at the end of the book.

volcanic belt in British Columbia is one and, as you know, part of the Cascadia Subduction Zone."

"My word! That's where the Black Tusk is."

"Umhmm. Do you have an idea what the crevice is characterizing?"

"I believe it's a fault, Doc, but, wait a second. Isn't there skiing at the Black Tusk?"

"Yes. It's a well-known ski area and, in fact, there are two mountains above Garibaldi known for alpine skiing: Whistler and Blackcomb. But I must say your dream is leaning toward Black Tusk."

"It bothers me, Dr. Steno, that when I come to the crevice, *I'm looking down into a big open hole.* I worry that people may actually be skiing over a dangerous opening that can't be seen by the naked eye. That could be a real trap. It sounds like the fault is next to a crater and a volcano is building there in the bottom of the crater where all the rocks are."

My dreams were looking like Swiss cheese with holes all over. Again, I wondered why all the holes, noticing that they matched honest-to-goodness places. What did they have in common? Were they all craters?

As directed, I tried connecting the dots, considering that holes could be volcanic craters or volcanic openings in the earth's crust. Dreams pointed to Yellowstone Plateau — Teton Fault, the Lower St. Lawrence Seismic Zone and now the Cascadia Subduction Zone.

Maybe geologists know about the big holes — or maybe they know and don't see danger — and then again, maybe I'm overreacting to this whole idea of volcanism.

"Steno waved his magic spyglass, "Let us walk through the dream and see if you are.

"Now for your *cute, fuzzy old spider.* Tarantula species are found in southwestern United States, Central America, South America and other New World tropical regions. The hairy tarantula crawled into your dream web to validate the Cordilleras, which share those geographic areas.

"Since you've developed a relationship with andesite, it won't surprise you to learn that the oldest and most striking andesite volcano in Garibaldi Lake is Black Tusk. In line with the personification of your cousin Andi, andesites are rocks, usually yellow or brown in color, like your spider, and are found in nearly all volcanic areas. That links to nearly the same colors that describe the cone being built, undoubtedly a volcanic cone. Your dreams are rising up in you much like mountains rising from the earth and pointing to andesites, named for the Andes Mountains, which, incidentally, rose up during the Chilean earthquakes in 2010.

"You see, Clueso, no matter how far you roam you will find our connections to be gloriously infinite."

I feared I was on the right track. The *wig with the whiplike pieces* resonated with the analogy of Mother Earth; the wig ... the covering of the Earth; the whip-like pieces ... Pele hair, the volcanic glass spun by lava and blown by the wind.

"Penelope, here's a little profile of your fuzzy spider. While the bites of many New World tarantula species are reported to be no worse than a wasp sting, some from South America are reputed to be deadly or to cause severe pain, swelling, vomiting, cramps and shock – reactions analogous to what Mother Earth endures during a violent volcanic eruption."

"The boss swinging on a rope, spuming, cocky and jerking his head around typifies the symptoms resulting from a European wolf spider's bite, which in the Middle Ages, were thought to cause hysterical ailments or tarantism for which dancing was the cure. It lent its name to a dance called the 'tarantella.'"

"I don't understand why the dream says *he's too cute to be dangerous,* if a volcano is being built under where people are skiing."

"You're earning your name, Clueso. Since the dream is portraying volcanic activity, we have to think of the plates involved.

"The Cascadia Subduction Zone which extends under Garibaldi Park, is between the oceanic Juan de Fuca plate and the North American plate. These plates are currently locked together, building up strain in the earth's crust and causing hundreds of small earthquakes. Eventually the plates will snap loose, which will generate a huge offshore 'subduction' earthquake."

"But, Doc, that's an earthquake, and my dream talks about building a volcano."

"Good point. They can go together. A volcano-tectonic earthquake can occur as rock is moving to fill in spaces where magma is no longer present; it can cause land to collapse and produce large ground cracks. Unfortunately, for Earth geologists, these quakes don't indicate that the volcano will be erupting; they can occur anytime."

"Wow, Doc! My dream tells the story! *The rocks I was skiing over – the lava on the bottom – the crevice.*"

"Well done, Clueso.

"Between the present slow rate of convergence and a debatable decline in volcanic activity Earth geologists may view the Juan de Fuca plate – the smallest of Earth's tectonic plates – as too small to be dangerous or, in dream lingo, *too cute to be dangerous.*"

Steno was still caught up in a massive spider web. "The European wolf spider's bite is painful but never, so far as records show, dangerous or fatal to humans. Of course, you realize that if it posed no threat at all we wouldn't have bothered to transmit this elaborate dream web."

"Why, Dr. Steno, is this dream so specific to the Tarantula?"

Beaming approval, he responded. "Well, Penelope, you have now stepped on the fringes of paleontology. The tarantula represents the Ordovician Period, when early plants and the first invertebrate animals related to today's insects and spiders appeared. It is the second division of the Paleozoic era and lasted from about 500 million to 435 million years ago."

I sensed a connection between the forming of mountain ranges and the chains of volcanoes during the Paleozoic Era and conditions in the twenty-first century.

"'Scuse me. 'Scuse me, Dr. Steno. Wasn't it in the Paleozoic era when chains of volcanoes were formed?"

"Yes, Penelope. The early Ordovician also corresponds to when the shallow seas that covered much of North America withdrew, leaving behind thick deposits of limestone. Returning later in the Ordovician, the seas deposited thick blankets of quartz, sand and more limestone like the *greenish-pink rocks you skied over.*"

(Gulp.) "Doc. I shudder at the mention of Paleontology. I'm just limping along the vast plains of geology, and when I think of the silos of astronomy and anthropology dreams waiting to be sorted, I get weak."

"Not to worry. We've only touched on it. Peggymoonbeam told us of your tendency to doze off and suggested we charge you with new subjects once in a while to keep you alert."

"My pal Peggymoonbeam seems to have forgotten that sleeping is something we need to do on Earth. I've been burning the midnight oil for the last decade trying to absorb so much information, so of course I'd get drowsy from time to time. I'm only human, y'know.

When the boss comes in, the store closes was a puzzler. I focused on the word spuming: spume means foam or froth. Is *the boss* parodying the frothing of lava?"

Peggymoonbeam whirled in on a peach-scented puff. "Penelope, read my lips: who do you call The Boss down there? I'll give you a tip: it's where I used to work."

Where she used to work?

I wracked my brain. Where did she work? The Boss? What was her bosses' name? It was typically American. Something like Roberts.

"Oh! I don't know. I don't get it."

Then a flash of recognition burned through.

"Oh, for Heaven's sake! She worked for a recording company. It's Bruce Springsteen, nicknamed by his fans, 'The Boss.'"

"Whew!" Her peach tinged essence vanished.

The dream presence of the famed American rock-and-roll singer flamboyantly dancing around a fault in the Cordilleras, spun right into the rocks I was skiing over, as well as the rolling motions found in mountain building.

"Penelope, my dear, methinks we've made our point with the 'rock 'n' roll' theme. You're becoming quite adept at deciphering our clues."

I thrived on gratis nods and winks. Some days, I was fighting my way out of a paper bag, so a give-away clue now and again gave me hope.

Hmm. Could the age of the spider be the age of a volcano? I started to think more about tarantism and how it's characterized by an extreme impulse to dance. That would mean a volcano could suddenly erupt.

"The message that *when the boss comes in, the store closes* has me worried sick, for store means what is 'in store.' If the boss is code for a volcano, then the closing of the store may be code for future disaster.

"Closing can mean terminating, finishing, putting an end to, expiring, dying. A dream instructing *Repetition for children*[524] echoed across vast mountains formed by volcanic action."

"Now that we've performed a dissection of the Cordilleras dream, Penelope, do you still think you're overreacting to volcanism?"

Nearly in tears and my stomach wound into a pretzel, I answered, "No, Doc, I don't. And I'm petrified. Science will never listen to a dreamer. Science has to be proven. How will they know if any of these theories are accurate? They have to be tested. They'll just think this is a fantasy and now I know it's not. How many times do I have to communicate this and in how many ways?"

"I get a migraine when I think of all the seafloor spreading and the hotspots and now volcano-tectonic earthquakes. The throbbing increases with the warnings – the hammering, head-pounding warnings about the Children ... the Playground. Oh, help. If they're not monitoring these areas, they can't see what's smoldering underneath. Please ask someone to listen! Please, Dr. Steno. Please get us some help!"

Steno responded, "My child, we've enlisted many people who will listen when you have connected all the dots." He then enfolded me in his larger than life spirit. "And you have been given an extra shot of valor to see you through."

The warmth of his caring guidance bolstered my waning energy.

Wafting above was the faint flutter of a songbird. It was Peggymoonbeam chanting her aria, "Be Strong. Have Courage."

As we left the Garibaldi area, I held close the hope of vegetation and rebirth I had unearthed at Black Tusk.

---

524 6/11/99.

CHAPTER ONE HUNDRED FOURTEEN

CONNECTING THE DOTS

Steno and I were almost like Siamese twins. I had grown to love this fatherly mentor, scholar and friend who knew what I should do and when I should do it. "Penelope," mused Steno, "now that you're advancing in your earthly class, why don't you connect the geological and spiritual dots that highlight how your related discoveries fit the Mission? This will help your readers to reflect on the mechanics you've learned while adventuring in the unseen and the unknown."

"Good idea, Doc. I'll start with the Labrador journey, which though virtual, was unexpectedly productive.

"The dream's great talent for simile revealed shocking analogies between the Hebron oil field in Labrador and the British Petroleum oil spill in the Gulf of Mexico. Marie Curie forewarned us of chemical toxicity urgently demanding change in the way we harvest energy. Dreams linking *Keystone restaurant* – to *Mexican restaurant* – to the Gulf of Mexico came alive with hope for renewal and resurrection. The classic geologic concept: *'the present is the key to the past,'* was fully illustrated.

"One of our most important discoveries was around the mutual magnetic pull of acid rain to carboniferous rocks. Such magnetism could result in contamination of both sea and air.

"The spirit of Vancouver led us to the Horseshoe Bay Ferry which linked to a dream where I take a *ferry* and meet a *mechanic on the other side.* That mechanic was the spirit team which came to teach me technical aspects of geology.

"While scouting for junk in Alert Bay in pursuit of the message, *earthquake sites are great resources for junk,* I realized that in my dreams, *junk* represents nuclear waste and *sites* – nuclear dump sites – should not be in earthquake zones like Yucca Mountain beneath which exist thirty-five active faults. Whether in the earth or in the oceans we don't want to put a waste disposal site on top of a fault line, where now or years into the future an earthquake or volcanic eruption will occur, releasing buried radioactive waste into the environment.

Footnotes contain dream dates and references to prior pages where the dream appeared.

Endnotes contain bibliographical references, are marked with "ε" in the text, and appear at the end of the book.

"By journey's end, the message *I know where the fault line is,* registered overwhelming concern, for fault lines are everywhere, not only underlying the terrain mapped by Mission Lavender. The geologic fault line encircles the Earth; the metaphoric fault line represents the Industrial Mafia playing Russian Roulette with our precious home. This shock electrified me into seeing that the combination of seismic zones, nuclear waste and drilling for oil, gas or metal is a recipe for unmitigated disaster. We must, eventually, lose this roulette game.

"Repetitions and hidden coding of the words "*back*" and "*architect*" taught me about island arcs – belts of volcanic islands where fault lines exist. I learned back-arc spreading and stress in island arc systems can make the systems move toward an incoming plate. My dreams connected island arc systems to the Mid-Atlantic ridge under Newfoundland/Labrador and Vancouver – and possibly other island areas not yet revealed. My dreams suggest such areas are susceptible and warn that our wanton disregard for the earth is making them more so.

"I discovered that the Africa plate and the Indo-Australian plate are in zones where plates are moving apart and that piezoelectricity – resulting from the squeezing and stretching of the rocks – plays a part in the spreading. The connection of andesite, piezo-electricity and electromagnetic energy wound back to quartz crystal, galena, and nonlocal communication.

"A network of complex geologically based dreams implies that plate movement in seafloor spreading zones is impinging on the North American plate. For instance, a dream suggests a strike-slip fault where *a car slips on some metal discs or plates on the ground, goes over the edge and lands underwater.*[525] The car, symbolic of the tectonic engine, set off an alarm. Such dreams point to vulnerability of the North American plate, implying that it's being crowded out by the Eurasian plate. Hundreds of dreams spanning nearly two decades caused me to question whether earthquake activity in the lower St. Lawrence Seismic Zone, volcanic activity in the Avalon Zone in Eastern Newfoundland and volcano-build-ing in the Cascadia Subduction Zone in Vancouver Island were prototypical and could set off such a fatality on a global basis.

"And in Alert Bay – *Success Wake Lake* – my drowning Angela star introduced me to the supernova and the mystery of the Big Bang in the presence of Gideon."

Unbeknownst to us, dear Reader, we had been invited to Honeymoon Bay for a metaphorical wedding where we learned the true meaning of the marriage of science and spirit, first in thought, then in feeling, finally merging in bold, concrete certainty of mate-rial evidence of both a geological and spiritual presence. It was as though they had at one time, perhaps very long ago, taken their nuptial vows.

From my world on Earth to distant Terracrust and Starsight, I've found myself liv-ing in a mystical multidimensional bubble. Mission Lavender ushered me beyond my

---

525 3/3/99. See Ch. 84 – American Currency A La Origami, p. 399

microscopic existence in New York to the inner-workings of Earth and the Mission's profound concern for Her survival. The weight of the message is heavy and dark and solid; yet the vitality and illumination infused in me by all of you speaks to a new day where hope will pave the way back to civility.

Tears fell to my feet like raindrops, my heart throbbed soulful strains of joy and sorrow, my voice fell lower and lower, fading into the bittersweet memory of fantasy, fantasy hardened from a wisp of a dream to a new reality. I was unable to utter the rest.

"Doc, I'm sorry. I just can't find the words."

"Keep going, Penelope. Just write your feelings: you needn't speak them. Though the journey continues, every now and again, you must pause and appreciate how far you've traveled. You'll reach points that break your excursion into segments that will help you to understand where you are."

I found solace in his words as I tried to compose myself for the denouement.

I departed Garibaldi Lake, which held my dream image of the *Black Tusk,* with great misgiving that innocent vacationers are skiing over dangerous crevices where volcano building is proceeding – unseen.

It became clear at journey's end that Telegraph Cove, population twenty, was our lightship for the entire Vancouver expedition. From all outward appearances, it was the most inconspicuous stop along the way but repeated the most compelling of messages: a *cigarette burning deep in the ground;*[526] again, reminding us that a *cigarette is burning in a rug.*[527]

The rug is the Earth. THE EARTH IS ABOUT TO CATCH FIRE!

As pieces of dreams flew about, growing in number with each disaster, animals and people flee here and there while we humans cling to our own little vision in our own little world and follow our own sets of rules. And all over creation, the invisible shepherds of the Earth clamor for our attention shouting in inaudible voice, "We see the destruction. We know it's happening. The clock is ticking. Time is running out. You must shift course!" and they plead with us to listen.

Are we, humankind, the metaphorical ship of fools about ready to capsize as Titanic did? The arrogance of shipping magnates who drove the Titanic into a darkened chasm a century ago mirrors the oil barons who drove a bleeding hole in the earth. The Dream, in true archetypal form, had mirrored two crimes against humanity, each driven by near insanity for the acquisition of money and power, blindly plotting their respective downfalls. As Titanic's death knell echoes in memory, so too will the footprints of British

---

526 10/8/99. See Ch. 93 – Home Plate, p. 461
527 11/11/98. See Ch. 107 – Telegraph Cove, p. 565

Petroleum and the U.S. government's oil-soaked massacre in the ocean's depths. Such reprehensible crimes will remain circulating in our waters, on our shores and in our psyches – much as they came to me in my dreams.

An ocean liner could be replaced. Our Earth – our Ecosystem – our Species cannot be.

Memories of my innocent Raggedy doll wearing her perpetual smile tugged at my heartstrings. Values of kindness, generosity, cooperation, friendship and love engendered by her invincible spirit are imbued in all of us when we arrive. They are seemingly lost to many of us now, but surely, one day we will recover them.

The string of geologic clues made clear in Dream metaphor that the symbol of the Volcano is warning of destruction that we, the children, can expect if we don't hearken.

The invisible telegraphers who see consequences we cannot see are demanding we lay down our venomous toys of industrial appetite, political power, war mongering and fanatical profiteering. They see the addictive oils of narcissism squeezed dry. They know our transient world and the fleeting rewards of indulgence. Their omnipresent wisdom has unveiled the reflection of our human faults in the weakness of the earth.

These beneficent mechanics of the night came to awaken us to the atrocities we have committed upon our Earth and each other. WE MUST WAKE UP! Mother Earth is tired. She is angry. She does not deserve this. This is not a game! She is pleading with her children to save her – to save themselves, for they are part of her.

Steno spoke quietly. "Penelope, your journey to Alert Bay began with a *mechanic from the other side* and ended with Telegraph Cove. You have read our telegram and have heard our message: *Success Wake Lake*. Humankind can succeed if it awakens."

CHAPTER ONE HUNDRED FIFTEEN

A ROYAL SEND-OFF

Day Ten: Vancouver City

Shaken by the disquieting, but revelatory wrap-up with Steno, I was ready to return home and engage in some deep thinking. Smilingshadow and I concluded as much physical exploration as time allowed, but there were still unvisited areas nagging at me.

Clinton, for example.

In one dream, *Clinton pairs with a corroded pipe.* In another, *Clinton appears with an article on Waste and a mountain of scrap.* Still another dream tells of *a uranium link to Clinton* and attaches a description *of a twisty tie.*[528]

"Twisty" described the Coast Mountains of British Columbia. Though we didn't make the trip, the map showed a serpentine stretch of mountainous road from Brittania Beach to Clinton. The most commonplace clues were perfectly executed; the *twisty tie* tied every fragment to the next.

Ten days had sped by and it was time to head home. Yet there was one last call before we went to the airport: the Canada Geological Survey.

I asked if they had maps of Clinton and expressed interest in the Garibaldi area, explaining to the office manager that I was teaching myself about geology.

Louise, the manager, went overboard showing me maps, geological etiquettes, ecological and environmental reports. A gentleman overheard my requests and asked what my area of interest was.

How could I say I was led here by dreams? When I reluctantly answered "Clinton," he exuberantly offered worlds of information that made my head spin.

He told me the area was heavy in basalt and how volcanic it was. He gave me designations of rocks. He talked about a landslide in the Garibaldi area. He gave me information on Black Tusk: that it was from the Jurassic period and that Mt. Garibaldi was younger,

---

528 Clinton dreams: 1//20/00, 10/18/99, 7/12/99.

Footnotes contain dream dates and references to prior pages where the dream appeared.

Endnotes contain bibliographical references, are marked with "Ɛ" in the text, and appear at the end of the book.

from the Eocene. He said Vancouver Island's largest earthquake and Canada's largest on shore earthquake was a M7.3 in 1946.

Overwhelmed at the depth of knowledge and generosity of this stranger, I sensed a familiar feeling of guardianship.

Louise joked about us owing him a consulting fee. I thanked him profusely for all his help. After he left, I asked Louise who he was. She said, "A geologist."

I was hurriedly deciding what materials to get from the Survey's collection, rushing to gather up all I needed in time to get to the airport but I was confused; I didn't know what I lacked. Distracted, once more, by the feeling of a nearby presence, I looked up, but it was not one of the usual spirits. The stranger had returned.

"I was thinking," he said to Louise. "You might have the book on volcanic rock - the Vancouver Geology that has the bedrock map and – oh! What about the little pamphlet on Garibaldi Geology? That might be good for her. And check to see if you have the book on Southern Vancouver Island. She could use that."

They did cartwheels, assembling materials, gathering references and packing everything just so. I would later reflect on the blissful interconnectedness of the experience. Almost predictably, their selections were exactly what I needed.

It was truly extraordinary. A deep fraternal bond was forged. We exchanged cards. The angelic geologist turned out to be a geotechnical engineer.

For one dense moment, I wondered why he came back. In gurgled the laugh I knew so well. Peggymoonbeam injected, "You gotta be kidding!"

Just then I noticed something floating toward Earth. It was Agneswiseheart's Oneiroball making a delivery.

"Good job, Agneswiseheart," swirled in Steno, positioning his spyglass over the epistle that had just landed.

"Now, tell them what she sent, Penelope."

"OK, Dr. Steno. It's a map with lots of mountains – it looks like a belt of land that extends from the Adirondacks into Canada. Oh, my goodness! It IS the Adirondacks. There's another Clinton in Upper New York!"

Nicolaus Steno, happily warbled, "That's called the Northern New York-Western Quebec Seismic Zone."

Another seismic zone? I dialed back to the Lower St. Lawrence Seismic Zone[Ɛ118] in the estuary of the St. Lawrence River and my new horror at plans to build an LNG terminal along the river.[Ɛ119] Then there was the Laurentian Slope Seismic Zone, where the 7.2 Grand Banks earthquake-landslide-tsunami occurred in 1929.[529] And now, a third seismic zone – the Northern New York – Western Quebec.

---

529 See Ch. 83 – A Hidden Key, pp. 396–97

Three seismic zones, all in Canada! They must connect. I reflected back on the Gestalt concept of a unified whole and how my lessons convinced me that the complete structure could only be understood by looking at the vast seismic network.[530]

Steno responded, "There are more than three seismic zones in Canada, Clueso, but these have caught your eye. Then, in a flurry of silvery scientific dream dust, he broke out of scholarly character, singing and dancing, spinning and spiraling over, under and all around us. Flapping in the wind like a whirlybird, he transmitted pure unbridled joy at having seen the fruits of his labor. He'd taught his novice well. He then turned to Smilingshadow.

"Now, Miss Smilingshadow, did this adventure meet your expectations? I would like to know your impressions so we may prepare a syllabus for future recruits."

"Sparkle. I think Steno is talking to me."

"Good. Just listen and respond."

Smilingshadow had picked up my nervous habit.

(Gulp.) "Meet my expectations, Doc? It exceeded all my expectations! I knew it wouldn't be an ordinary trip, but I had no idea how extraordinary it would be. I didn't really understand what we were looking for. Sparkle said she didn't know what we'd find, but it would become apparent as we followed the dream clues, and follow we did.

"As we wended our way across the island, I realized it didn't matter that I lacked understanding of the quest; I was meant to be part of it. There were times when I was not at all in charge of my part in the adventure but was led in different directions. There were times I felt I needed to be in a particular place by a certain time. Since I was the designated driver, Sparkle couldn't persuade me to divert from the 'Mission.'

"As we went on, my knowledge of the quest sharpened, and I was able to help Sparkle find clues and answers, but I know it had nothing to do with my skills because I had been loaned to her for whatever was needed in her quest.

"It was a magical, amazing and weird experience that I wouldn't trade for the world."

"Good to hear, Smilingshadow. Your intuitive skills are magnificent. You have more than fulfilled our requirements. On behalf of Terracrust and Starsight, we offer you carte blanche on any upcoming Missions.

"It is now time for a recess. We wish you girls a safe journey home and trust you will communicate the knowledge you've gained to those who will listen."

Whereupon our Heaven-sent chaperons ballooned into the stratosphere, spyglass, peach glow, celestial scrabble, paint cans, totem pole and all.

Smilingshadow and I were floored. Together we chimed, "They must have tapped Louise! They must have sent the geologist!"

530 See Ch. 81 – Gestalt and the Chair, pp. 391–92

Bottled inside that one measured hour were the supreme forces of the cosmos in perfect harmony, astral angels and Earth angels working hand in hand. The music of the spheres had manifested a royal sendoff, braced with hope that the battle would not be as solitary as it appeared. It was a floodlit moment forever sealed in our memories.

As he joined the exodus, Steno added proudly, "When you settle down back in New York, Penelope, I'll show you the finishing threads in my sacred rug. Hidden in it are some colorful gifts from your mentors which, I must say, sparkle with perfection. We've been riding this blessed carpet for a while now and I'm pleased to say that the seers at Terracrust have officially named it Steno's Magic Carpet."

A rush of symbols, codes and keys hidden in obscure messages in endless dreams had come to life in each of these ordinary places. Mysteriously, this pattern of information appearing so random and scattered knew exactly how to self-organize.

The ancient sages were teaching us their silent language and providing the keys for decryption. So we could hear the inaudible and see the invisible, they chose the quiet solitude of the pristine Canadian landscape as their backdrop. Their kaleidoscopic language was transmitting more puzzles and riddles than the human mind could consciously absorb. It spanned all time and distance and was telegraphed in mind and in matter, in a splash of paint, a picket fence, a pole and hydrant, an orb of light, a lavender map, an enchanted park, a Word on a sign, a Word in a hole.

The Hole. Labrador! Oh, my Lord! We left Percival and Simon in Labrador!

"Oh, Doc, I've been so entranced with all the miraculous happenings in Vancouver, I nearly forgot our pets. I don't even know if we left enough milk and cookies for them. We've been gone so long! What if they're starving? I could never live with myself! And now we're ready to depart Vancouver! What to do? I feel like an errant mother. How could I be so remiss? How could I forget and just leave them there?"

"Not to worry, my child," wired Steno. "They, too, have been assigned to Mission Lavender, and living by the principles of your spirit team, the concept of time, as you know it, does not exist for Percival and Simon. Nor do they require much food. Of course, treats like milk and cookies they'll lap right up, but their real sustenance is manna from Heaven.

"I've looked in on them and they're happy as can be, romping about and tending to their tasks. You may not have realized it, but they are also helping you in your discoveries, no matter the distance between you. You and Percival and Simon have come together with a common objective. Your minds have created a common field. Trust that you will know when it's time to fetch them. Remember, as Andre Gide said, you have consented 'to lose sight of the shore for a very long time.'"

We were being shown by the custodians of the Earth how to observe, to listen, to trust and to follow. If we obeyed, we would heed their foreboding message born of love and protection. We would grasp this mystical experience and know the forgotten riches of the world were still within our reach. Our seers beneficently telegraphed a message of survival. It was our job to receive it.

Then we had to inform. Scientists predict earthquakes – to a degree. They frequently gauge oncoming tsunamis. Submarine volcanoes need to be observed as studiously. Problem is, science won't listen to the dreams of an unknown, unacknowledged person, but the Truth is in the dreams – in the invisible. Still, *as we were going under, I felt we could make it back up.*[531]

My Dream had received the message and took a long walk that stretched to Newfoundland and Vancouver, a real-life demonstration in fragmentation and connection. Fragments of dreams would appear: (the lavender and yellow paint appearing separately in Newfoundland), then connected as a unit: (forming a twosome in Vancouver) – a verifiable reenactment of the Dream. The spreading of clues, time and again, took on a physical form within a seemingly prescribed radius in each of the places we visited corresponding with Rupert Sheldrake's theory of morphic fields. My field of geologic dreams had reached beyond my mind to link to physical fields, the environs where such geology exists.

Thus, the language of spirit comes to us in fragments that are seeking connection. By understanding the fragmentation in our dreams, we become aware of the fragmentation in our lives. By connecting different aspects of the Earth, we take in a larger picture of where we stand in relation to our planet. In so doing, we perceive both our smallness and our "wholeness" in this grand design called Life. By understanding how connected we are – to each other, to the Earth and to the Universe at large – we begin to fulfill our purpose: peace, harmony and oneness. We learn that only by connecting the smallest slivers – in dreaming and in waking – will we eventually see the big picture.

Telegraph Cove would have been a blur had we not been alert to the miracles surrounding us.

Smilingshadow and I – and before that Karensurefoot and I – had soared together beyond the mundane to return with eyes and hearts wide open to the infinite possibilities within our human grasp.

---

531 3/3/99. See Ch. 84 – American Currency a la Origami, p. 399

CHAPTER ONE HUNDRED SIXTEEN

AND SO IT IS WRITTEN

You cannot travel on the path
until you become the path itself.
                                                Buddha

I returned to New York deeply introspective and awed by our findings. Sharply contrasted with the joy of illumination realized on these adventures were the alarming truths of what we faced. My busy year of travel was winding down. Of course I'd continue to dream, but now the days were my own. I could finally clean my closets, catalogue bundles of unattended dreams and reconnect with family and friends. I thought about Steno's sacred rug and what other gifts might be hidden in it. It sounded intriguing but I needed a break.

The message of the children and their toys haunted me. I stepped outside for a breath of air. The air, however, was not still and I sensed a strong current of Terracrustian wind. Sure enough, it was Nicolaus Steno, spyglass in one hand, a scroll in the other. I was familiar with the spyglass, but had no idea why he carried a scroll.

"Good day, Penelope. I'm here to advise you, on behalf of the Terracrust Geologic Survey in conjunction with Starsight Lab, that Mission Lavender is delving further into the depths of geology and chemistry, referred to by earthlings as geochemistry. That is the science dealing with chemical changes in the earth and composition of the earth's crust. Our Mission, in which a special post for you has been reserved, will eventually reach far beyond the North American plate and certainly beyond your findings thus far.

"My findings? Even with a whole boatload of clues, I still don't know what really happened to the Titanic. I can speculate but what I do know is that it took me to the lower depths."

Steno chuckled, then, cleared his throat. "Penelope. The first dream in your Titanic series introduced itself with the *Girl Scout motto, 'Be Prepared,'* which means you are always to be in a state of readiness in mind and body to do your DUTY."

Footnotes contain dream dates and references to prior pages where the dream appeared.

Endnotes contain bibliographical references, are marked with "Ɛ" in the text, and appear at the end of the book.

"I just don't know, Doc. I completely respect the meaning of the motto, but so many clues are left to decode and now, you want to leave Canada and travel the world. I don't even know the fate of the North American plate yet – and oh! What about the Himalaya? And what about that Japanese instructor whose name I can't pronounce?"

Steno cleared his throat again, this time with greater authority.

"Ahem. My precious, weary Penelope. I feel we've overtaxed you. In traveling to Newfoundland, Labrador and Vancouver you uncovered solid evidence that corroborated your dreams. In seeing the truth, waves of ecstasy and undercurrents of fear have overwhelmed you. We were laying the groundwork for what promises to be a much larger case, one which will unearth even further evidence to unravel Titanic's mysterious threads and rocket you far above the Earth where your *Half Circle, Full Star, Clog*[532] puzzle will become clear. At the moment, you have only a sketchy and unfinished picture.

"As we've traversed the multi-natured landscape of your dreams, we've made visible to you imagery enfolded in your tapestry, but not yet perceptible to the naked eye. This process spread over two decades in Earth time mirrors the cosmos and contains a timeless microcosm of eternity.

"Every dream theme we've revealed on this journey, Penelope, contains a total structure enfolded within it. Despite the endless number of disordered possibilities, we've stayed true to the ordered pattern where, eventually, all the pieces will fit together. As your dreams become one at journey's end, you'll be delighted at the perfect symmetry you've achieved. Much of our dream gathering will continue to present itself in the physical world. Quite simply, you'll find that our two worlds are connected."

"Come to think of it, many of my dreams about geology actually did come true and I certainly remember those head-spinning spells of excitement when I found pieces of my dreams in the form of matter. So, Dr. Steno, does that mean my personal dreams can also come true?" I wondered about Johnnie Pianissimo.

"Your personal dreams can come true in a different way. They will erupt out of feelings rising to the surface when you uncover a private truth. In your scientific dreams, when facts rise to the surface, the impact of discovery triggers feelings associated with humankind. You are learning that the images of all you see – in waking and in dreaming, material and spiritual, personal and scientific, in human behavior and earth behavior – are cut of the same cloth and exist as a unified whole.

"And while you have learned much, we're not yet done. Your deep and committed concern for your fellow man has led to a solid foundation and the Terracrust Geologic Survey has selected you to steward its global project, which will transmit vital communications to all of humankind. The job has been, de facto, yours, ever since you were honored with the sacred Branches. Now we'd like you to formally sign on for the post.

---

532 See Ch. 21 – Half Circle, Full Star, Clog, pp. 93–94
        Ch. 42 – Geology: The Second Branch, p. 194

"Madame Curie and I will be your tour guides on a flagship expedition to uncover important aspects of the geochemical infrastructure of earth as we view it from Terracrust. You will also be taking a deeper cosmological look into Earth's beginnings and your chief guides for that portion of the mission will be your darling Twink Ptolemy and the ever-insightful Lord Galen.

"Your Branches of Vision, Geology and Chemistry afford you the ability to perceive, as we do, reactions deep within the Earth and far, far above it. You see, Penelope, we receive information from many sources about conditions there. We do everything in our power, which is considerable, to moderate the effects of social and physical forces creating havoc on Earth.

"Terracrust requires that our guides on Earth be willing to undertake new and complex projects with a sense of personal dedication and great endurance, both physical and mental and be aware of their surroundings. Of course, the essential precondition for our enlistees rests in the knowledge of the heart which is that of 'Trust.'"

"But … But … Dr. Steno, I really don't have much physical endurance. I tire easily and am lazy by nature. I should be a lizard sunning on a big mossy rock all the day long. I know nothing more about geology or geography or matters universal than what you've taught me. I can't even read a map. I know I've been generously and beneficently gifted with the three Branches, the Psymometer and the Timelessness Glasses and for those, I'm ever grateful. My amazing experiences of uncovering Lava Under and portions of the Titanic will be with me forever. It took a while to learn that the Dream is a symbolic language, which is why I call it Oneiromantics. It was shocking to think that the areas we visited are symbolic of what's happening all over the world. Once I knew what to look for, I dug up reams of knowledge I never knew existed. I'm glad I was able to translate your dire concerns about all that's occurring in the earth and I hope with all my heart that science will heed the warnings and continue the work. But honestly, Doc, I have already given ten years to Mission Lavender and desperately yearn to return to a normal life. I've only just now set foot back in New York. If we're going to cover the world, it will certainly take many more years.

"I've lost contact with my family and am only in touch with a handful of friends because my time has been so consumed with this work. If only I could meet a man of flesh and go to the movies on a Saturday night or have a romantic candlelight dinner or escape for a weekend in the mountains. Ptolemy is supposed to send Johnnie Pianissimo, and I've been looking for him, Dr. Steno, but I haven't seen a single solitary man who wears a ring with the insignia of infinity, like Marie Curie said he would. He's nowhere in sight and I think he's just a fantasy anyhow. Besides, where would I meet him?

"Surely, I can't fill the bill for so glorious an honor. There must be other earthlings with far superior credentials to mine. I'm just an average person with only two years of college."

"Now you can take some time to think about this, but actually, Penelope, you are just what we're looking for. We seek earthlings with no preconceived ideas, no biases, no learning habits to unlearn – just pure unfiltered intelligence," said Steno, as he began to unfurl the mysterious scroll.

"And as you've been able to receive our messages, so can anyone who's open to them. But we have pre-screened you and you meet all our qualifications, and then some. Are there others who might do as well? Certainly. But your emotional profile, history and friends and family are important factors. And you have met our requirements and have passed our tests. We now have a vested interest in you for you are learning to see the shapes of all things visible and invisible. You are learning to decode the inextricably bound languages of Dreams and Nature.

"Much of what we look for will remind you of the skills you acquired as a Girl Scout – things like backpacking, camping, a love of high adventure and digging through the past.

"The writings are contained right here in this scroll from the Akashic Records, also known as the Book of Life. You might recall that earlier in your journey, Peggymoonbeam shared with you her viewing of the Emerald Tablet, a secret formula which she witnessed in the Akashic Records.[533] As that was a while ago in Earth time, I shall re-introduce you to this infinite body of scientific and spiritual knowledge."

"I have some vague recall, Doc, about being able to see beyond the veil, but I don't think I grasped the entire meaning."

"That's understandable, Penny. You see, as souls journey through time, from one lifetime to the next, all of their deeds are recorded. The records of all these lives, past and present, as well as information concerning the life of your planet is kept in the Library of Akasha."

"You mean all my actions, all my deeds and misdeeds are on record for everyone to see? Isn't there any privacy? I don't want every single body knowing my business.

"No, no, Miss Penny. Nothing like that at all. Tu-whit is actually a devout seeker of Truth and a leading authority on the Akashic Records."

ÕÕ "'The Akashic Records are written on Scrolls or Books, in the language of the civilization and time period during which you've lived. These lives may have been on Earth or anywhere else in the cosmos. As you think, speak and act, everything you experience, and everything you do, is written. Souls who incarnated very early in history naturally have more written accounts of their lifetimes; souls that chose to incarnate less frequently have fewer lifetimes to record.'"[Ɛ120]

---

533 See Ch. 52 – A Little Night Music, p. 237

"Penny, it's not just about souls," Steno added. Tu-whit will explain how it envelops everything in the Universe."

ÕÕ "'Akasha has been brilliantly described by the great Indian Yogi Swami Vivekananda:

"'Everything that has form, everything that is the result of combination, is evolved out of this Akasha. It is the Akasha that becomes the air, that becomes the liquids, that becomes the solids; it is the Akasha that becomes the Sun, the Earth, the Moon, the stars, the comets; it is the Akasha that becomes the human body, the animal body, the plants, every form that we see, everything that can be sensed, everything that exists. It cannot be perceived; it is so subtle that it is beyond all ordinary perception; it can only be seen when it has become gross, has taken form. At the beginning of creation there is only this Akasha. At the end of the cycle the solid, the liquids, and the gases all melt into the Akasha again ε121

"'The records connect each of us. They contain the sources of every archetypal symbol or mythic story which have ever deeply touched patterns of human behavior and experience. They are the inspiration for dreams and invention. They mold and shape levels of human consciousness.'"ε122

Steno noted: "The personal records Tu-whit has borrowed from the library of Akasha are largely a review of deeds ending with the twentieth century life of one Penelope Peacock."

Glancing at the scroll, he reviewed: "It is written here that you joined Mission Lavender without so much as a starting point. You have followed the path. You've been listening to what can't be heard and seeing what can't be seen.

"Having an empty mind means that you can't see what's in front of it because what's in front will only distract you from the real knowledge you seek. This is the beginning of what we call transcendence, which embodies all that is true. You can look at a calendar and get a date, but a calendar cannot impart to you the timelessness of the Universe which you've experienced on Mission Lavender.

"You have opened your heart and let it speak, freely, clearly and honestly. You've stared across hundreds of blank manuscript pages not knowing what might be written next and blindly chased your dreams across Canada to learn why you were having them. Your freedom has allowed you to face mortality, which has intimately connected you to us in the Astral realm. You have intuitively known that one day you may face suspicion, fear and ridicule because of this experience which you are slated to share. Yet this has not stopped you from trusting, because you know you are like everyone else – that this knowledge has been designed for the collective whole with the hope of fostering a more humane society on Earth. You have not shaped yourself or your message to fit anything other than your own instinctive nature and trust in the Mission. You are shifting right along with Mother Earth to a higher frequency because you are attuned to her energies.

"Your dreams have come full circle, Penelope. You have reconnected with the Earth. You are the child from the mother – the Great Mother Earth. The convergence of the material and the spiritual is what Pierre Teilhard de Chardin called the ultimate reunion at the Omega Point – the maximum level of consciousness – giving direction to the whole evolutionary process.

"Because humankind is at a turning point in evolutionary history, we are recruiting those having great respect for the natural world and a feeling of oneness with the planet. This attribute is not held by time or space, for such humans can sense energy frequencies and are able to recognize even the subtlest changes, which are virtually undetectable to the naked eye or the five senses. We tap those who, from lifetime to lifetime, have learned from their mistakes and not allowed them to erode their true nature.

"And the records note acts of compassion, for the quality of caring for others is foremost to the Mission."

"Well, Doc, this all sounds very noble and I'm sure there are great humanitarian souls on Earth who rise to those lofty standards, but I'm sure as sure can be that I'm not one. You've pegged me wrong, Doc. I'm just another traveler. I'm full of foibles – and mistakes! Holy moley! I've made more than my share.

"The values you speak of are in those who have lived far more commendably than I."

"Penelope, all the details of every being who has ever existed on Earth is recorded in the Akashic Records. The sum of these records tells of the state of evolution you are in as you progress toward perfection. There will always be people more or less developed than you, but it is not for you to judge your own evolution nor to weigh one deed against another. The totality of your life experience holds you accountable when your days on Earth come to a close and when it is time to cross over to the spiritual world. I daresay you are not yet ready for such a crossing. Nor are you ready to take on a task you can't fully understand while embodied. Just trust that we know what we're doing.

"You see, Penelope, we have been monitoring your evolution long before you ever knew of Mission Lavender. In fact, I see in this scroll a dream you had in 1992. You dream of *Noah's Ark; then you see a camel. The rest is fuzzy. You are reading from two scrolls of purplish wool fabric. One scroll has a small stone at the very end.*[534] You have likely forgotten this dream but we have not.

"You unknowingly began this work through remembering such dreams. Signing on to the global phase of Mission Lavender will broaden your horizons in ways inconceivable to you. You will set sight on shores beyond unimaginable boundaries. Your masters will teach you the rudiments of the combined sciences. Through these lessons, you'll gather scientific data with which to nurture your flowering tree, except that your study will out-

---

534 10/31/92.

distance any typical field study on Earth. This sweeping underground investigation will focus your attention on the cosmos through our Astral Court system."

"Astral Court system?"

"Yes, Penelope. Your findings will someday lead to a hearing in the Astral Courts."

"Dr. Steno. I can't imagine how there would be anything legal to what I'm learning. That sounds so weird. I never even heard of an Astral Court."

"When it is time for you to know more, rest assured you'll be informed. Just trust that you will be accessing worlds of data through universal connections and your dreams may bring those inhabitants on Earth who are ready to listen to a place of healing through higher thought."

"Do you mean when I had the epiphany of Lava Under, this umm – global part of the Mission was already in the works?"

"Correct, Penelope. You have been in our orientation program and we have supplemented the record with first-hand knowledge of your endurance.

"We included the *Girl Scouts* in your *Half Circle* dream because you needed to *practice the Girl Scout motto 'Be Prepared'*; that is, knowing the right thing to do at the right time and being willing to do it. The Girl Scout Promise and the Girl Scout Law may seem ordinary to you now, but they are defining models in adolescence that instill in young girls principles they hold to throughout their lives.

'Do you recall when you were trying to earn your sewing badge? Do you remember how long it took you?"

"I'd rather not, Doc. It took me years because the first dress I made fell apart while I was wearing it. I was mortified! Then I had to do it again. The next time I sewed the dress inside out and all the seams were showing. To get a grade, we had to wear what we made to Home Ec class. Everyone laughed at me. I swore I'd never again sew – or even try to stitch another scrap of material."

"That's right, Penelope. But you did! And you earned the badge. It's here in the records under Perseverance.

Well, this project is much like sewing – sewing a tapestry as vast as the world. And its rewards are far greater than the satisfaction of making even a whole wardrobe of dresses. By continuing on Mission Lavender's global path, you will belong to something larger. It will empower you to make a difference. The determination stamped on your lives, Penelope Peacock, was developed to full potential in your twentieth century adolescence."

"Well … Just how long is this part of the project, Dr. Steno? How much more of my earthly time would it consume?"

"Unfortunately, I can't give you the answer to that. It would be unwise to make a decision based on such worldly concerns, for Mission Lavender has been taking place outside of your ordinary concepts of time and space and will continue to do so."

Oh, no! What am I to do now? Why did he have to remind me of the Girl Scout Promise? Years of repeating the pledge echoed across time ...

> "On my honor, I will try:
> To serve God and my country,
> To help people at all times
> And to live by the Girl Scout Law."

And if I remember right, the Girl Scout Law talks about making the world a better place. Oh help! Thoughts of my Girl Scout honor, my devotion to Steno, my days happily spent with Mission Lavender and my yearning to just live in the world as I used to were spinning around in my head. Why was I so torn? Why did I feel so panicky? I had been ready to resume my life. Now this! Sure, it's been exciting, but what about my niece? My family? My friends? What about the everyday hobbies I've missed: the concerts, the ballet, the theater, the stacks of books and magazines I haven't touched for years? What about taking a trip that didn't connect to Mission Lavender? What about visiting France, again, the country I love most — or traveling to parts of the world I haven't seen?

This is probably the toughest decision I've ever faced, and it sure doesn't feel like it's from some other life. I was paralyzed with indecision. How could I choose? To choose one future is to forsake the promise of the others? Either way, I might never fully recover.

And then it came to me in a flash! I couldn't take another trip that wouldn't connect. I couldn't do another thing that was not related because everything does connect and is infinitely interrelated. And deep in my heart, I still held a glimmer of hope that Johnnie Pianissimo would appear someday, wearing the promised ring of infinity. I reflected on my days with my mentors, who invited me to sip the nectar of joy from their fountain of knowledge. I was just beginning to feel the everlasting effects of their divine protection.

Maybe if I signed on I'd learn about the mystifying pole and why I got all those dreams about DNA. I couldn't forget that we left Percival and Simon in Hopedale with a *dirty sock*. I knew Hopedale held a surprise. What I didn't know was whether it was good or bad. Hidden messages like Twink's Valentine with the cryptic *Optica -Optico pages 16, 17, 18, 19, 20, 21* were finally revealed. But what of the *blue rubbery logs — a missing piece of a board game and — a hole at the base of a skull?*[535] The dream said *all the information would be in the logs.* Perhaps, you dear Reader, could help.

There were many clues left to unravel, secrets to unlock, connections to be made. The Yellow Slab dream that advised: "Be patient. You will learn everything you need to know." That was one. Maybe I would even learn about the people in the jars someday. And I wondered if the Greek code would ever be fully deciphered. I dared not even ask, for I knew there was an unwritten law about asking for knowledge we're not ready to

---

535 2/14/97. See Ch. 25 – Remembering Osiris, p. 116

receive. One question as big as the world revolved around the Big Bang of evolution and the most mystifying of all was the Word is code for key enigma.

Most pressing was the metal and crystal compound that would banish the *swarms of bugs infecting the tree*.[536] If we could learn about that, it could be a cure for the Earth and all its creatures so dependent on it for nourishment.

I remembered the great pains Marie Curie took to teach me about the butterfly and how it could be something beautiful but also poisonous. I thought about how *one branch of the tree was weak* and the great difficulty we had in stopping the *spread of those awful swarms of bugs*.

It was as though a big horrible outbreak was coming and all the children and animals of the Earth were making pathetic whimpering sounds because they didn't know what to do or where to go.

I see the children as one mass of humanity – elders and babies – the innocent multitudes, huddled together in one small room. Their stories are so sad, and they are so frightened and my heart is breaking as I fight back the tears. They know their house is about to explode; they know something terrible is coming, and there's nothing they can do. The only sound I hear is one long wailing sob eerily echoing through the vast tunnels of time. They want to smell the flowers and hear the birds sing and feel the wind just one more time, but they were too scared to even think of that; they were sure it was too late. I wept and I wept some more because I knew that in reality, my dream about the exploding oven is happening. I felt so helpless. I could not tell them in time and I knew I would carry this sorrow with me to my grave, lifetime after lifetime for all eternity. It would remain permanently etched in my soul.

And as I reflected on all of this, a vision broke out of the blackness of my thoughts. Peggymoonbeam fluttered wildly, emerging from a beautiful cloud of yellow sulfur butterflies. Suddenly, a penetrating golden blue sphere of light from the heavens momentarily lifted that sinking void of suffering and loss.

I reflected on Percival's *begging cup* – his hallowed Grail cup – begging in my dream and, in all likelihood, the dreams of every being on the planet to save ourselves and our Earth. *Success Wake Lake* rang in my ears. *We are running late. There won't be time to eat.*

And what about the children? They are all of us and need to be awakened. The circle was widening. I saw it wide as the Earth and bright as the Sun, and in its center, Peggymoonbeam's almighty tree grew in Heaven but reached down to Earth, providing all the children food and shelter.

That calmed me and took me back to my center, but then I thought about the Oneiroball. Agneswiseheart said it held my purpose. I lifted up my eyes and could see the softness of her being. She had come to explain:

---

536 3/29/98. Ch. 76 – Chemistry: The Third Branch, p.

"Penelope, one part of your purpose is to deliver this message, but your purpose is not yet complete for hundreds of dreams are waiting for you to tell the story. Even when you have achieved your purpose you will not speak of the depth of this experience no matter how hard you try, because, my sweet Penelope, it is ineffable. That means it is not for words."

I cried and cried some more because I knew that when I was all finished telling what I could, it would be time to join my guides and nothing would worry me anymore and maybe some of the sorrow would fade. But then I might find out what is not for words. And as I wept, flashbacks swirled 'round me. Memories ricocheted, sparking new Ahas! The first signal at Signal Hill connected to Morse code and followed our footsteps to the last signal at Telegraph Cove. A Signal in Newfoundland – a Telegraph in Vancouver.

Our multilayered truer-than-life adventure still begged the question: Why Placentia? Was it a symbol of birth? Was Newfoundland, a new land discovered, dream shorthand for a new way of being? Was the motto, "Spirit of Vancouver"– another coincidence? Or, was it a new kind of vision – a new spiritual outlook – seeing undercover – seeing the invisible? Three branches: Vision – Geology – Chemistry now entwined, made perfect sense. These masters of light and spirit were trying to show us what was underground – imperceptible to the naked eye.

I would always remember the local and regional maps revealing dozens of surprise codes that told us to follow the invisible. The epiphanies were imprinted in my mind, in my heart, in my gut, most deeply, in my soul; in Branch, the paint-splashed fishing village that matched my dreams; in Placentia, the mysterious branch protruding from the water; in Vancouver Island, the dream mechanics who sped us toward the 7 *o'clock shadow*, who pointed us to island arc systems, arranging for rooms and merrily beeping the way to our next stop, and in Labrador, the actual mining of metals with which the story began: a dime in one eye, a penny in the other.

It struck me that the transformations of these nocturnal messages to daytime realities were the initiation. I knew that, if I continued, the journey would lead to the sum of knowledge and experience I had been seeking.

Had I been drawn to a plane from which I could never return? My choice is absolute knowledge imparted by my mentors, requiring me to give up life as I know it – or returning to my normal plane and struggling to increase my knowledge and awareness with my limited human senses.

Not only that. How could I say no to the great Steno? How could I abandon my guiding spirits?

Steno responded. "A word about your guiding spirits, Penelope ... we will always be with you, whether or not you resume Mission Lavender. Your higher self will know this."

"My Higher Self? I've mused over that for a long time. Is it like my doppelganger, the self writing the story with me? How many higher selves do I have?"

Steno's laughter scattered dream dust all over the place.

"What a curious little cat, you are, Penelope. Your Higher Self or your doppelganger are one. Think of it as the overseer of the Soul that holds wisdom beyond the human limits of the Ego. It is eternal, conscious, and intelligent: a part of yourself that has ventured beyond your personal province with a desire for discovery in other worlds. Your yearning for wholeness among all your fellow earthlings is what decided you on first joining Mission Lavender. This is because you found a secret in your dreams that you had to share."

Peggymoonbeam's words rang out. "We see you as one planet .. one people."

"Dr. Steno, do you think that with all this repetition in my dreams and the way one connection validates the next that I've come to some kernel of truth: my theory being that our dreams contain all the information in the Universe, even though I've only seen a smidgen in my own dreams?"

"Yes, Penelope. We at Terracrust and Starsight know the dream is a courier carrying messages of truth to the world soul. Your *Upanishads* dream and its mystic wisdom taught you about an underlying unity. But it's not all that simple on the Earth plane. It's a matter of paradigms – the generally accepted models of how ideas relate and form a framework within which scientific research is carried out.

"Today's earthly paradigm for reasoning is science and mathematics, with their hypotheses and theories, proofs and laws, that converge on Truth. Your impassioned foray through many branches of science illustrates your devotion to the Truth which you've married to the Dream by using research, intuitive and inductive reasoning, association and observation. We see field evidence provided by Mission Lavender as an hypothesis of an underlying interconnectivity in the universe – one that transcends the world of physics, including psyche as well as matter. Our goal is that one day it shall be respected as its paradigm for proving truth."

"But, Doc, you know truths that humans do not."

"Ummhmm. Our omniscience discerns truth as well as falsehoods.

"You've discovered that the cosmic imprints of Timelessness and Consciousness are shared. That is, that dreaming and waking live in the same house, but in different parts, as do Heaven and Earth.

"Many of your Earth scientists are working on a unified theory. Your experiential body of psi phenomena illustrates the relationship of mind and matter in a circumscribed geographical area. The insights from this methodology exemplify the dual nature of consciousness in waking and in dreaming; both forms of thought are initially fragmentary – one in focus, one not. Through your Timelessness Glasses, your focus converged in one singular vision – one cohesive whole.

You've grasped the oneness of the thinking process through associative reasoning. You were confused with the entanglement of so many fragments: which ones went where, which were different and which, the same. You observed how fragmentation self-organizes according to its own rules of time and space, systematically unfolding to wholeness. Through association and joining the pieces together, they became inseparable; first in your own life, then on the Canadian landscape in village after village, province after province, to reveal the oneness of Man and Nature – Mother and Mother Earth – Mother Earth and the Universe. What could be more unified?

"In the words of David Bohm … 'fragmentary content and fragmentary process have to come to an end together.'

"You arrived at this truth, Penelope, because you trusted Consciousness – that non-local transcendent field not bound to the space-time continuum. You couldn't see it because it was the seer. You knew it was real, yet neither concrete nor abstract. In quantum language, it would be called the Observer and the Observed.

"When you pass over to our side, the energy stream will be withdrawn from your physical body and completely absorbed back into your Higher Self. This happens when your incarnations have achieved their intended purpose and at that point, all will merge.

"You have grappled with the question of how all of this science was coming your way. Well, dear Penelope, you, the being who has journeyed with us on Mission Lavender, are one of the incarnations that your Higher Self, which is the real you, has sent to Earth to garner experiences in this time and place. Your current life builds on its own past, on the memory of what was learned – then forgotten – then relearned. Those experiences include the body of science we've been helping you relearn to further your crusade for Truth. Coming back to your choice, it is up to you to decide how much more you want to upload in your energy stream. Do not fear, my lass. There will be no final judgment for you are your own judge. You wrote your contract before you returned to Earth and your actions while there will determine the options you'll have next. If you desire more, then your masters will heartily welcome you and rejoice in your decision to advance Mission Lavender's noble calling. And if not, they will humbly respect your choice and remain a part of you forevermore."

I was so nervous, I could hear my heart clicking and clacking to the beat of La Cucaracha and I was scared it would awaken all the angels at Starsight and Terracrust. Signing on for an extended tour of Mission Lavender was a lot to commit to, but I thought about the ascended masters and how they enlightened my knowledge of their dimension. In a swirl of kaleidoscopic flashes, I could see Steno's great love for the earth and Marie's devotion to chemistry; I saw Galen's noble efforts in teaching me to see and dear sweet funny Ptolemy, my eternal love and maestro astronomer of the galaxies waiting to take me on the cosmic spin of my life. While I learned the mechanics of their disciplines, their core teaching focused on Listening. This had a lot to do with information recall. If you don't listen, you can't remember. They all taught it, and taught it well.

My choice loomed. My cadre of loved ones stood by: Peggymoonbeam, Agneswiseheart, Charlesbigstar, while Simon and Percival waited patiently in Labrador.

I would run the risk of biases toward abstract thinking and people saying, "Oh, that's just a bunch of dreams," but if they realized the concreteness and gravity of the message, it would be a great day, a great awakening and bring great happiness to all the children.

I turned the focus ring on the kaleidoscope and, in a brilliant cascade of science, I saw clear as day: Geology – Chemistry – Vision. The starry messengers of Mission Lavender had filled the Oneiroball with hundreds of dreams and thousands of disconnected dots spelling out an urgent communiqué of truth and fact. The big dreams came first as though they were descending from Heaven on a long flight. As they approached Earth, the smaller pieces drifted into view. My vision became clearer and clearer, so clear I could see right into the center of the Earth.

The booming voice of the ancients rang out. "Someday, someone will be able to uncover all that went before. Someone will understand the meaning of the hieroglyphics."

In the language of Oneiromantics, the mentors were making known a chemical reaction in the earth not visible to the naked eye, a reaction that could impact all of God's creatures during passages of Earth time we couldn't begin to count. Peggymoonbeam's tree was growing in heaven with new leaves coming into bloom on the Branches bestowed me. A new stem – Astrophysics – was just beginning to sprout.

I could not turn away.

With a monster lump in my throat, I quivered, "OK, Doc. Sign me on – but what will I have to do? What is required of me?"

"We ask that you continue to dutifully record your dreams, observe the subtle signs and secrets from the universe, keep listening, watching, questioning, learning, and pay close attention your lessons. Your intuitive nature will, through science, show you the true nature of reality. At times, you may be bored with our teachings and at other times, exasperated and frightened, but you must stay alert and concentrate, for the abundance flowing your way will exceed any of your imaginings."

"Oh, well. That's not a problem. It's what we've been doing. But ... but ... will I .. um... will I be able to get a release if it doesn't work out?"

"Of course, dear Penny. You always have free will."

"Well ... uh .. Will I finally be able to understand how this all works – about all the mystical and magical things that have happened and how we're able to communicate?

"You know, Doc, I've been having a new kind of sensation while I'm dreaming. It feels like a fluttering vibration is traveling through me. You told me about electromagnetic radiation – waves that radiate from electrically charged particles and confessed that you transmit information to me through light waves. I wonder if I'm feeling energy being transmitted from you and my other masters through the electromagnetic spectrum or if it's my own body's electrical impulses at work. Am I getting closer to learning how our energies get transferred?"

Well, Penelope, spirit communication and all paranormal phenomena is a rather complicated process requiring a dramatic transition in planetary consciousness for earthlings to understand it. Paradigm shifts are never easy and the more major ones can take centuries of speculation to become accepted. Agreement of plate tectonics in the twentieth century really began with my work in 1669. At present, most earthlings are only able to know the mechanistic details of paranormal happenings when they are over here with us. However, your experience with us is putting you on the fringe of a deeper understanding. With this, you will gain insight into Mission Lavender's multiple objectives. We at Terracrust and Starsight have spent lifetimes accruing the universal knowledge we are attempting to impart to you on an elementary level. This cannot happen overnight. That is why we ask that you 'Be Patient.'"

"I have one last question, Dr. Steno, but it could disqualify me because of the rule of patience. I'm still trying to understand the – umm, er – um – the 'Word is code for key' puzzle."

His brows knit into a frown I'd not seen before. He was becoming impatient. "All right, Miss Peacock. Why don't you enlighten me?"

Oh God! I knew I shouldn't have asked. The ball was in my court. My memory was clicking like a metronome. OK, Penny. Think hard. Think hard. You know the answer. Remember Percival's question, "Whom does the Grail serve?" Think of the Grail legend of a mysterious stone that fell from the heavens. Remember, *"You're in real estate and you're also an alchemist."* The dream said you have the clues – the clues are in the Word. OK. Spell it out. He's waiting.

(Gulp). "I think the key is in trusting the logos – the Word of God – the divine ordering principle of the Universe – Akasha. A picture is framed in metal, the symbol for Uranium – a radioactive, toxic element – the main source of heat inside the earth and an abundant source of nuclear energy. *Something new* is mentioned twice: *Keystone and self-turning eggs.* The key: stone – gravel – uranium. *Self-turning eggs:* sulfur cooking in the earth – a sulfurous transmutation occurring in the earth. An emergent hypothesis: the heat of uranium decay leads to a transmutation of sulfur producing more sulfur. I coin this transmutation, 'Sulfuranium,' possibly a radioactive gas.[E123] To expand on this supposition, much research is required in various branches of science particularly geochronology, geochemistry, ecology and seismology.

"The Bible directs humankind to replenish the Earth. The Dream shows humankind depleting the Earth. Human excesses, dissipation, anger and upheaval are mirrored in the Earth and reflected back on man. The Word of God centers on a hole, a metaphor for holes drilled deep in the earth's crust. They are violent wounds in a living organism that is part of us. Day by day we watch in frozen horror the poisons strangling our ocean, our species, our lives. Logos has been ignored and defiled. The dream avatars have offered us the branches of science, truth and knowledge needed to achieve salvation, to understand that Empathy for the Earth and one another is our only answer."

"Quite astute. My resplendent magic carpet awaits you, Miss Penelope Peacock. We can embark on a new era for humankind, but we must do so now. The choice is yours."

(Gulp.) (Gulp.)

"Hmm. (Gulp.) Well – um – Where will we wind up when the Mission is over?"

"You won't be disappointed, Penny, but do remember … the destination is never more important than the journey."

I reflected. Was this a glimpse of the choice we all inevitably face?

I had to obey the precept of "not asking" but I wondered if, on the next mission I'd learn more about the anonymous architect …

Who presented the metal frame.

Who was busy on February 18 arranging for a family get-together.

Who sent bouquets of roses, each scent imparting a different mystery.

Who dispatched MOMOM – SAVE OUR EARTH.

Who saw the crime but could not incriminate the criminal.

Who laid masses of irregular pieces on my chest. They were tectonic plates.

Who sent a floating metal wrench; a strike slip fault.

Who painted the settings of sulfurous gases and sleeping volcanoes in yellow and lavender.

Who guided us to volcanic activity extending from the Yellowstone Plateau to Jackson Hole, Wyoming.

Who painted a hole with glue. The glue was lava.

Who knew all along that "yellow lexicon" was Sulfur.

Who heard the noisy boy and declined to endorse the nickel smelter in Voisey's Bay.

Who delivered us beyond all boundaries to a Keystone Restaurant known for its home-baked bread.

Who taxied me in my dirty socks to Grace Lines and the Moravian Mission.

Who sent a fuzzy spider to show us volcano building in the Cordilleras.

Who witnessed Angela's drowning. Gideon was present.

Who introduced a Japanese instructor to remind us of our vulnerabilities.

Who taught us the language of the Dream ... the language of the gods.

Who instilled in us Trust.

Who led us to the Bethany church where Lazarus was raised from the dead.

Who sent the guiding wisdom of a heavenly owl.

Who pled for Lovingkindness and transformation through the symbol of a begging cup.

Who sent supreme emissaries of the Universal Unconscious to help decipher the message.

As I stood with one foot firmly planted in that which is Known, I cautiously placed my other foot on the welcome mat of the Unknown. The thrill of the unexplored danced before me, taunting me with Steno's invitation to swim in the eternal ocean of universal knowledge. Waves of excitement encircled me as I was drawn deeper and deeper into a vortex of light within which spiraled the keys to the unseen. I wondered, as I always had about the transmission of light. Did it flutter as a wave in the cosmos? Was my heart aflutter because such a wave was passing through me when I dreamt? What would the next part of the journey hold? I was curious as my Percival cat and not at all convinced I was up to the task. As though a million strings were reverberating across the star-studded galaxies, chords of the Girl Scout oath rang out true and clear: "On my honor, I will try, To serve God and my country." I would take this giant leap and trust that a net would appear. I would reach for the stars and believe that if I reached high enough, I could touch just one.

The Beginning

EPILOGUE

This spiritual pilgrimage has guided me to the mysterious transformation between matter and spirit, between time and eternity and the fluctuating scales of human and earth behavior. The journey would have been impossible without the conviction that Lavender was something that you, my Readers would share. I am humbled by your perseverance and unflagging support. It is you who have driven this golden chariot heavenward toward its destination and for that, I give back to you all the love I have received on this wondrous mission. It is my great wish that Lavender has served as a portal for your own dreams and that you'll join our heavenly band of mentors on our continuing mission toward wholeness.

AN APPEAL TO SCIENCE

You cannot hope to build a better world without improving the individuals. To that end, each of us must work for our own improvement and, at the same time, share a general responsibility for all humanity, our particular duty being to aid those to whom we think we can be most useful.

Marie Curie

Using cosmic dreaming as its bedrock, this tome enfolds an urgent message to Science.

After fifteen years of research and assembly, I found that Lavender – Lava Under – was showing us occurrences in the earth which may not be monitored by Science. Many dreams point to the past and resounding warnings point to the future.

My conclusions on Sulfuranium derive from the theory of disintegration in which piezoelectrically charged quartz passing through magma in a field where sulfur giving off a gaseous substance (indirectly from uranium decay) is continuously disintegrating while the gaseous discharge is being produced. The emanation is not permanent, for it is gradually transmuted into other radioactive substances, which - if the emanation comes into contact with solid bodies - are deposited on them in a so-called active precipitation.

Elemental sulfur is found in volcanic regions. When in indirect contact with the heat of uranium decay it continuously turns back on itself, producing more sulfur. I suggest this disintegration to be the cause of an alchemical transmutation which I call Sulfuranium, a radioactive gas not yet fully defined.

Though I don't claim that my investigations have made me an expert, my appeal is that scientific research be conducted to determine a common denominator, and that those in control share in the responsibility. Nowhere has the urgency for truth and cooperation been more evident than that witnessed by the 2010 oil disaster in the Gulf of Mexico. An immediate call-to-action has been prompted by the 2011 9.0 Tōhoku earthquake and tsunami in Japan which devastated the city of Sendai threatening a nuclear meltdown and causing growing alarm over a potential spread of radiation.

Mission Lavender's conclusions reveal global prototypes which are reminders of catastrophic volcanic eruptions in Yellowstone – Teton Range (Wyoming) – Colima, (Mexico) – Krakatoa (Indonesia) – Mt. Kilimanjaro (Tanzania). Warnings of earthquakes pointed to Tabriz (Iran) – Alaska (Prince William Sound) – St. Lawrence – the Himalaya – Vancouver Island.

Other dreams point to more recent earthquakes – India, Haiti, Chile, Japan and to locations not yet revealed.

It is worth mentioning that the 2010 fissure eruption of Eyjafjallajokull volcano in Iceland mirrored dream images of ash clouds in the Surtsey, Iceland, eruption when that volcanic island popped up in the ocean in 1963; the British Petroleum oil spill in the Gulf of Mexico off Louisiana was symbolized in a dream mirroring the 1989 Exxon Valdez spill.[537] Both events are wake-up calls to the fact that adequate monitoring is sorely needed.

Dear Reader, geologists will be able to ascertain trends associated with historic activity as well as to current global events. The team members, as I came to know them, masterminded this operation with precision and deliberation. They had a reason for focusing on these events.

As I write, only about one hundred of the 1,545 known active volcanoes worldwide are outfitted with monitoring equipment, according to Rick Wunderman of the Smithsonian Institution's Global Volcanism Program.[E124]

Mission Lavender urges that geophysical and geo-chemical exploration of areas containing common characteristics similar to those in the book, if not underway, begin immediately.

Seismic zones requiring attention are:

° Lower St. Lawrence Seismic Zone - Eastern Canada
° Avalon Zone in Eastern Newfoundland
° Cascadia Subduction Zone - Vancouver Island
(The Cascade Range has very high threat volcanoes with inadequate monitoring.)

Other areas requiring monitoring are:
° Island Arc Systems: Aleutian Trench – Vancouver,
    possibly Newfoundland/Labrador. Sunda Strait – Krakatoa, Indonesia

° Oilfields: Radium testing for radioactivity

° Gas and Oil Drilling:
Complete overhaul of industry standards and government regulatory enforcement. Inspection for leaks in abandoned oil and gas wells

A worst-case scenario involves a gas or oil leak from a pipeline rupture or faulty oil rig as happened in 2010 in the Gulf of Mexico would be compounded in an area of magmatic disturbances or where other hydrocarbon gases are found in deep rock fractures. Adding in gases from volcanoes, radioactive waste and interaction with gases and chemical dispersants

---

537 3/13/00. See Ch. 93 – Home Plate, p. 459

in ground and meteoric waters,[125] creates an historically unprecedented and widespread ignition threat endangering wildlife, humans, our oceans and our land. Add in the still unknown impact of dispersants used in an impulsive effort to defuse the impact of floating oil, and the prospects are even more catastrophic.

For environmental, ecological and humanitarian reasons, it is urgent that every alternative be carefully scrutinized and that precautionary measures be taken in all geographical areas before pipelines, oceanic and terrestrial, are built and prior to the commencement of drilling for oil, gas, minerals or metals. While certain measures may be in place in some areas, my studies say it is a dire necessity to employ the following in all cases:

- Seismic real-time monitoring of deep-sea volcanoes

    Volcanic gas detection systems.
    Multibeam sonar mapping of the seafloor to detect underwater volcanoes.
    Acoustic monitoring stations to detect sound waves associated with volcanic activity.
    Technologies that can measure changes in temperature and composition of gases escaping from the earth.
    Technology that can detect magma moving closer to the surface.
    Global Positioning System receivers to monitor ground deformation.
- Analysis of seismic gap potential.
- Study of rocks to determine if magma has been gaining in silicate content.
- Soil-testing for hydrocarbon gases and hazardous chemicals.
- Fractional crystallization studies to determine the chemical composition of any involved magma
- Studies of crystal formation to calculate the timescale between the trigger of volcanic activity and the volcano's eruption. (Such a study was conducted in Santorini, Greece.)
- Oxygen isotope testing for the mixing of magmatic and meteoric waters.
- Surficial geology mapping to study groundwater, sediment characteristics and to locate geologic hazards.
- Geochronological determination of magnetism of acid rain to carboniferous rocks.
- Biotoxin testing. See Cawthron Institute, NZ for water management and the largest natural toxin monitoring program in the world.[126]

I go forward, at this hour in our struggle for wholeness, with the hope that – with the help of Science – humankind will awaken to our symbiotic relationship with Planet Earth, the only home we have. Our survival depends on Hers.

SYNCHRONOUS EXPERIENCES

Synchronous experiences are when seemingly unrelated events appearing to be meaningful parallels take place outside of space and time. The intuitive, spiritual function in waking and dreaming consciousness cultivates the potential of transcendence where parallel meanings in a mental state with physical events are realized.

Listed are various locations in Mission Lavender and corresponding manifestations of dream particles (italicized). These meaningful parallels appear to have been organized by an underlying pattern ranging across time and space to and from local and nonlocal regions in the cosmos.

Rupert Sheldrake's morphogenetic fields may have been actualized in these areas.

Newfoundland

St. John's:

> Cabot Tower - Marconi exhibit (*museum*, *Morse code*)
> Titanic Exhibit
>> Passenger Manifest - Helen Loraine *Allison*
>> Cargo Manifest — *Sero*

Placentia: *Church of the Sacred Heart*
Church of Our Lady of Angels
Dead kitten – (Kitty Darling Child of Robert Jardine
Freebairn, Died September 3rd, 1895, Aged 4 years)

Castle Hill: *Ambrose* (Ambrose Shea Bridge)
lavender painted *bricks*
logs, *yellow* paint
picket fence
pirate sign, M. Noel
Pauline Maher
Maher's Polypipe
> Maher's Collision Center gas supplier (*gas pipe*line) *upside-down boat* (ties to Chicago Titanic exhibit)

Argentia   *gymnasium* (Avalon Fitness Center)
Branch   *yellow initials on rock, lavender* paint on rocks
Burin   *Bethany Church*
Cape Chapeau Rouge
         red hat, pink rose (rose quartz)
Three Capes   Cape Chapeau Rouge, Cape St. Mary, Cape Shore area

Grand Bank   Yellowstone trailer park
                 (*yellow stones*)
Isthmus of Avalon
                 neck
Lawn   *lavender poles and hydrants*
SE Arm   *blue glove*
St. Brides   *bride, wedding gown*
Swift Current   *curly cue doodle on rock*
Trinity Bay   *Spread Eagle*

Labrador
       Moravian Mission stations:
       Nain   Voisey's Bay (*noisy boy*)
       Hebron   *Rabbi*
       Hopedale   oldest *framed houses* in Canada

Vancouver, British Columbia
Alert Bay:
       7 o'clock shadow
       back porch
       blue logs
       cinder blocks
       picket fence
       totem pole

Beaver Creek:
       lavender map

Garibaldi Lake:
       Black Tusk mountain

ELECTRONIC ANOMALIES

During the writing of this book, typed text changed spontaneously in a variety of ways revealing a systematic logic in relation to the overarching message. This occurred usually during writing, but occasionally after the file was closed and then reopened.

Information Technology may explain various electronic functions; it, however, cannot explain the congruence of these implantations and specificity at key points where they occurred. Following are examples, some of which appear in their changed form; others, in their original form.

Greek Implantations

3/18/00   Agneswiseheart, p. 84-5
"mother to me in my early years, she" replaced with the Greek.

6/23/00   Galen, p. 462
"On the Function of the Parts of the Body," replaced with the Greek.

7/25/00   St. Lawrence, Newfoundland, pp. 438-39
Avalon Tectonic zone would be where disaster would originate..., replaced with the Greek.

11/06/00   Tanzania, p. 411
"vegetation ... that mesh with your descriptions of the patchwork quilt." replaced with the Greek.

11/16/00   Cape Shore, Newfoundland,
I was under Sally's wing wearing a cape decorated with bird feet and ὦΩΥ´ϑΩ´ "feathers" replaced with the Greek. (not in book)

Bolded Words

black hole in the microwave, p. 557

gut which flows into the waters, p. 269

legend embodied in three ancient beliefs: p. 252

Manufactured in 1989 - Made in Thailand, p. 557

Tectonic Zone ...where disaster would originate, p. 448

TOXIN, DESTRUCTION, p. 449

triumvirate arch, p. 584

"Carbon is black. My socks were dirty, almost black. Sulfuric Acid? **The chemical symbol for sulfur is S. Carbon is coal – black and dirty. Dirty sock: drop the s. Change sock to rock and we have a sulfurous rock.** If the *outer edges of the socks are dirty,* and if socks symbolize **sulfurous** rocks, certain rocks **along the coast of Labrador might** contain sulfur. **Remarkable! A dirty sock is a sulfurous rock!** p. 485

Color Changes
Blue/Lavender
  Illusion, p. 17
Gray
        Past life, p. 45
        faulting, exhibit stress going on within the continent's crust. They occur between pairs of mountain chains that cross the great shields. p. 200
Green
        Radioactive Clock, p. 452
        Word of God is the means by which He is present and working in the world, p. 507
        Electronic in the title of this appendix
        Grail – Chrétien de Troyes' 'Perceval, the Story of the Grail,' p. 300
        Omega – set, abstract objects, p. 439
        Speed of Light – **miles, foot, nanosecond,** p. 184

Reversed order

Upside-down exclamation point, p. 155
        a cone device that connected to a boat graced by the presence of Abraham Lincoln. f320,,¡

Font size reductions
Zone, p. 522

Separated letters
S U B D U C T I O N, p. 522

if you on Earth can compress many dreams into one why can't we do the r e v e r s e a n d s p r e a d o u t t h e c l u e s . A f t e r a l l , f r o m o u r v a n t a g e p o i n t t h e r e i s n o d i f f e r e n t i a t i o n b e t w e e n n e i g h b o r h o o d s . . . . . . e v e n c o n t i n e n t s b l u r . p. 586

Garbled citations
Origin of the Elements – How a Supernova Explodes – Gideon , p. 563
Steganography – secret writing, p. 349

Number code insertions
        280,, *Part of a wall has been broken through,* p. 328
        280,, the collision dream, p. 439
        280,, triumvirate arch, p. 584

Fax printing spontaneously
Hearts: 1999-2004 (Over fifty hearts appeared as signs from Peggymoonbeam encouraging this work.)
Bi-directional arrow, smiley face p. 462

LIST OF ILLUSTRATIONS

PART ONE – ENDNOTES

CHAPTER 1

ε_1 Montague Ullman, M.D, *The Transformation Process In Dreams*, The American Academy of Psychoanalysis Journal, Vol. 79, No. 2, May 1975.

ε_2 Australian Museum *<http://australianmuseum.net.au/Indigenous-Australia-Spirituality/>*

ε_3 James R. Lewis, *The Dream Encyclopedia*, (Visible Ink Press, 1995) p. 25.

ε_4 Natue Nancy Parsifal-Charles, *The Dream. 4,000 Years of Theory and Practice*, (Locust Hill Press, 1986) p. Gardiner/169. (*Gardiner (Alan H.). Hieratic Papyri in the British Museum*. 3rd Series. Chester Beatty Gift. Papyrus No. III. [Papyrus Facsimile +text and annotations] London, 1935.)

As the editor notes, the Chester Beatty papyrus considerably enhances Egypt's claim to be the place of origin of all later dream books, though he does admit that Babylonia has perhaps a stronger claim of being the original home of dream books. Dreams are categorized as either good or bad (of evil omen), the hieroglyph for bad being written in red, the color of blood.

ε_5 Op. cit. Parsifal-Charles, *The Dream. 4,000 Years of Theory and Practice*, (Locust Hill Press, 1986) p. Gardiner/169.

ε_6 Catholic Encyclopedia: The Holy Grail <http://www.newadvent.org/cathen/06719a.htm>

ε_7 *Galen. On The Usefulness Of The Parts Of the Body*, trans. Intro. and Comm. by Margaret Tallmadge May (Ithaca, NY: Cornell University Press, 1968.) Vol. 1, pp. 392-393.

CHAPTER 5

ε_8 Ibid. Vol. II, pp. 490-491.

ε_9 Op. cit. Parsifal-Charles, p. Gardiner/169.

ε_{10} Rudolph E. Siegel, M.D., *Galen. On Sense Perception* (S. Karger, Basel, Switzerland, 1970) pp. 67, fig.5.

ε_{11} With thanks to Richard Rodgers and Lorenz Hart for "Dancing on the Ceiling."

CHAPTER 9

ε_{12} www.faqs.org/faqs/astronomy/faq/part7

ε_{13} Ibid.

ε_{14} O. Richard Norton, *Rocks From Space*, 2nd ed. (Mountain Press Publishing, 1998) p. 232.

ε_{15} http://en.wikipedia.org/wiki/Type_II_supernova

CHAPTER 10

ε_{16} Paul J. Achtemeier, Harper's Bible Dictionary, Ed., (HarperSanFrancisco, 1985) pp. 347.

ε_{17} Ouwerkerk N, Steenweg M, de Ruijter M, Brouwer J, van Boom JH, Lugtenburg J, Raap J., *One-pot two-step enzymatic coupling of pyrimidine bases to 2-deoxy-D-ribose-5-phosphate. A new strategy in the synthesis of stable isotope labeled deoxynucleosides.*(J Org Chem. 2002 Mar 8;67(5):1480-9) <http://www.ncbi.nlm.nih.gov/pubmed/11871876>

Footnotes contain dream dates and references to prior pages where the dream appeared.

Endnotes contain bibliographical references, are marked with "ε" in the text, and appear at the end of the book.

CHAPTER 11

ℰ18   Merriam-Webster's Online Dictionary <http://www.aolsvc.merriam-webster.aol.com/dictionary/ genetic percent20drift>

CHAPTER 13

ℰ19   Leon E. Long, *Geology,* Ninth Edition, (Pearson Custom Publishing, 1999) p. 455.

ℰ20   Brain Greene, *The Elegant Universe*, (Vintage Books, 2000), p. 14.

CHAPTER 14

ℰ21   http://en.wikipedia.org/wiki/Nicolas_Steno

ℰ22   Op. cit., Long, pg. 38.

ℰ23   Nicolaus Steno, *Sample of the Elements of Myology* 1667, (Creation 23(4):47–49 September 2001 by Ann Lamont).

CHAPTER 17

ℰ24   J.C. Cooper, *An Illustrated Encyclopaedia of Traditional Symbols,* (Thames and Hudson, 1978) pg. 48.

CHAPTER 20

ℰ25   Variable Star Astronomy Chapter 7: Observing Variable Stars in the Real Sky <http://www.scribd. com/doc/34954747/>

ℰ26   OBSERVING VARIABLE STARS, Observing Delta Cephei, The American Association of Variable Star Observers <http://www.eso.org/public/outreach/eduoff/aol/market/collaboration/var-star/pg1.html>

ℰ27   The Center for Psychology and Social Change was renamed the John E. Mack Institute after Mack's death in 2004.

ℰ28   World ITC, The New Technology of Spiritual Contact <http://www.worlditc.org/>

ℰ29   Carl Sagan, The Best of Cosmos, VHS. *Cosmos* was produced in 1978 and 1979 by Los Angeles PBS affiliate KCET.

ℰ30   John Tyerman Williams*, Pooh and the Philosophers,* (Methuen, 1995) pg. 37.

PART TWO – ENDNOTES

CHAPTER 23

ℰ1   J. Stevenson, Ph.D., and Sharon Rutman, *The Complete Idiot's Guide to The Titanic* (Alpha Books, 1998), p. 125.

ℰ2   Ibid. pp. 118, 126.

ℰ3   Ibid. p. 52.

ℰ4   John P. Eaton and Charles A. Haas, *Titanic, A Journey Through Time* (W.W. Norton & Company, 1999) p. 60.

ℰ5   D. E. Bristow, *Titanic: Sinking the Myths* (Katco Literary Group, 1995), pp. 59-60.

ℰ6   Ibid. p. 60.

ε7 Lee W. Merideth, *1912 Facts About Titanic* (Savas Publishing Company, 1999), p. 213.

ε8 http://en.wikipedia.org/wiki/William_McMaster_Murdoch, *Sinking of the RMS Titanic*

ε9 Op. cit. Stevenson and Rutman, p. 106.

ε10 Don Lynch, *Titanic* (Madison Press Books, 1992) p. 80.

ε11 Op. cit., Merideth, p. 22.

ε12 Susan Wels, *TITANIC, Legacy of The Worlds' Greatest Ocean Liner* (Time Life Books, 1956) p. 84.

ε13 Op. cit., Eaton and Haas, pp. 65, 67.

ε14 Ibid.

ε15 Op.cit., Merideth, p. 44.

ε16 Op.cit., Stevenson and Rutman, p. 100.

ε17 Ibid. p. 69.

ε18 *Answers from the Abyss,* 104 min. videotape, Discovery Channel, April 1999.

ε19 Op. cit., Bristow, pp. 132, 140.

ε20 Op. cit., *Answers from the Abyss.*

CHAPTER 24

ε21 The American Scholar <http://www.theamericanscholar.org/buoyancy/>

ε22 William Shakespeare, The Tempest, 224:21.

CHAPTER 25

ε23 *Sound and Light at Karnak Temples* videotape, The Egyptian Ministry of Culture.

ε24 John Van Auken, *Ancient Egyptian Mysticism*, (A.R.E. Press, 1999).

ε25 Robert Hume and George Haas, translator, *The Thirteen Principal Upanishads* translated from the Sanskrit, (Oxford University Press, 1931).

CHAPTER 31

ε26 *Calculating the threat of tsunami*, Australian Academy of Science <http://www.science.org.au/nova/045/045key.htm>

CHAPTER 34

ε27 Op cit., Bristow, p. 135.

ε28 *Titanic – A Voyage of Discovery* <http://www.euronet.nl/users/keesree/rusticle.htm>

ε29 Titanic Reference Map. (Hedberg Maps, Inc., 1998).

ε30 Alan Cutler, *The Seashell on the Mountaintop: How a Humble 17th Century Genius Solved the Greatest Geological Riddle of His Time and Forever Changed the World* (Dutton: Penguin Group USA, 2003).

CHAPTER 36

ε31 Op. cit., *Answers from The Abyss.*

CHAPTER 37

ε32 William Wordsworth, I Wandered Lonely As a Cloud, st. 2.

ε33   Richard Walzer and Michael Frede, translators, *Galen. Three Treatises On The Nature of Science* (Hackett Pub. Co., 1985), p. 27.

ε34   Microsoft Encarta Encyclopedia, 2001. Partial quote from the *Odyssey: Penelope*. Source: Homer, translated by Albert Cook. *The Odyssey.* (New York: *W.W. Norton & Co.*, 1974).

CHAPTER 38

ε35   Norma Jean Katan with Barbara Mintz, *Hieroglyphs, The Writing of Ancient Egypt* (Atheneum Publishers, 1981), p. 7.

ε36   Microsoft Encarta Encyclopedia 2001. "Ptolemy V."

ε37   Manfred Lurker, *The Gods and Symbols of Ancient Egypt* (Thames and Hudson, 1974), p. 116.

CHAPTER 40

ε38   Alan H. Cutler, *In the Beginning: Religion and Geology in the Era of Nicolaus Steno* (The Geological Society of America, 2003).

CHAPTER 41

ε39   Rudolph E. Siegel, M.D, *Galen. On Sense Perception* (S. Karger, Basel, Switzerland, 1970) p. 61.

ε40   Ibid. pp. 10-11.

ε41   Robert Frost, *Two Tramps in Mud Time 1936, st. 9.*

ε42   Miguel de Cervantes, Don Quixote, John Ormsby translator, Part 1, Chapter 8.

ε43   John Keats, *Ode to a Nightingale*, st. 8.

CHAPTER 42

ε44   *Song of the Sky Loom*, Anonymous, Tewa (Native American).

CHAPTER 44

ε45   Luigi Palmieri. (1807-1896), physicist and meteorologist, was a pioneer in the detection of volcanic eruptions.

ε46   Fusakichi Omori, (1911): Report on the observation of pulsatory oscillations in Japan, Bull. Imp. Earthquake Inv. Comm., 5, 109-137.

CHAPTER 45

ε47   Dr. John R. Delaney. PBS Online *<www.pbs.org/wgbh/nova/abyss/mission/delaney.html>* Updated October 2000.

CHAPTER 48

ε48   Margaret Tallmadge May, translation, introduction and commentary. *Galen. On The Usefulness Of The Parts Of The Body* (Ithaca, NY: Cornell University Press, 1968.) p.400.

ε49   <http://en.wikipedia.org/wiki/Pneumatology>

ε50   Op. cit., Siegel, p.40.

ε51   Tilling, *Volcanoes*: USGS General Interest Publication, 1985.

<http://vulcan.wr.usgs.gov/Glossary/PlateTectonics/description_plate_tectonics.html>

[52] Titanic Sunk Faster Than Thought. December 12, 2005 <http://www.physorg.com/news8959. html>

[53] Danko Dimchev Georgiev, MD, *Bose-Einstein condensation of tunnelling photons in the brain cortex as a mechanism of conscious action.* Division of Electron Microscopy, Medical University of Varna, Bulgaria, 2004 <http://cogprints.org/3539/>

[54] *Scientists Model Words as Entangled Quantum States in our Minds,* Feb. 18, 2009, Lisa Zyga <http://www.physorg.com/news154180635.html>

The aim of "quantum cognition" is to use quantum theory to develop radically new models of a variety of cognitive phenomena ranging from human memory to decision making. A recent study reveals that words can become entangled in the human mental lexicon."

[55] Montague Ullman, *The Dream: In Search of A New Abode.* Presented at the twenty-third Annual Meeting of the International Association for the Study of Dreams, July 22, 2006.
<http://siivola.org/monte/papers_grouped/index.htm>

[56] Edgar Mitchell, Sc.D, *Nature's Mind: the Quantum Hologram <www.edmitchellapollo14.com/naturearticle. htm>*

[57] D. Bohm and B.J. Hiley, *The Undivided Universe*, 1993. (Routledge; 1st ed.) November 12, 1993.

[58] Lynne McTaggart, *The Field: The Quest for the Secret Force of the Universe* (HarperCollins Publishers, 2002) p. 26.

CHAPTER 50

[59] S. Judson and S.M. Richardson, Illustrated Glossary of Geologic Terms. Based on the glossary in Earth: An Introduction to Geologic Change (Englewood Cliffs, NJ, Prentice Hall, 1995).

CHAPTER 51

[60] Op. cit., Stevenson and Rutman, pp. 125-6.

[61] Op cit., Wels, pp. 83-4.

[62] Op. cit., Eaton and Hass, p. 61.

[63] Op. cit., Bristow, p. 159.

[64] Hotspots: Mantle Thermal Plumes <http://pubs.usgs.gov/gip/dynamic/hotspots.html>

[65] Wikipedia, List of Hotspots <http://en.wikipedia.org/wiki/Hotspot_ percent28geology percent29>

CHAPTER 52

[66] Op. cit., Stevenson and Rutman, pp. 52, 162.

[67] Graham Hancock, *Fingerprints of the Gods, 1995,* Thoth, the Great God of Science and Writing *<http://www.think-aboutit.com/Spiritual/thoth.htm>*

PART THREE – ENDNOTES

CHAPTER 53

ε_1 *Encyclopedia of Newfoundland and Labrador* <http://www.cuff.com/enl/Anext.htm>
Commissioned by Joey Smallwood, first Premier of Newfoundland.

CHAPTER 60

ε_2 David Bohm, Wholeness and The Implicate Order, (Routledge & Kegan Paul, 1980), pp. 225, 229.

CHAPTER 61

ε_3 Op. cit., *Encyclopedia of Newfoundland and Labrador*, Castle Hill.

CHAPTER 62

ε_4 Translation by Jabir ibn Hayyan < http://www.hermetics.org/pdf/ontablet.pdf>

CHAPTER 64

ε_5 Jeremy W. Hayward, Letters to Vanessa, (Shambala Publications, 1997, p. 138).

ε_6 Gevin Giorbran, *Everything Forever - Two Kinds of Order* <http://everythingforever.com>

ε_7 Ibid.

CHAPTER 66

ε_8 Op. cit. The Telegram, September 7, 1999.

ε_9 B. Sherwood Lollar, T. Westgate, J. Ward, G.F. Slater, and G. Lacrampe-Couloume, *Abiogenic formation of alkanes in the Earth's crust as a minor source for global hydrocarbon reservoirs*. **Nature** Vol. 416:522-
524 (2002) <bsl@quartz.geology.utoronto.ca> Also discussed in National Geographic, April 5,
2002, and other publications, and at <http://www.mail-archive.com/meteorite-list@meteoritecentral.
com/msg03283.html>

ε_{10} Chloroflourocarbons are air pollutants blamed for the depletion of atmospheric ozone.

ε_{11} calcium carbonate.

CHAPTER 67

ε_{12} Wendy Martin, Once Upon a Mine, Chapter VI <http://www. heritage.nf.ca/environment>

CHAPTER 68

ε_{13} Op. Cit., *Encyclopedia of Newfoundland and Labrador*, Argentia.

CHAPTER 69

ε_{14} Bartlett's Familiar Quotations, 16th Ed., 1992, John Bartlett, High Diddle Diddle.

ε_{15} United States Geological Survey, University of Utah, The BBC
< http://www.solcomhouse.com/yellowstone.htm>

CHAPTER 71

ε_{16} The Dehumanization of Art (1925).

ε_{17} Nicholas Pinter and Mark T. Brando, *Our Everchanging Earth, How Erosion Builds Mountains,* Scientific American, Special Edition 2005, Vol. 15, No. 2, pp. 74-80.

CHAPTER 72

ε_{18} James R. Lewis, *The Dream Encyclopedia*, (Visible Ink Press, 1995) p. 353.

ε_{19} Ibid.

ε_{20} Num 21:4-9. Note that Moses made the serpent at God's direction only after an attack upon his people by deadly serpents.

ε_{21} J.C. Cooper, *An Illustrated Encyclopaedia Of Traditional Symbols,* (Thames and Hudson, 1978), p.188.

ε_{22} Ibid, p.147-8.

ε_{23} http://www.worlditc.org/f_02_macy_spirit_world_realms_0.htm

CHAPTER 73

ε_{24} Bruno Latour, translated by Alan Sheridan and John Law, *The Pasteurization of France, Irreduction of "the Sciences"* 4.5.7.2 (Harvard University Press, 1988) pp. 226-7.

ε_{25} Ecclesiastes 3:1-4.

CHAPTER 74

ε_{26} Husky Energy News Release, March 28, 2002.

ε_{27} Offshore Atlantic Canada Update, May 18, 2004.

ε_{28} Frank Sobiech, *Natural-History Research and Science of the Cross,* Australian EJournal of Theology, August 2005 - Issue 5 - Issn 1448 – 632, <http://dlibrary.acu.edu.au/research/theology/ejournal/aejt_5/Sobiech.htm>

CHAPTER 76

ε_{29} Francis Bacon, *Novum Organum*, (Liberal Arts Press, Inc., New York, 1960) p. 93.

ε_{30} "Sulfur on Flower." *Microsoft® Encarta® Encyclopedia 2001.*

ε_{31} Op. cit., *Encyclopedia of Newfoundland & Labrador*, Fluorspar.

ε_{32} St. Lawrence's part in the Allied war effort during World War II. Echoes of Valour <http://www.stemnet.nf.ca/monuments/nf/nf8.htm> [dead link] Retrieved 2009.

ε_{33} James Neil Hollingworth (1933-1996) wrote under the pseudonym Ambrose Redmoon.

ε_{34} <http://texinfo.library.unt.edu/texasregister/html/1998/Jun-19/adopted/environmental-quality.html>

CHAPTER 77

ε_{35} *Science,* Oct. 12, 1962: Vol. 138. no. 3537, pp. 136 – 138.

CHAPTER 78

[36]   *Magnetic Reversals and Glaciation* <http://www.iceagenow.com/Magnetic_Reversal_Chart.htm>

[37]   With apologies to the late Dean Martin for the slight modification.

[38]   http://www.aip.org/history/curie/brief/03_radium/radium_6.html

CHAPTER 79

[39]   Op. cit., B. Sherwood Lollar, et al.

[40]   Op. cit., D. Bohm, 1980, p. 233.

CHAPTER 80

[41]   C.F. O'Driscoll, C.J. Collins and J. Tuach, Selected publications at the Geological Survey of Newfoundland and Labrador: 1988 Volcanic-hosted, high-alumina, epithermal environments and the St. Lawrence fluorite deposit in the Avalon Zone, eastern Newfoundland.

[42]   encyclopedia.farlex.com/sulfur

[43]   Op. cit. C. F. O'Driscoll et al.

CHAPTER 83

[44]   John 12:13

[45]   Op. cit., *Encyclopedia of Newfoundland and Labrador*, Meteorites.

CHAPTER 84

[46]   Kenneth C. Macdonald and Paul J. Fox, *The Mid Ocean Ridge* <http://www.geol.ucsb.edu/faculty/macdonald/ScientificAmerican/sciam.html>

The Mid Ocean Ridge is the longest mountain chain, the most active volcanic area and until recently, the least accessible region on the earth. New maps reveal striking details of how segments of the Ridge form and evolve.

CHAPTER 85

[47]   Lawrence .W, Fagg, *Electromagnetism and the Sacred*, (The Continuum Publishing Company, 1999), pp. 75, 79.

[48]   Op. cit., *Encyclopedia of Newfoundland and Labrador*, Geologic history.

CHAPTER 88

[49]   Op. cit., *Encyclopedia of Newfoundland and Labrador*, Placentia.

CHAPTER 91

[50]   Life expectancy: 77.9 years. On average, we breathe 23,000 times a day. <http://www.cdc.gov/nchs/fastats/lifexpec.htm>

[51]   See Ch 20 – Agneswiseheart. Set of 17 Greek characters.

[52]   The Cosmic Plenum: Bohm's Gnosis: The Implicate Order <http://www.bizcharts.com/stoa_del_sol/plenum/plenum_3.html>

ε_{53} Mining in Newfoundland and Labrador, March 2010 <http://www.nr.gov.nl.ca/mines&en/min-ing/Overview percent20March percent2010, percent202010 percent20PDF percent20for percent-20website.pdf>

ε_{54} *LNG Transshipment Port Planned for Newfoundland* <http://www.rigzone.com/news/article.asp?a_id=38600>

ε_{55} Offal News, January 22, 2007, Liquefied Natural Gas in Atlantic Canada <http://offalnews.blogspot.com/2007/01/5-top-stories-of-2006-in-abm-2-of-4.html>

ε_{56} http://www.netl.doe.gov/publications/factsheet (dead link) Retrieved March 26, 2007.

ε_{57} Environmental Assessment Registration, Project Description in accordance with the requirements of the Canadian Environmental Assessment Agency, 2.2.1 LNG Background Information, November 22, 2006.

ε_{58} Calgary Energy <http://wn.com/s/calgaryenergy/index.htm> This site notes that *Canada is a net exporter of oil, natural gas, coal, uranium, and hydropower. It is one of the most important sources of U.S. energy imports.*

ε_{59} *Liquefied Natural Gas Worldwide*, The California Energy Commission <http://www.energy.ca.gov/lng/international.html>

ε_{60} NCEP Staff Background Paper – *The Safety of Liquefied Natural Gas* <http://www.energycommission.org/files/finalReport/IV.1.f percent20- percent20Safety percent20of percent20LNG.pdf>

ε_{31} http://en.wikipedia.org/wiki/List_of_countries_by_total_length_of_pipelines

ε_{62} Op. cit., B. Sherwood Lollar, et al.

ε_{63} John Tyerman Williams, *Pooh and the Philosophers*, (Methuen, London, 1997), p. 37-38, 40.

CHAPTER 92

ε_{64} *Is the Super Volcano Beneath Yellowstone Ready to Blow?* <http://www.unmuseum.org/supervol.htm>

ε_{65} As You Like It (II, vii, 139-143).

ε_{66} Mark Chirnside and Sam Halpern, Encyclopedia Titanica, Sunday 29 April 2007, *Olympic and Titanic: Maiden Voyage Mysteries* <http://www.encyclopedia-titanica.org/maiden voyagemysteries.html>

CHAPTER 93

ε_{67} Concerning the Early History of Planet Earth <http://ldolphin.org/Early.html>

ε_{68} Reuters U.K., *Denali starts open season on $35 bln Alaska line*, Tue Jul 6, 2010 <http://uk.reuters.com/article/idUKN0611646620100706>

ε_{69} Feldspar is a tectosilicate within the silicate family.

ε_{70} Op. cit, *Encyclopedia of Newfoundland and Labrador*, Merewether Crater.

CHAPTER 96

ε_{71} CBC News, *N.L. announces $16B Hebron oilfield deal* <http://www.cbc.ca/canada/newfoundland-labrador/story/2007/08/22/hebron-deal.html>

ε_{72} Newfoundland Business Directory, *The Hebron Oil Project* <http://www.newfoundlandbusinesses.ca/article.php?id=12>

ε_{73} Ibid.

ε74   *N.L. announces $16B Hebron oilfield deal* <http://www.cbc.ca/canada/newfoundland-labrador/
      story/2007/08/22/hebron-deal.html>

ε75   Op.cit., Newfoundland Business Directory.

ε76   Moravian Church in North America <http://www.moravian.org/>

ε77   John Quincy Adams.

ε78   Though construction began on a US$2.2-billion nickel processing plant at Long Harbour on Aug.
      26, 2010, Hydromet research and development has been conducted at Argentia. The project is mov-
      ing forward despite a worldwide recession and arguments from those opposed to the use of a nearby
      pond for the disposal of residue from the hydromet plant, the first commercial operation of its kind
      in the world.

      Terry Roberts, Transcontinental Media, Daily Business Buzz, *Construction begins on $2.2B nickel
      plant in Long Harbour* <http://www.dailybusinessbuzz.ca/2009/04/17/construction-begins-
      on-22b-nickel-plant-in-long-harbour/>

ε79   http://en.wikipedia.org/wiki/One_Hundred_Years_of_Solitude

ε80   IC Monthly Headlines, 12-21-2009 Atlantic Canada Oil and Gas Activity: Update and Outlook
      2009.

ε81   Chemical: NICKEL CAS Number: 7440-02-0

      Scorecard. The Pollution Information Site. <http://www.scorecard.org/chemical-profiles/summary.
      tcl?edf_substance_id=7440-02-0>

ε82   Voisey's Bay Project, Government of Newfoundland & Labrador
      <http://www.nr.gov.nl.ca/voiseys/state_princ.htm>

ε83   Chemical: COPPER CAS Number 7440-50-8 <http://www.scorecard.org/chemical-profiles/sum-
      mary.tcl?edf_substance_id=7440-50-8>

ε84   Peter van der Krogt, *Elementymology & Elements Multidict* <http://elements.vanderkrogt.net/>

ε85   The New York Times, *Radiation Danger Found in Oilfields Across the Nation*, December 3, 1990, Front
      page.

CHAPTER 97

ε86   A Mineral and Management Services review in 2009 found 41 deaths and 302 injuries out of 1,443
      oil-rig accidents from 2001 to 2007.

ε87   *Environmental Health Perspectives* Vol 108, No 12, December 2000 (National Institute of Environmental
      Health Sciences), pp. 1203-1207. <http://ehpnet1.niehs.nih.gov/docs/2000/108p1203-1207weisglas-
      kuperus/abstract.html>

CHAPTER 98

ε88   Creation 23(4):47–49, September 2001, Ann Lamont, *Great Creation Scientists: Nicolaus Steno* <http://
      www.answersingenesis.org/creation/v23/i4/steno.asp>

ε89   Luke 6: 27-31.

CHAPTER 101

ϵ_{90} R Müller, M. Sdrolias, *Back-arc Basins: Spreading and Convergence History,* (American Geophysicsl Union, 12/2003) SAO/NASA ADS Physics Abstract Service <http://adsabs.harvard.edu/abs/2003AGUFM.T51F0220M>

ϵ_{91} Op. cit., *Encyclopedia of Newfoundland and Labrador* (2005).
     The Avalon Zone is older and has a different geological history from the rest of the Newfoundland Appalachians. It is believed to be a far-travelled terrain similar to rocks in southern Europe and northwestern Africa that collided with the Gander Zone about 400,000,000 years ago.

ϵ_{92} Australian slang for "a long way from civilization."

ϵ_{93} Robert Gilman, *Morphogenetic Fields and Beyond, an interview with Rupert Sheldrake,* In Context, A Quarterly of Humane Sustainable Culture, #12, Winter 1985/86, <http://www.context.org/ICLIB/IC12/TOC12.htm>

ϵ_{94} Wim Kayzer, *A Glorious Accident*, 1995, (W. H. Freeman and Company, 1999) p. 156.

ϵ_{95} David Pratt, *Rupert Sheldrake: A Theosophical Appraisal Part 1: Morphic Fields and the Memory of Nature* <http://www.theosophy-nw.org/theosnw/science/prat-shl.htm>
     Rupert Sheldrake, *A New Science of Life: The Hypothesis of Formative Causation* (J.P.Tarcher, 1981).

ϵ_{96} Op. cit. Wim Kayzer, p. 153.

ϵ_{97} <http://www.sheldrake.org/Resources/glossary>

ϵ_{98} John Polkinghorne, *Quarks, Chaos & Christianity*, (The Crossroad Publishing Company, 1994). Speaking of Faith Newsletter, Krista's Journal, April 20, 2006 <http://speakingoffaith.publicradio.org/programs/quarks/>

ϵ_{99} R.L.Armstrong, J.E. Muller, J.E. Harakal, and K. Muehlenbachs, *The Neogene Alert Bay Volcanic Belt of Northern Vancouver Island, Canada: Descending-plate-edge Volcanism in the Arc-trench Gap;* Journal of Volcanology and Geothermal Research, Volume 26, Issues 1-2, October 1985, pp. 75-97.

ϵ_{100} Edgar Cayce, *The End Times, Prophecies of Coming Changes*, A.R.E. Press, Reprint edition (December 1, 1996).

ϵ_{101} With apologies to McLandburgh Wilson, fl. 1915, Optimist and Pessimist.

ϵ_{102} Targ's notes from *My Big Toe* (Theory Of Everything), by Thomas Campbell Weekend workshop, Campbell, Calif., February 20-21, 2010.

CHAPTER 105

ϵ_{103} Microsoft® Encarta® Encyclopedia 2001, *The Origin of the Elements.* © 1993-2000. Citation changed to garbled code.

ϵ_{104} Wikipedia, *Metallicity, Population I and II stars* <http://en.wikipedia.org/wiki/Metallicity>

ϵ_{105} Microsoft® Encarta® Encyclopedia *2001, How a Supernova Explodes.*© 1993-2000. Citation changed to garbled code.

ϵ_{106} Montague Ullman, *The Transformation Process In Dreams,* The American Academy of Psychoanalysis, Paper delivered at a Conference of Scientists with J.Krishnamurti at Brockwood Park, October 14, 1974 <http://siivola.org/monte/papers_grouped/index.htm>

ℇ107   Jakob D. Bekenstein, *Information in the Holographic Universe,* Scientific American, August 2003, p. 60.

ℇ108   Jenny Hogan, *Hawking cracks black hole paradox*, New Scientist, July 14, 2004 <http://www.newscientist.com/article/dn6151-hawking-cracks-black-hole-paradox.html>

CHAPTER 106

ℇ109   Microsoft® Encarta® Encyclopedia 2001, *Gideon.* © 1993-2000. Citation changed to garbled code.

ℇ110   Op. cit., Wim Kayzer, p. 161.

ℇ111   D. Bohm, *Fragmentation And Wholeness*, (The American Academy of Psychoanalysis, Vol. 17 No. 1, February 1973, p. 19).

CHAPTER 107

ℇ112   Robert Frost, Writers at Work, The Paris Review Interviews, Second Series (The Viking Press, 1963).

CHAPTER 108

ℇ113   Will Keepin, *Lifework of David Bohm, River of Truth,* <http://www.vision.net.au/~apaterson/science/david_bohm.htm>

       D. Bohm*, Wholeness and the Implicate Order (*London Routledge & Kegan Paul, 1980).

ℇ114   Bruce Obee, *Tsunami!,* Canadian Geographic, Feb. March 1989 <http://www.canadiangeographic.ca/tsunami/tsunami_cg1989.asp>

CHAPTER 110

ℇ115   *Yellowstone's Quiet Power, A Volcano Forcefully Shapes the Land, Even between Eruptions*, University of Utah, March 1, 2007 <http://unews.utah.edu/p/?r=020507-1>

ℇ116   Shakespeare. Twelfth Night. Act ii. Sc. 4.

CHAPTER 111

ℇ117   "Clocks and Watches." *Microsoft® Encarta® Encyclopedia 2001.*

CHAPTER 115

ℇ118   Natural Resources Canada, *Earthquake zones in Eastern Canada* <http://earthquakescanada.nrcan.gc.ca/zones/eastcan-eng.php>

ℇ119   Op. cit, CALGARY ENERGY - January 30, 2010 <http://archive.wn.com/2010/01/30/1400/calgaryenergy>

ε120   Roberta S. Herzog, *The Akashic Records*, 2004 <http://www.robertaherzog.com/>

ε121   Ervin Laszlo, *Science and the Akashic Field*, 2nd Ed. (Inner Traditions, 2007) pg. 76.

ε122   Edgar Cayce, *Akashic Records, The Book of Life* (A.R.E.®, Inc., 2003).

ε123   My conclusions on Sulfuranium derive from the theories of disintegration and transmutation. See Appeal to Science, p. 626.

Appeal-to-Science

ε124   Christine Dell'Amore, *Mount St. Helens Still Highly Dangerous, 30 Years Later*, National Geographic News, May 18, 2010.

ε125   Harmon Craig, *Isotopic Variations in Meteoric Waters*, Department of Earth Sciences, University of California, La Jolla. (*Science,* May 26, 1961, Vol. 133. no. 3465) pp. 1702 – 1703.

The relationship between deuterium and oxygen-18 concentrations in natural meteoric waters from many parts of the world has been determined with a mass spectrometer. The isotopic enrichments, relative to ocean water, display a linear correlation over the entire range for waters which have not undergone excessive evaporation.

ε126   http://www.cawthron.org.nz/

BIBLIOGRAPHY

Bekenstein, Jakob D. *Information in the Holographic Universe.* Scientific American, August 2003, p. 60.

Baumann, M.D. T. Lee. *God at the Speed of Light.* Virginia Beach: A.E.E. Press, 2001.

Bohm, David. *Fragmentation and Wholeness.* The American Academy of Psychoanalysis, Vol. 17 No. 1, February 1973, p.19.

Bohm, D. *Unfolding Meaning.* London and New York: ARK Paperbacks, 1987.

Bohm, David. *Wholeness and The Implicate Order.* London: Routledge & Kegan Paul, 1980.

Bohm, D. and Hiley, B.J., *The Undivided Universe.* London: Routledge & Kegan Paul, 1993.

The Cosmic Plenum: Bohm's Gnosis: The Implicate Order http://www.bizcharts.com/stoa_del_sol/plenum/plenum_3.html

Briggs, John. *Fractals.* New York: Touchstone, 1992.

Cayce, Edgar. *The End Times, Prophecies of Coming Changes.*, Virginia Beach: A.R.E. Press, Reprint edition (December 1, 1996).

Davies, Paul. *About Time.* New York: Simon & Schuster, 1995.

Fagg, Lawrence .W. *Electromagnetism and the Sacred.* New York: Continuum Publishing, 1999.

Gardiner, Alan H., trans. *Hieratic Papyri in the British Museum.* 3rd Series. Chester Beatty Gift. Papyrus No. III. [Papyrus Facsimile +text and annotations] London, 1935.

Greene, Brian. *The Elegant Universe.* New York: Vintage Books, a Division of Random House, 2000.

Hayward, Jeremy W. *Letters to Vanessa.* Boston & London: Shambhala Publications, Inc., 1997.

Hoff, Benjamin. *The Tao of Pooh.* New York: Penguin Books, 1983.

Hogan, Jenny. *Hawking cracks black hole paradox.* New Scientist, July 14, 2004. http://www.newscientist.com/article/dn6151-hawking-cracks-black-hole-paradox.html

Hutton, William. *Coming Earth Changes.* Virginia Beach, Va. A.R.E. Press, 1996.

Kaku, Michio. *Parallel Worlds.* New York, London, Toronto, Sydney, Auckland: Doubleday, a division of Random House, 2005.

Kayzer, Wim. *A Glorious Accident.* New York: W. H. Freeman and Co., 1999.

Laszlo, Ervin. *Science and the Akashic Field 2nd Ed.* Rochester, Vermont: Inner Traditions, 2007.

LeDoux, Joseph. *The Emotional Brain.* New York: Simon & Schuster, 1996.

Long, Leon E. *Geology,* Ninth Edition. U.S.A: Simon & Schuster, 1997.

Lurker, Manfred. *The Gods and Symbols of Ancient Egypt.* London: Thames and Hudson Ltd, London, 1882.

Mascaro, Juan. *The Upanishads.* England: Penguin Books, 1965.

May, Margaret Tallmadge, trans. intro. and commentary. *Galen. On The Usefulness Of The Parts Of the Body.* I Vol. 1, pp. 392-393. Ithaca, NY: Cornell University Press, 1968.

McLaughlin, Samuel Clarke. *On Feeling Good.* Brookline, Mass: Autumn Press, Inc., 1978.

McTaggart, Lynne. *The Field: The Quest for the Secret Force of the Universe.* New York: Harper Collins, 2002.

Milner, A. David and Goodale, Melvyn A. *The Visual Brain in Action.* Oxford, New York, Tokyo: Oxford University Press, 1995.

Mitchell, Edgar. *Nature's Mind: the Quantum Hologram. www.edmitchellapollo14.com/naturearticle.htm*

Mitchell, Edgar. *The View From Space - A Message of Peace* (DVD). SMPI/Sheila Mitchell Productions, Inc., 2006.

Neihardt, John G., as told through. Intro by Vine DeLoria, Jr. *Black Elk Speaks.* Lincoln and London: University of Nebraska Press, 1988.

Parsifal-Charles, Nancy The Dream. 4,000 Years of Theory and Practice. West Cornwell, CT: Locust Hill Press, 1986.

Peat, F. David. *Einstein's Moon.* Chicago: Contemporary Books, 1990.

Polkinghorne, John. *The Quantum World.* Princeton, N. J: Princeton University Press, 1984.

Polkinghorne, John. *Quarks, Chaos & Christianity.* New York: Crossroad Publishing, 1994

Pratt, David. Rupert Sheldrake: A Theosophical Appraisal Part 1: Morphic Fields and the Memory of Nature. http://www.theosophy-nw.org/theosnw/science/prat-shl.htm

Primack, Joel R. and Abrams, Nancy Ellen. *The View from the Center of the Universe,* New York: Riverhead Books, 2006.

Radin, Dean. *Entangled Minds.* New York, London, Toronto, Sydney: Paraview, 2006.

Rosen, Steven M. *The Self-Evolving Cosmos.* New Jersey, London, Singapore, Beijing, Shanghai, Hong Kong, Taipei, Chennai: World Scientific Publishing Co., Pte. Ltd., 2008.

Sagan, Carl *The Best of Cosmos.* (DVD) Cosmos Studios, 2000.

Sheldrake, Rupert. *The Presence Of The Past.* New York: Random House, First Vintage Books Edition, 1989.

Shepherd, A.P., *Scientist of The Invisible – Rudolf Steiner.* Foreword by Owen Barfield. Rochester Vt: Inner Traditions International, 1983.

Siegel, Rudolph E., ed. *Galen. On Sense Perception.* Basel, Switzerland: S. Karger, 1970.

Ullman, Montague. "*Dreams as Exceptional Human Experiences.*" ASPR Newsletter, The American Society for Psychical Research, Inc., Volume XVIII Number 1993.

Ullman, Montague. *On the Relevance of Quantum Concepts to Dreaming Consciousness.* Date unknown, between 2001-2005. http://www.siivola.org/monte/papers_grouped/uncopyrighted/Dreams/on_the_relevance_of_quantum_concepts_to_dreaming_consciousness.htm

Ullman, Montague. "The *Dream: In Search of A New Abode.*" Paper presented at the twenty-third Annual Meeting of the International Association for the Study of Dreams, July 22, 2006.

Ullman, Montague. *The Transformation Process In Dreams,* The American Academy of Psychoanalysis Journal, Vol. 79, No. 2, May 1975.

Ullman, Montague. *Wholeness in dreaming.* Essays in honour of David Bohm. Edited by B.J. Hiley, and F. David Peat, London and New York: Routledge & Kegan Paul, 1987.

Ullman, Montague, Krippner, Stanley with Vaughan, Alan. *Dream Telepathy. New York:* Macmillan Publishing Co., Inc., 1973.

Van Auken, John. *Ancient Egyptian Mysticism.* Virginia Beach, Va.: A.R.E. Press, 1999.

Wachsmuth, Guenther. *Reincarnation.* Translated by Olin D. Wannamaker. New York: Anthroposophic Press, 1937.

Walzer, Richard and Frede, Michael, trans. *Galen. Three Treatises On The Nature of Science.* Indianapolis, In: Hackett Publishing. Co.,1985.

Williams, John Tyerman. *Pooh and the Philosophers.* London: Methuen, 1997.

Zajonc, Arthur. *Catching the Light.* New York: Oxford University Press, 1993.

8

INDEX TO FRAGMENTATION
AND WHOLENESS

Some entries are generic in nature. The actual word may
not appear in the reference but the context will be present.

Dream images are italicized; waking images are not.
Illustrations and photos are indicated by an asterisk*

Lavenderisms

One
Logos
Consciousness
Patience for adults.
Repetition for children.
Freedom from the past.
The Word is in the Hole.
Heaven is a children's nursery.
Truth, like cork, always rises to the top.
We see you as one planet … one people.
Listen. He has something important to say.
Life's experience departs with the enteric soul.
Humankind must learn the meaning of Empathy.
Be Patient. You will learn everything you need to know.
The cosmic imprints of Timelessness and Consciousness are shared.
Mother Earth is pleading with her children to save her – to save themselves

Dreams

Circularity

Circles in Lavender illustrate how dream fragments connect to make one circle at a time, each circle widening to reflect the circularity of time and consciousness.

Paranormal

Physics

Quantum Theory according to Lavender

Cosmic Dreaming

Quantum Consciousness

Dual Nature of Consciousness

Connectivity

Congratulations! You have reached the last page of Lavender which began with one dream on a blank page.

Perhaps this blank page will encourage you to jot down your own connections or inspire you to record a dream of your own. Remember, the most outwardly meaningless dream often conveys the greatest meaning.

Proof

8502815R1

Made in the USA
Charleston, SC
15 June 2011